# Delilah Dirk

### and the
## KING'S SHILLING

First Second

Copyright © 2016 by Tony Cliff

Produced primarily using pencil on paper with intermediate
digital processes and digital lettering and coloring.

Published by First Second
First Second is an imprint of Roaring Brook Press,
a division of Holtzbrinck Publishing Holdings Limited Partnership
175 Fifth Avenue, New York, New York 10010
All rights reserved

Cataloging-in-Publication Data is on file at the Library of Congress.

ISBN 978-1-62672-155-5

Our books may be purchased in bulk for promotional, educational, or business use. Please
contact your local bookseller or the Macmillan Corporate and Premium Sales Department
at (800) 221-7945 ext. 5442 or by e-mail at MacmillanSpecialMarkets@macmillan.com.

FIRST
EDITION

First edition 2016
Book design by John Green

Printed in China by RR Donelley Asia Printing Solutions Ltd., Dongguan City, Guandong Province
10 9 8 7 6 5 4 3 2 1

# Delilah Dirk

### and the
## KING'S SHILLING

## Tony Cliff

# :01

First Second

*New York*

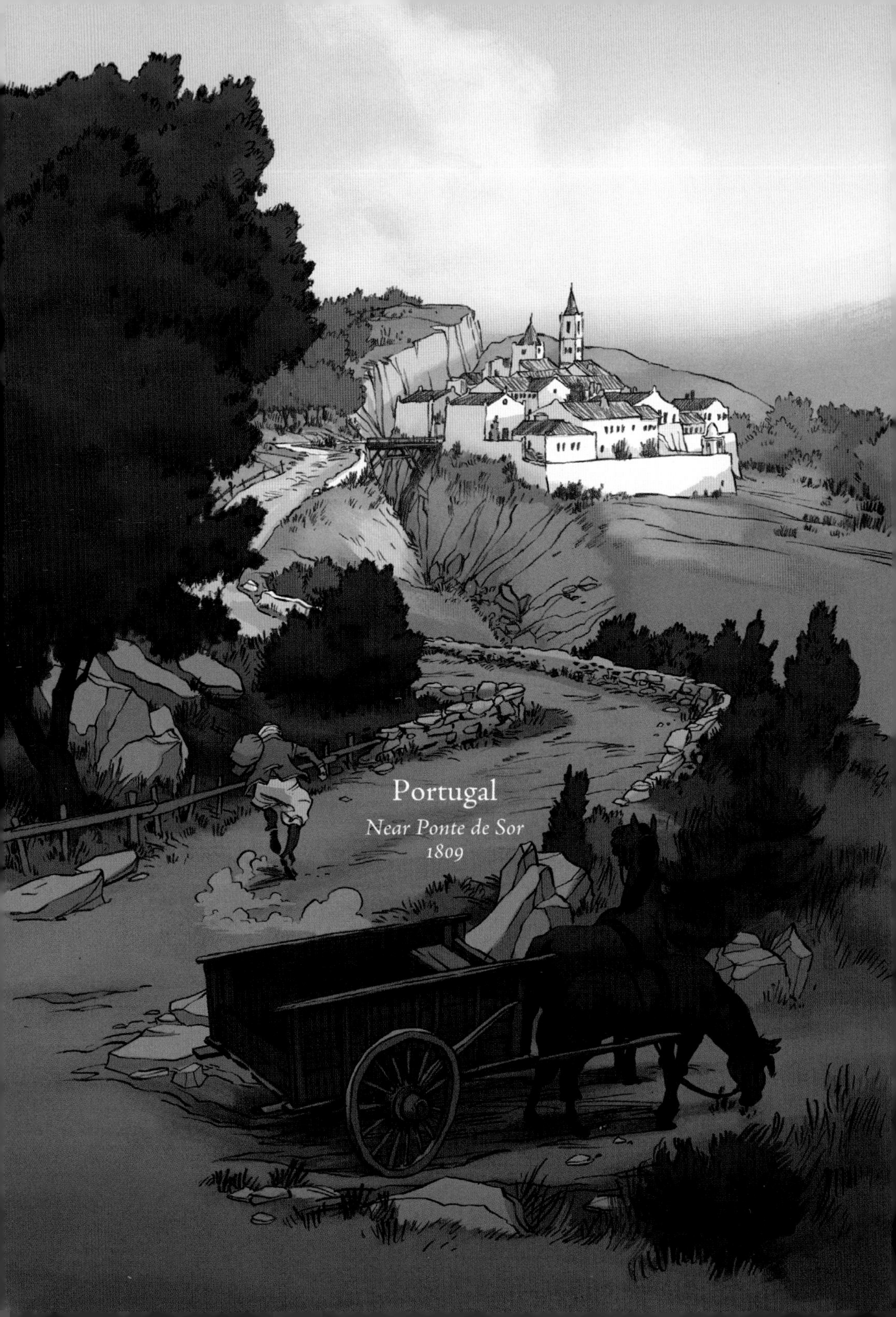
Portugal
Near Ponte de Sor
1809

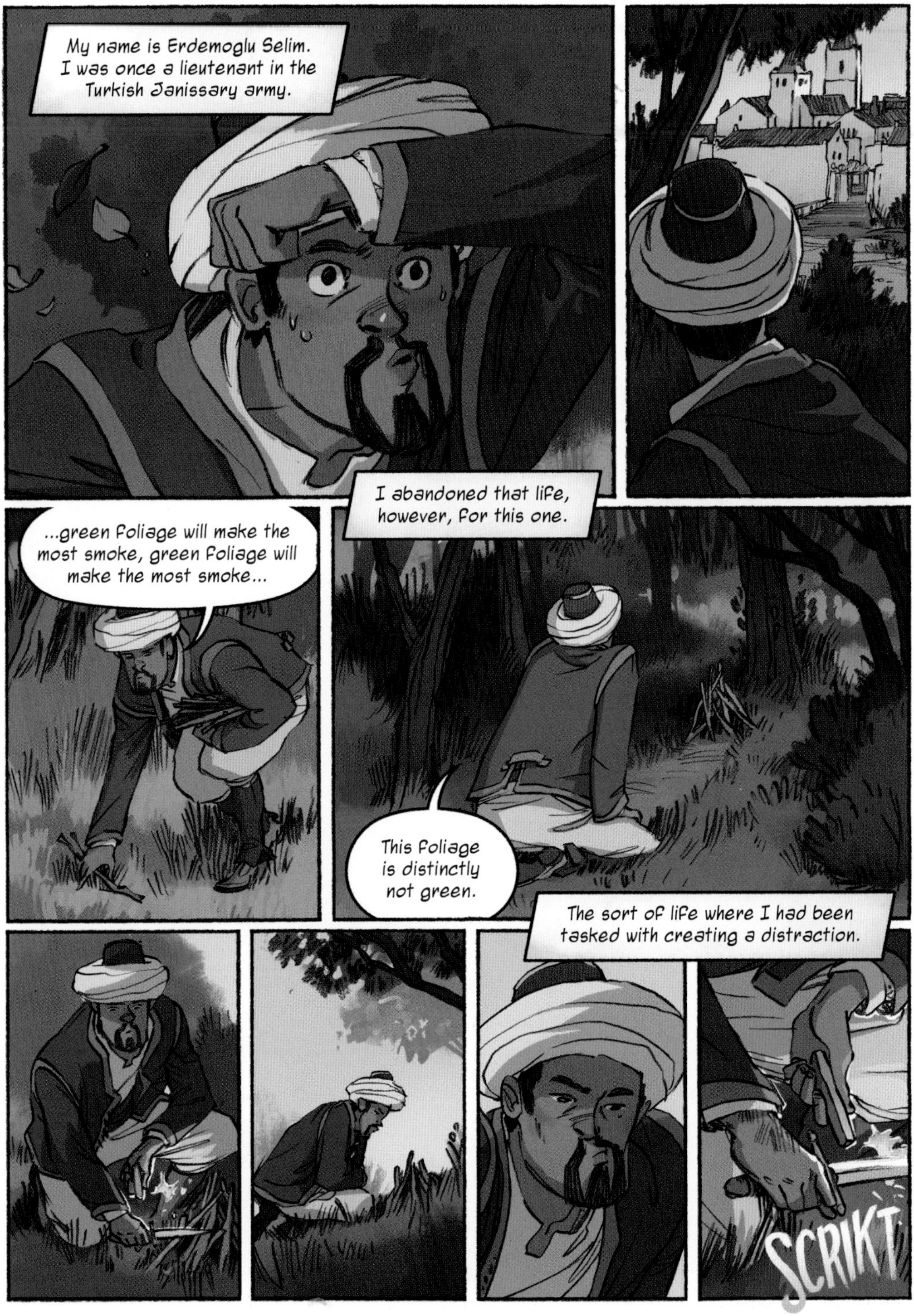
My name is Erdemoglu Selim. I was once a lieutenant in the Turkish Janissary army.
I abandoned that life, however, for this one.
...green foliage will make the most smoke, green foliage will make the most smoke...
This foliage is distinctly not green.
The sort of life where I had been tasked with creating a distraction.
SCRIKT

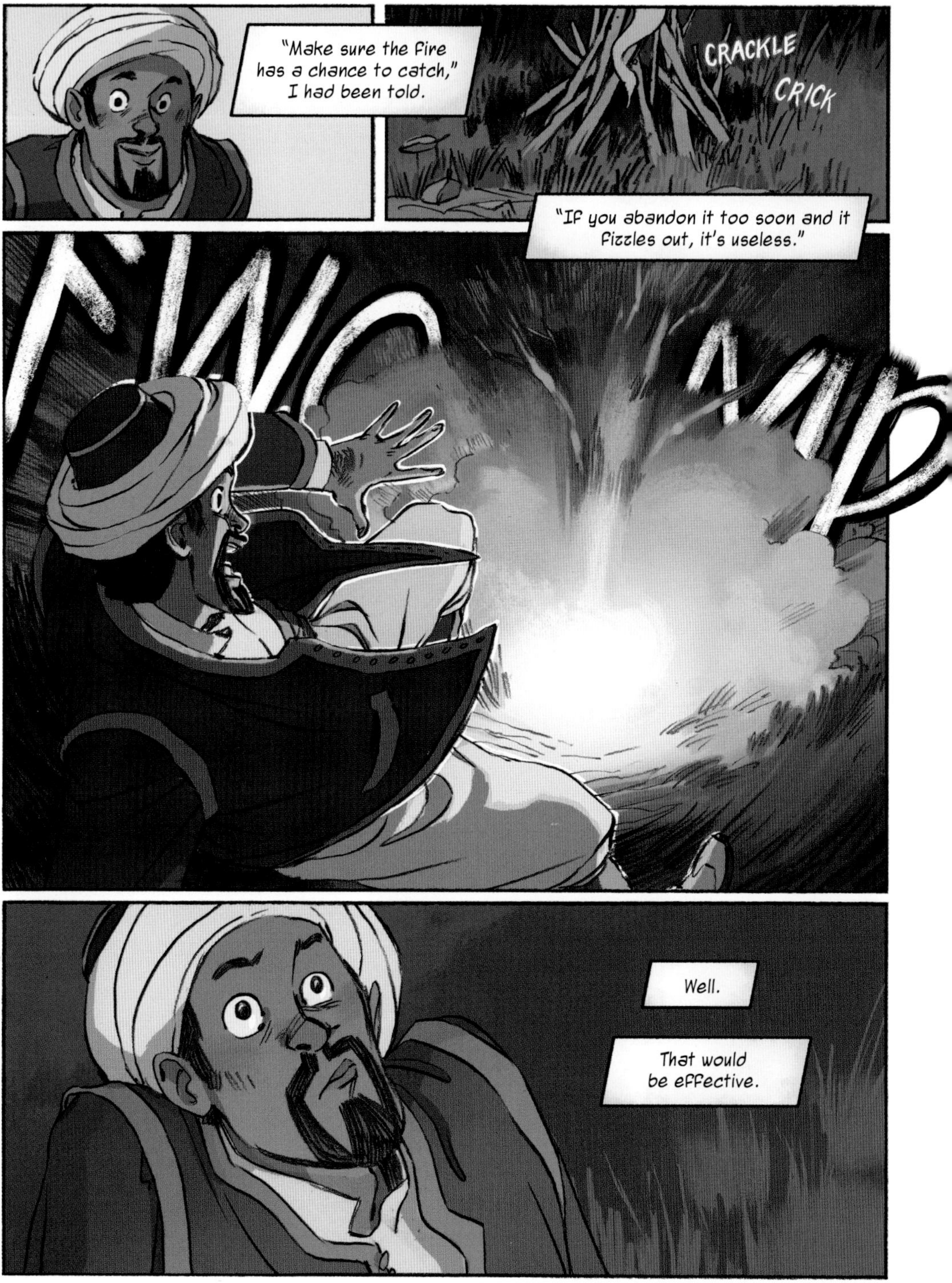
"Make sure the fire has a chance to catch," I had been told.
CRACKLE
CRICK
"If you abandon it too soon and it fizzles out, it's useless."
Well.
That would be effective.

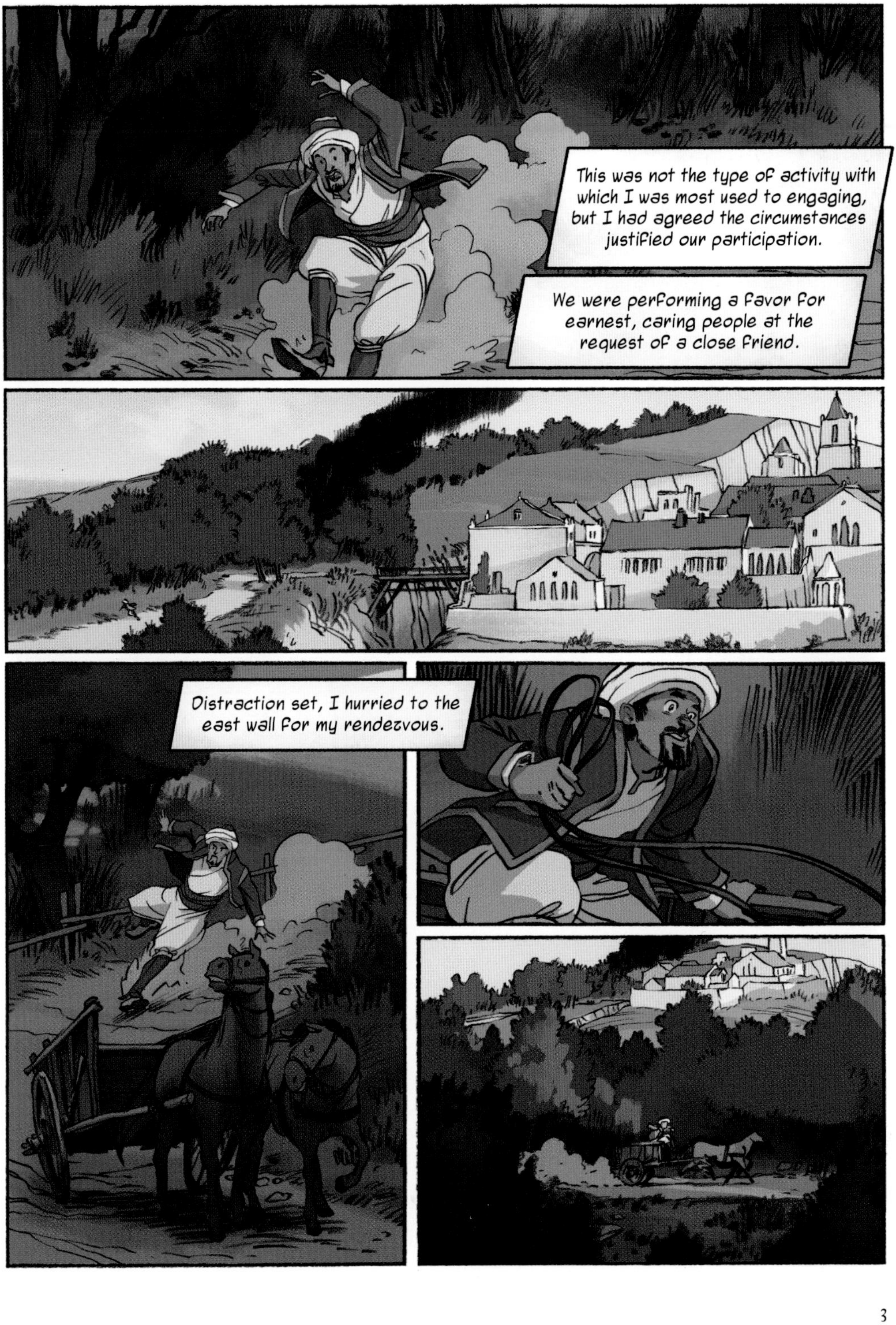
This was not the type of activity with which I was most used to engaging, but I had agreed the circumstances justified our participation.
We were performing a favor for earnest, caring people at the request of a close friend.
Distraction set, I hurried to the east wall for my rendezvous.

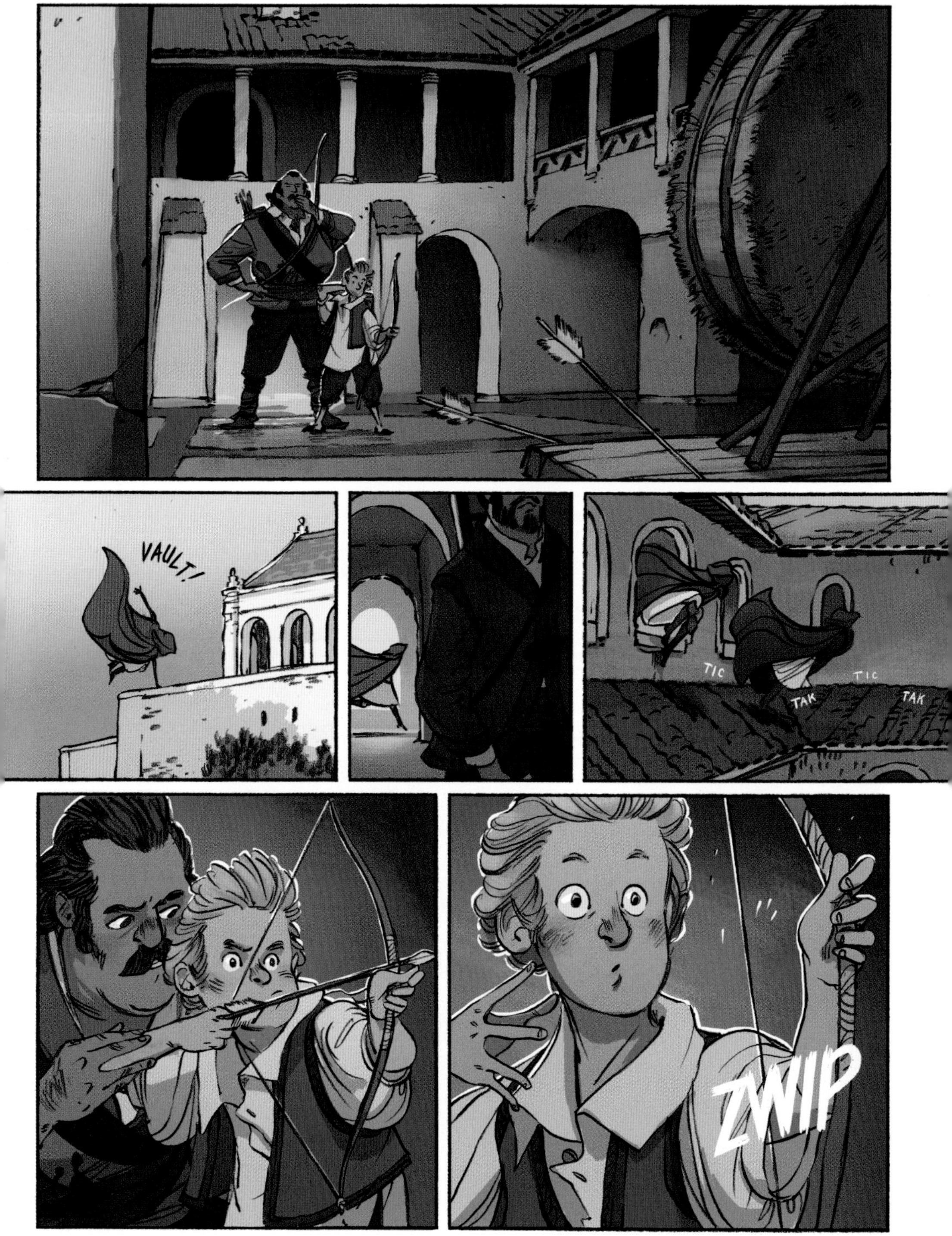
VAULT!
TIC
TAK
TIC
TAK
ZWIP

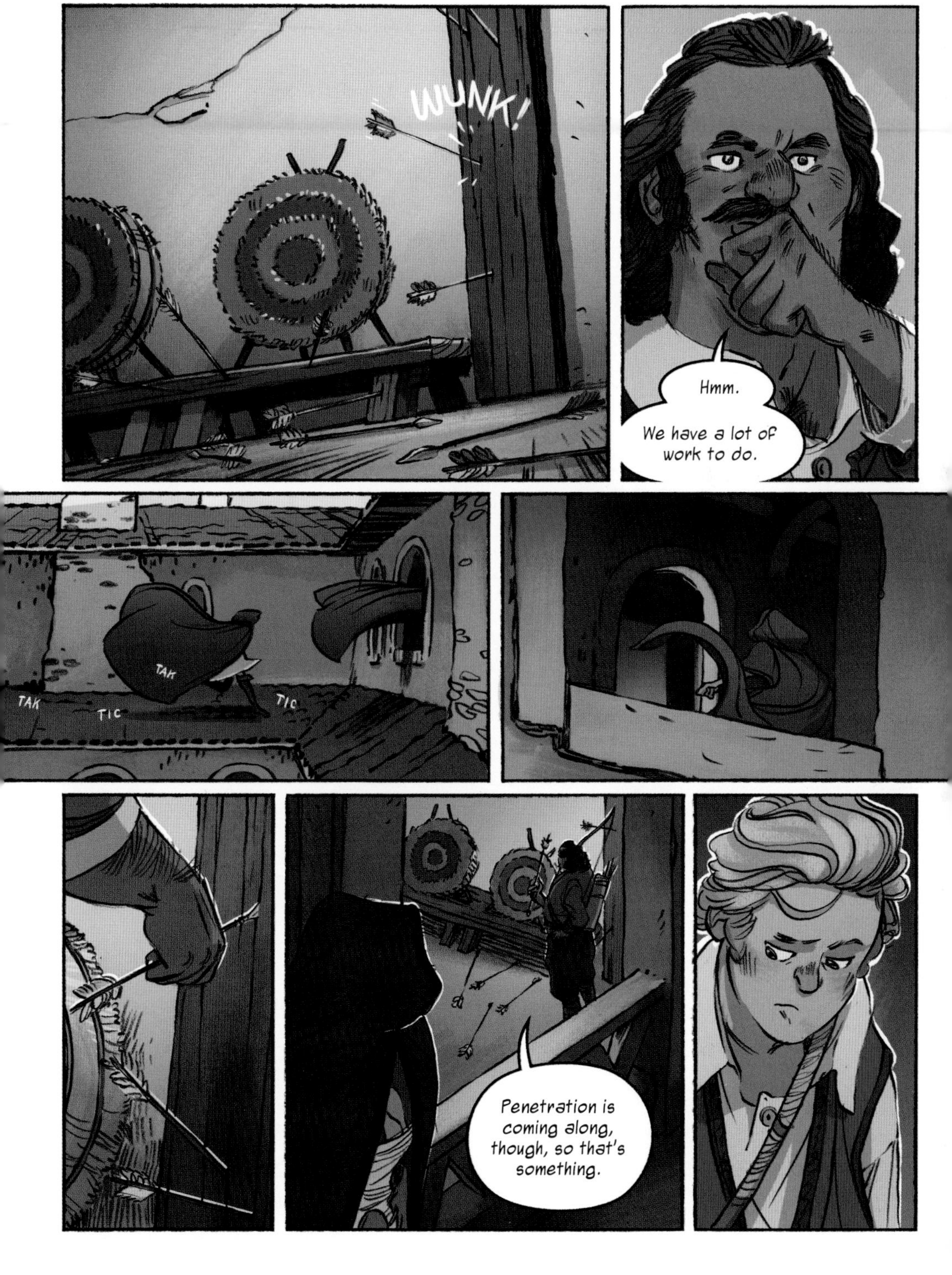
WUNK!
Hmm.
We have a lot of work to do.
TAK
TIC
TAK
TIC
Penetration is coming along, though, so that's something.

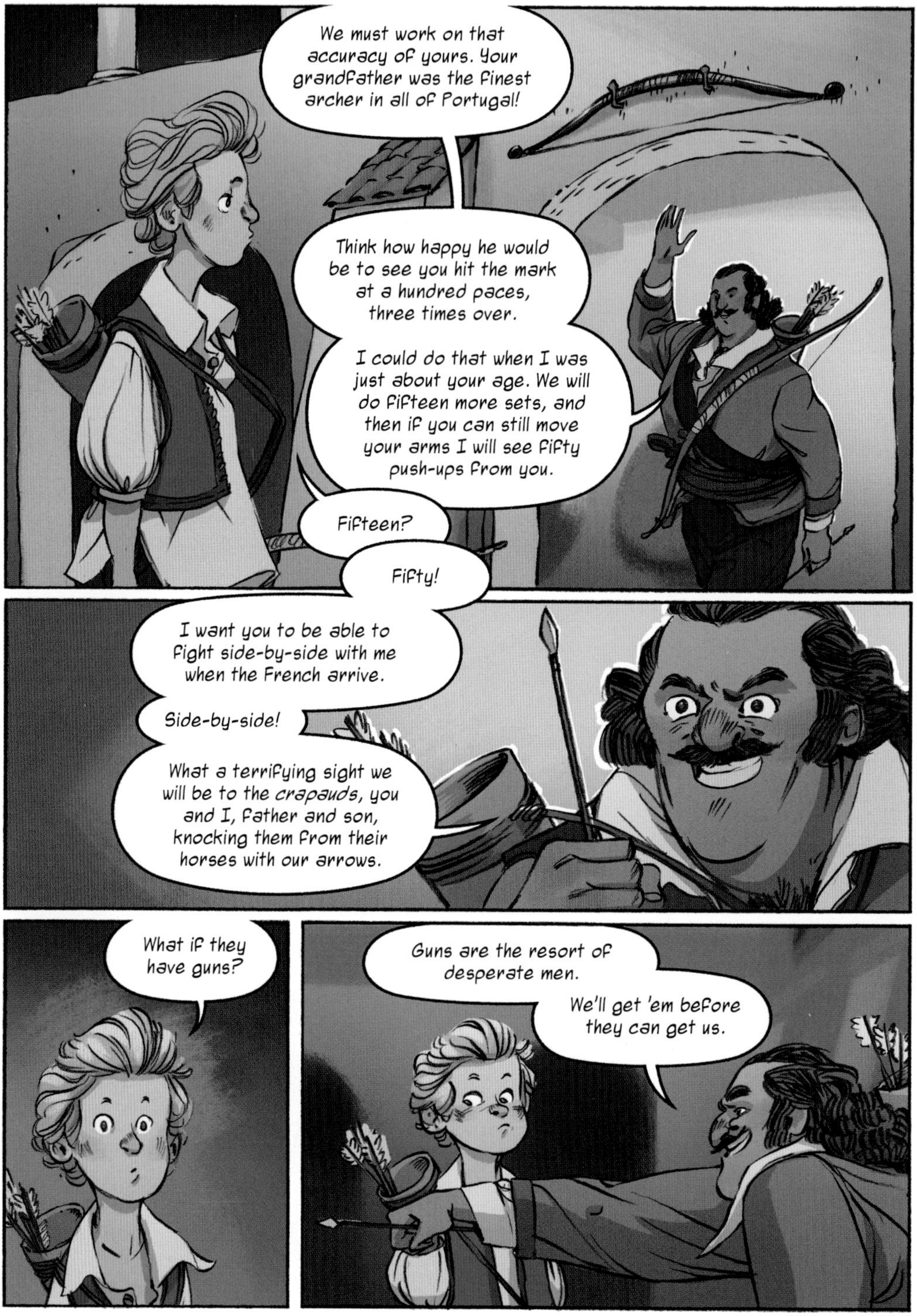
We must work on that accuracy of yours. Your grandfather was the finest archer in all of Portugal!
Think how happy he would be to see you hit the mark at a hundred paces, three times over.
I could do that when I was just about your age. We will do fifteen more sets, and then if you can still move your arms I will see fifty push-ups from you.
Fifteen?
Fifty!
I want you to be able to fight side-by-side with me when the French arrive.
Side-by-side!
What a terrifying sight we will be to the *crapauds*, you and I, father and son, knocking them from their horses with our arrows.
What if they have guns?
Guns are the resort of desperate men.
We'll get 'em before they can get us.

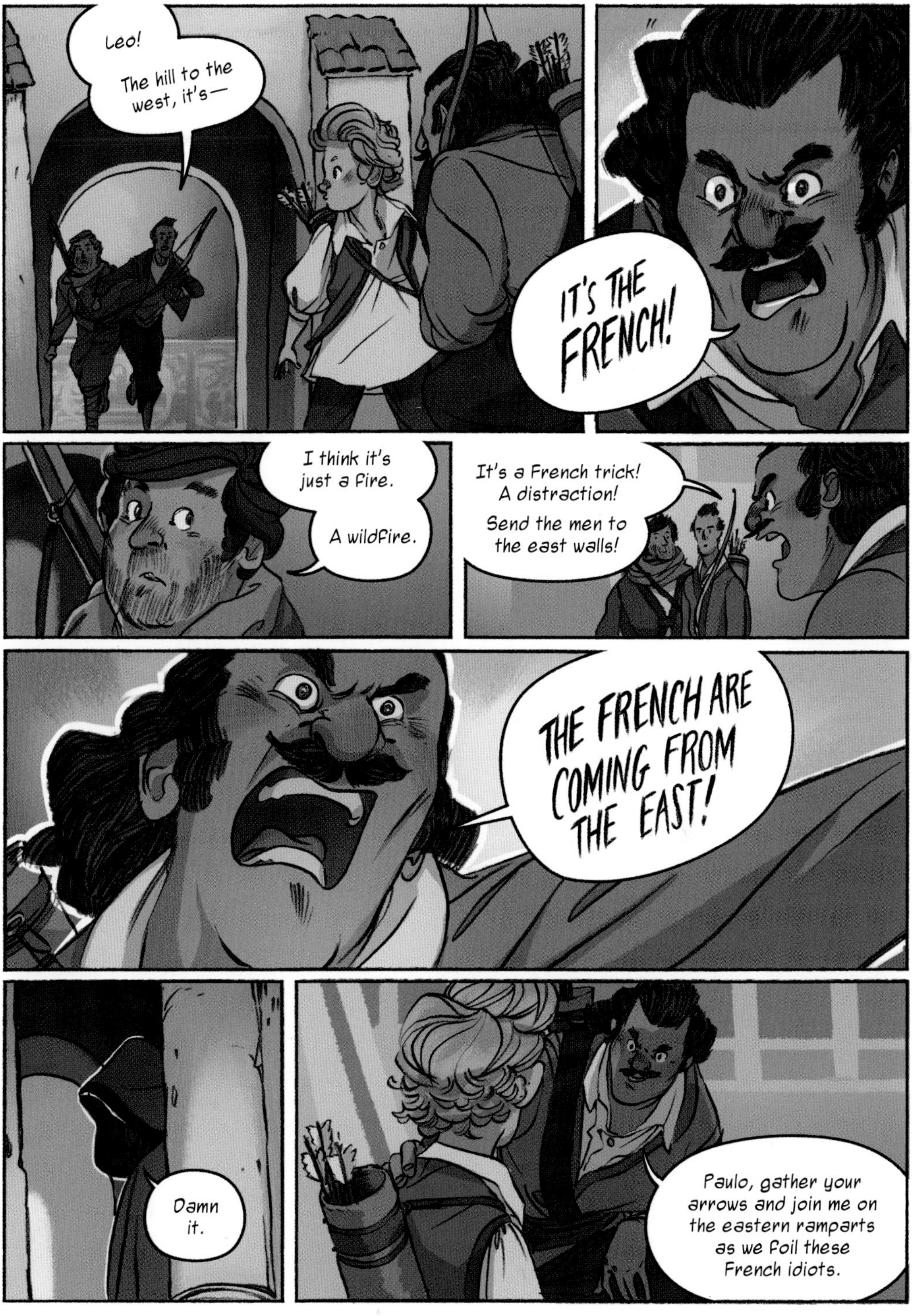
Leo!
The hill to the west, it's—
IT'S THE FRENCH!
I think it's just a fire.
A wildfire.
It's a French trick! A distraction!
Send the men to the east walls!
THE FRENCH ARE COMING FROM THE EAST!
Damn it.
Paulo, gather your arrows and join me on the eastern ramparts as we foil these French idiots.

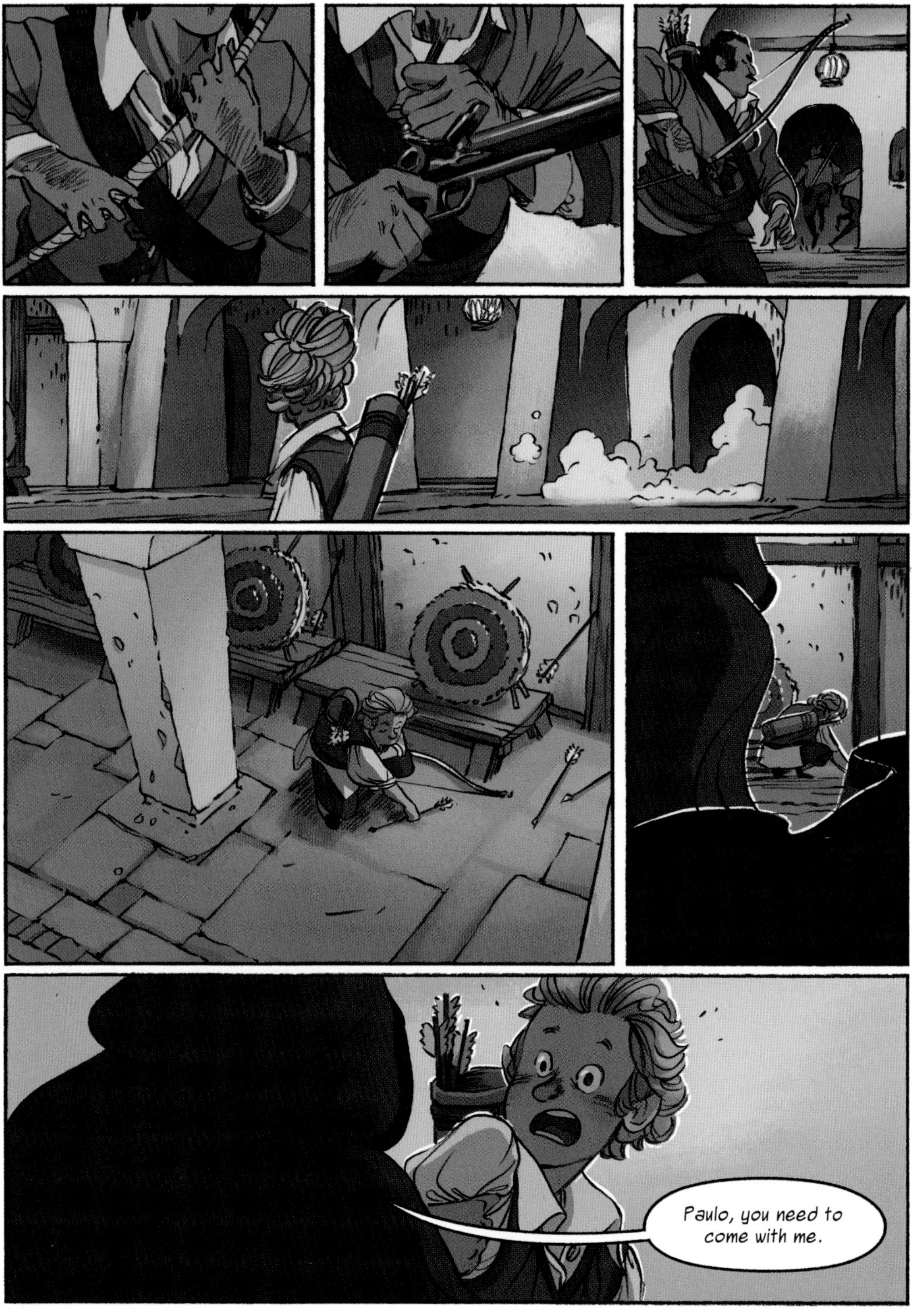
Paulo, you need to come with me.

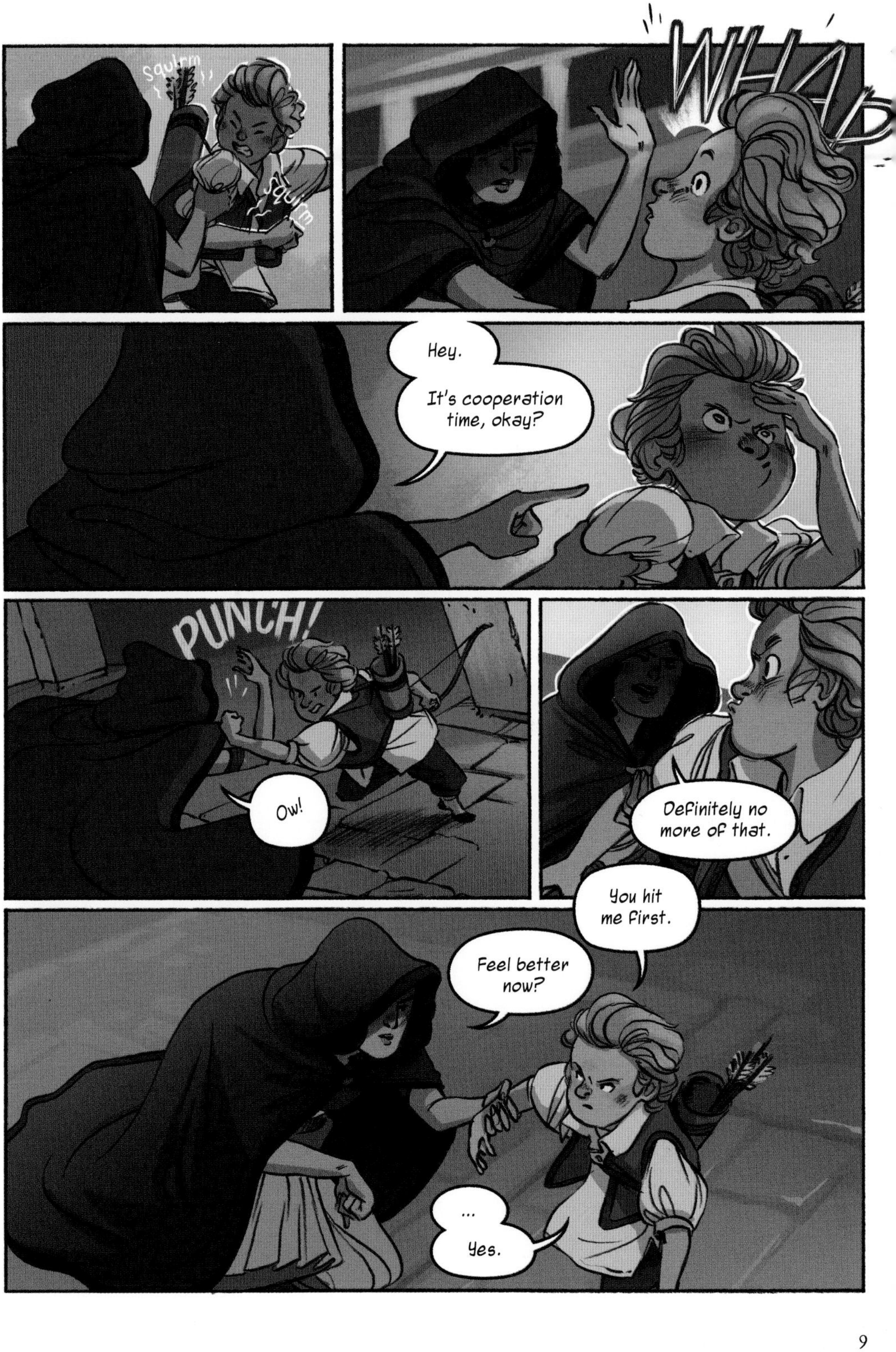
squirm
squirm
WHAP
Hey.
It's cooperation time, okay?
PUNCH!
Ow!
Definitely no more of that.
You hit me first.
Feel better now?
...
Yes.

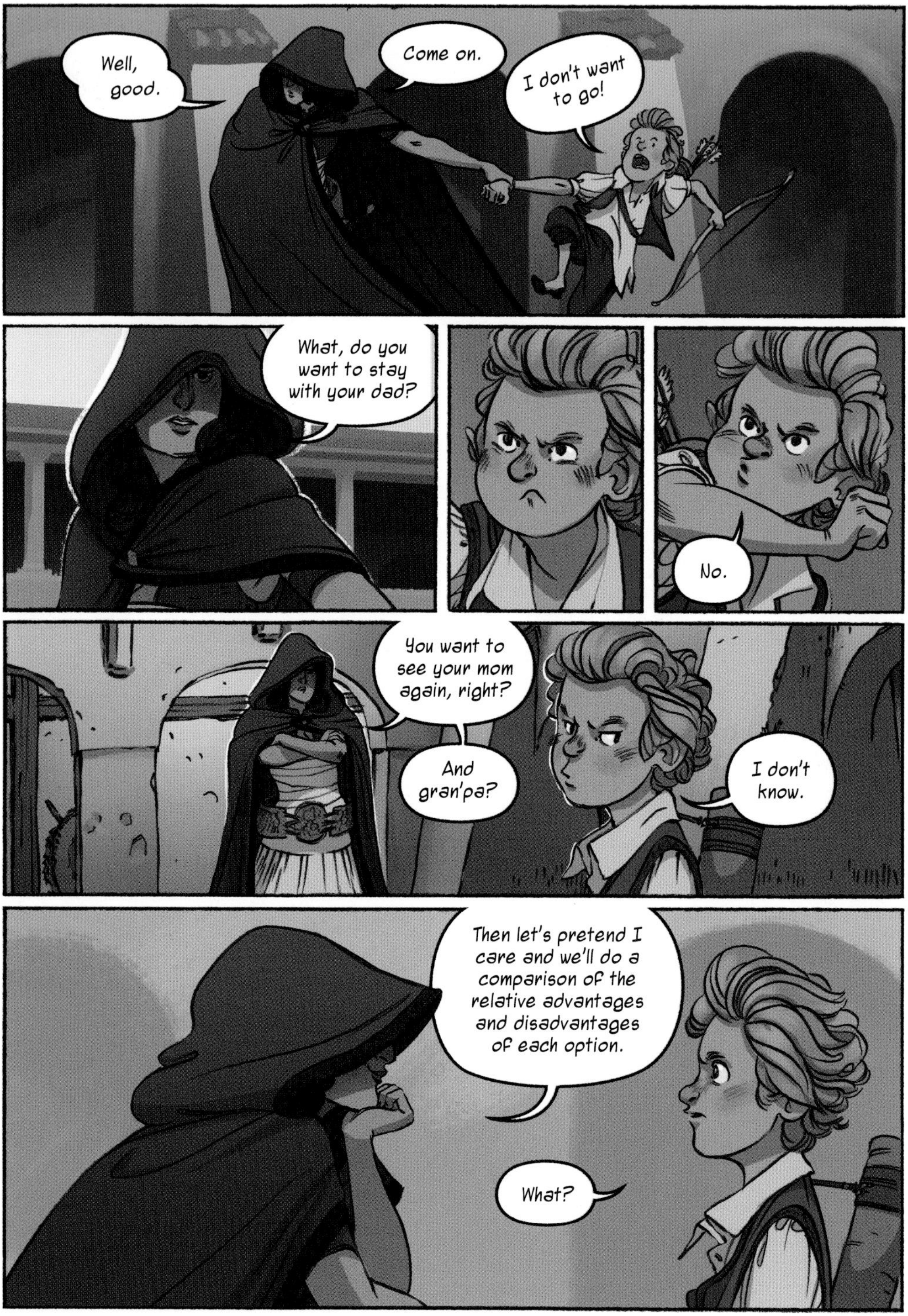
Well, good.
Come on.
I don't want to go!
What, do you want to stay with your dad?
No.
You want to see your mom again, right?
And gran'pa?
I don't know.
Then let's pretend I care and we'll do a comparison of the relative advantages and disadvantages of each option.
What?

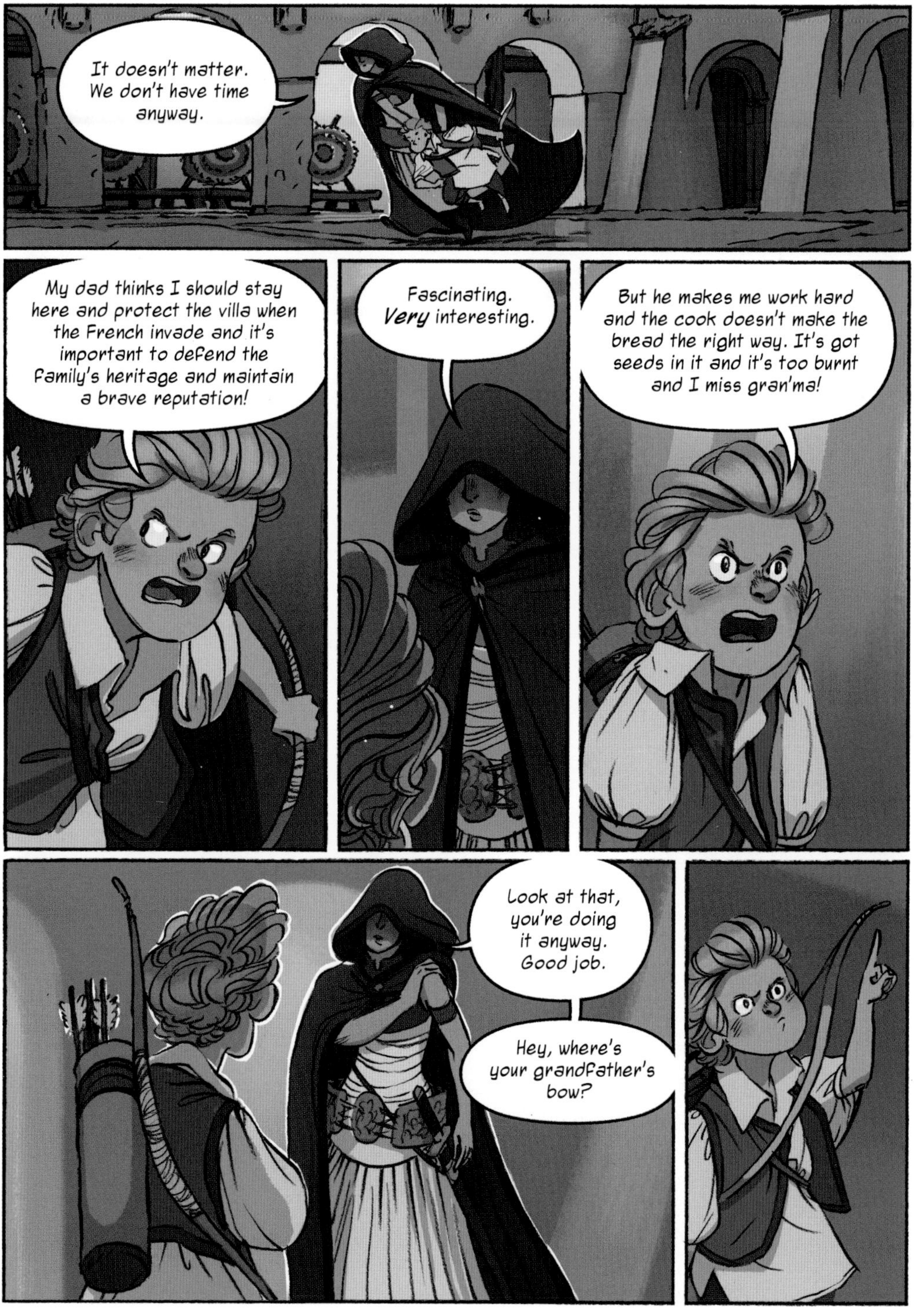

It doesn't matter. We don't have time anyway.
My dad thinks I should stay here and protect the villa when the French invade and it's important to defend the family's heritage and maintain a brave reputation!
Fascinating. *Very* interesting.
But he makes me work hard and the cook doesn't make the bread the right way. It's got seeds in it and it's too burnt and I miss gran'ma!
Look at that, you're doing it anyway. Good job.
Hey, where's your grandfather's bow?

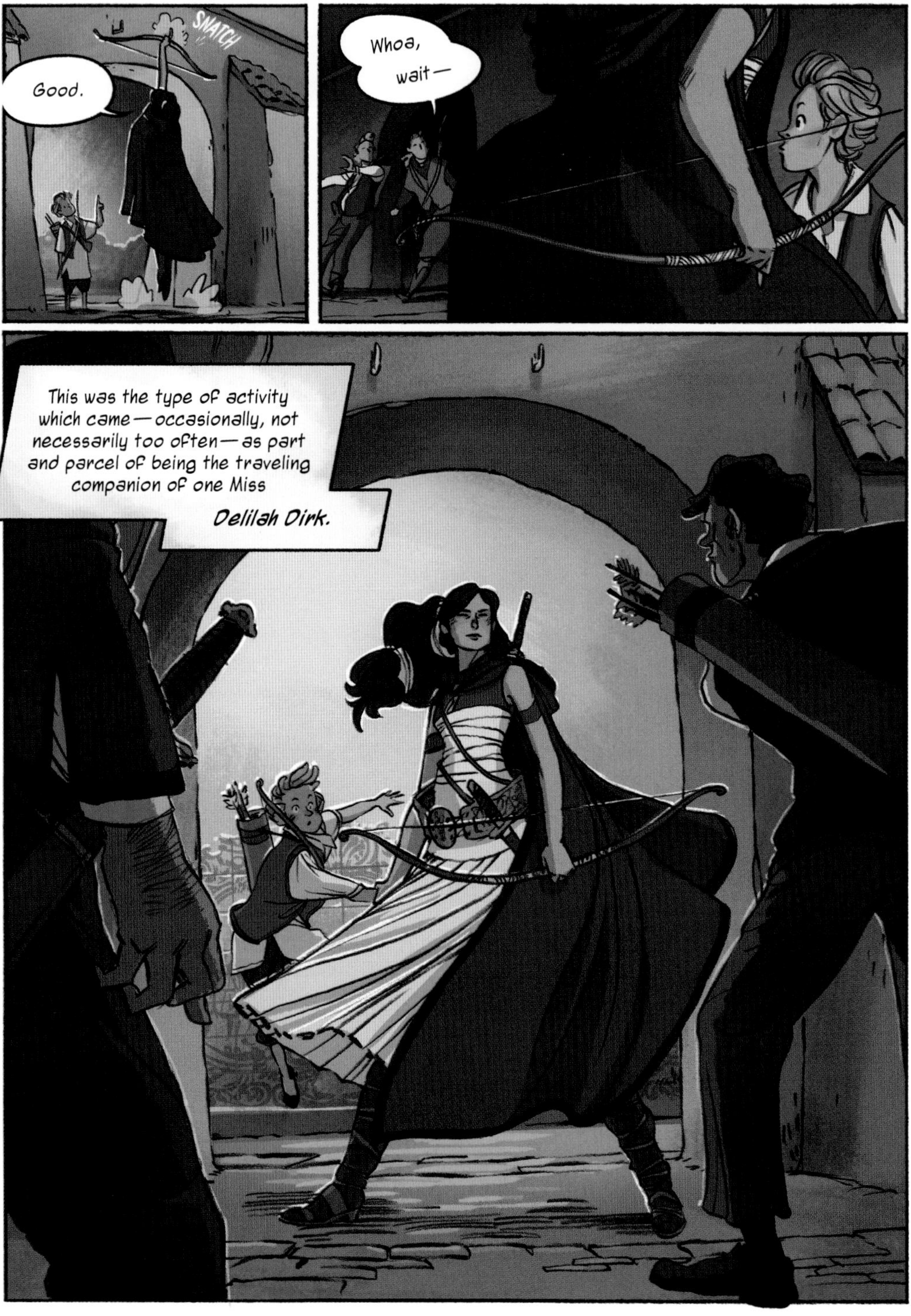
SNATCH
Good.
Whoa, wait—
This was the type of activity which came—occasionally, not necessarily too often—as part and parcel of being the traveling companion of one Miss
Delilah Dirk.

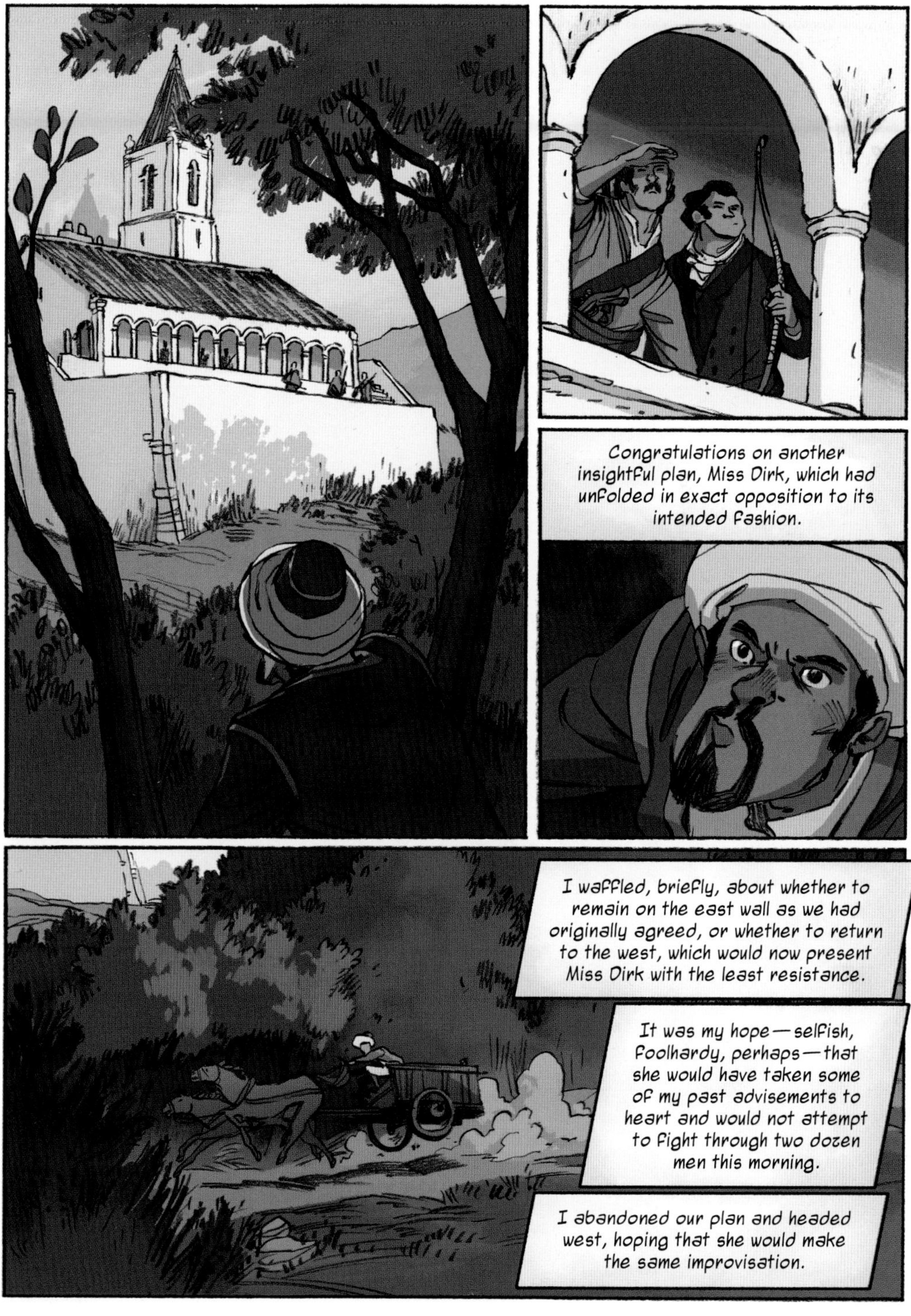
Congratulations on another insightful plan, Miss Dirk, which had unfolded in exact opposition to its intended fashion.
I waffled, briefly, about whether to remain on the east wall as we had originally agreed, or whether to return to the west, which would now present Miss Dirk with the least resistance.
It was my hope—selfish, foolhardy, perhaps—that she would have taken some of my past advisements to heart and would not attempt to fight through two dozen men this morning.
I abandoned our plan and headed west, hoping that she would make the same improvisation.

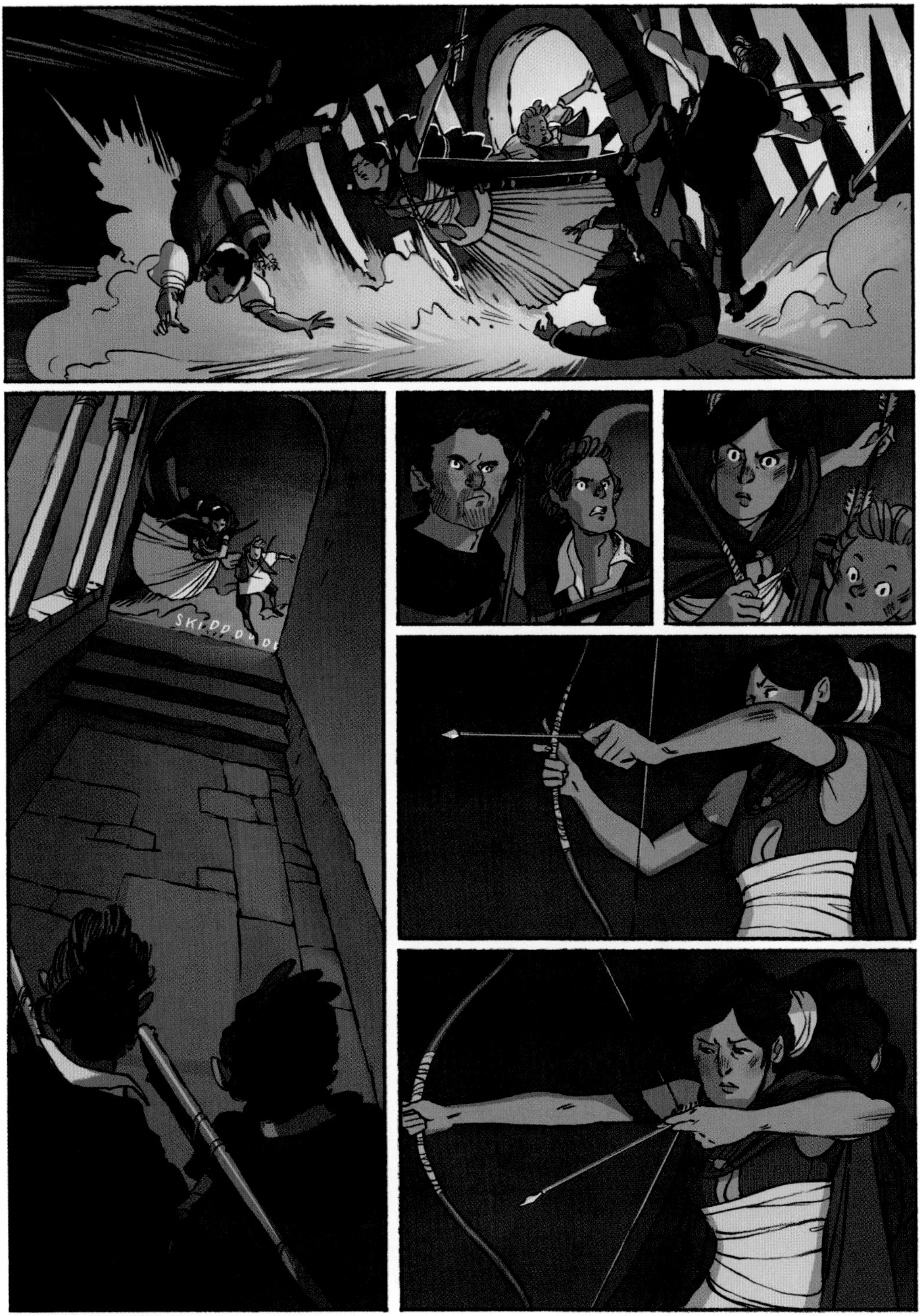
SKIDDOODDE

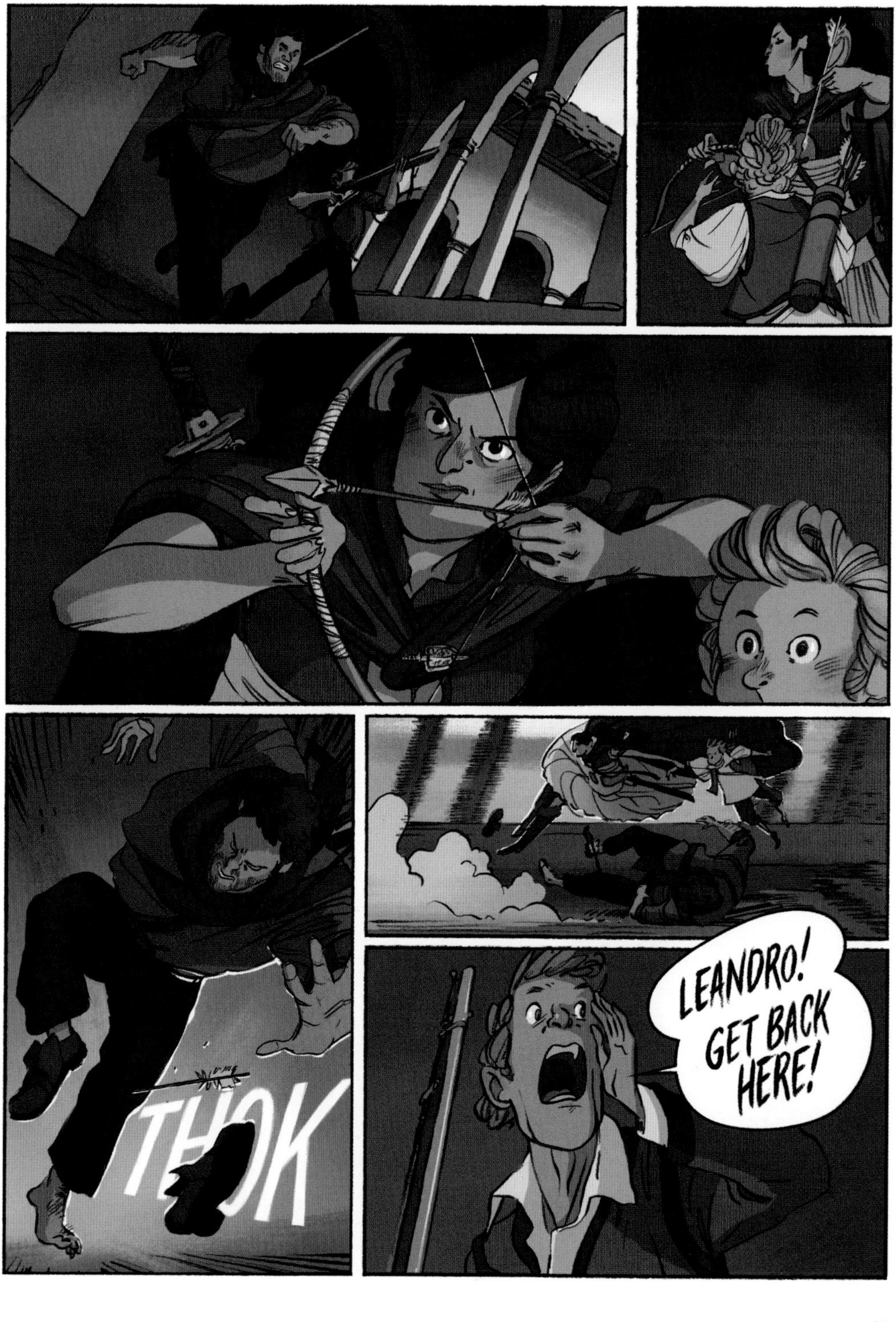
THOK
LEANDRO! GET BACK HERE!

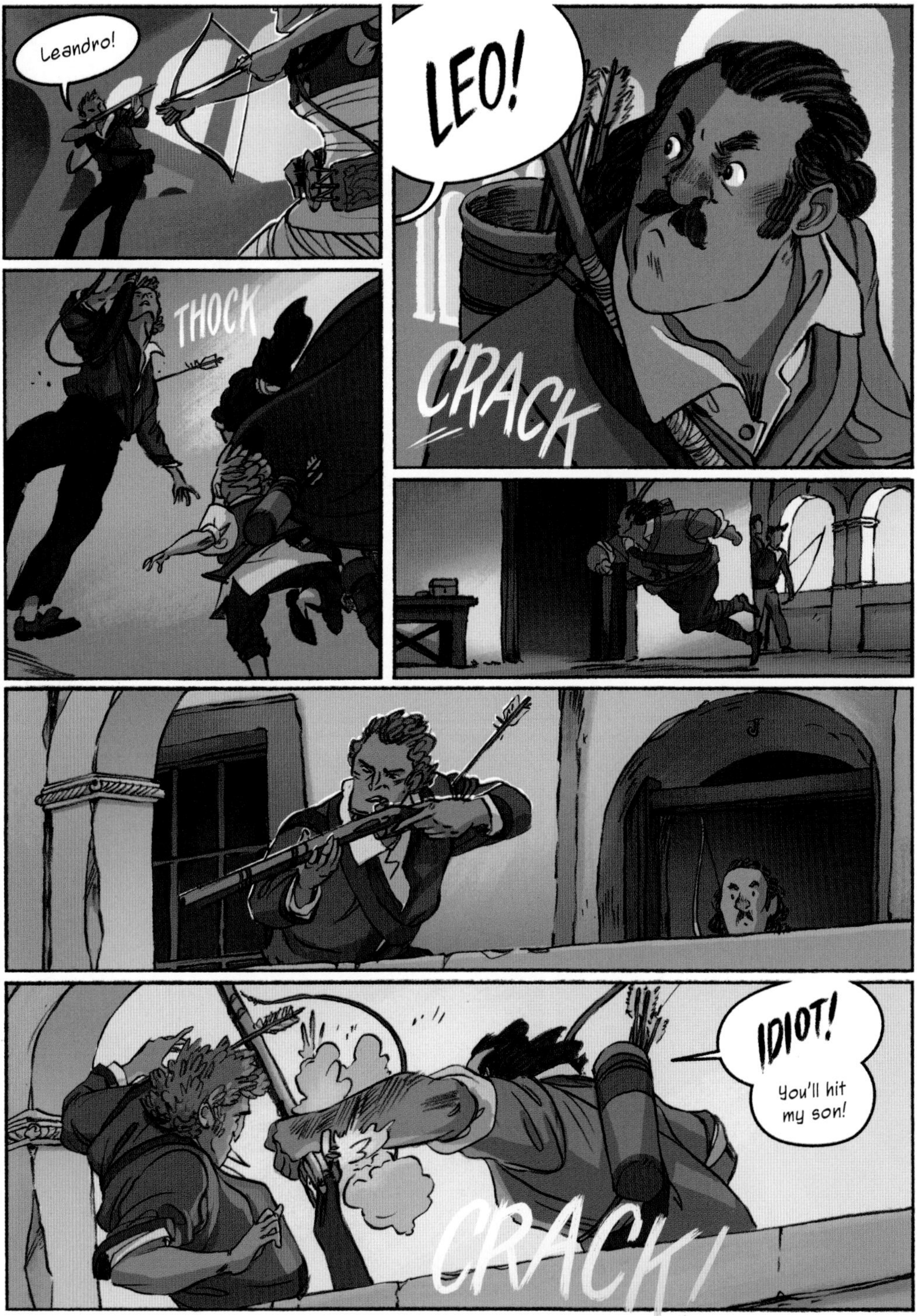
Leandro!
LEO!
CRACK
THOCK
IDIOT!
You'll hit my son!
CRACK!

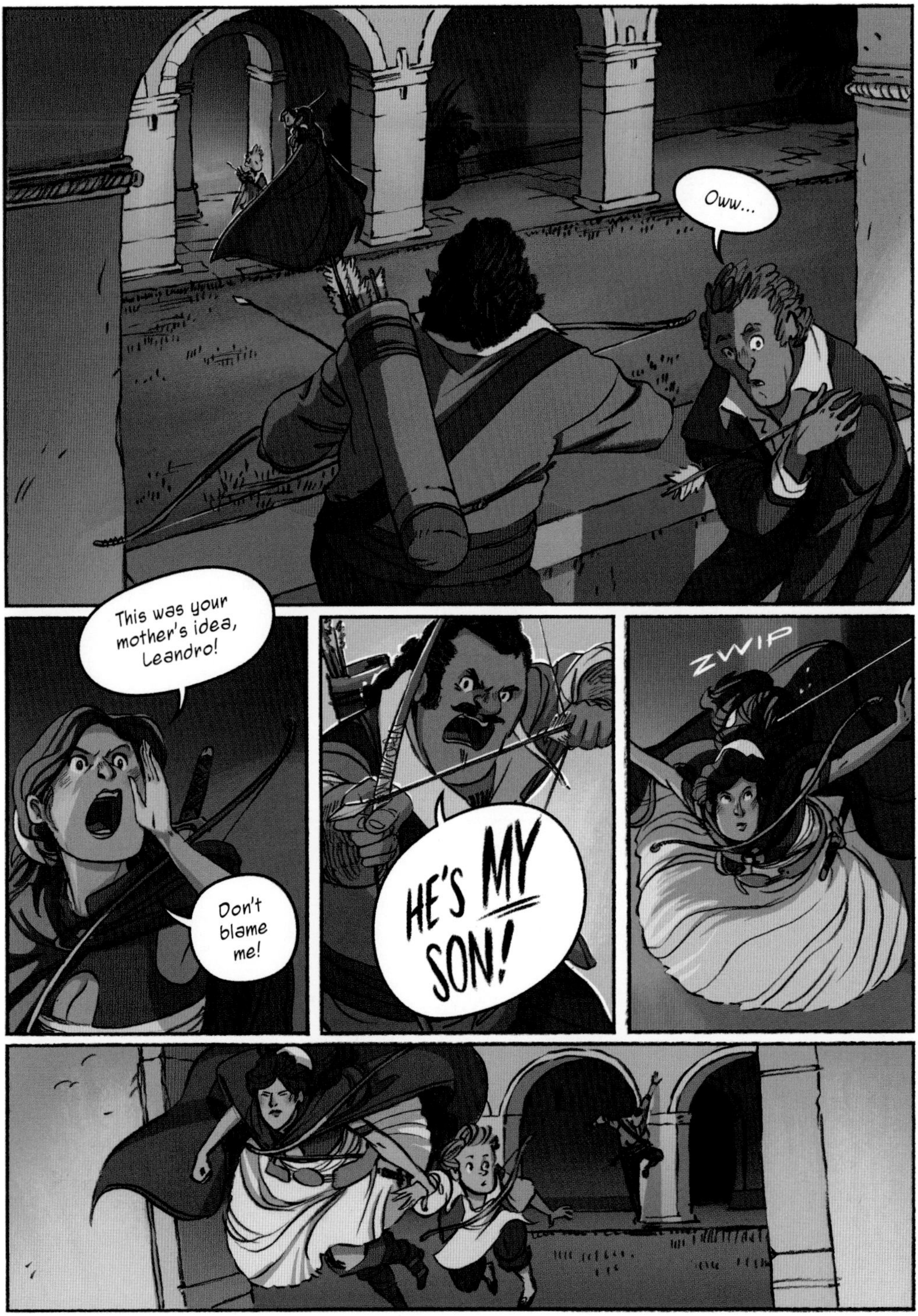
Oww...
This was your mother's idea, Leandro!
Don't blame me!
HE'S MY SON!
ZWIP

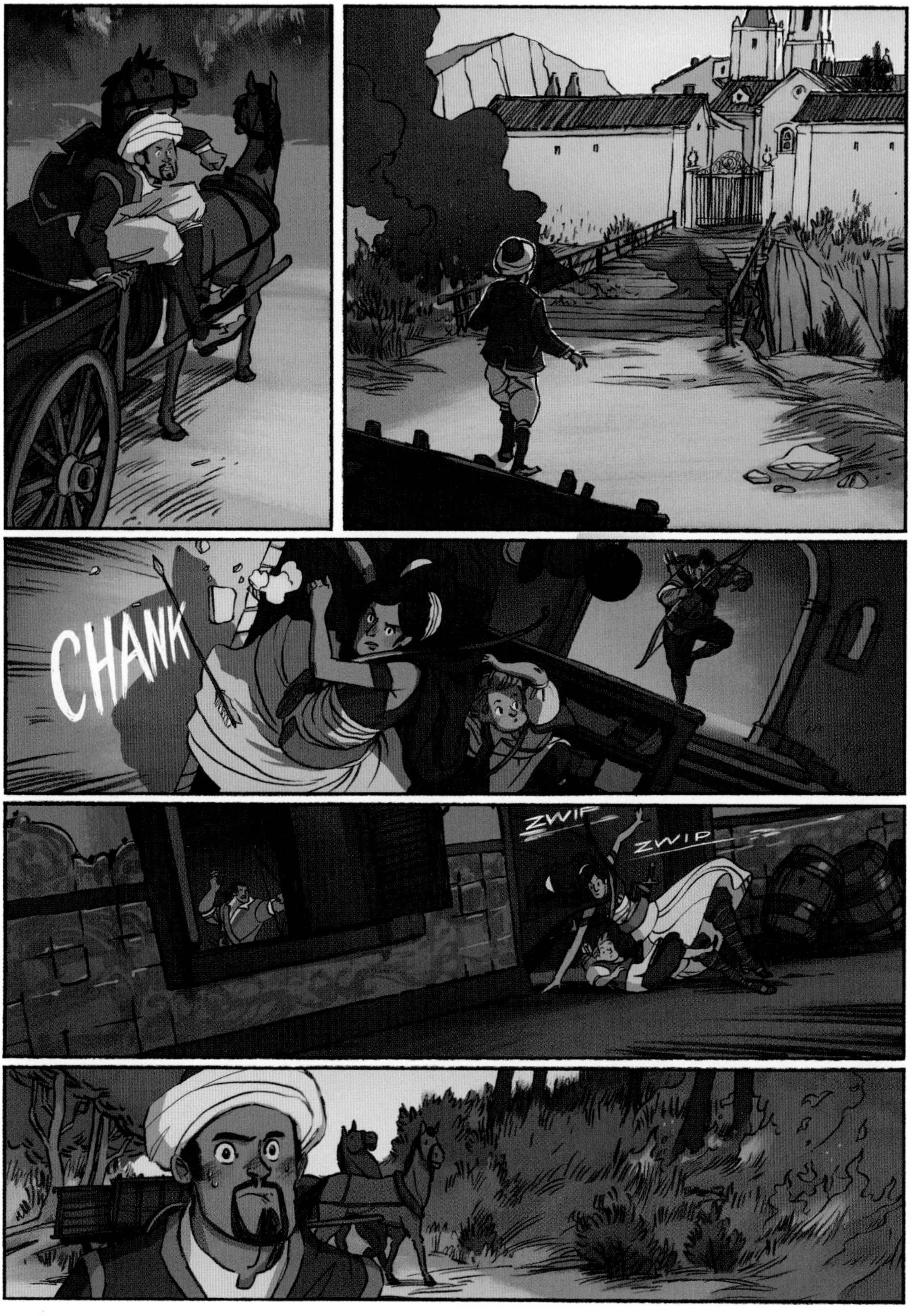
CHANK
ZWIP
ZWIP

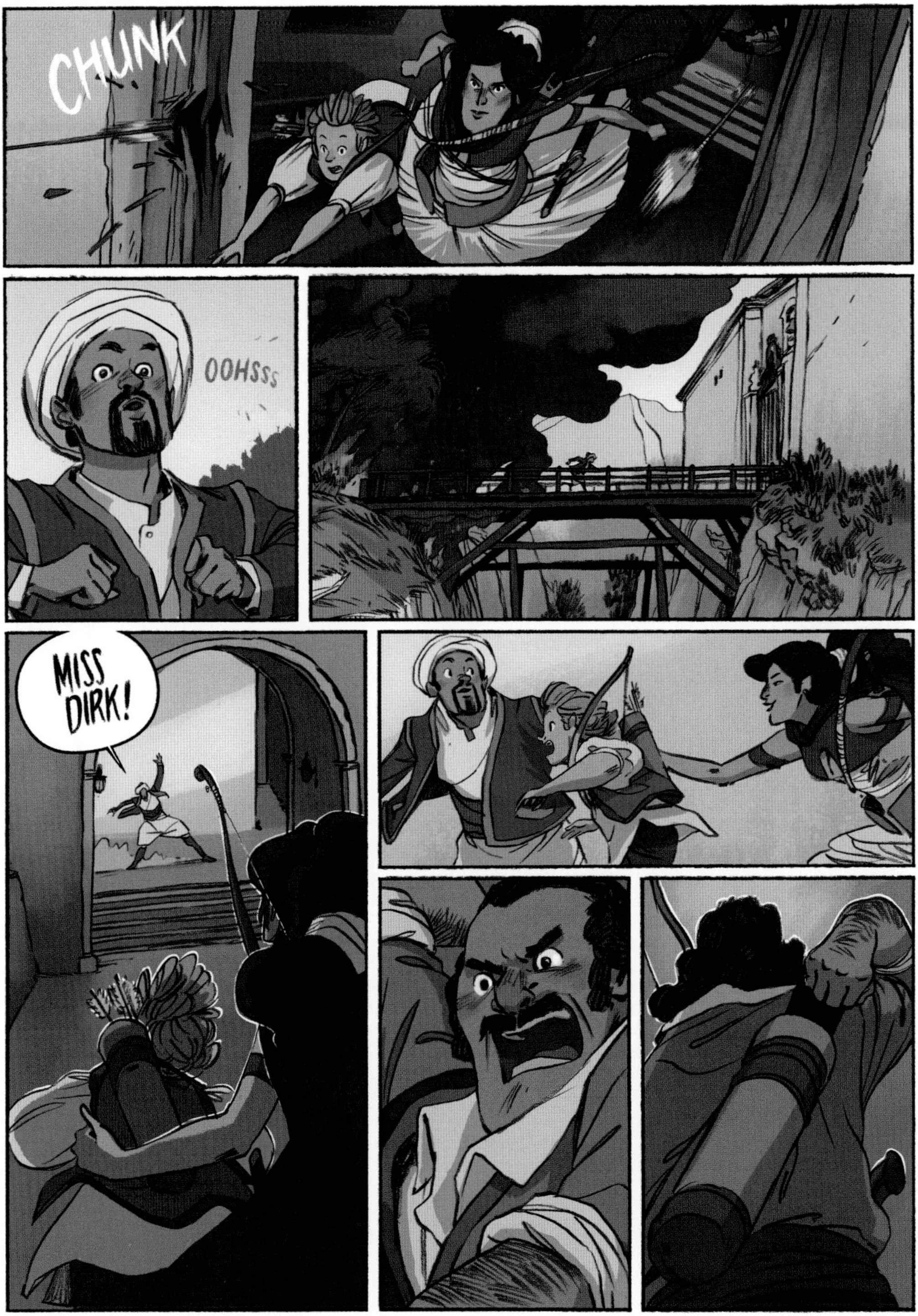
CHUNK
OOHSSS
MISS DIRK!

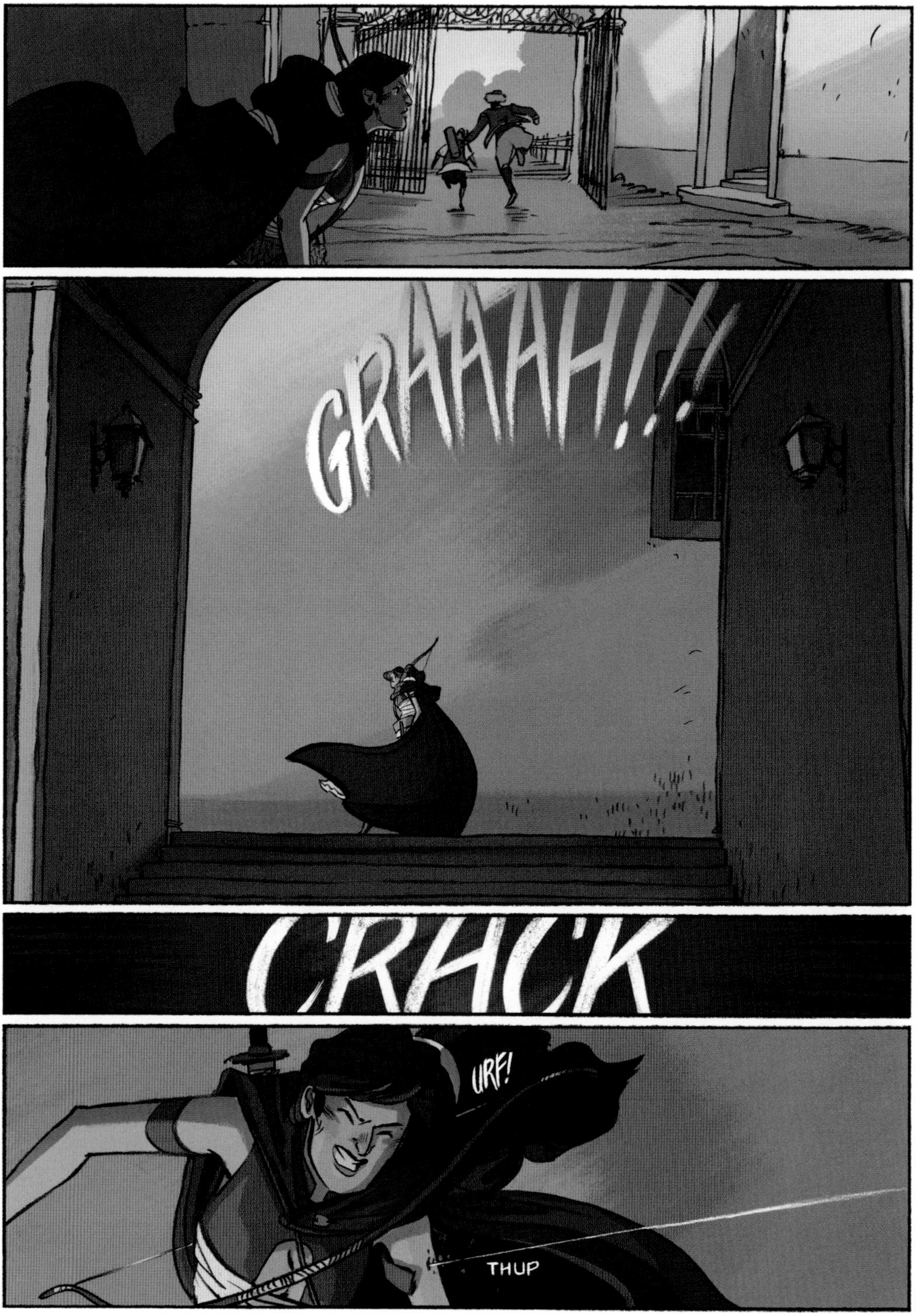
GRAAAH!!!
CRACK
URF!
THUP

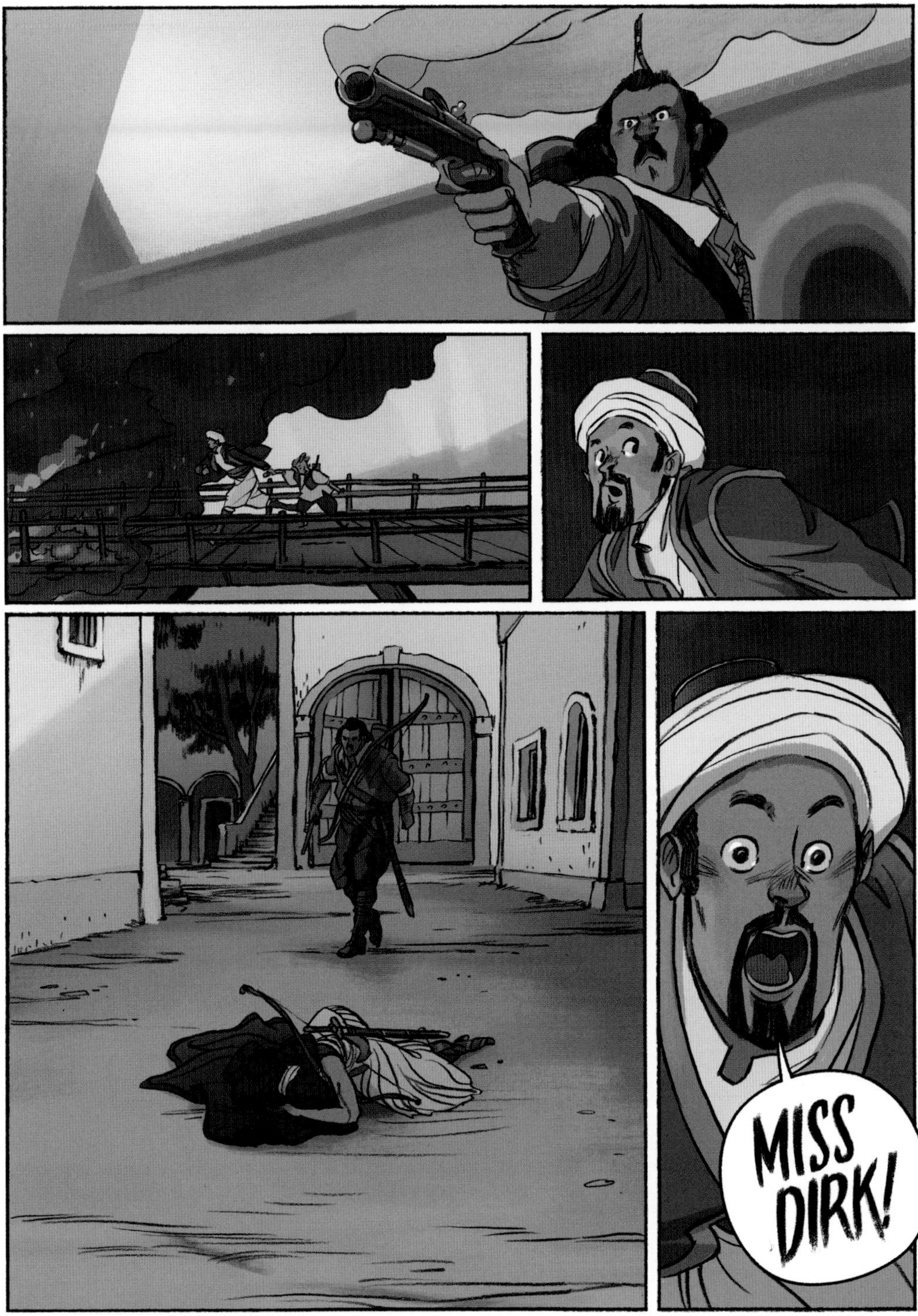
MISS DIRK!

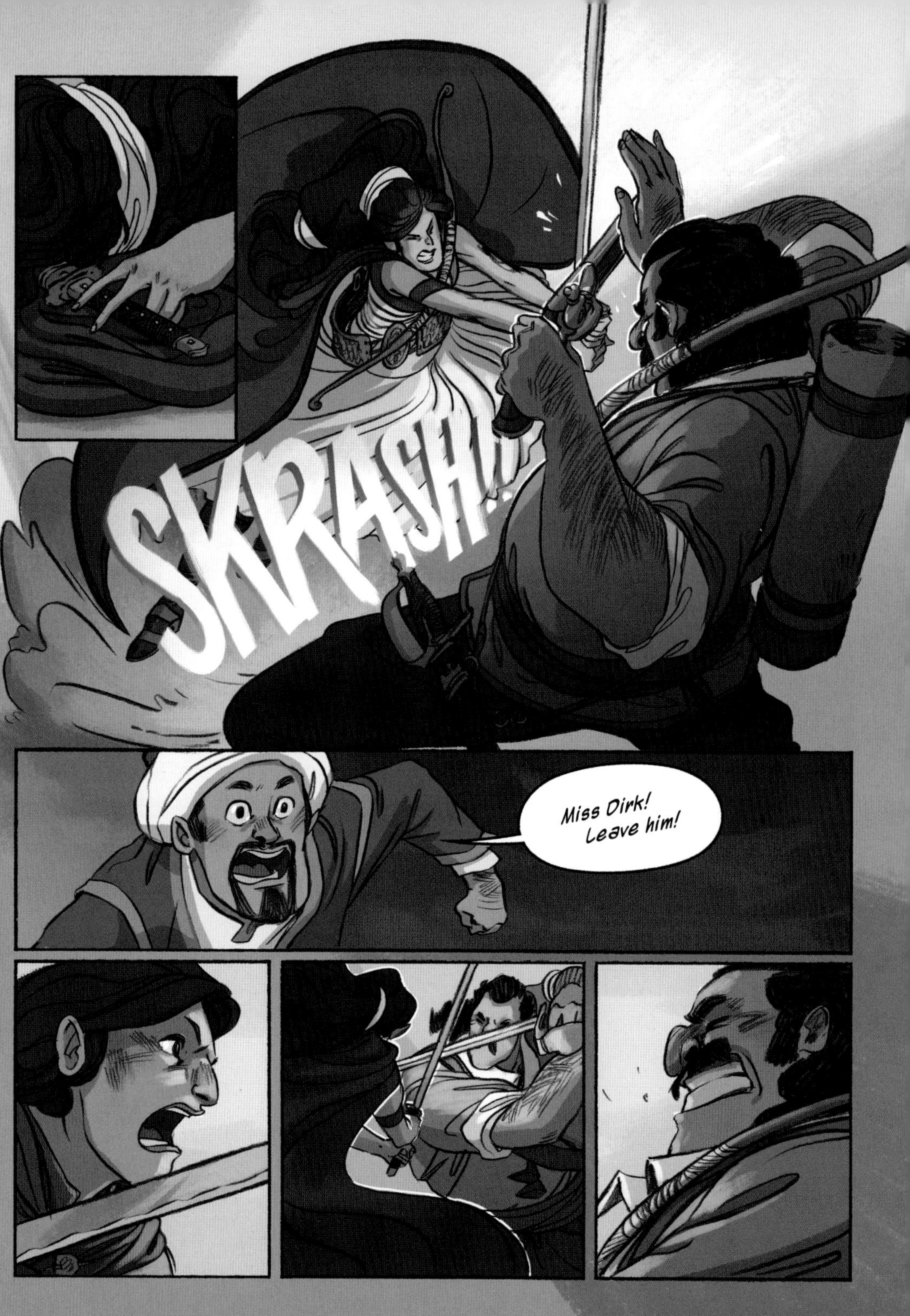
SKRASH!!
Miss Dirk! Leave him!

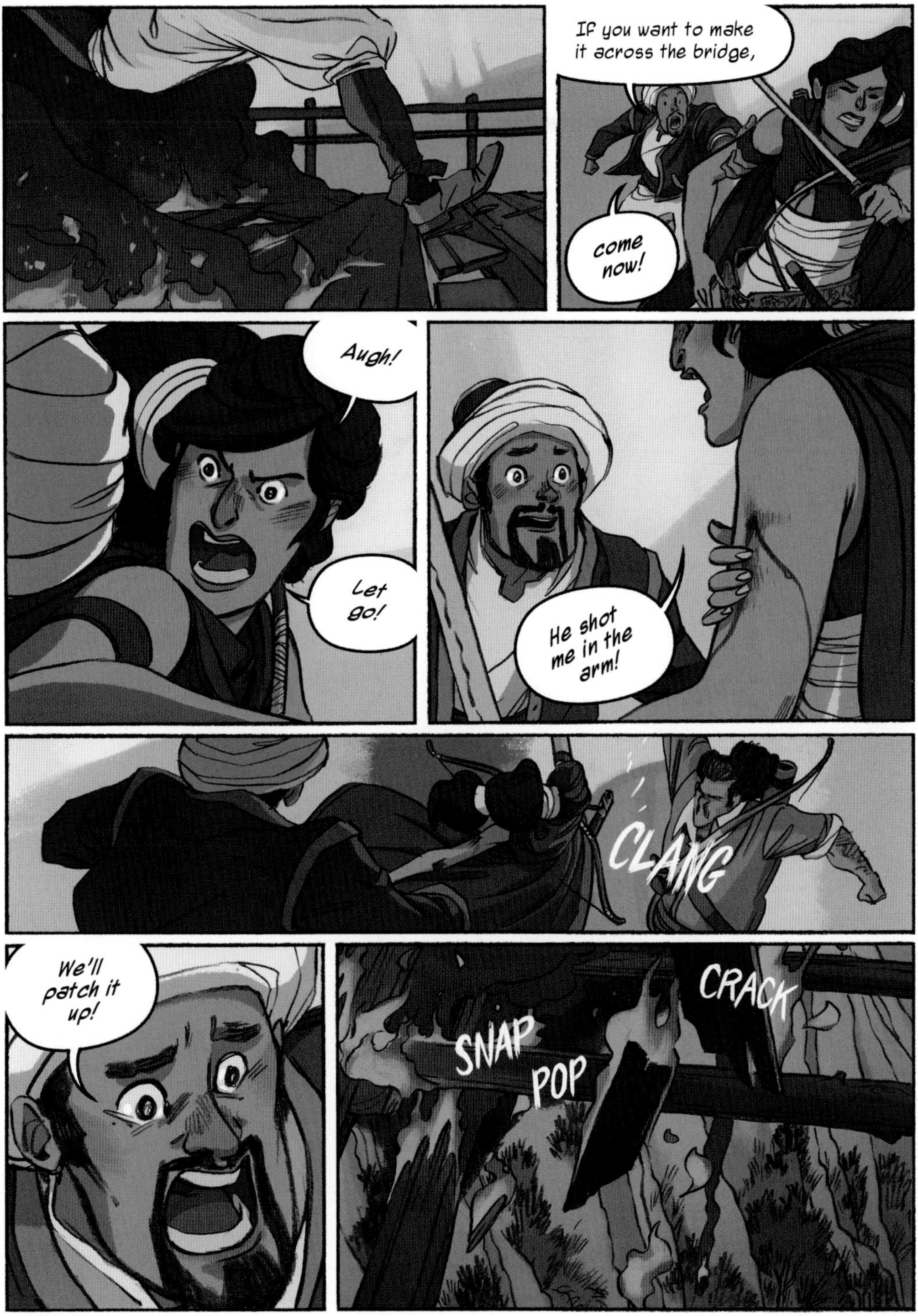

If you want to make it across the bridge,
come now!
Augh!
Let go!
He shot me in the arm!
CLANG
We'll patch it up!
CRACK
SNAP
POP

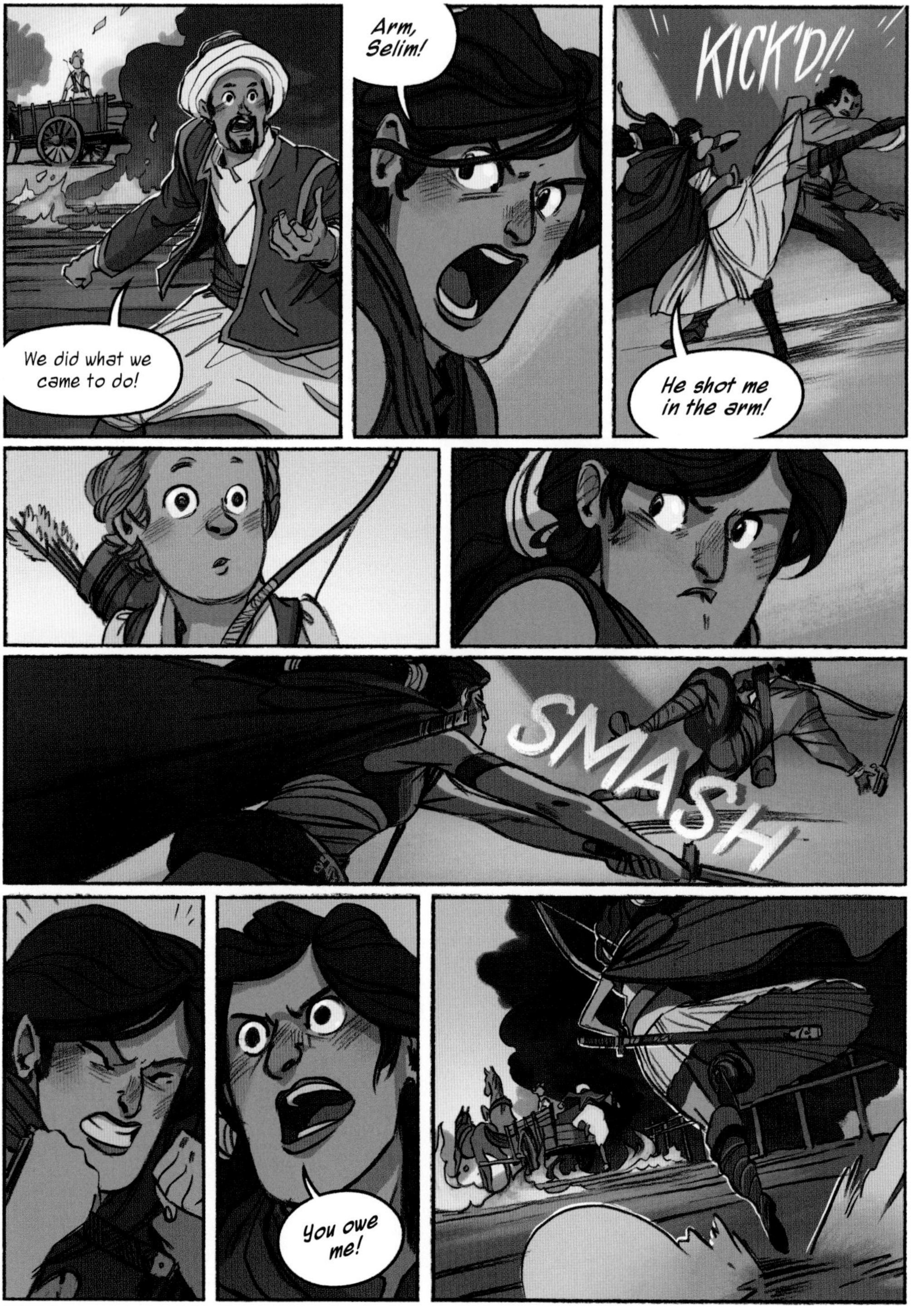
We did what we came to do!
Arm, Selim!
KICK'D!!
He shot me in the arm!
SMASH
You owe me!

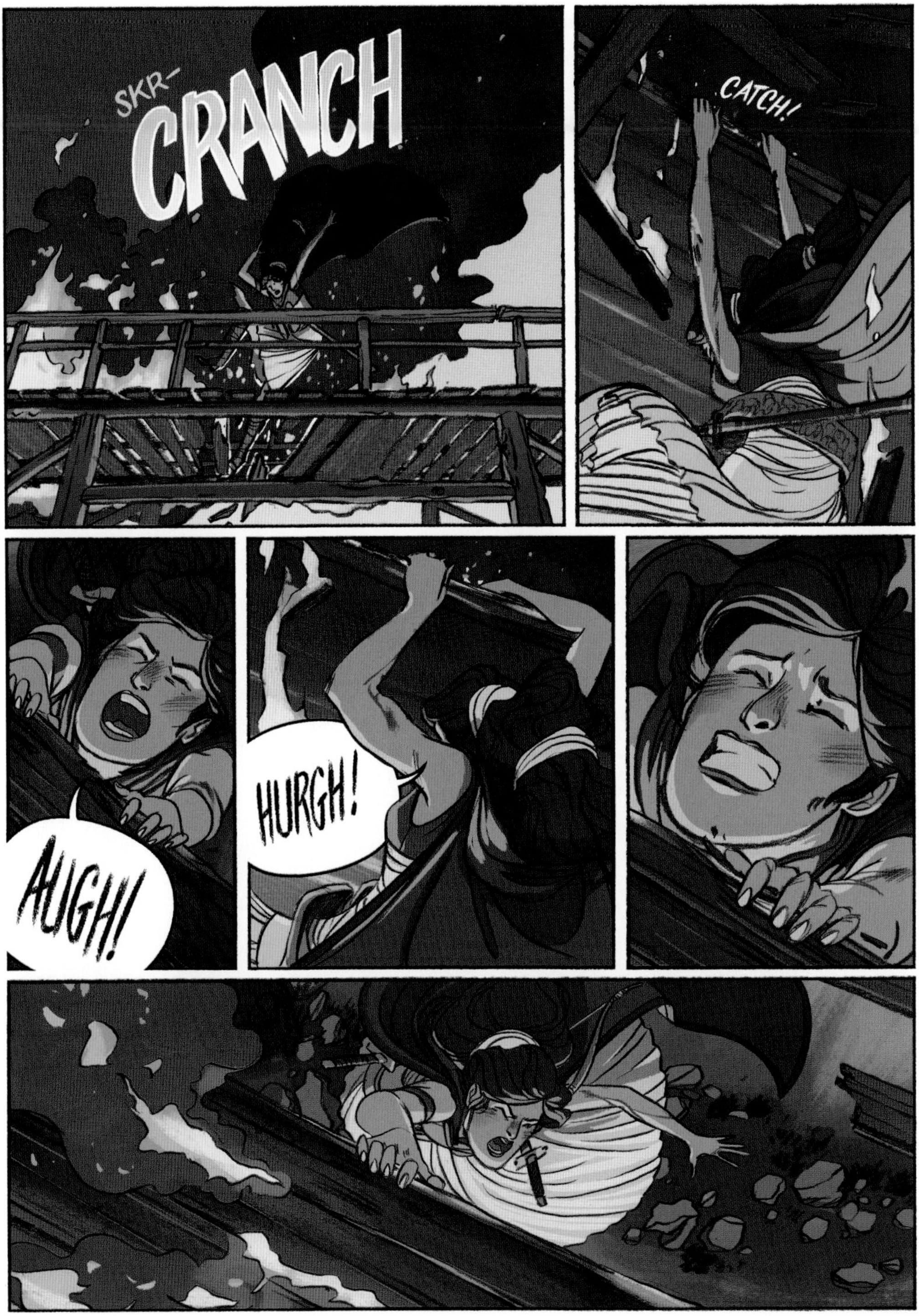
SKR-
CRANCH
CATCH!
AUGH!
HURGH!

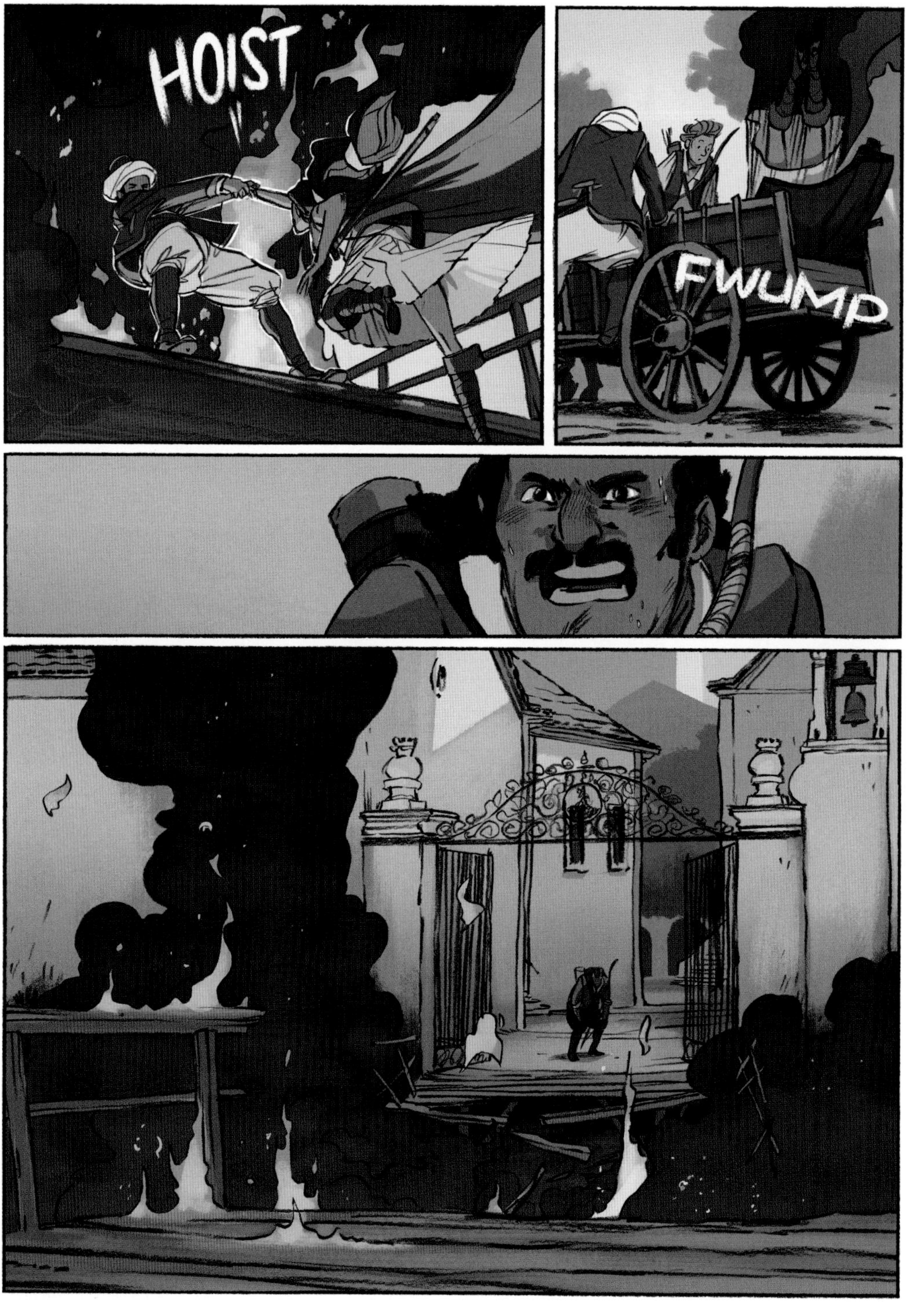
HOIST
FWUMP

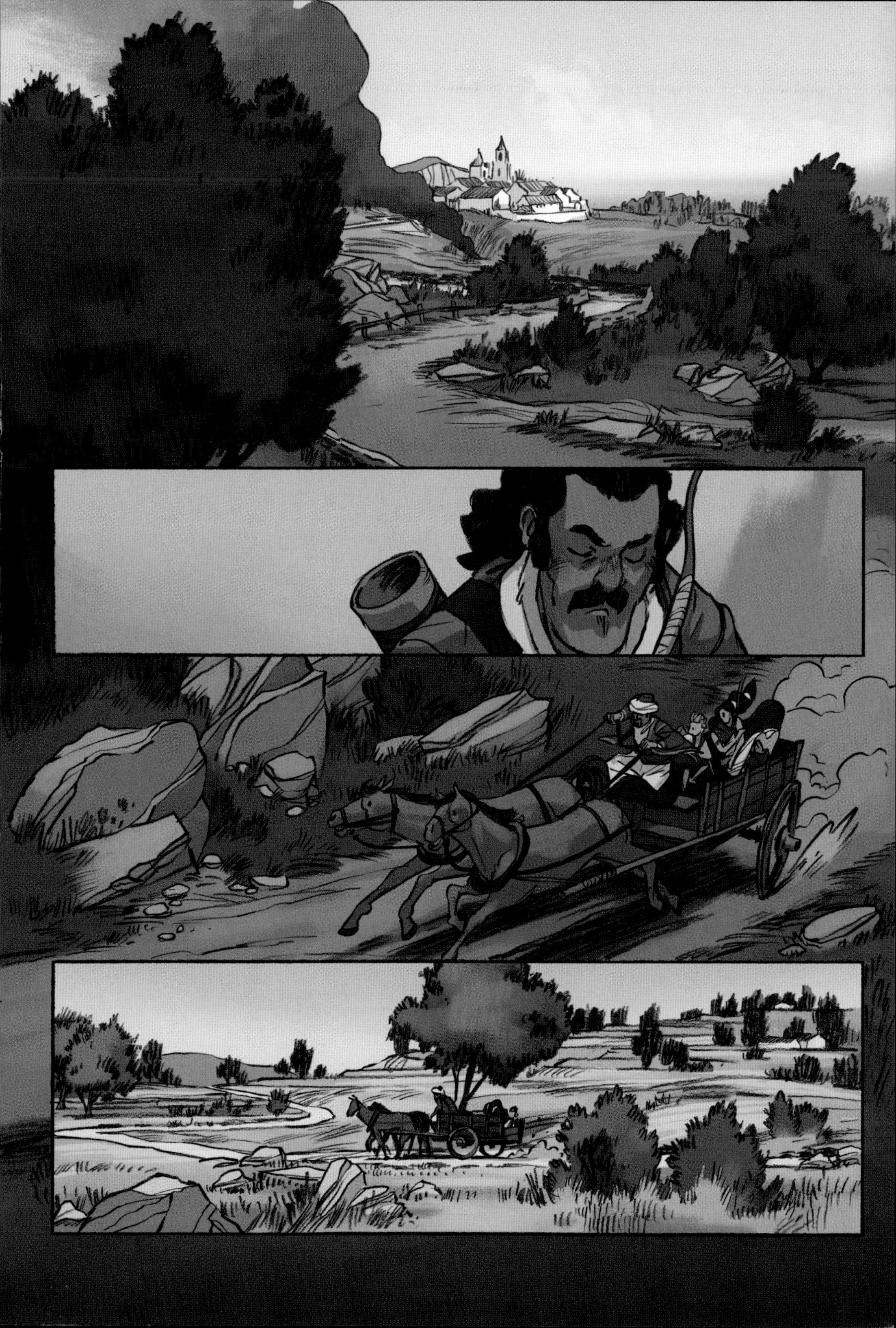

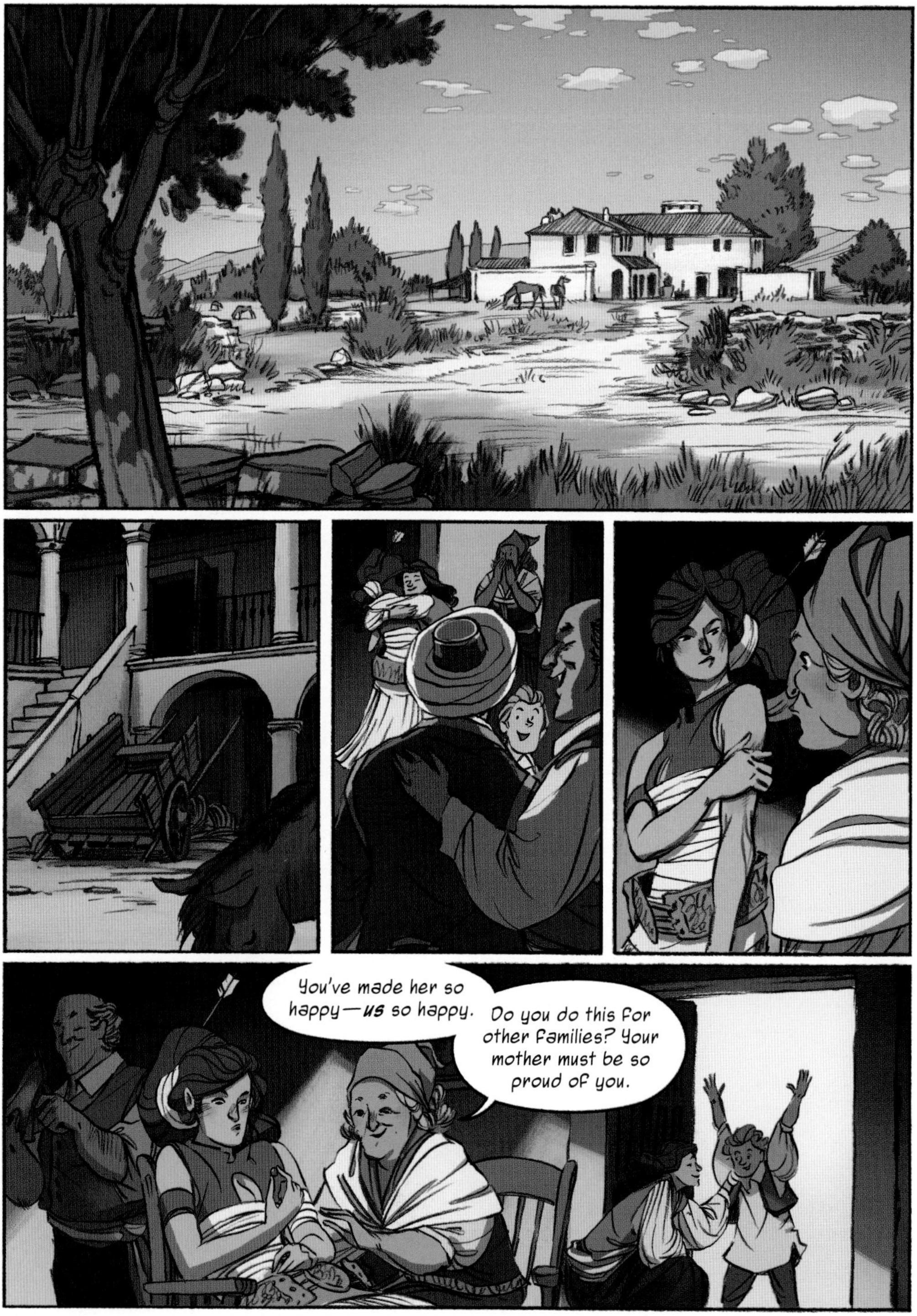
You've made her so happy—*us* so happy.
Do you do this for other families? Your mother must be so proud of you.

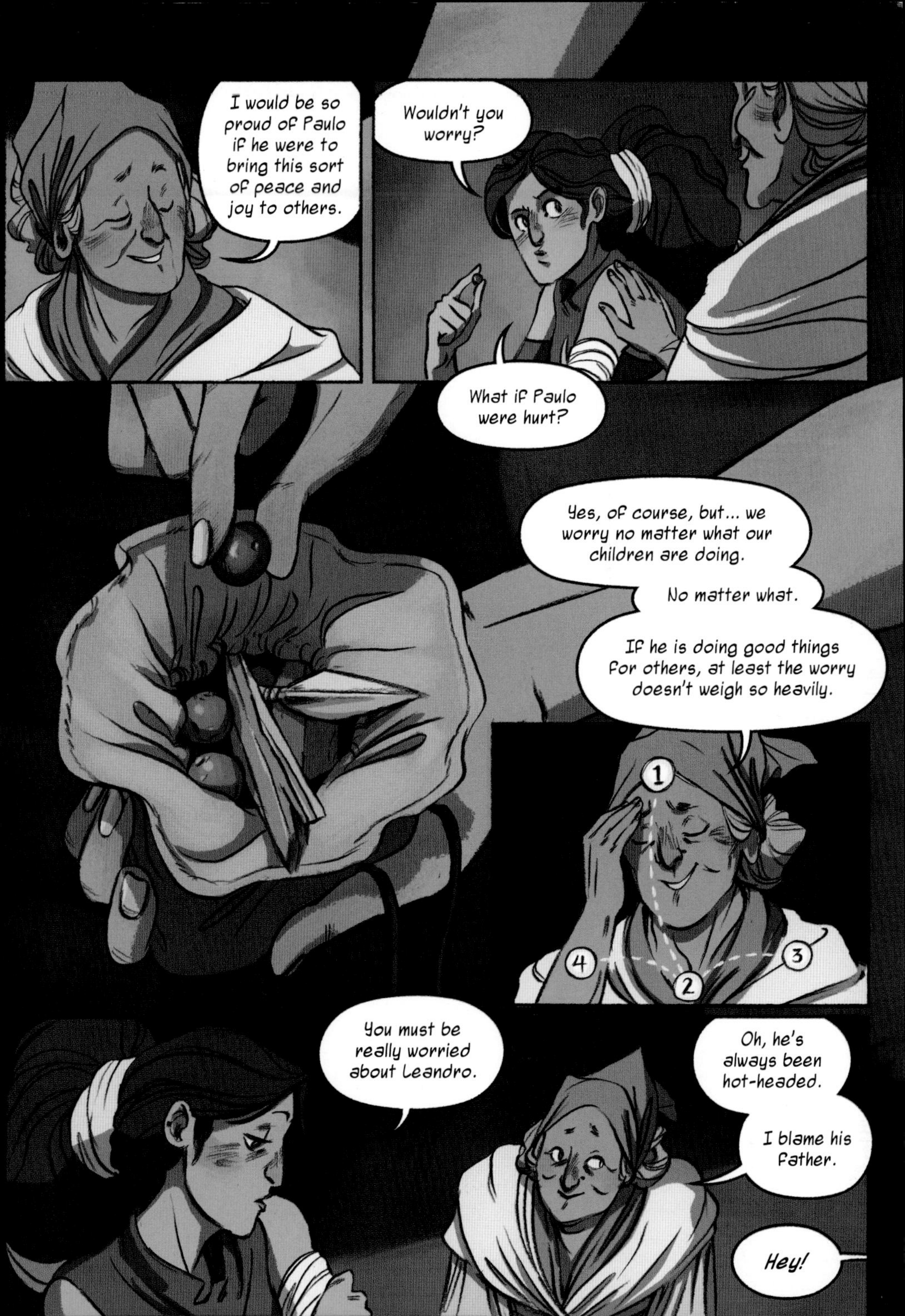

I would be so proud of Paulo if he were to bring this sort of peace and joy to others.
Wouldn't you worry?
What if Paulo were hurt?
Yes, of course, but... we worry no matter what our children are doing.
No matter what.
If he is doing good things for others, at least the worry doesn't weigh so heavily.
1
2
3
4
You must be really worried about Leandro.
Oh, he's always been hot-headed.
I blame his father.
Hey!

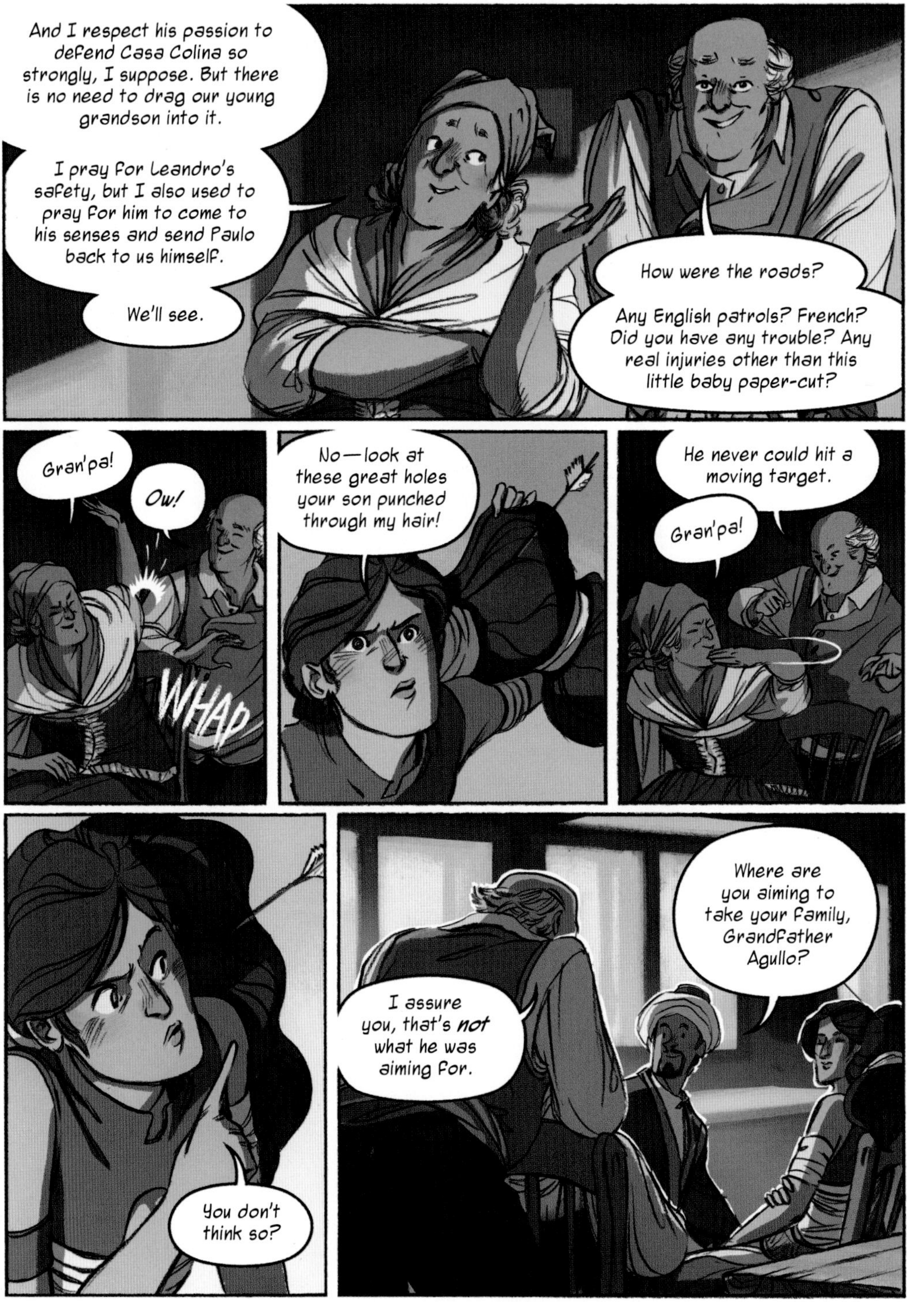
And I respect his passion to defend Casa Colina so strongly, I suppose. But there is no need to drag our young grandson into it.
I pray for Leandro's safety, but I also used to pray for him to come to his senses and send Paulo back to us himself.
We'll see.
How were the roads?
Any English patrols? French? Did you have any trouble? Any real injuries other than this little baby paper-cut?
Gran'pa!
Ow!
WHAP
No—look at these great holes your son punched through my hair!
He never could hit a moving target.
Gran'pa!
You don't think so?
I assure you, that's *not* what he was aiming for.
Where are you aiming to take your family, Grandfather Agullo?

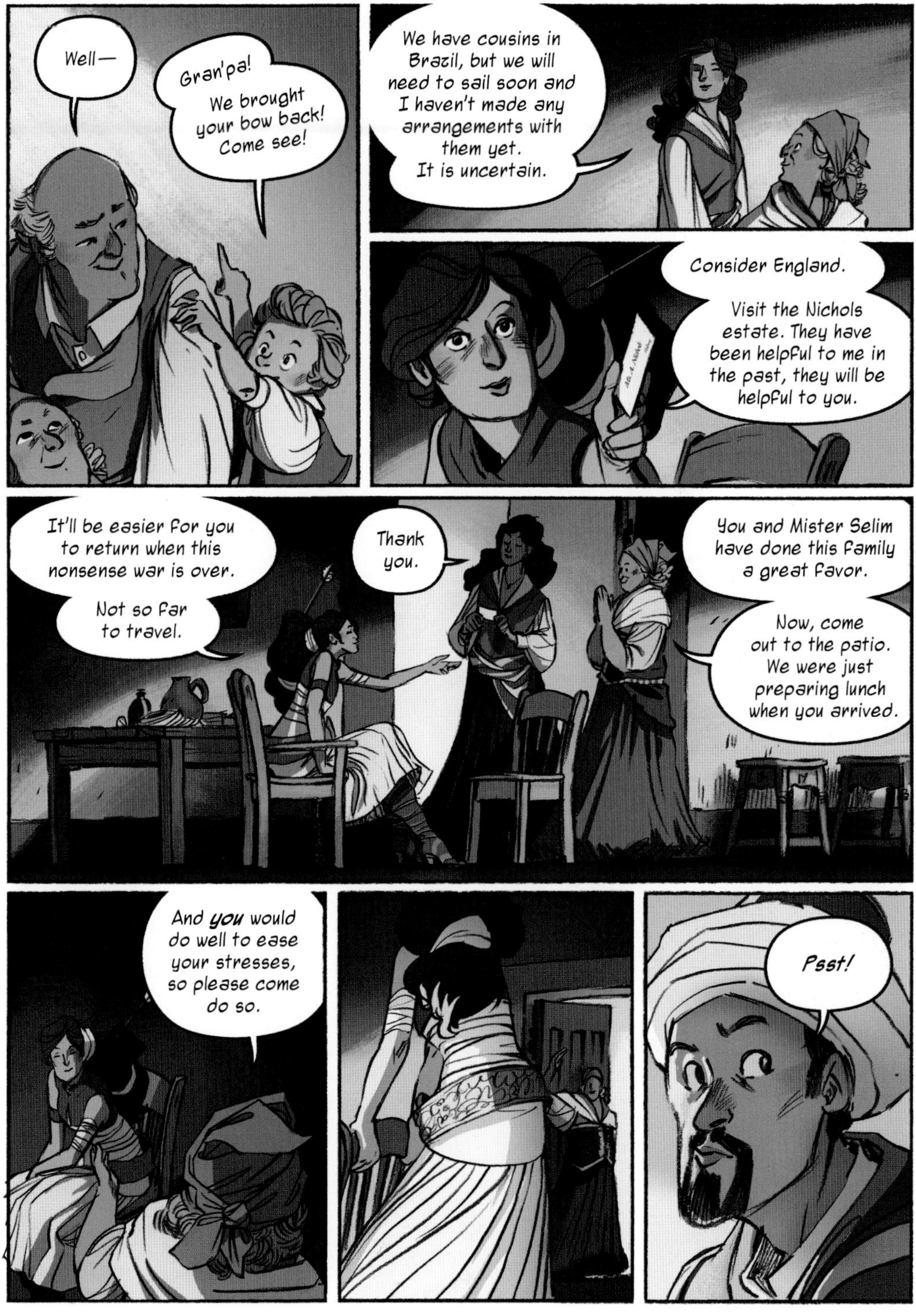
Well—
Gran'pa!
We brought your bow back! Come see!
We have cousins in Brazil, but we will need to sail soon and I haven't made any arrangements with them yet.
It is uncertain.
Consider England.
Visit the Nichols estate. They have been helpful to me in the past, they will be helpful to you.
It'll be easier for you to return when this nonsense war is over.
Not so far to travel.
Thank you.
You and Mister Selim have done this family a great favor.
Now, come out to the patio. We were just preparing lunch when you arrived.
And *you* would do well to ease your stresses, so please come do so.
*Psst!*

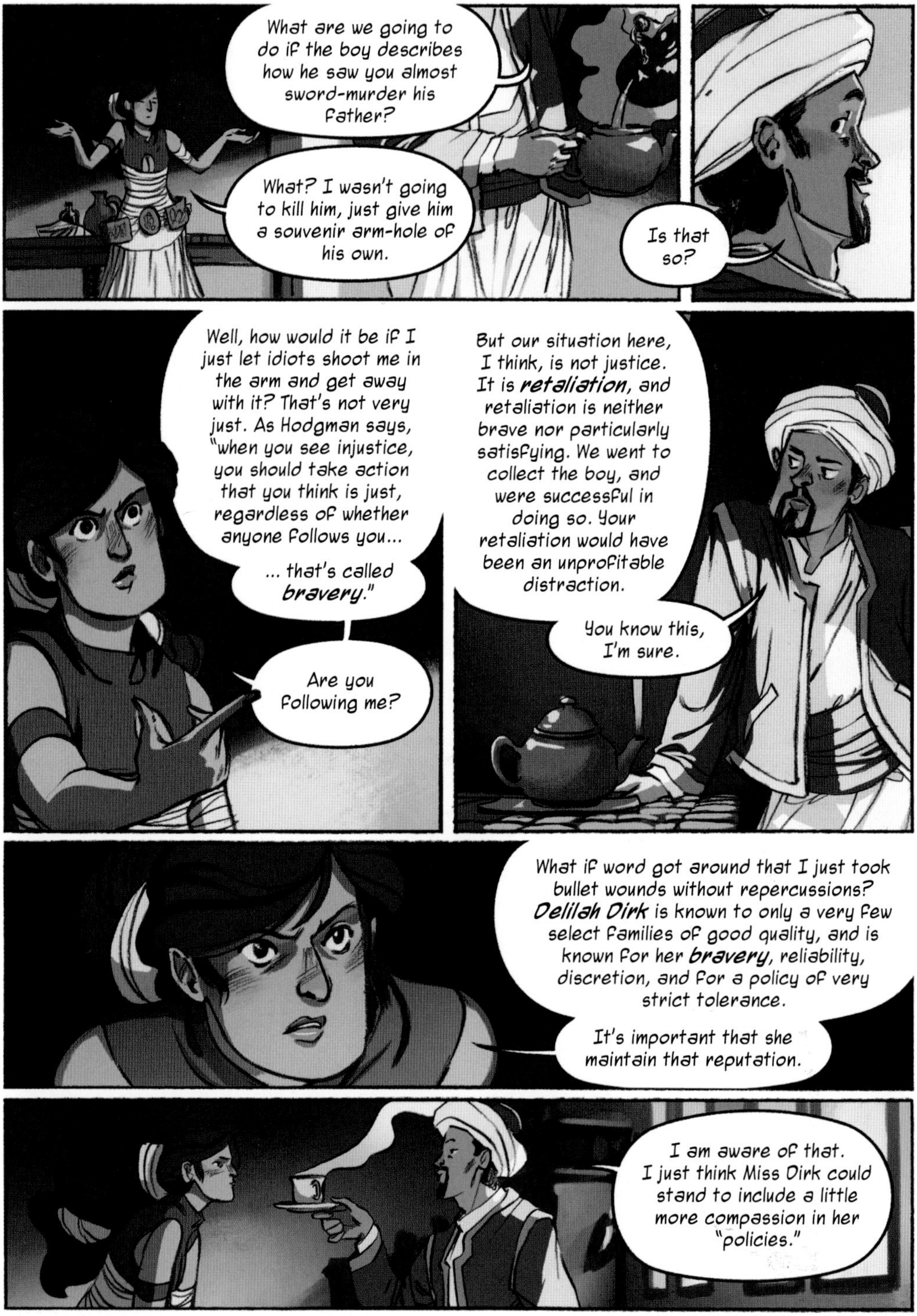
What are we going to do if the boy describes how he saw you almost sword-murder his father?
What? I wasn't going to kill him, just give him a souvenir arm-hole of his own.
Is that so?
Well, how would it be if I just let idiots shoot me in the arm and get away with it? That's not very just. As Hodgman says, "when you see injustice, you should take action that you think is just, regardless of whether anyone follows you...
... that's called *bravery*."
Are you following me?
But our situation here, I think, is not justice. It is *retaliation*, and retaliation is neither brave nor particularly satisfying. We went to collect the boy, and were successful in doing so. Your retaliation would have been an unprofitable distraction.
You know this, I'm sure.
What if word got around that I just took bullet wounds without repercussions? *Delilah Dirk* is known to only a very few select families of good quality, and is known for her *bravery*, reliability, discretion, and for a policy of very strict tolerance.
It's important that she maintain that reputation.
I am aware of that. I just think Miss Dirk could stand to include a little more compassion in her "policies."

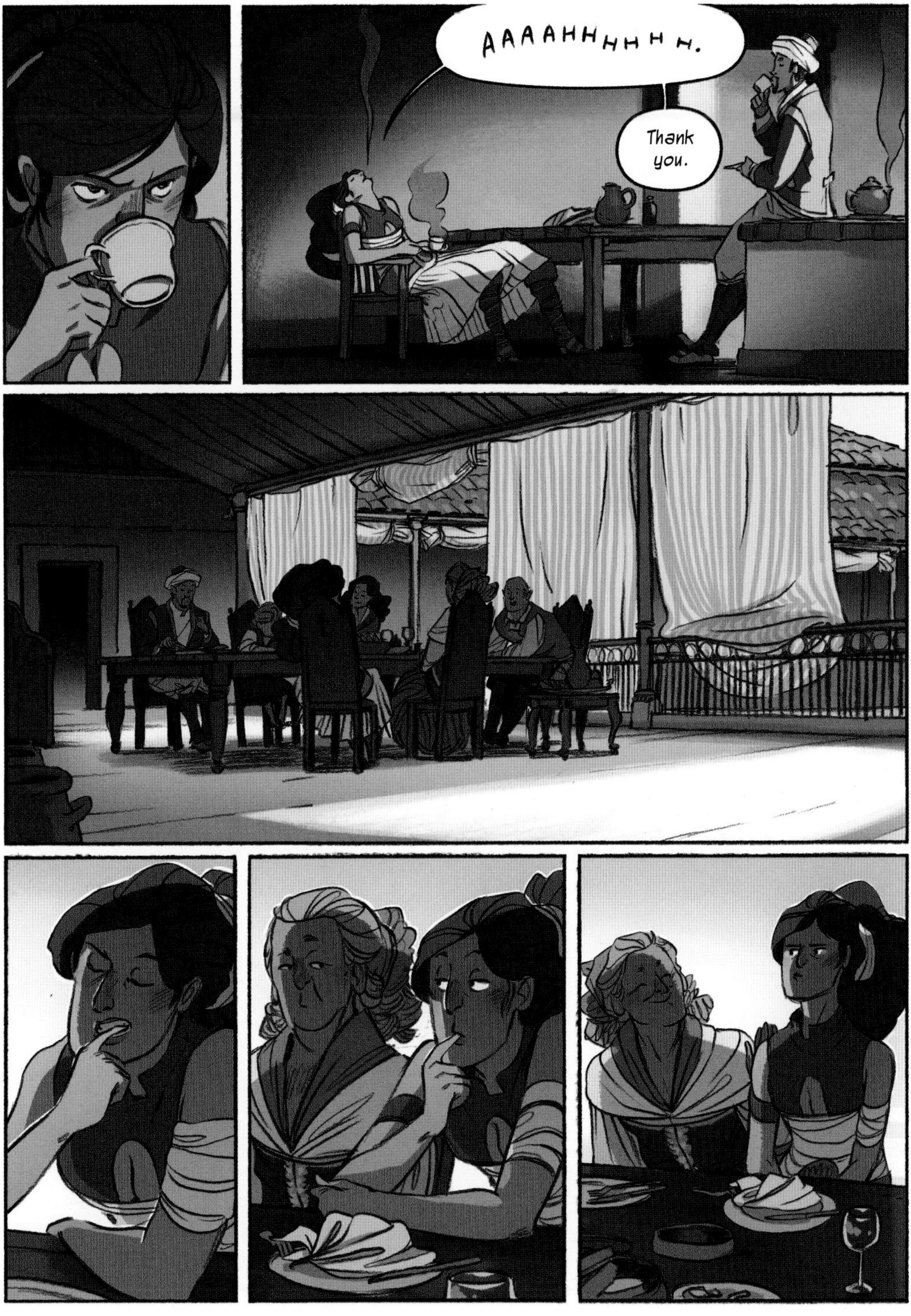
AAAAHHHHHH H.
Thank you.

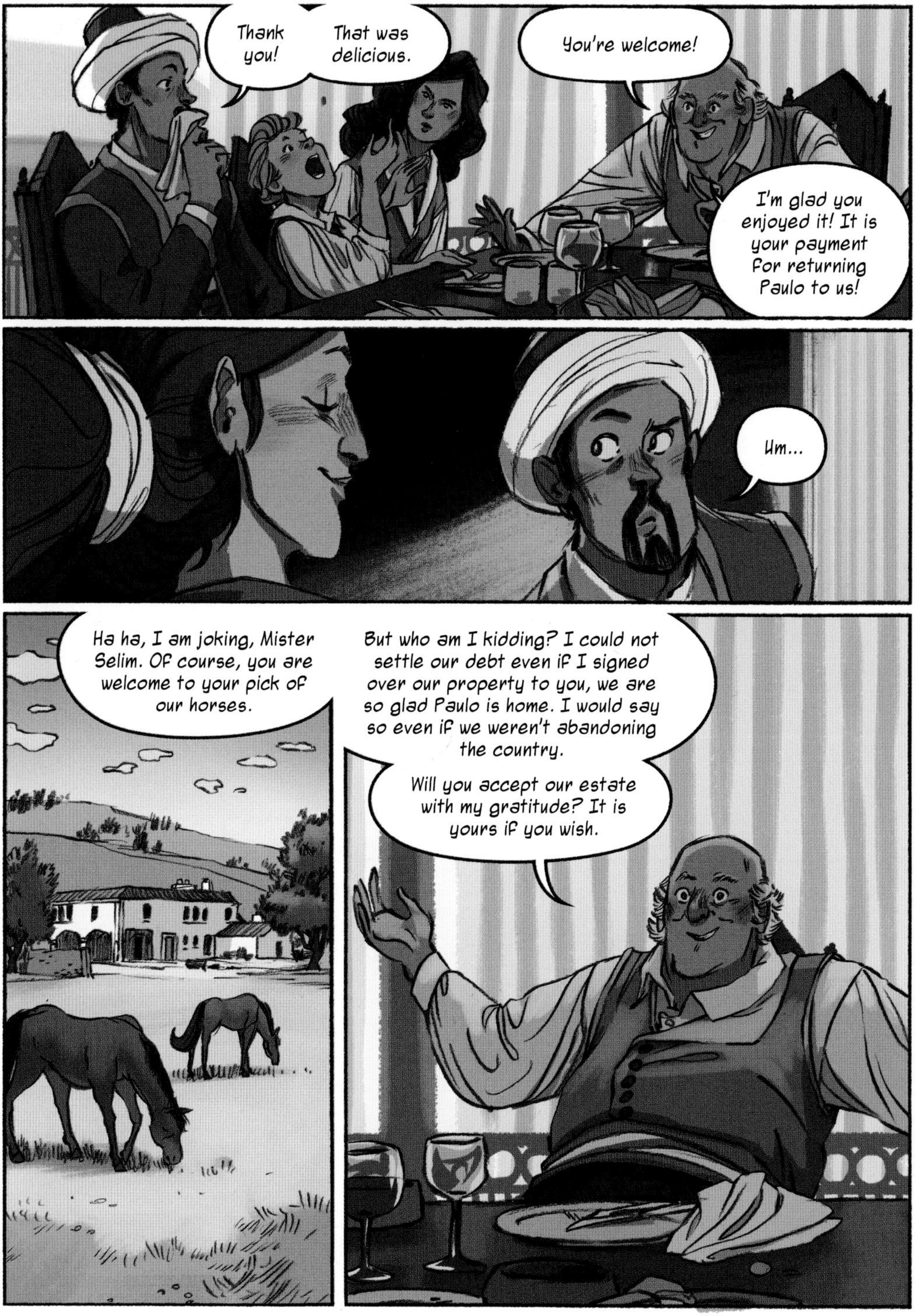
Thank you!
That was delicious.
You're welcome!
I'm glad you enjoyed it! It is your payment for returning Paulo to us!
Um...
Ha ha, I am joking, Mister Selim. Of course, you are welcome to your pick of our horses.
But who am I kidding? I could not settle our debt even if I signed over our property to you, we are so glad Paulo is home. I would say so even if we weren't abandoning the country.
Will you accept our estate with my gratitude? It is yours if you wish.

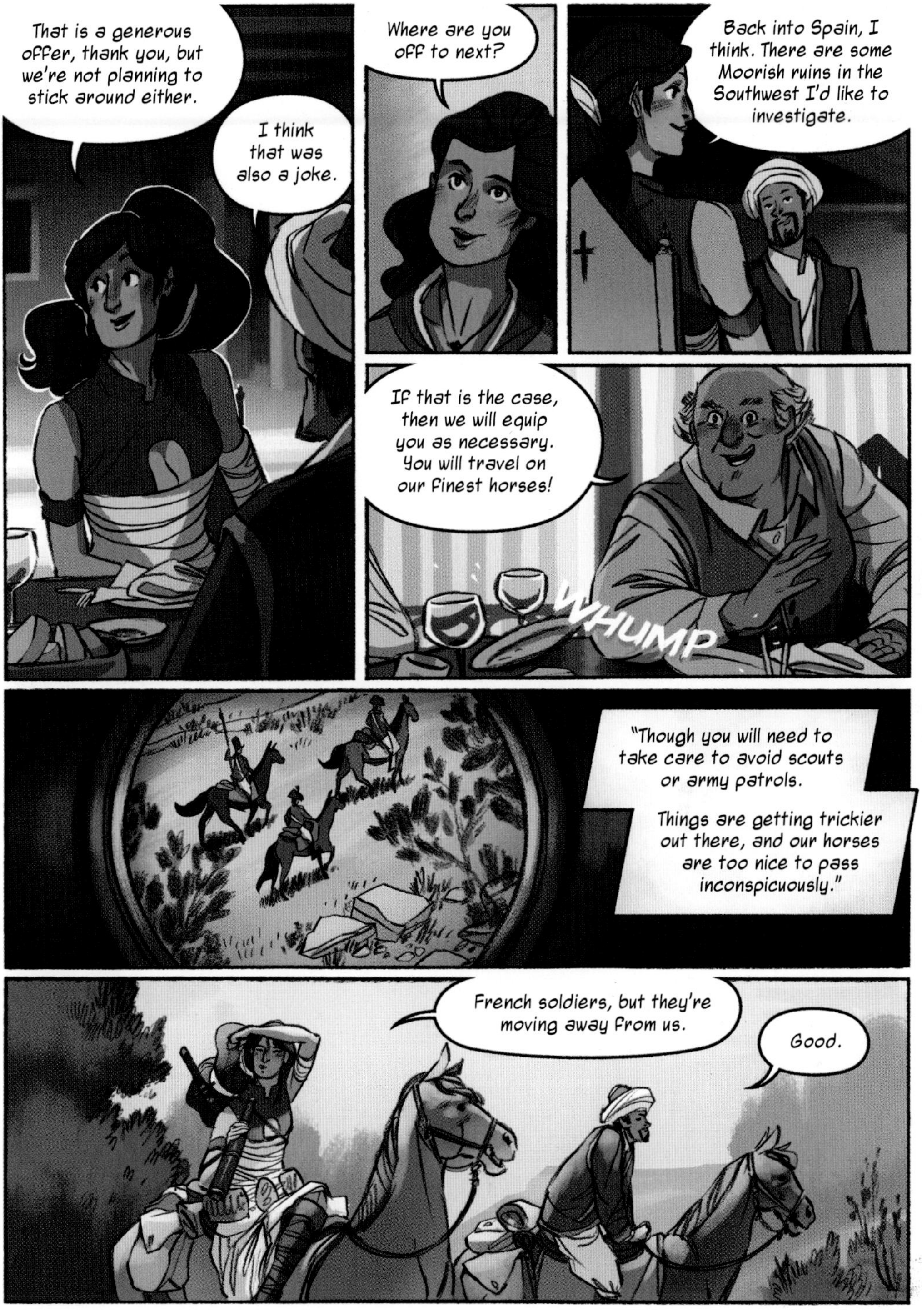
That is a generous offer, thank you, but we're not planning to stick around either.
I think that was also a joke.
Where are you off to next?
Back into Spain, I think. There are some Moorish ruins in the Southwest I'd like to investigate.
If that is the case, then we will equip you as necessary. You will travel on our finest horses!
WHUMP
"Though you will need to take care to avoid scouts or army patrols.
Things are getting trickier out there, and our horses are too nice to pass inconspicuously."
French soldiers, but they're moving away from us.
Good.

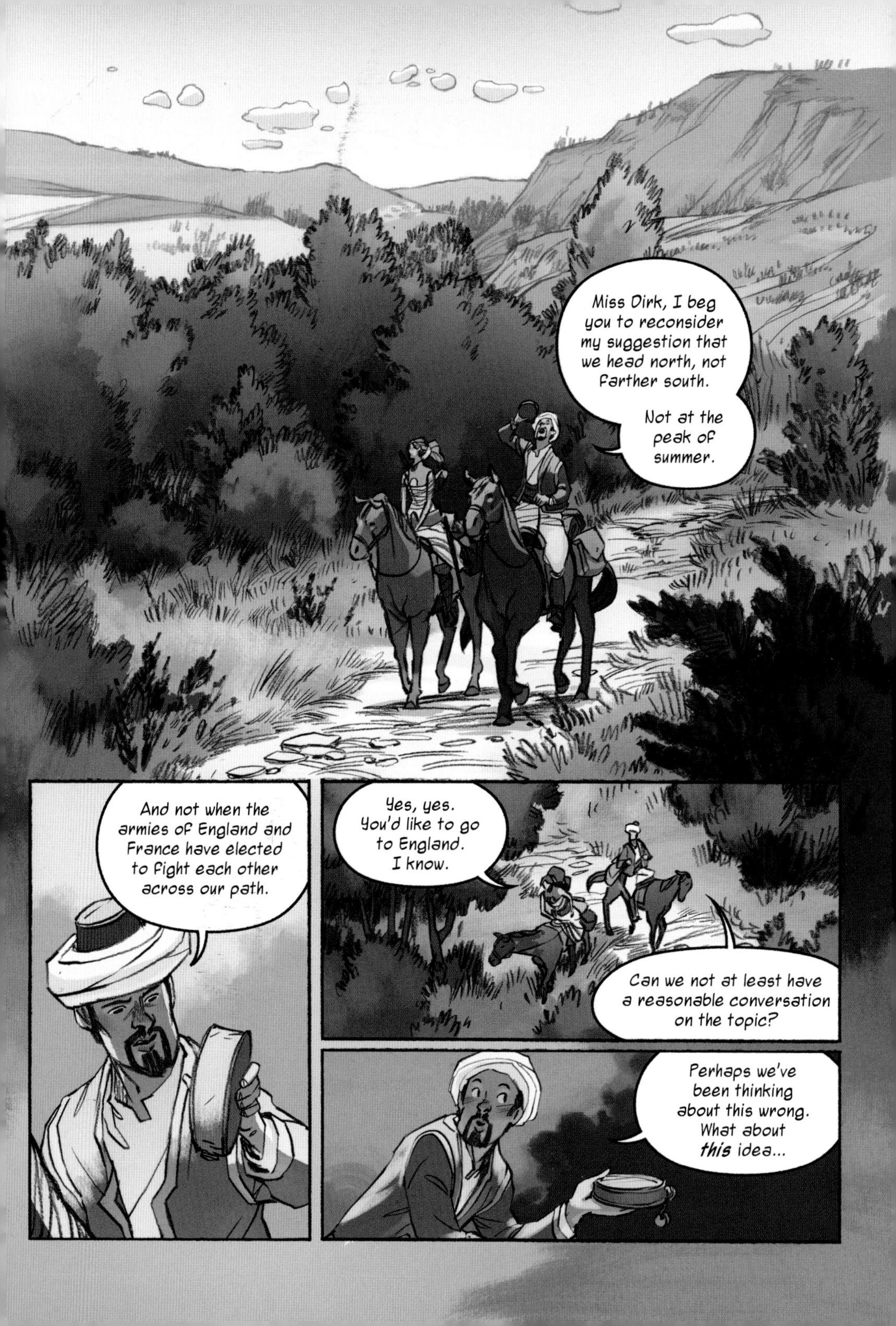
Miss Dirk, I beg you to reconsider my suggestion that we head north, not farther south.
Not at the peak of summer.
And not when the armies of England and France have elected to fight each other across our path.
Yes, yes. You'd like to go to England. I know.
Can we not at least have a reasonable conversation on the topic?
Perhaps we've been thinking about this wrong. What about *this* idea...

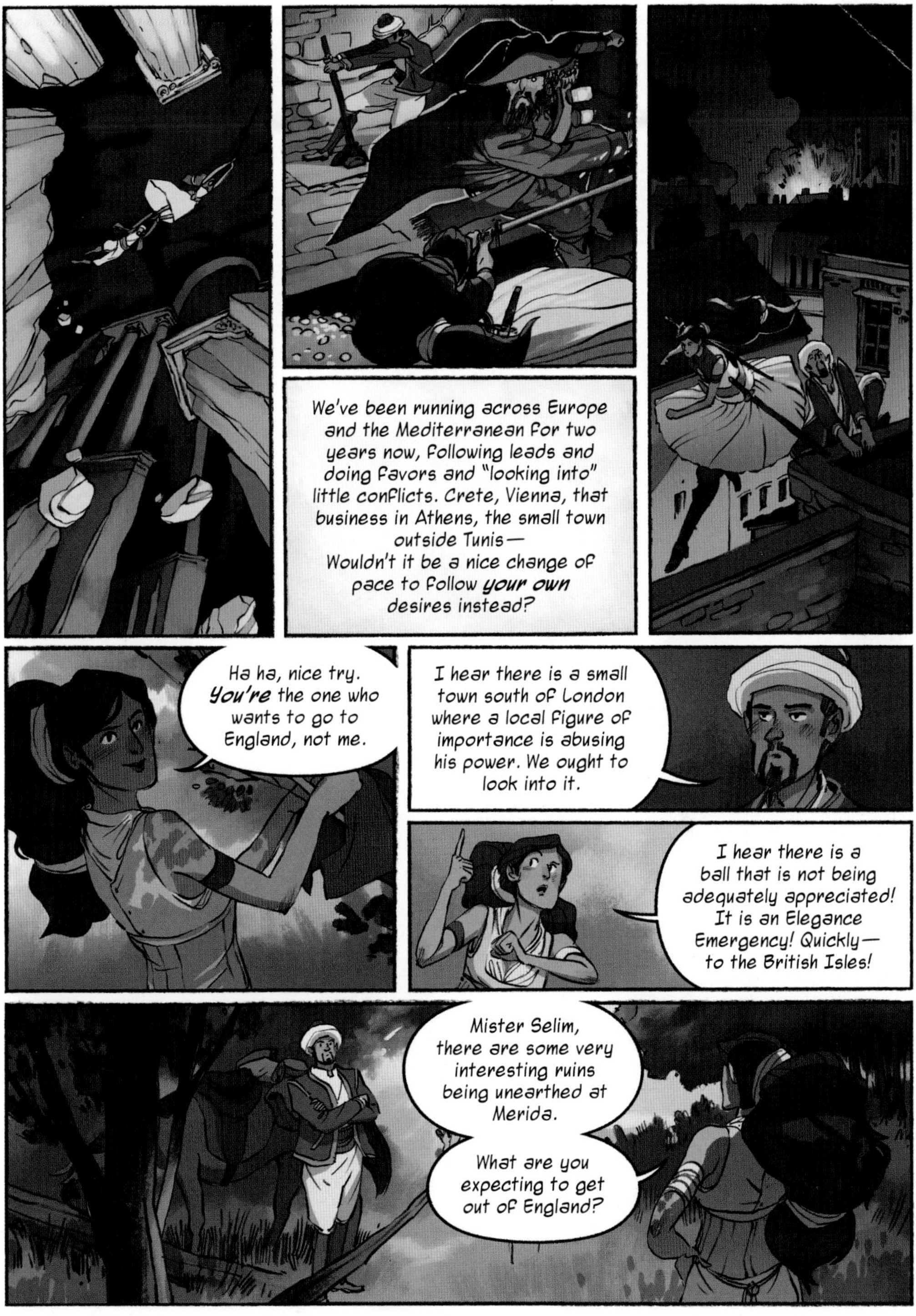
We've been running across Europe and the Mediterranean for two years now, following leads and doing favors and "looking into" little conflicts. Crete, Vienna, that business in Athens, the small town outside Tunis— Wouldn't it be a nice change of pace to follow ***your own*** desires instead?
Ha ha, nice try. ***You're*** the one who wants to go to England, not me.
I hear there is a small town south of London where a local figure of importance is abusing his power. We ought to look into it.
I hear there is a ball that is not being adequately appreciated! It is an Elegance Emergency! Quickly— to the British Isles!
Mister Selim, there are some very interesting ruins being unearthed at Merida.
What are you expecting to get out of England?

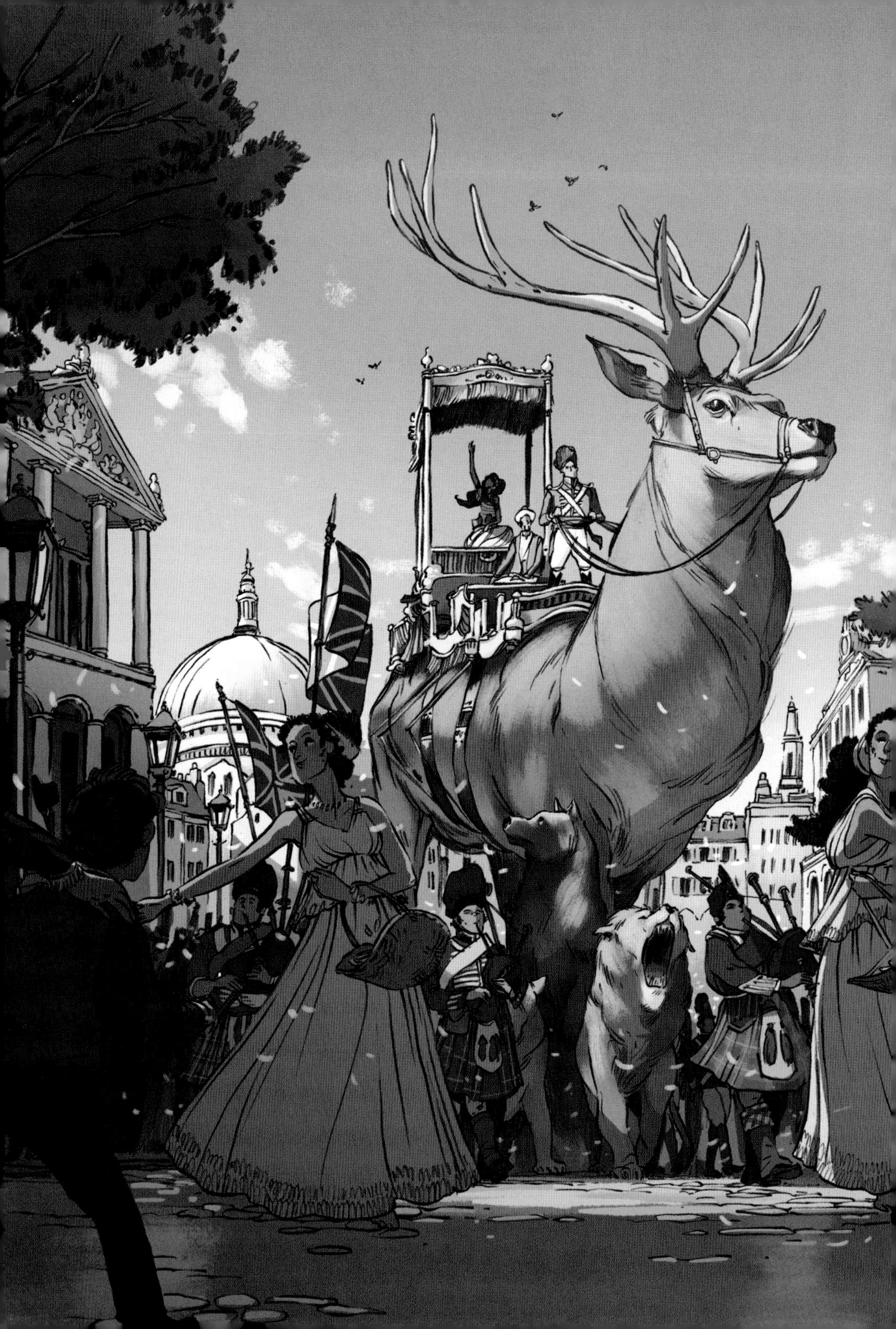

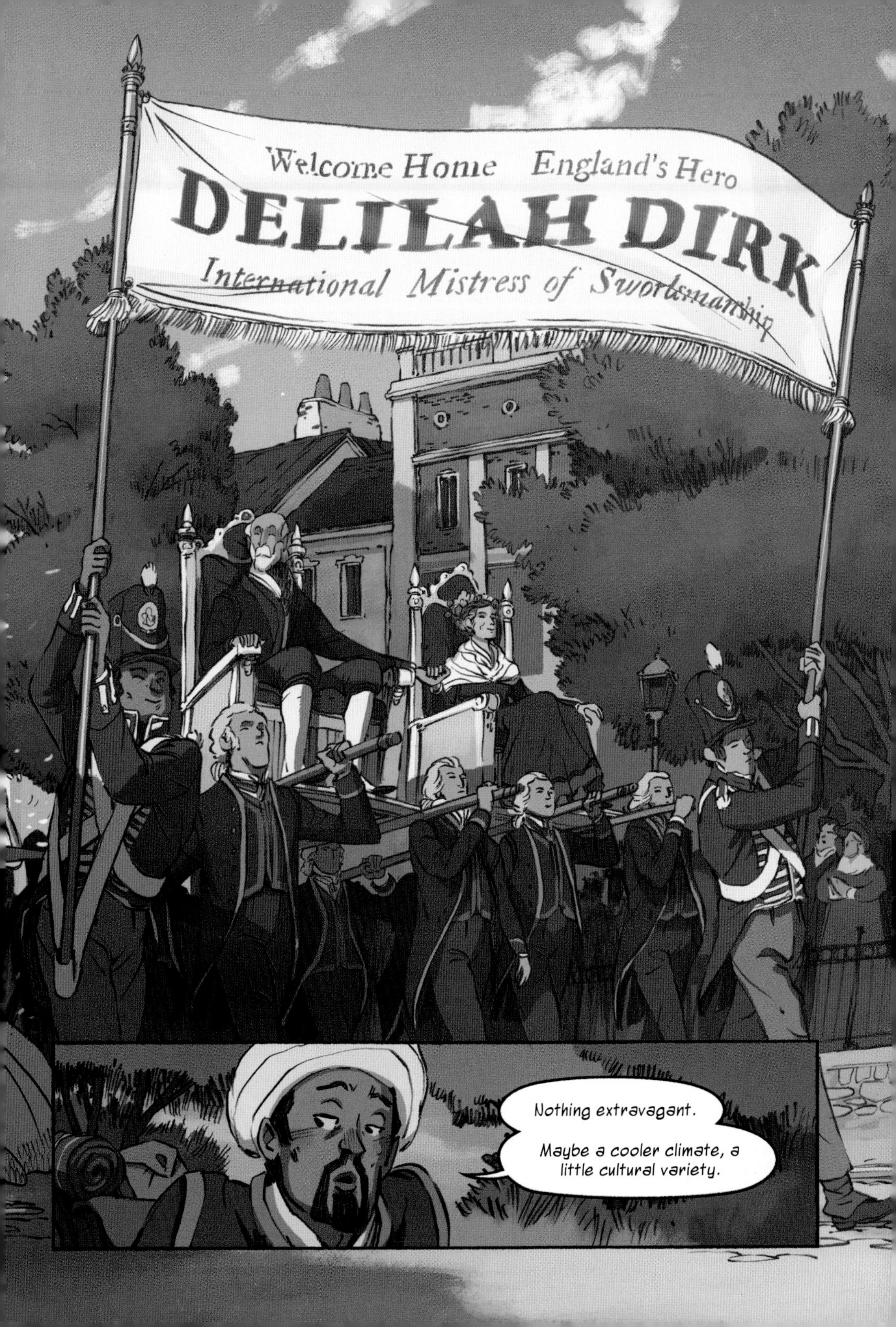
Welcome Home England's Hero
DELILAH DIRK
International Mistress of Swordsmanship
Nothing extravagant.
Maybe a cooler climate, a little cultural variety.

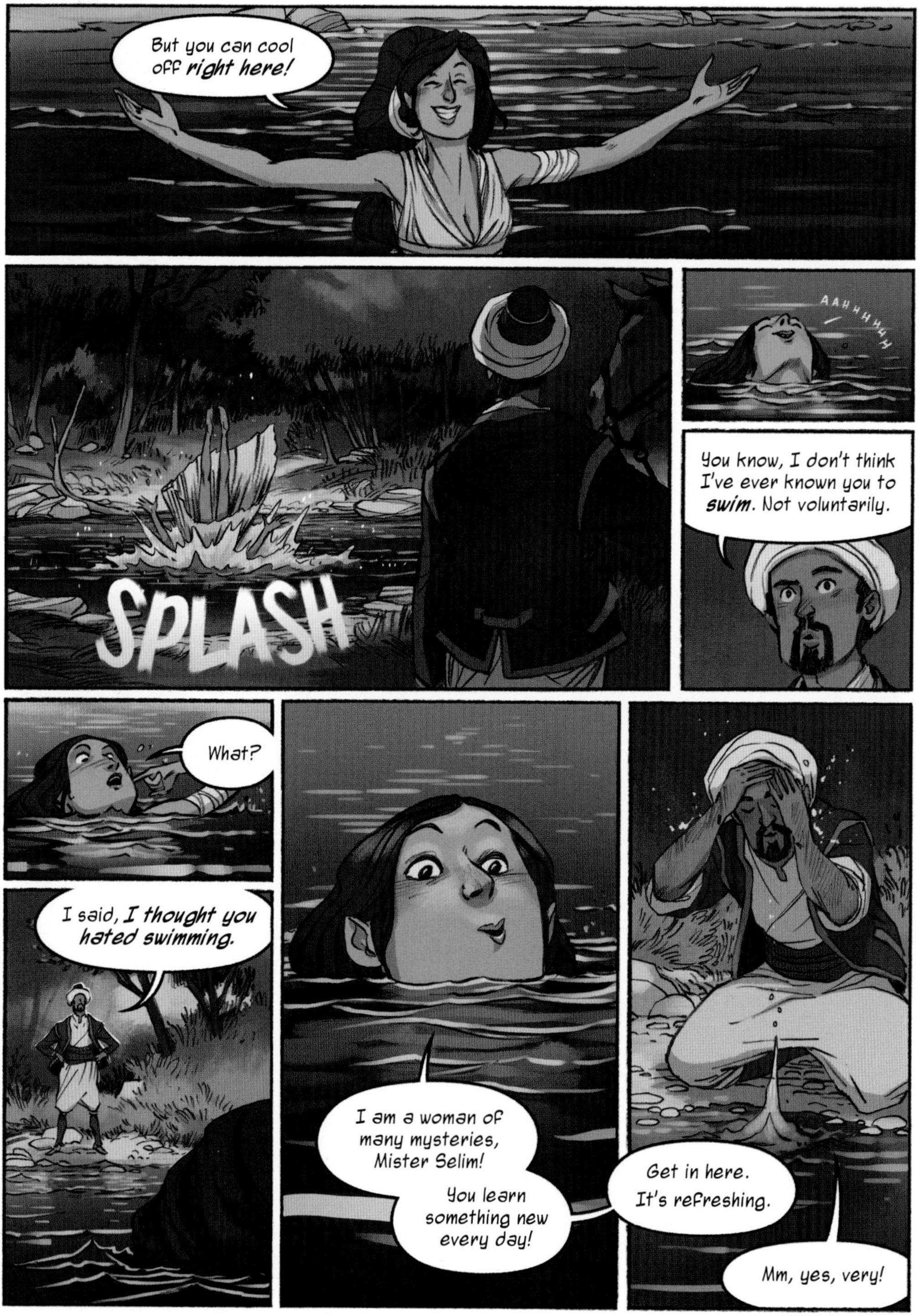

But you can cool off **right here!**
SPLASH
AAHHHHHH
You know, I don't think I've ever known you to **swim**. Not voluntarily.
What?
I said, **I thought you hated swimming.**
I am a woman of many mysteries, Mister Selim!
You learn something new every day!
Get in here. It's refreshing.
Mm, yes, very!

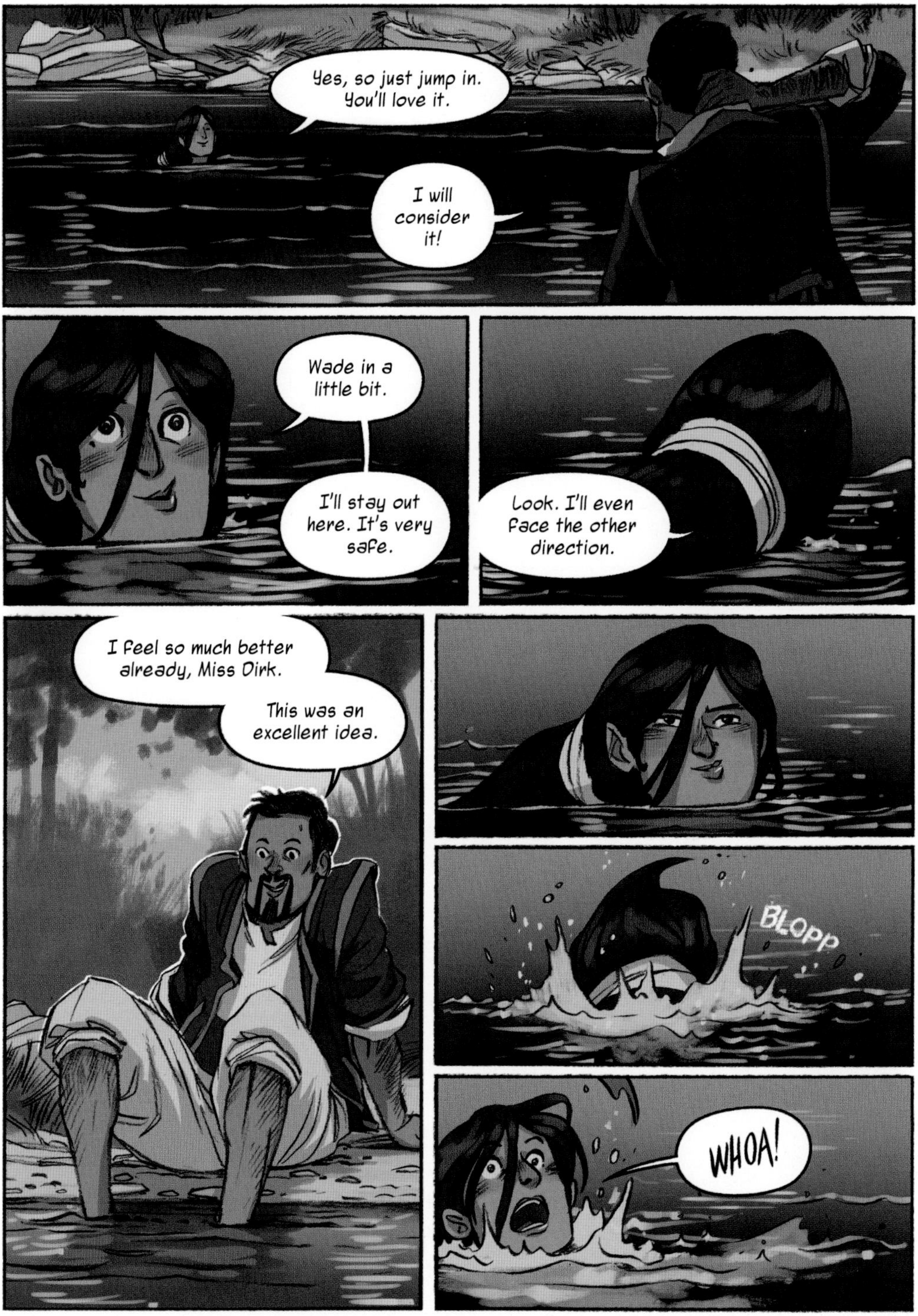
Yes, so just jump in. You'll love it.
I will consider it!
Wade in a little bit.
I'll stay out here. It's very safe.
Look. I'll even face the other direction.
I feel so much better already, Miss Dirk.
This was an excellent idea.
BLOPP
WHOA!

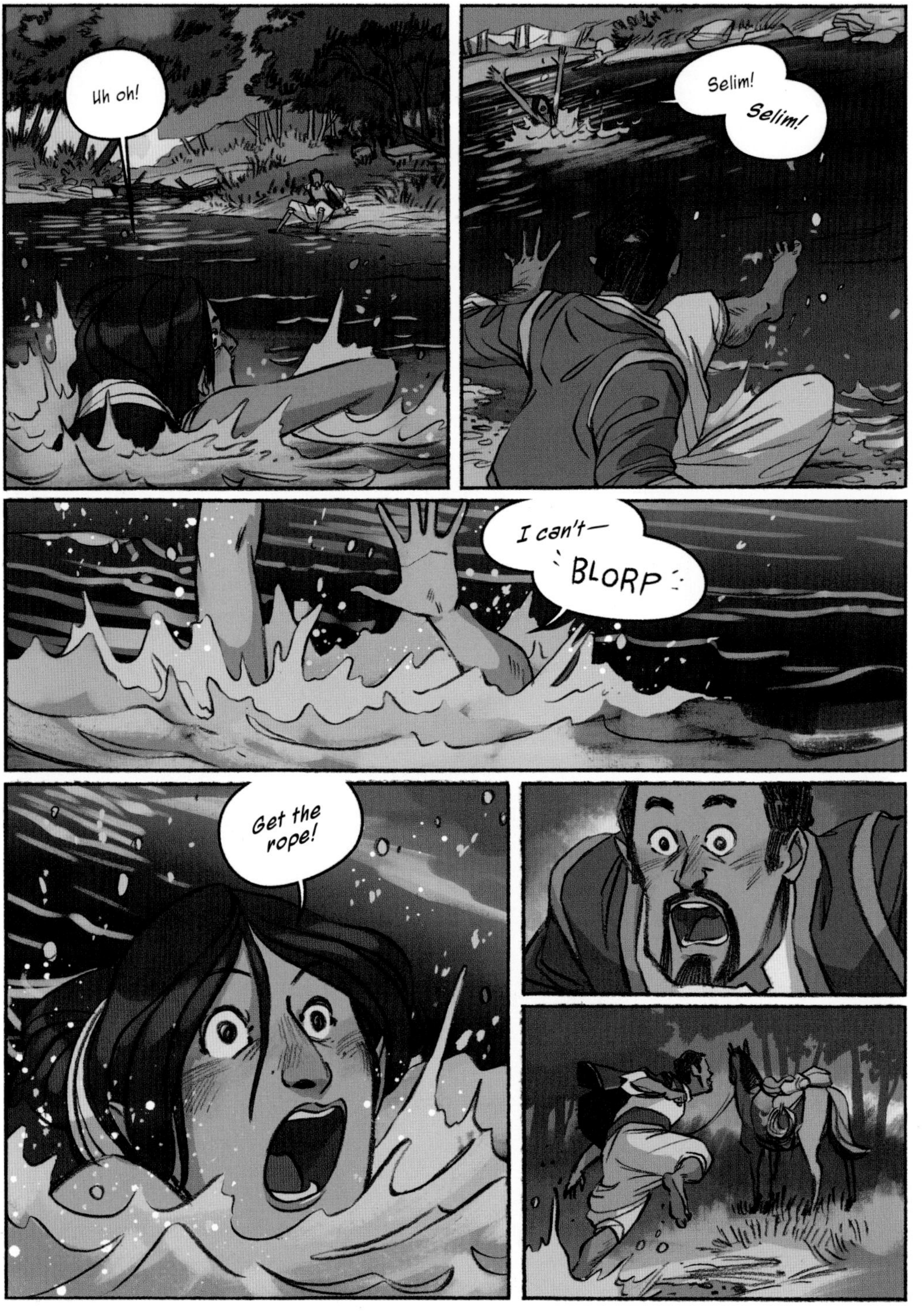
Uh oh!
Selim! Selim!
I can't—
BLORP
Get the rope!

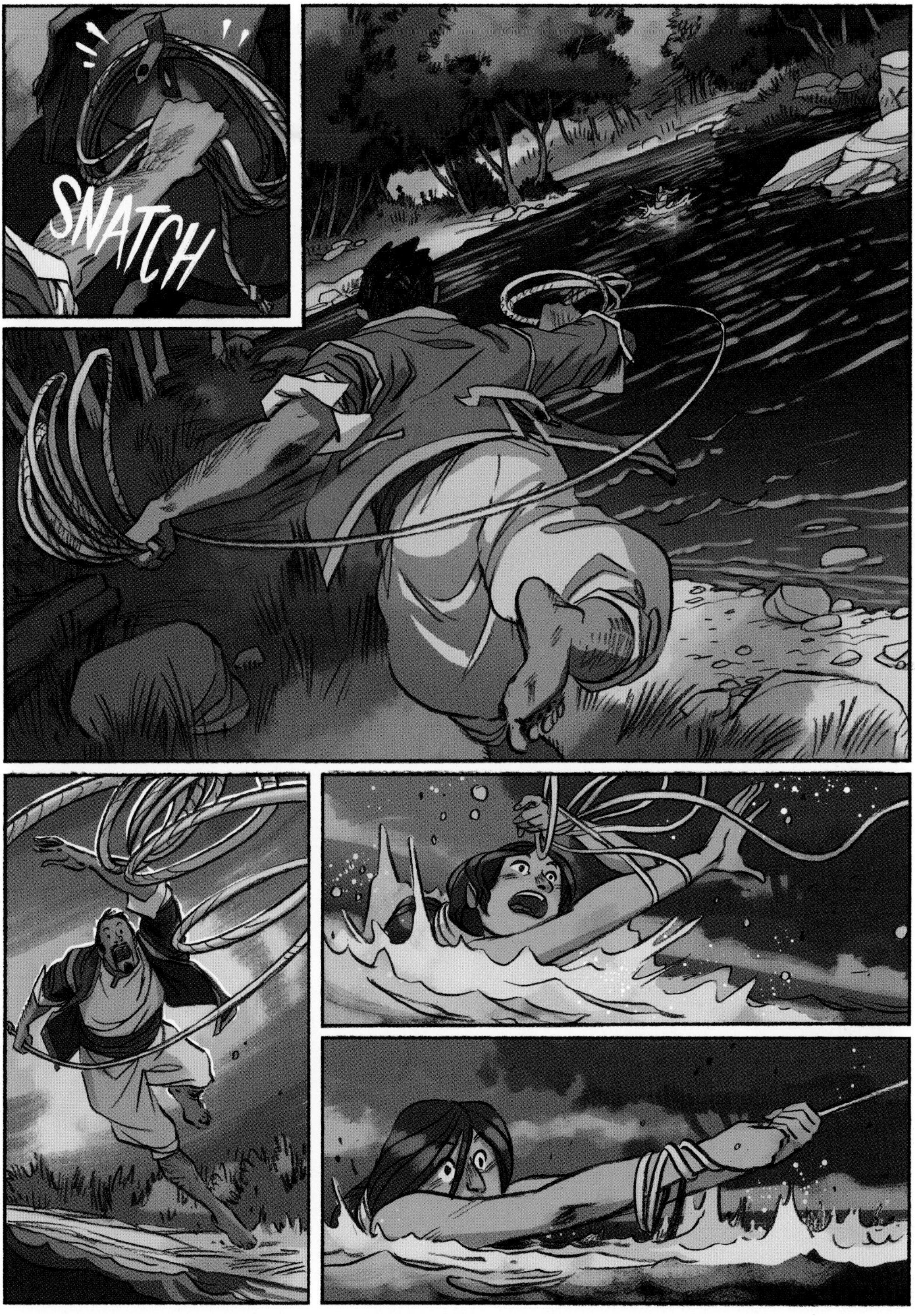
SNATCH

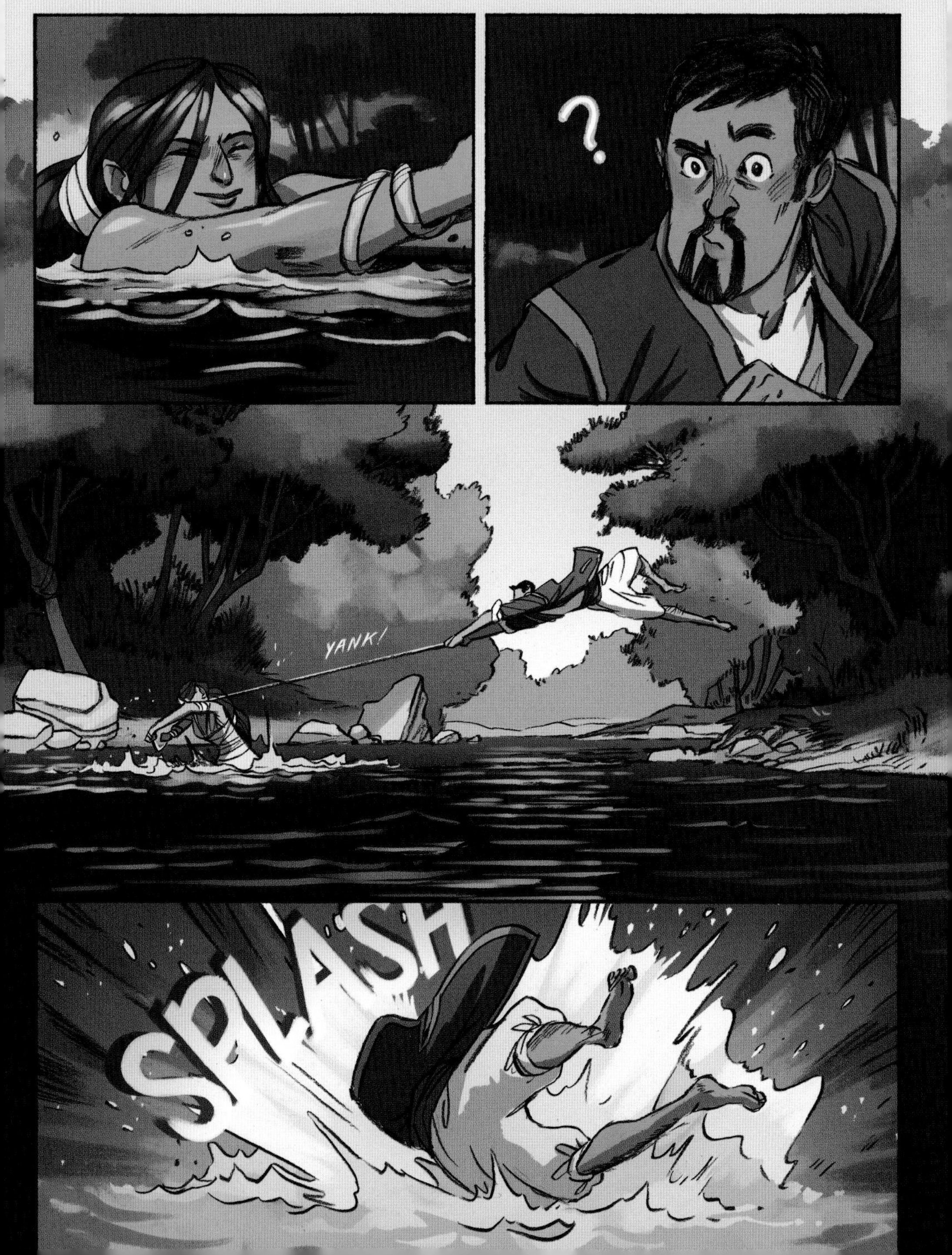
?
YANK!
SPLASH

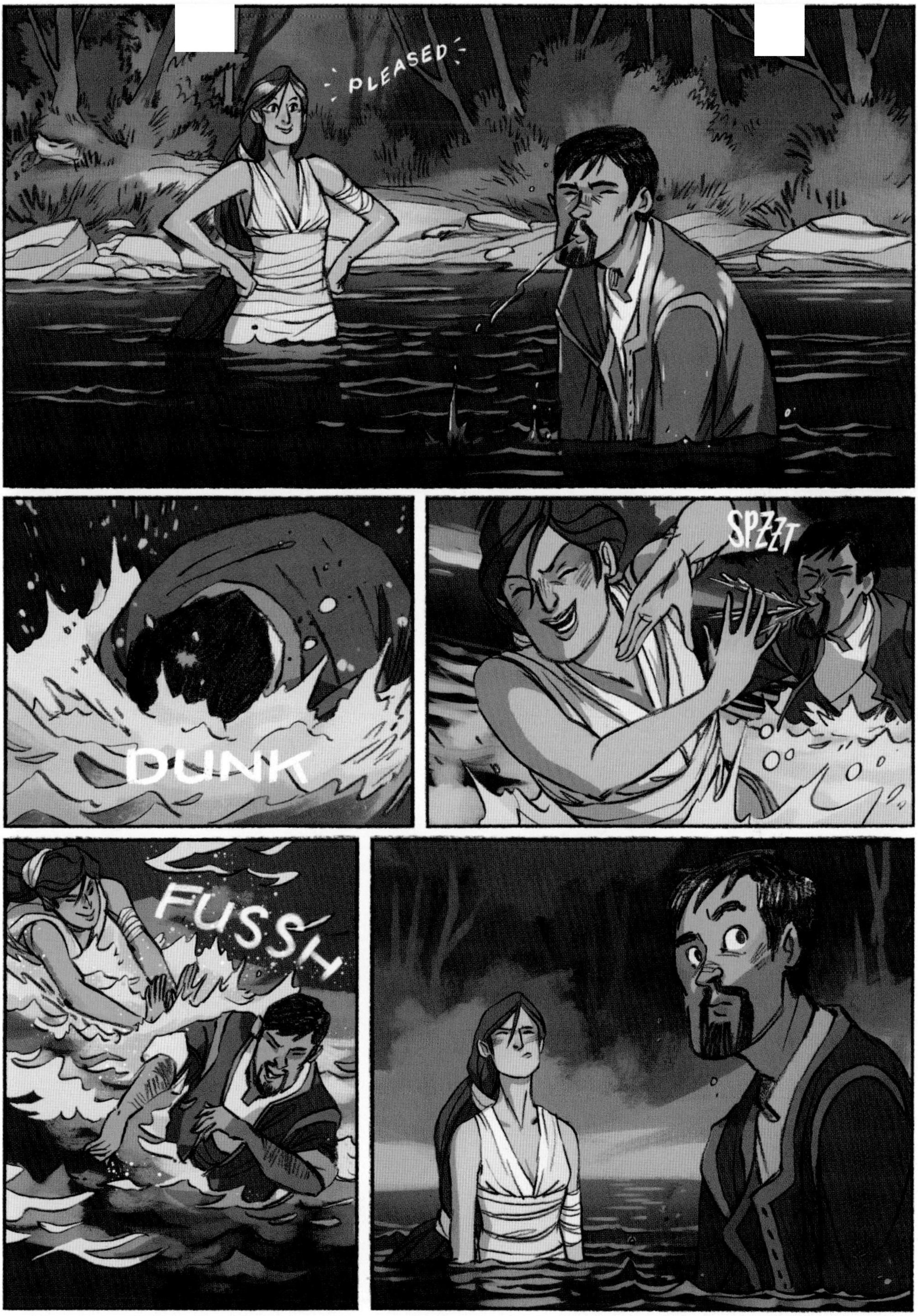
PLEASED
DUNK
SPZZT
FUSSH

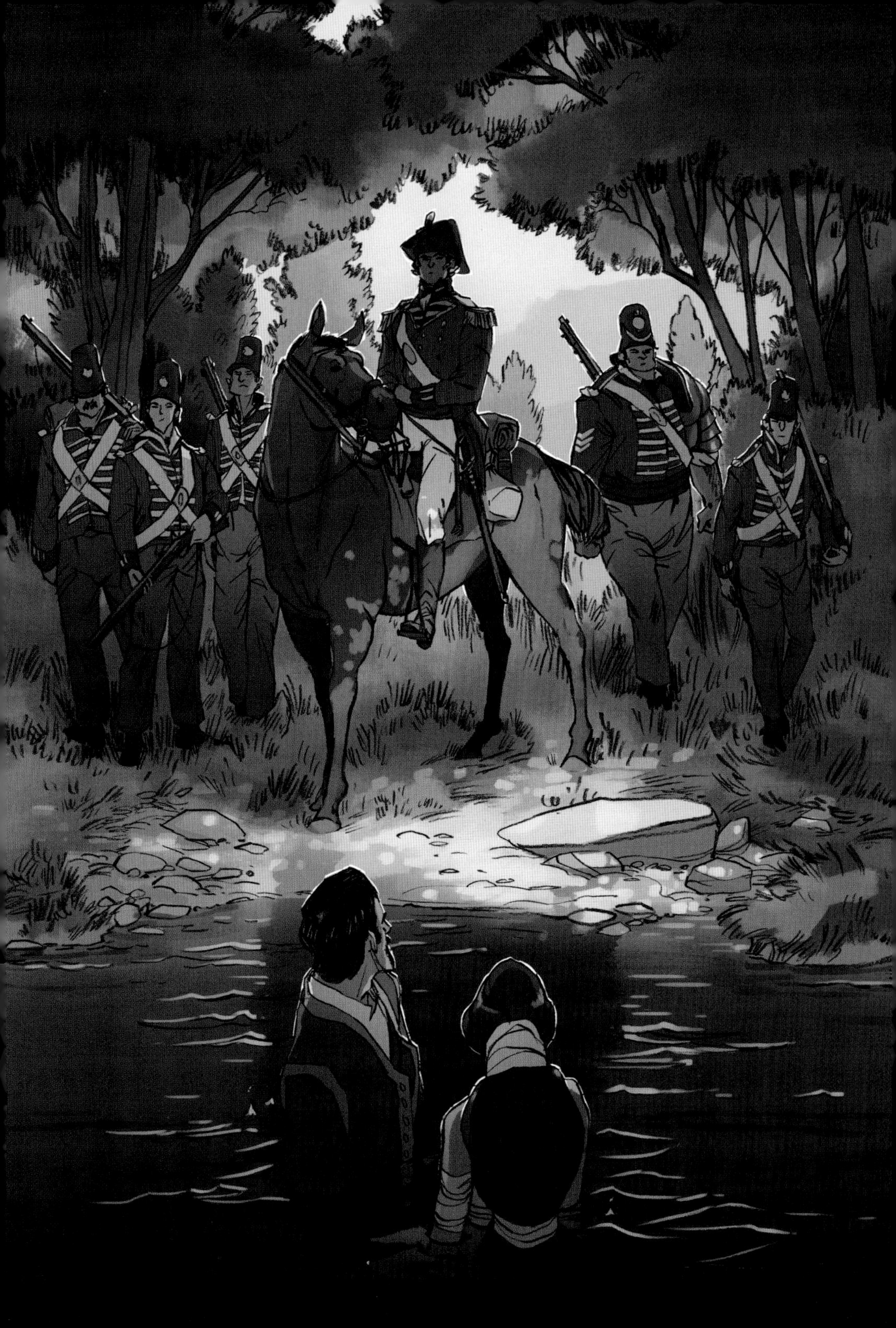

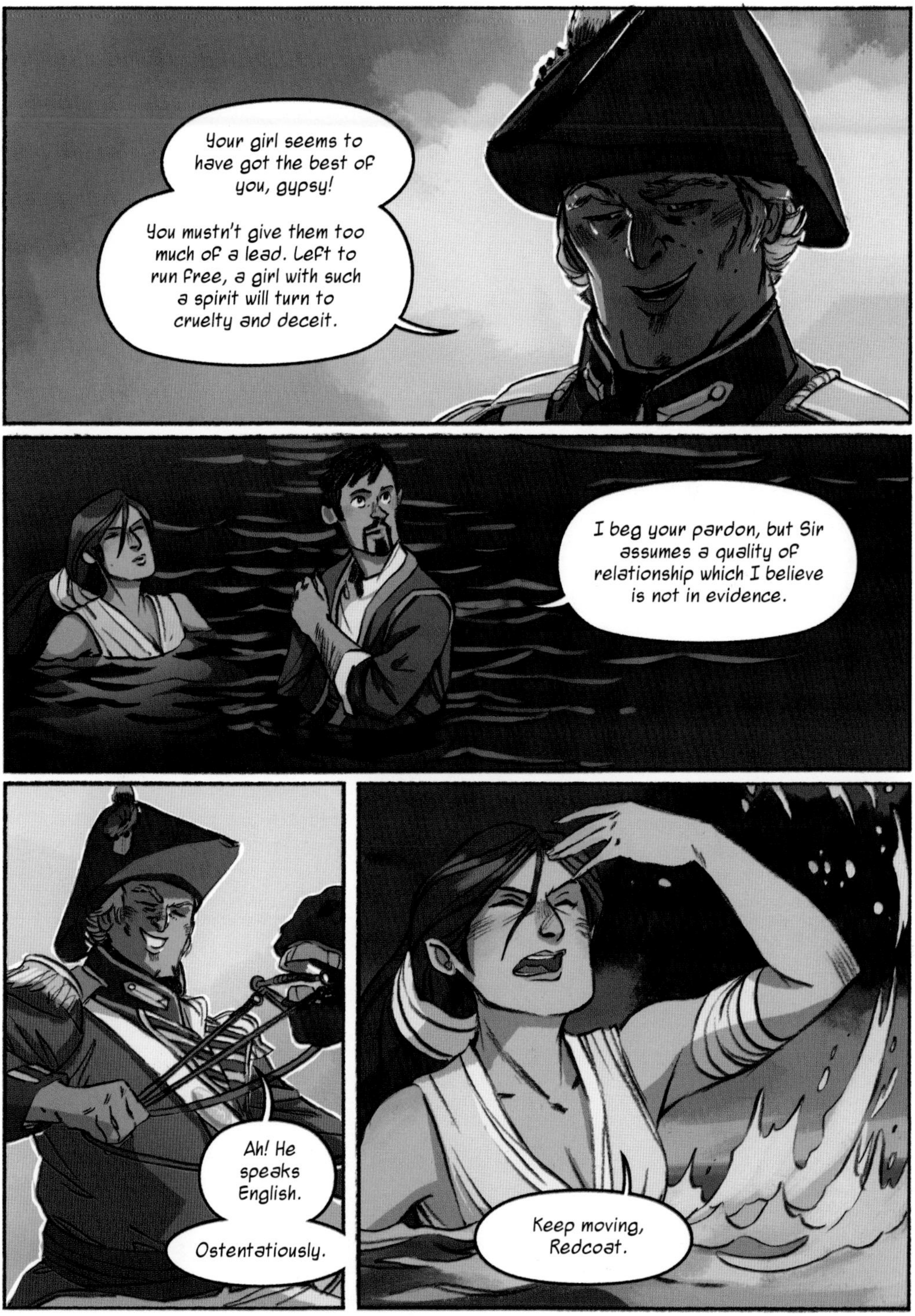
Your girl seems to have got the best of you, gypsy!
You mustn't give them too much of a lead. Left to run free, a girl with such a spirit will turn to cruelty and deceit.
I beg your pardon, but Sir assumes a quality of relationship which I believe is not in evidence.
Ah! He speaks English.
Ostentatiously.
Keep moving, Redcoat.

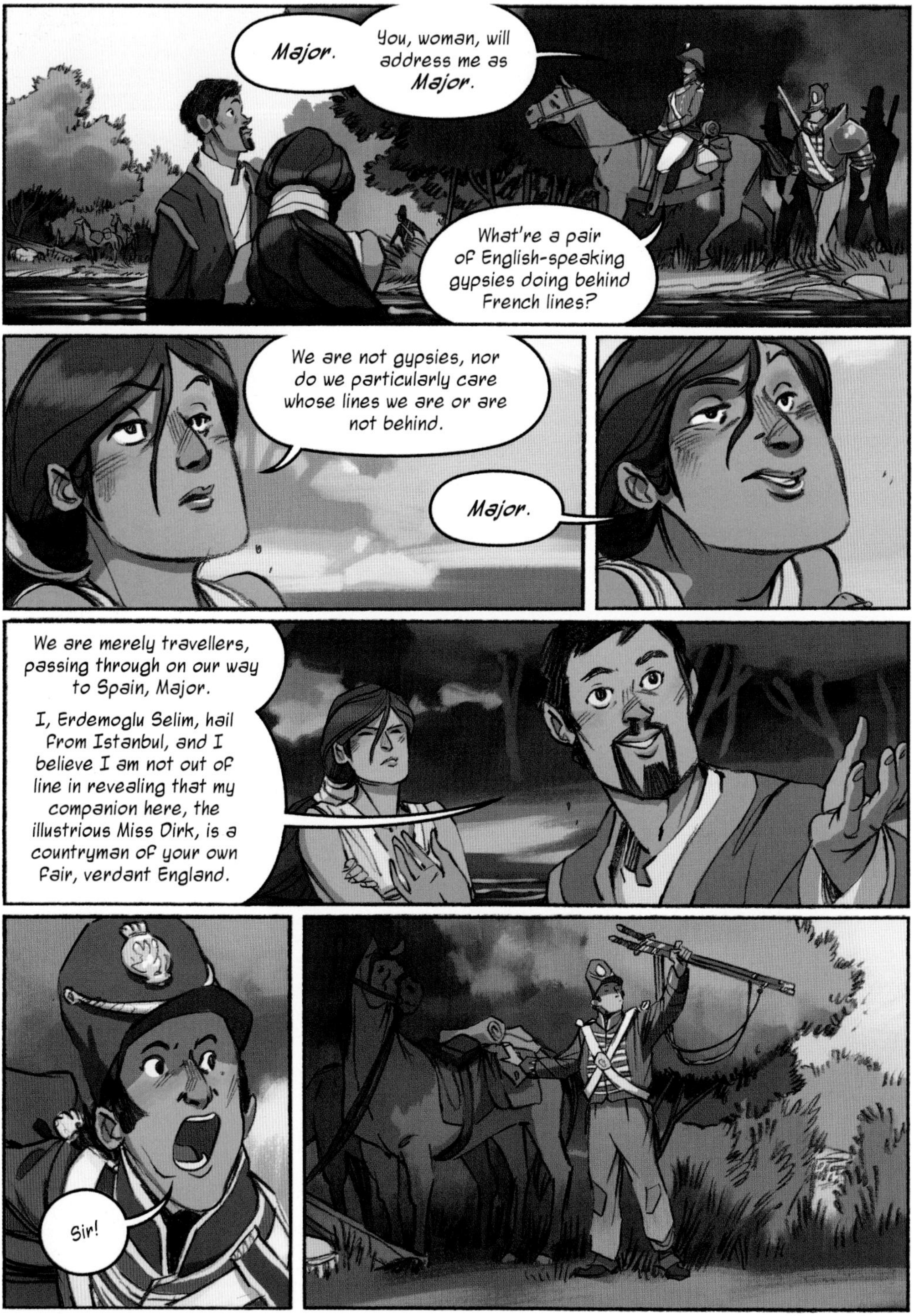
Major.
You, woman, will address me as Major.
What're a pair of English-speaking gypsies doing behind French lines?
We are not gypsies, nor do we particularly care whose lines we are or are not behind.
Major.
We are merely travellers, passing through on our way to Spain, Major.
I, Erdemoglu Selim, hail from Istanbul, and I believe I am not out of line in revealing that my companion here, the illustrious Miss Dirk, is a countryman of your own fair, verdant England.
Sir!

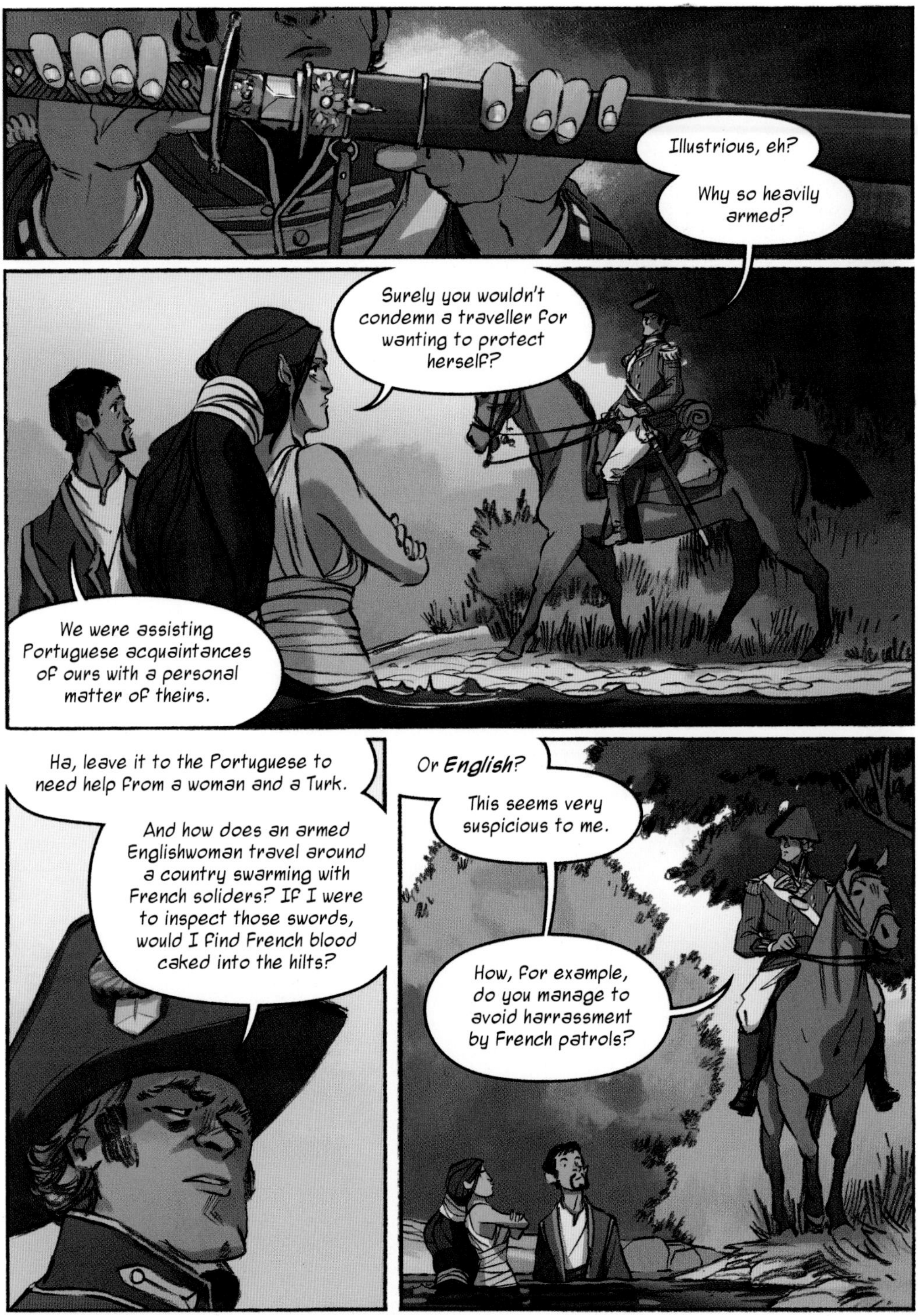

Illustrious, eh?
Why so heavily armed?
Surely you wouldn't condemn a traveller for wanting to protect herself?
We were assisting Portuguese acquaintances of ours with a personal matter of theirs.
Ha, leave it to the Portuguese to need help from a woman and a Turk.
And how does an armed Englishwoman travel around a country swarming with French soliders? If I were to inspect those swords, would I find French blood caked into the hilts?
Or ***English***?
This seems very suspicious to me.
How, for example, do you manage to avoid harrassment by French patrols?

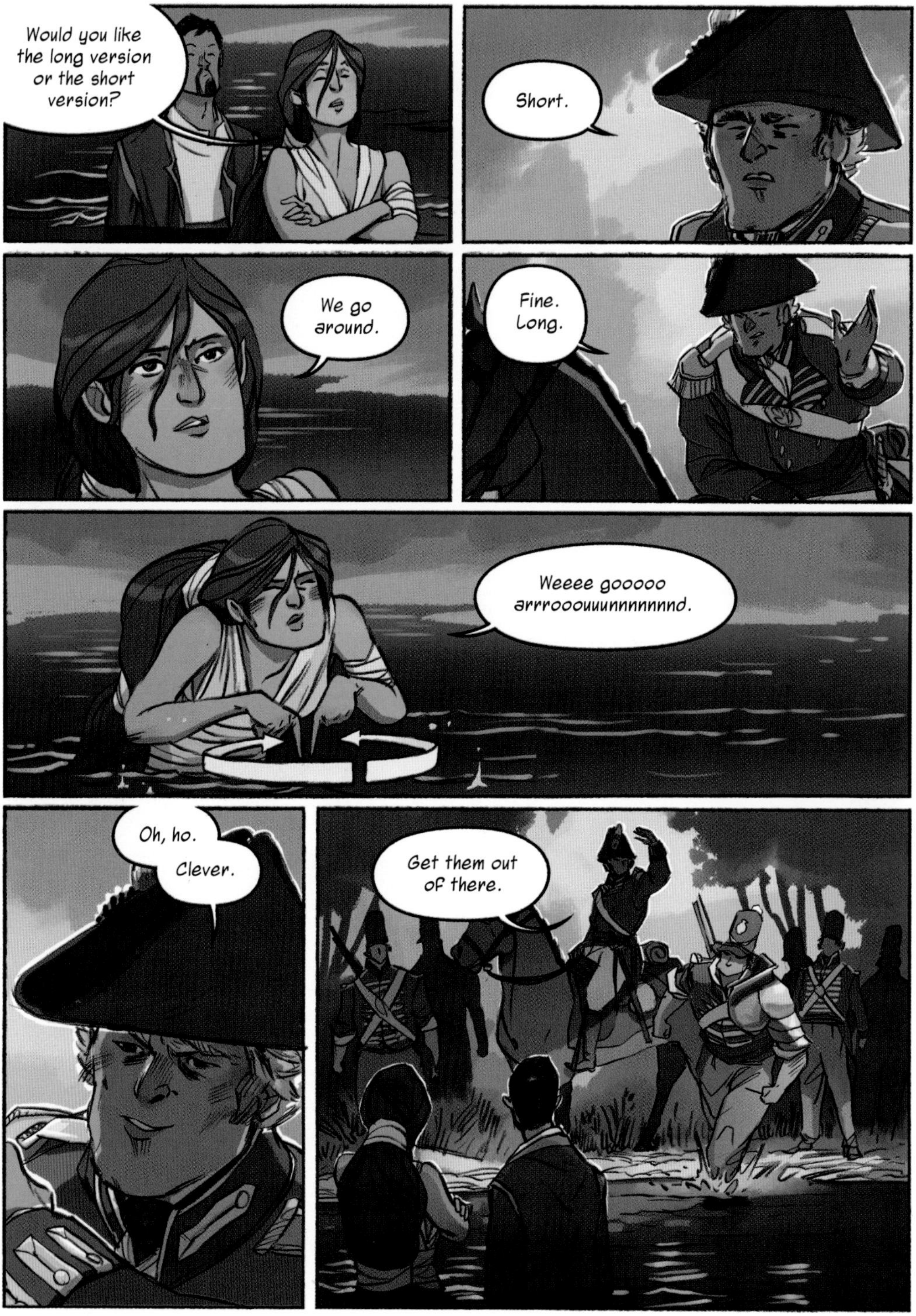
Would you like the long version or the short version?
Short.
We go around.
Fine. Long.
Weeee gooooo arrrooouuunnnnnnnd.
Oh, ho.
Clever.
Get them out of there.

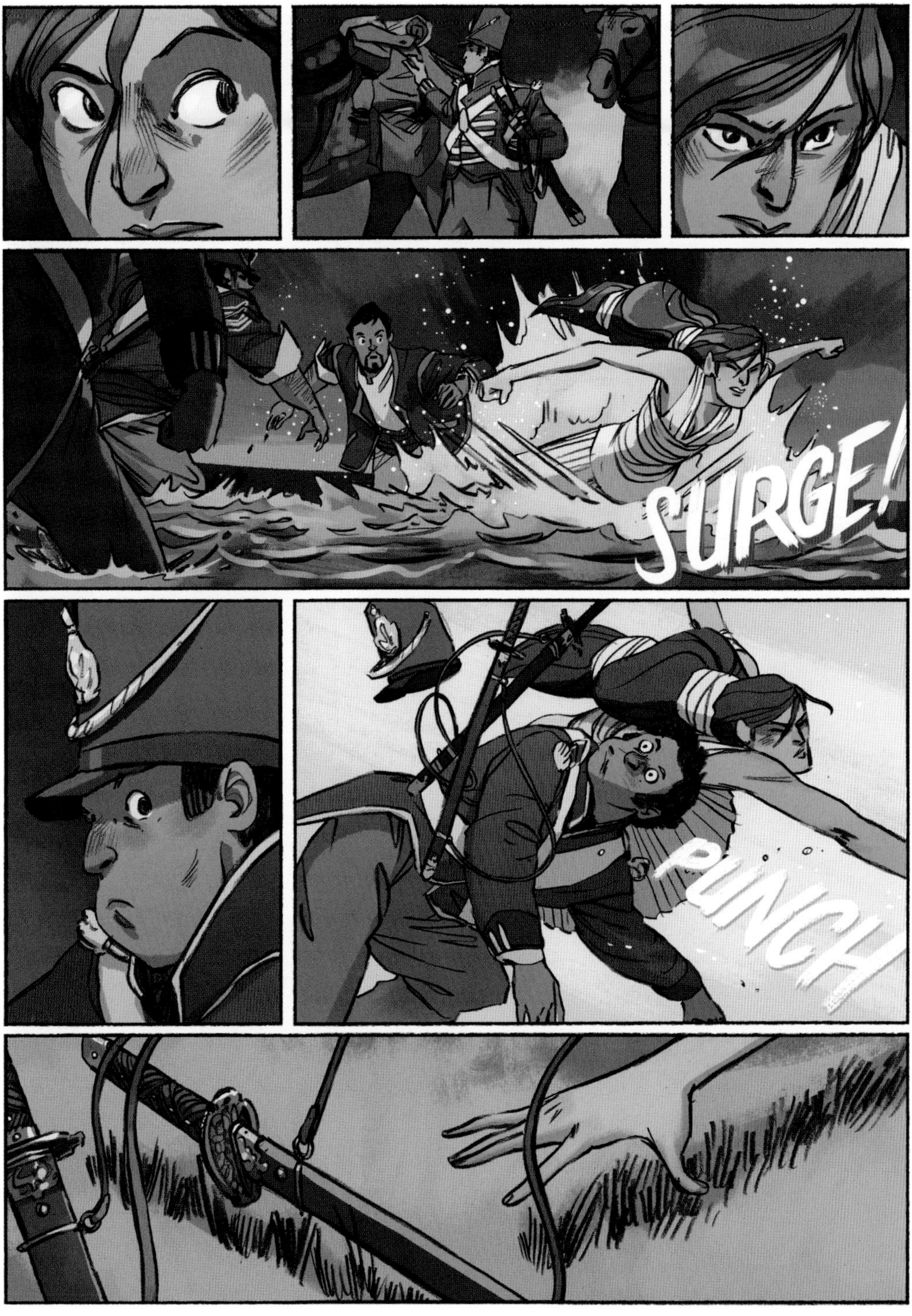
SURGE!
PUNCH

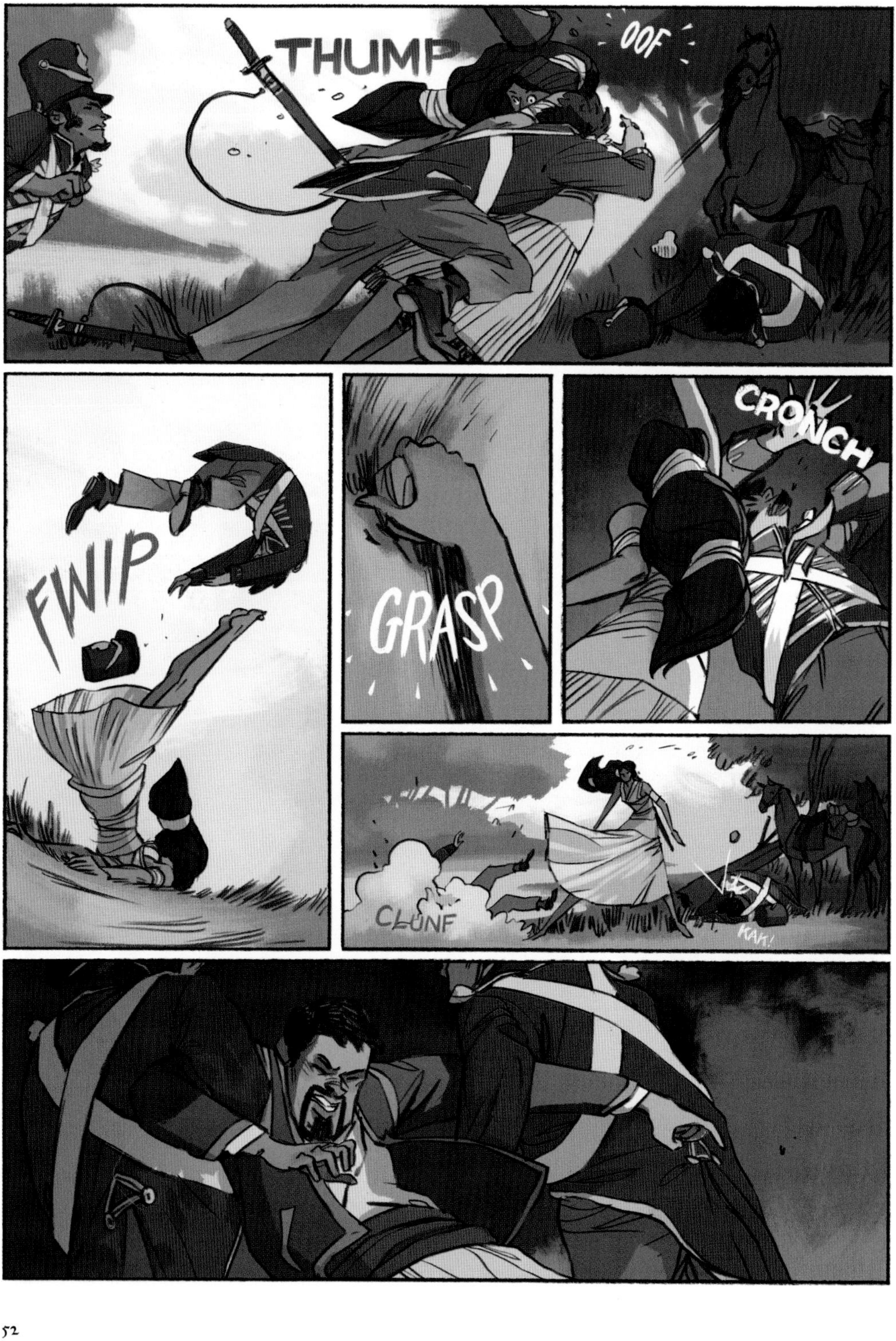
THUMP
OOF
FWIP
GRASP
CRONCH
CLUNF
KAK!

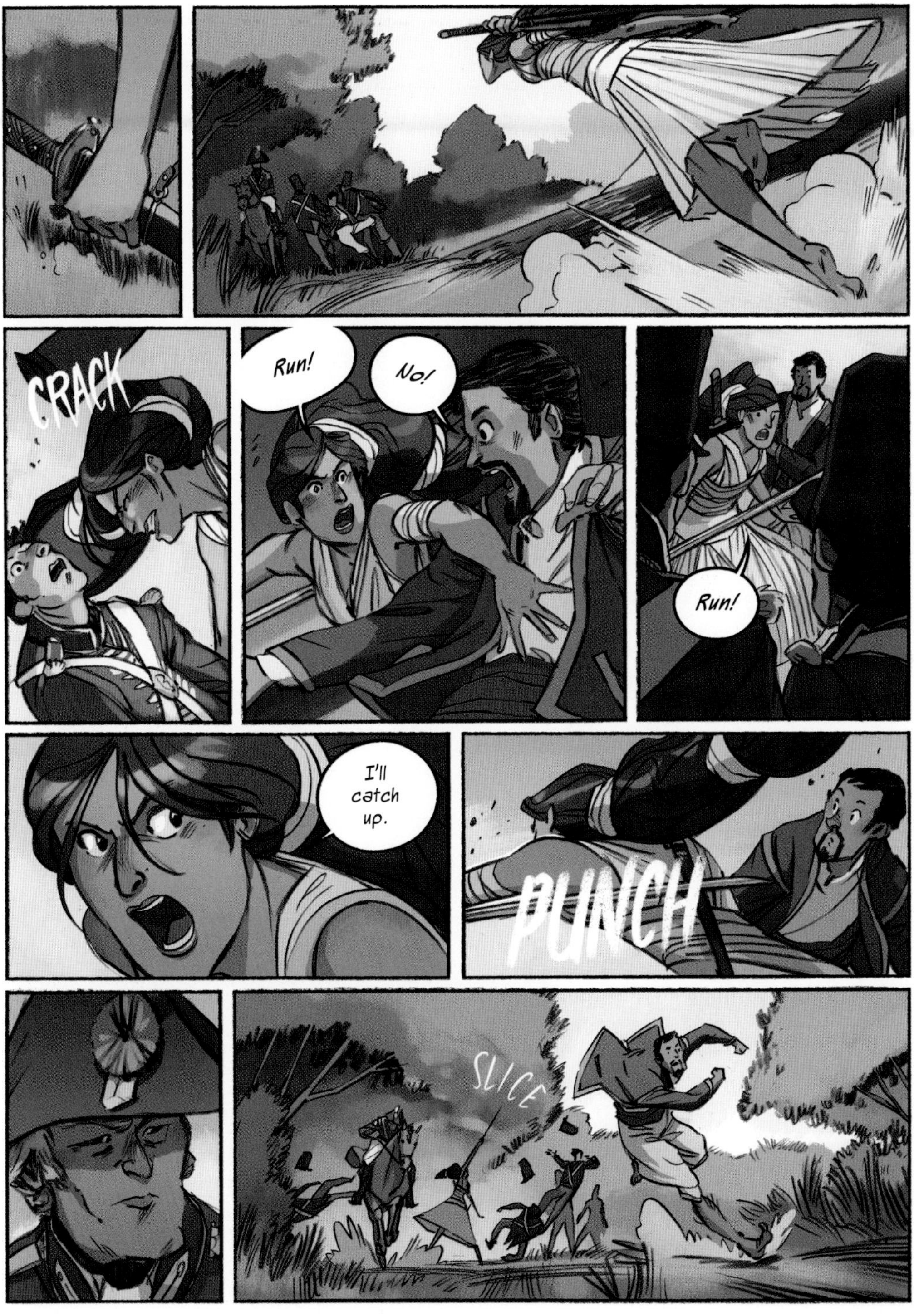
CRACK
Run!
No!
Run!
I'll catch up.
PUNCH
SLICE

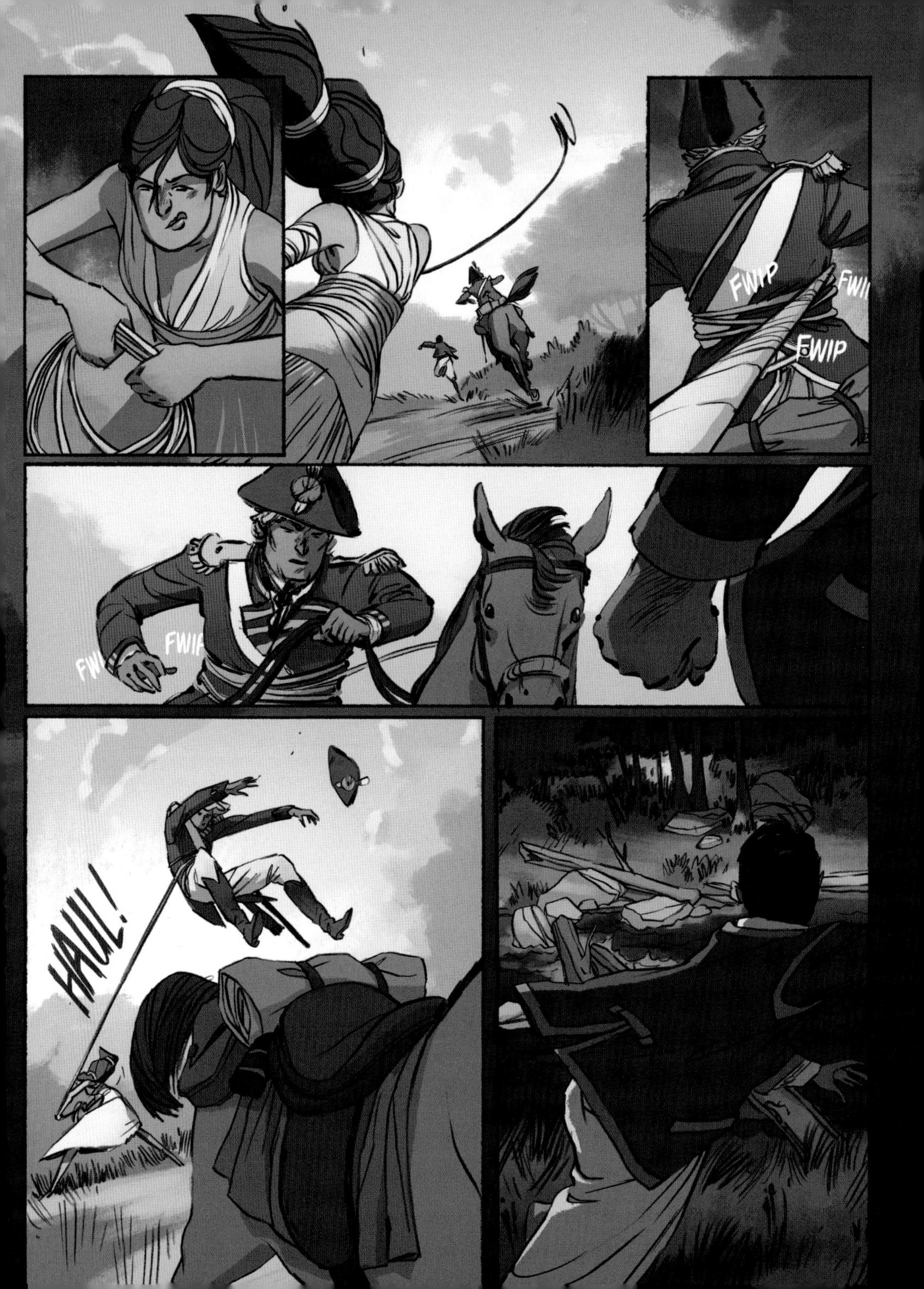
FWIP
FWII
FWIP
FWII
FWIF
HAUL!

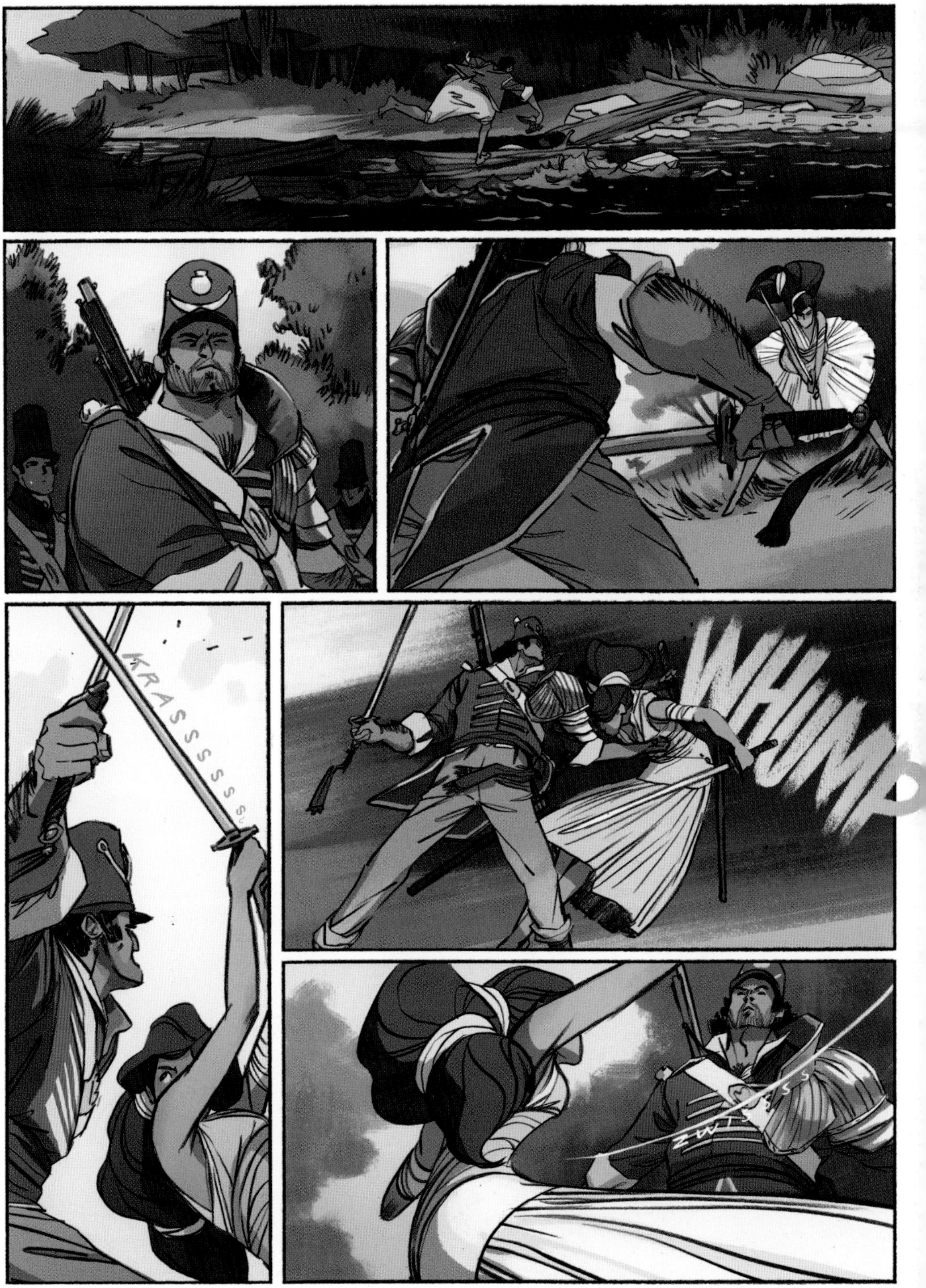
KRASSSSSS
WHUMP
ZWISSSS

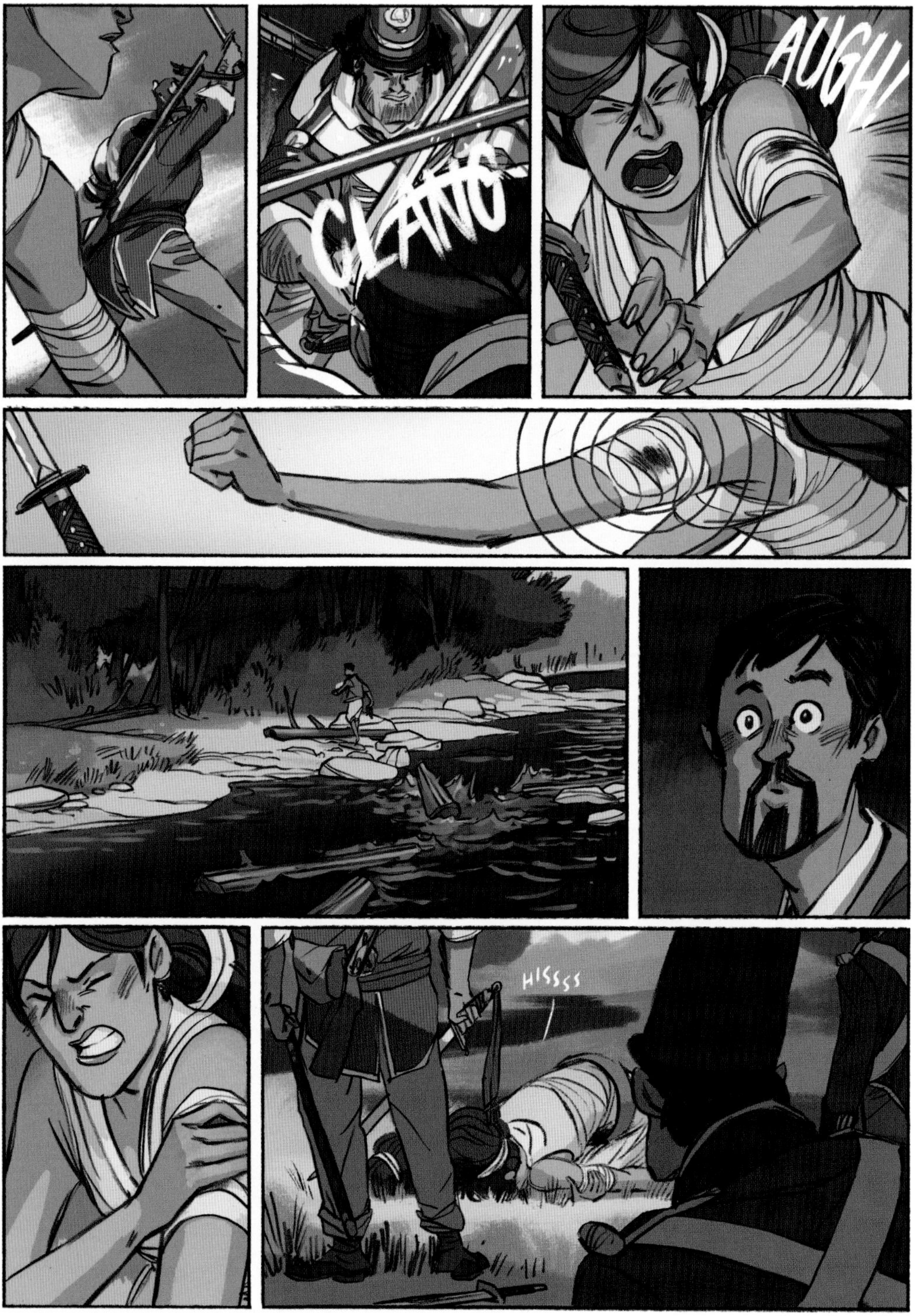
CLANG
AUGH!
HISSSS

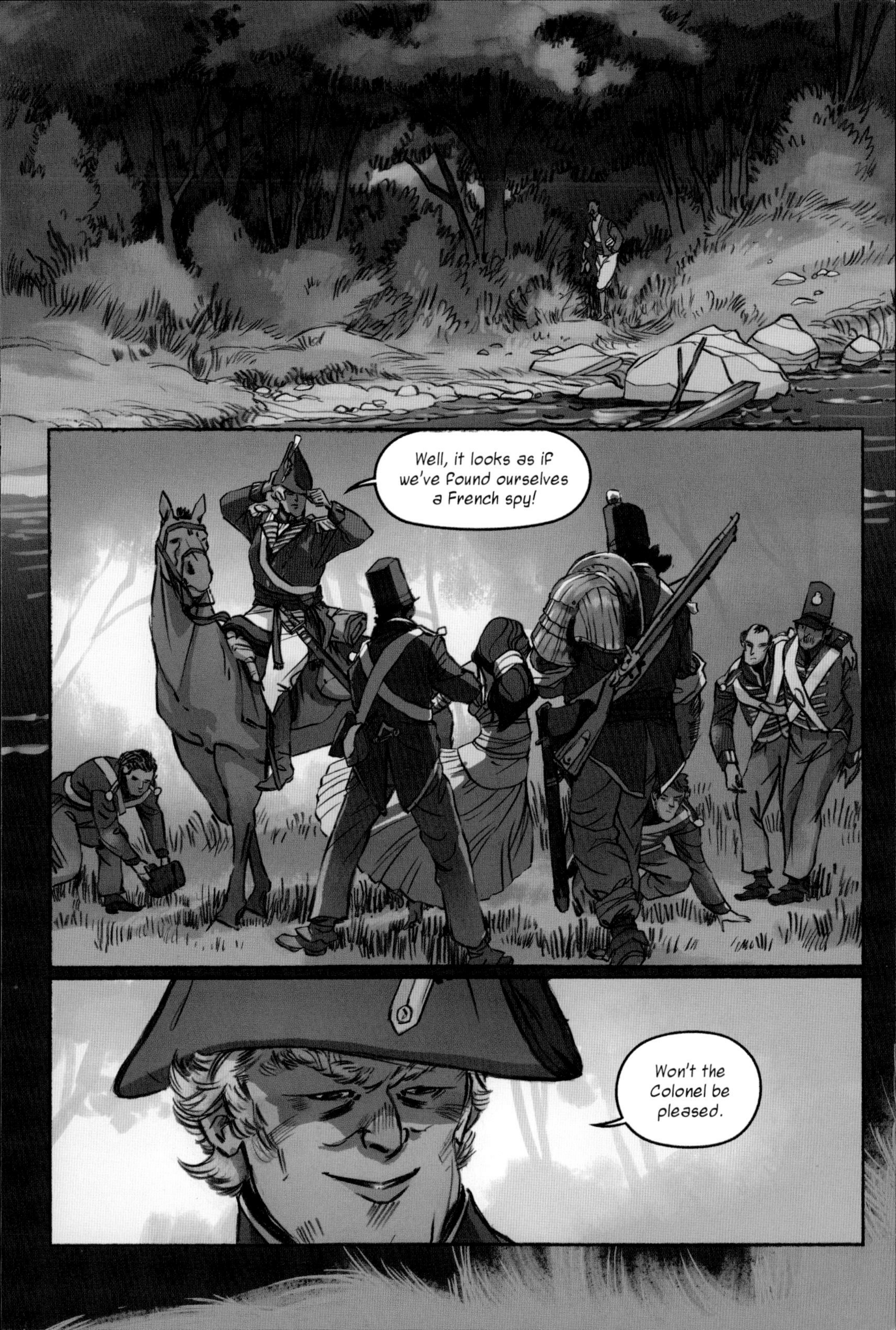
Well, it looks as if we've found ourselves a French spy!
Won't the Colonel be pleased.

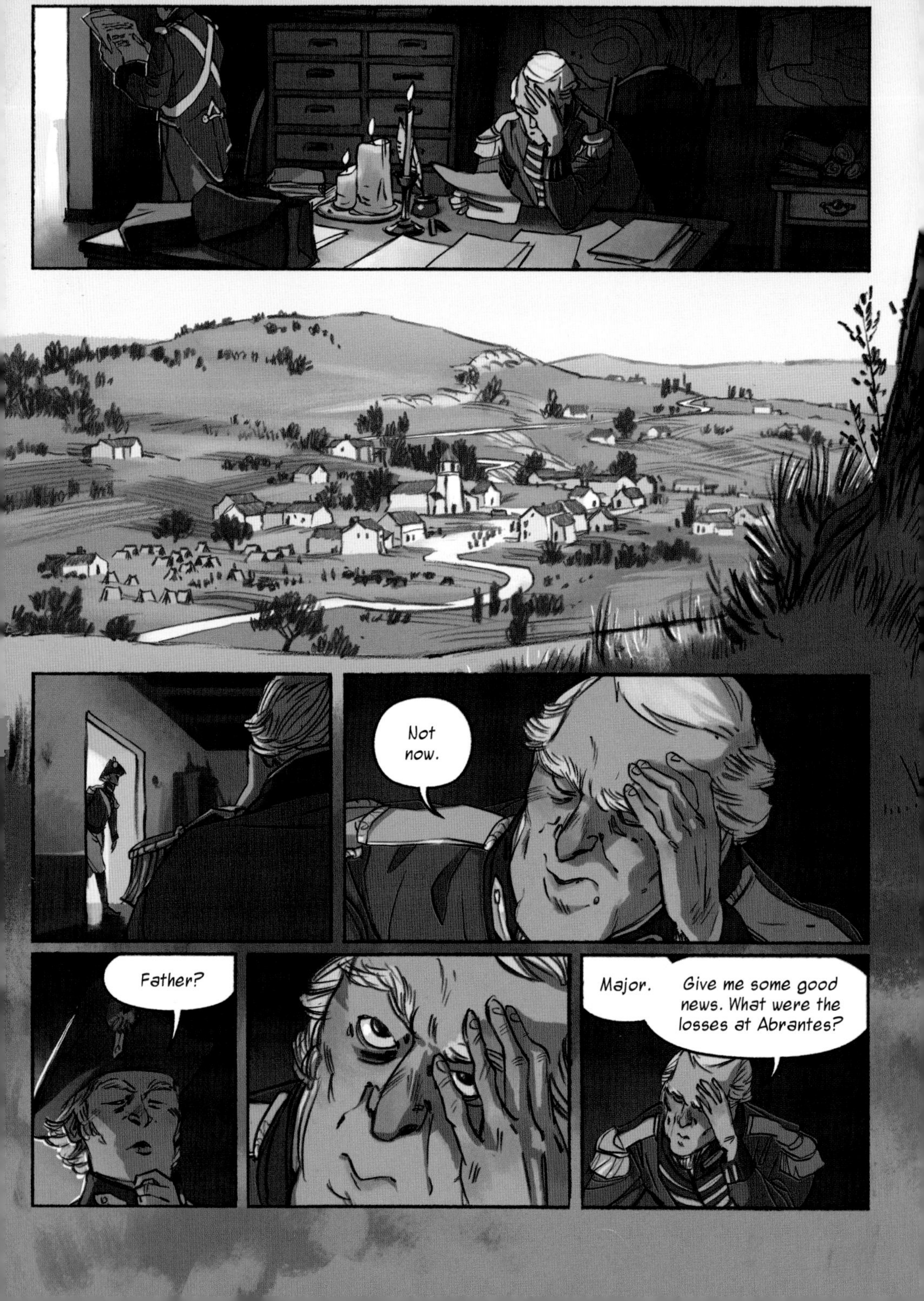
Not now.
Father?
Major.
Give me some good news. What were the losses at Abrantes?

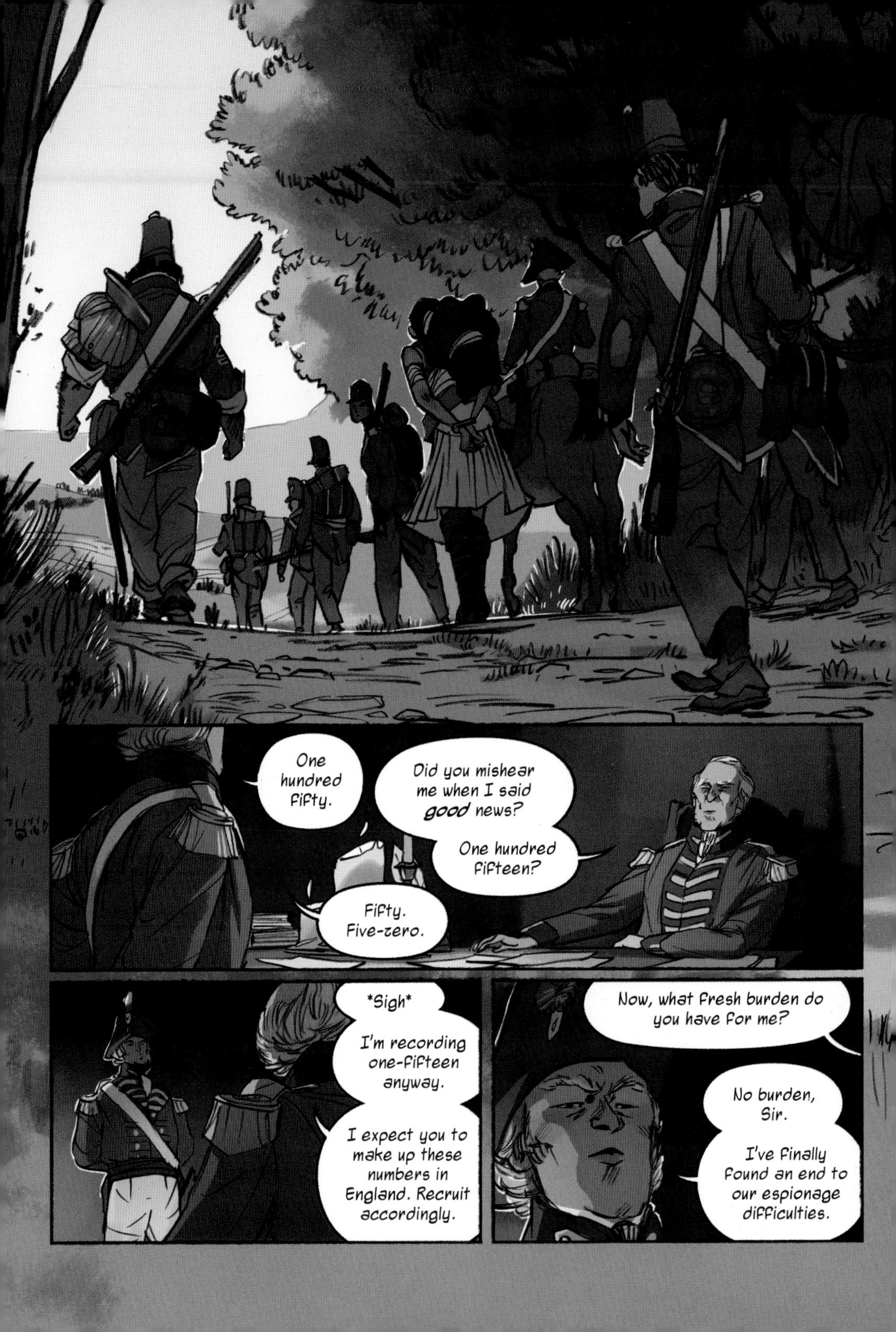

One hundred fifty.
Did you mishear me when I said *good* news?
One hundred fifteen?
Fifty. Five-zero.
*Sigh*
I'm recording one-fifteen anyway.
I expect you to make up these numbers in England. Recruit accordingly.
Now, what fresh burden do you have for me?
No burden, Sir.
I've finally found an end to our espionage difficulties.

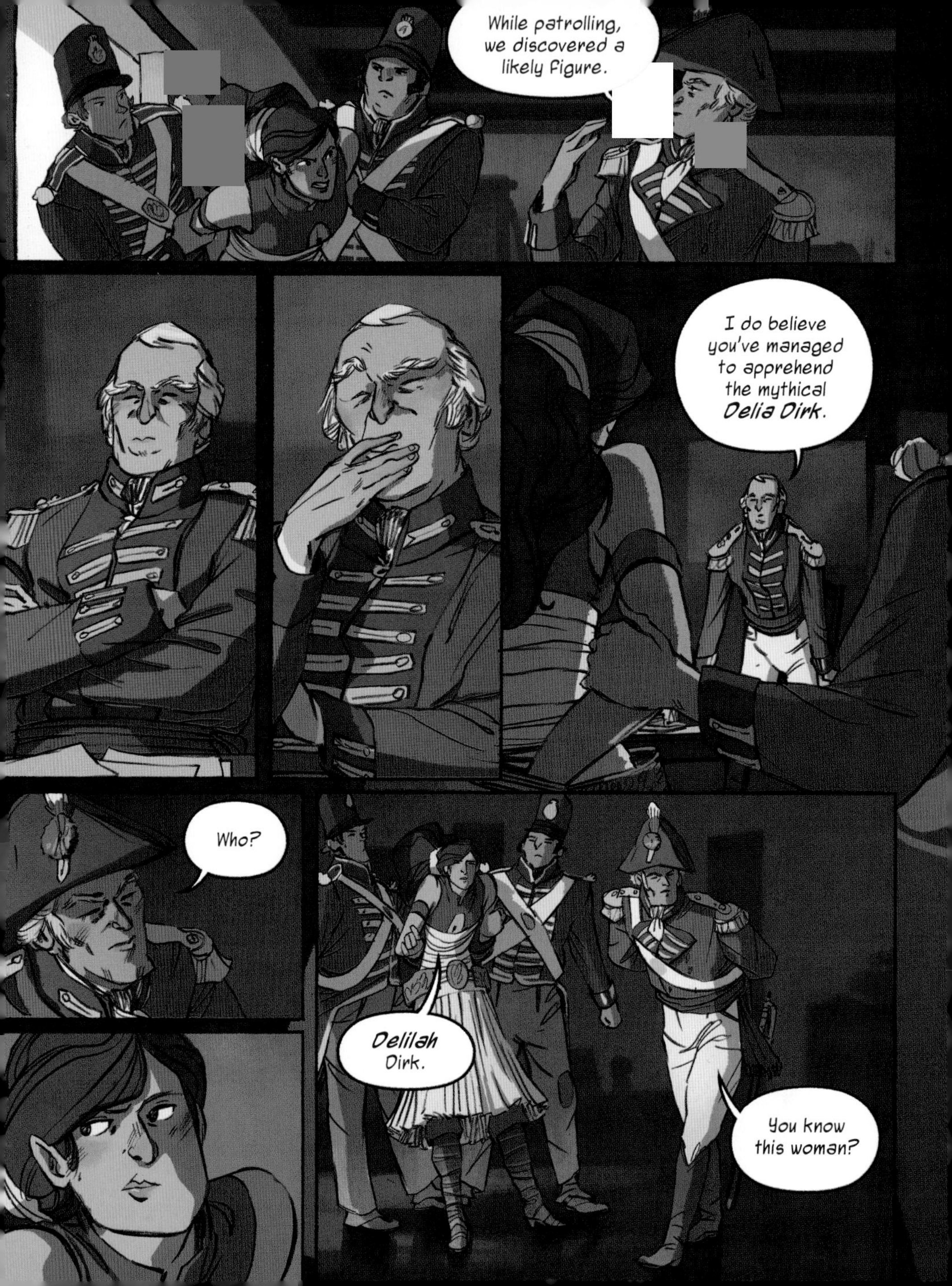
While patrolling, we discovered a likely figure.
I do believe you've managed to apprehend the mythical *Delia Dirk*.
Who?
*Delilah* Dirk.
You know this woman?

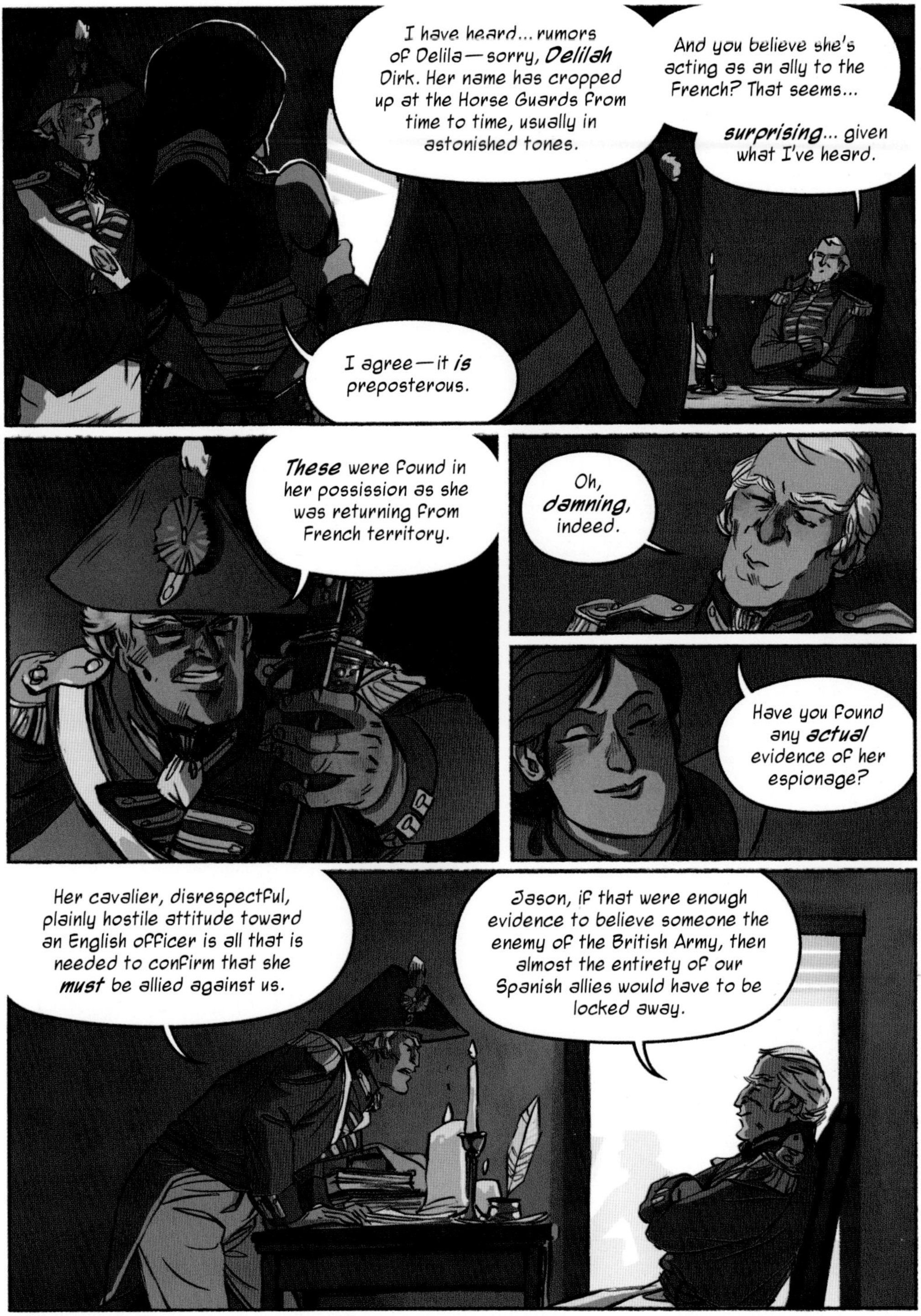
I have heard... rumors of Delila—sorry, *Delilah* Dirk. Her name has cropped up at the Horse Guards from time to time, usually in astonished tones.
And you believe she's acting as an ally to the French? That seems...
*surprising*... given what I've heard.
I agree—it *is* preposterous.
*These* were found in her possission as she was returning from French territory.
Oh, *damning*, indeed.
Have you found any *actual* evidence of her espionage?
Her cavalier, disrespectful, plainly hostile attitude toward an English officer is all that is needed to confirm that she *must* be allied against us.
Jason, if that were enough evidence to believe someone the enemy of the British Army, then almost the entirety of our Spanish allies would have to be locked away.

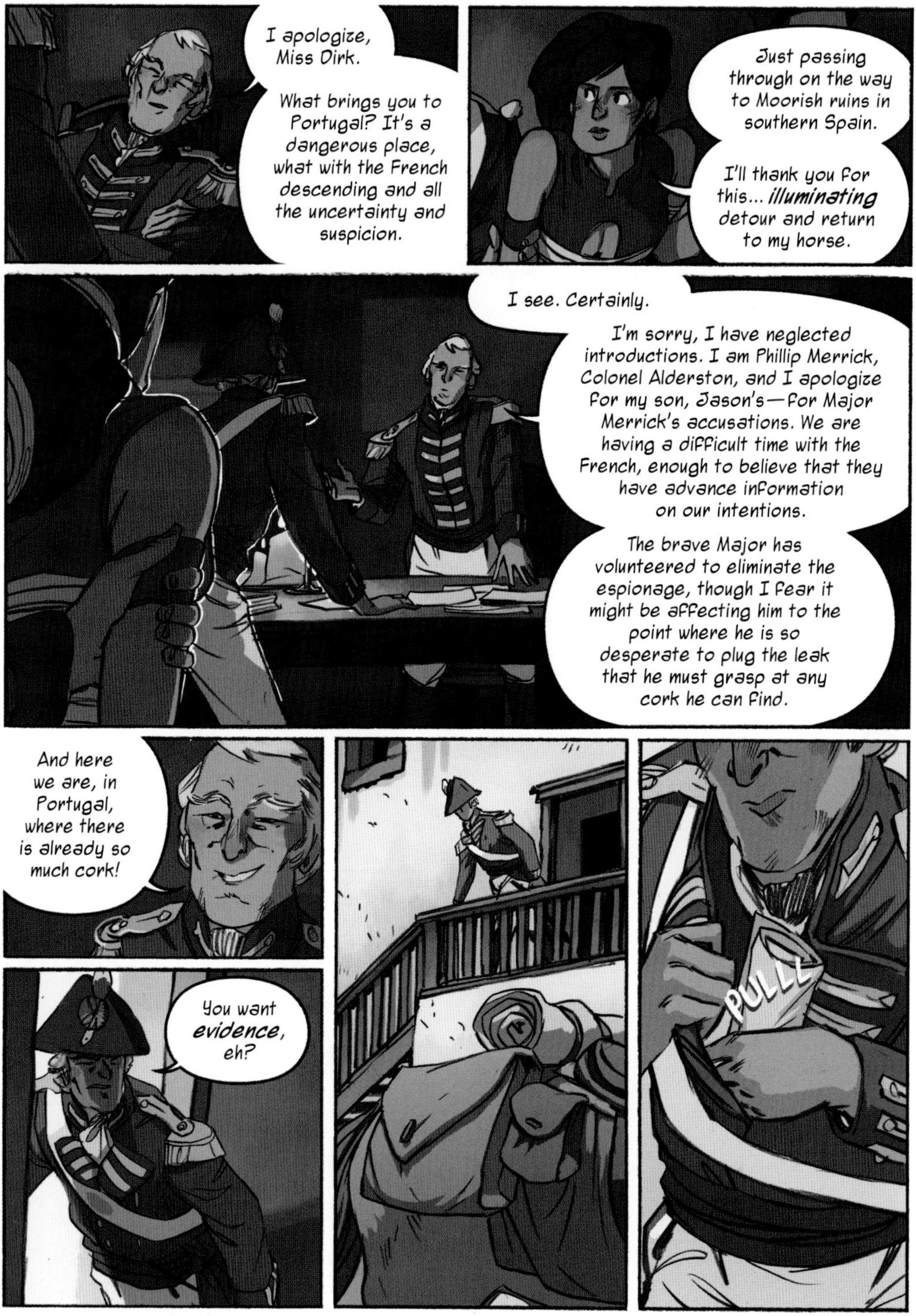
I apologize, Miss Dirk.
What brings you to Portugal? It's a dangerous place, what with the French descending and all the uncertainty and suspicion.
Just passing through on the way to Moorish ruins in southern Spain.
I'll thank you for this... ***illuminating*** detour and return to my horse.
I see. Certainly.
I'm sorry, I have neglected introductions. I am Phillip Merrick, Colonel Alderston, and I apologize for my son, Jason's—for Major Merrick's accusations. We are having a difficult time with the French, enough to believe that they have advance information on our intentions.
The brave Major has volunteered to eliminate the espionage, though I fear it might be affecting him to the point where he is so desperate to plug the leak that he must grasp at any cork he can find.
And here we are, in Portugal, where there is already so much cork!
You want ***evidence***, eh?
PULLL

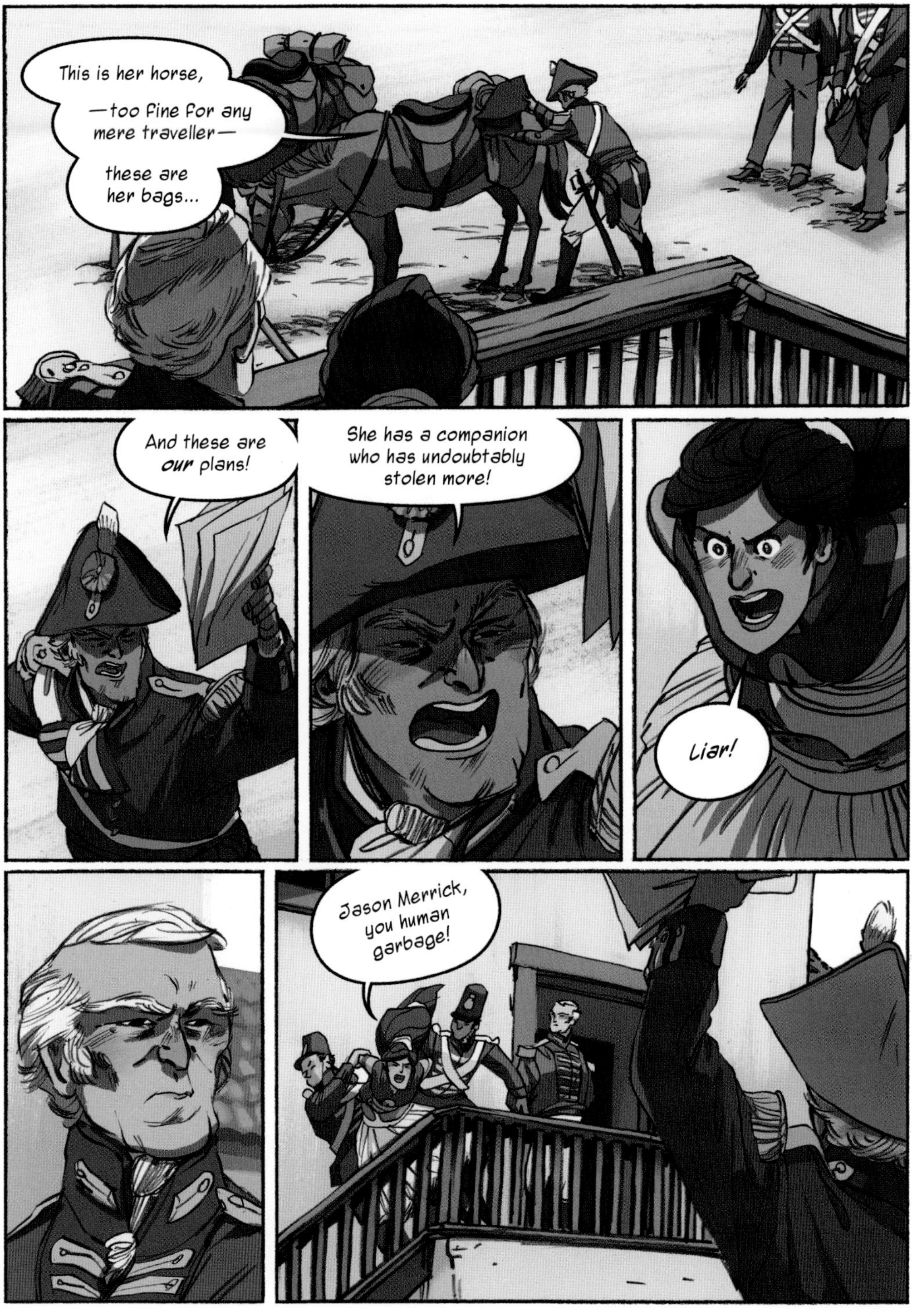
This is her horse,
—too fine for any mere traveller—
these are her bags...
And these are our plans!
She has a companion who has undoubtably stolen more!
Liar!
Jason Merrick, you human garbage!

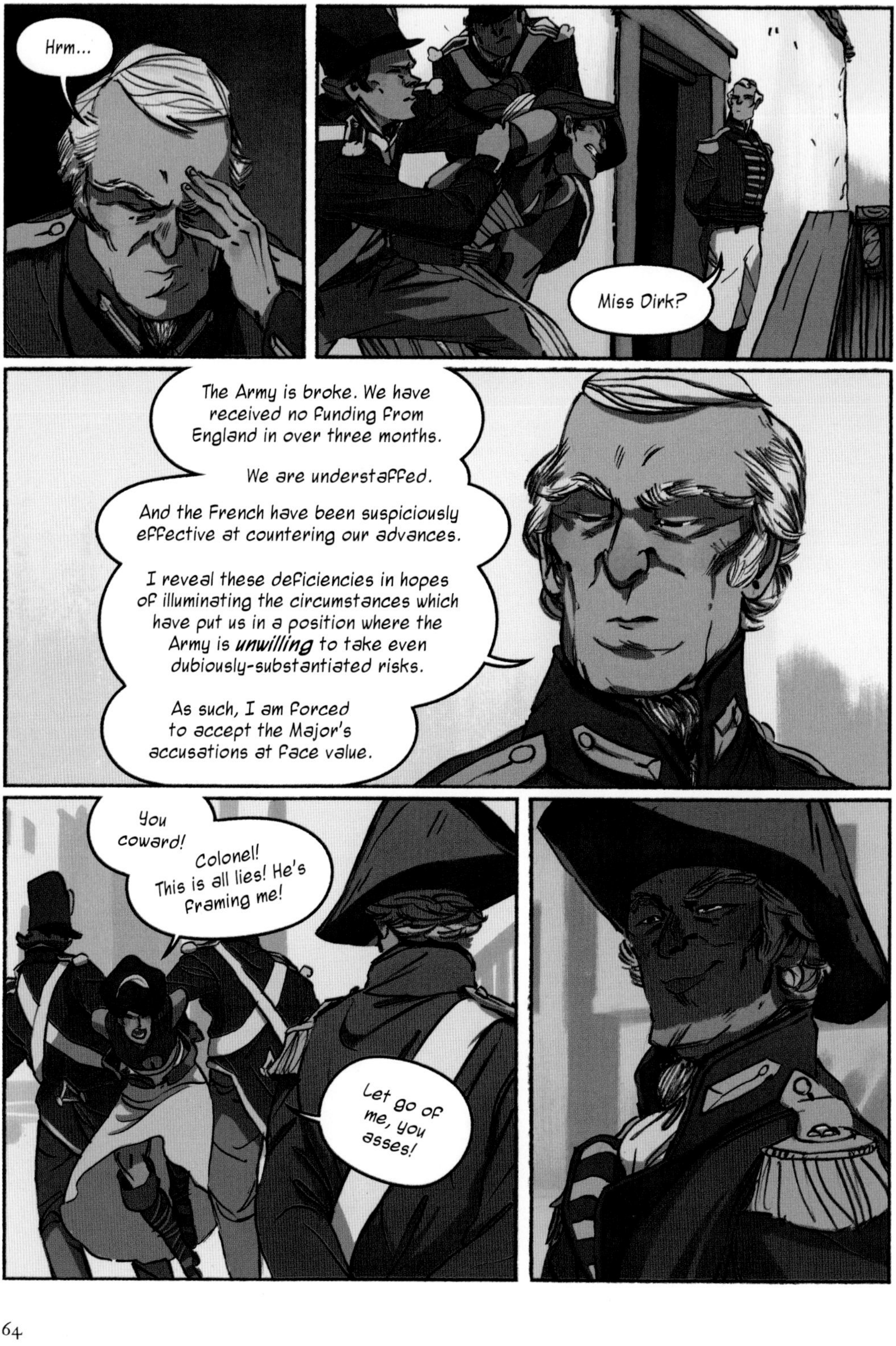
Hrm...
Miss Dirk?
The Army is broke. We have received no funding from England in over three months.
We are understaffed.
And the French have been suspiciously effective at countering our advances.
I reveal these deficiencies in hopes of illuminating the circumstances which have put us in a position where the Army is unwilling to take even dubiously-substantiated risks.
As such, I am forced to accept the Major's accusations at face value.
You coward!
Colonel! This is all lies! He's framing me!
Let go of me, you asses!

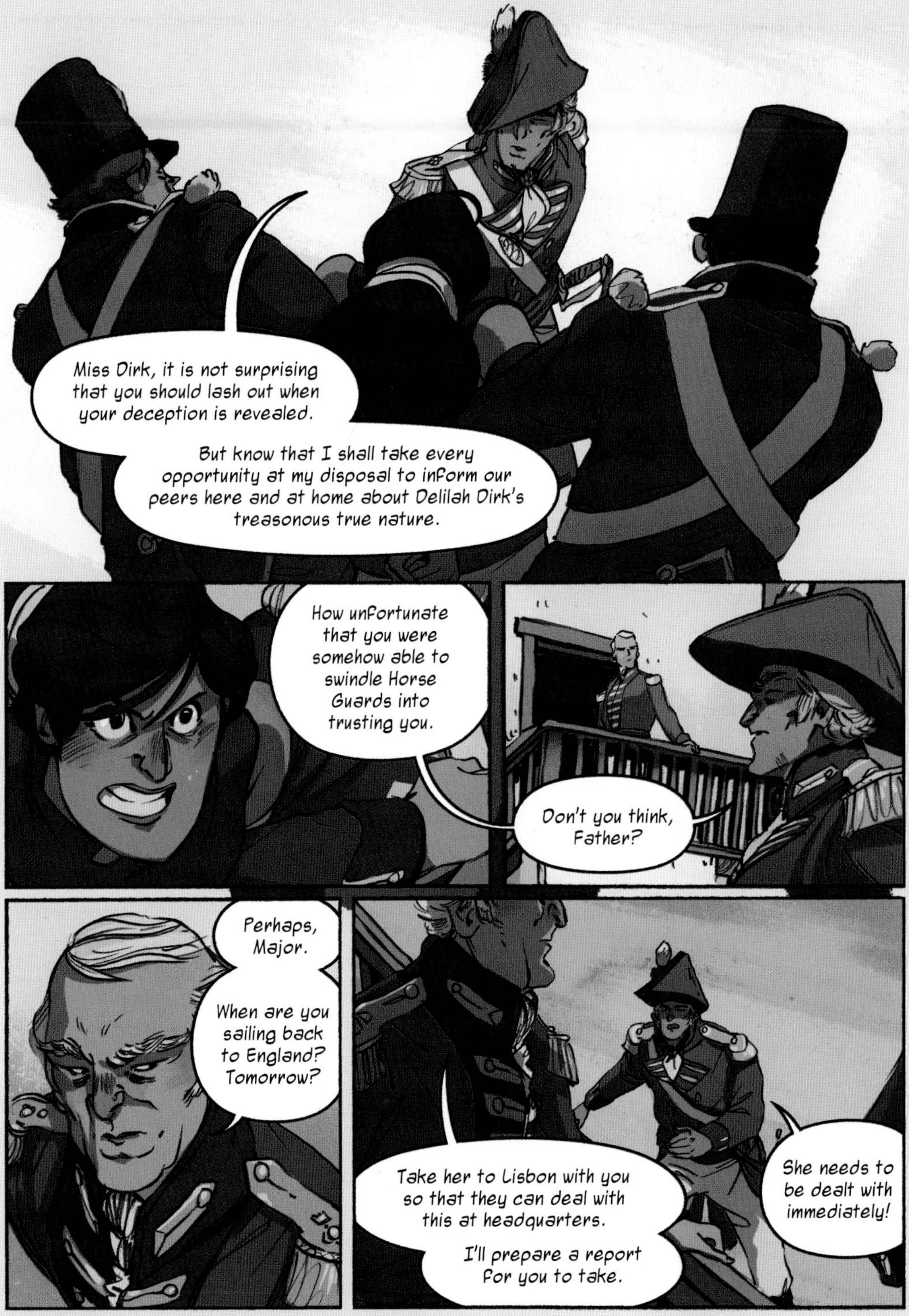
Miss Dirk, it is not surprising that you should lash out when your deception is revealed.
But know that I shall take every opportunity at my disposal to inform our peers here and at home about Delilah Dirk's treasonous true nature.
How unfortunate that you were somehow able to swindle Horse Guards into trusting you.
Don't you think, Father?
Perhaps, Major.
When are you sailing back to England? Tomorrow?
Take her to Lisbon with you so that they can deal with this at headquarters.
I'll prepare a report for you to take.
She needs to be dealt with immediately!

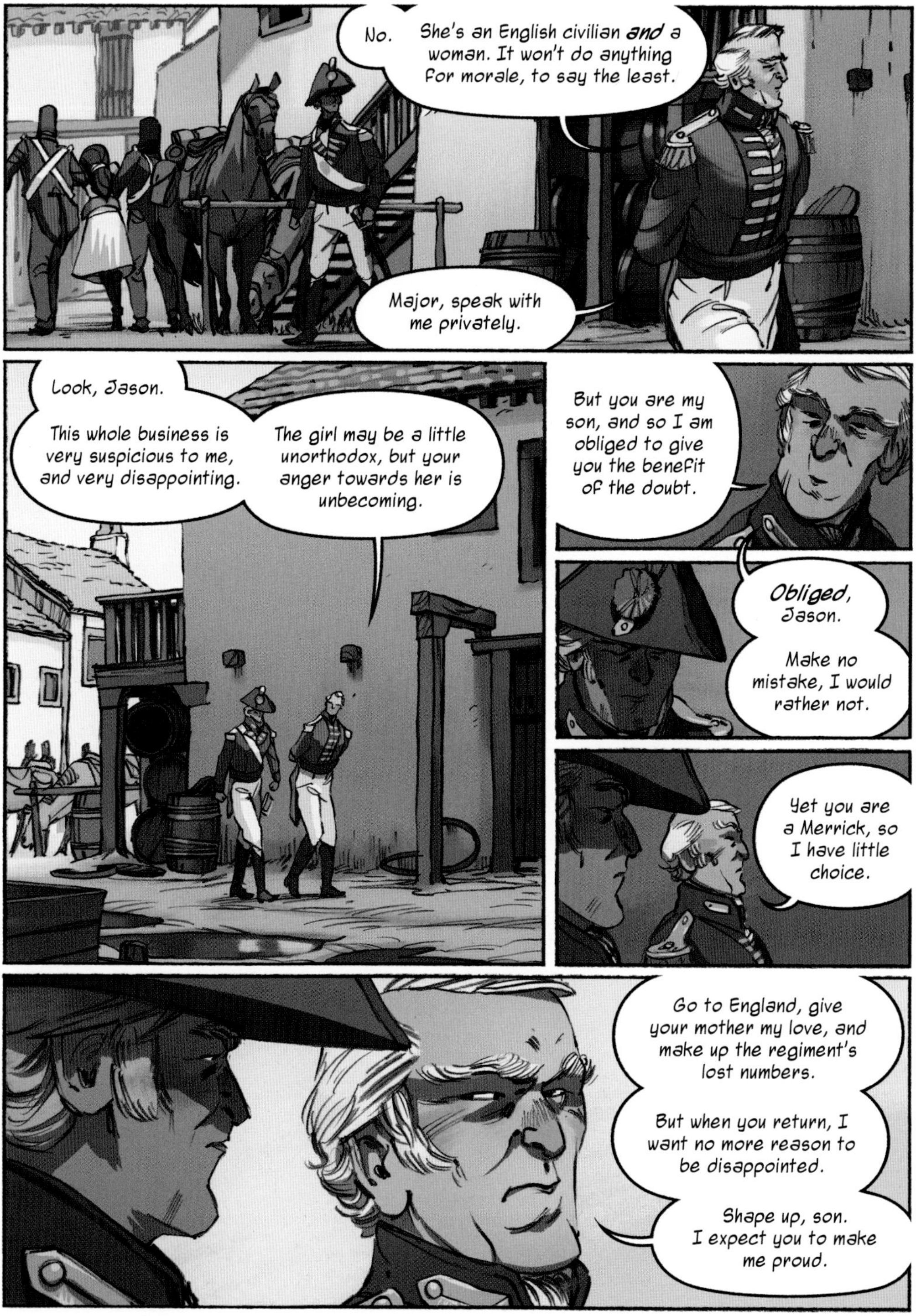
No.
She's an English civilian *and* a woman. It won't do anything for morale, to say the least.
Major, speak with me privately.
Look, Jason.
This whole business is very suspicious to me, and very disappointing.
The girl may be a little unorthodox, but your anger towards her is unbecoming.
But you are my son, and so I am obliged to give you the benefit of the doubt.
*Obliged*, Jason.
Make no mistake, I would rather not.
Yet you are a Merrick, so I have little choice.
Go to England, give your mother my love, and make up the regiment's lost numbers.
But when you return, I want no more reason to be disappointed.
Shape up, son. I expect you to make me proud.

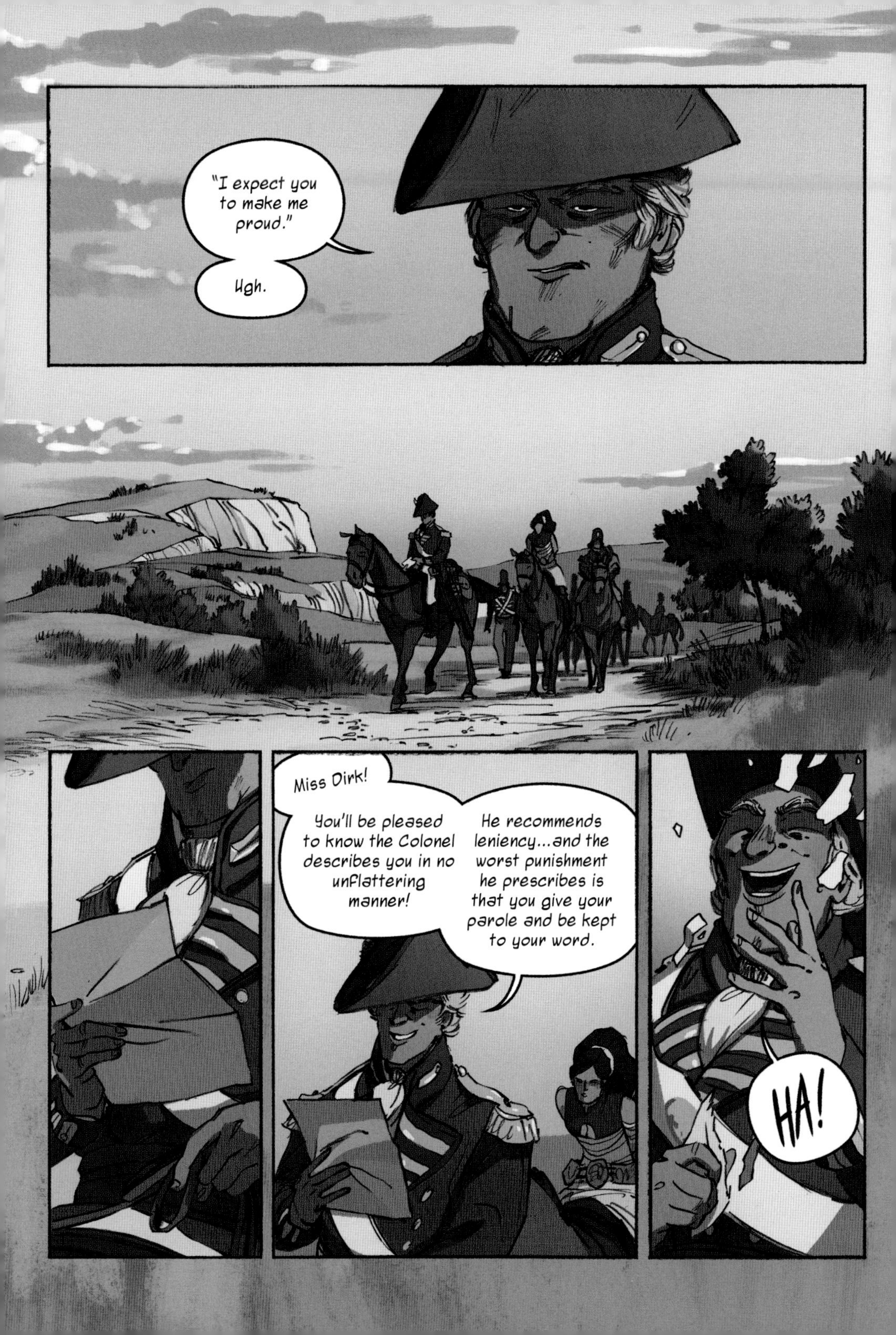
"I expect you to make me proud."
Ugh.
Miss Dirk!
You'll be pleased to know the Colonel describes you in no unflattering manner!
He recommends leniency...and the worst punishment he prescribes is that you give your parole and be kept to your word.
HA!

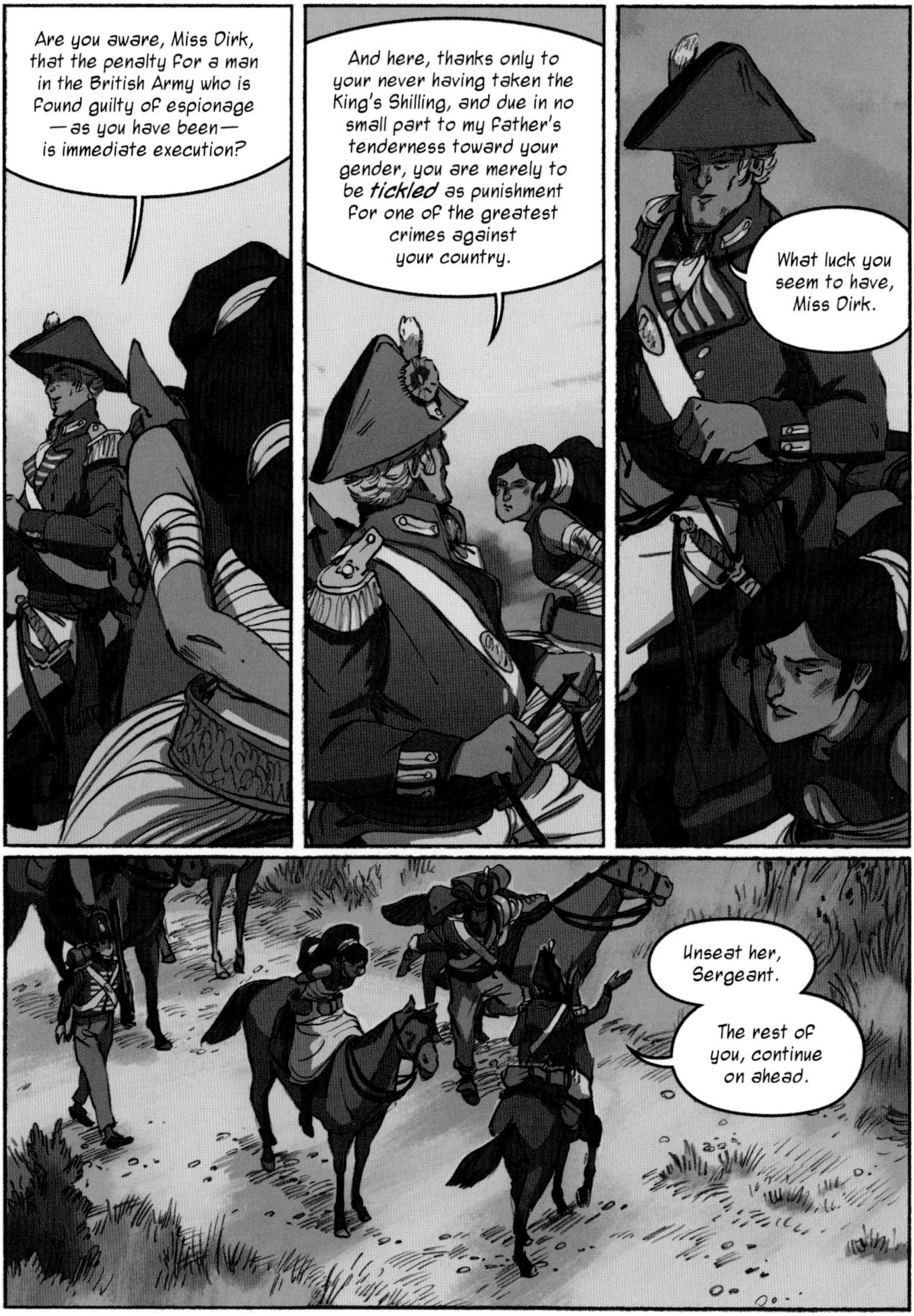
Are you aware, Miss Dirk, that the penalty for a man in the British Army who is found guilty of espionage —as you have been— is immediate execution?
And here, thanks only to your never having taken the King's Shilling, and due in no small part to my father's tenderness toward your gender, you are merely to be *tickled* as punishment for one of the greatest crimes against your country.
What luck you seem to have, Miss Dirk.
Unseat her, Sergeant.
The rest of you, continue on ahead.

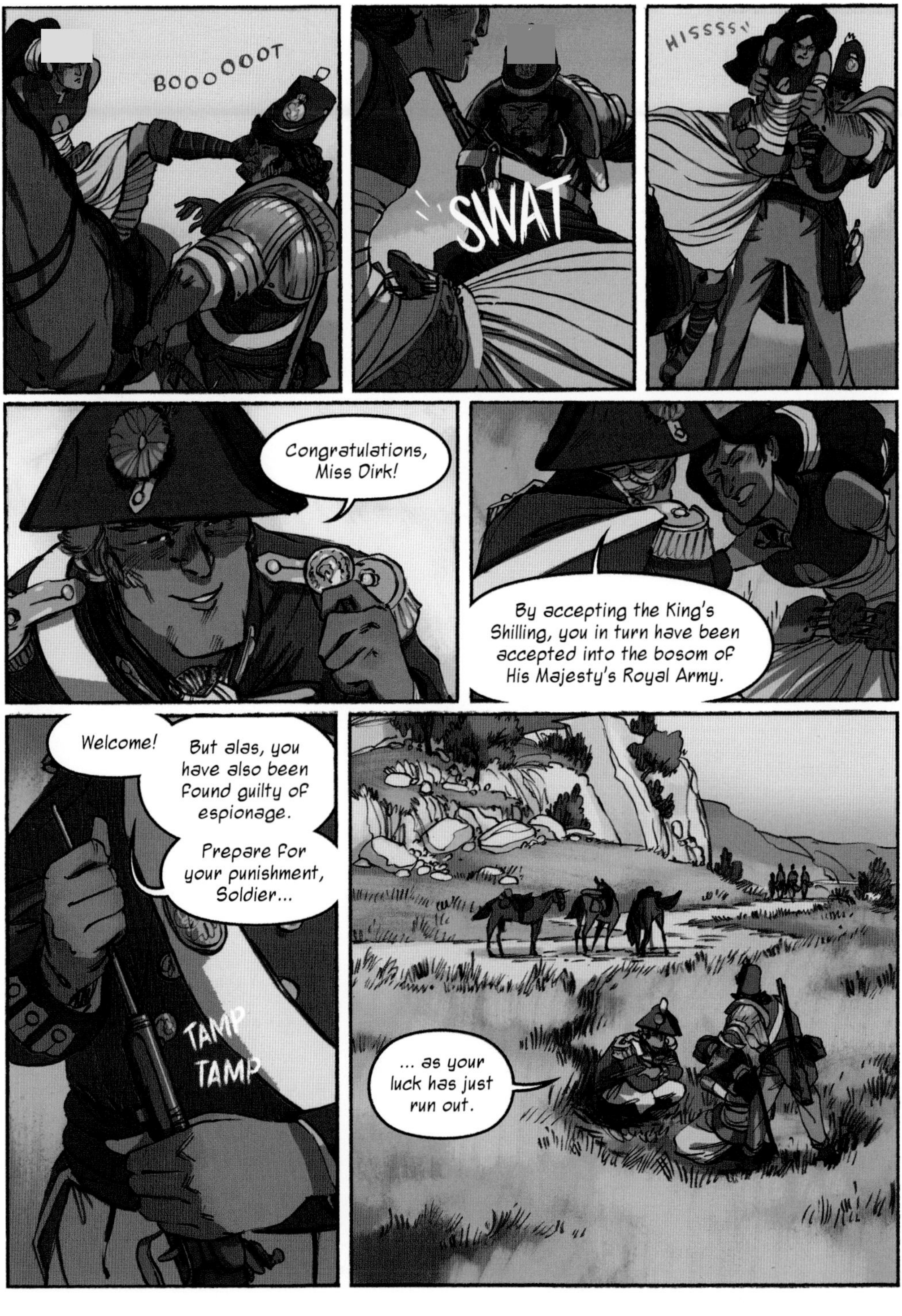
BOOOOOOT
SWAT
HISSSS
Congratulations, Miss Dirk!
By accepting the King's Shilling, you in turn have been accepted into the bosom of His Majesty's Royal Army.
Welcome!
But alas, you have also been found guilty of espionage.
Prepare for your punishment, Soldier...
TAMP TAMP
... as your luck has just run out.

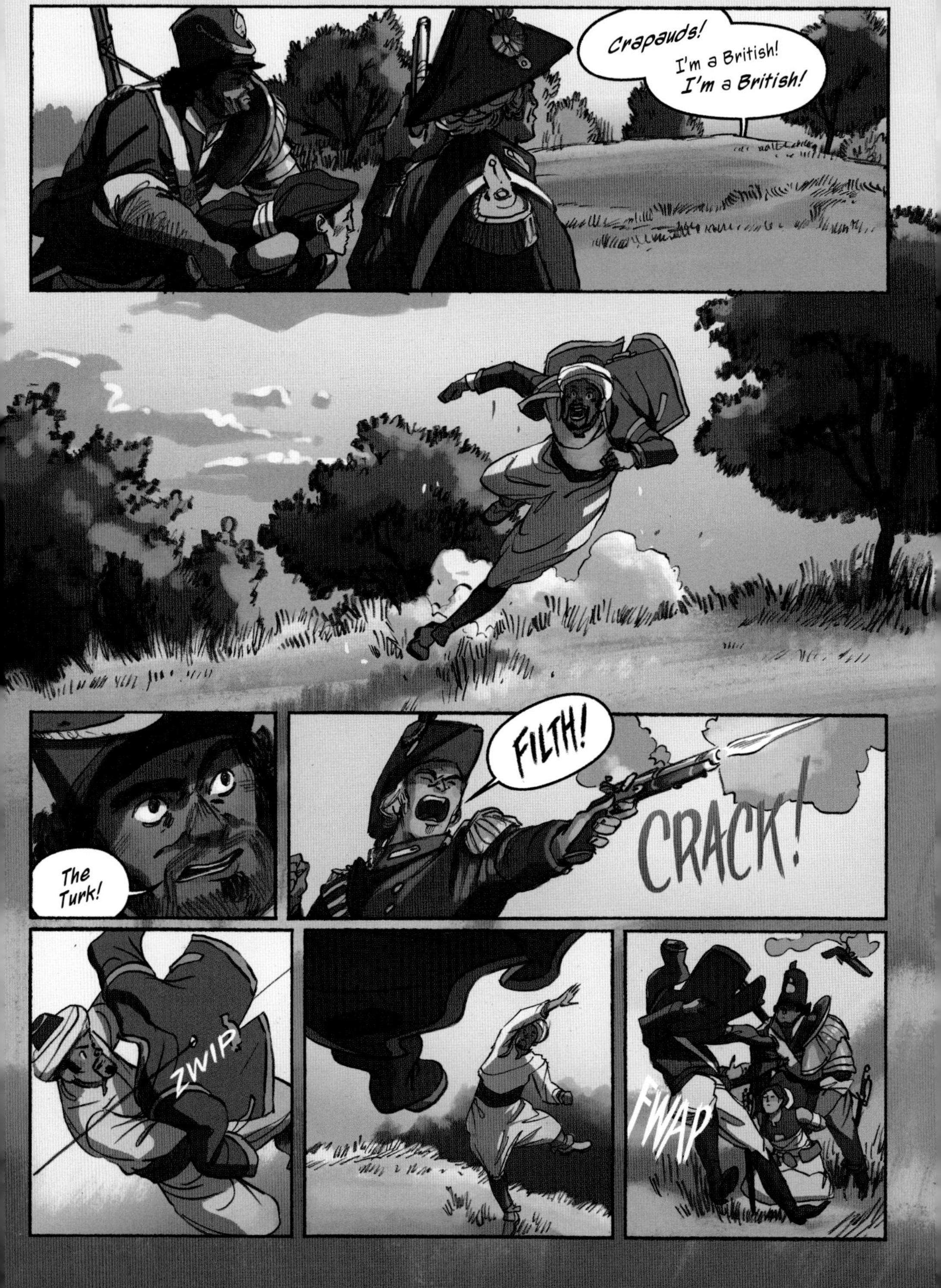
Crapauds!
I'm a British!
I'm a British!
The Turk!
FILTH!
CRACK!
ZWIP
FWAP

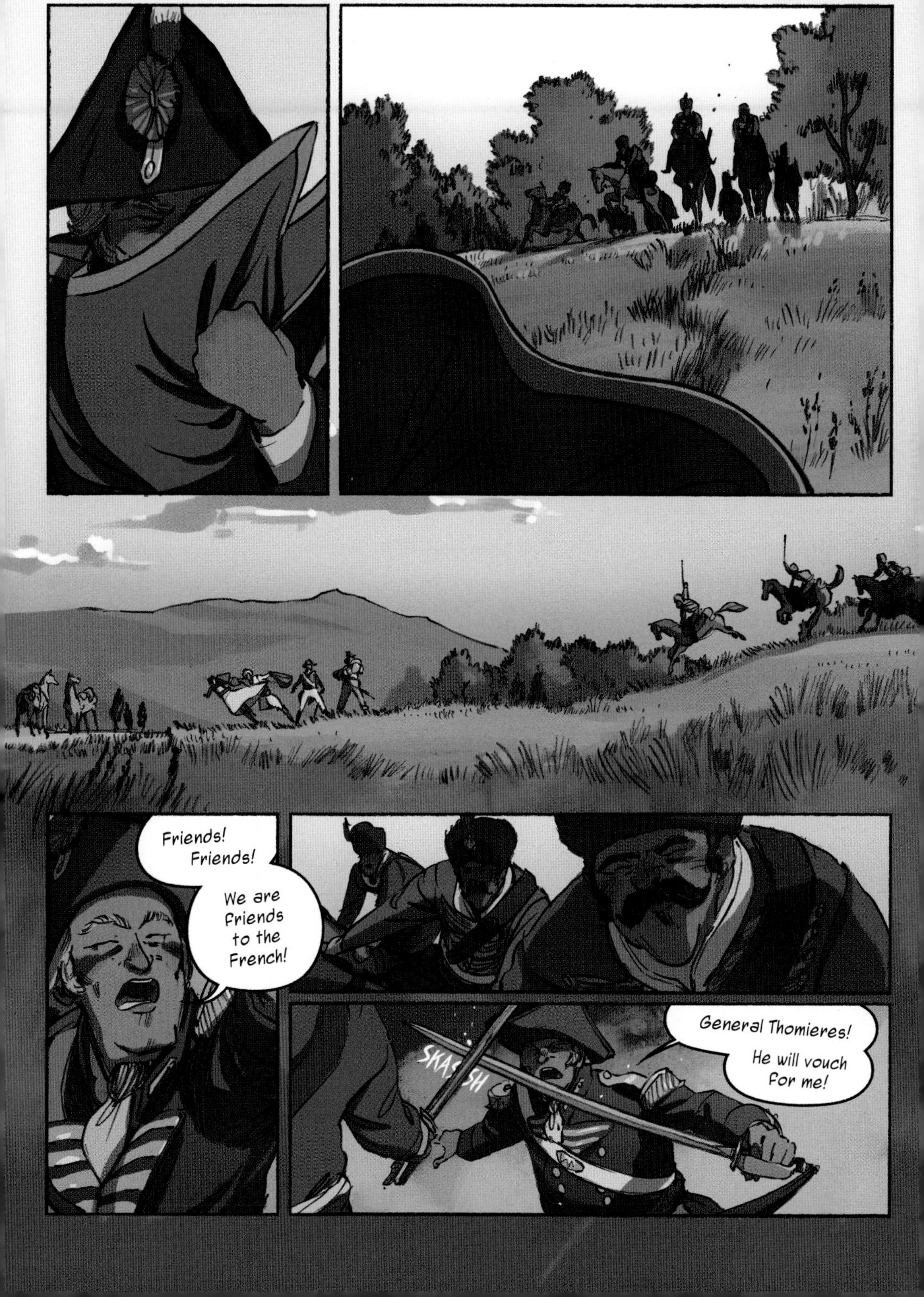
Friends! Friends!
We are friends to the French!
SKASSH
General Thomieres!
He will vouch for me!

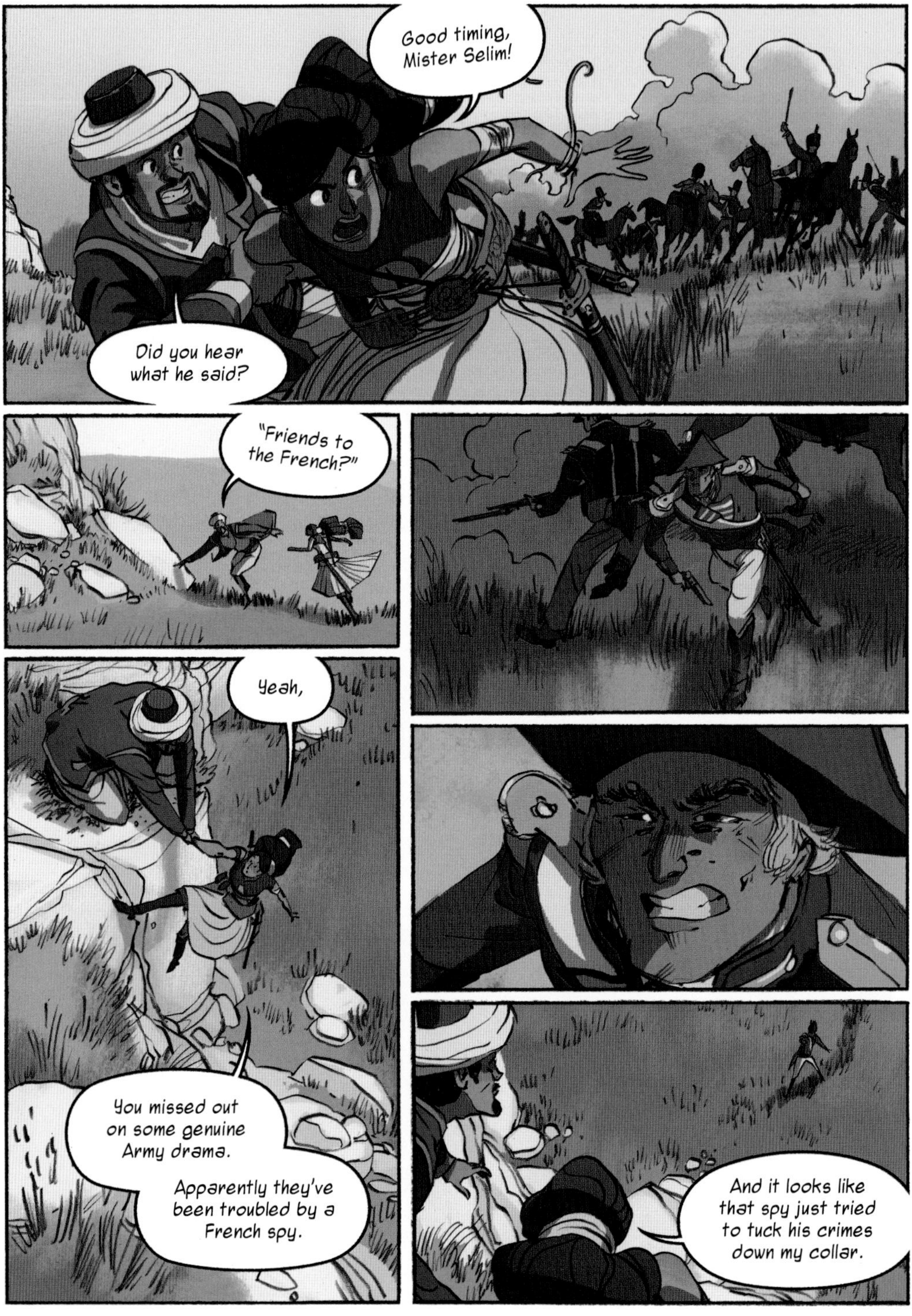
Good timing, Mister Selim!
Did you hear what he said?
"Friends to the French?"
Yeah,
You missed out on some genuine Army drama.
Apparently they've been troubled by a French spy.
And it looks like that spy just tried to tuck his crimes down my collar.

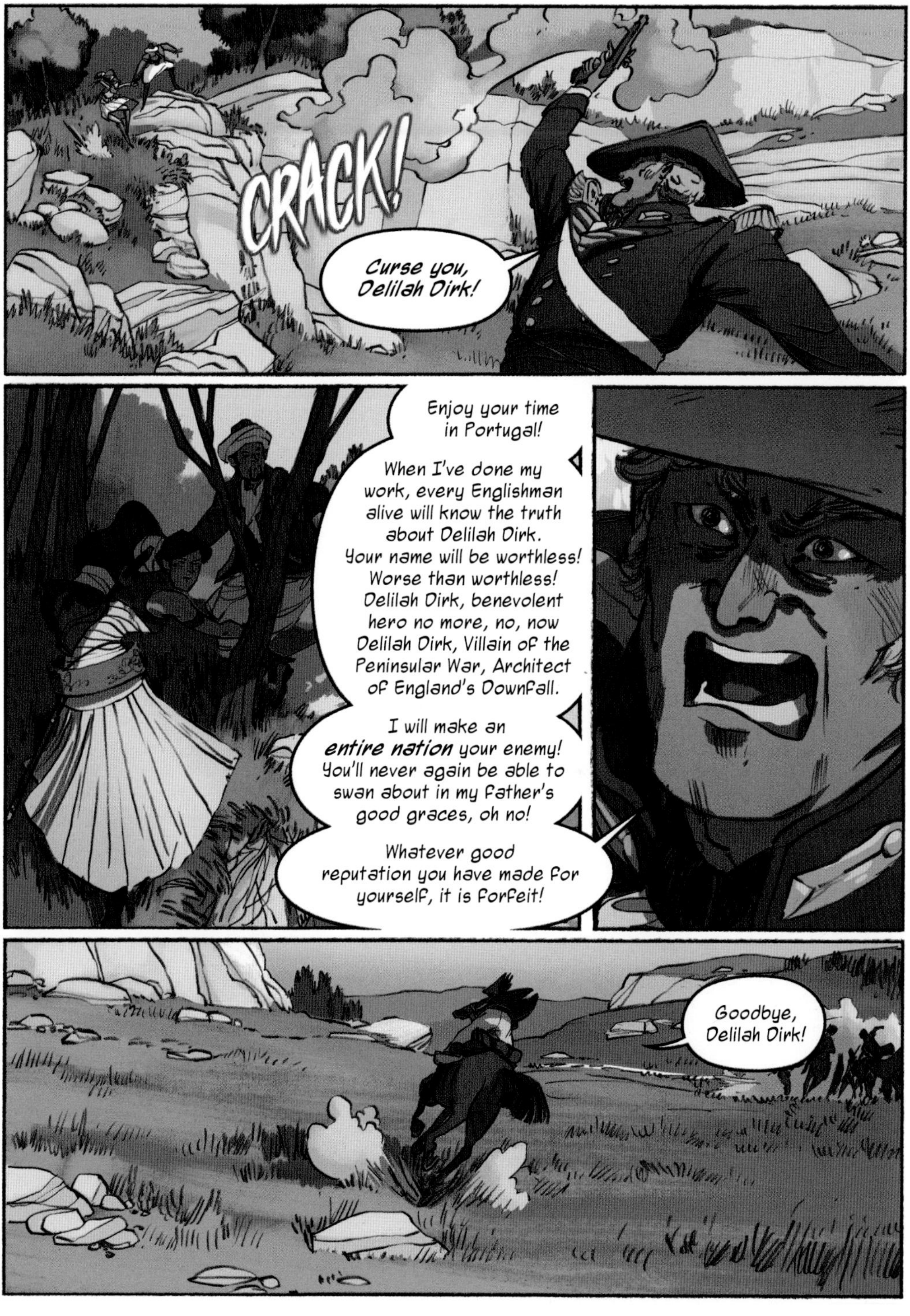
CRACK!
Curse you, Delilah Dirk!
Enjoy your time in Portugal!
When I've done my work, every Englishman alive will know the truth about Delilah Dirk. Your name will be worthless! Worse than worthless! Delilah Dirk, benevolent hero no more, no, now Delilah Dirk, Villain of the Peninsular War, Architect of England's Downfall.
I will make an *entire nation* your enemy! You'll never again be able to swan about in my father's good graces, oh no!
Whatever good reputation you have made for yourself, it is forfeit!
Goodbye, Delilah Dirk!

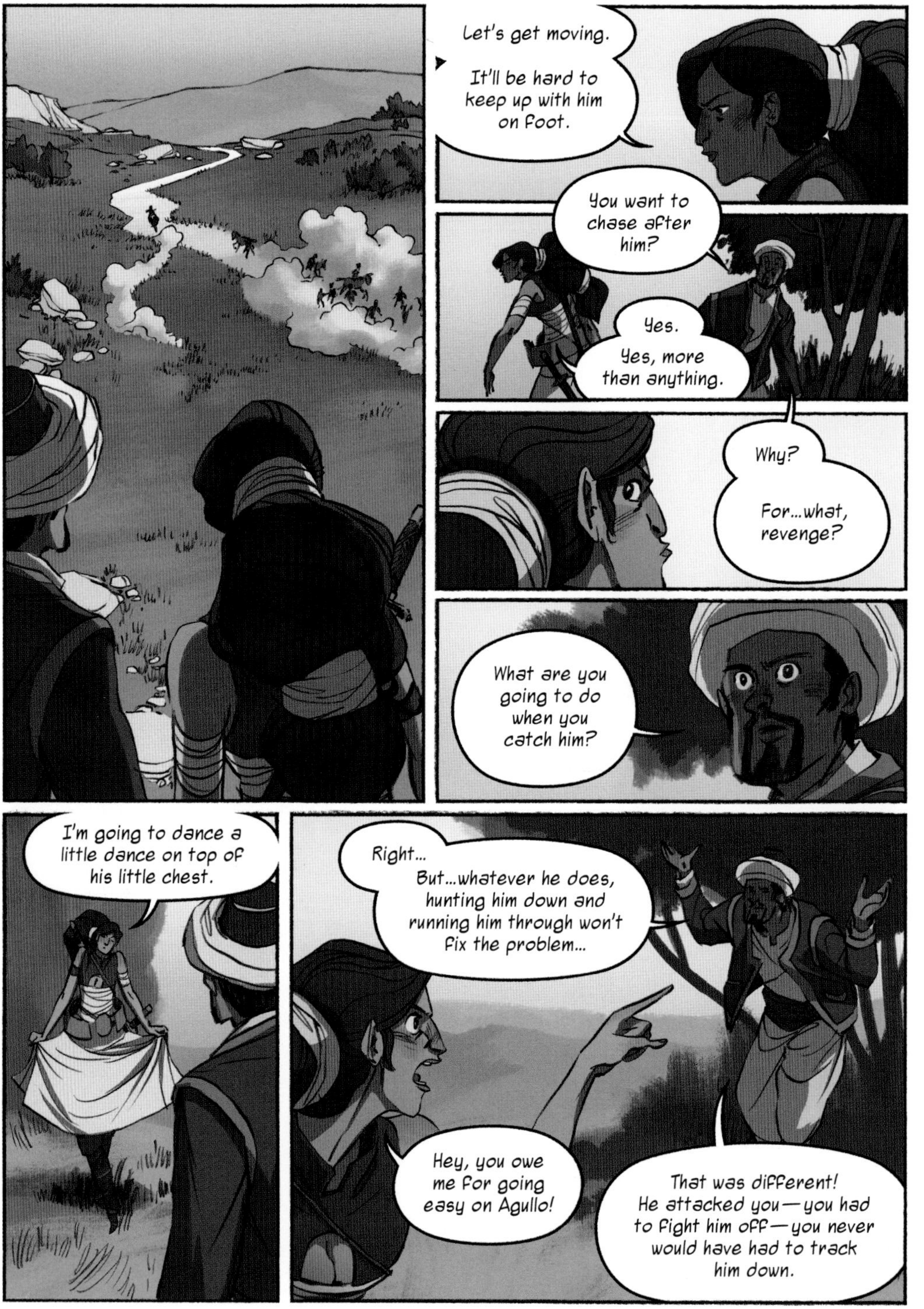
Let's get moving.
It'll be hard to keep up with him on foot.
You want to chase after him?
Yes.
Yes, more than anything.
Why?
For...what, revenge?
What are you going to do when you catch him?
I'm going to dance a little dance on top of his little chest.
Right...
But...whatever he does, hunting him down and running him through won't fix the problem...
Hey, you owe me for going easy on Agullo!
That was different! He attacked you—you had to fight him off—you never would have had to track him down.

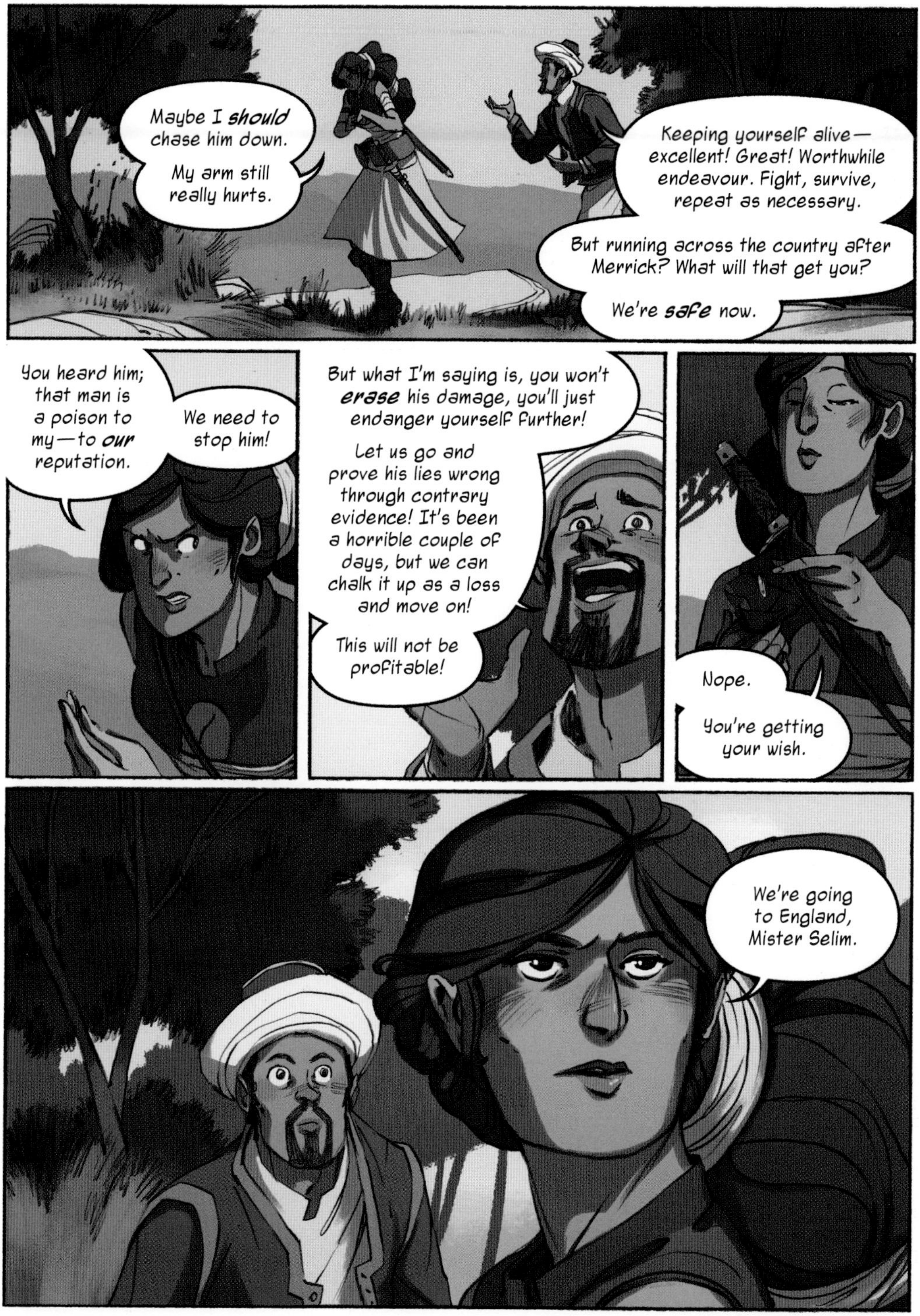
Maybe I *should* chase him down.
My arm still really hurts.
Keeping yourself alive—excellent! Great! Worthwhile endeavour. Fight, survive, repeat as necessary.
But running across the country after Merrick? What will that get you?
We're *safe* now.
You heard him; that man is a poison to my—to *our* reputation.
We need to stop him!
But what I'm saying is, you won't *erase* his damage, you'll just endanger yourself further!
Let us go and prove his lies wrong through contrary evidence! It's been a horrible couple of days, but we can chalk it up as a loss and move on!
This will not be profitable!
Nope.
You're getting your wish.
We're going to England, Mister Selim.

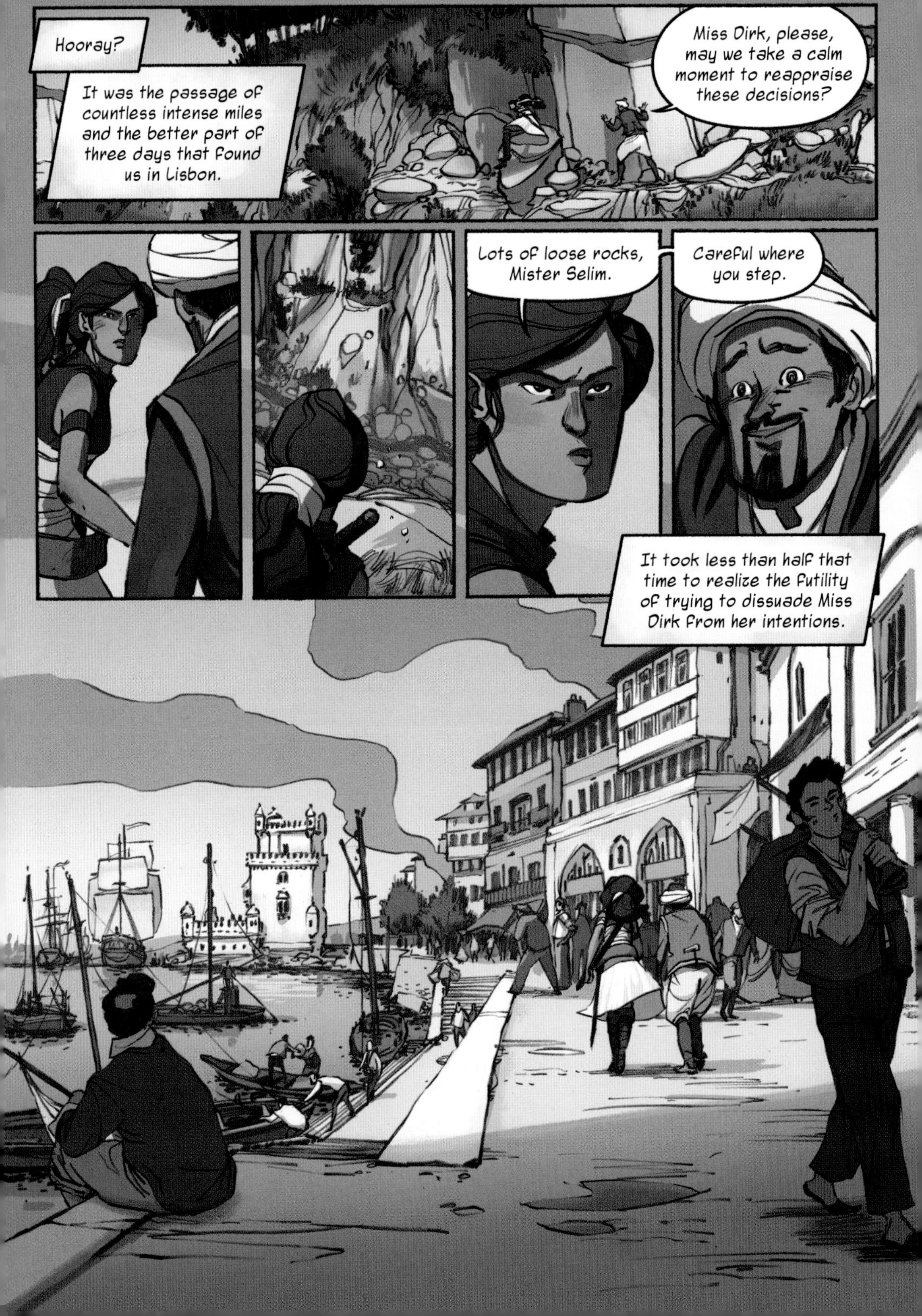
Hooray?
It was the passage of countless intense miles and the better part of three days that found us in Lisbon.
Miss Dirk, please, may we take a calm moment to reappraise these decisions?
Lots of loose rocks, Mister Selim.
Careful where you step.
It took less than half that time to realize the futility of trying to dissuade Miss Dirk from her intentions.

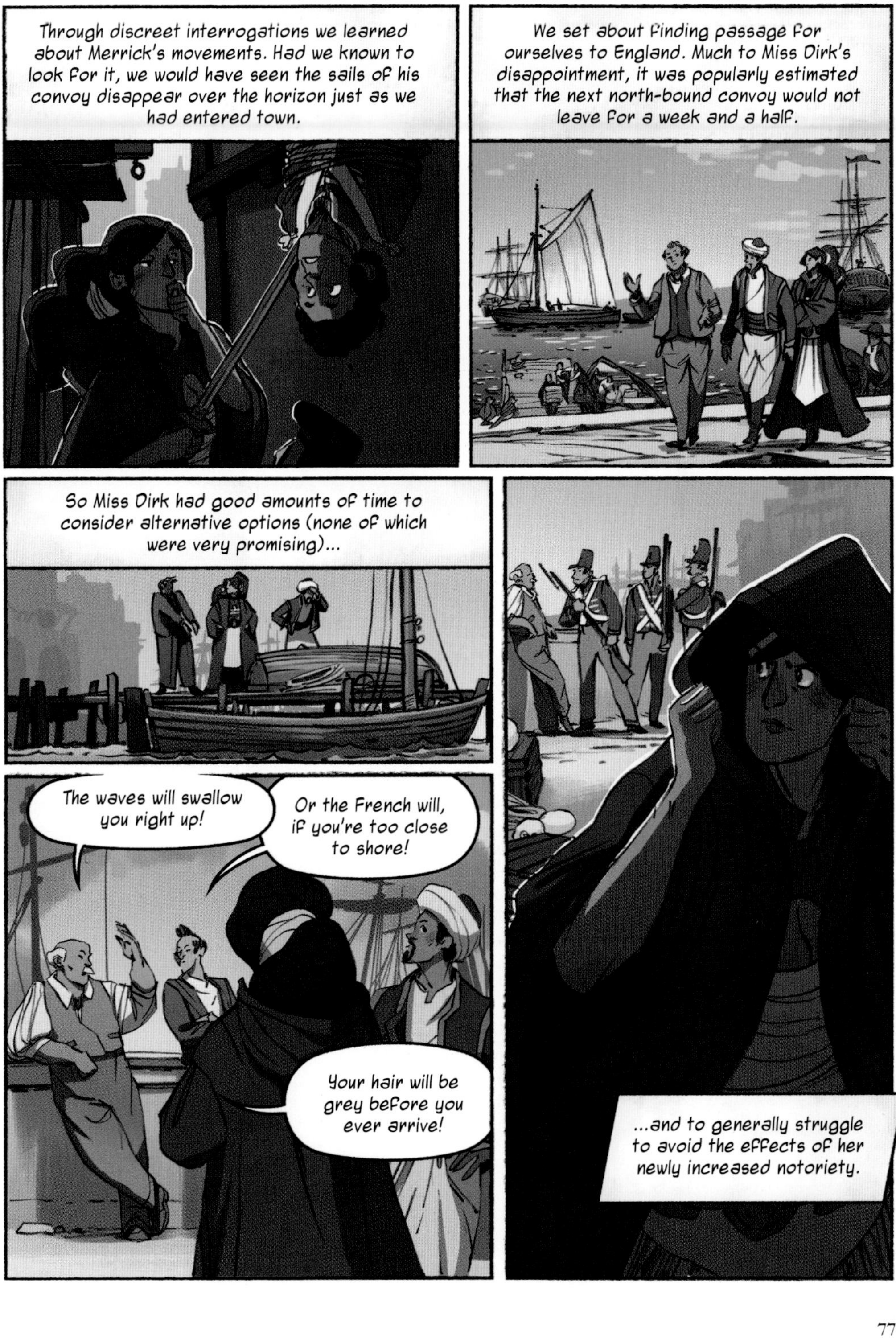
Through discreet interrogations we learned about Merrick's movements. Had we known to look for it, we would have seen the sails of his convoy disappear over the horizon just as we had entered town.
We set about finding passage for ourselves to England. Much to Miss Dirk's disappointment, it was popularly estimated that the next north-bound convoy would not leave for a week and a half.
So Miss Dirk had good amounts of time to consider alternative options (none of which were very promising)...
The waves will swallow you right up!
Or the French will, if you're too close to shore!
Your hair will be grey before you ever arrive!
...and to generally struggle to avoid the effects of her newly increased notoriety.

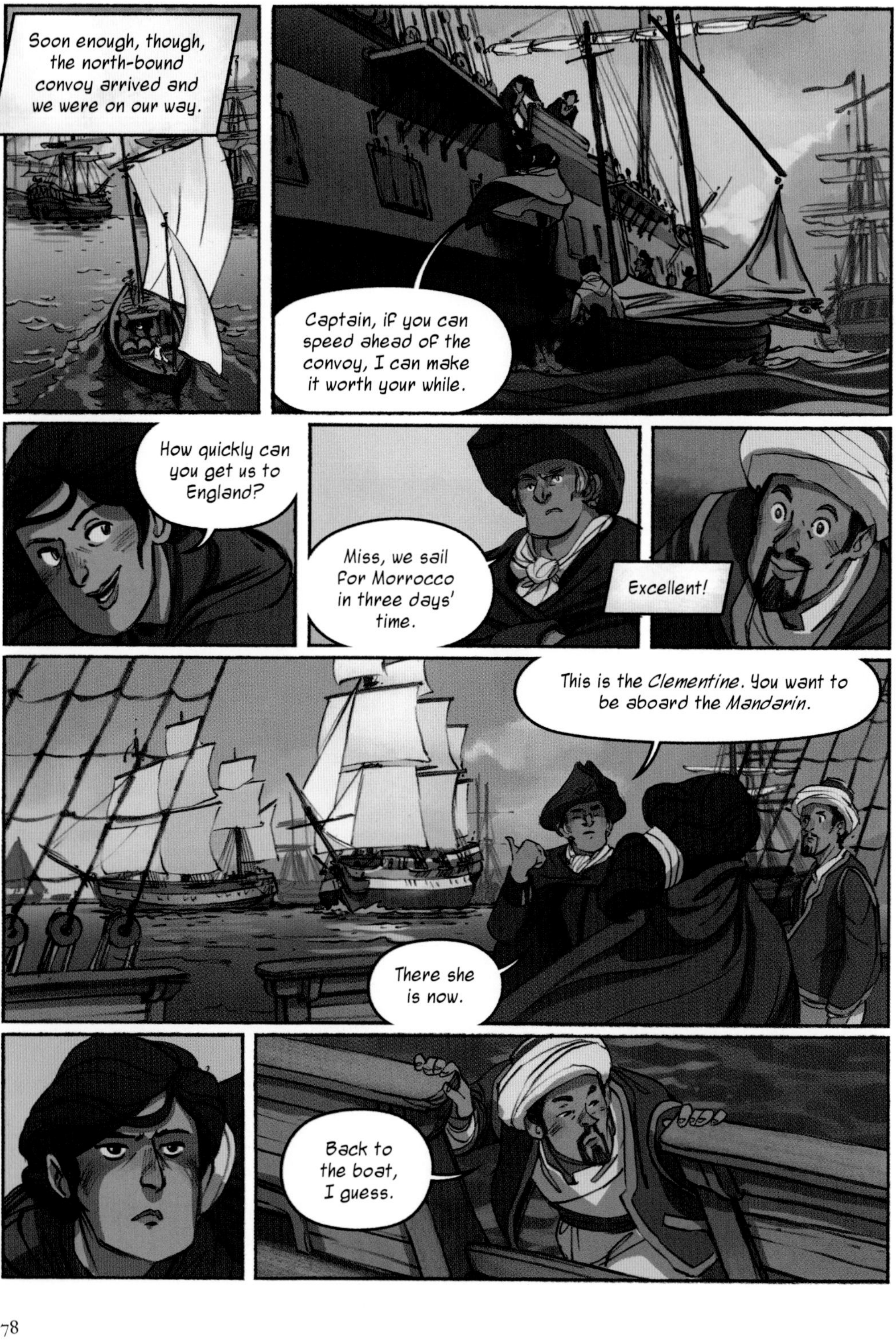
Soon enough, though, the north-bound convoy arrived and we were on our way.
Captain, if you can speed ahead of the convoy, I can make it worth your while.
How quickly can you get us to England?
Miss, we sail for Morrocco in three days' time.
Excellent!
This is the *Clementine*. You want to be aboard the *Mandarin*.
There she is now.
Back to the boat, I guess.

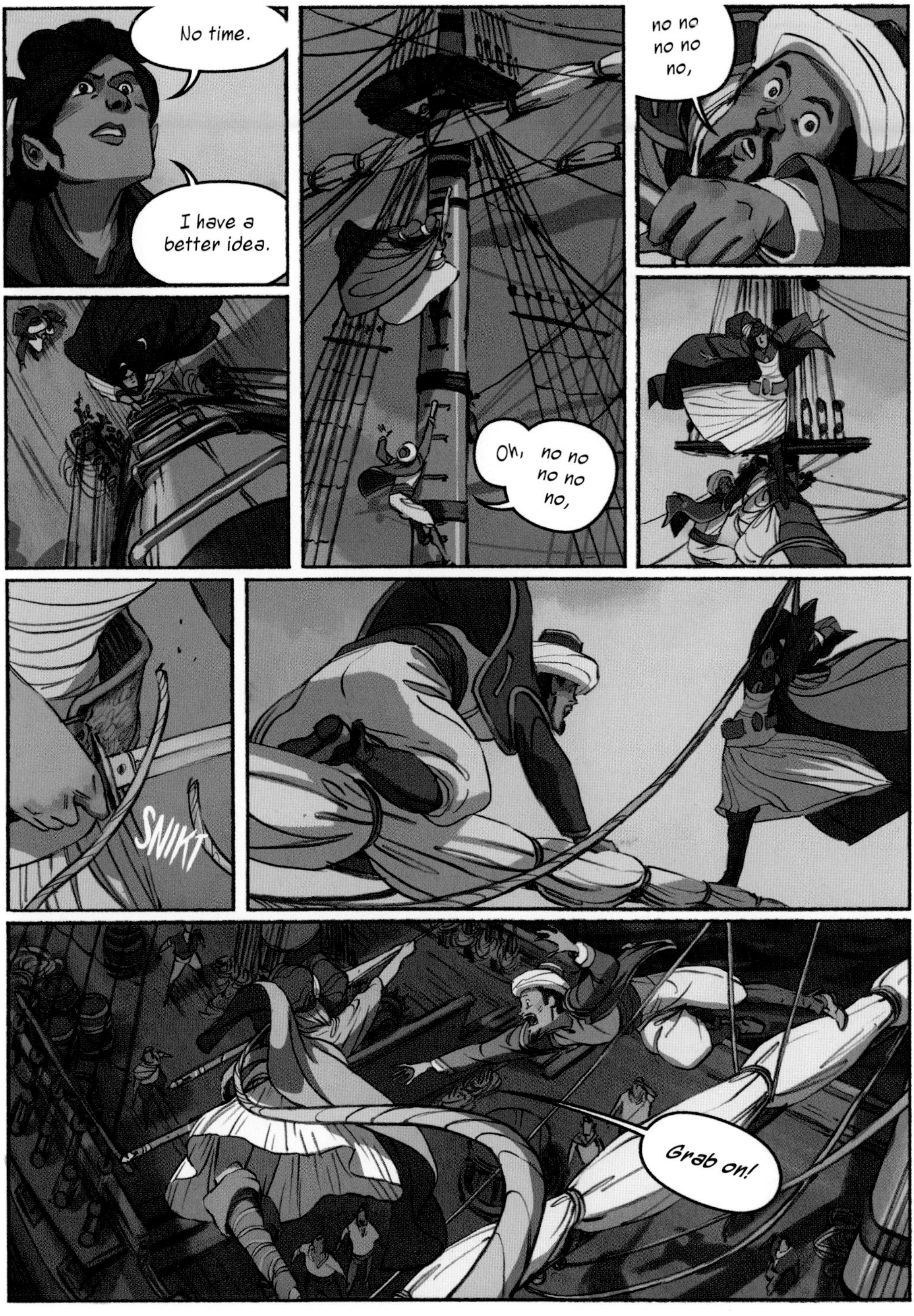
No time.
I have a better idea.
no no no no no,
Oh, no no no no no,
SNIKT
Grab on!

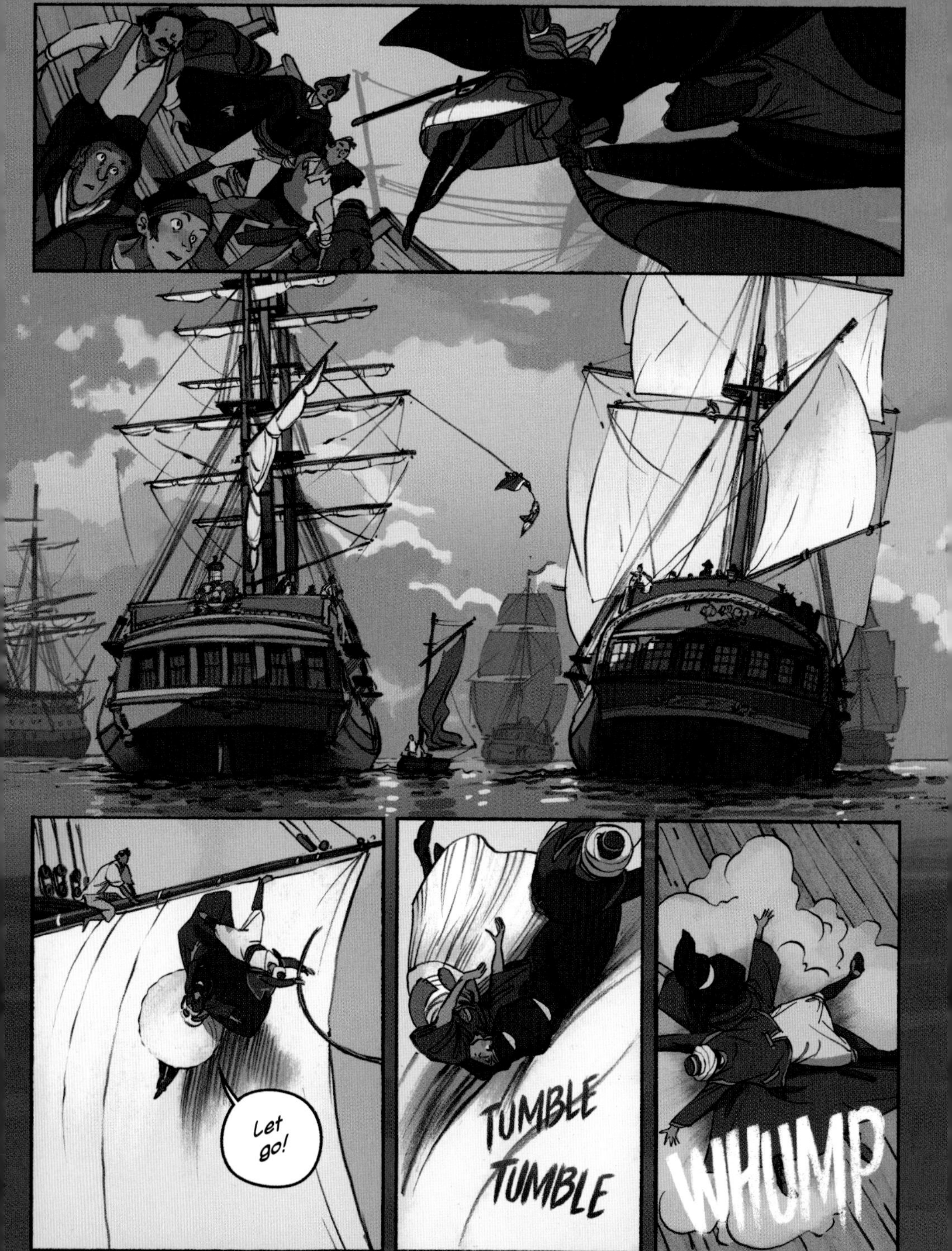
Let go!
TUMBLE
TUMBLE
WHUMP

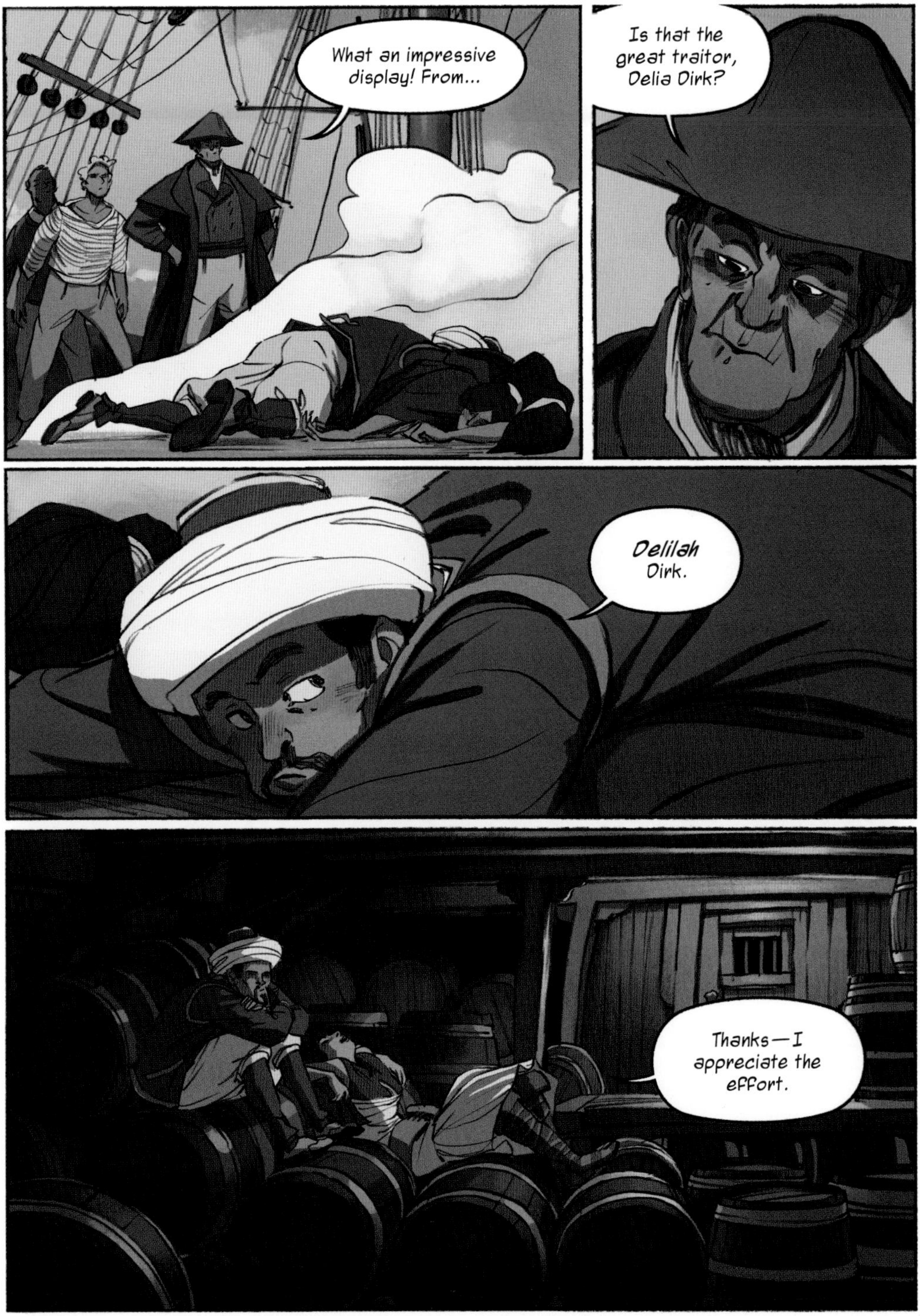
What an impressive display! From...
Is that the great traitor, Delia Dirk?
*Delilah* Dirk.
Thanks—I appreciate the effort.

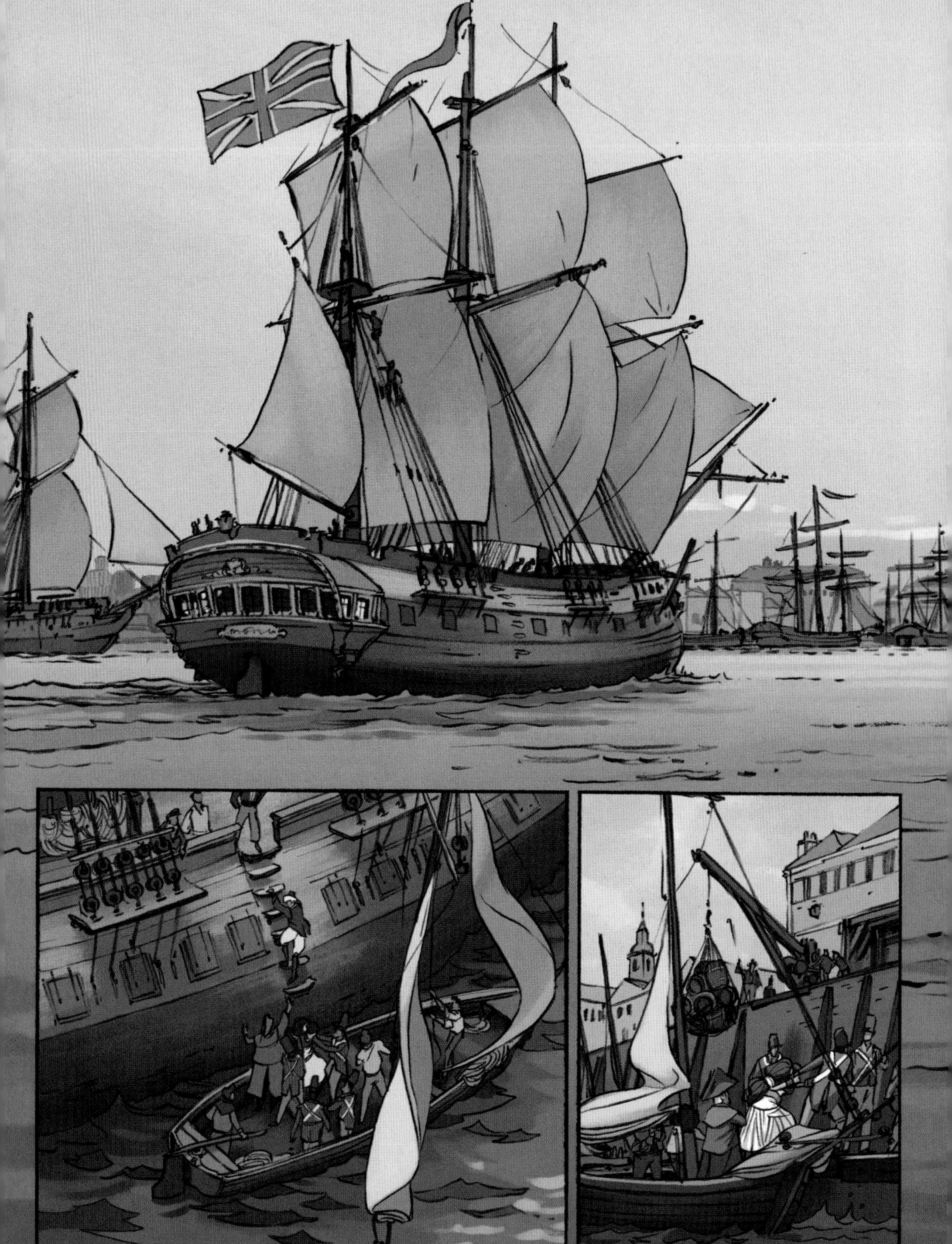

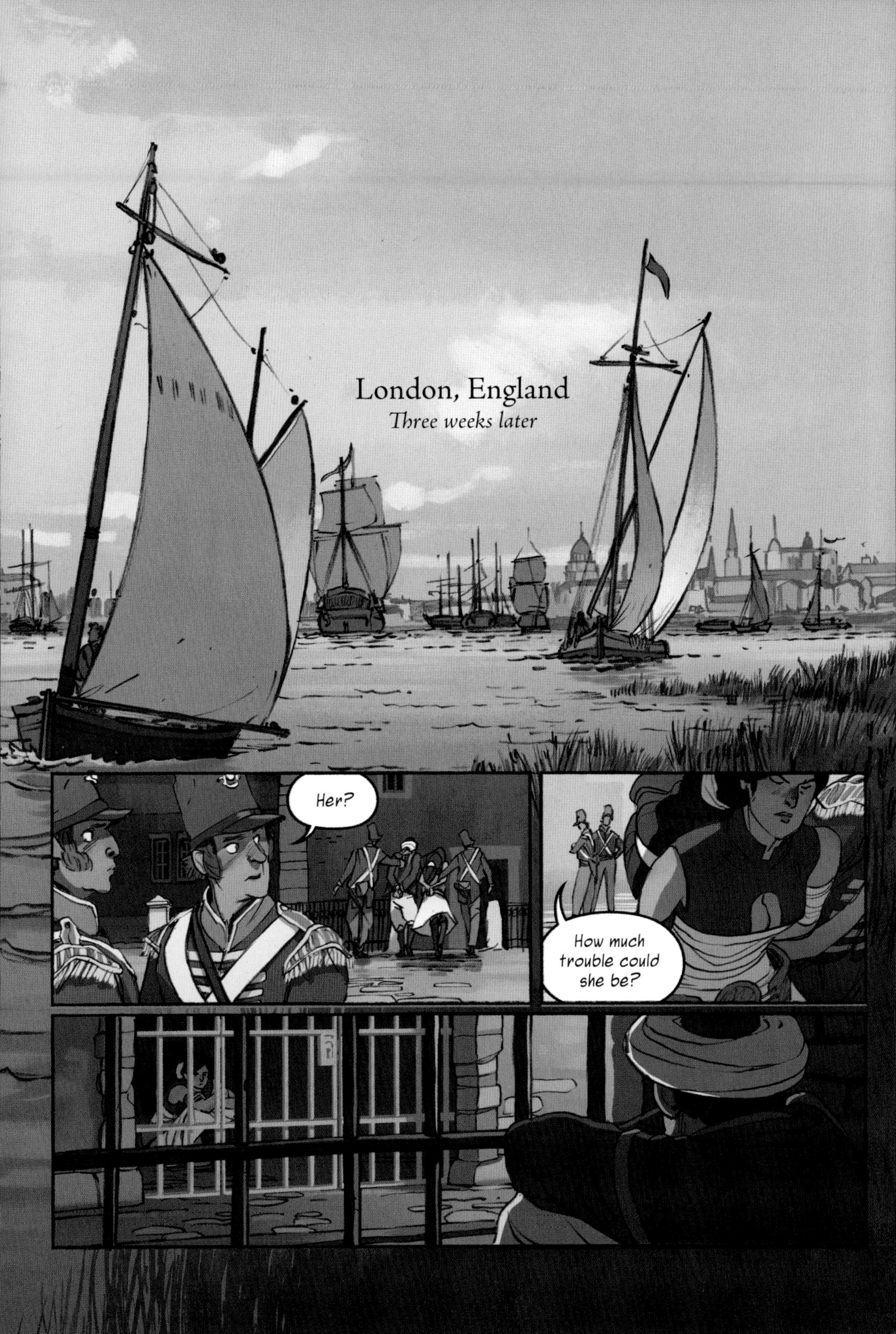
London, England
Three weeks later
Her?
How much trouble could she be?

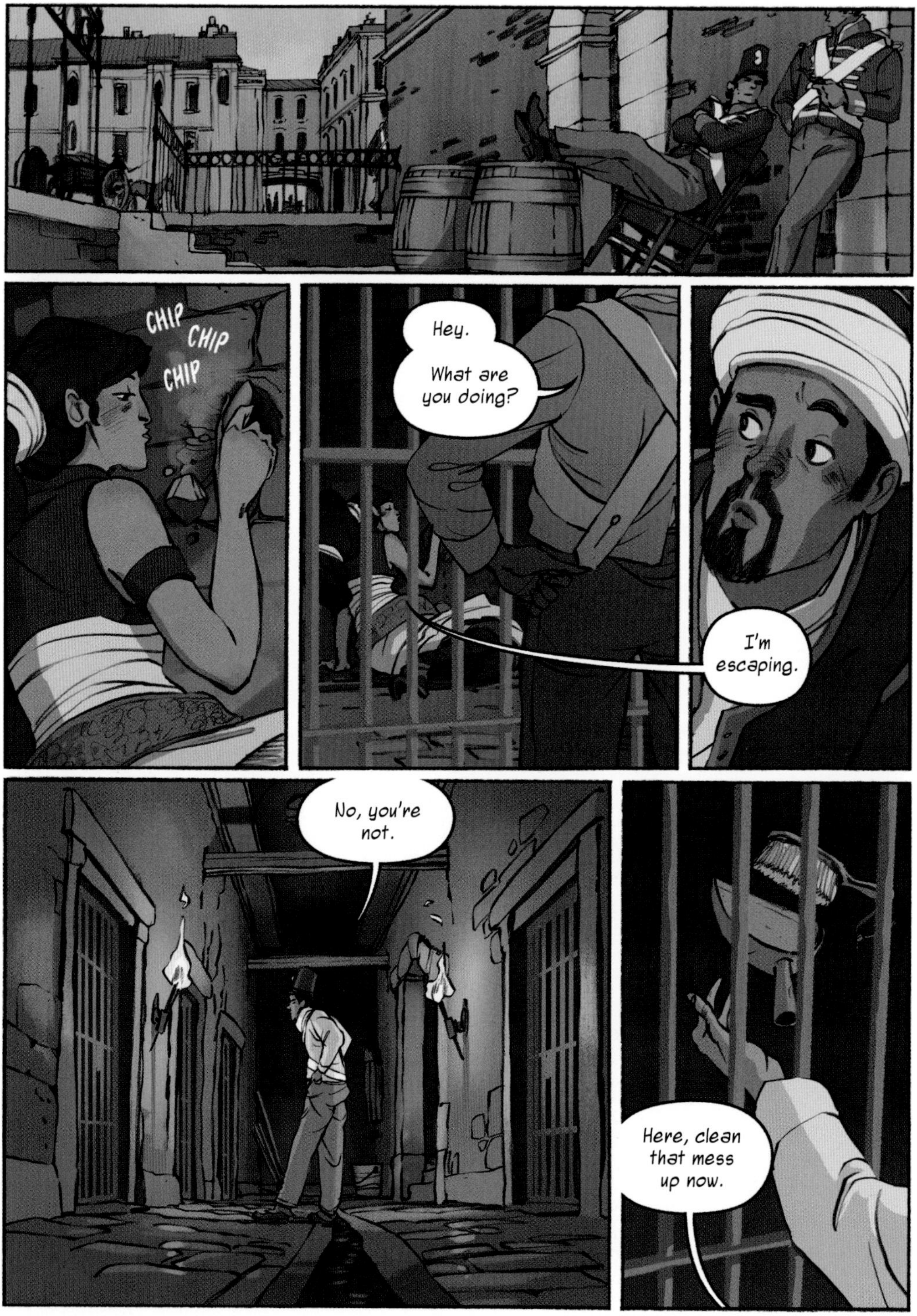
CHIP
CHIP
CHIP
Hey.
What are you doing?
I'm escaping.
No, you're not.
Here, clean that mess up now.

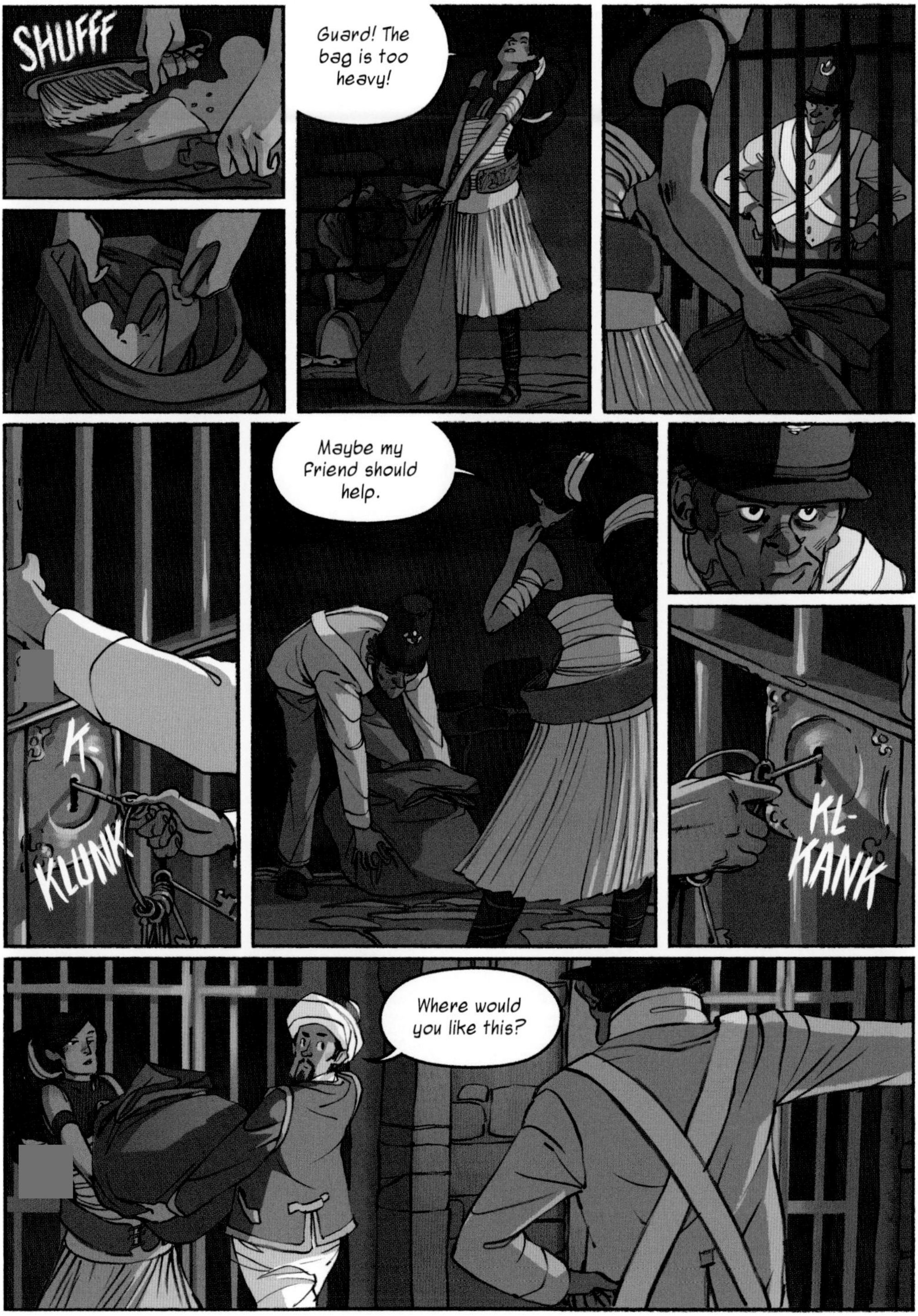
SHUFFF
Guard! The bag is too heavy!
Maybe my friend should help.
K-KLUNK
KL-KANK
Where would you like this?

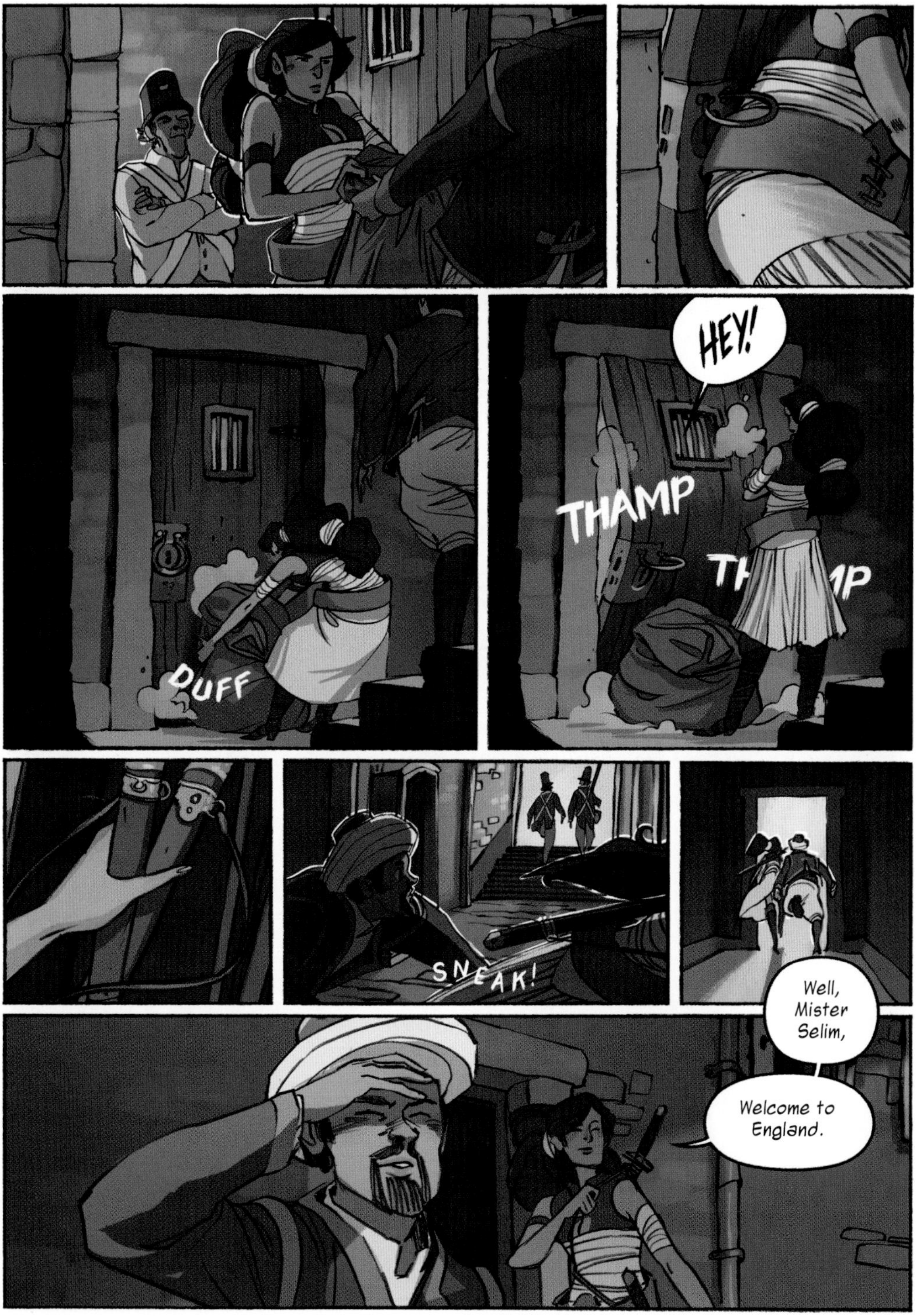
DUFF
HEY!
THAMP
THAMP
SNEAK!
Well, Mister Selim,
Welcome to England.

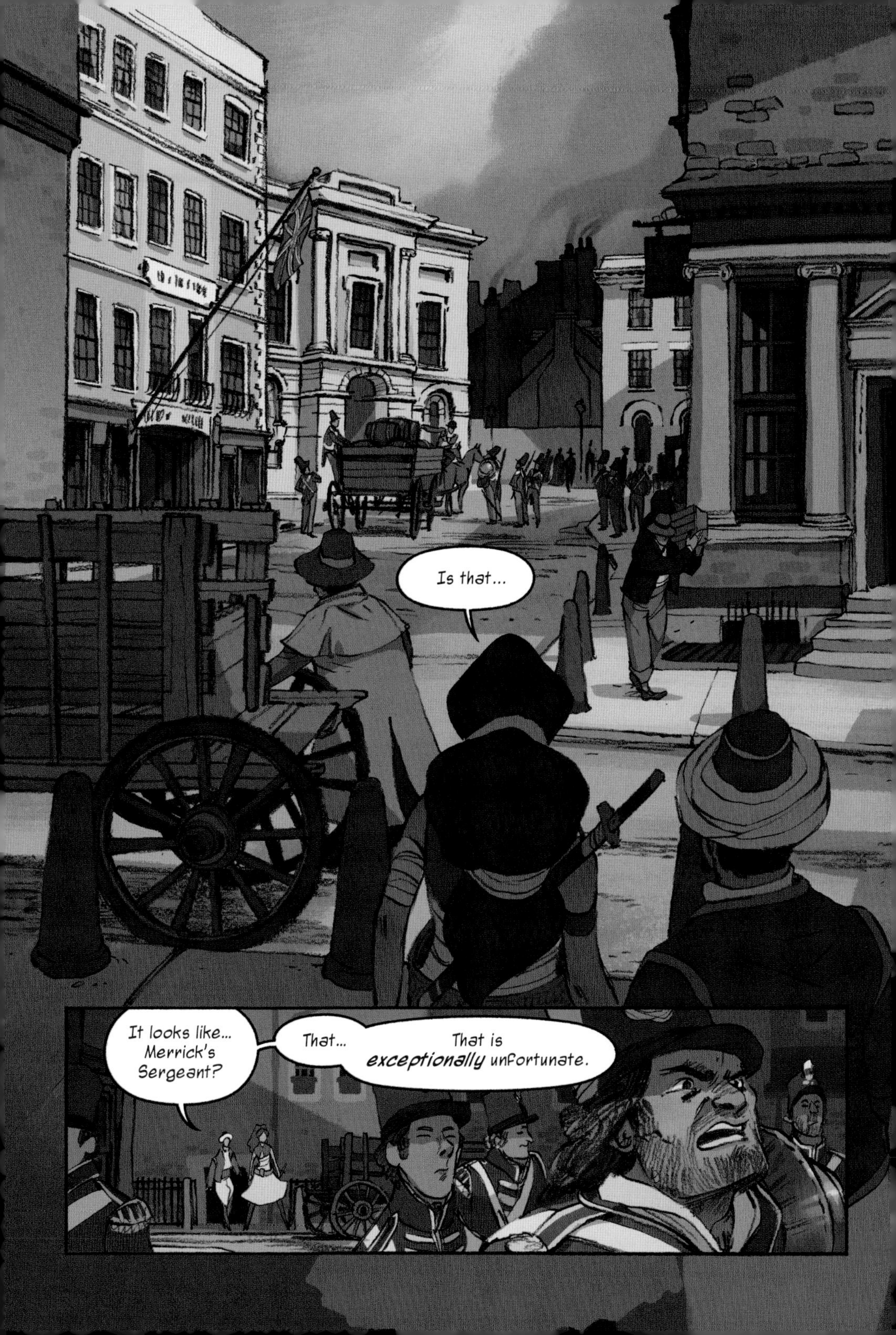

Is that...
It looks like... Merrick's Sergeant?
That...
That is *exceptionally* unfortunate.

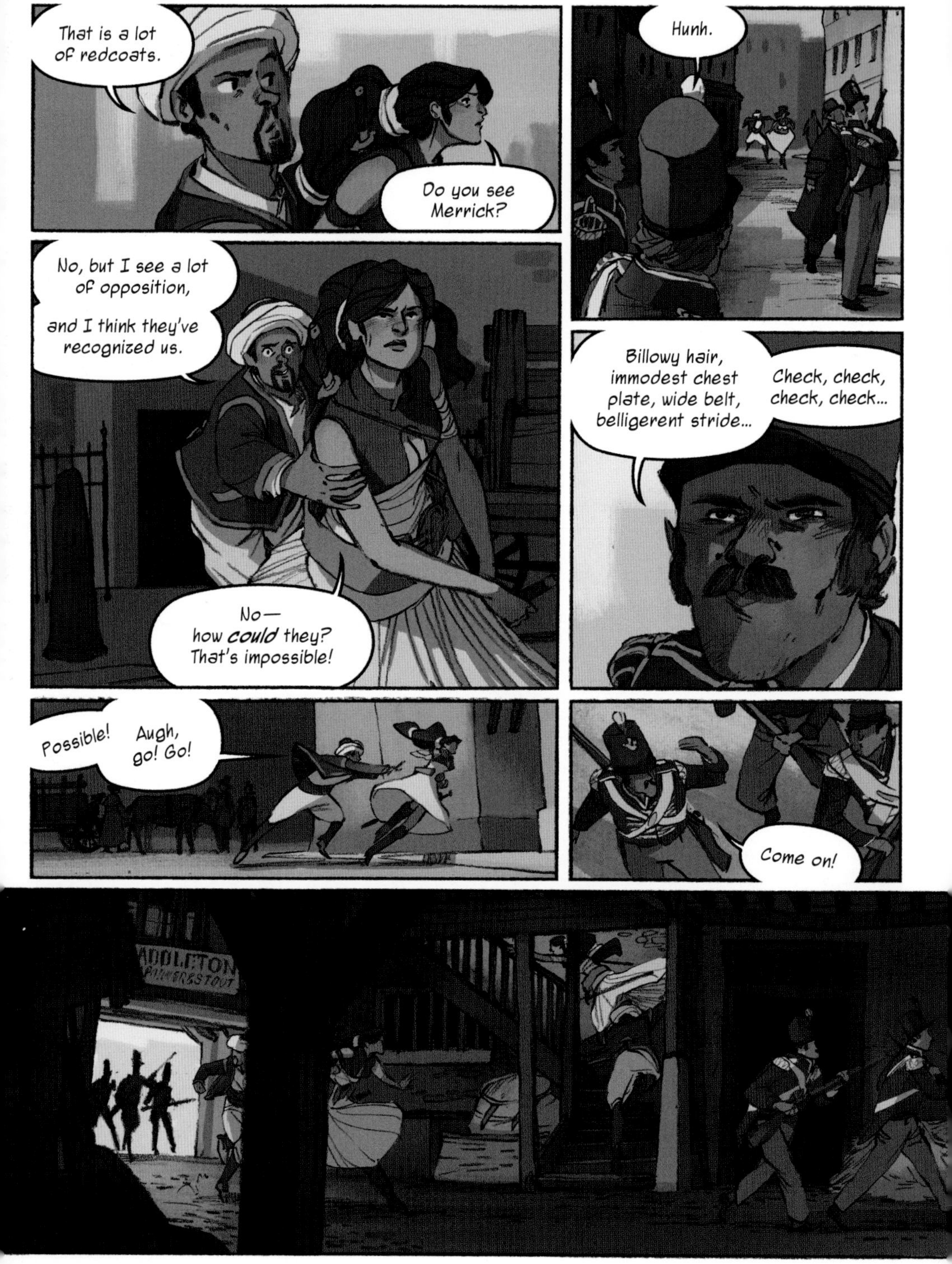
That is a lot of redcoats.
Do you see Merrick?
Hunh.
No, but I see a lot of opposition,
and I think they've recognized us.
No— how *could* they? That's impossible!
Billowy hair, immodest chest plate, wide belt, belligerent stride...
Check, check, check, check...
Possible!
Augh, go! Go!
Come on!

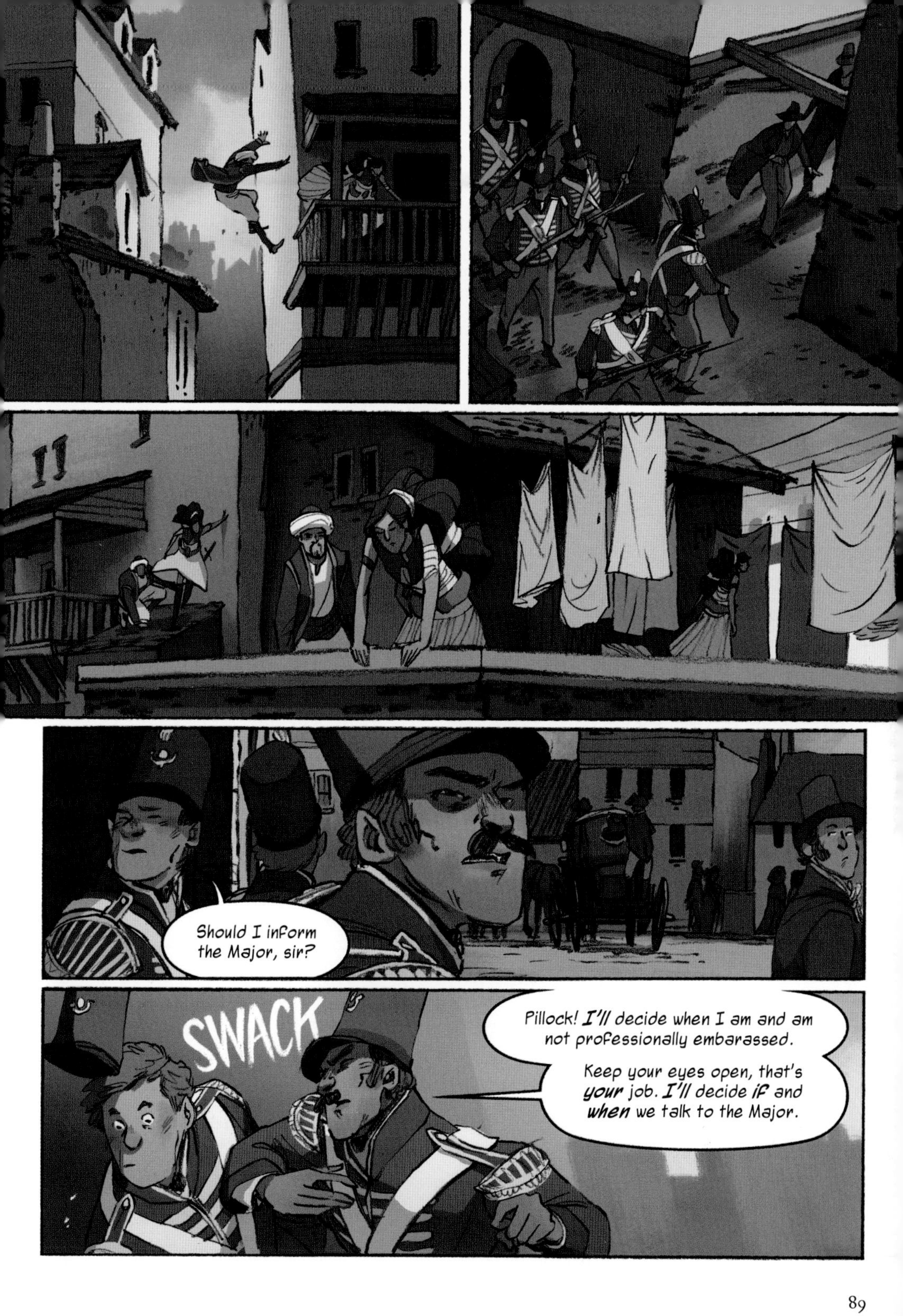
Should I inform the Major, sir?
SWACK
Pillock! I'll decide when I am and am not professionally embarassed.
Keep your eyes open, that's your job. I'll decide if and when we talk to the Major.

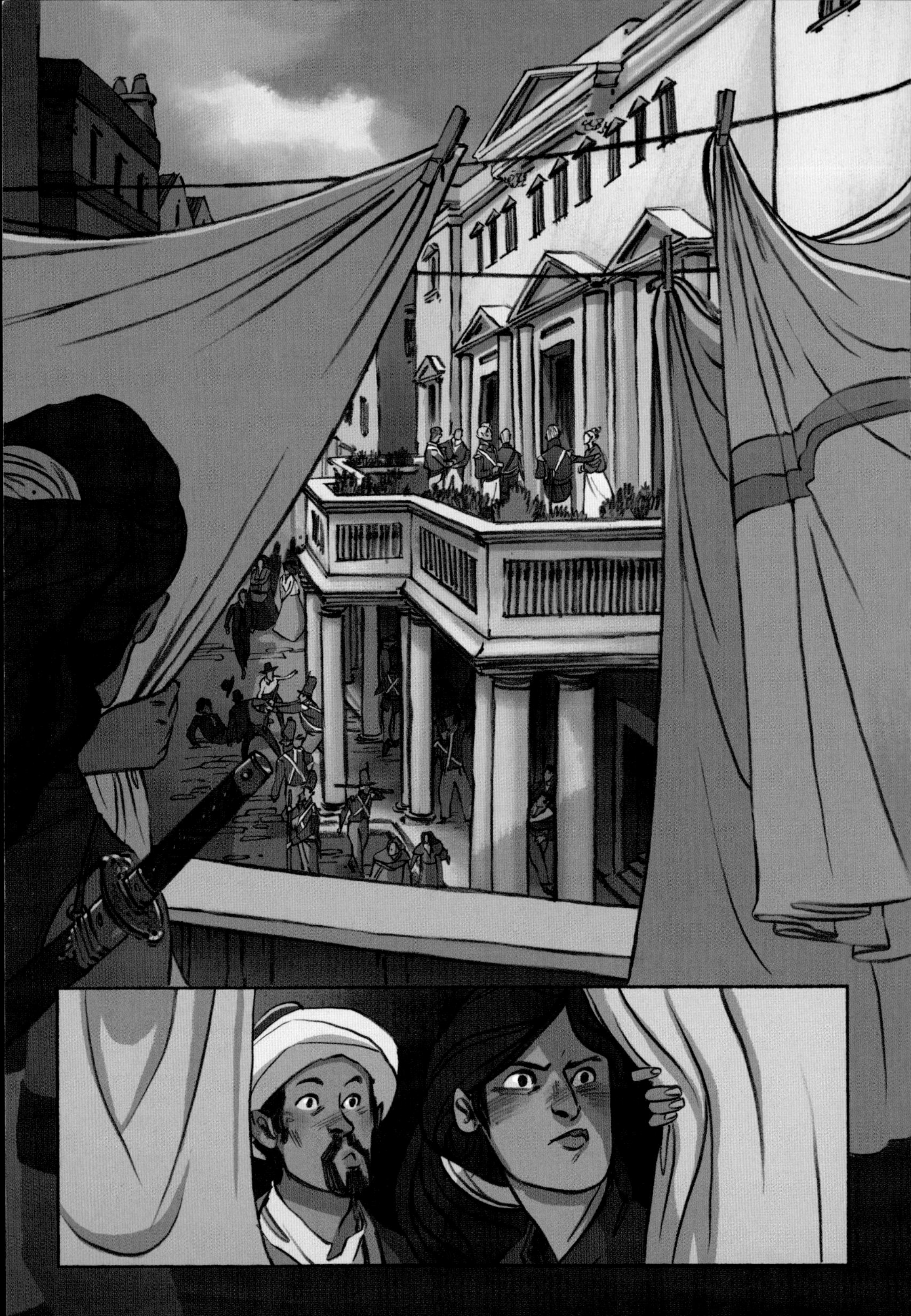

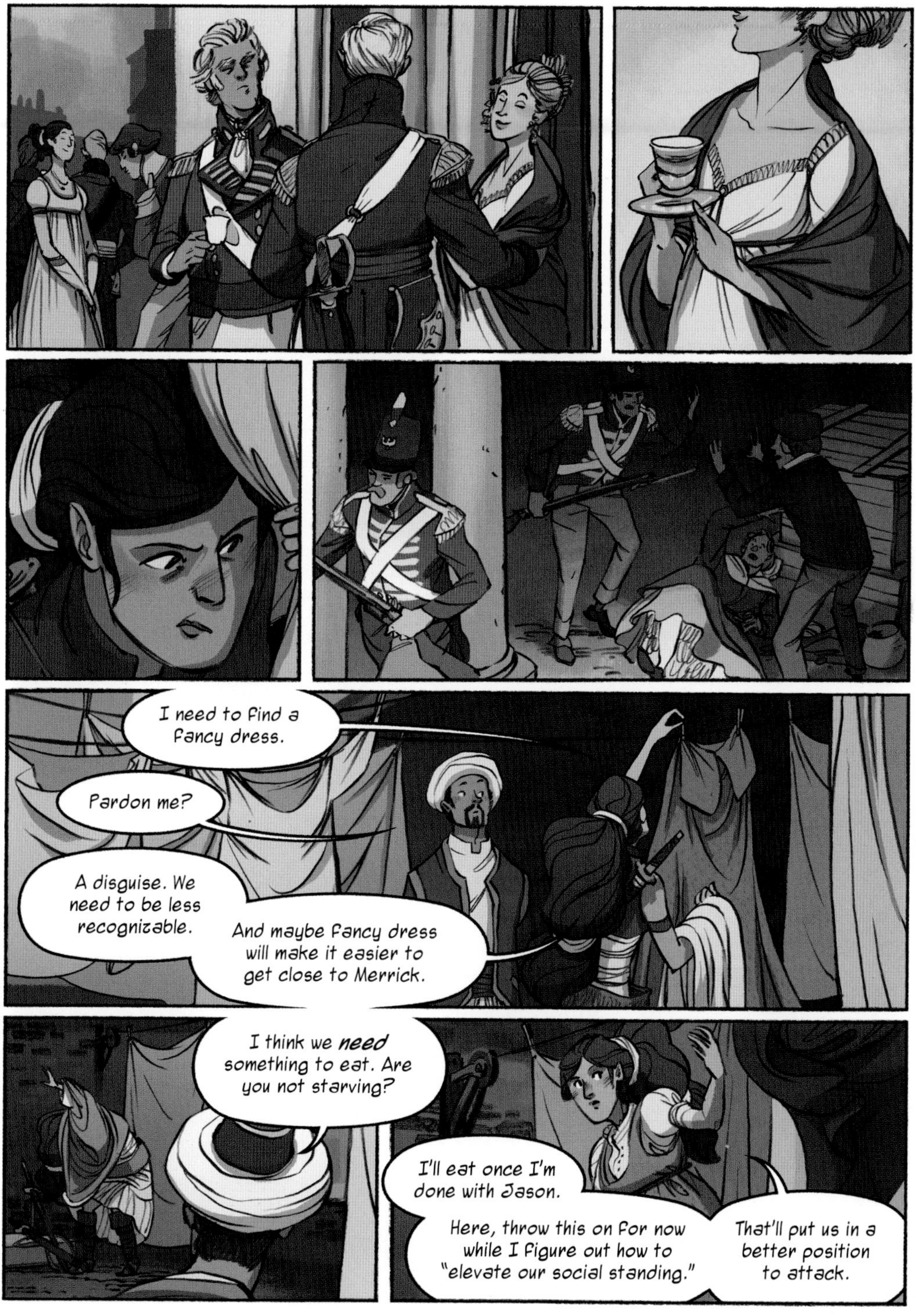
I need to find a fancy dress.
Pardon me?
A disguise. We need to be less recognizable.
And maybe fancy dress will make it easier to get close to Merrick.
I think we *need* something to eat. Are you not starving?
I'll eat once I'm done with Jason.
Here, throw this on for now while I figure out how to "elevate our social standing."
That'll put us in a better position to attack.

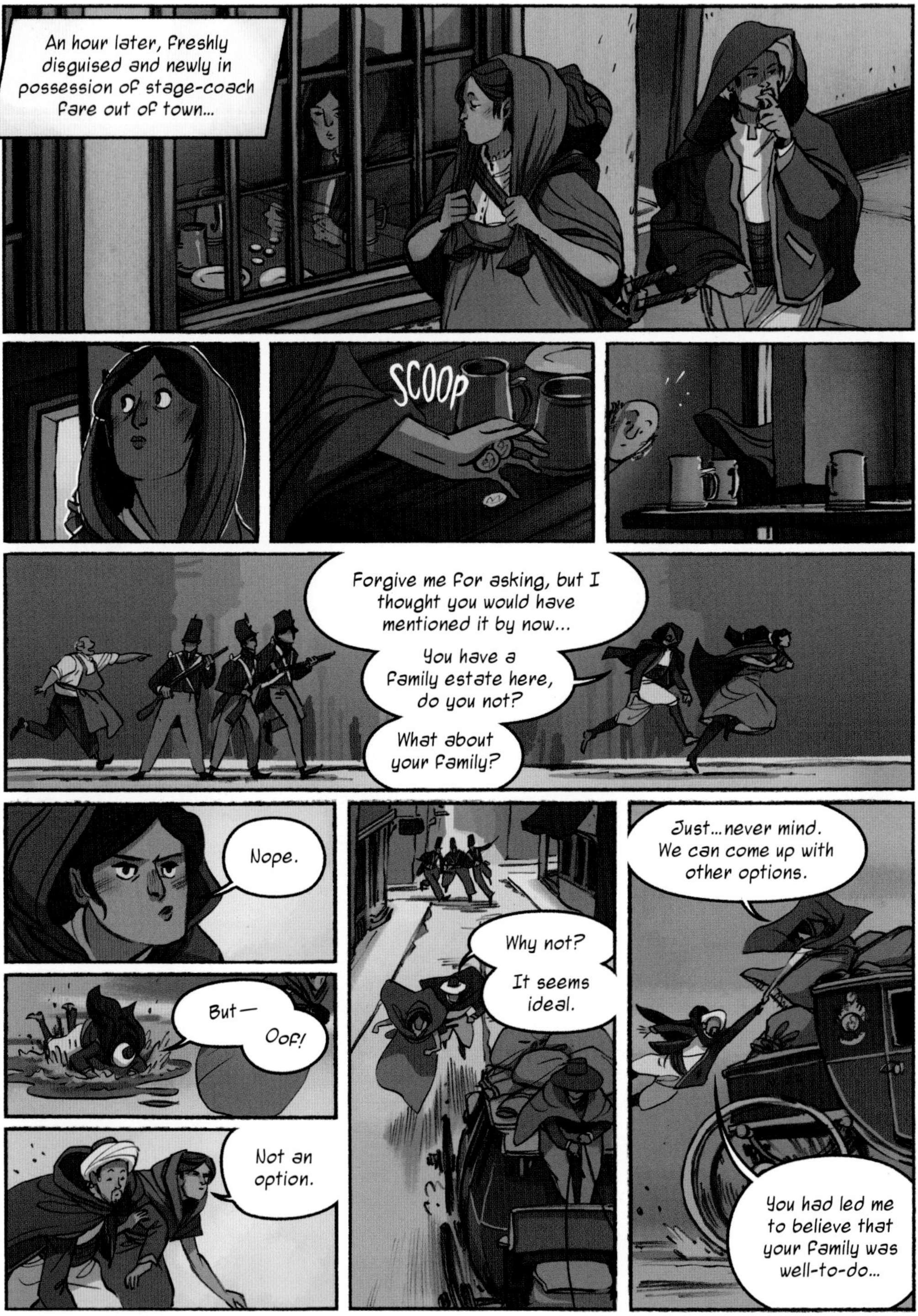
An hour later, freshly disguised and newly in possession of stage-coach fare out of town...
SCOOP
Forgive me for asking, but I thought you would have mentioned it by now...
You have a family estate here, do you not?
What about your family?
Nope.
But—
Oof!
Not an option.
Why not?
It seems ideal.
Just...never mind. We can come up with other options.
You had led me to believe that your family was well-to-do...

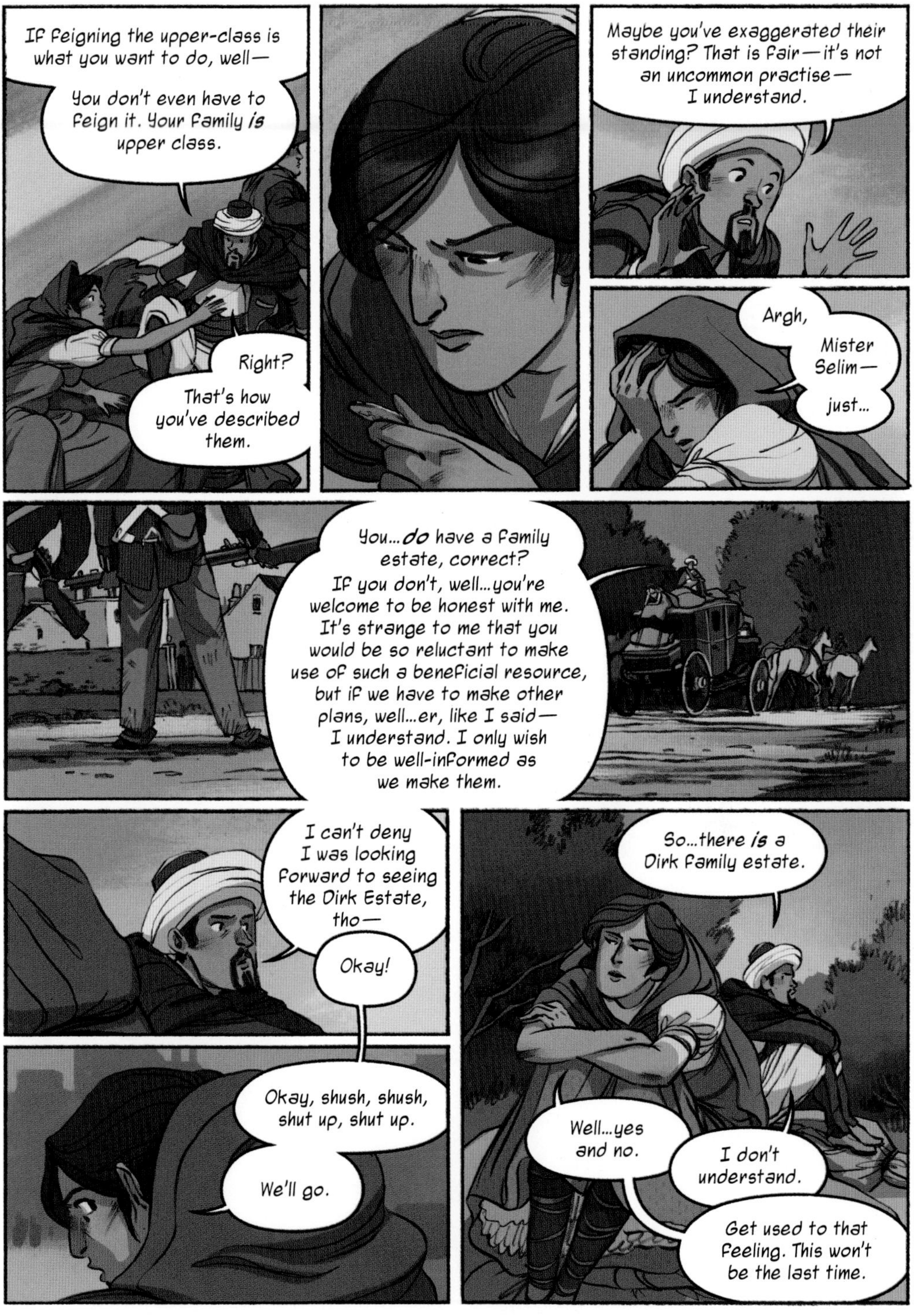
If feigning the upper-class is what you want to do, well—
You don't even have to feign it. Your family *is* upper class.
Right?
That's how you've described them.
Maybe you've exaggerated their standing? That is fair—it's not an uncommon practise—I understand.
Argh,
Mister Selim—
just...
You...*do* have a family estate, correct? If you don't, well...you're welcome to be honest with me. It's strange to me that you would be so reluctant to make use of such a beneficial resource, but if we have to make other plans, well...er, like I said—I understand. I only wish to be well-informed as we make them.
I can't deny I was looking forward to seeing the Dirk Estate, tho—
Okay!
Okay, shush, shush, shut up, shut up.
We'll go.
So...there *is* a Dirk family estate.
Well...yes and no.
I don't understand.
Get used to that feeling. This won't be the last time.

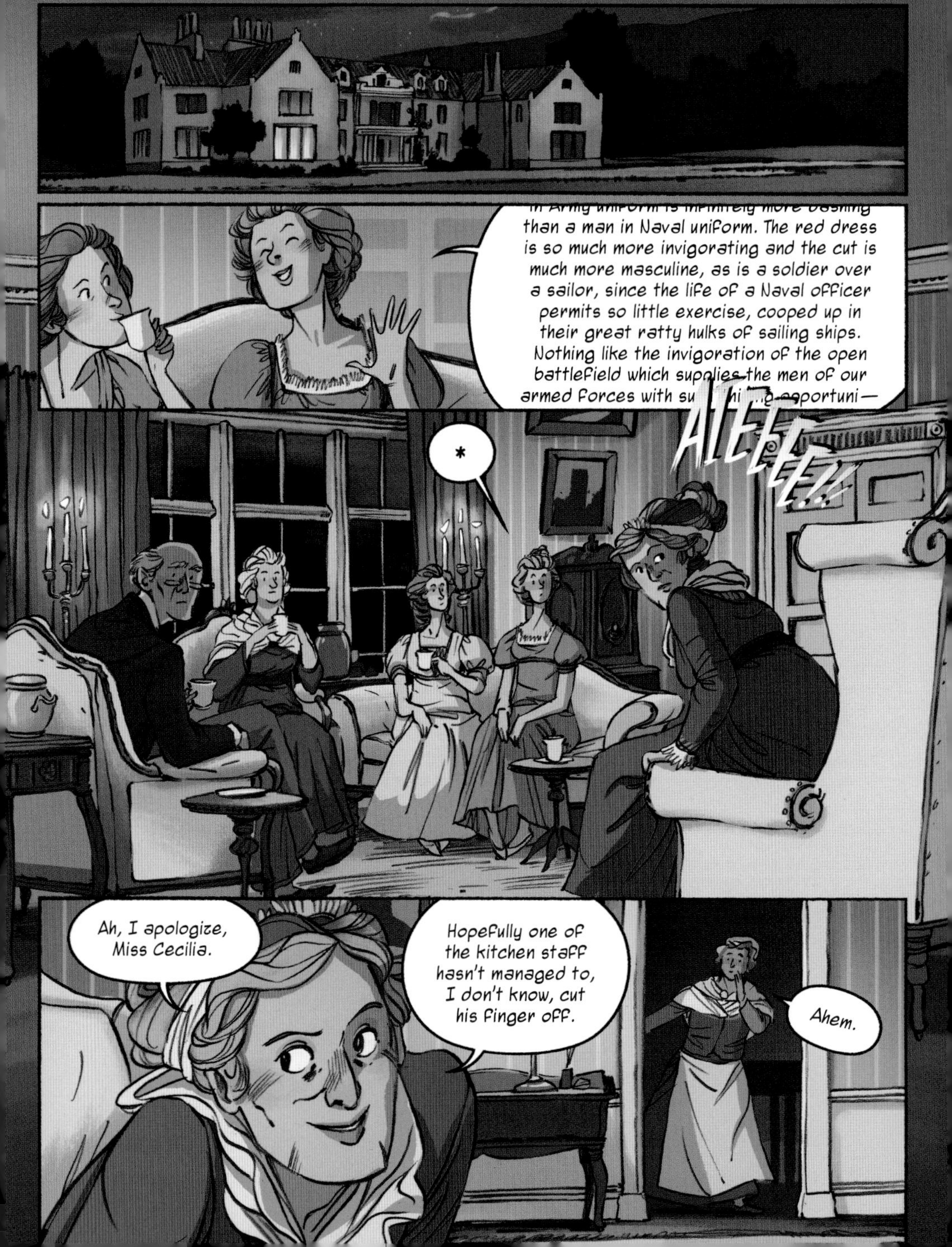
than a man in Naval uniform. The red dress is so much more invigorating and the cut is much more masculine, as is a soldier over a sailor, since the life of a Naval officer permits so little exercise, cooped up in their great ratty hulks of sailing ships. Nothing like the invigoration of the open battlefield which supplies the men of our armed forces with su opportuni—
AIEEEE!!
*
Ah, I apologize, Miss Cecilia.
Hopefully one of the kitchen staff hasn't managed to, I don't know, cut his finger off.
Ahem.

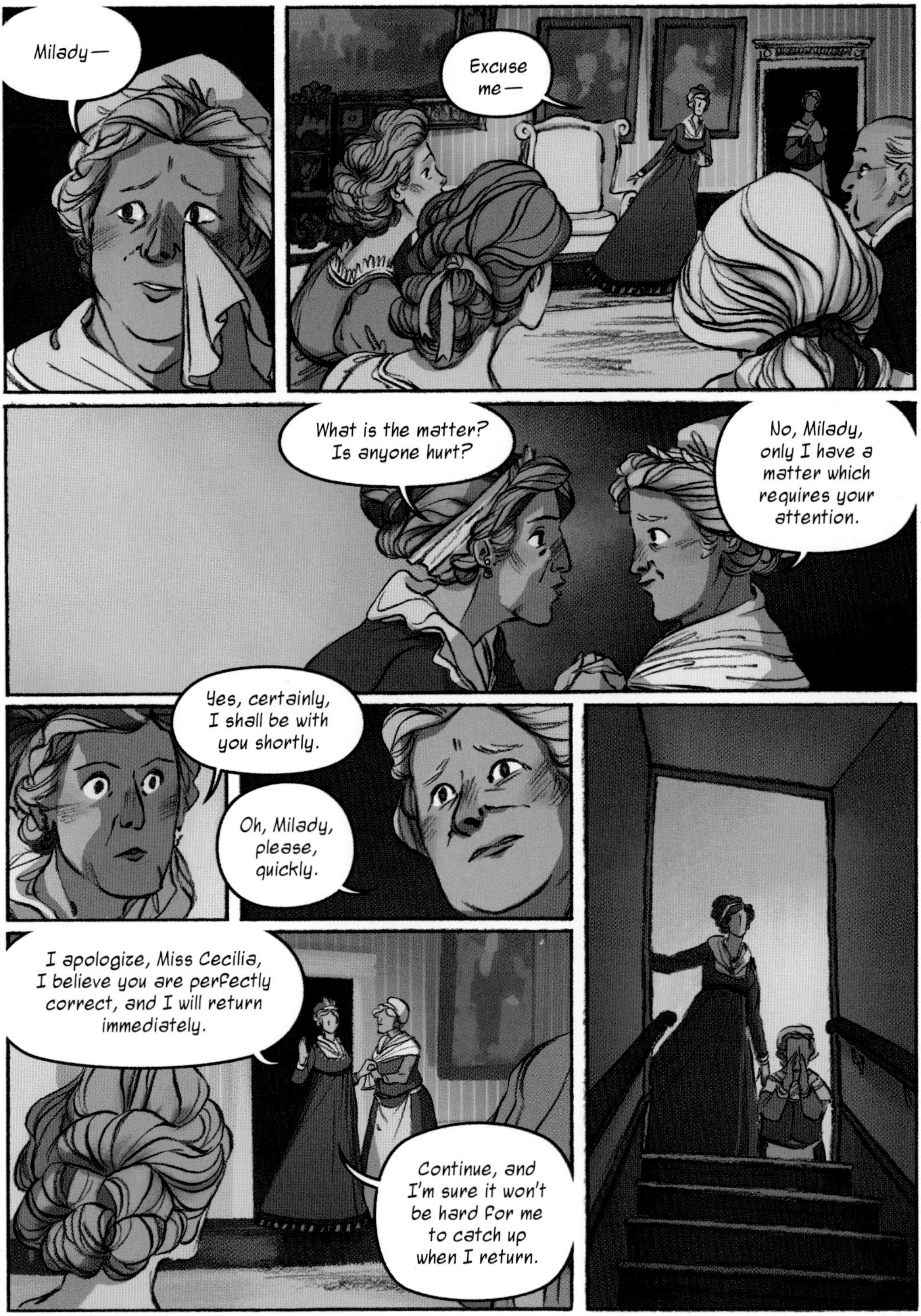
Milady—
Excuse me—
What is the matter? Is anyone hurt?
No, Milady, only I have a matter which requires your attention.
Yes, certainly, I shall be with you shortly.
Oh, Milady, please, quickly.
I apologize, Miss Cecilia, I believe you are perfectly correct, and I will return immediately.
Continue, and I'm sure it won't be hard for me to catch up when I return.

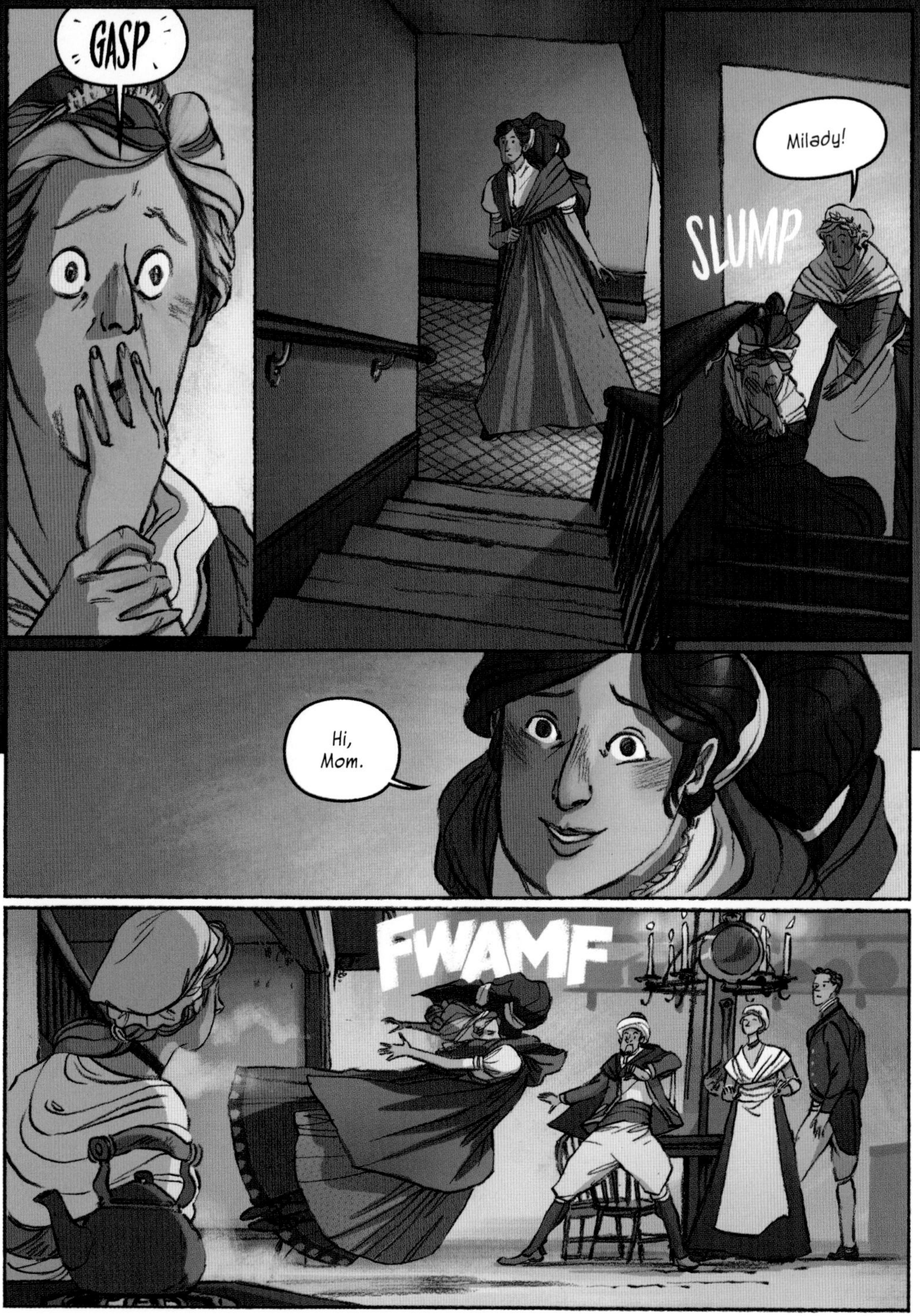
GASP
Milady!
SLUMP
Hi, Mom.
FWAMF

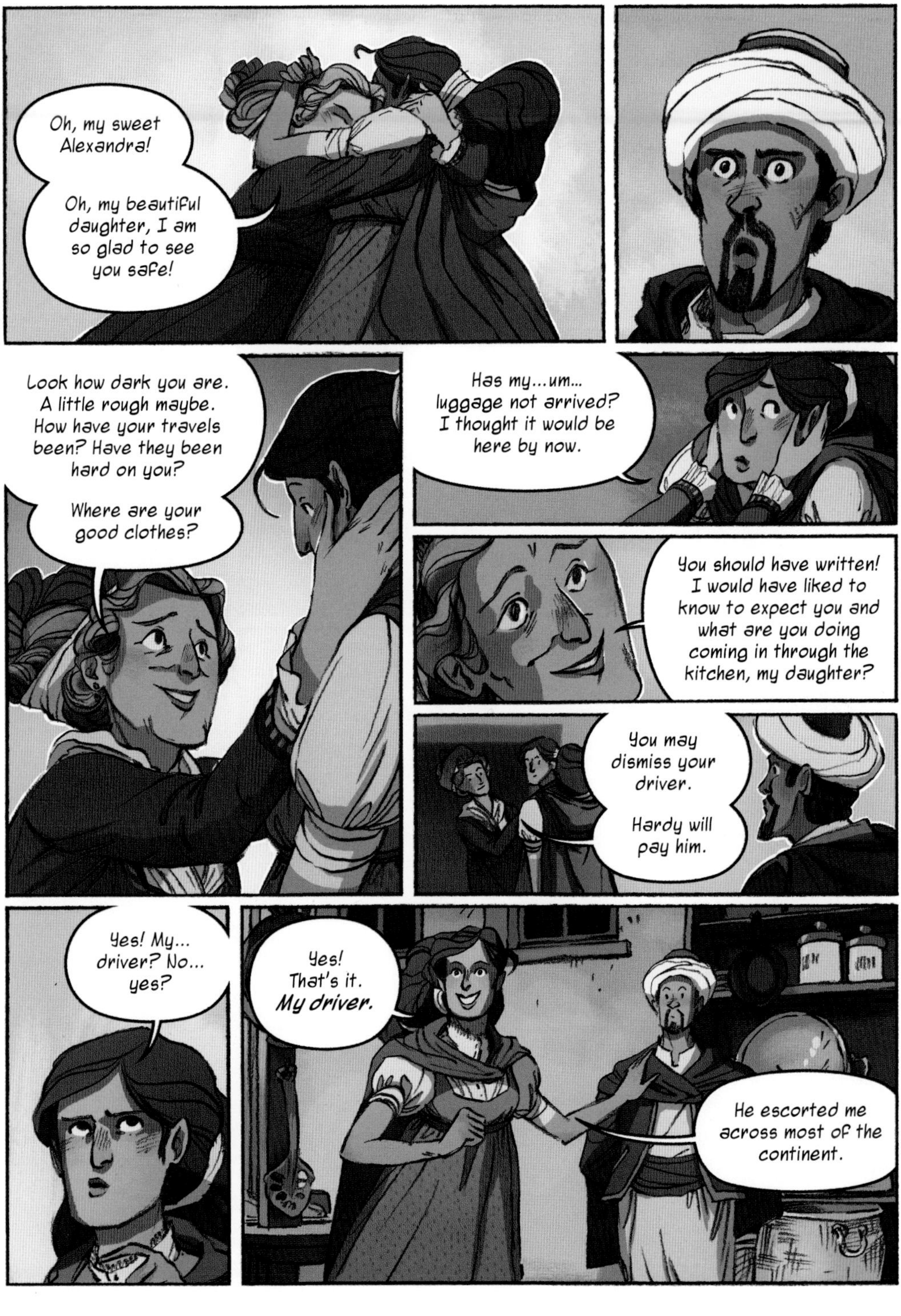
Oh, my sweet Alexandra!
Oh, my beautiful daughter, I am so glad to see you safe!
Look how dark you are. A little rough maybe. How have your travels been? Have they been hard on you?
Where are your good clothes?
Has my...um... luggage not arrived? I thought it would be here by now.
You should have written! I would have liked to know to expect you and what are you doing coming in through the kitchen, my daughter?
You may dismiss your driver.
Hardy will pay him.
Yes! My... driver? No... yes?
Yes! That's it. *My driver.*
He escorted me across most of the continent.

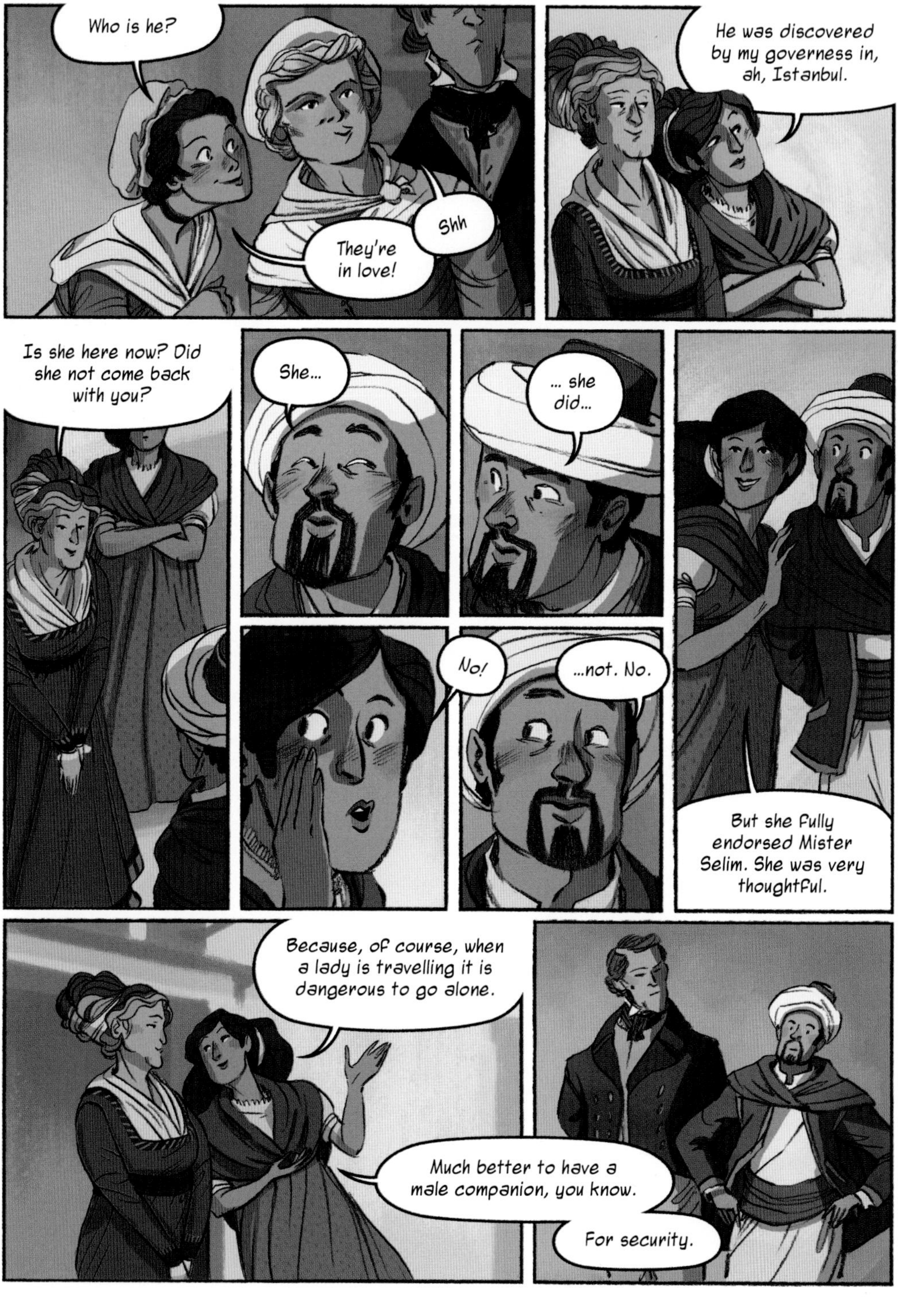
Who is he?
They're in love!
Shh
He was discovered by my governess in, ah, Istanbul.
Is she here now? Did she not come back with you?
She...
... she did...
No!
...not. No.
But she fully endorsed Mister Selim. She was very thoughtful.
Because, of course, when a lady is travelling it is dangerous to go alone.
Much better to have a male companion, you know.
For security.

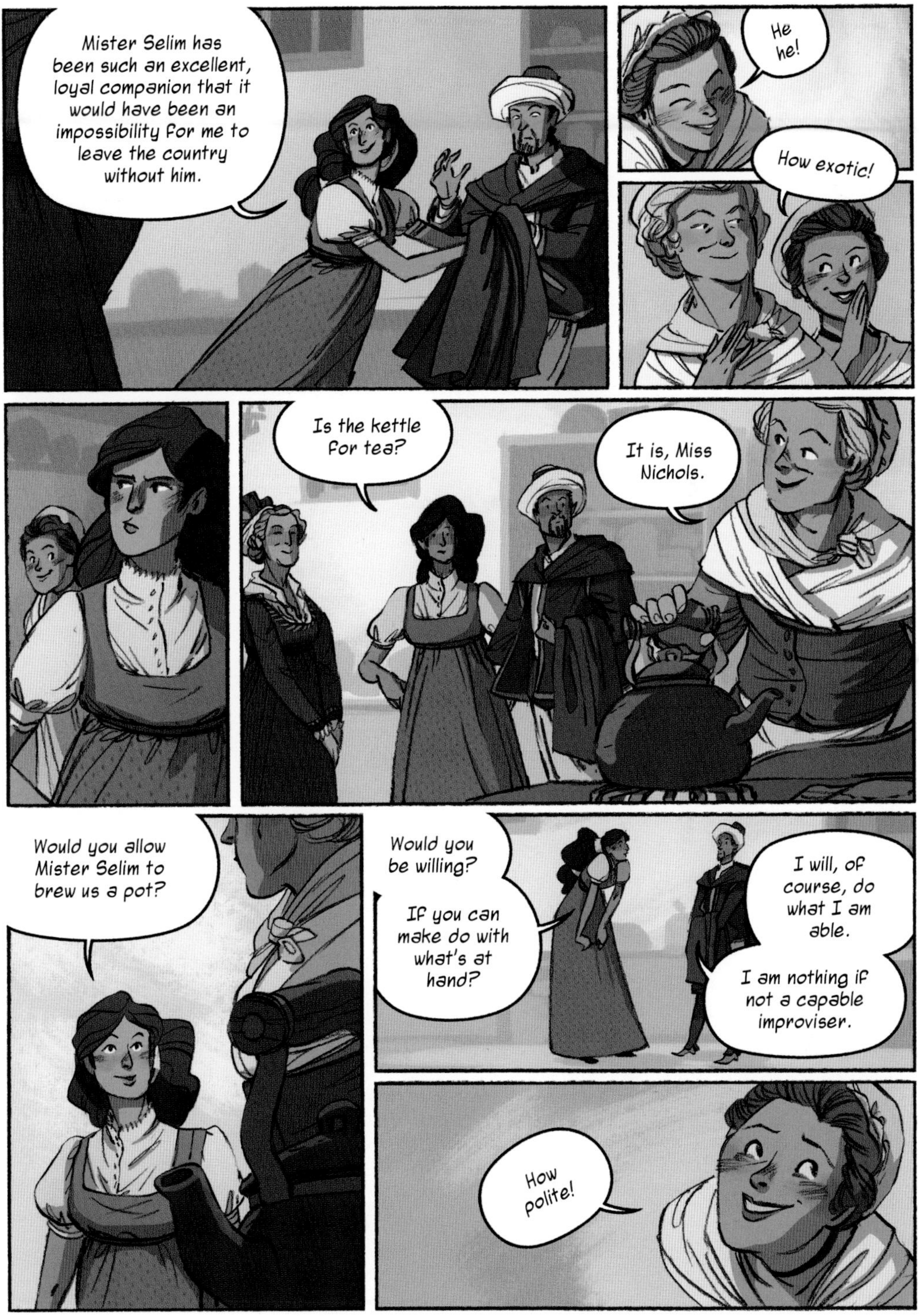
Mister Selim has been such an excellent, loyal companion that it would have been an impossibility for me to leave the country without him.
He he!
How exotic!
Is the kettle for tea?
It is, Miss Nichols.
Would you allow Mister Selim to brew us a pot?
Would you be willing?
If you can make do with what's at hand?
I will, of course, do what I am able.
I am nothing if not a capable improviser.
How polite!

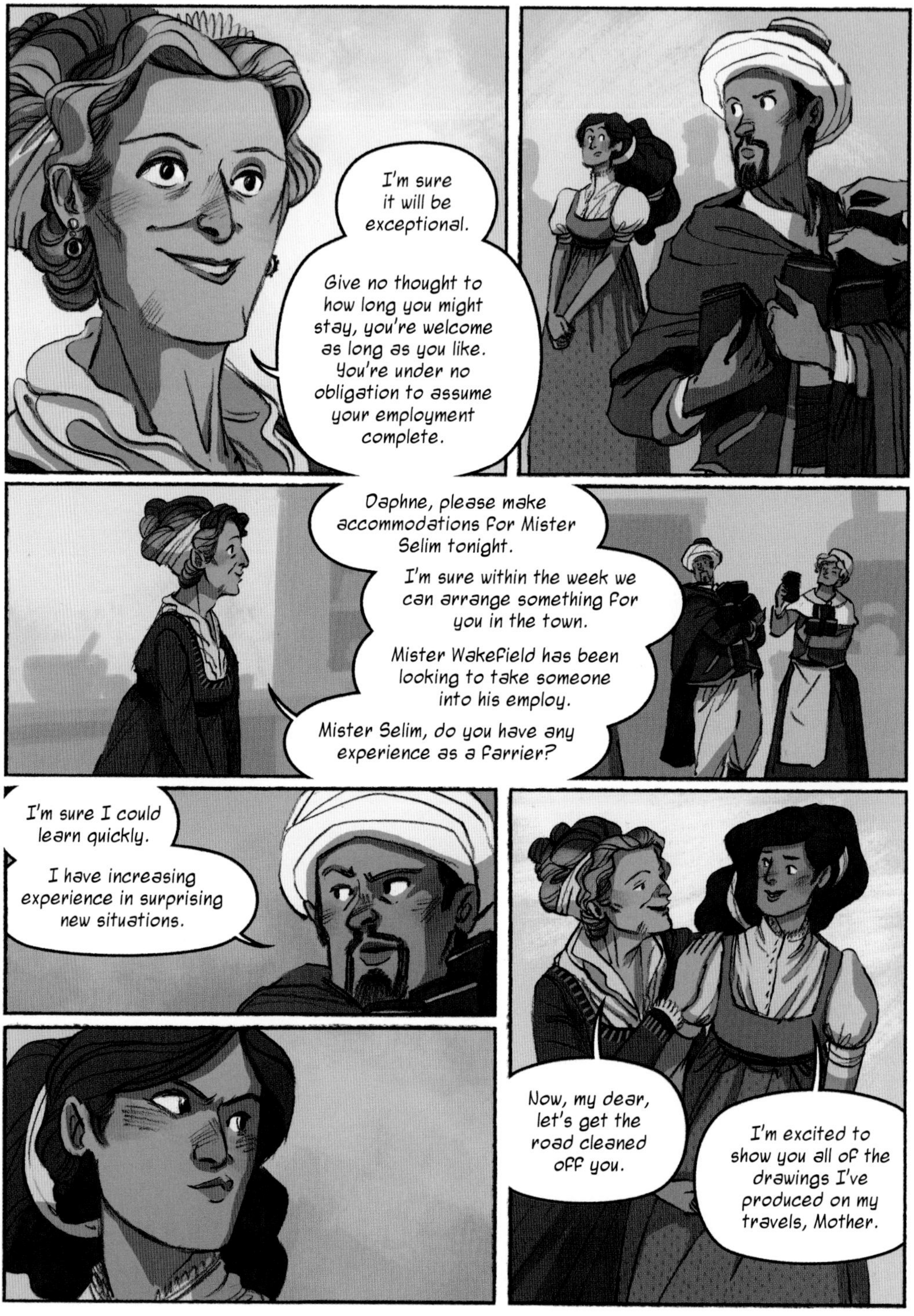
I'm sure it will be exceptional.
Give no thought to how long you might stay, you're welcome as long as you like. You're under no obligation to assume your employment complete.
Daphne, please make accommodations for Mister Selim tonight.
I'm sure within the week we can arrange something for you in the town.
Mister Wakefield has been looking to take someone into his employ.
Mister Selim, do you have any experience as a farrier?
I'm sure I could learn quickly.
I have increasing experience in surprising new situations.
Now, my dear, let's get the road cleaned off you.
I'm excited to show you all of the drawings I've produced on my travels, Mother.

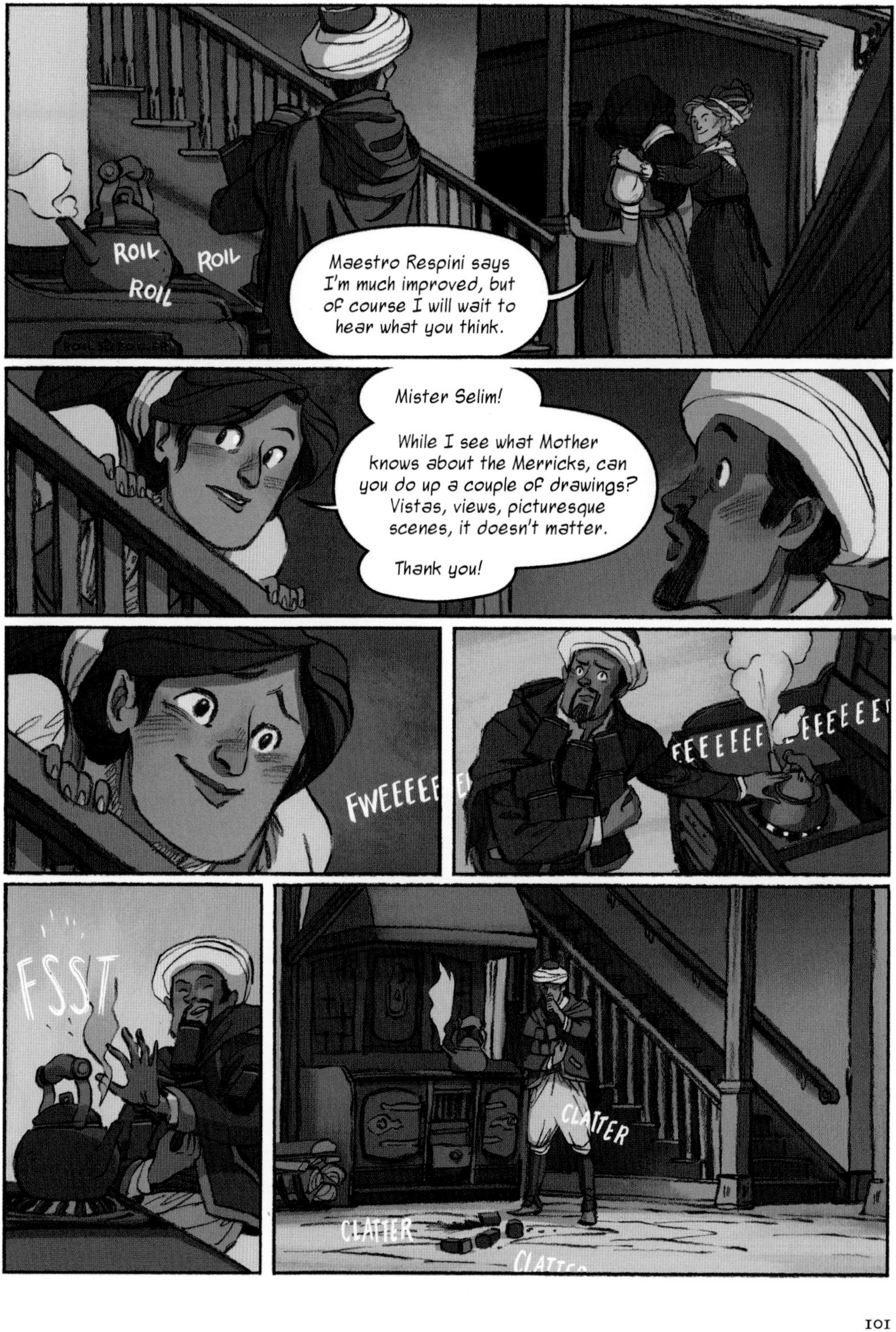
ROIL
ROIL
ROIL
Maestro Respini says I'm much improved, but of course I will wait to hear what you think.
Mister Selim!
While I see what Mother knows about the Merricks, can you do up a couple of drawings? Vistas, views, picturesque scenes, it doesn't matter.
Thank you!
FWEEEEE
EEEEEE
FSST
CLATTER
CLATTER

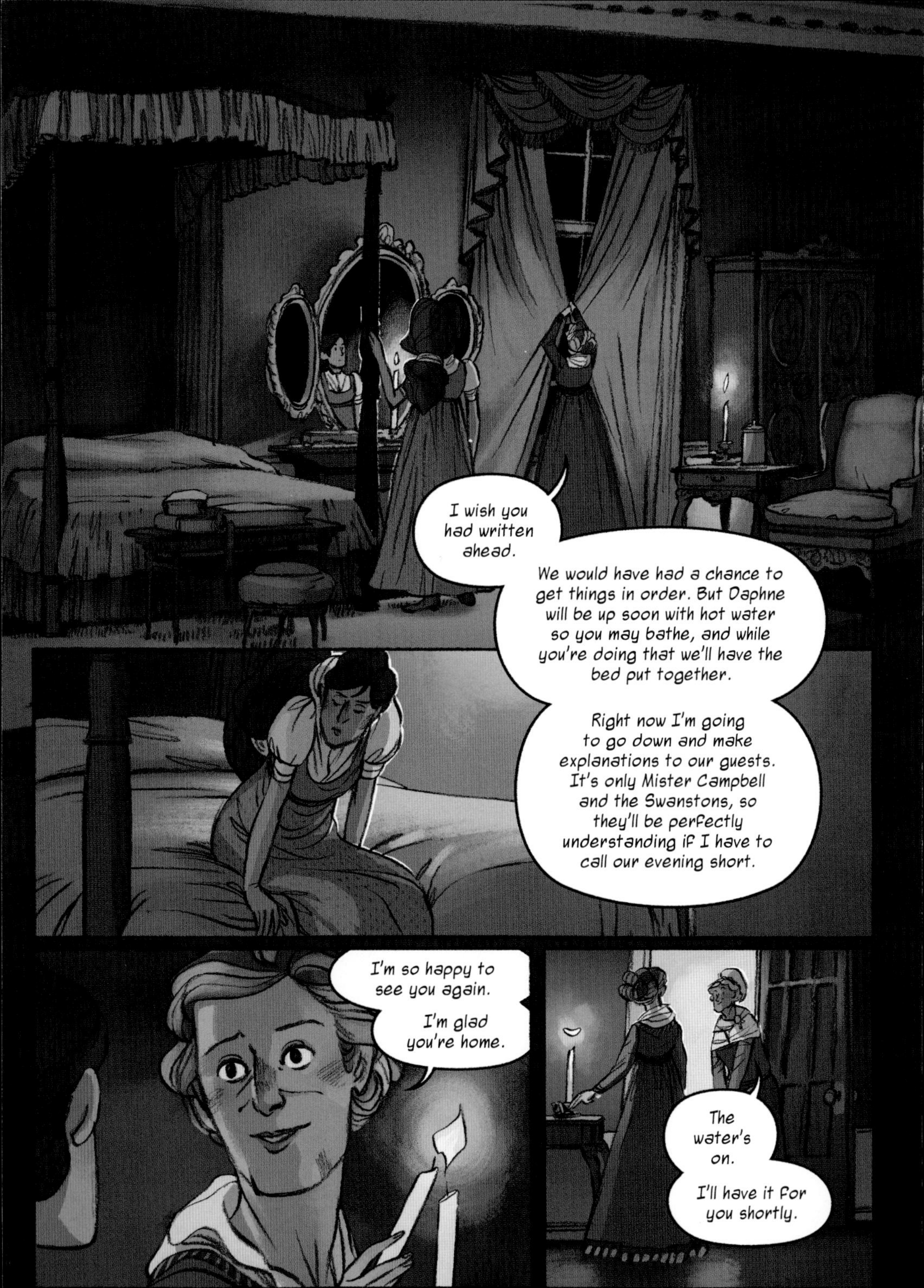
I wish you had written ahead.
We would have had a chance to get things in order. But Daphne will be up soon with hot water so you may bathe, and while you're doing that we'll have the bed put together.
Right now I'm going to go down and make explanations to our guests. It's only Mister Campbell and the Swanstons, so they'll be perfectly understanding if I have to call our evening short.
I'm so happy to see you again.
I'm glad you're home.
The water's on.
I'll have it for you shortly.

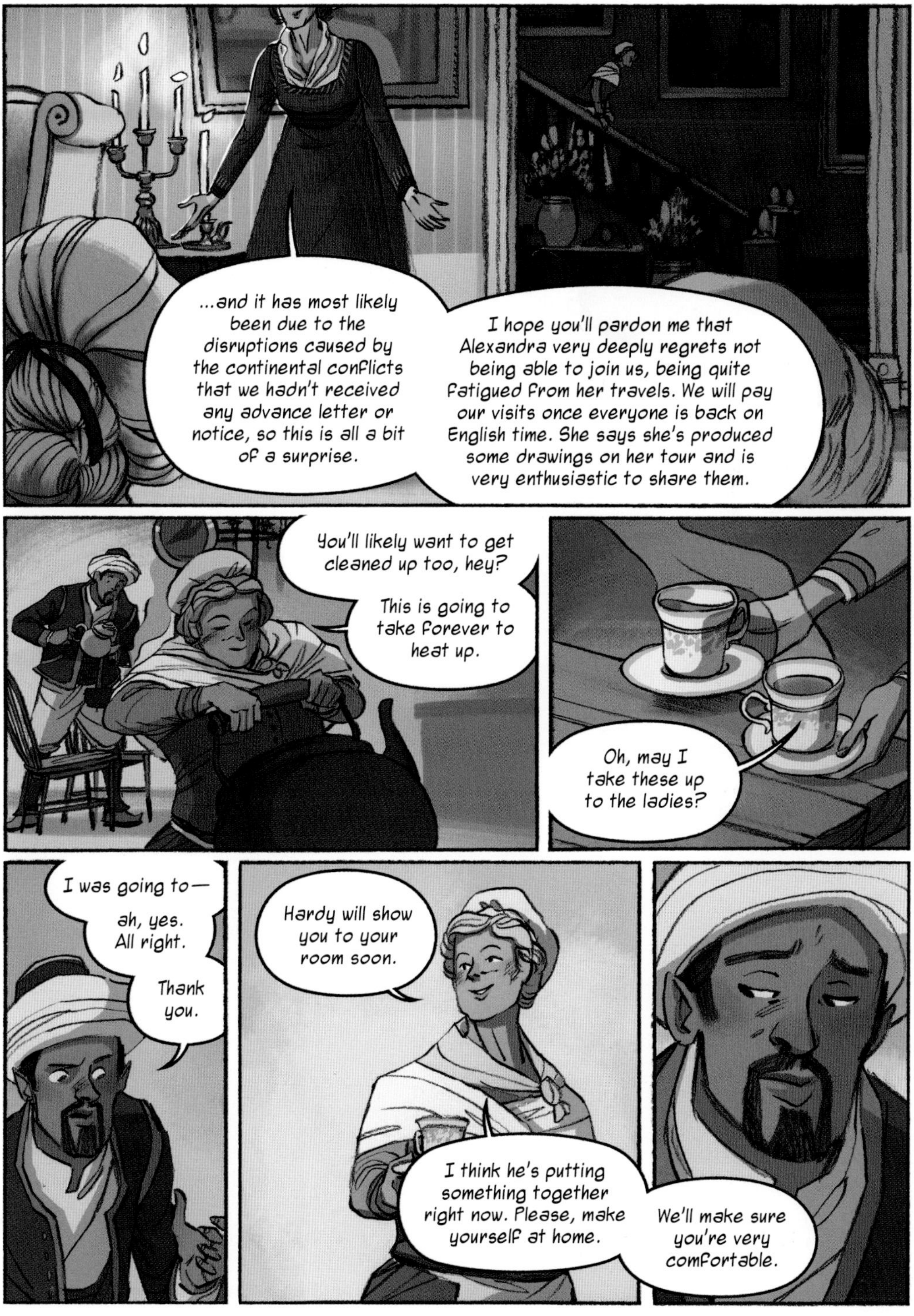
...and it has most likely been due to the disruptions caused by the continental conflicts that we hadn't received any advance letter or notice, so this is all a bit of a surprise.
I hope you'll pardon me that Alexandra very deeply regrets not being able to join us, being quite fatigued from her travels. We will pay our visits once everyone is back on English time. She says she's produced some drawings on her tour and is very enthusiastic to share them.
You'll likely want to get cleaned up too, hey?
This is going to take forever to heat up.
Oh, may I take these up to the ladies?
I was going to—
ah, yes. All right.
Thank you.
Hardy will show you to your room soon.
I think he's putting something together right now. Please, make yourself at home.
We'll make sure you're very comfortable.

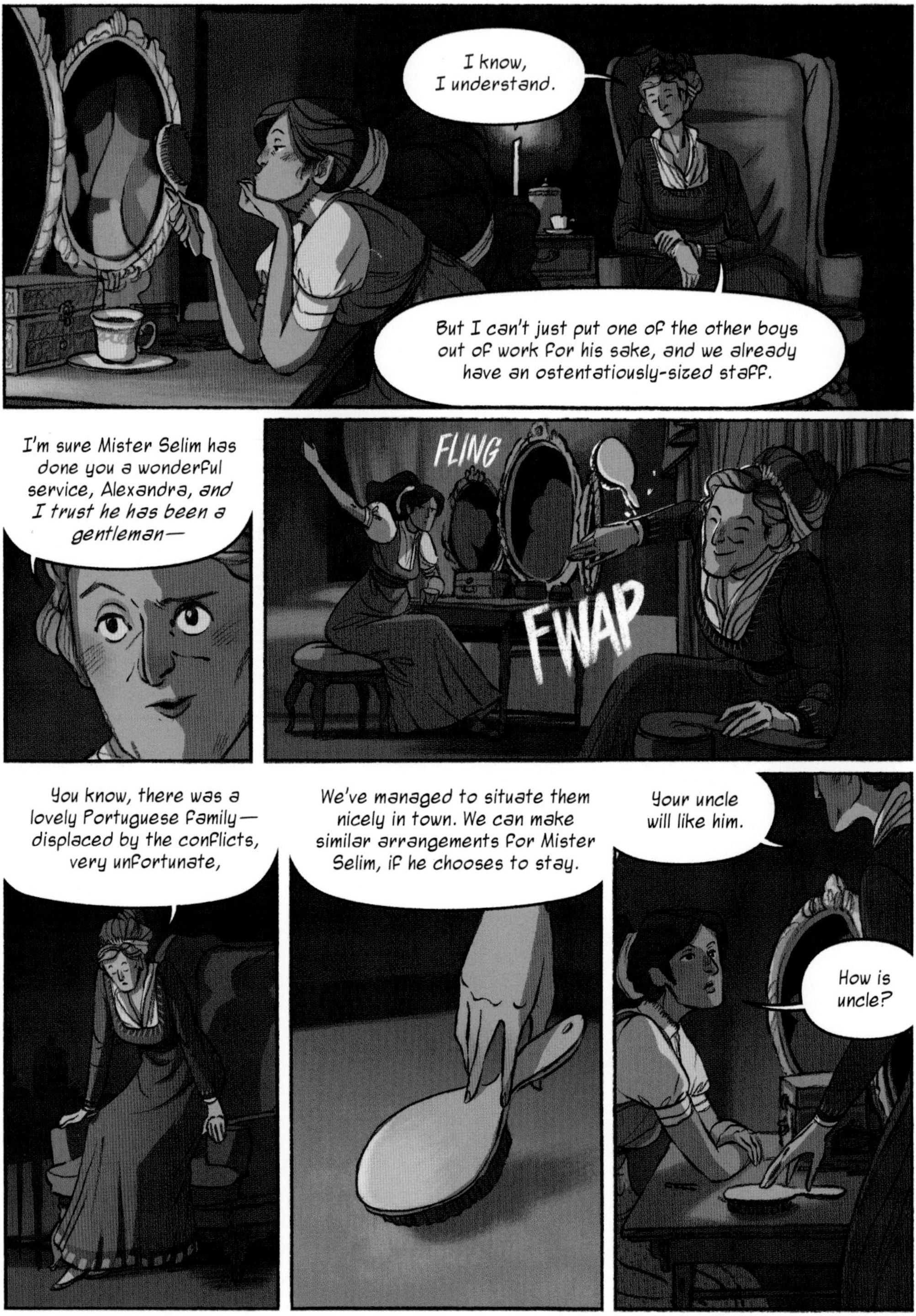
I know, I understand.
But I can't just put one of the other boys out of work for his sake, and we already have an ostentatiously-sized staff.
I'm sure Mister Selim has done you a wonderful service, Alexandra, and I trust he has been a gentleman—
FLING
FWAP
You know, there was a lovely Portuguese family—displaced by the conflicts, very unfortunate,
We've managed to situate them nicely in town. We can make similar arrangements for Mister Selim, if he chooses to stay.
Your uncle will like him.
How is uncle?

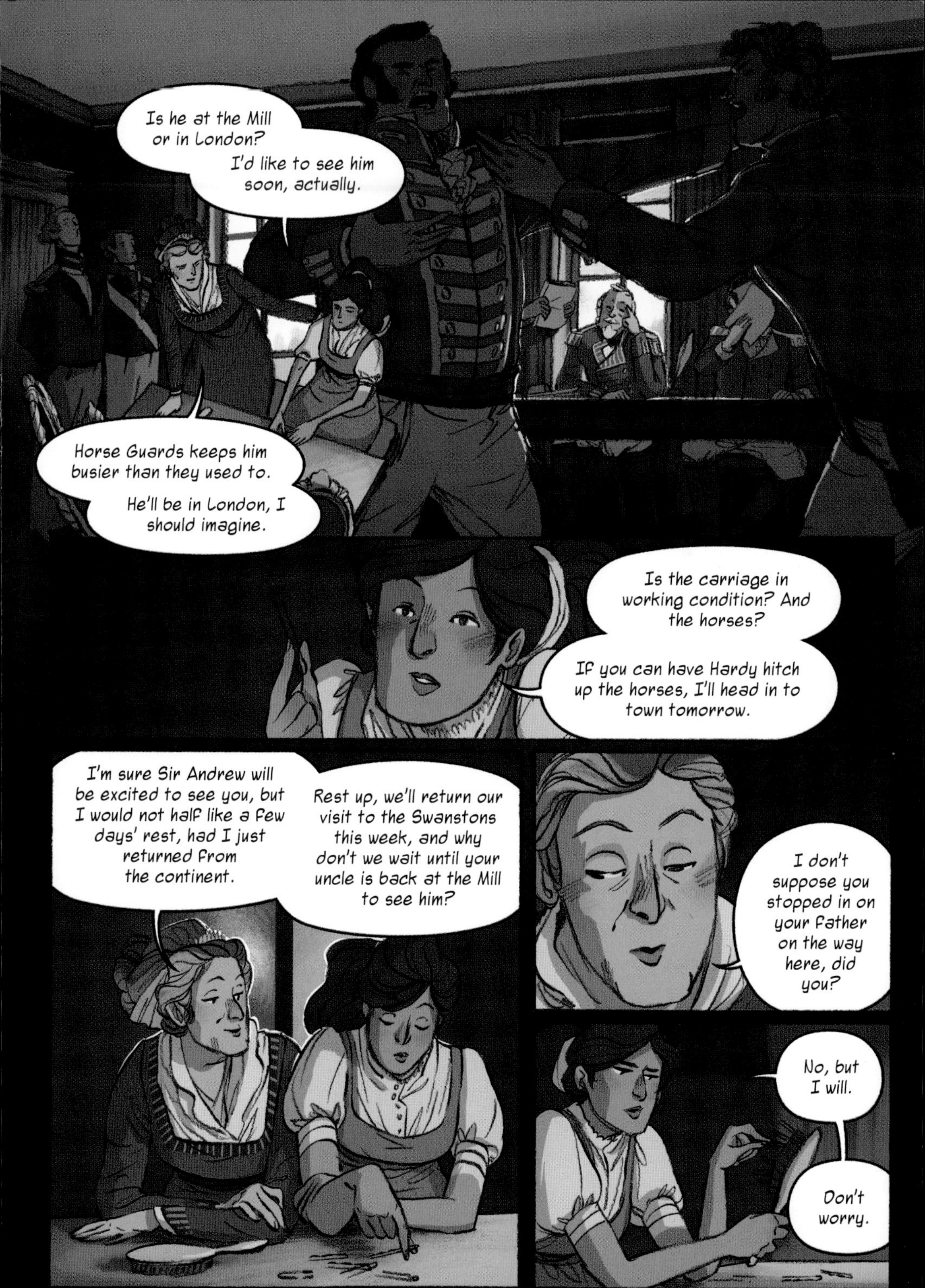
Is he at the Mill or in London?
I'd like to see him soon, actually.
Horse Guards keeps him busier than they used to.
He'll be in London, I should imagine.
Is the carriage in working condition? And the horses?
If you can have Hardy hitch up the horses, I'll head in to town tomorrow.
I'm sure Sir Andrew will be excited to see you, but I would not half like a few days' rest, had I just returned from the continent.
Rest up, we'll return our visit to the Swanstons this week, and why don't we wait until your uncle is back at the Mill to see him?
I don't suppose you stopped in on your father on the way here, did you?
No, but I will.
Don't worry.

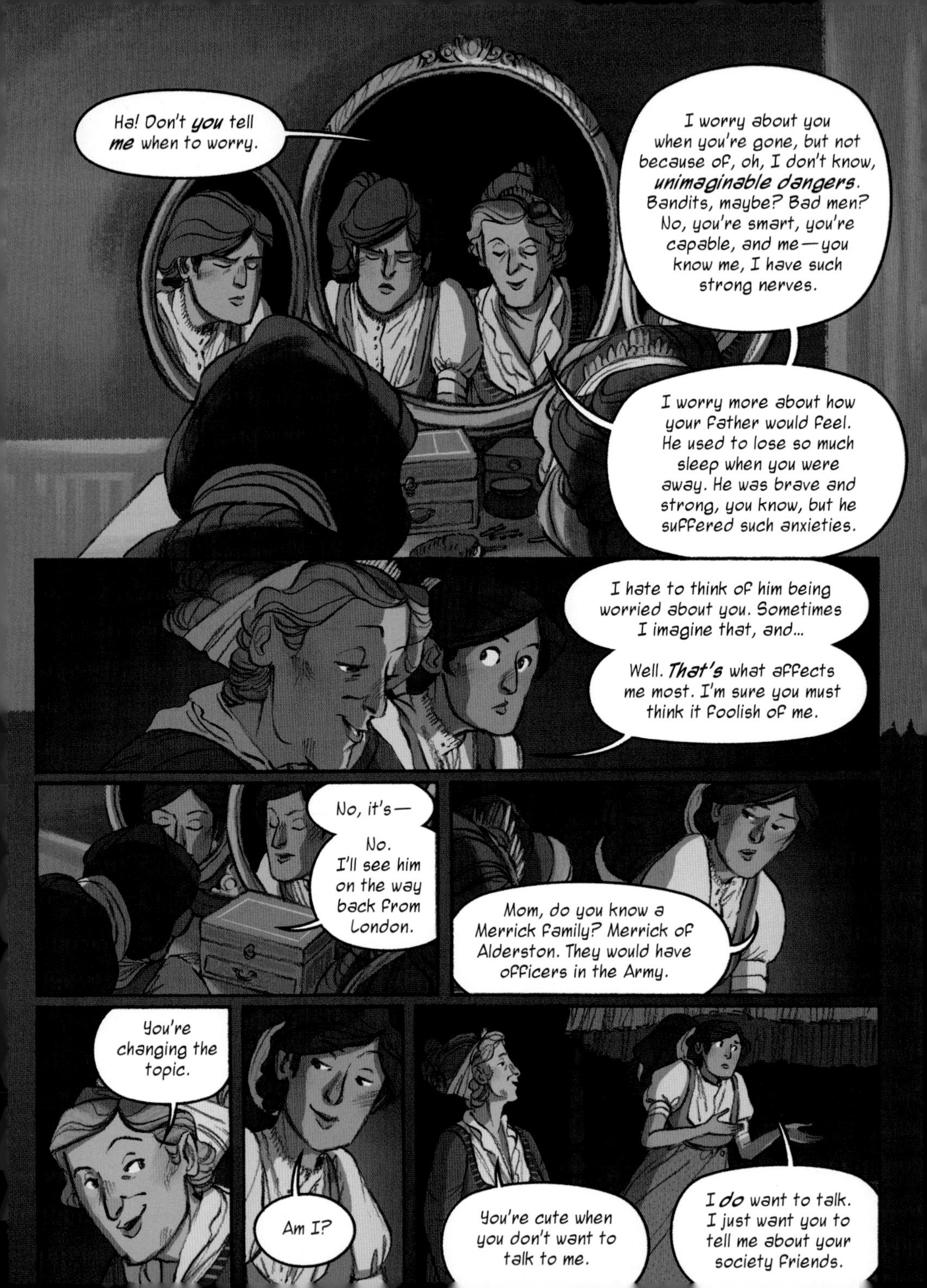
Ha! Don't *you* tell *me* when to worry.
I worry about you when you're gone, but not because of, oh, I don't know, ***unimaginable dangers***. Bandits, maybe? Bad men? No, you're smart, you're capable, and me—you know me, I have such strong nerves.
I worry more about how your father would feel. He used to lose so much sleep when you were away. He was brave and strong, you know, but he suffered such anxieties.
I hate to think of him being worried about you. Sometimes I imagine that, and...
Well. ***That's*** what affects me most. I'm sure you must think it foolish of me.
No, it's—
No. I'll see him on the way back from London.
Mom, do you know a Merrick family? Merrick of Alderston. They would have officers in the Army.
You're changing the topic.
Am I?
You're cute when you don't want to talk to me.
I *do* want to talk. I just want you to tell me about your society friends.

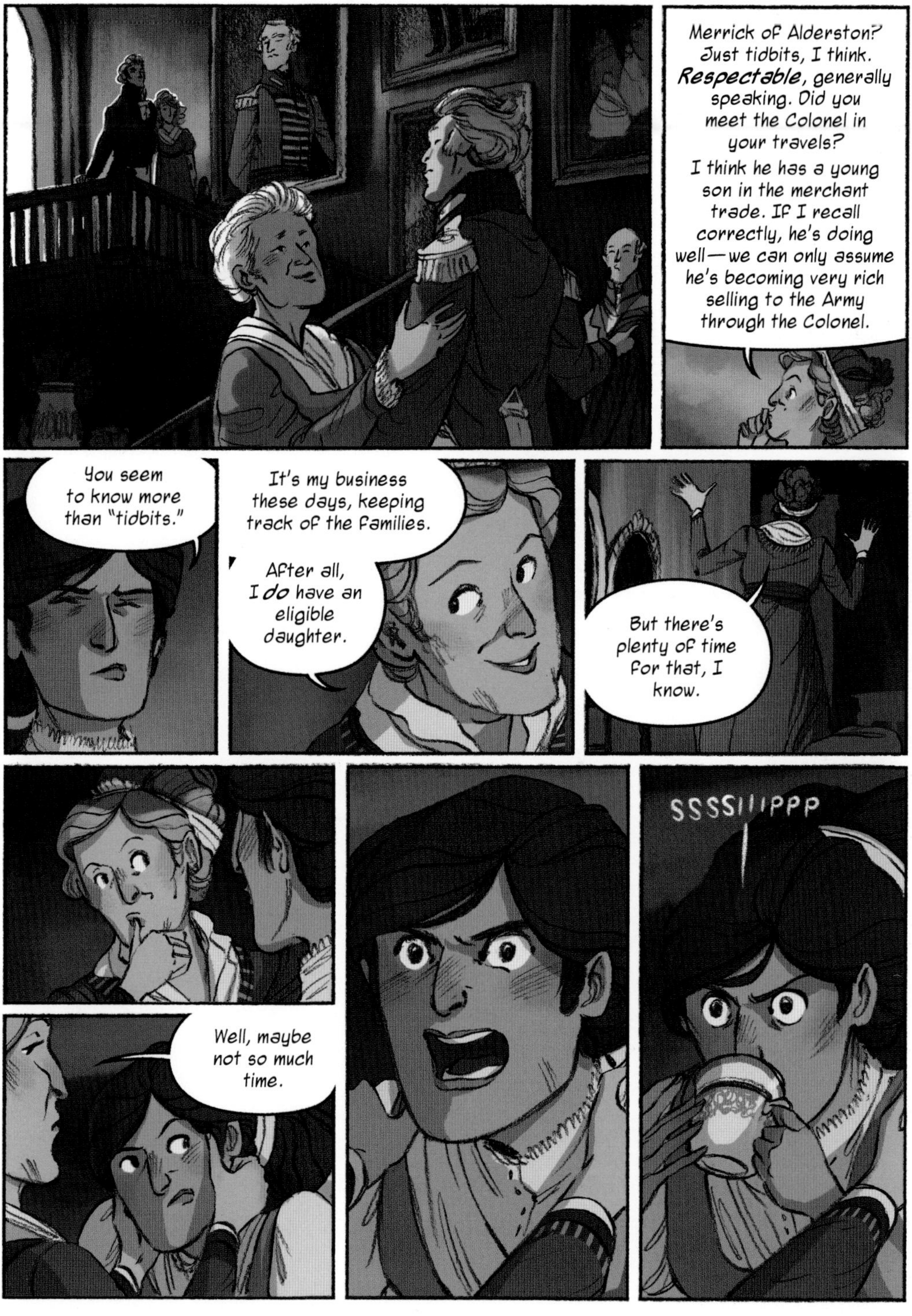
Merrick of Alderston? Just tidbits, I think. Respectable, generally speaking. Did you meet the Colonel in your travels?
I think he has a young son in the merchant trade. If I recall correctly, he's doing well—we can only assume he's becoming very rich selling to the Army through the Colonel.
You seem to know more than "tidbits."
It's my business these days, keeping track of the families.
After all, I do have an eligible daughter.
But there's plenty of time for that, I know.
Well, maybe not so much time.
SSSSIIIPPP

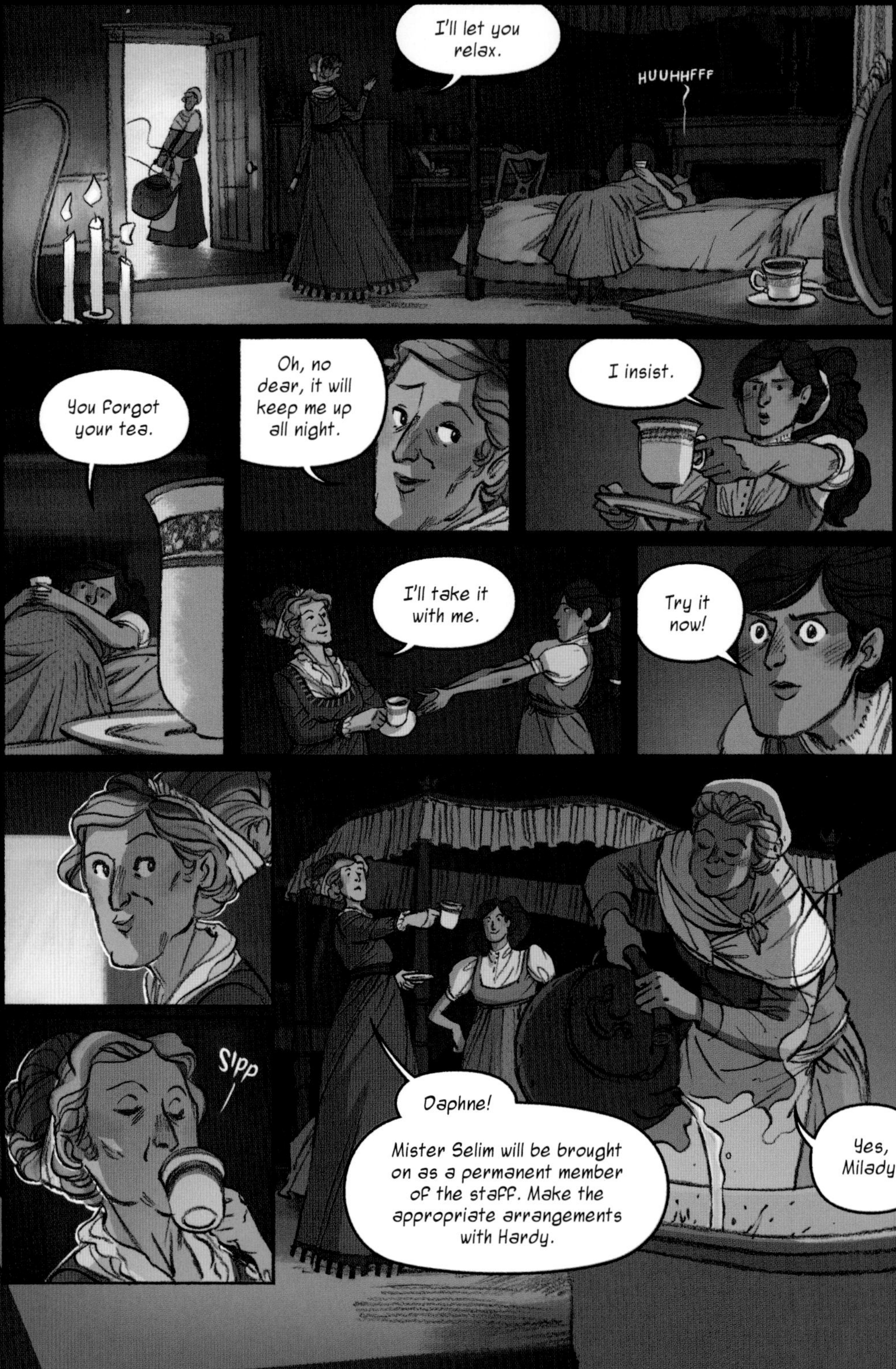
I'll let you relax.
HUUHHFFF
You forgot your tea.
Oh, no dear, it will keep me up all night.
I insist.
I'll take it with me.
Try it now!
SIPP
Daphne!
Mister Selim will be brought on as a permanent member of the staff. Make the appropriate arrangements with Hardy.
Yes, Milady.

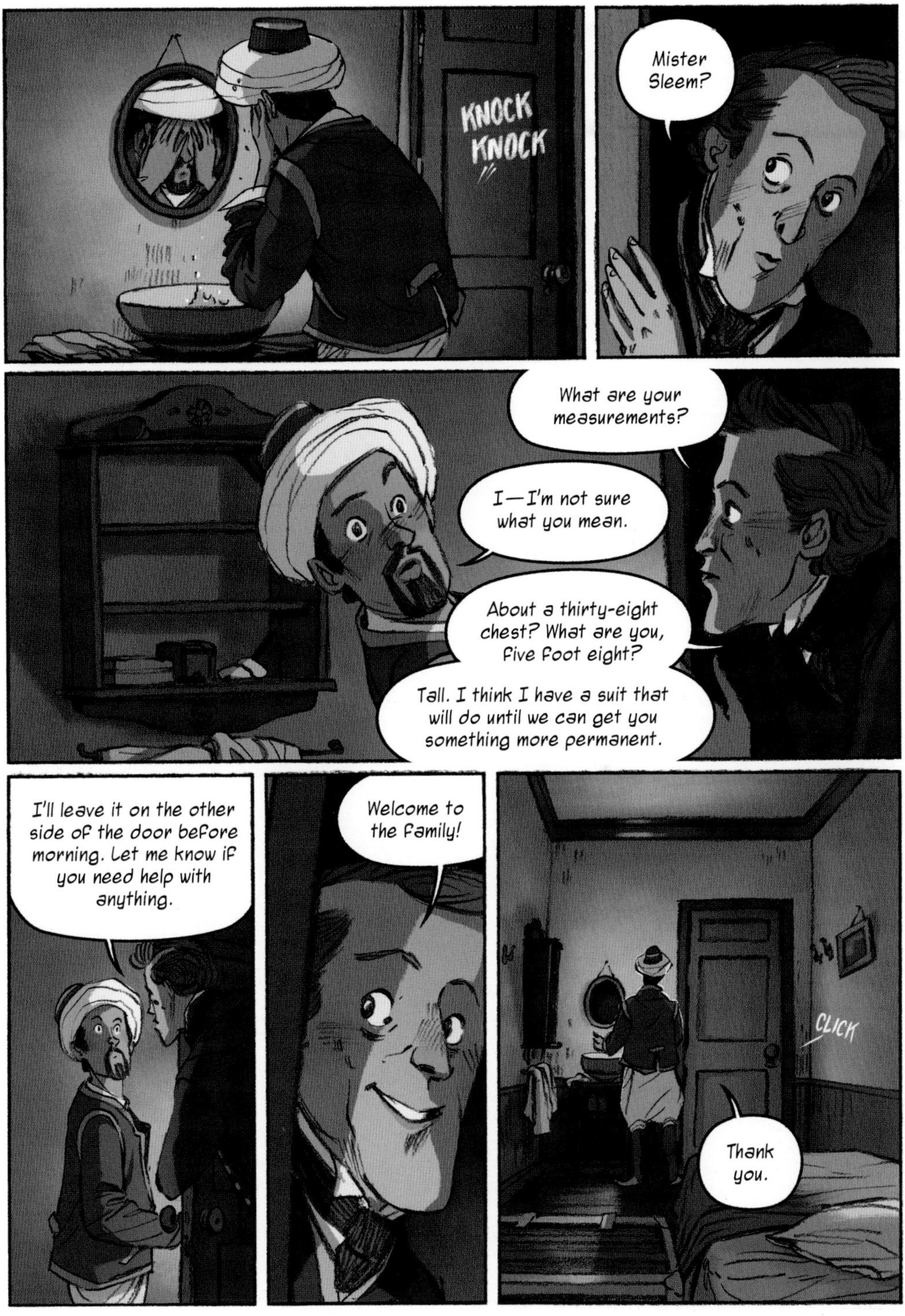
KNOCK KNOCK
Mister Sleem?
What are your measurements?
I—I'm not sure what you mean.
About a thirty-eight chest? What are you, five foot eight?
Tall. I think I have a suit that will do until we can get you something more permanent.
I'll leave it on the other side of the door before morning. Let me know if you need help with anything.
Welcome to the family!
CLICK
Thank you.

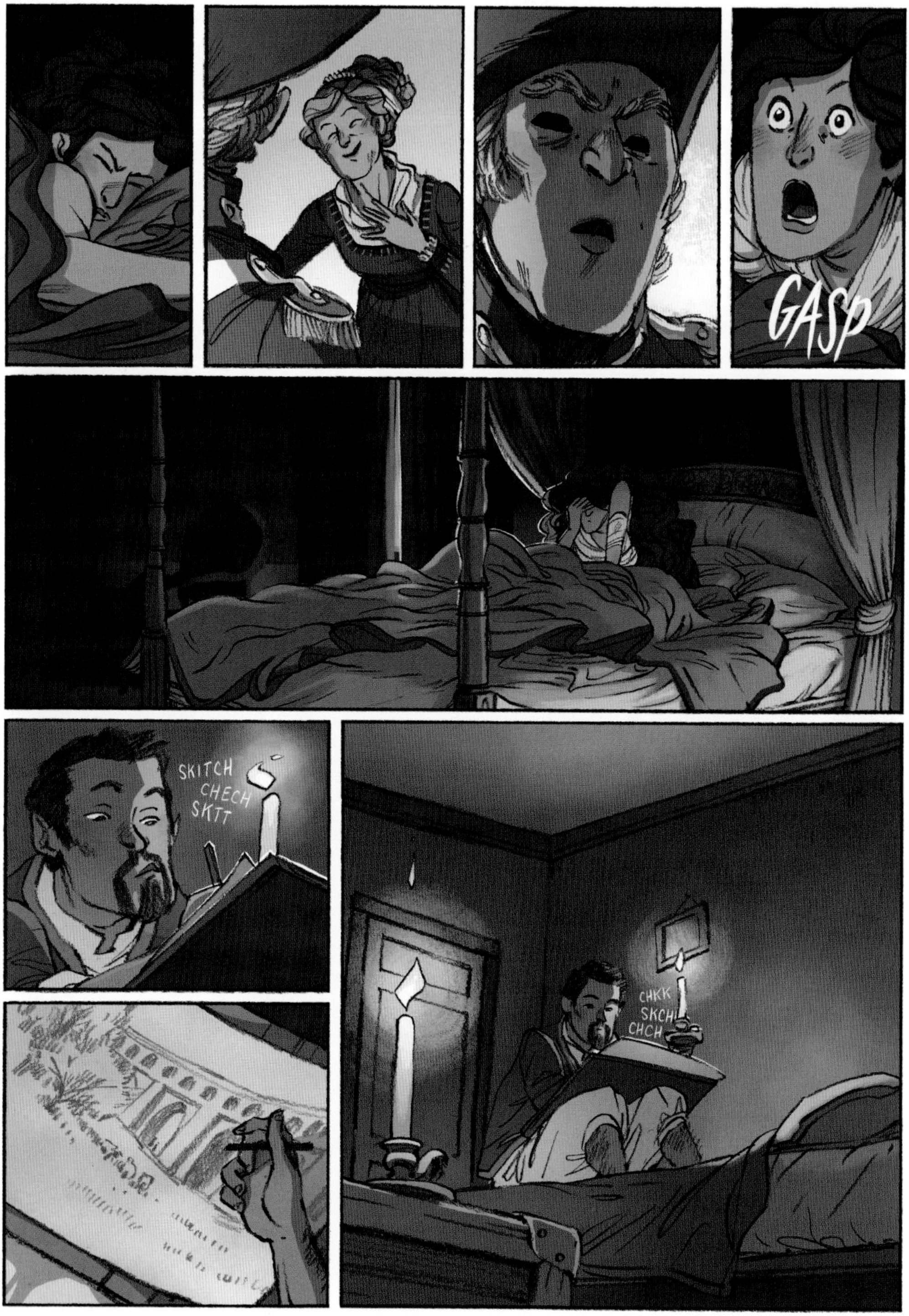
GASP
SKITCH
CHECH
SKTT
CHKK
SKCH
CHCH

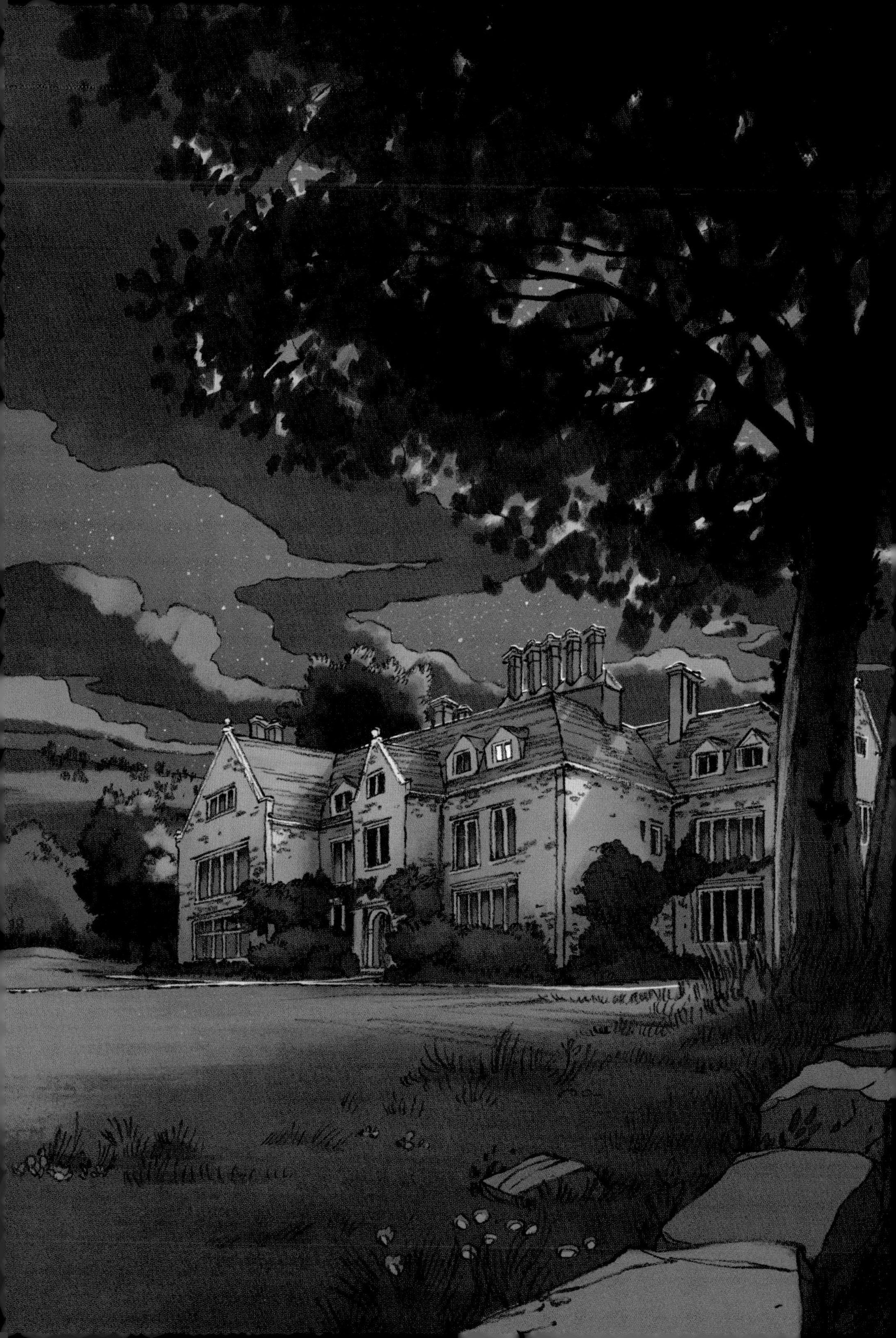

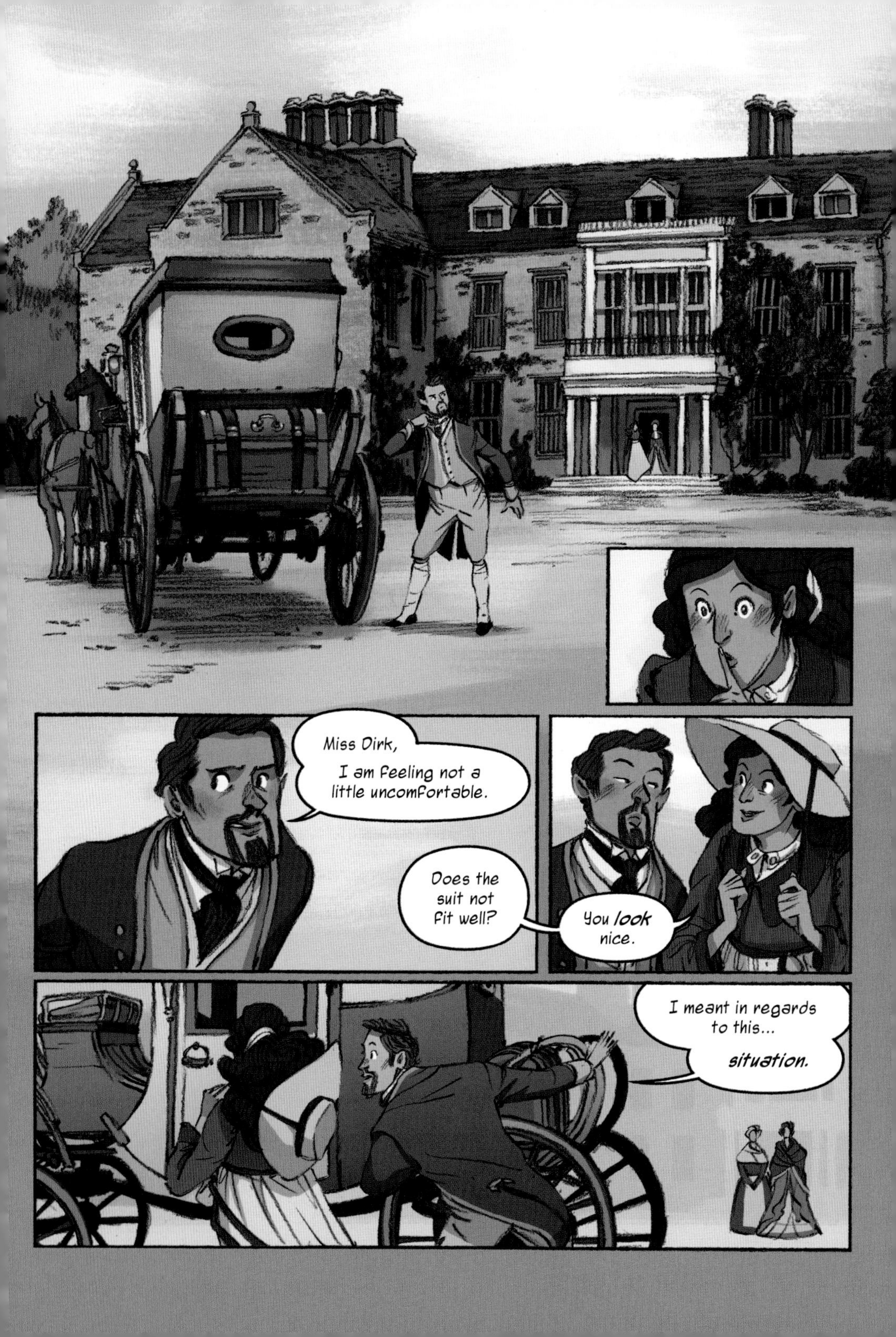
Miss Dirk,
I am feeling not a little uncomfortable.
Does the suit not fit well?
You *look* nice.
I meant in regards to this... *situation.*

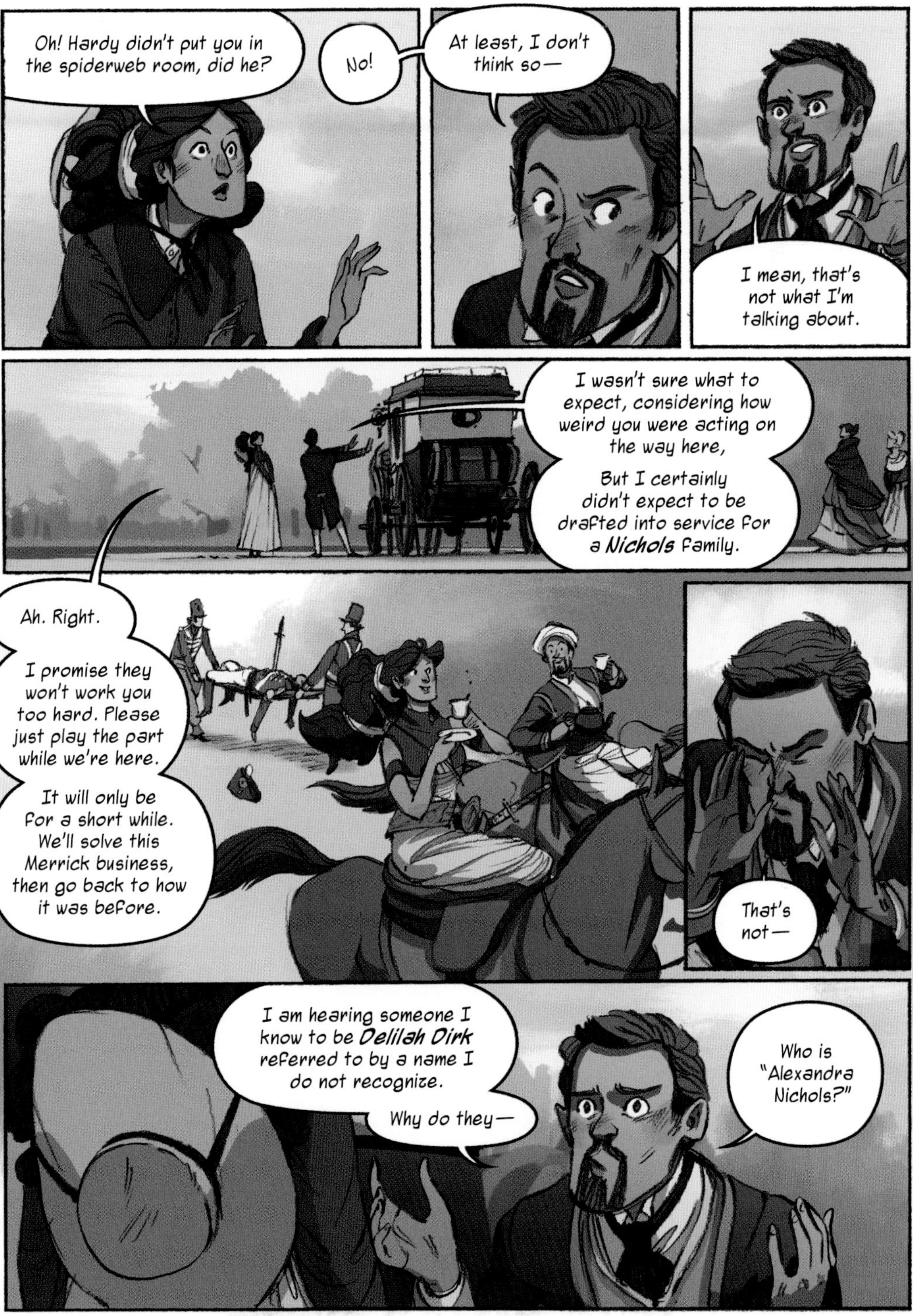
Oh! Hardy didn't put you in the spiderweb room, did he?
No!
At least, I don't think so—
I mean, that's not what I'm talking about.
I wasn't sure what to expect, considering how weird you were acting on the way here,
But I certainly didn't expect to be drafted into service for a Nichols family.
Ah. Right.
I promise they won't work you too hard. Please just play the part while we're here.
It will only be for a short while. We'll solve this Merrick business, then go back to how it was before.
That's not—
I am hearing someone I know to be Delilah Dirk referred to by a name I do not recognize.
Why do they—
Who is "Alexandra Nichols?"

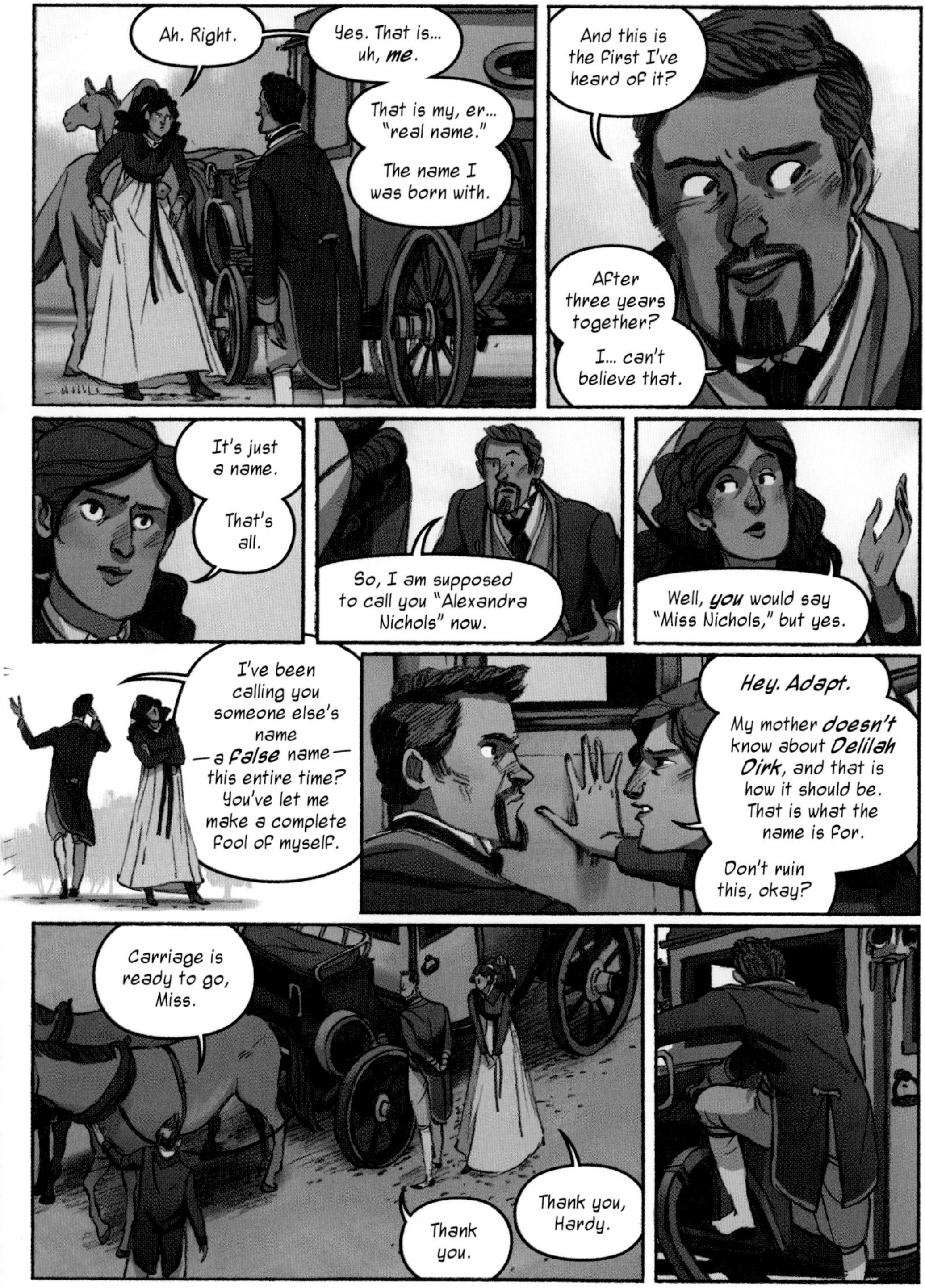
Ah. Right.
Yes. That is... uh, *me*.
That is my, er... "real name."
The name I was born with.
And this is the first I've heard of it?
After three years together?
I... can't believe that.
It's just a name.
That's all.
So, I am supposed to call you "Alexandra Nichols" now.
Well, *you* would say "Miss Nichols," but yes.
I've been calling you someone else's name —a *false* name— this entire time? You've let me make a complete fool of myself.
*Hey. Adapt.*
My mother *doesn't* know about *Delilah Dirk*, and that is how it should be. That is what the name is for.
Don't ruin this, okay?
Carriage is ready to go, Miss.
Thank you.
Thank you, Hardy.

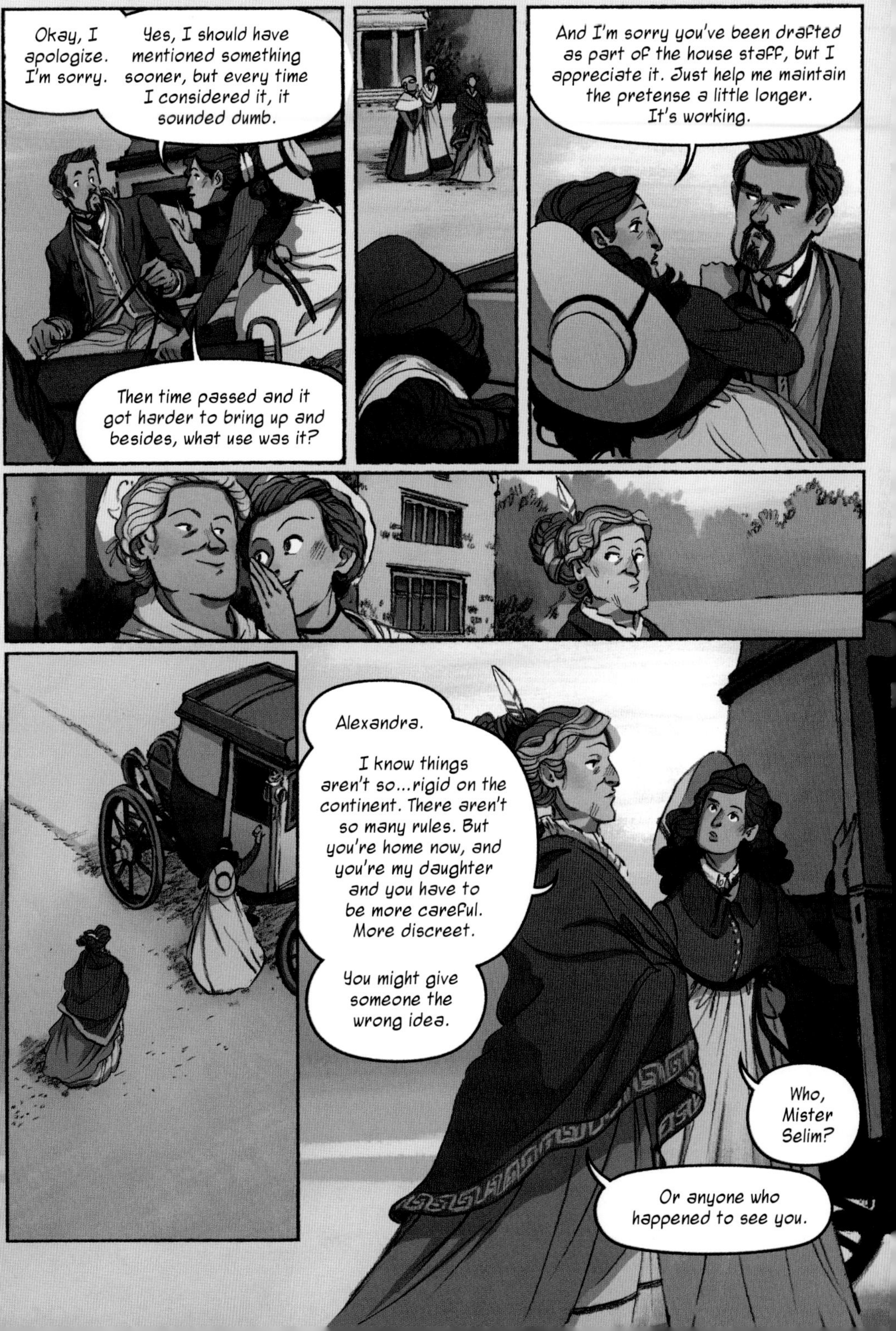
Okay, I apologize. I'm sorry.
Yes, I should have mentioned something sooner, but every time I considered it, it sounded dumb.
Then time passed and it got harder to bring up and besides, what use was it?
And I'm sorry you've been drafted as part of the house staff, but I appreciate it. Just help me maintain the pretense a little longer. It's working.
Alexandra.
I know things aren't so...rigid on the continent. There aren't so many rules. But you're home now, and you're my daughter and you have to be more careful. More discreet.
You might give someone the wrong idea.
Who, Mister Selim?
Or anyone who happened to see you.

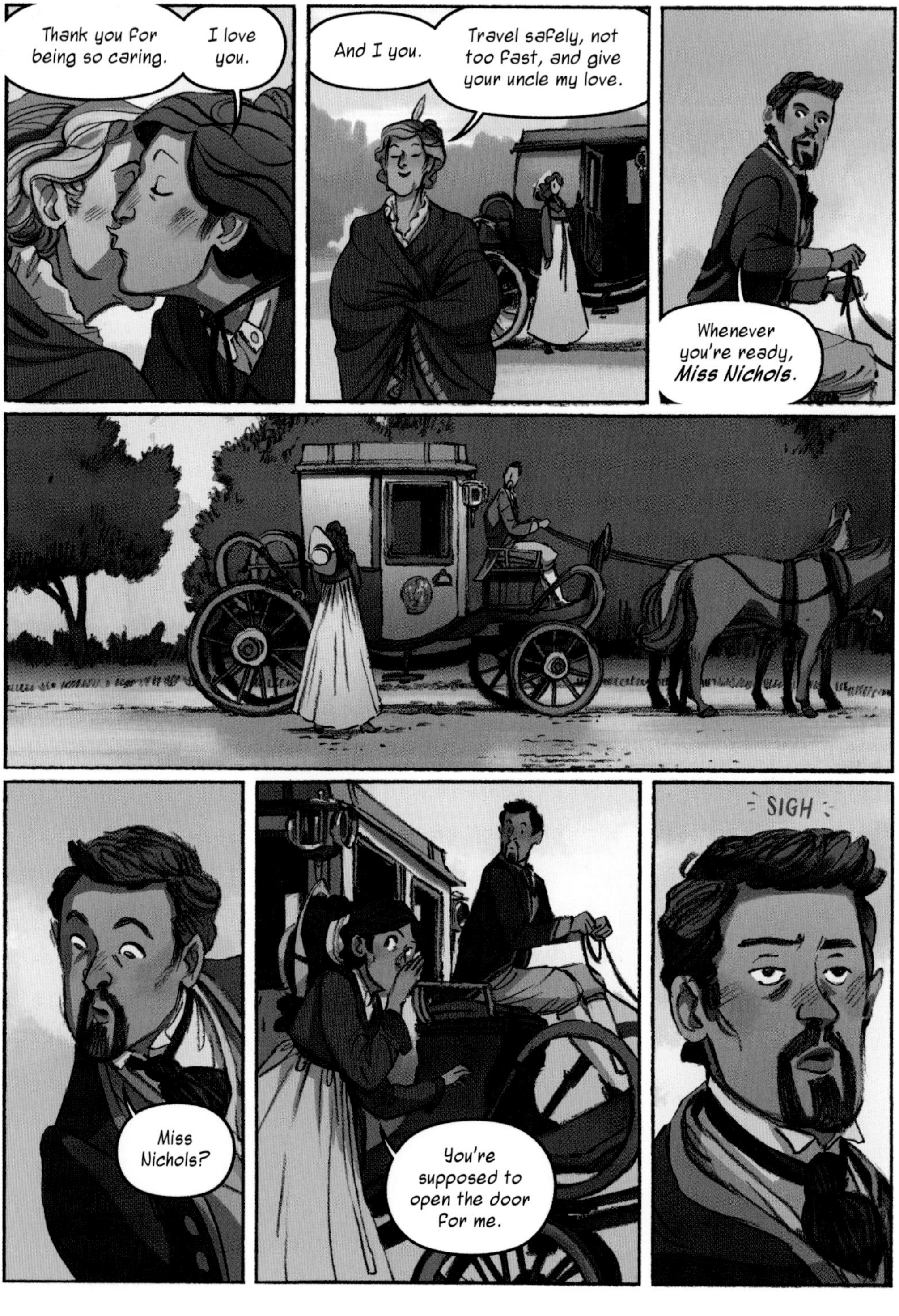
Thank you for being so caring.
I love you.
And I you.
Travel safely, not too fast, and give your uncle my love.
Whenever you're ready, Miss Nichols.
Miss Nichols?
You're supposed to open the door for me.
SIGH

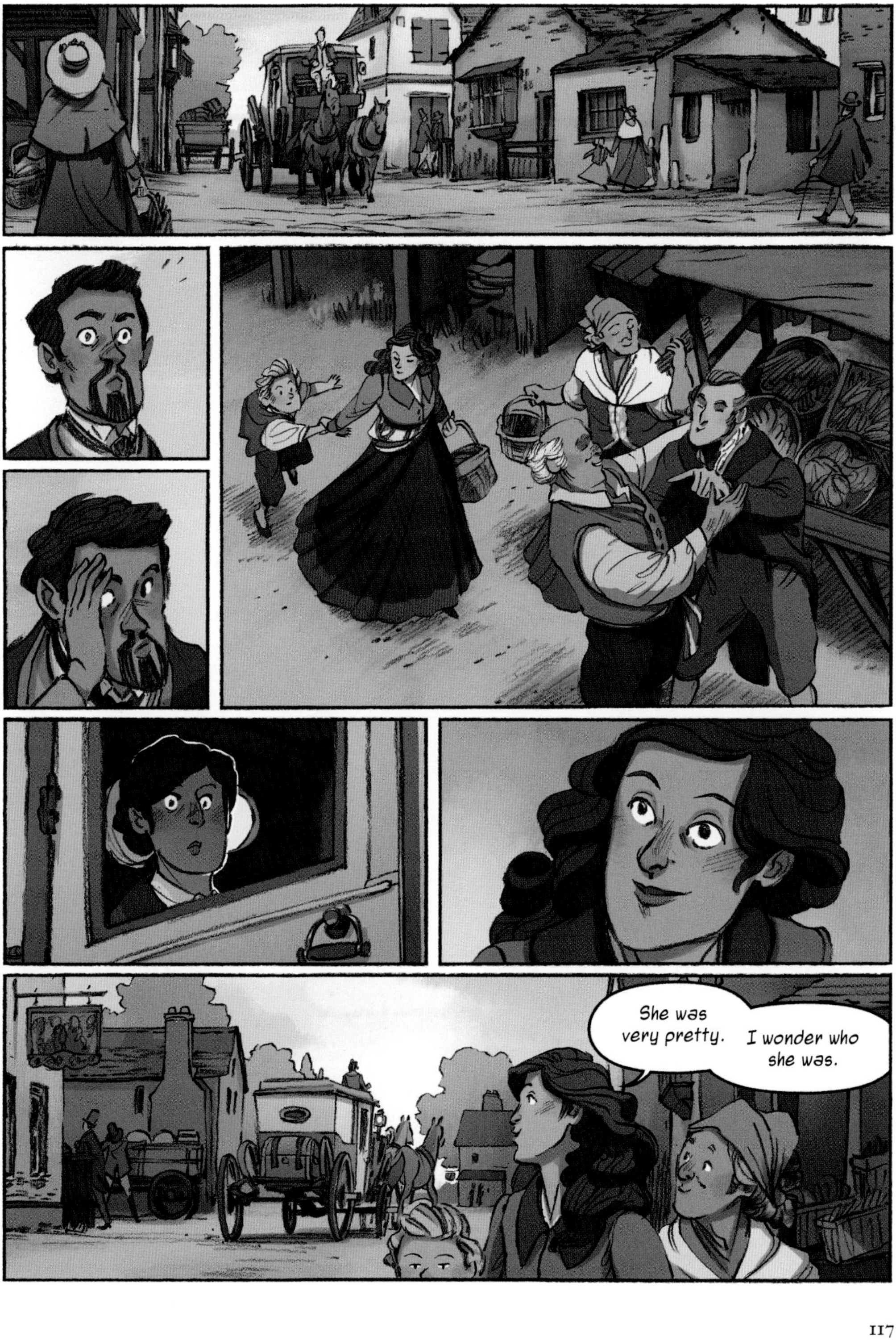
She was very pretty.
I wonder who she was.

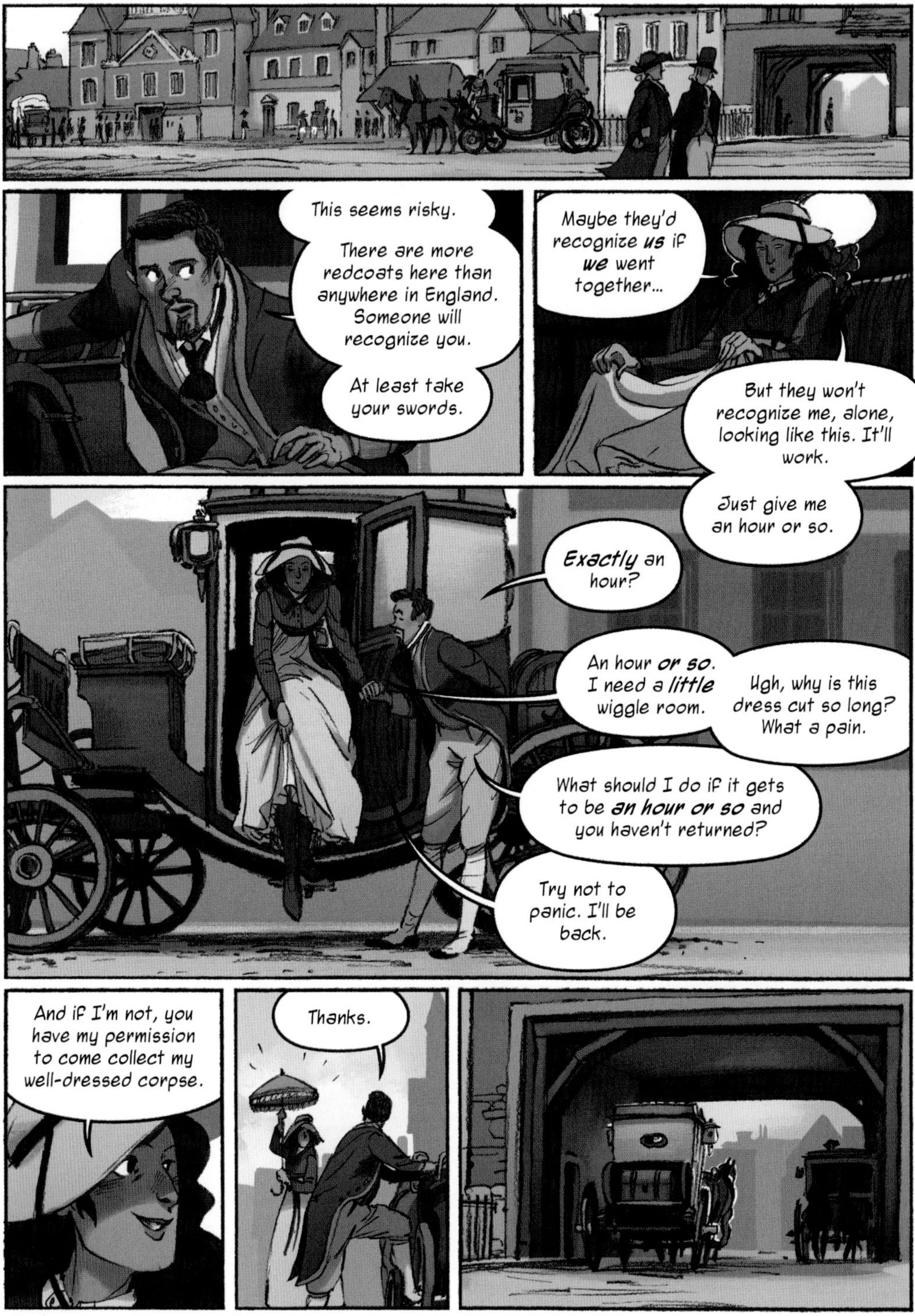
This seems risky.
There are more redcoats here than anywhere in England. Someone will recognize you.
At least take your swords.
Maybe they'd recognize *us* if *we* went together...
But they won't recognize me, alone, looking like this. It'll work.
Just give me an hour or so.
*Exactly* an hour?
An hour *or so*. I need a *little* wiggle room.
Ugh, why is this dress cut so long? What a pain.
What should I do if it gets to be *an hour or so* and you haven't returned?
Try not to panic. I'll be back.
And if I'm not, you have my permission to come collect my well-dressed corpse.
Thanks.

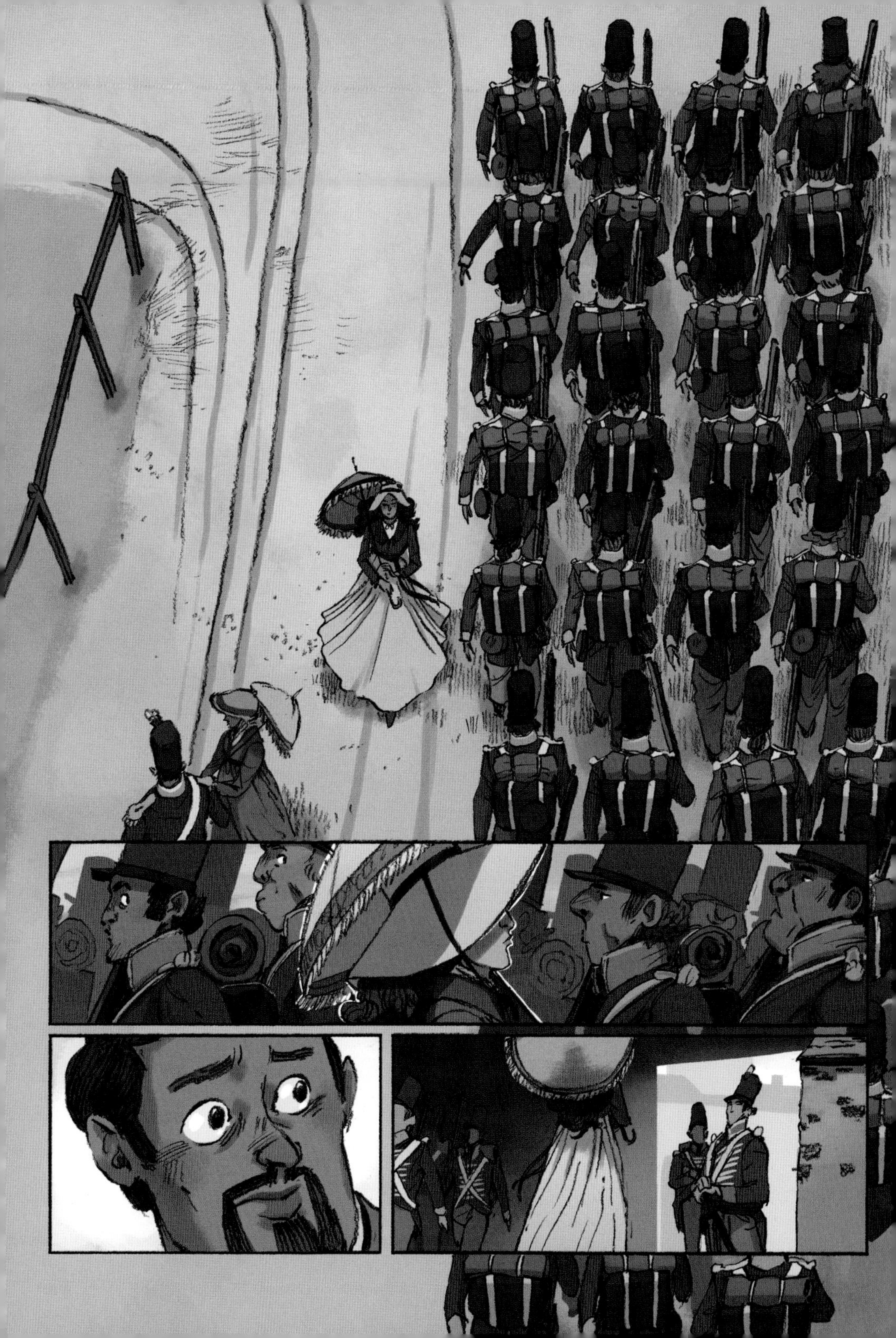

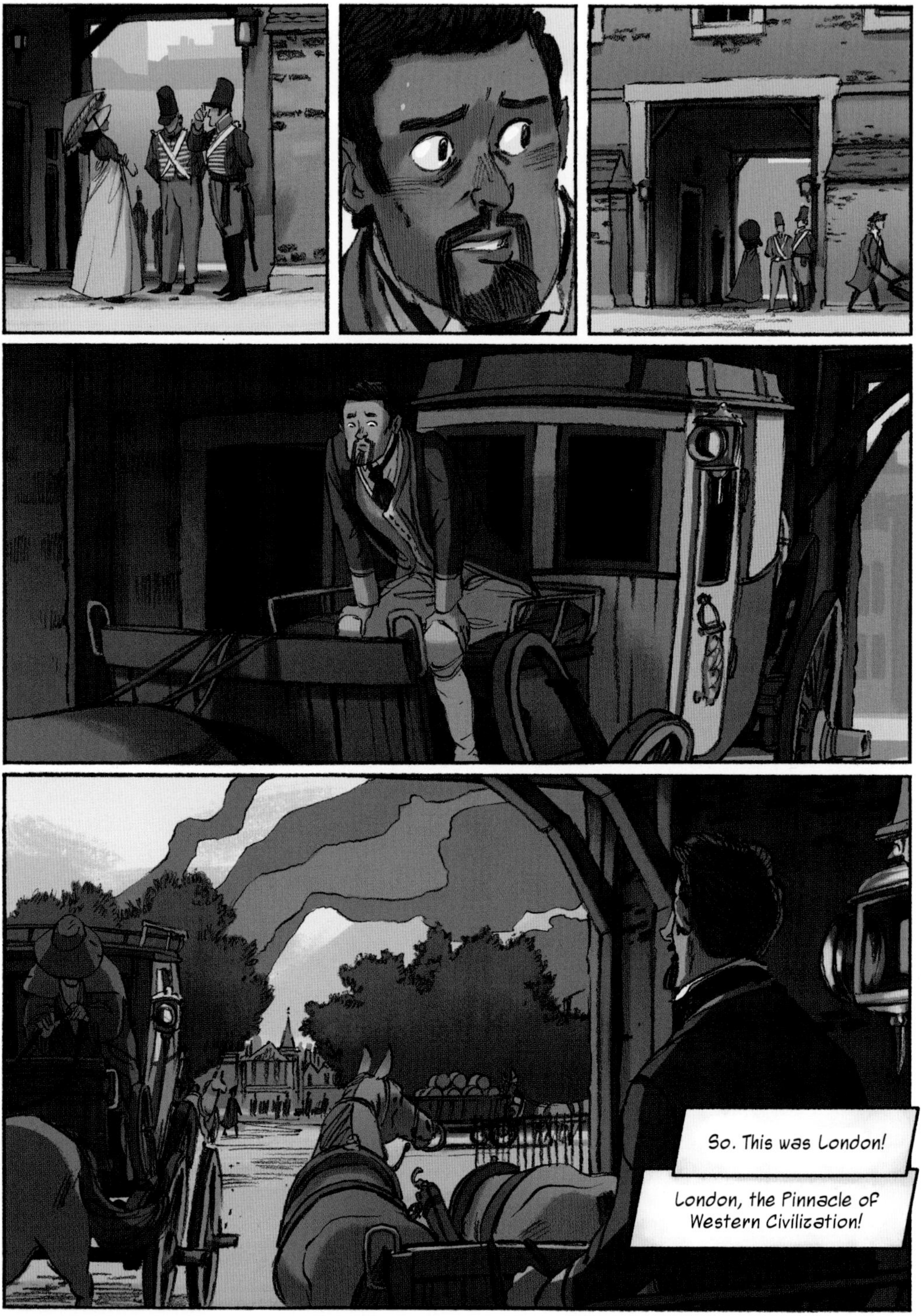
So. This was London!
London, the Pinnacle of Western Civilization!

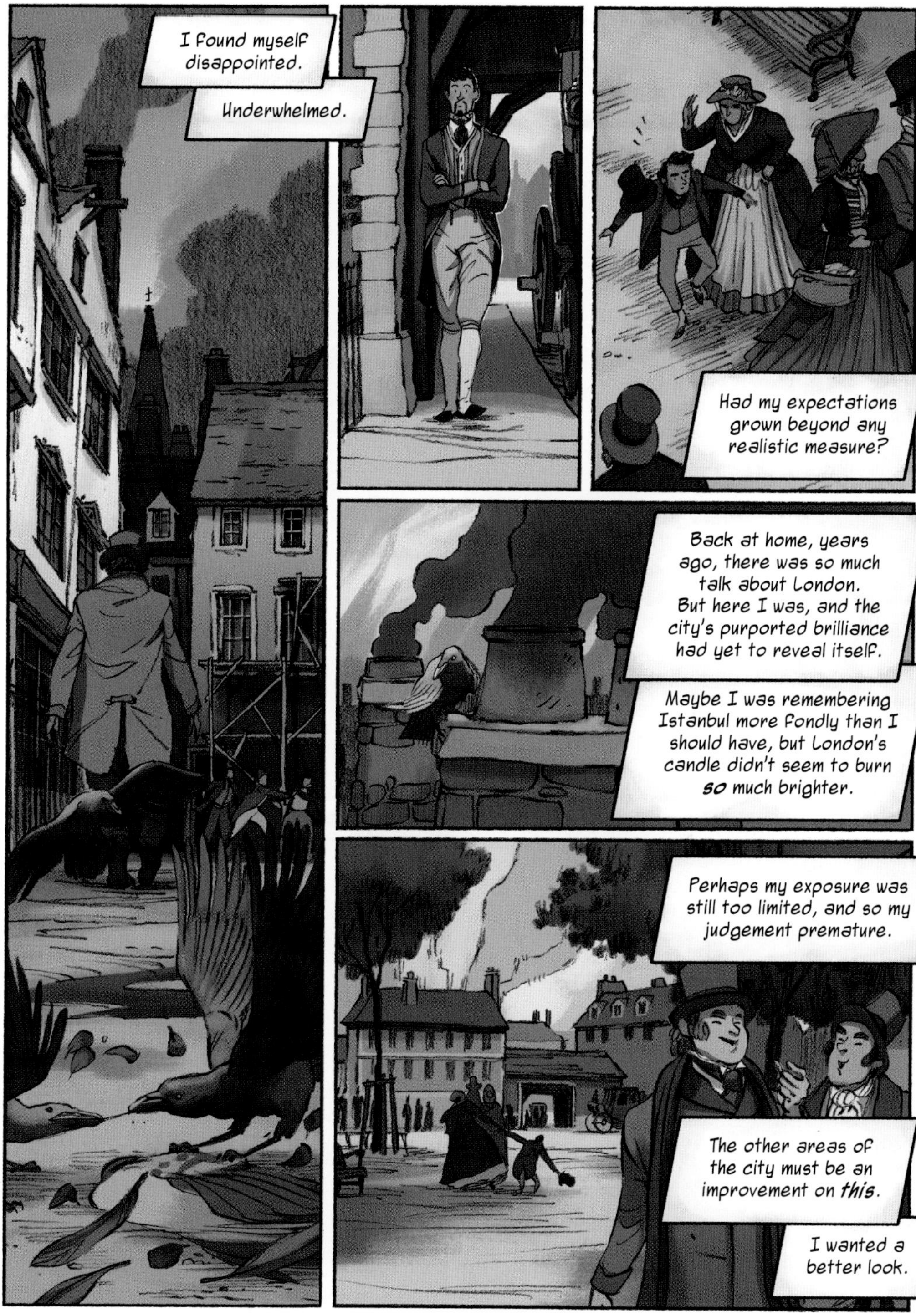
I found myself disappointed.
Underwhelmed.
Had my expectations grown beyond any realistic measure?
Back at home, years ago, there was so much talk about London. But here I was, and the city's purported brilliance had yet to reveal itself.
Maybe I was remembering Istanbul more fondly than I should have, but London's candle didn't seem to burn *so* much brighter.
Perhaps my exposure was still too limited, and so my judgement premature.
The other areas of the city must be an improvement on *this*.
I wanted a better look.

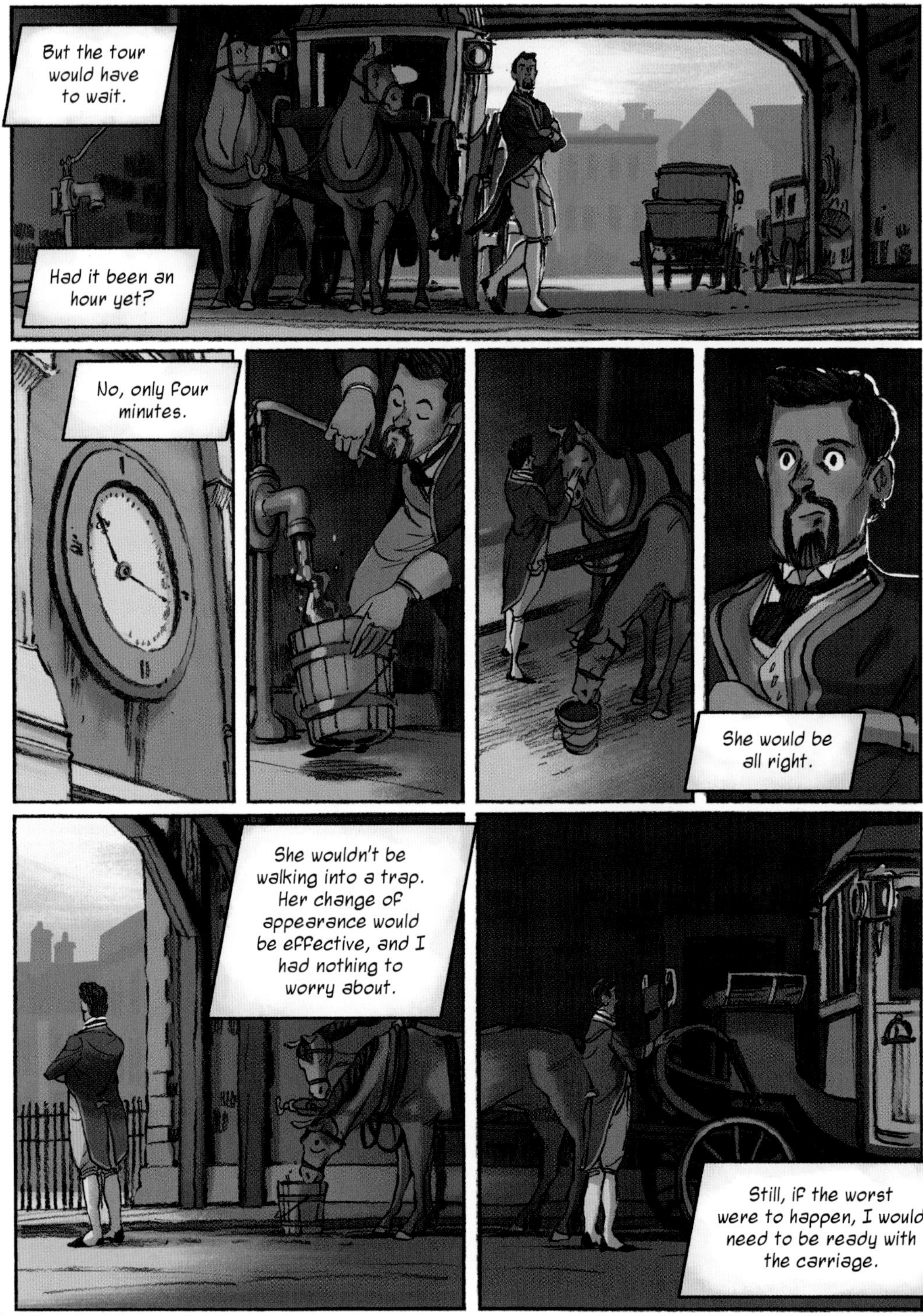
But the tour would have to wait.
Had it been an hour yet?
No, only four minutes.
She would be all right.
She wouldn't be walking into a trap. Her change of appearance would be effective, and I had nothing to worry about.
Still, if the worst were to happen, I would need to be ready with the carriage.

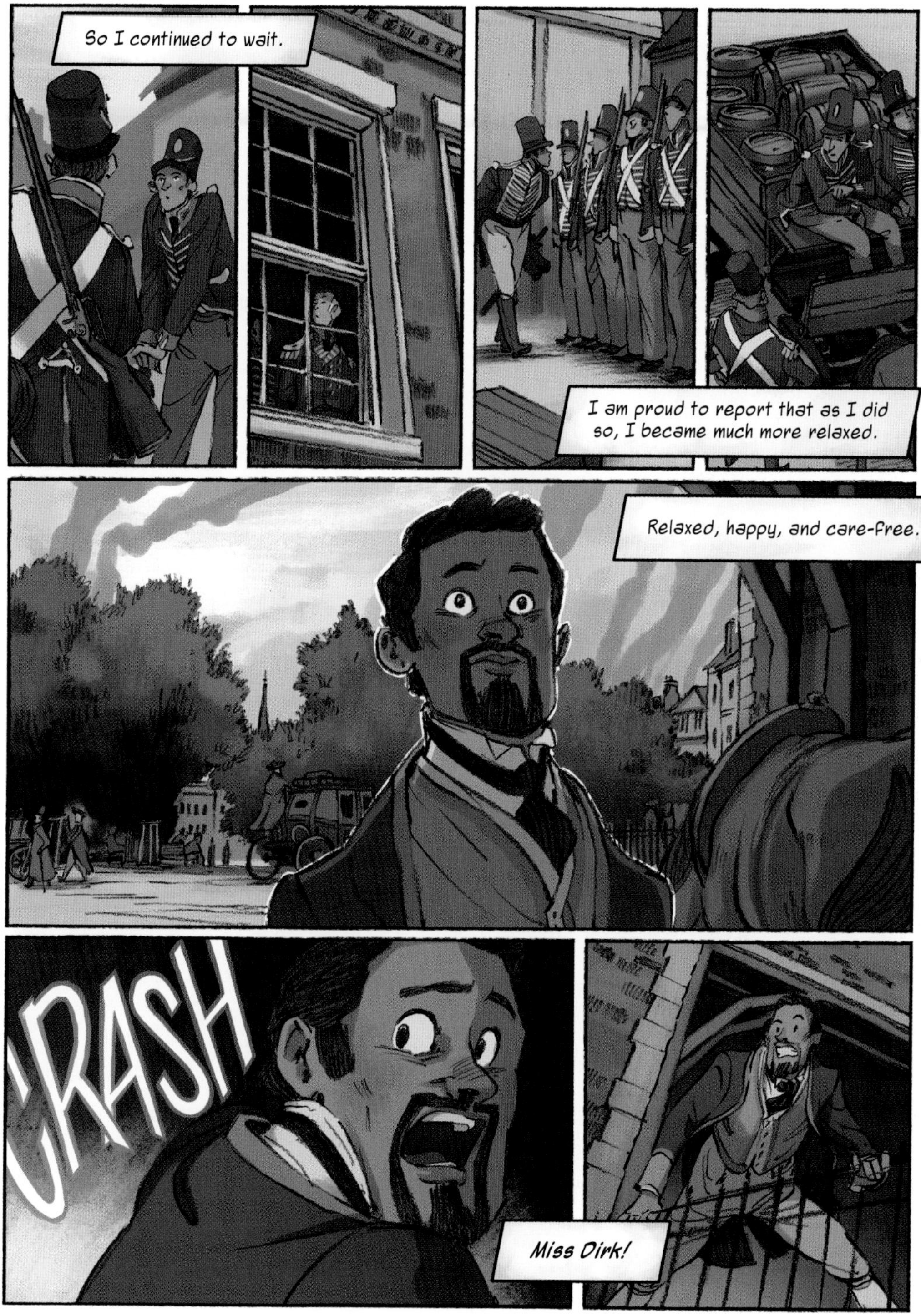
So I continued to wait.
I am proud to report that as I did so, I became much more relaxed.
Relaxed, happy, and care-free.
CRASH
Miss Dirk!

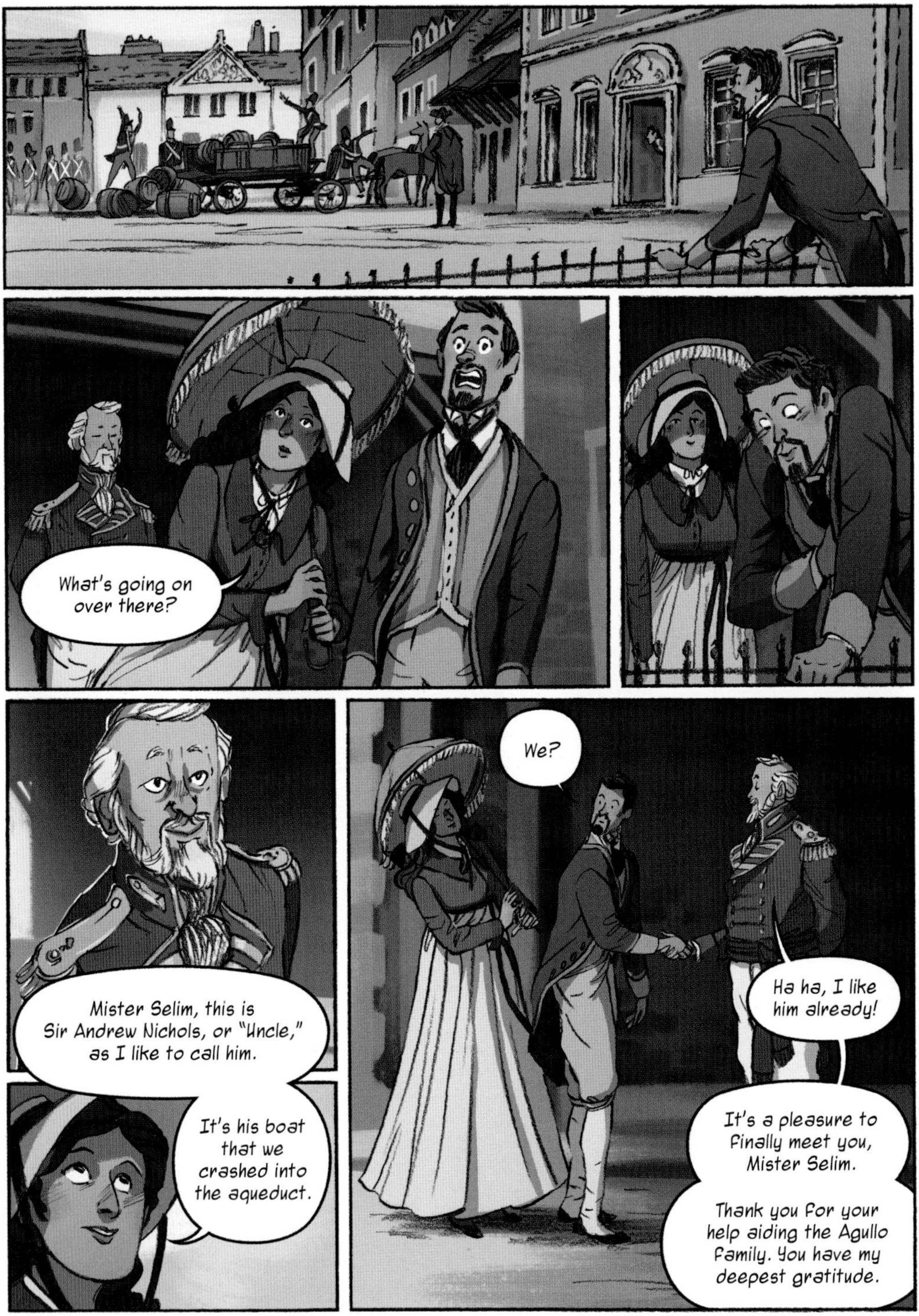
What's going on over there?
Mister Selim, this is Sir Andrew Nichols, or "Uncle," as I like to call him.
It's his boat that we crashed into the aqueduct.
We?
Ha ha, I like him already!
It's a pleasure to finally meet you, Mister Selim.
Thank you for your help aiding the Agullo family. You have my deepest gratitude.

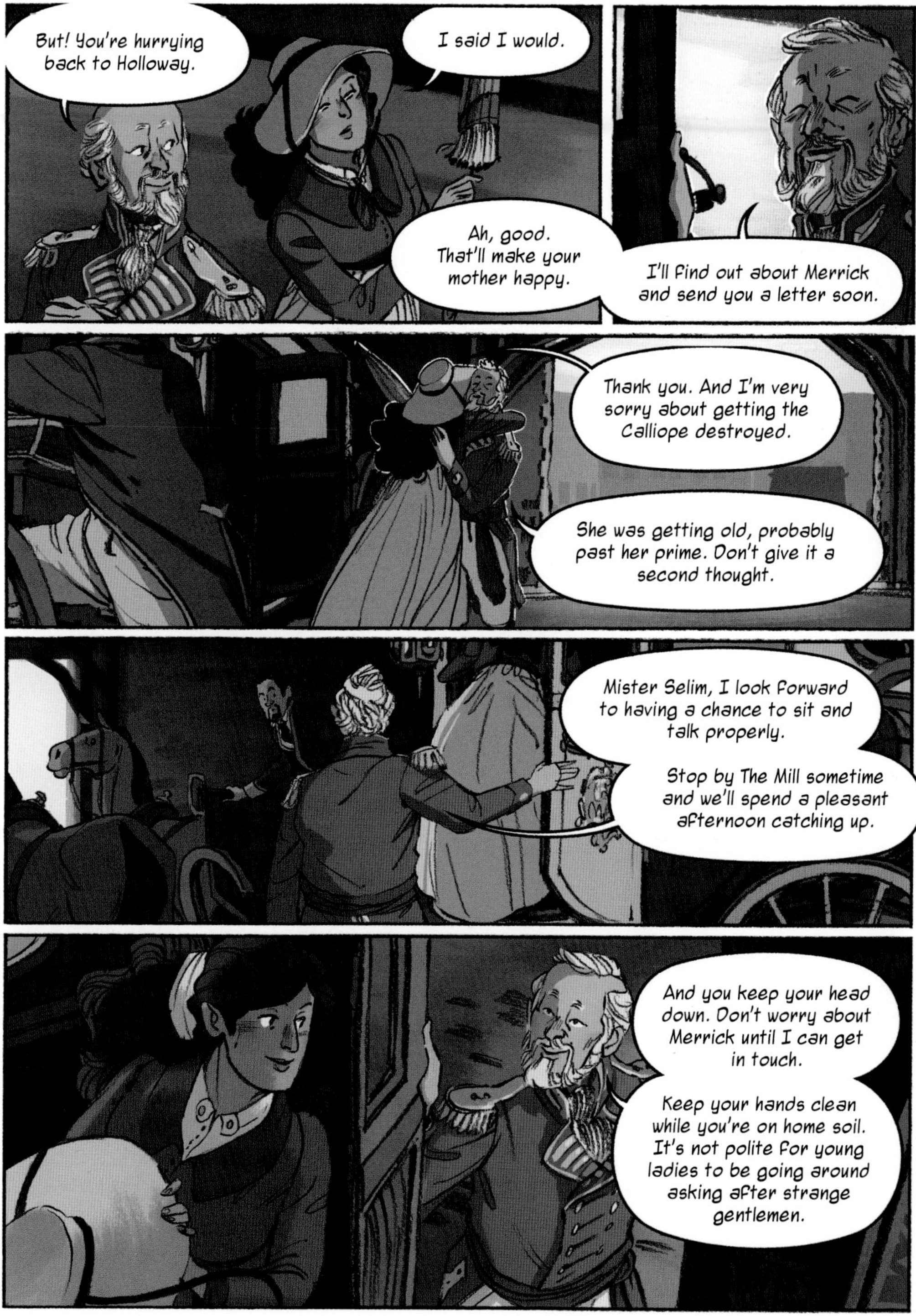
But! You're hurrying back to Holloway.
I said I would.
Ah, good. That'll make your mother happy.
I'll find out about Merrick and send you a letter soon.
Thank you. And I'm very sorry about getting the Calliope destroyed.
She was getting old, probably past her prime. Don't give it a second thought.
Mister Selim, I look forward to having a chance to sit and talk properly.
Stop by The Mill sometime and we'll spend a pleasant afternoon catching up.
And you keep your head down. Don't worry about Merrick until I can get in touch.
Keep your hands clean while you're on home soil. It's not polite for young ladies to be going around asking after strange gentlemen.

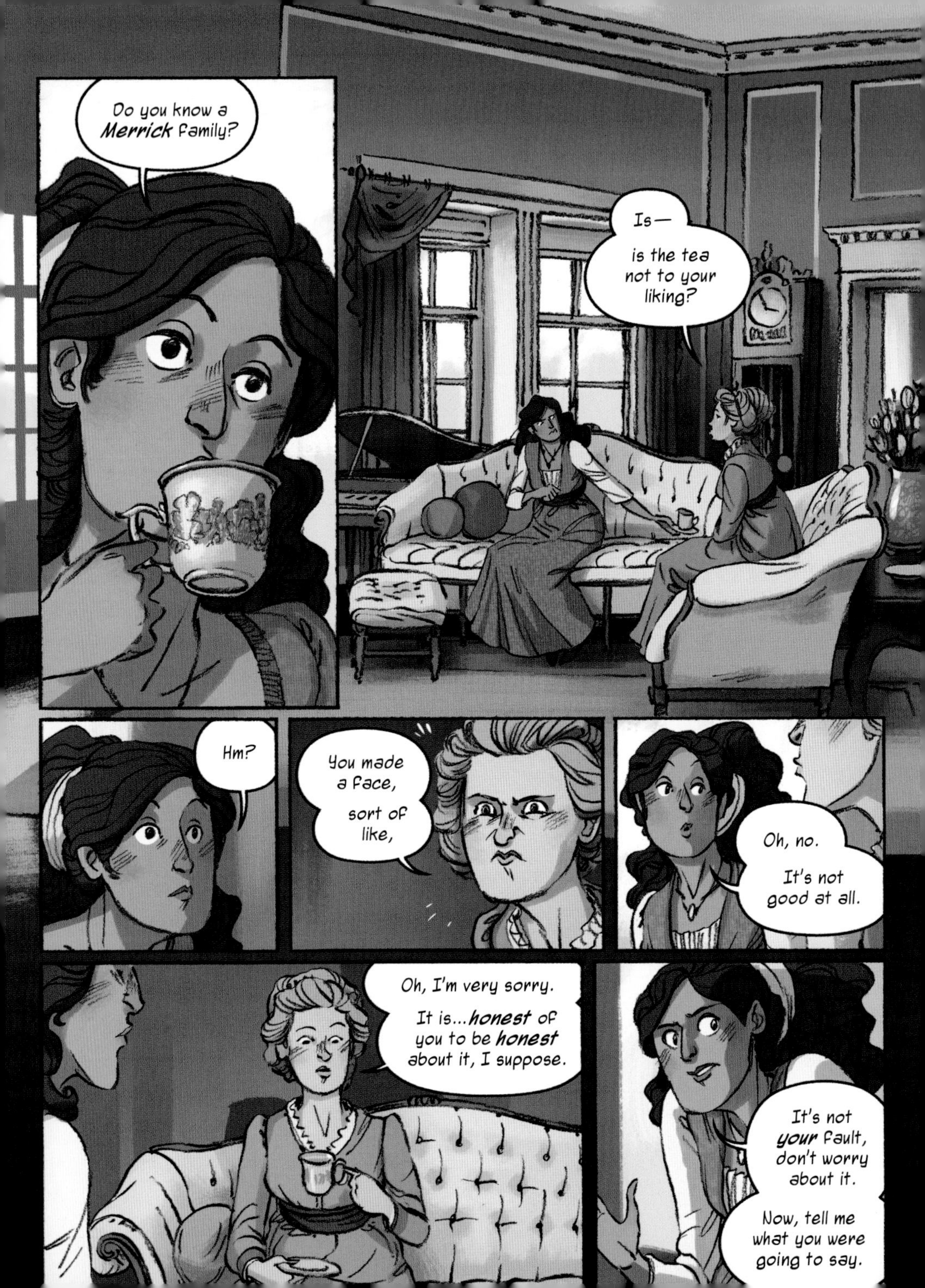
Do you know a Merrick family?
Is—
is the tea not to your liking?
Hm?
You made a face,
sort of like,
Oh, no.
It's not good at all.
Oh, I'm very sorry.
It is...honest of you to be honest about it, I suppose.
It's not your fault, don't worry about it.
Now, tell me what you were going to say.

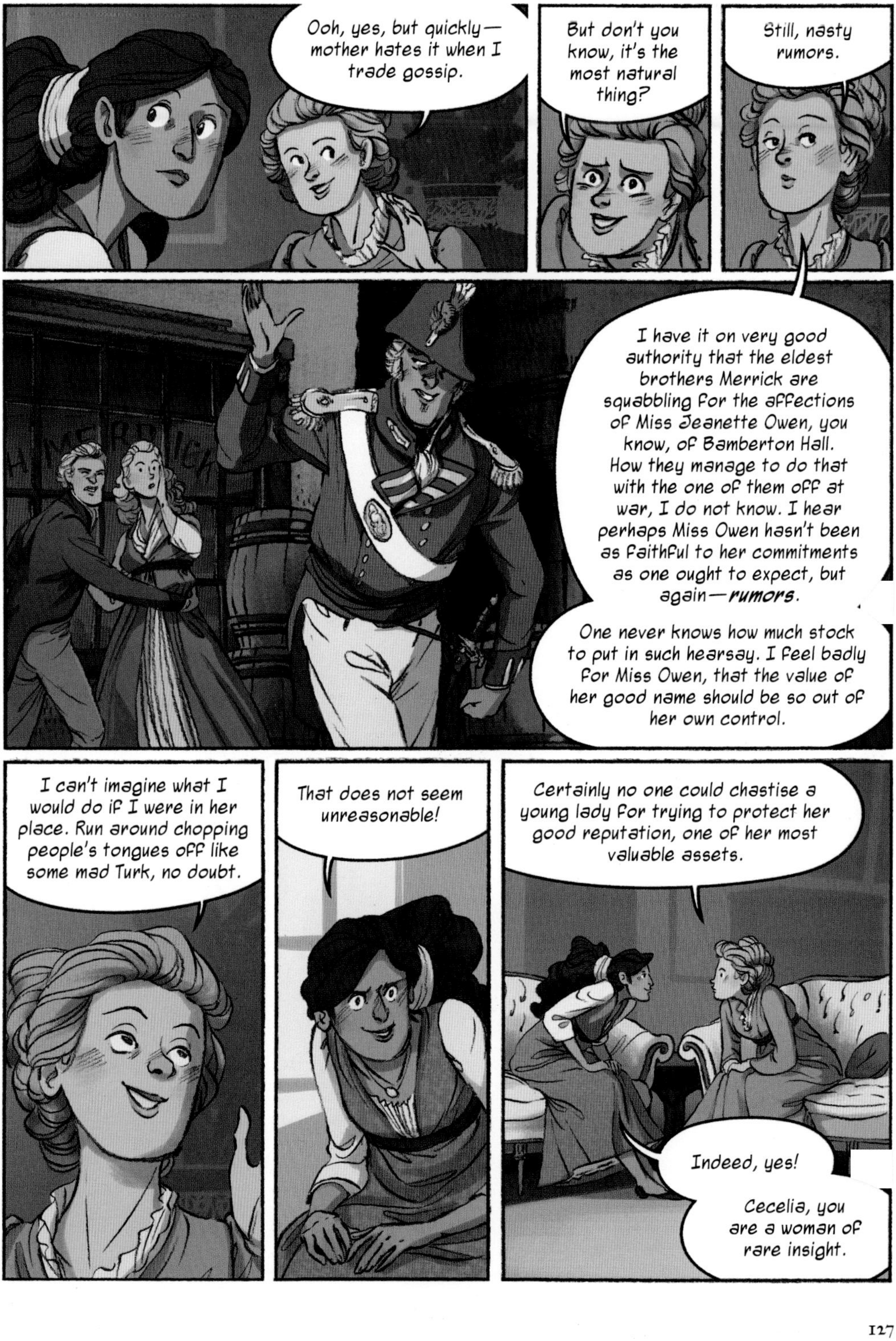
Ooh, yes, but quickly—mother hates it when I trade gossip.
But don't you know, it's the most natural thing?
Still, nasty rumors.
I have it on very good authority that the eldest brothers Merrick are squabbling for the affections of Miss Jeanette Owen, you know, of Bamberton Hall. How they manage to do that with the one of them off at war, I do not know. I hear perhaps Miss Owen hasn't been as faithful to her commitments as one ought to expect, but again—***rumors***.
One never knows how much stock to put in such hearsay. I feel badly for Miss Owen, that the value of her good name should be so out of her own control.
I can't imagine what I would do if I were in her place. Run around chopping people's tongues off like some mad Turk, no doubt.
That does not seem unreasonable!
Certainly no one could chastise a young lady for trying to protect her good reputation, one of her most valuable assets.
Indeed, yes!
Cecelia, you are a woman of rare insight.

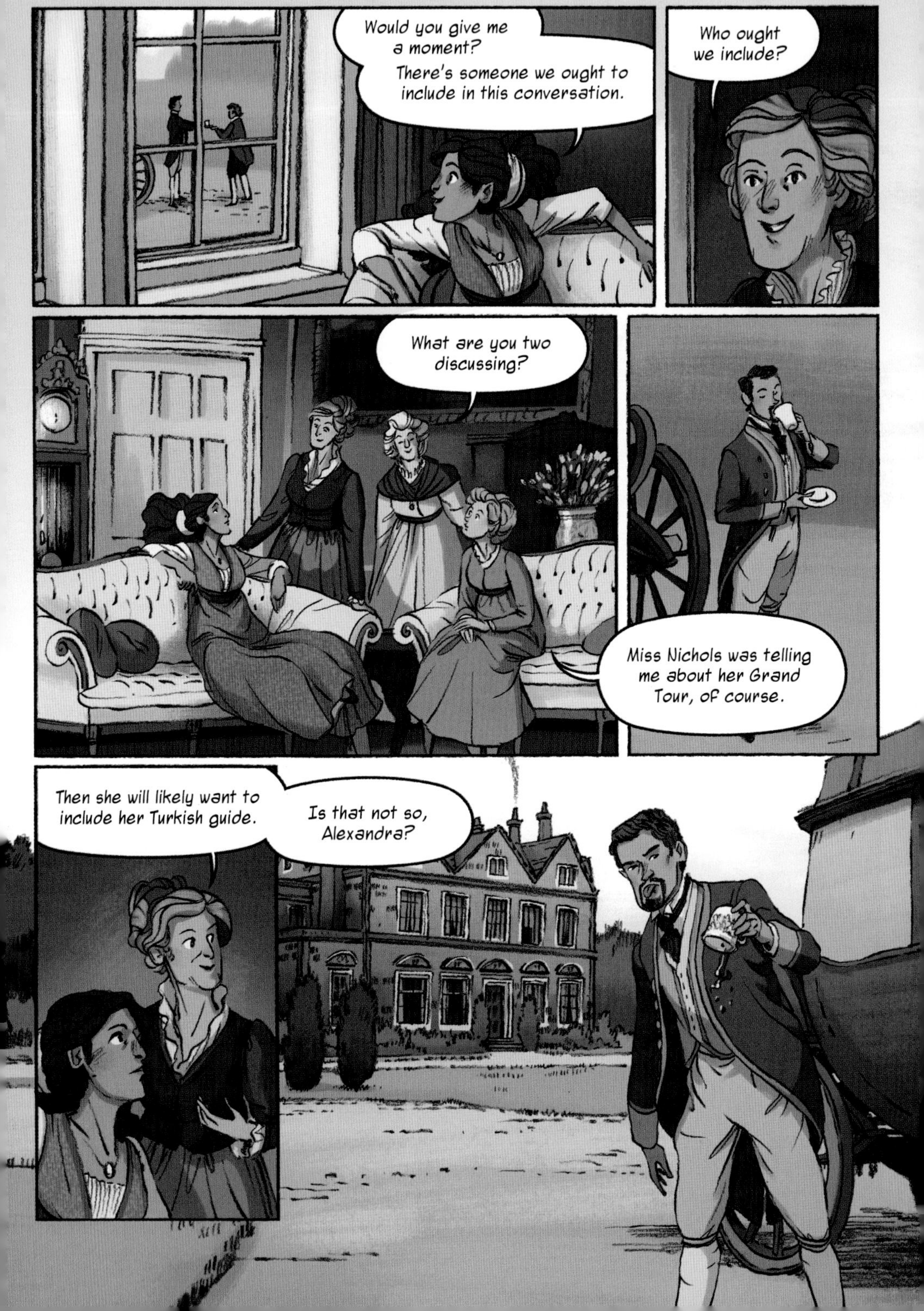
Would you give me a moment?
There's someone we ought to include in this conversation.
Who ought we include?
What are you two discussing?
Miss Nichols was telling me about her Grand Tour, of course.
Then she will likely want to include her Turkish guide.
Is that not so, Alexandra?

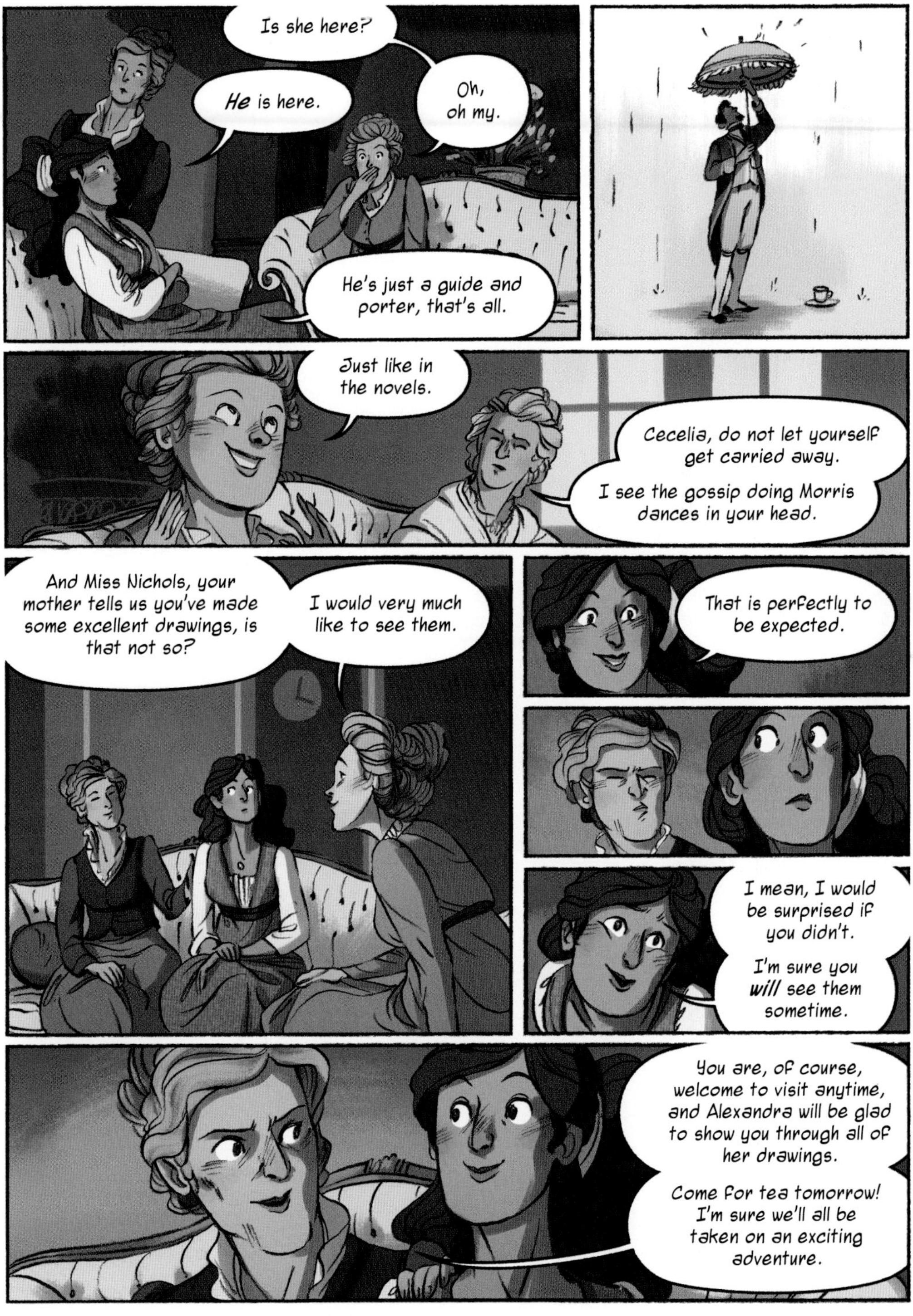
Is she here?
*He* is here.
Oh, oh my.
He's just a guide and porter, that's all.
Just like in the novels.
Cecelia, do not let yourself get carried away.
I see the gossip doing Morris dances in your head.
And Miss Nichols, your mother tells us you've made some excellent drawings, is that not so?
I would very much like to see them.
That is perfectly to be expected.
I mean, I would be surprised if you didn't.
I'm sure you ***will*** see them sometime.
You are, of course, welcome to visit anytime, and Alexandra will be glad to show you through all of her drawings.
Come for tea tomorrow! I'm sure we'll all be taken on an exciting adventure.

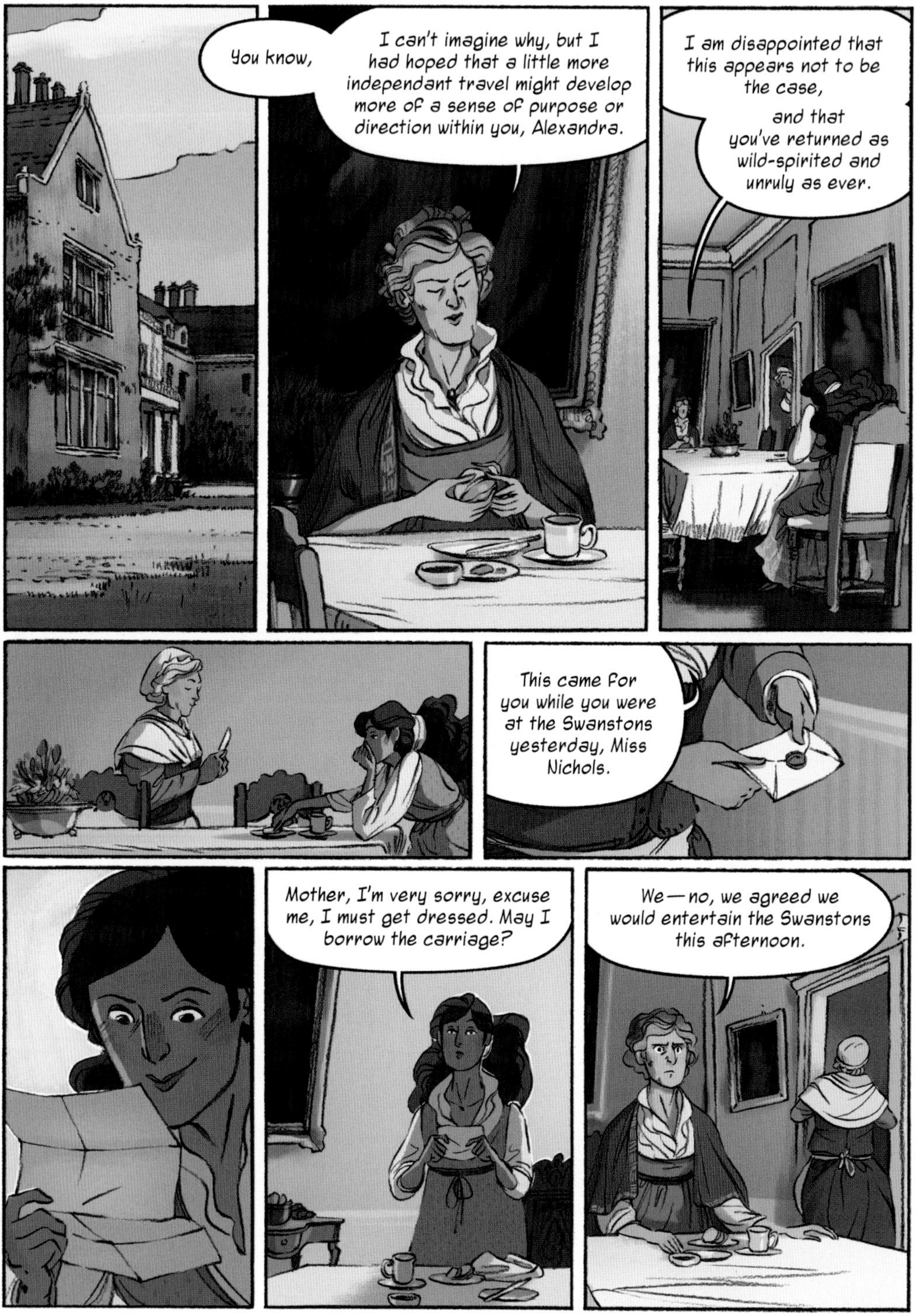
You know,
I can't imagine why, but I had hoped that a little more independant travel might develop more of a sense of purpose or direction within you, Alexandra.
I am disappointed that this appears not to be the case,
and that you've returned as wild-spirited and unruly as ever.
This came for you while you were at the Swanstons yesterday, Miss Nichols.
Mother, I'm very sorry, excuse me, I must get dressed. May I borrow the carriage?
We—no, we agreed we would entertain the Swanstons this afternoon.

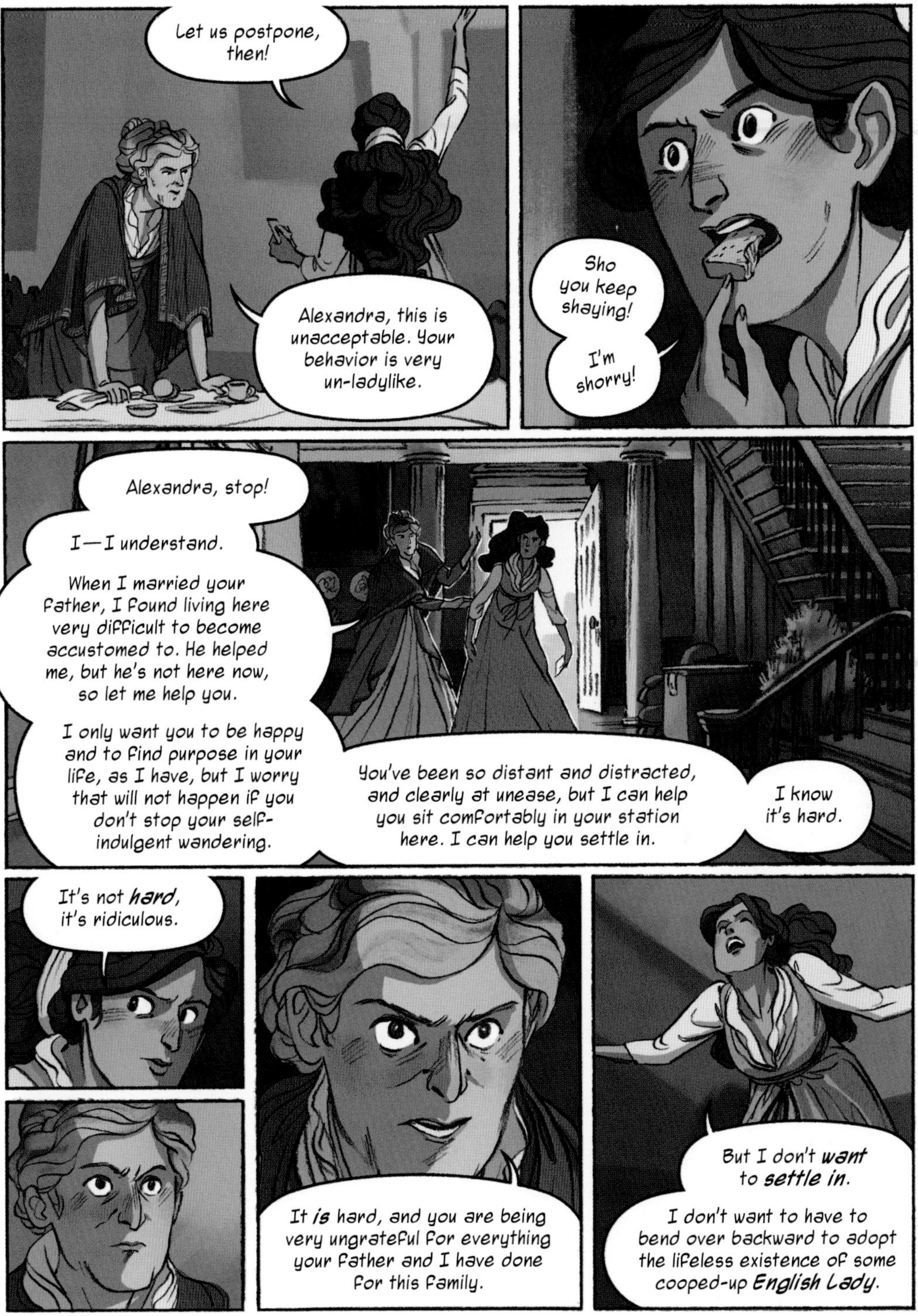
Let us postpone, then!
Alexandra, this is unacceptable. Your behavior is very un-ladylike.
Sho you keep shaying!
I'm shorry!
Alexandra, stop!
I—I understand.
When I married your father, I found living here very difficult to become accustomed to. He helped me, but he's not here now, so let me help you.
I only want you to be happy and to find purpose in your life, as I have, but I worry that will not happen if you don't stop your self-indulgent wandering.
You've been so distant and distracted, and clearly at unease, but I can help you sit comfortably in your station here. I can help you settle in.
I know it's hard.
It's not **hard**, it's ridiculous.
It *is* hard, and you are being very ungrateful for everything your father and I have done for this family.
But I don't ***want*** to ***settle in***.
I don't want to have to bend over backward to adopt the lifeless existence of some cooped-up ***English Lady***.

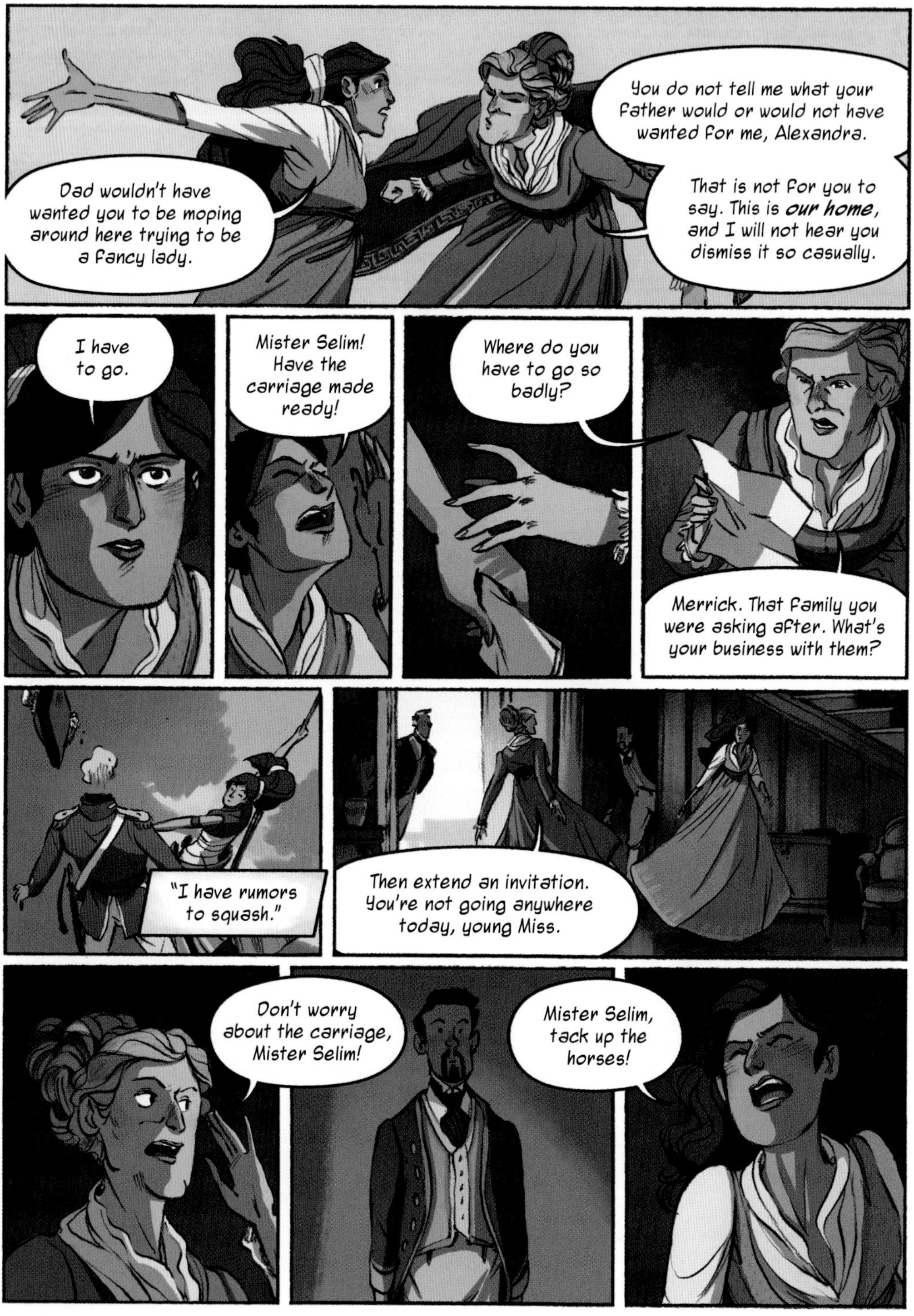
Dad wouldn't have wanted you to be moping around here trying to be a fancy lady.
You do not tell me what your father would or would not have wanted for me, Alexandra.
That is not for you to say. This is ***our home,*** and I will not hear you dismiss it so casually.
I have to go.
Mister Selim! Have the carriage made ready!
Where do you have to go so badly?
Merrick. That family you were asking after. What's your business with them?
"I have rumors to squash."
Then extend an invitation. You're not going anywhere today, young Miss.
Don't worry about the carriage, Mister Selim!
Mister Selim, tack up the horses!

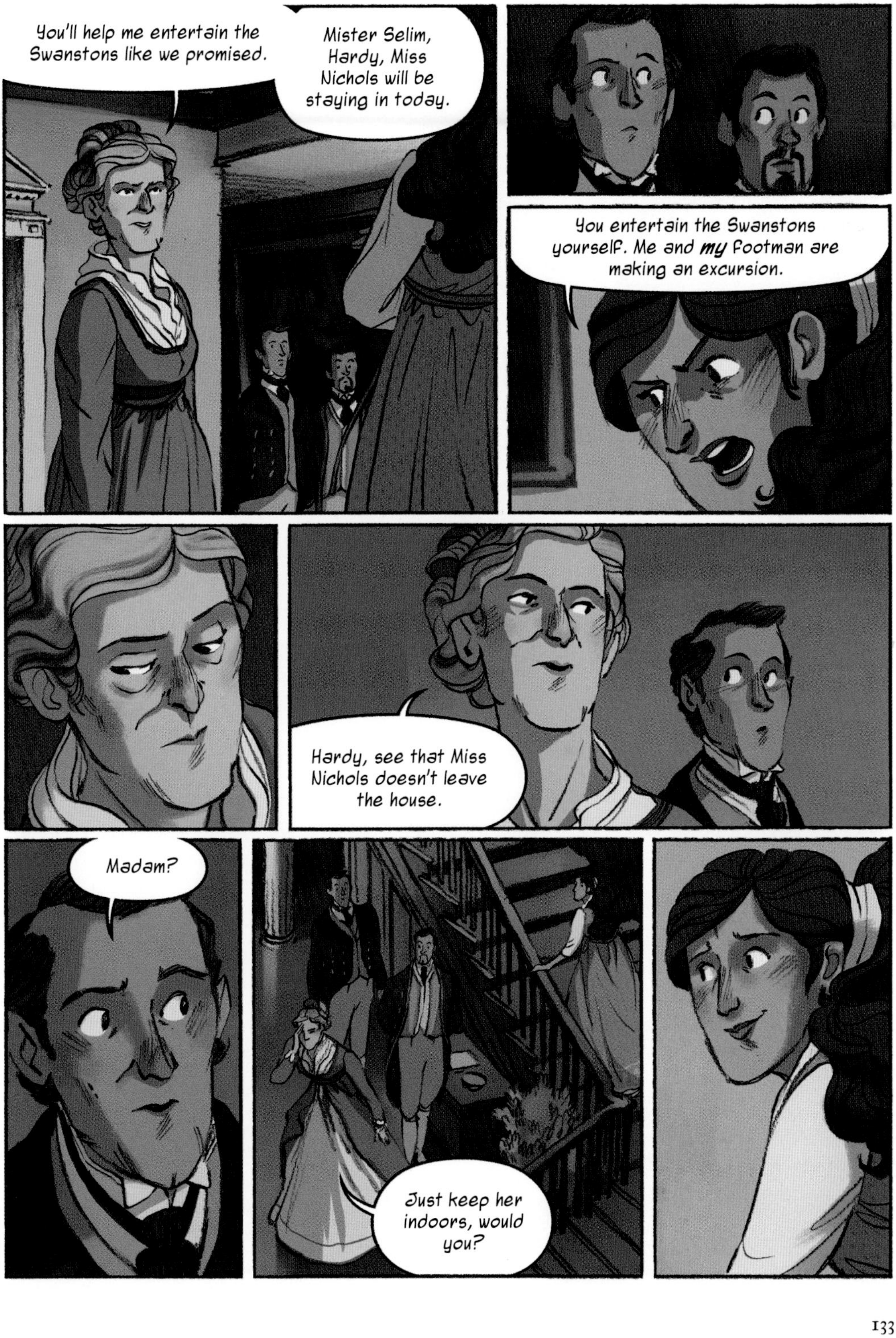
You'll help me entertain the Swanstons like we promised.
Mister Selim, Hardy, Miss Nichols will be staying in today.
You entertain the Swanstons yourself. Me and ***my*** footman are making an excursion.
Hardy, see that Miss Nichols doesn't leave the house.
Madam?
Just keep her indoors, would you?

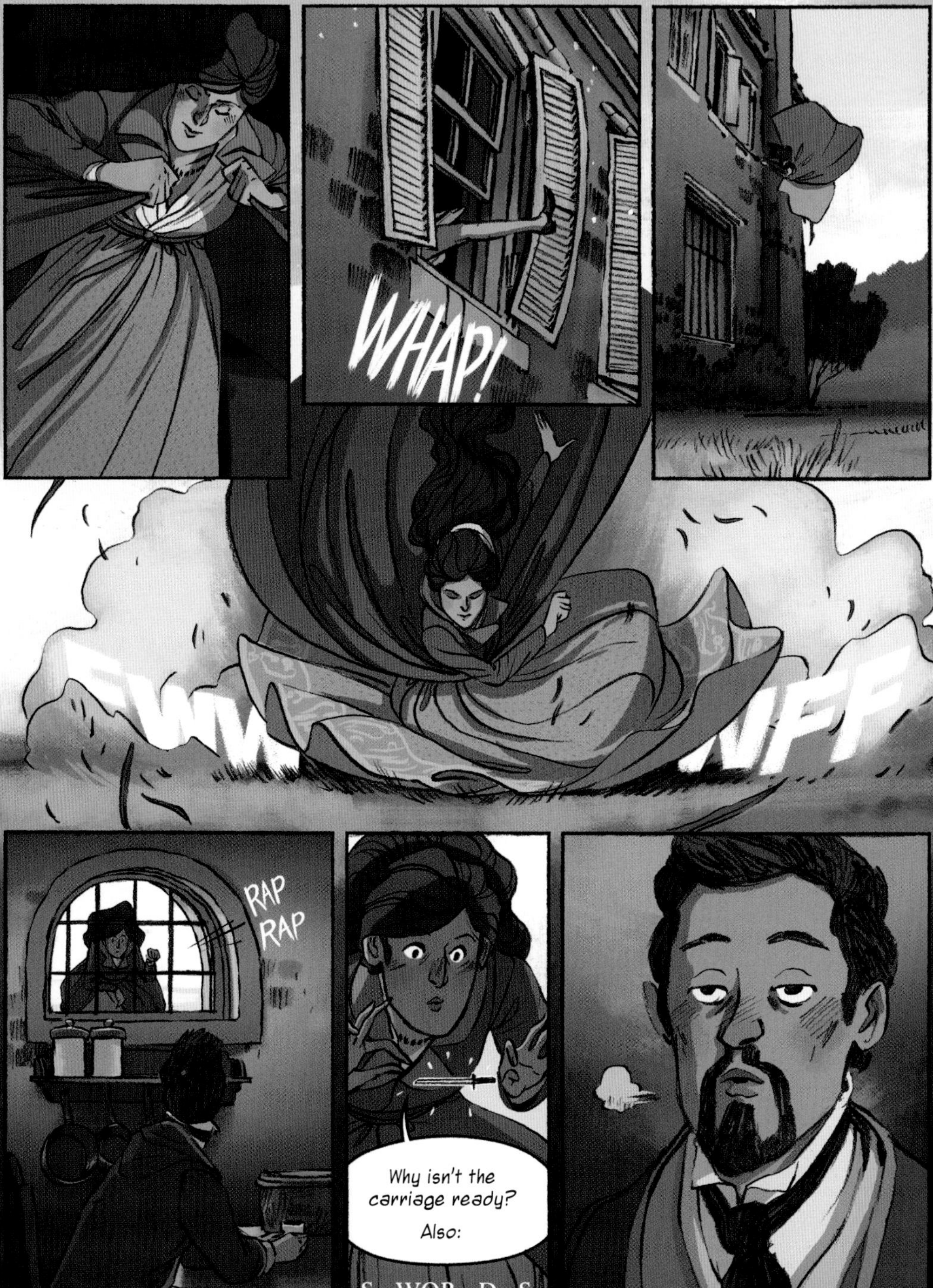
WHAP!
FWWWFF
RAP
RAP
Why isn't the carriage ready?
Also:

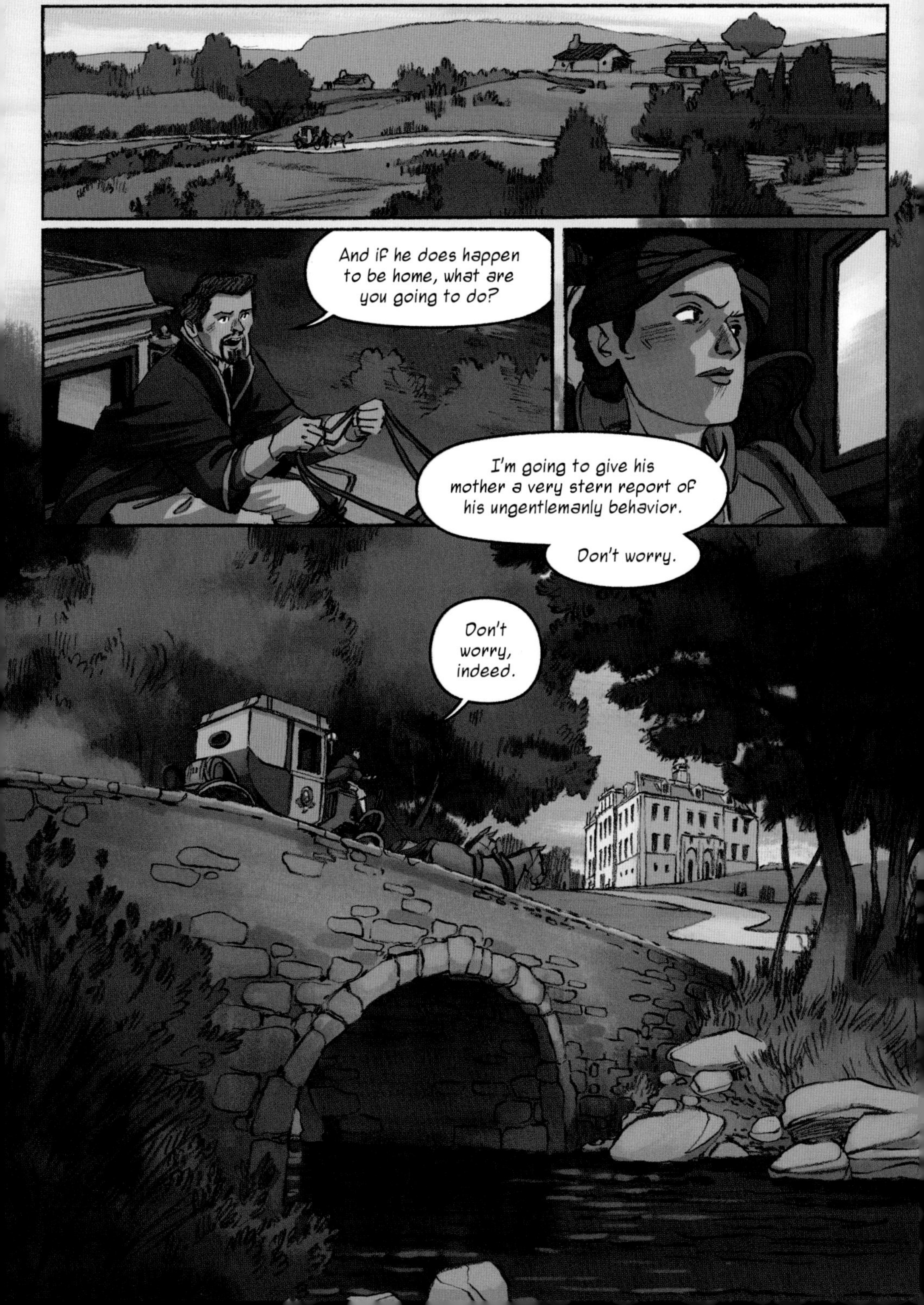
And if he does happen to be home, what are you going to do?
I'm going to give his mother a very stern report of his ungentlemanly behavior.
Don't worry.
Don't worry, indeed.

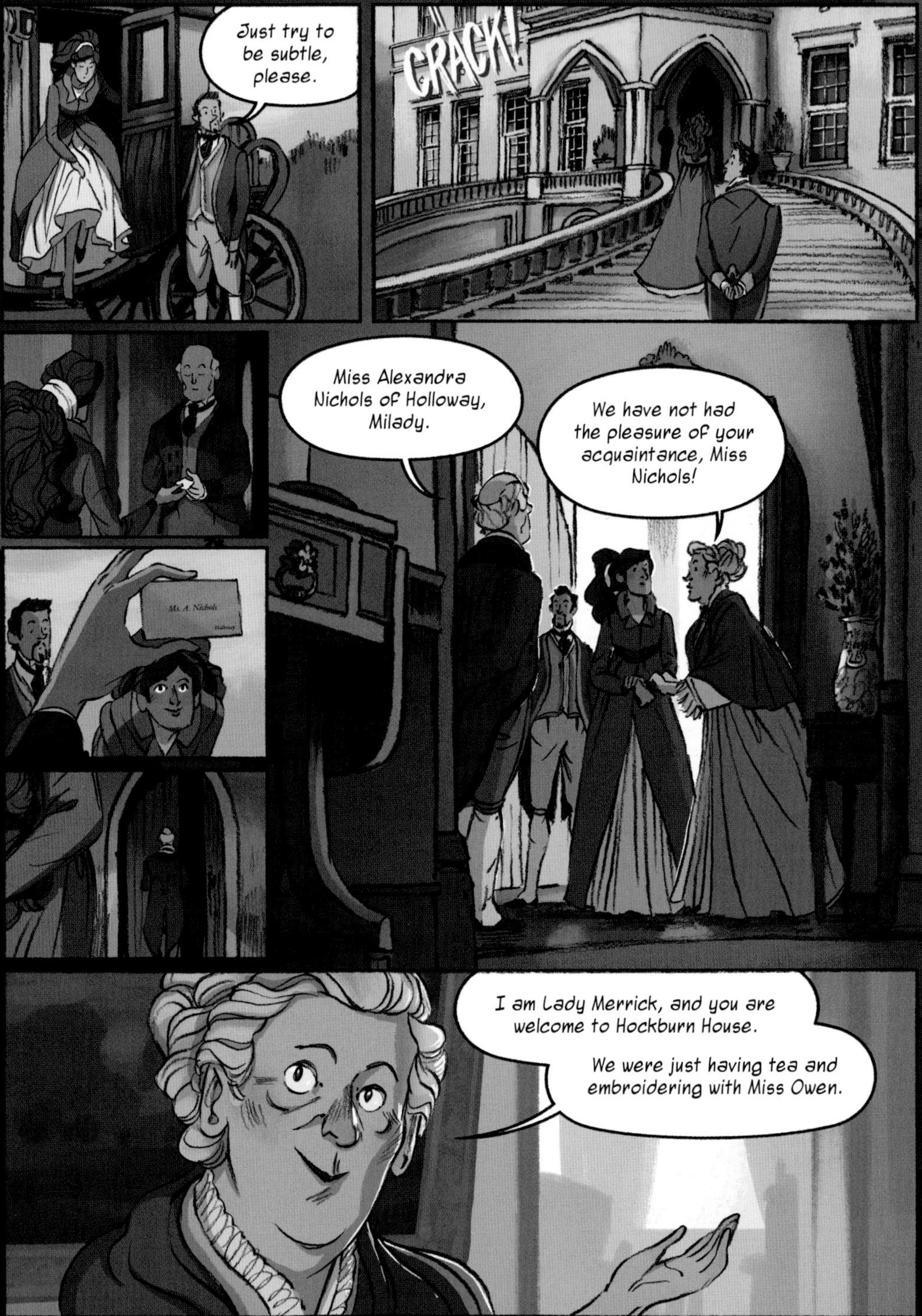
Just try to be subtle, please.
CRACK!
Miss Alexandra Nichols of Holloway, Milady.
Ms. A. Nichols
We have not had the pleasure of your acquaintance, Miss Nichols!
I am Lady Merrick, and you are welcome to Hockburn House.
We were just having tea and embroidering with Miss Owen.

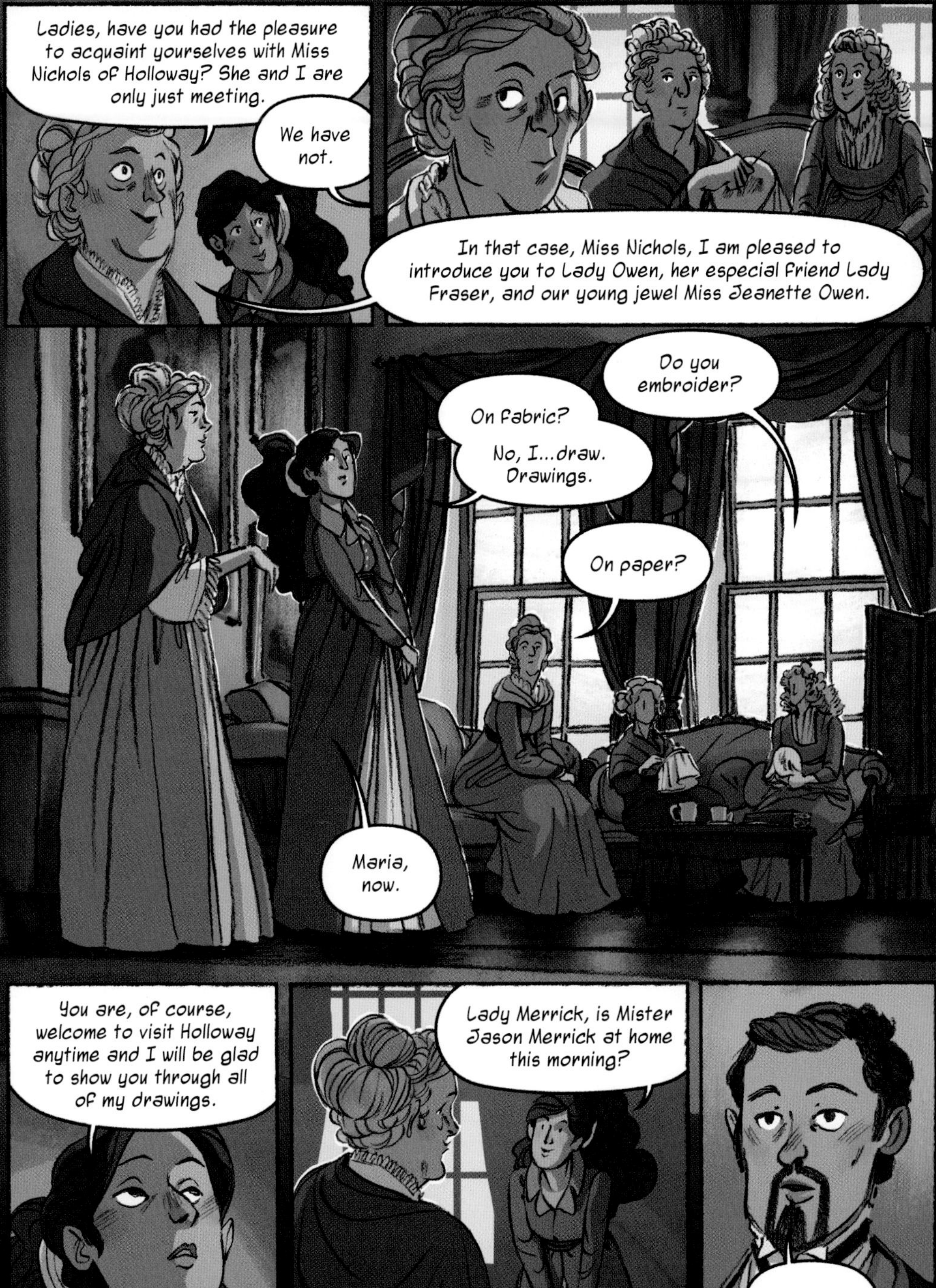
Ladies, have you had the pleasure to acquaint yourselves with Miss Nichols of Holloway? She and I are only just meeting.
We have not.
In that case, Miss Nichols, I am pleased to introduce you to Lady Owen, her especial friend Lady Fraser, and our young jewel Miss Jeanette Owen.
Do you embroider?
On fabric?
No, I...draw. Drawings.
On paper?
Maria, now.
You are, of course, welcome to visit Holloway anytime and I will be glad to show you through all of my drawings.
Lady Merrick, is Mister Jason Merrick at home this morning?
Subtle.

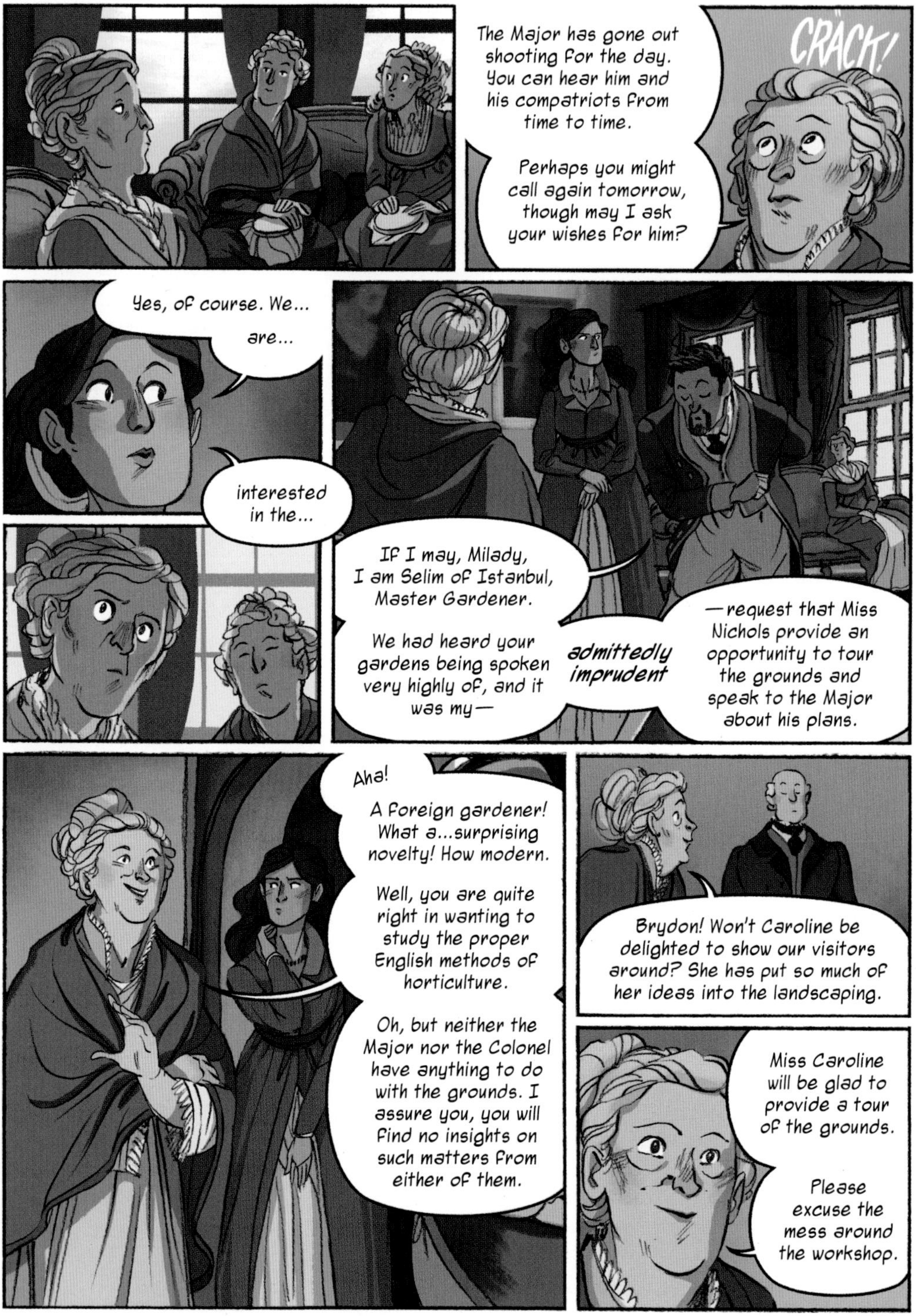
The Major has gone out shooting for the day. You can hear him and his compatriots from time to time.
Perhaps you might call again tomorrow, though may I ask your wishes for him?
CRACK!
Yes, of course. We...
are...
interested in the...
If I may, Milady, I am Selim of Istanbul, Master Gardener.
We had heard your gardens being spoken very highly of, and it was my—
admittedly imprudent
—request that Miss Nichols provide an opportunity to tour the grounds and speak to the Major about his plans.
Aha!
A foreign gardener! What a...surprising novelty! How modern.
Well, you are quite right in wanting to study the proper English methods of horticulture.
Oh, but neither the Major nor the Colonel have anything to do with the grounds. I assure you, you will find no insights on such matters from either of them.
Brydon! Won't Caroline be delighted to show our visitors around? She has put so much of her ideas into the landscaping.
Miss Caroline will be glad to provide a tour of the grounds.
Please excuse the mess around the workshop.

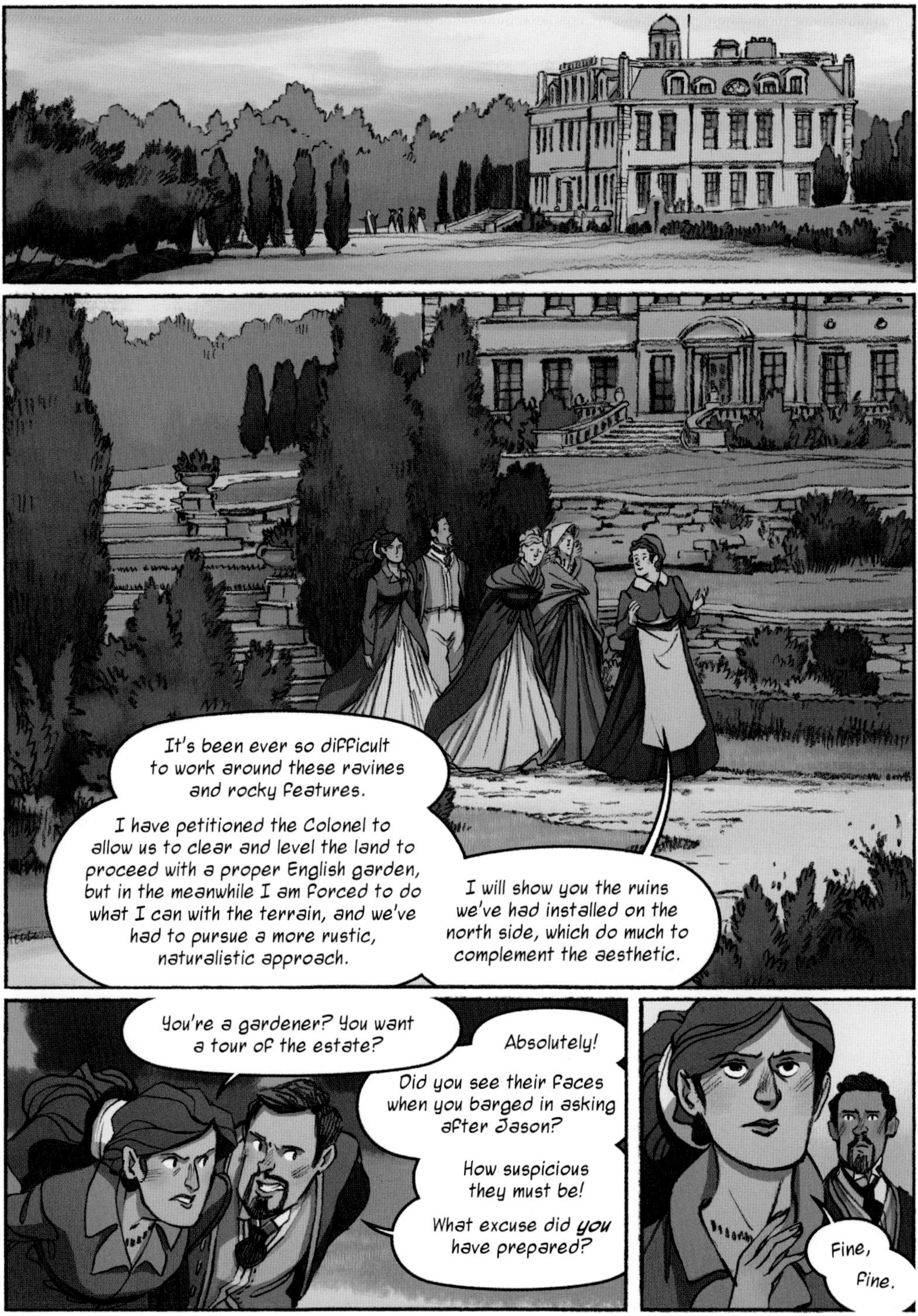
It's been ever so difficult to work around these ravines and rocky features.
I have petitioned the Colonel to allow us to clear and level the land to proceed with a proper English garden, but in the meanwhile I am forced to do what I can with the terrain, and we've had to pursue a more rustic, naturalistic approach.
I will show you the ruins we've had installed on the north side, which do much to complement the aesthetic.
You're a gardener? You want a tour of the estate?
Absolutely!
Did you see their faces when you barged in asking after Jason?
How suspicious they must be!
What excuse did *you* have prepared?
Fine,
Fine.

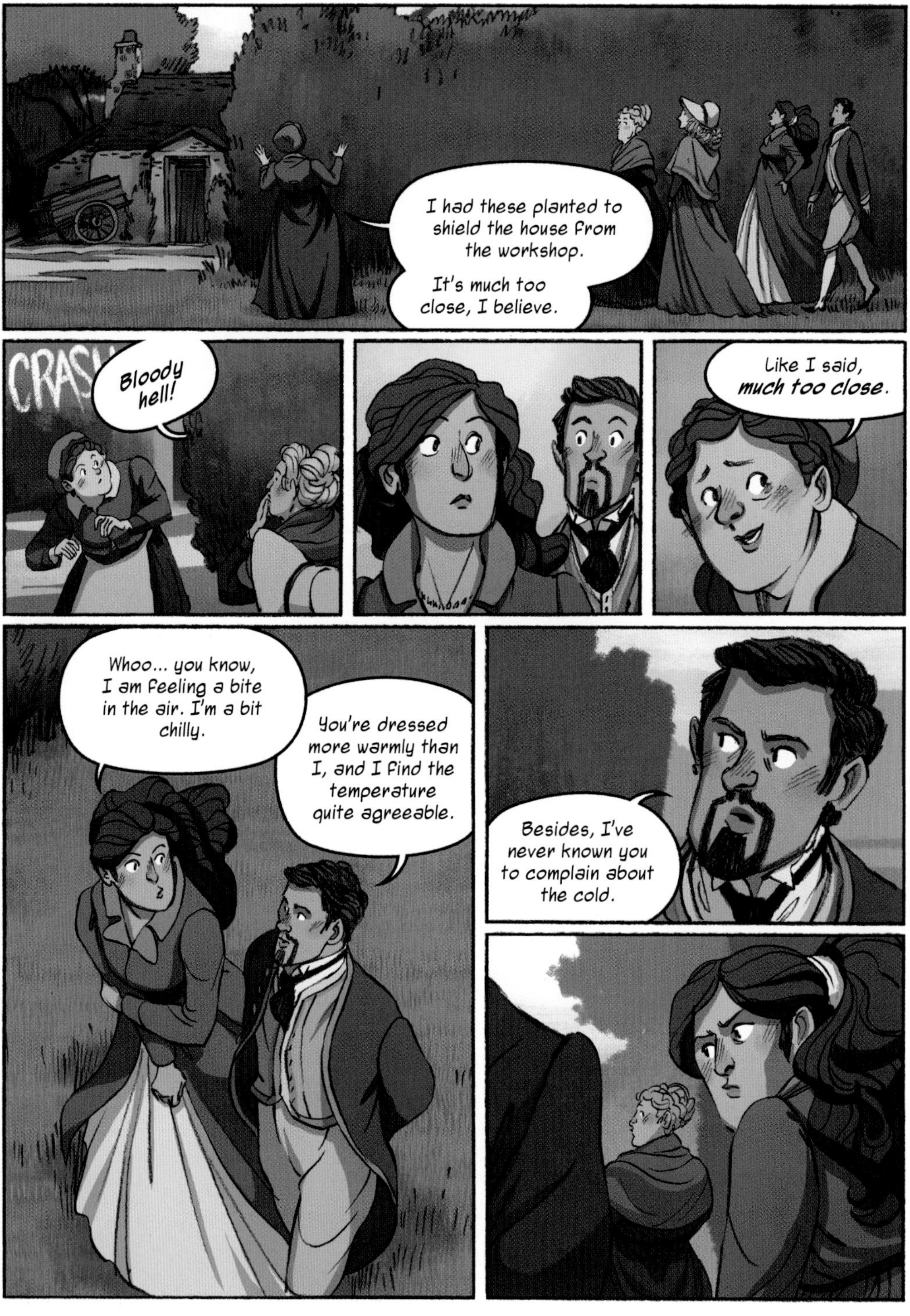

I had these planted to shield the house from the workshop.
It's much too close, I believe.
CRASH
Bloody hell!
Like I said, much too close.
Whoo... you know, I am feeling a bite in the air. I'm a bit chilly.
You're dressed more warmly than I, and I find the temperature quite agreeable.
Besides, I've never known you to complain about the cold.

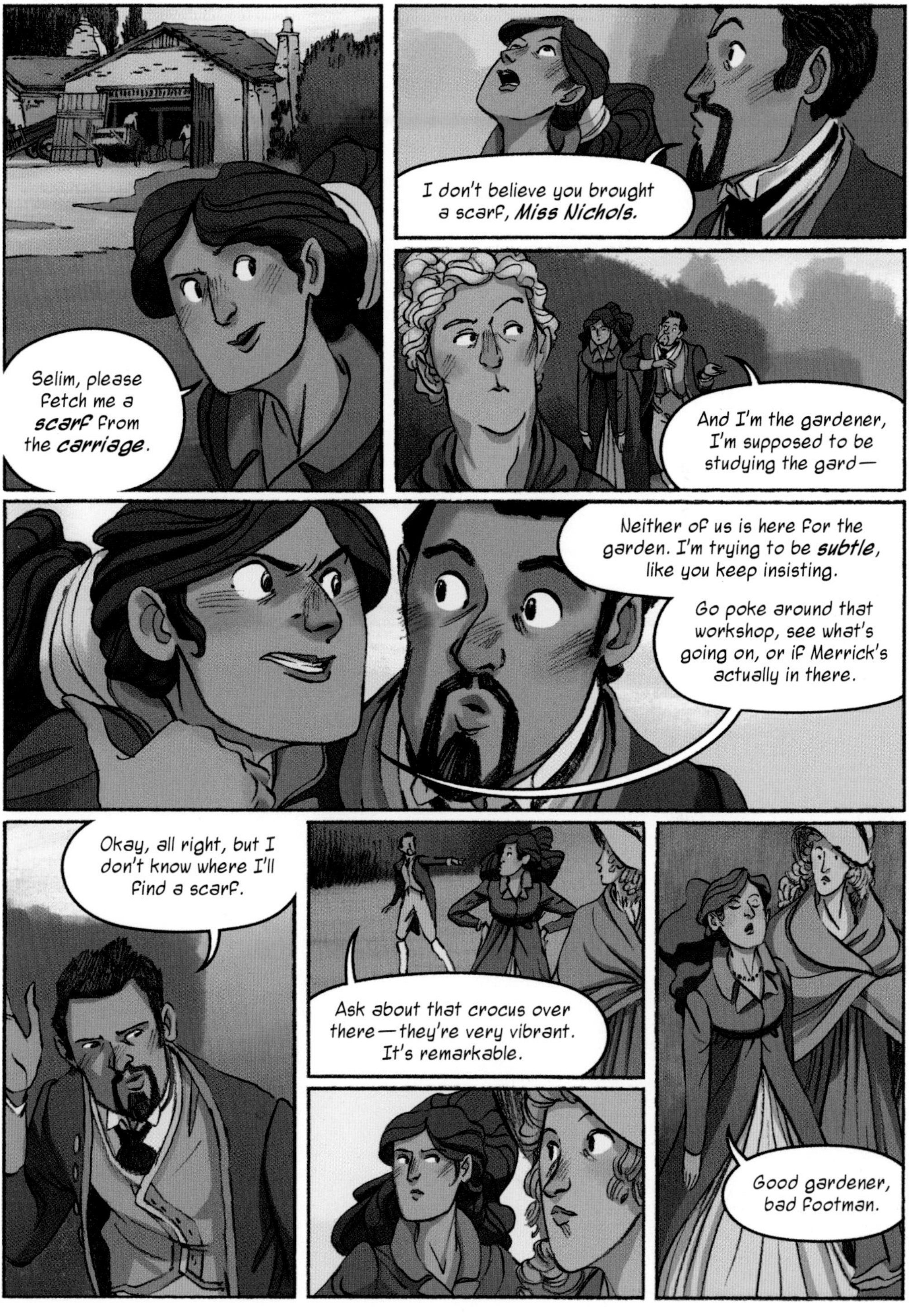
Selim, please fetch me a scarf from the carriage.
I don't believe you brought a scarf, Miss Nichols.
And I'm the gardener, I'm supposed to be studying the gard—
Neither of us is here for the garden. I'm trying to be subtle, like you keep insisting.
Go poke around that workshop, see what's going on, or if Merrick's actually in there.
Okay, all right, but I don't know where I'll find a scarf.
Ask about that crocus over there—they're very vibrant. It's remarkable.
Good gardener, bad footman.

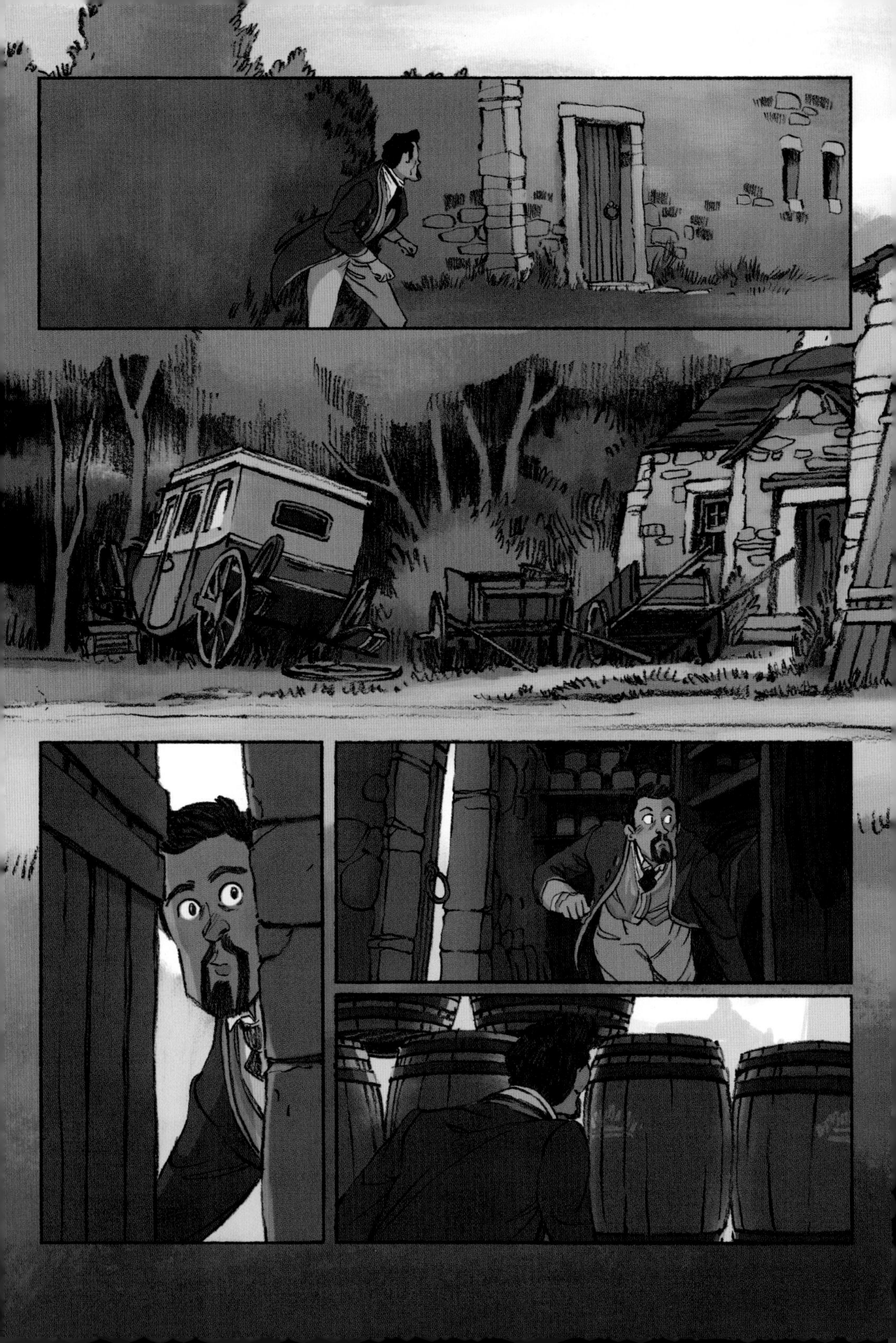

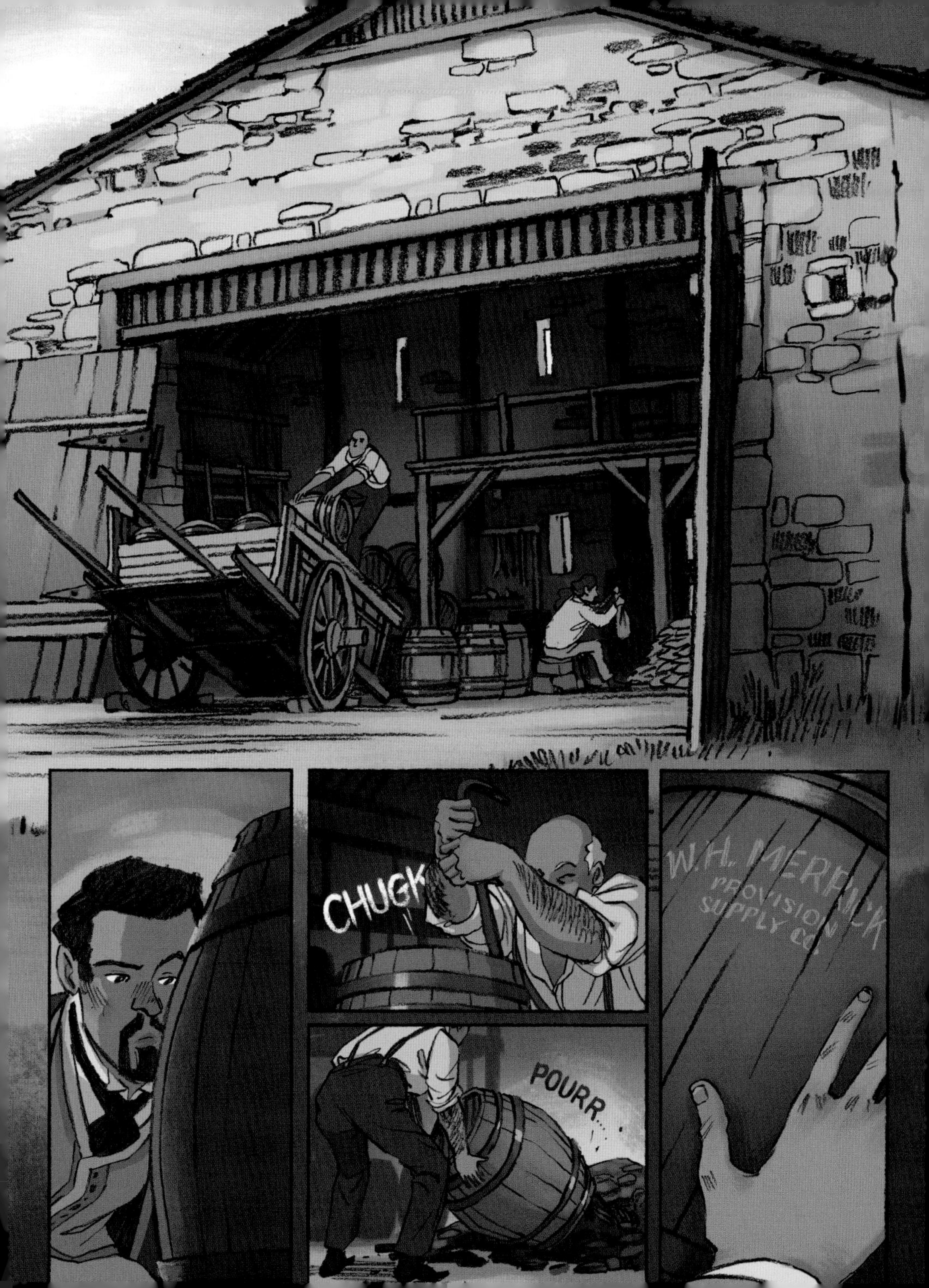
CHUGK
POURR...
W.H. MERRICK
PROVISION
SUPPLY CO.

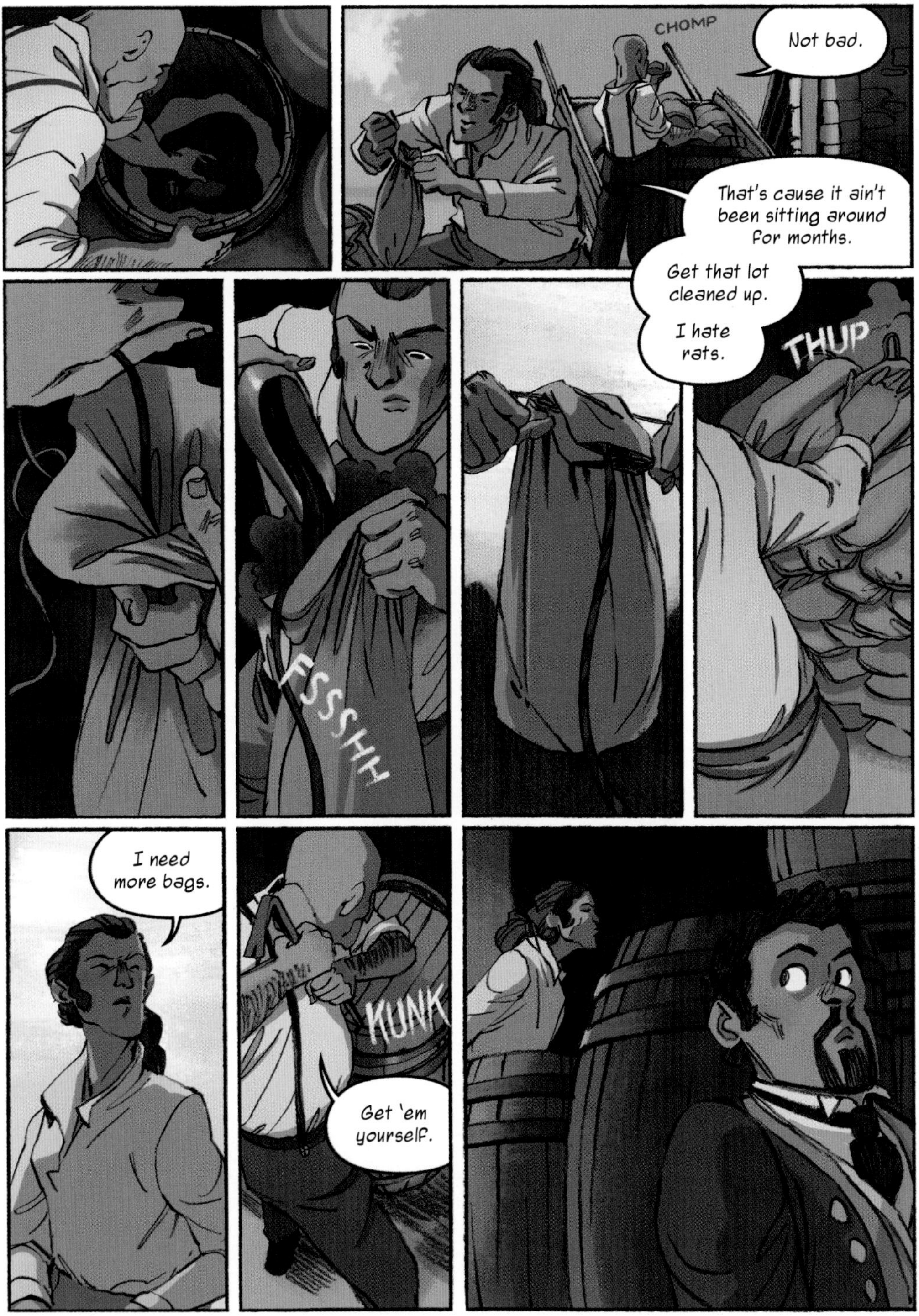
CHOMP
Not bad.
That's cause it ain't been sitting around for months.
Get that lot cleaned up.
I hate rats.
FSSSHH
THUP
I need more bags.
KUNK
Get 'em yourself.

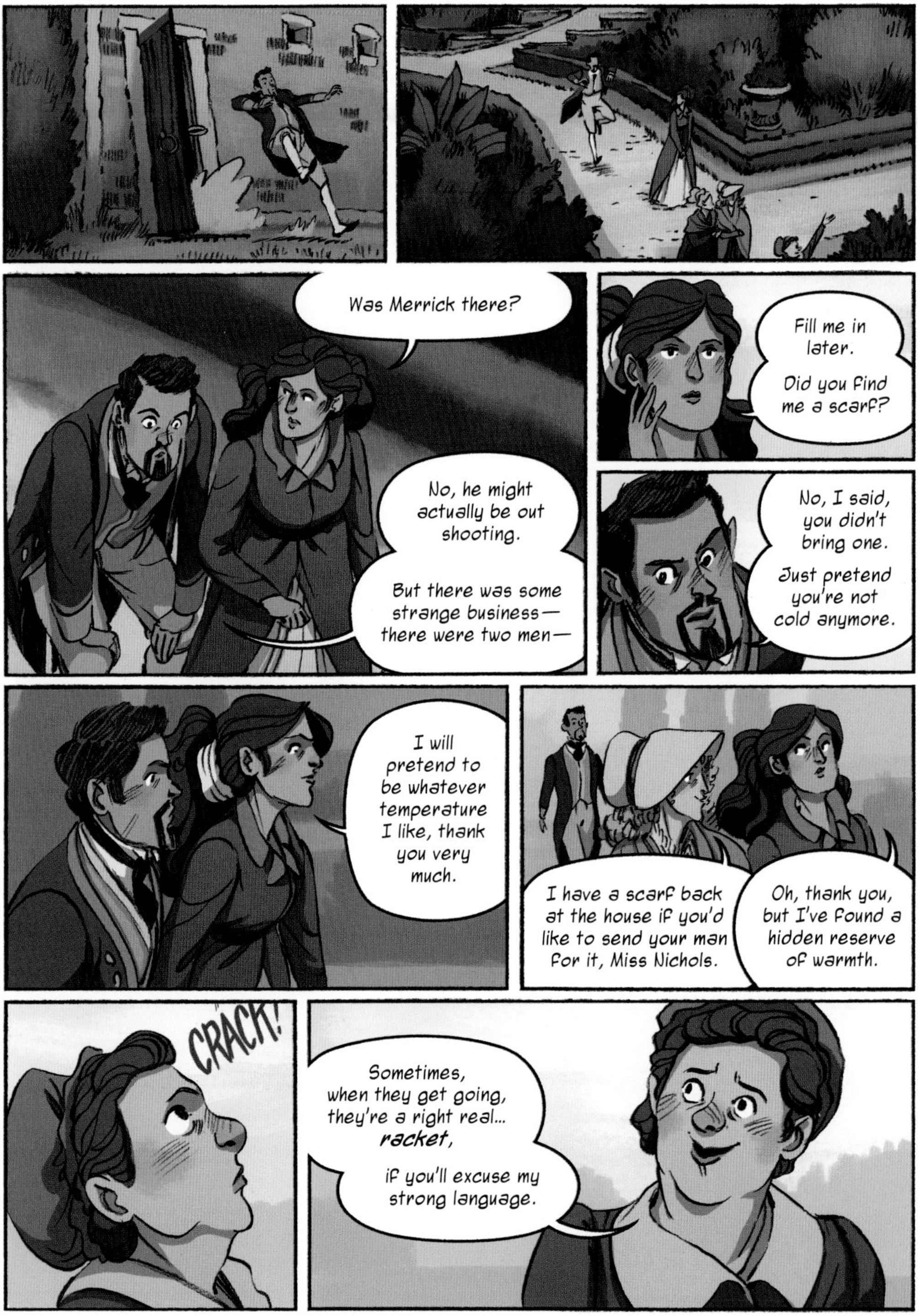
Was Merrick there?
No, he might actually be out shooting.
But there was some strange business— there were two men—
Fill me in later.
Did you find me a scarf?
No, I said, you didn't bring one.
Just pretend you're not cold anymore.
I will pretend to be whatever temperature I like, thank you very much.
I have a scarf back at the house if you'd like to send your man for it, Miss Nichols.
Oh, thank you, but I've found a hidden reserve of warmth.
CRACK!
Sometimes, when they get going, they're a right real... *racket*,
if you'll excuse my strong language.

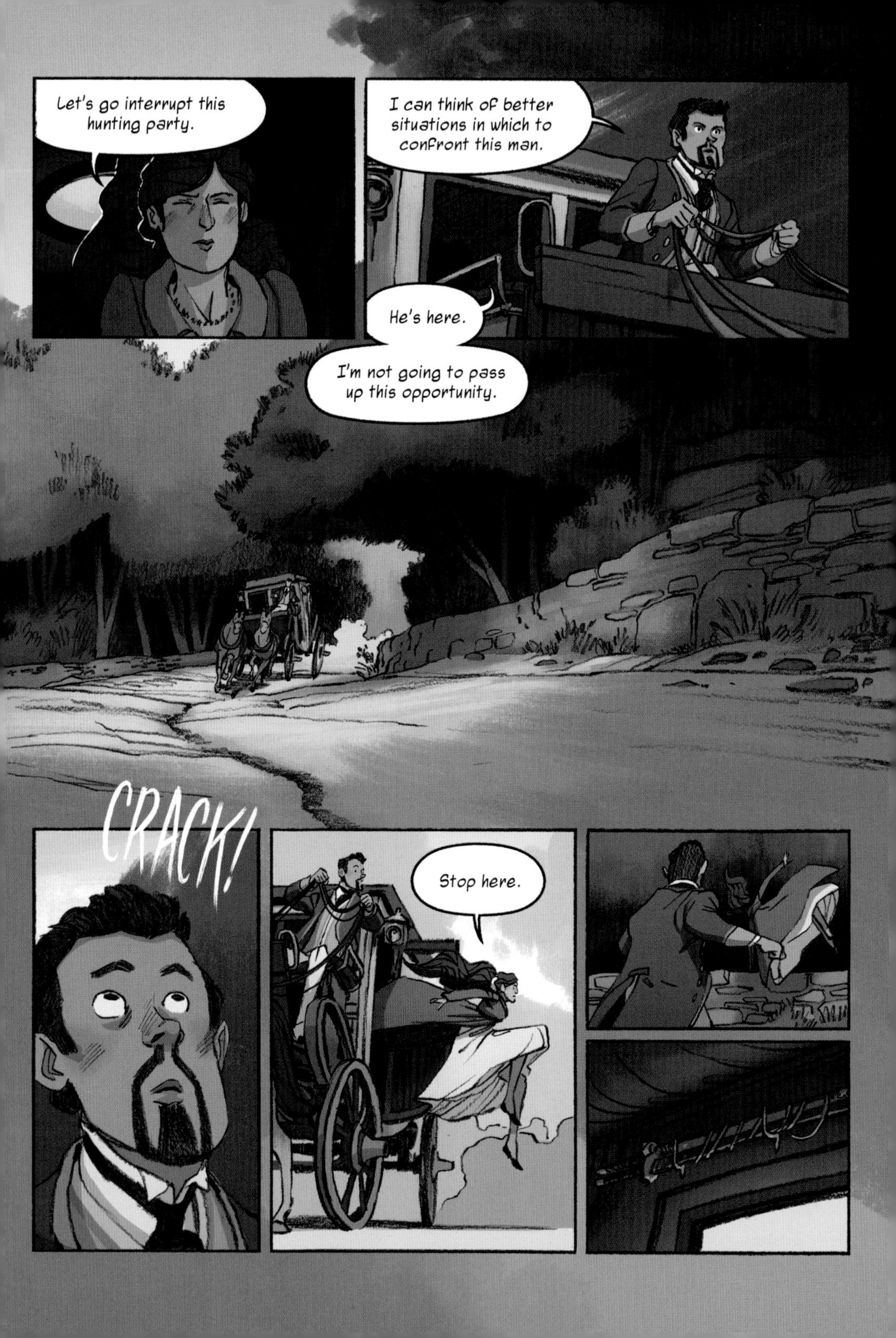
Let's go interrupt this hunting party.
I can think of better situations in which to confront this man.
He's here.
I'm not going to pass up this opportunity.
CRACK!
Stop here.

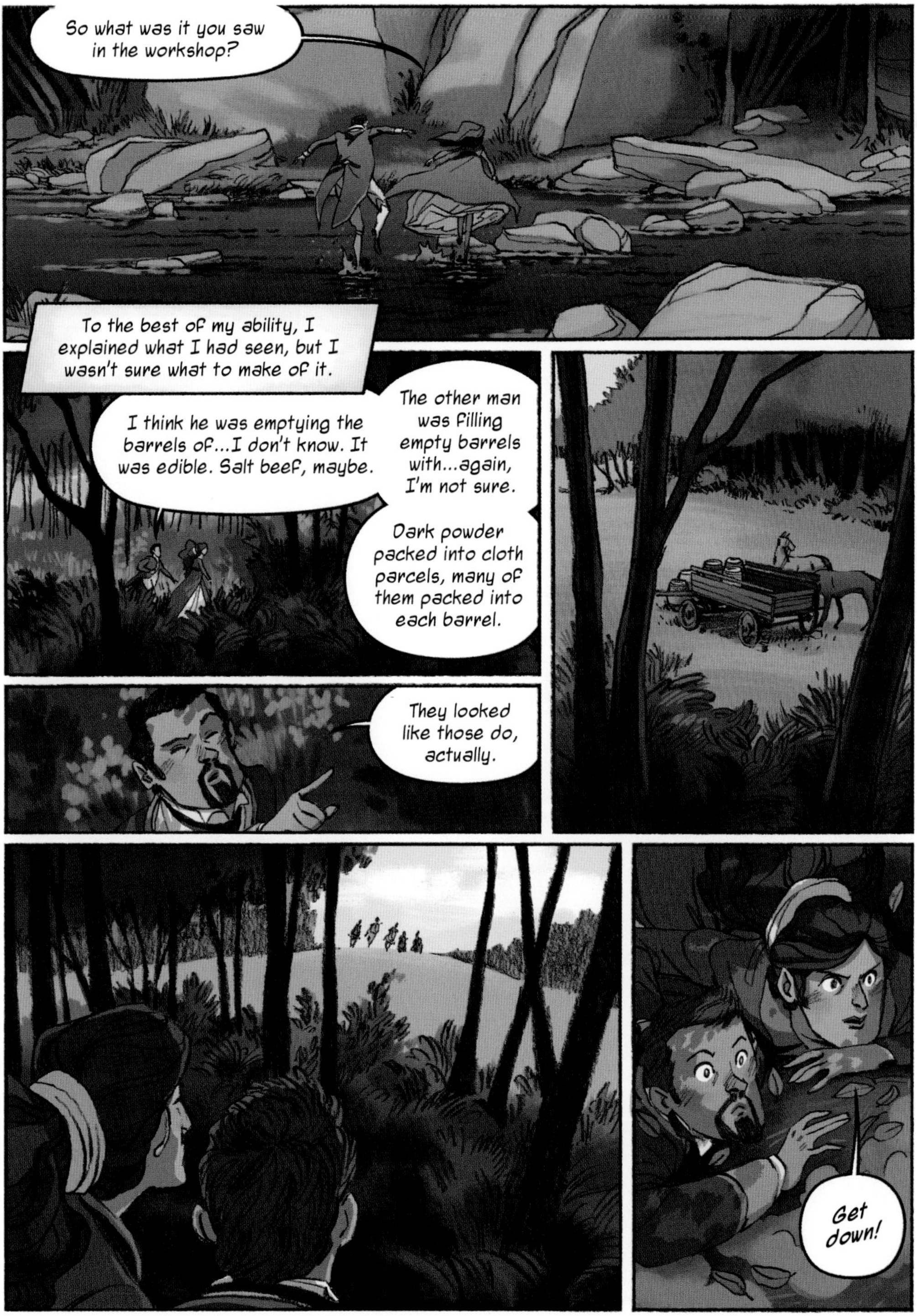

So what was it you saw in the workshop?
To the best of my ability, I explained what I had seen, but I wasn't sure what to make of it.
I think he was emptying the barrels of...I don't know. It was edible. Salt beef, maybe.
The other man was filling empty barrels with...again, I'm not sure.
Dark powder packed into cloth parcels, many of them packed into each barrel.
They looked like those do, actually.
Get down!

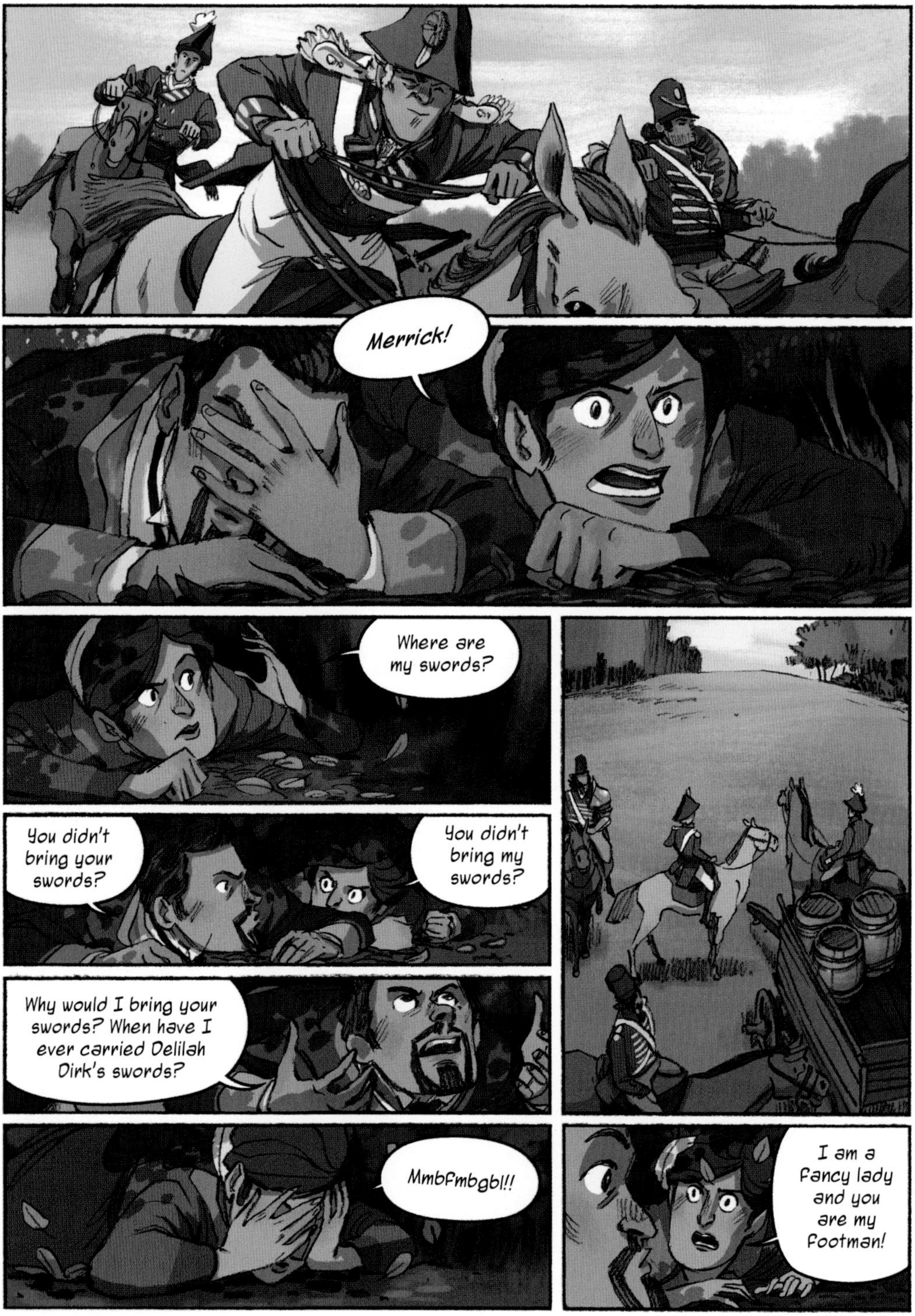
Merrick!
Where are my swords?
You didn't bring your swords?
You didn't bring my swords?
Why would I bring your swords? When have I ever carried Delilah Dirk's swords?
Mmbfmbgbl!!
I am a fancy lady and you are my footman!

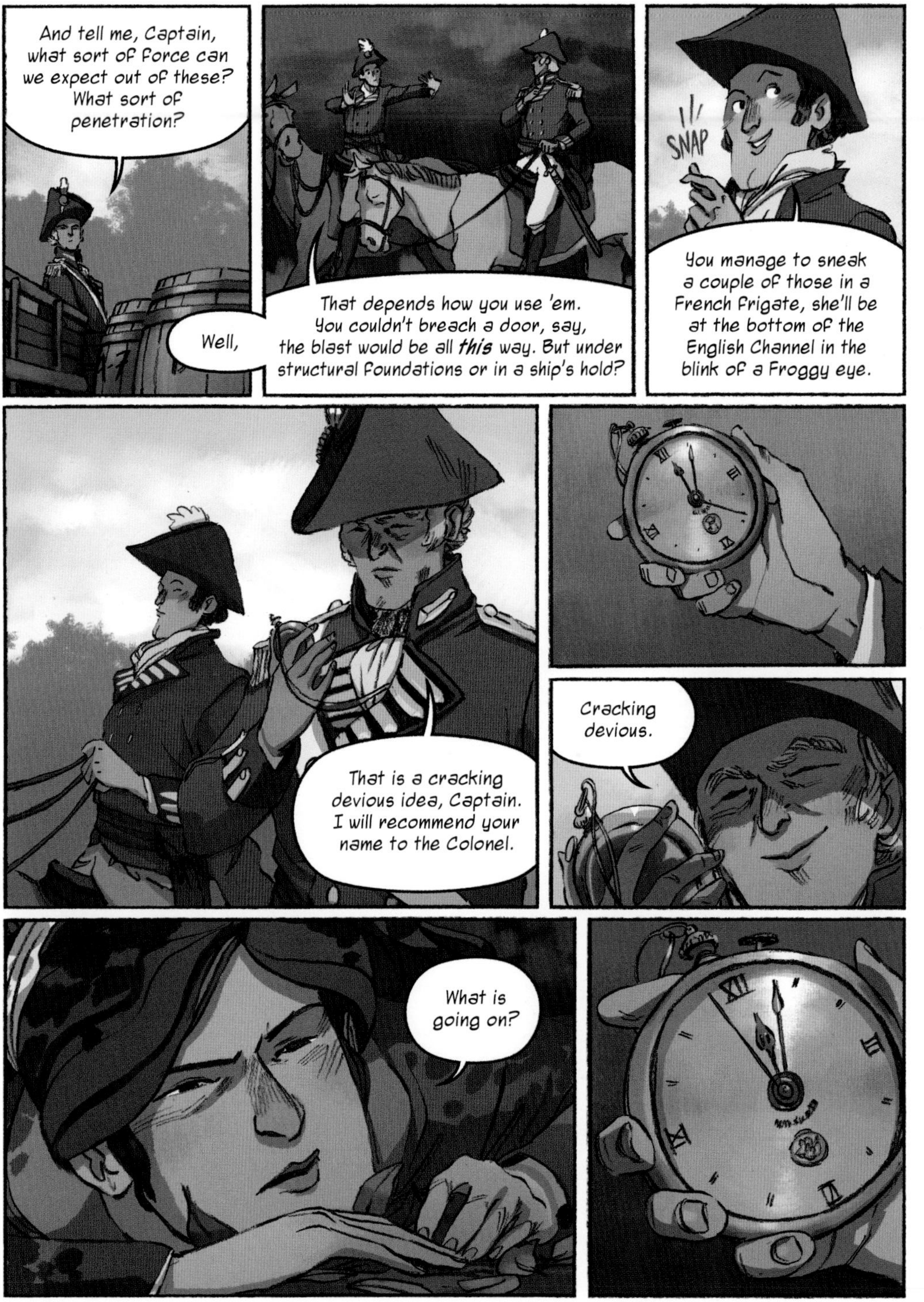
And tell me, Captain, what sort of force can we expect out of these? What sort of penetration?
Well,
That depends how you use 'em. You couldn't breach a door, say, the blast would be all *this* way. But under structural foundations or in a ship's hold?
SNAP
You manage to sneak a couple of those in a French frigate, she'll be at the bottom of the English Channel in the blink of a Froggy eye.
That is a cracking devious idea, Captain. I will recommend your name to the Colonel.
Cracking devious.
What is going on?

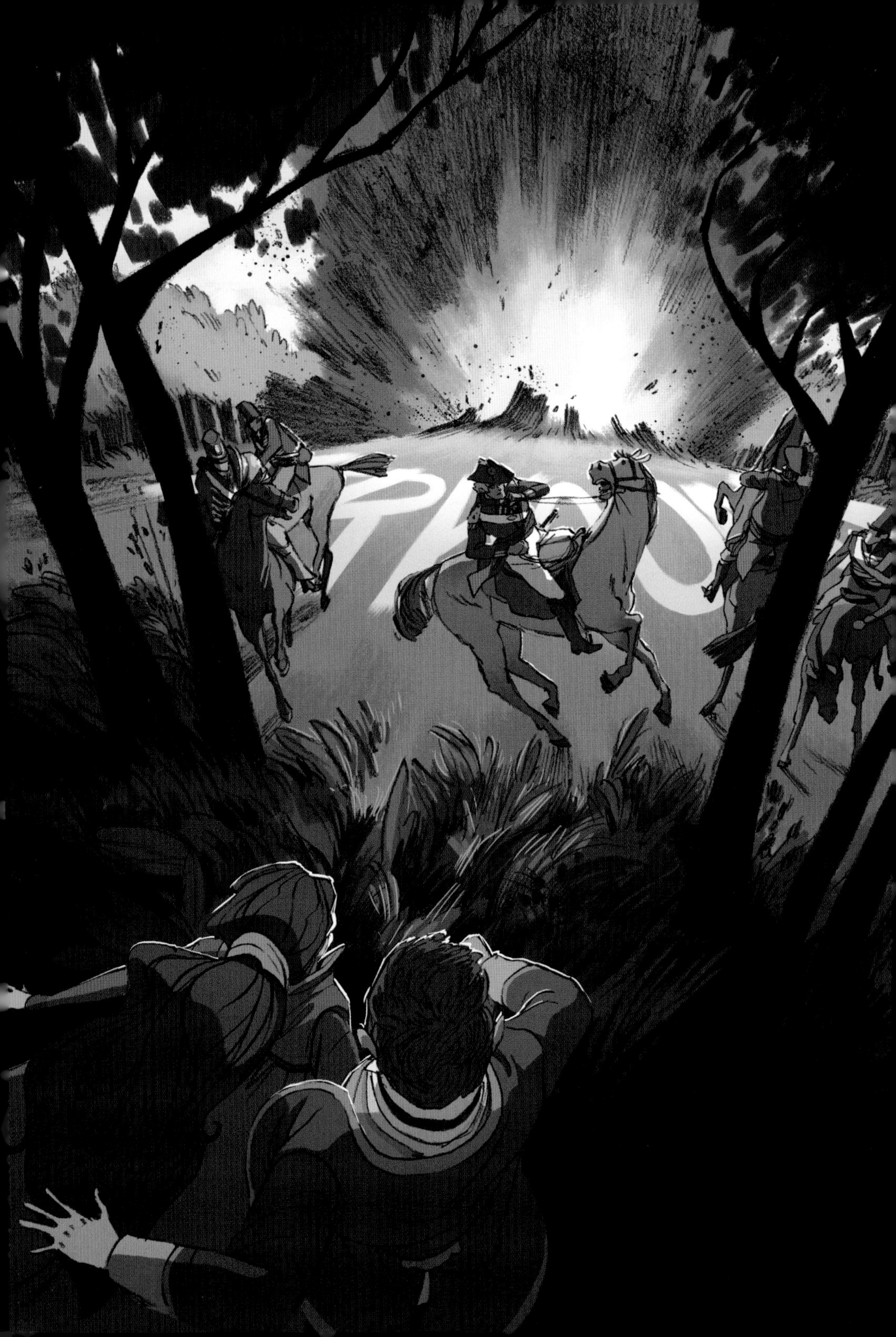

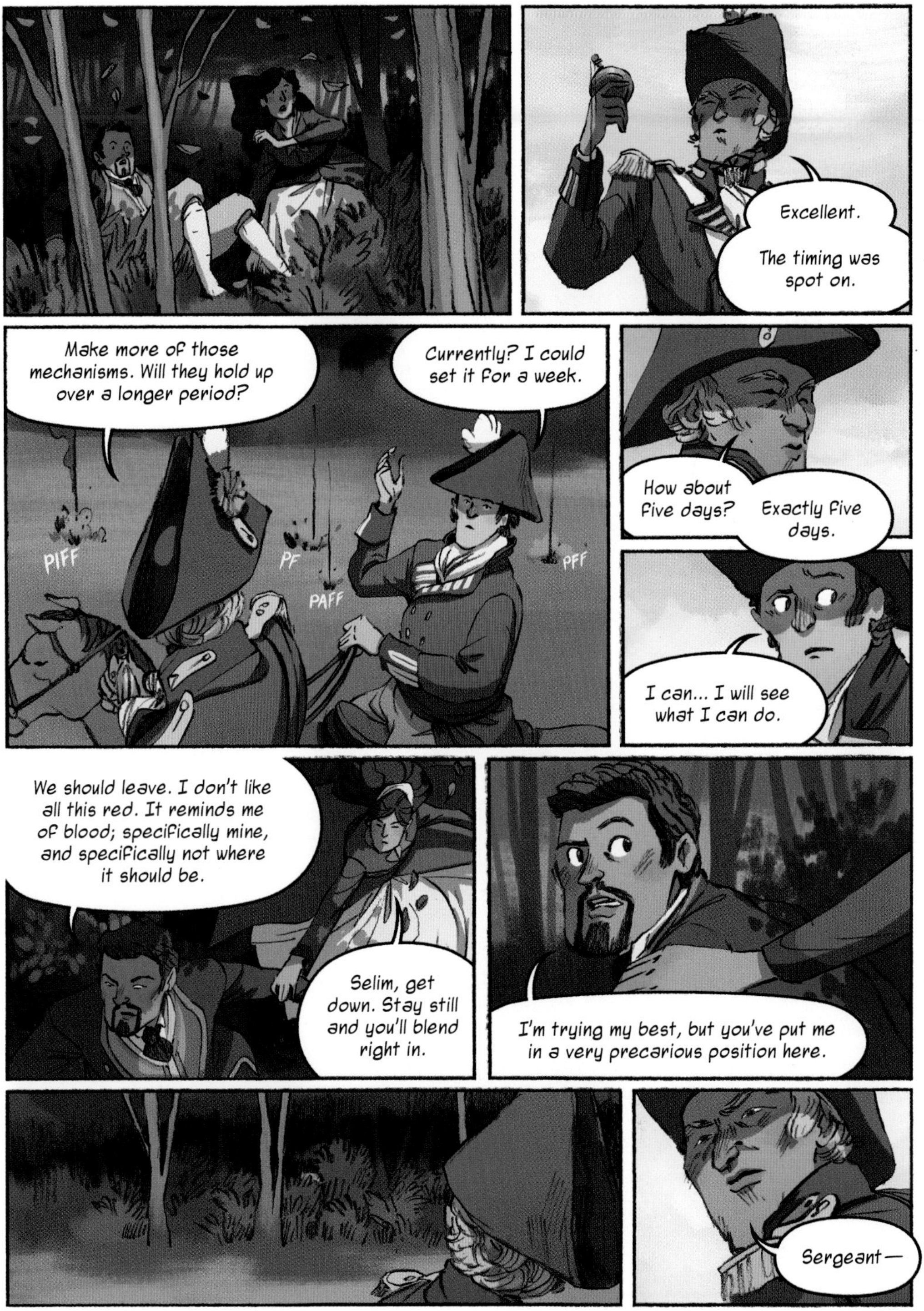
Excellent.
The timing was spot on.
Make more of those mechanisms. Will they hold up over a longer period?
Currently? I could set it for a week.
PIFF
PF
PAFF
PFF
How about five days?
Exactly five days.
I can... I will see what I can do.
We should leave. I don't like all this red. It reminds me of blood; specifically mine, and specifically not where it should be.
Selim, get down. Stay still and you'll blend right in.
I'm trying my best, but you've put me in a very precarious position here.
Sergeant—

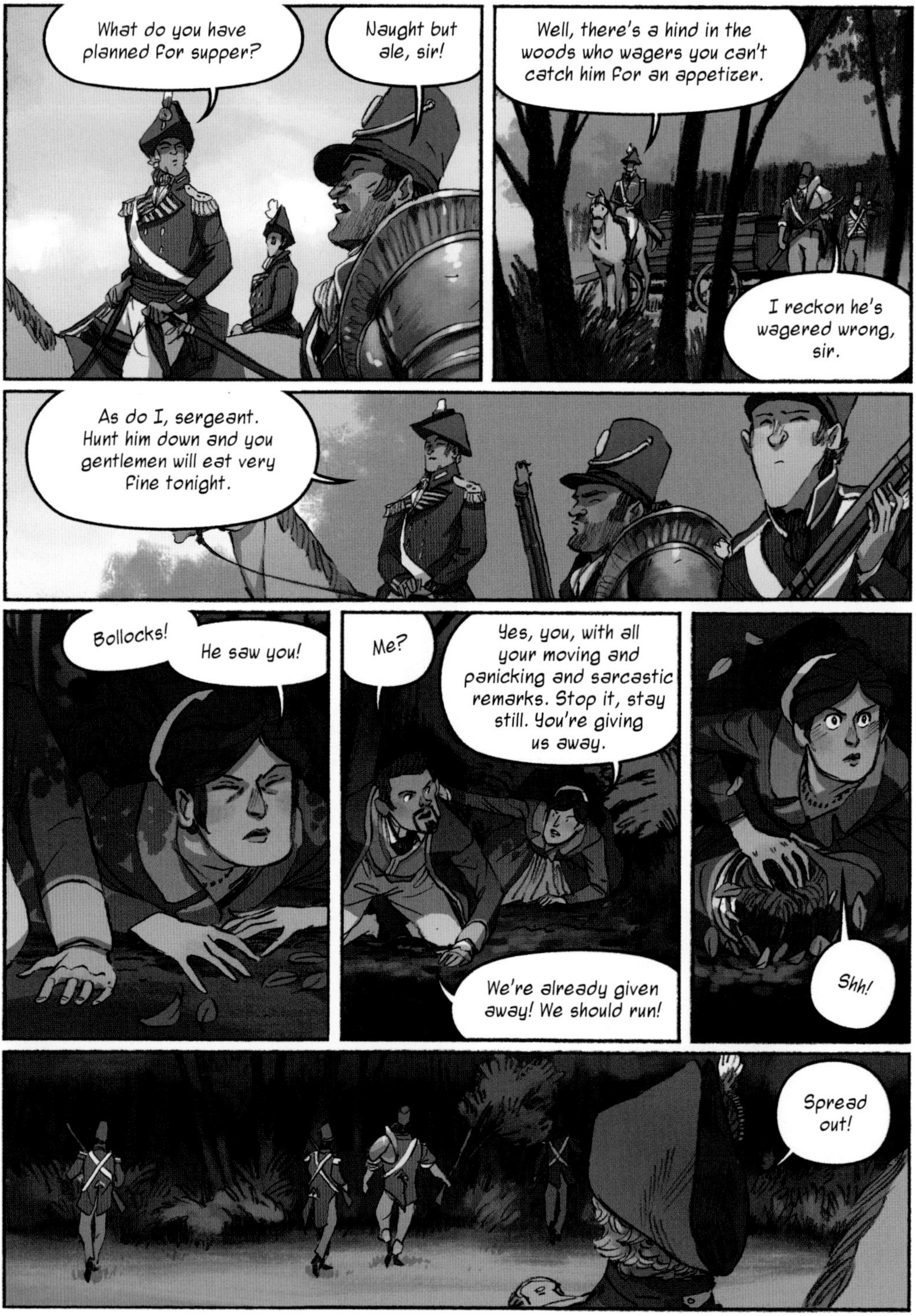
What do you have planned for supper?
Naught but ale, sir!
Well, there's a hind in the woods who wagers you can't catch him for an appetizer.
I reckon he's wagered wrong, sir.
As do I, sergeant. Hunt him down and you gentlemen will eat very fine tonight.
Bollocks!
He saw you!
Me?
Yes, you, with all your moving and panicking and sarcastic remarks. Stop it, stay still. You're giving us away.
We're already given away! We should run!
Shh!
Spread out!

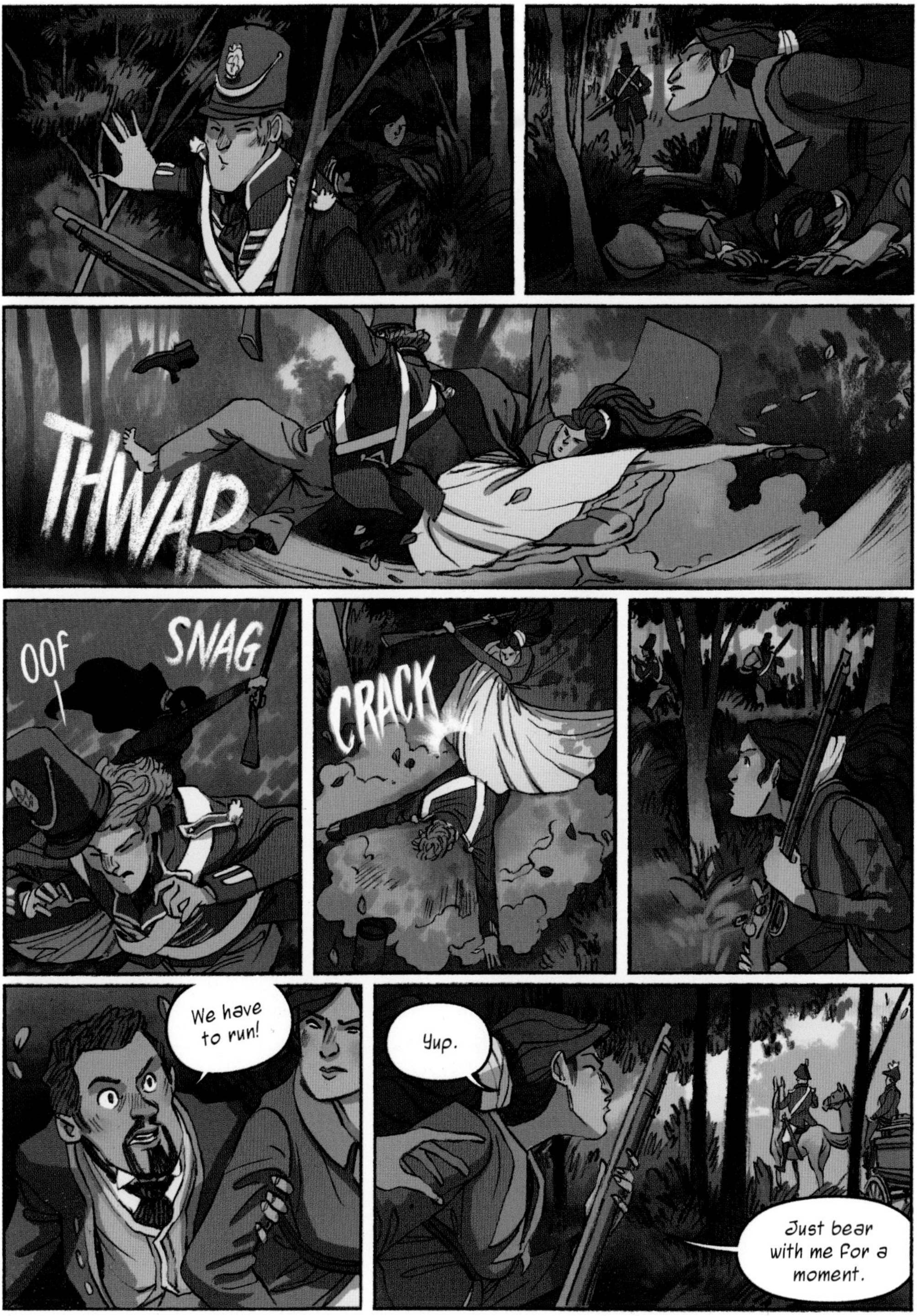
THWAP
OOF
SNAG
CRACK
We have to run!
Yup.
Just bear with me for a moment.

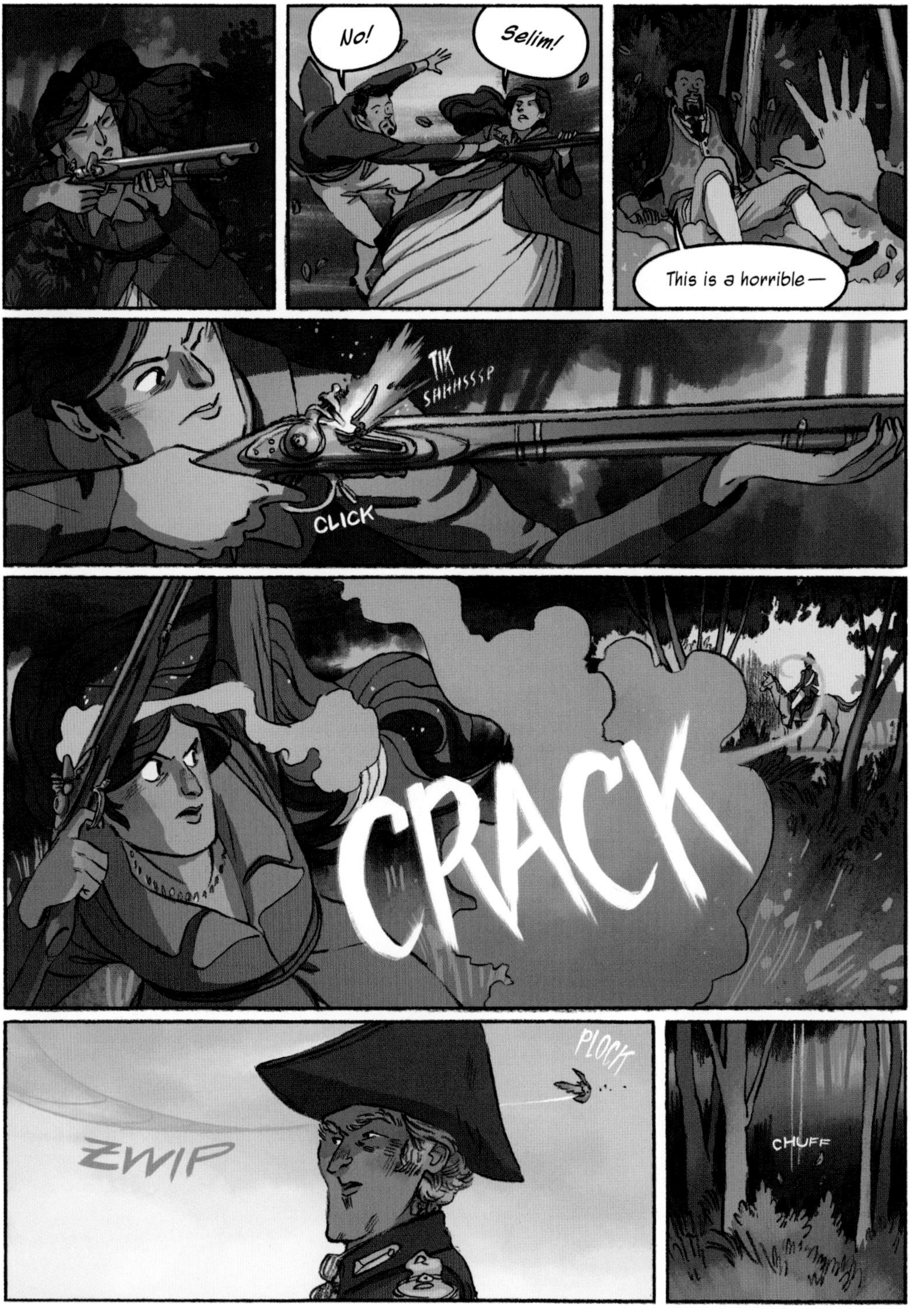
No!
Selim!
This is a horrible—
TIK
SHHHSSSP
CLICK
CRACK
ZWIP
PLOCK
CHUFF

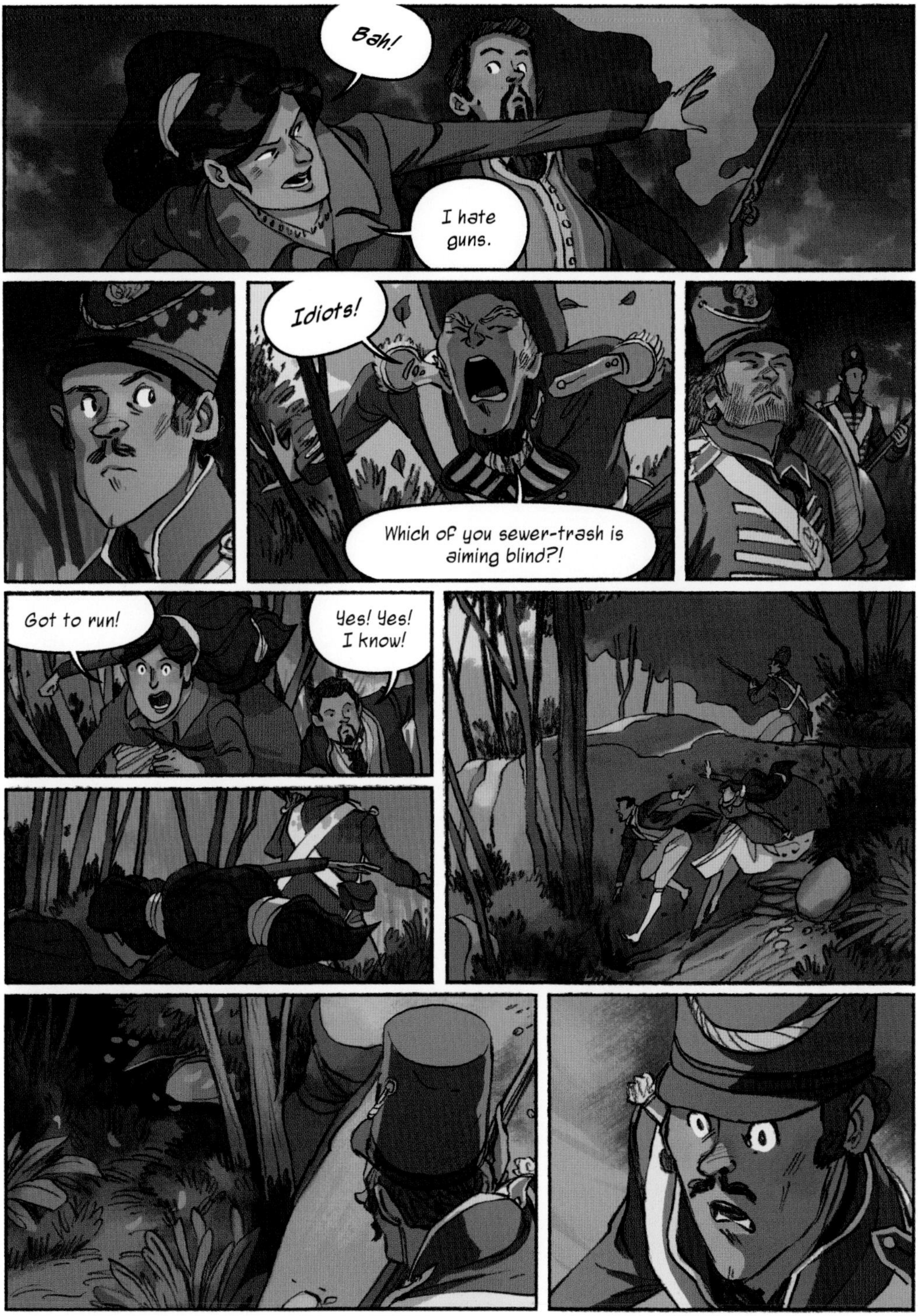
Bah!
I hate guns.
Idiots!
Which of you sewer-trash is aiming blind?!
Got to run!
Yes! Yes! I know!

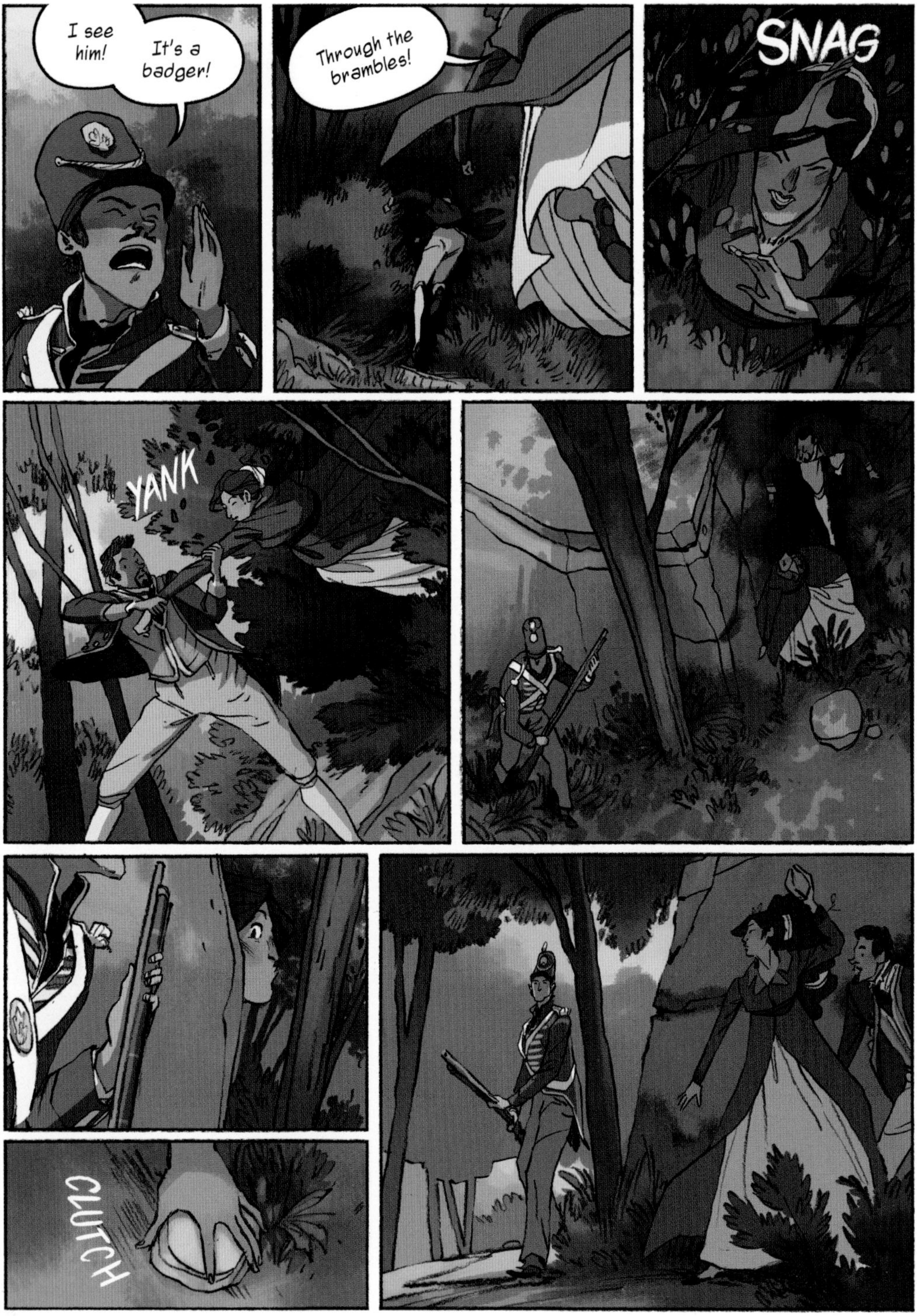
I see him!
It's a badger!
Through the brambles!
SNAG
YANK
CLUTCH

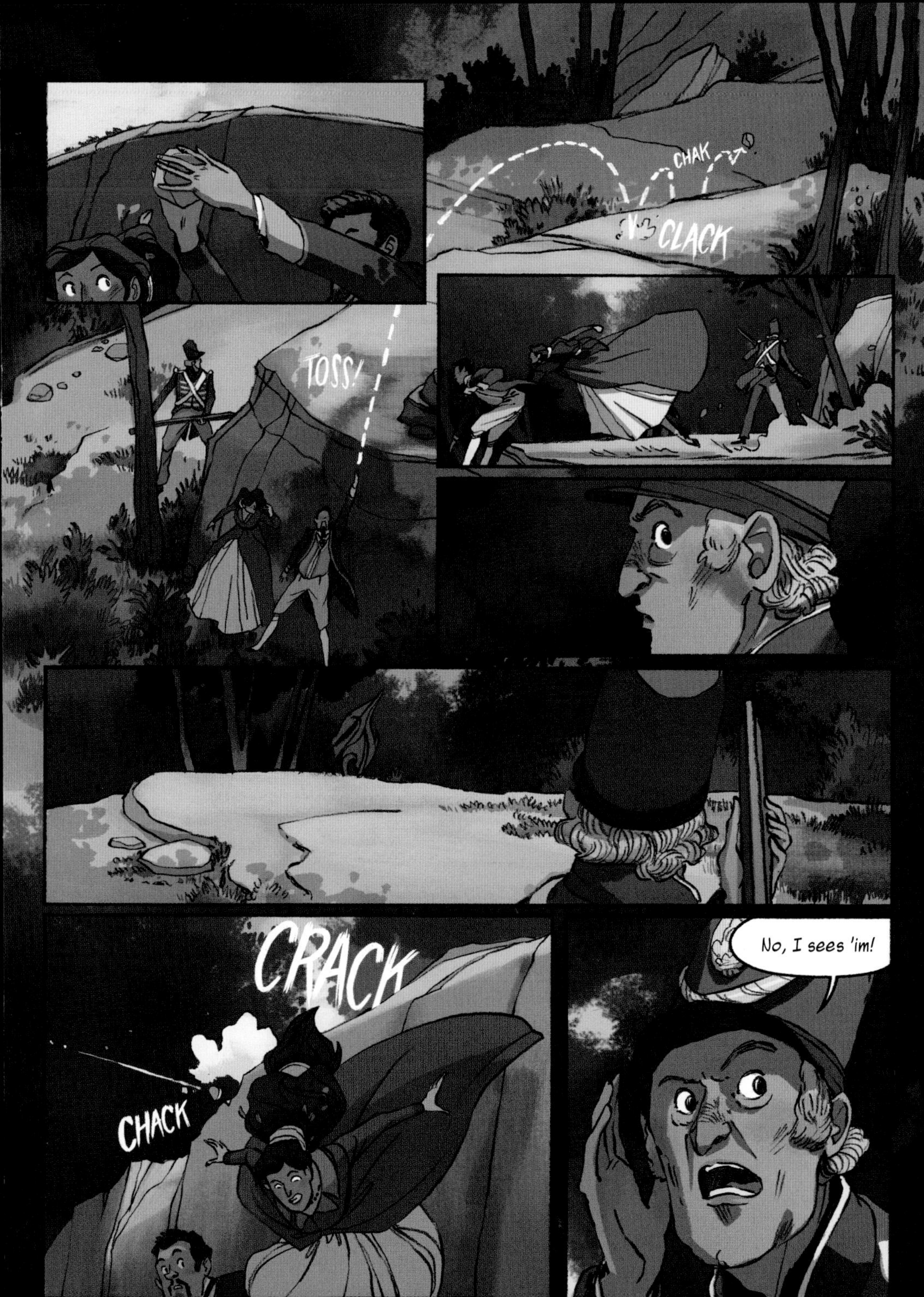
CHAK
CLACK
TOSS!
CRACK
CHACK
No, I sees 'im!

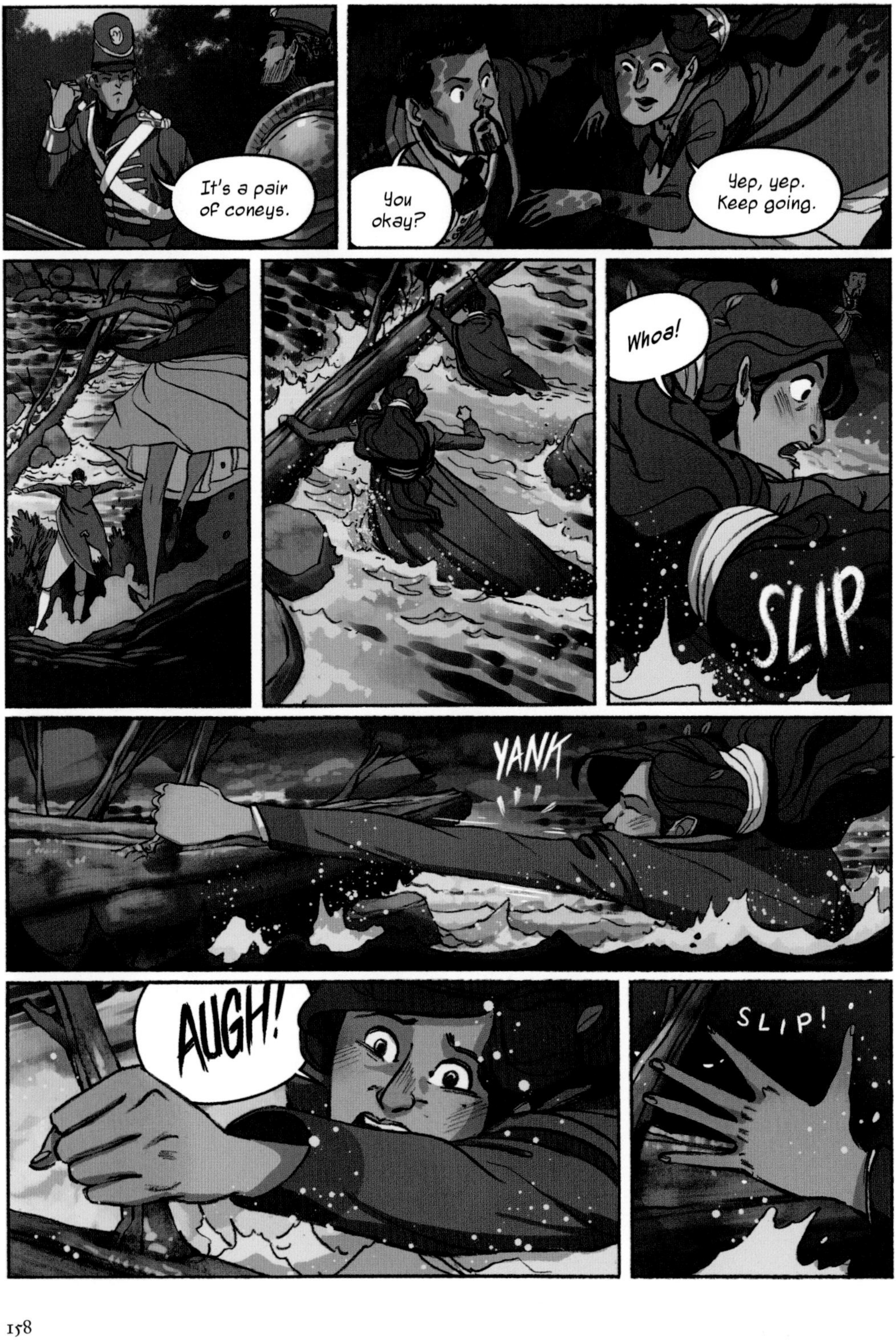
It's a pair of coneys.
You okay?
Yep, yep. Keep going.
Whoa!
SLIP
YANK
AUGH!
SLIP!

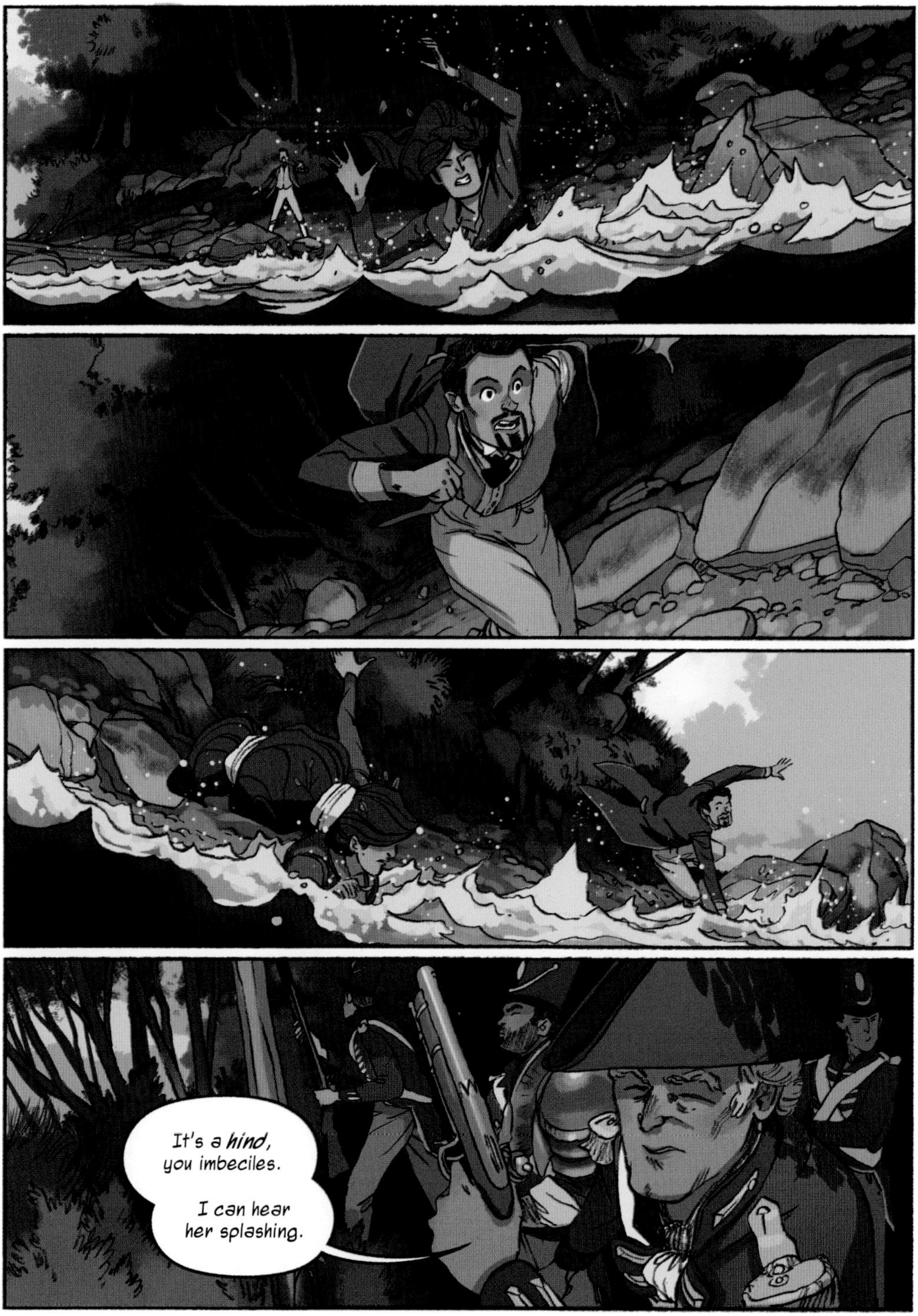
It's a *hind*, you imbeciles.
I can hear her splashing.

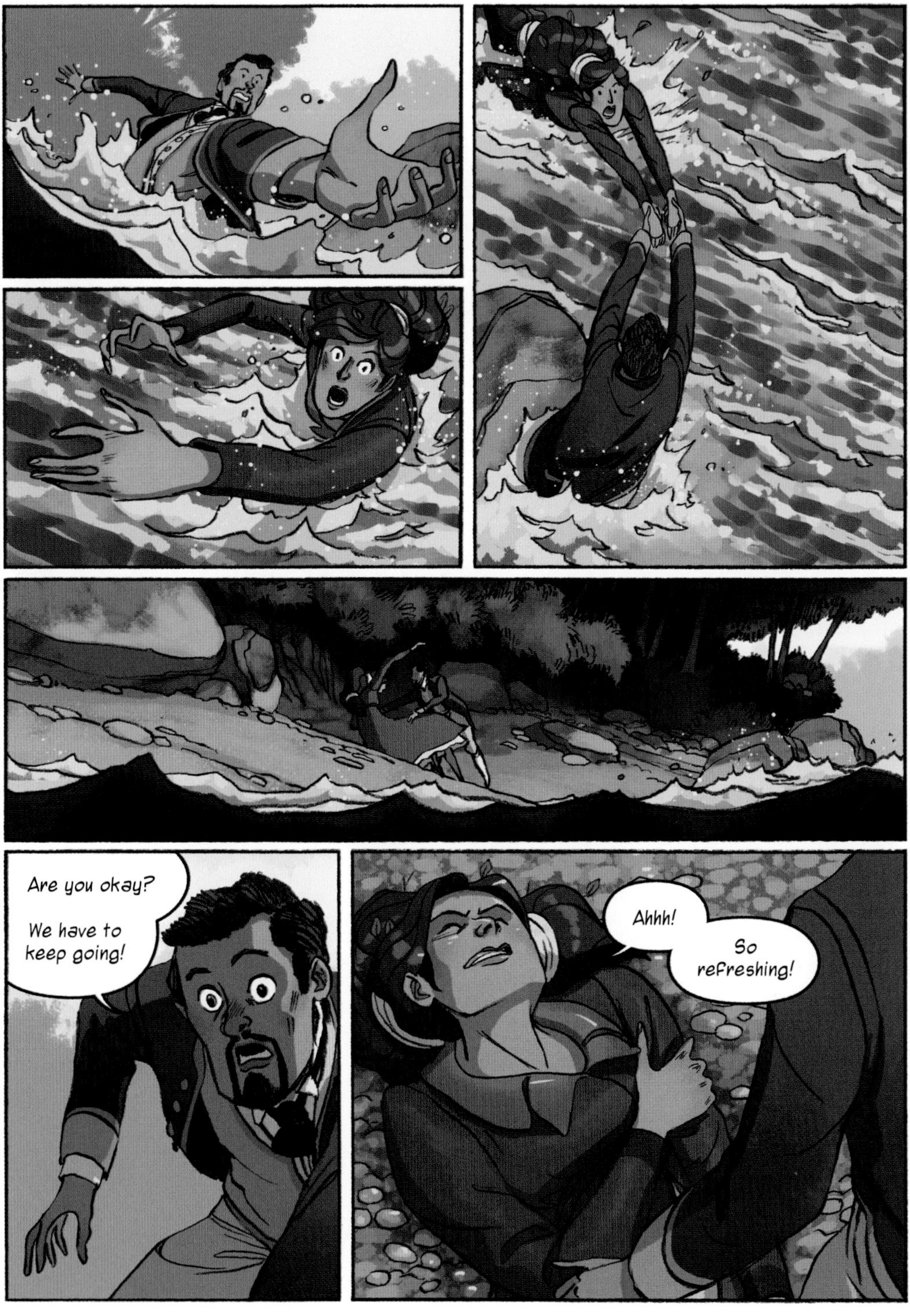
Are you okay?
We have to keep going!
Ahhh!
So refreshing!

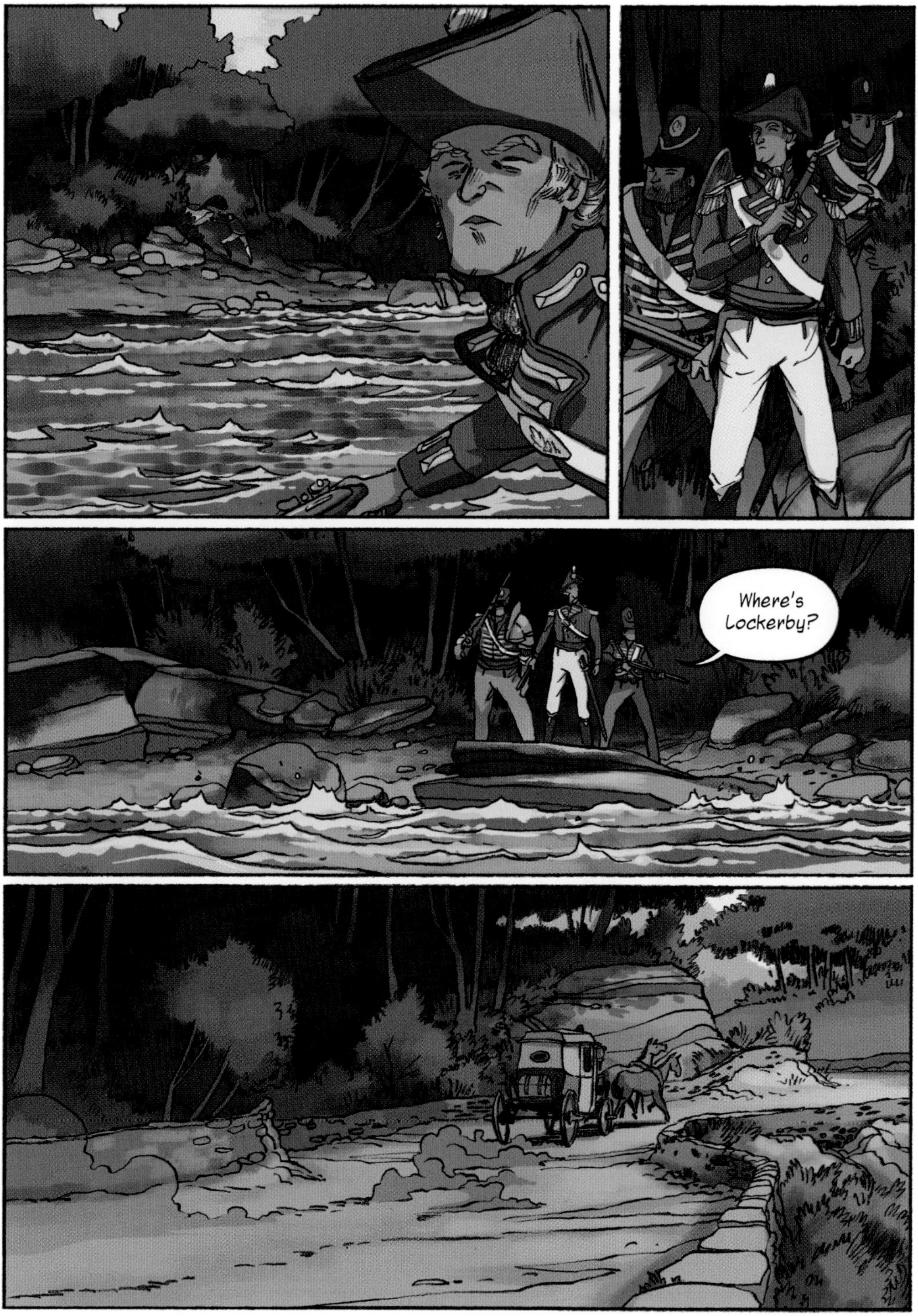
Where's Lockerby?

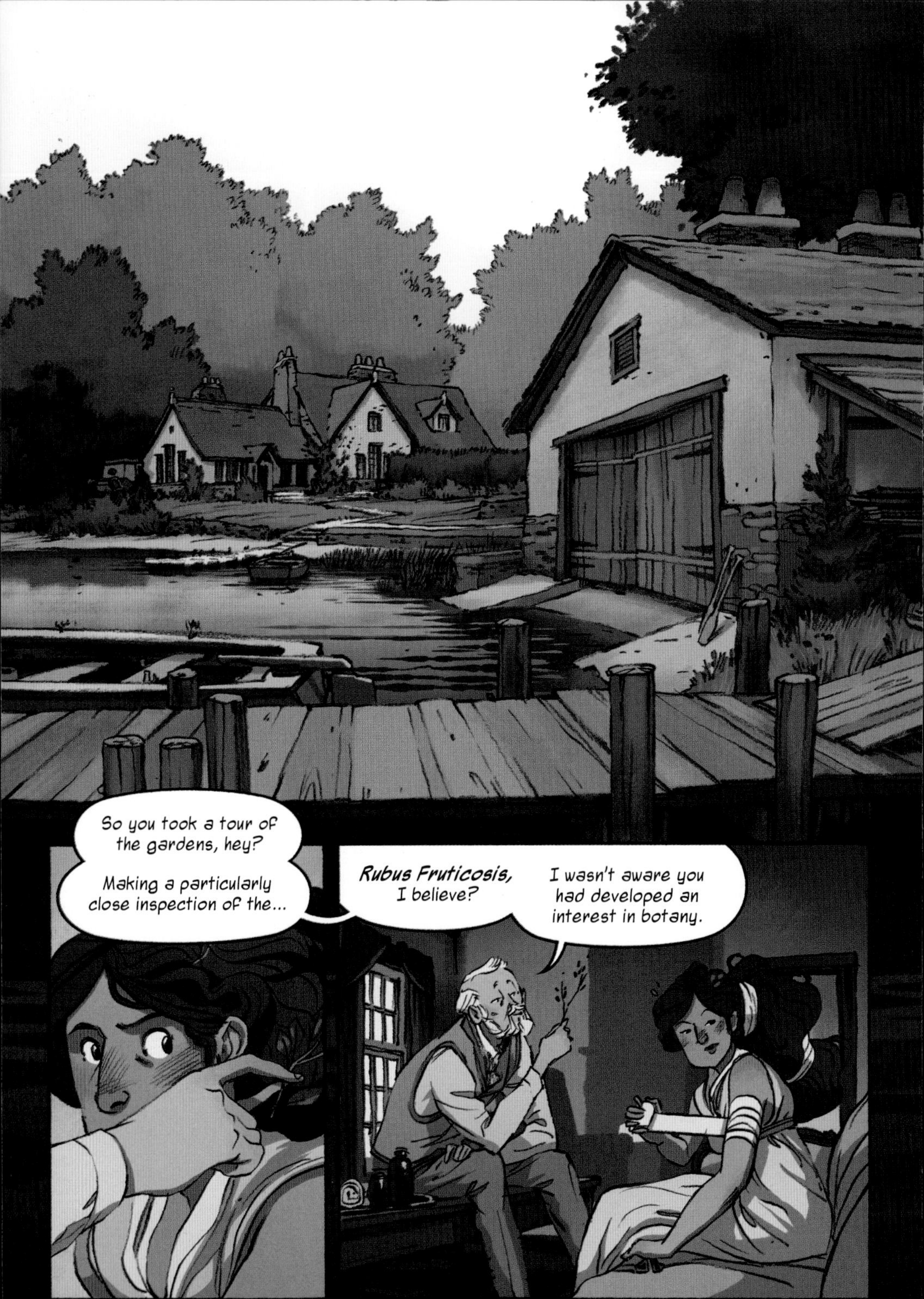
So you took a tour of the gardens, hey?
Making a particularly close inspection of the...
Rubus Fruticosis, I believe?
I wasn't aware you had developed an interest in botany.

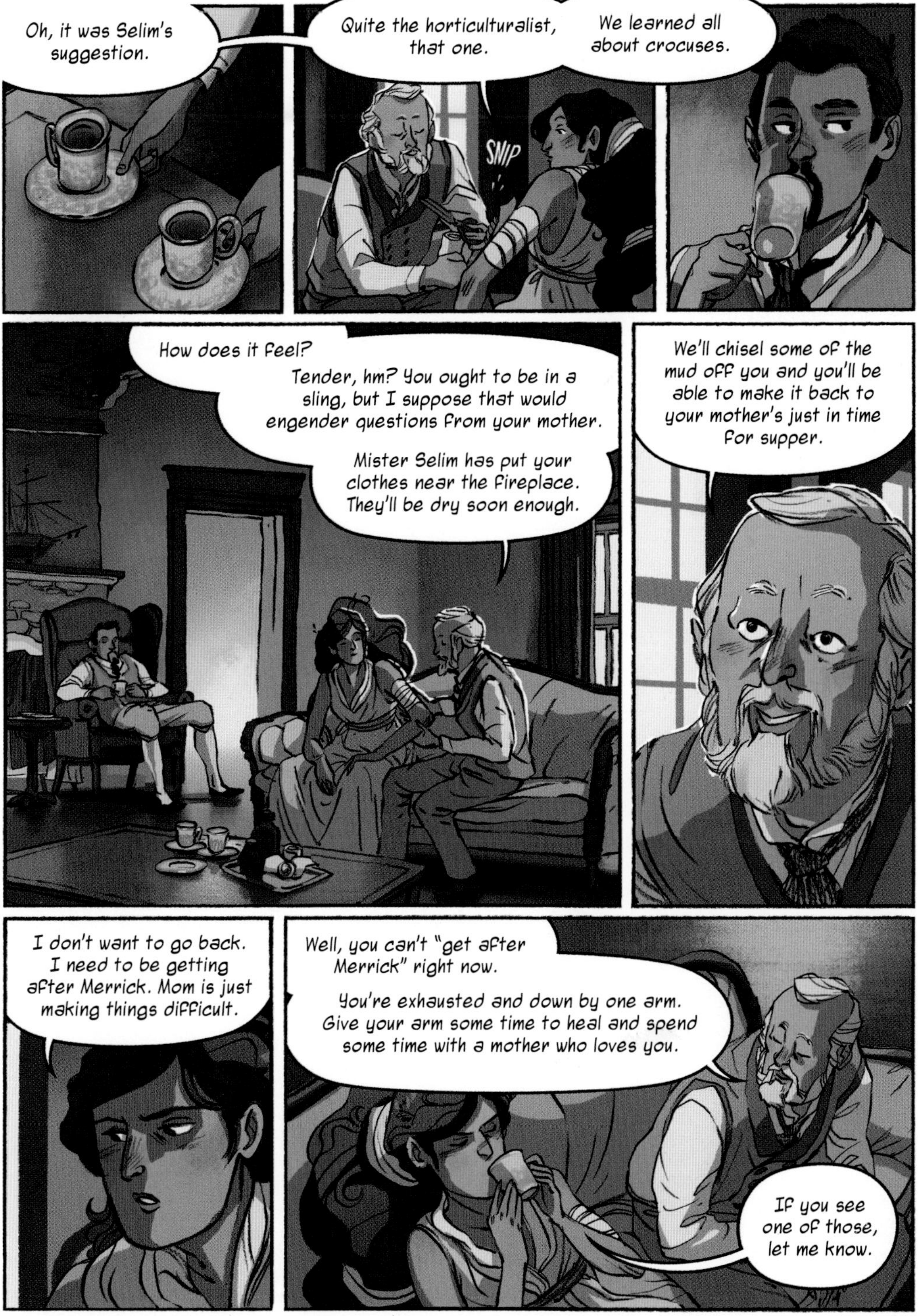
Oh, it was Selim's suggestion.
Quite the horticulturalist, that one.
We learned all about crocuses.
SNIP
How does it feel?
Tender, hm? You ought to be in a sling, but I suppose that would engender questions from your mother.
Mister Selim has put your clothes near the fireplace. They'll be dry soon enough.
We'll chisel some of the mud off you and you'll be able to make it back to your mother's just in time for supper.
I don't want to go back. I need to be getting after Merrick. Mom is just making things difficult.
Well, you can't "get after Merrick" right now.
You're exhausted and down by one arm. Give your arm some time to heal and spend some time with a mother who loves you.
If you see one of those, let me know.

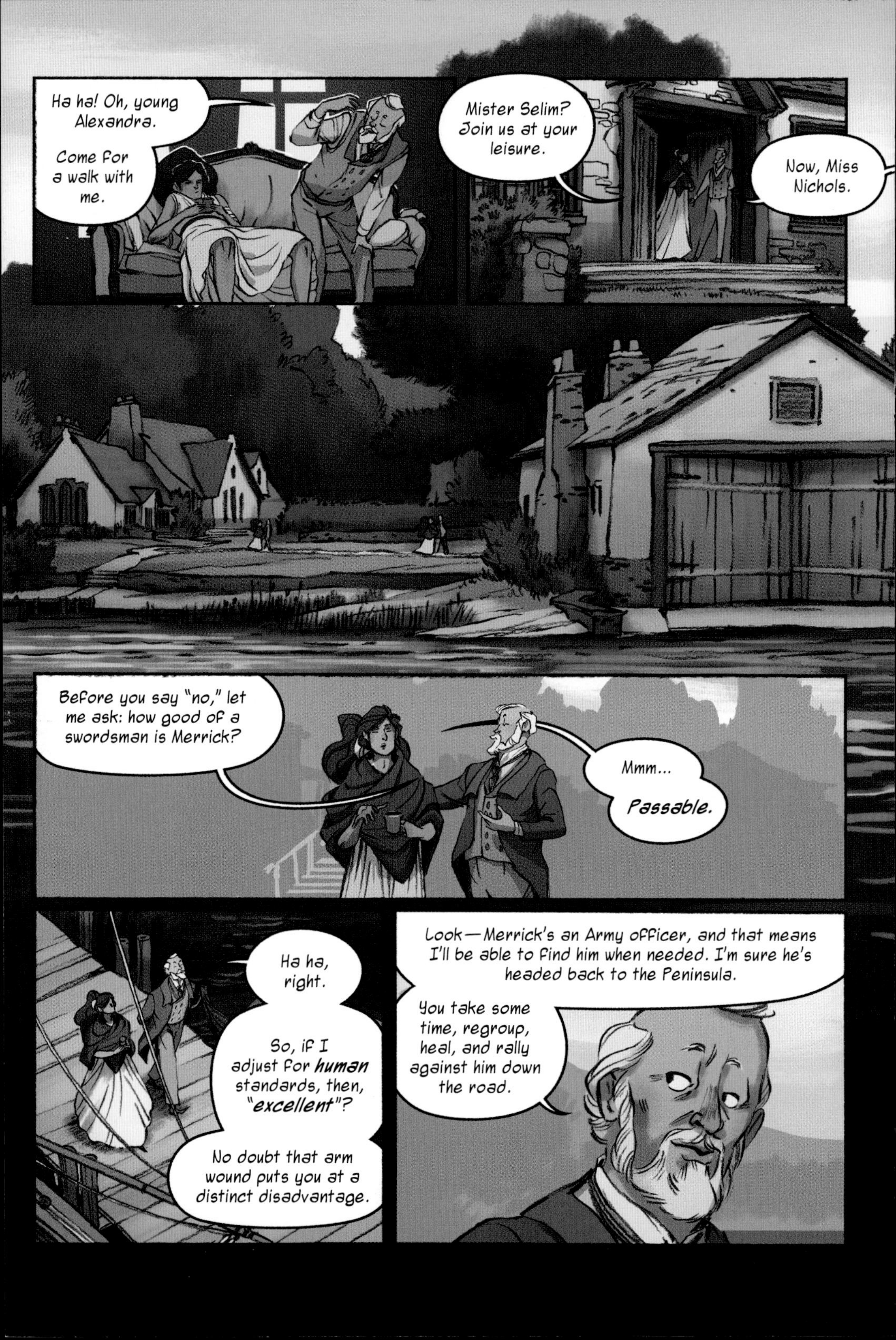
Ha ha! Oh, young Alexandra.
Come for a walk with me.
Mister Selim? Join us at your leisure.
Now, Miss Nichols.
Before you say "no," let me ask: how good of a swordsman is Merrick?
Mmm...
*Passable.*
Ha ha, right.
So, if I adjust for ***human*** standards, then, "***excellent***"?
No doubt that arm wound puts you at a distinct disadvantage.
Look—Merrick's an Army officer, and that means I'll be able to find him when needed. I'm sure he's headed back to the Peninsula.
You take some time, regroup, heal, and rally against him down the road.

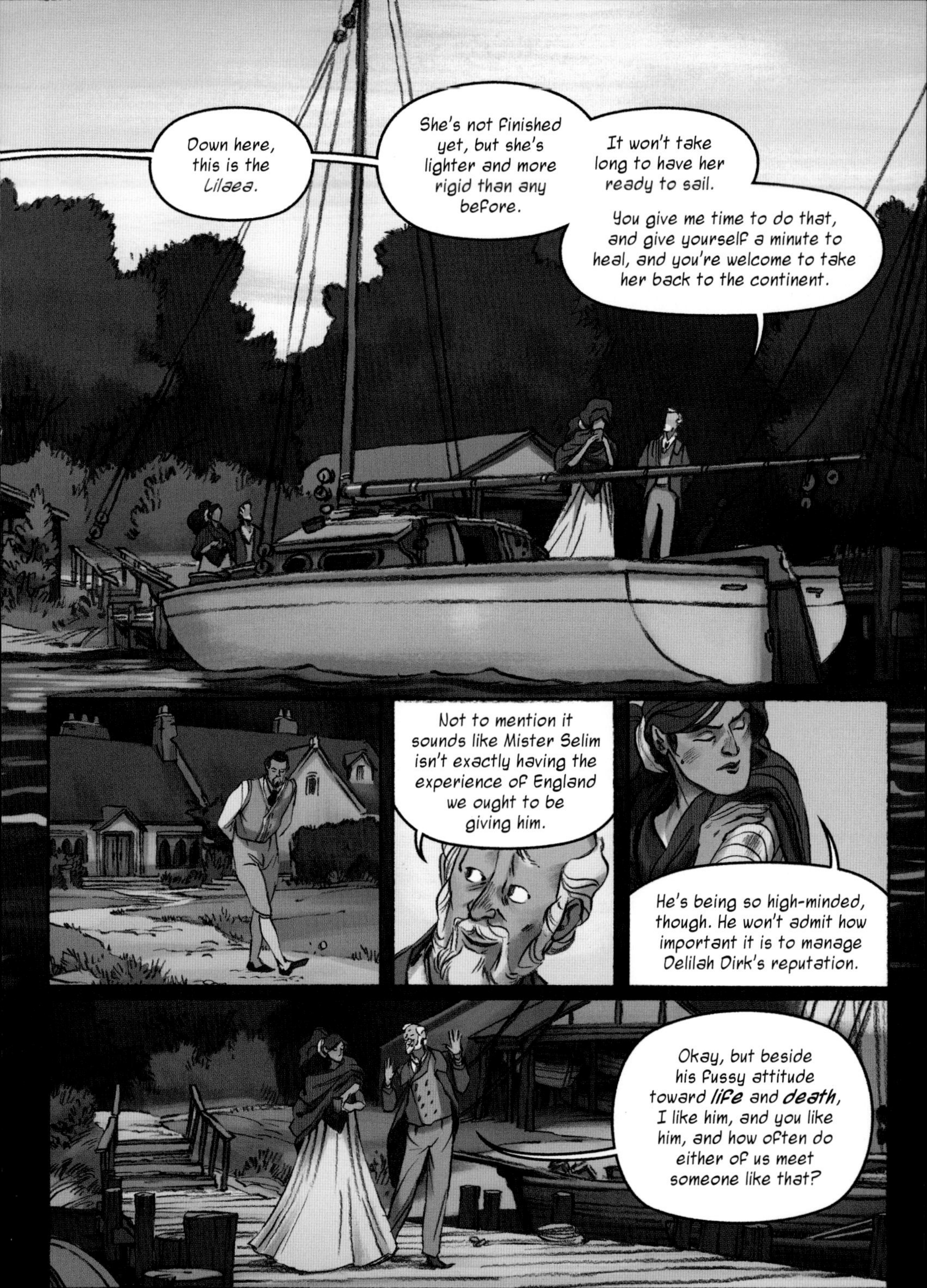
Down here, this is the *Lilaea*.
She's not finished yet, but she's lighter and more rigid than any before.
It won't take long to have her ready to sail.
You give me time to do that, and give yourself a minute to heal, and you're welcome to take her back to the continent.
Not to mention it sounds like Mister Selim isn't exactly having the experience of England we ought to be giving him.
He's being so high-minded, though. He won't admit how important it is to manage Delilah Dirk's reputation.
Okay, but beside his fussy attitude toward ***life*** and ***death***, I like him, and you like him, and how often do either of us meet someone like that?

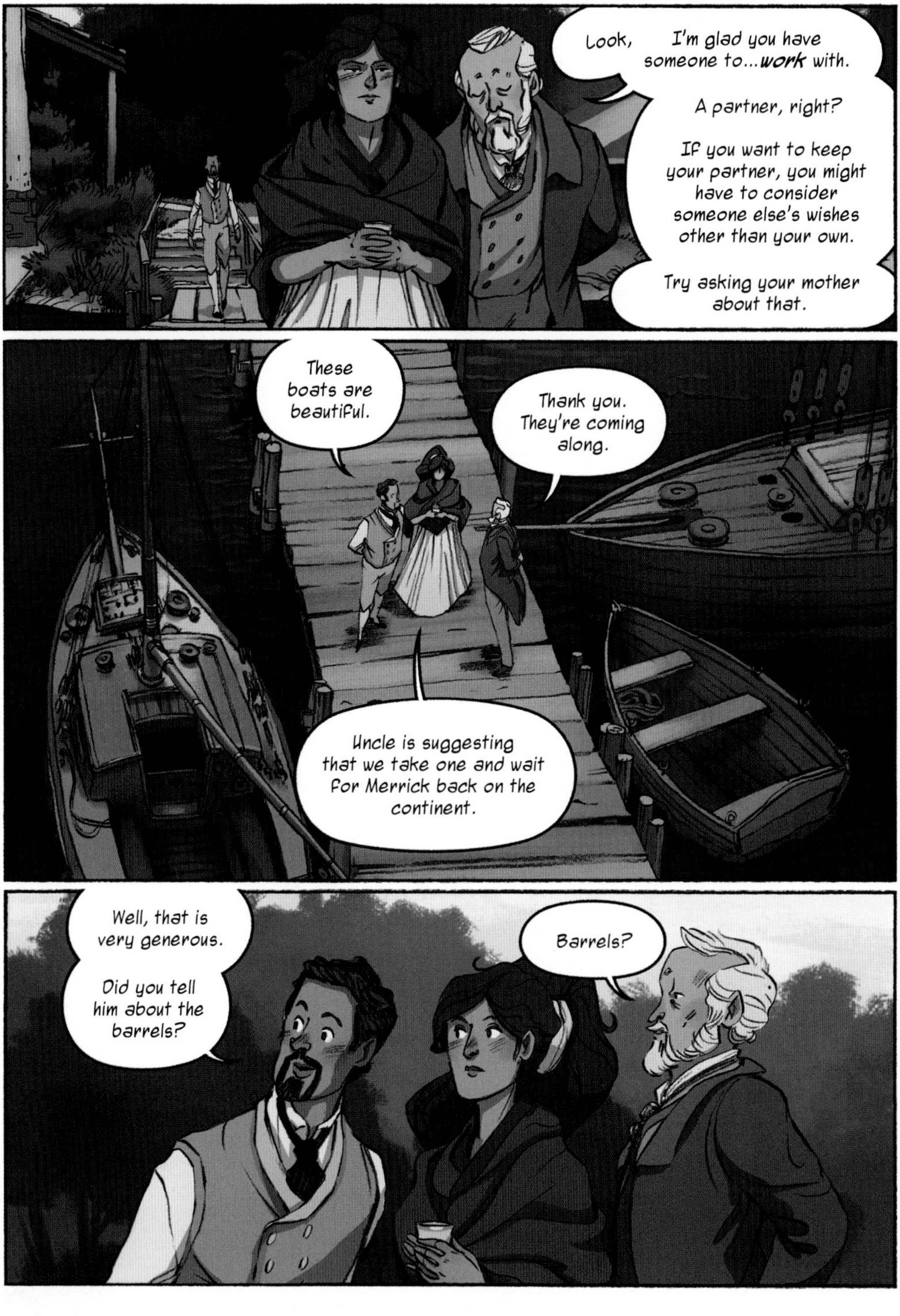
Look, I'm glad you have someone to...**work** with.
A partner, right?
If you want to keep your partner, you might have to consider someone else's wishes other than your own.
Try asking your mother about that.
These boats are beautiful.
Thank you. They're coming along.
Uncle is suggesting that we take one and wait for Merrick back on the continent.
Well, that is very generous.
Did you tell him about the barrels?
Barrels?

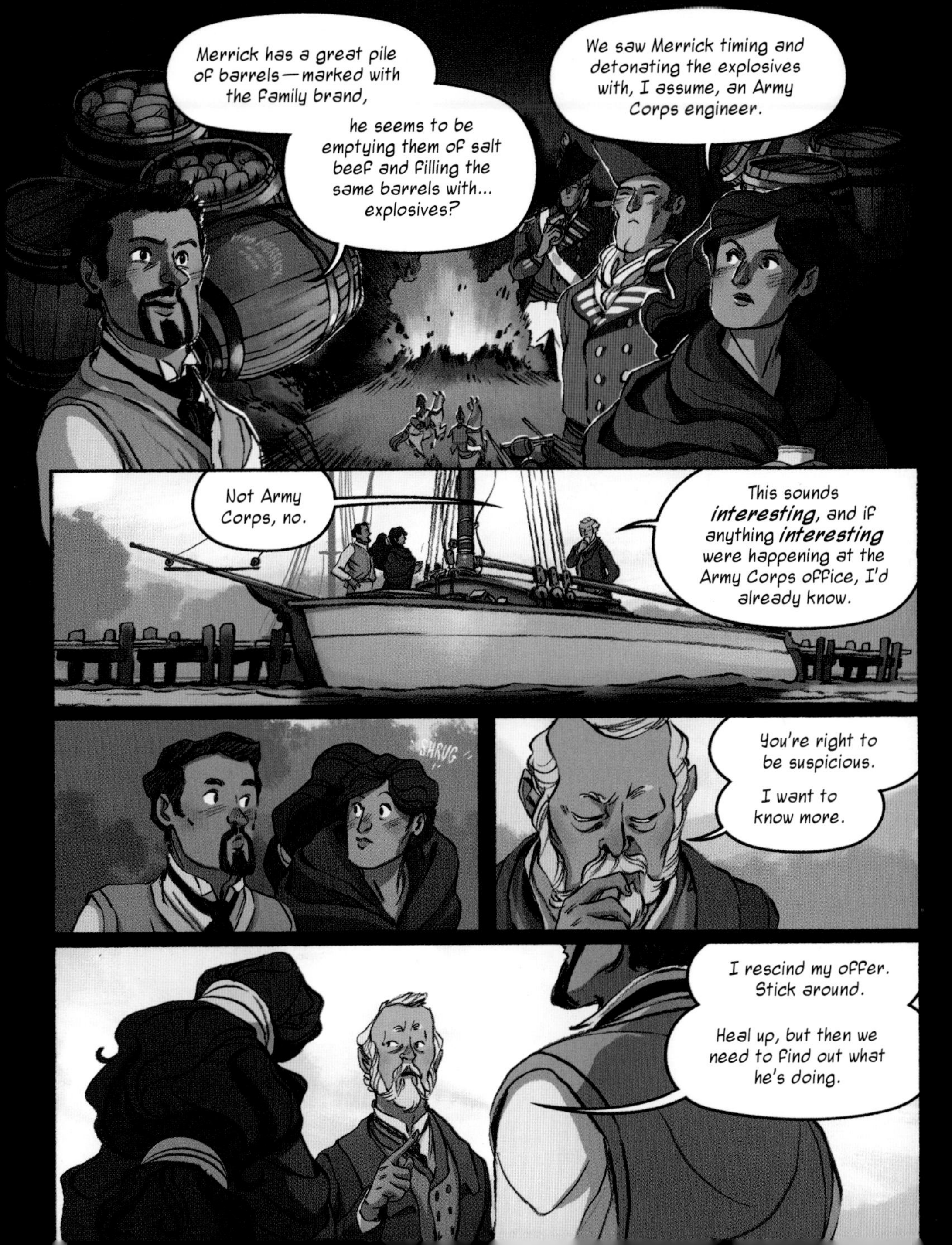
Merrick has a great pile of barrels—marked with the family brand,
he seems to be emptying them of salt beef and filling the same barrels with... explosives?
We saw Merrick timing and detonating the explosives with, I assume, an Army Corps engineer.
Not Army Corps, no.
This sounds *interesting*, and if anything *interesting* were happening at the Army Corps office, I'd already know.
SHRUG
You're right to be suspicious.
I want to know more.
I rescind my offer. Stick around.
Heal up, but then we need to find out what he's doing.

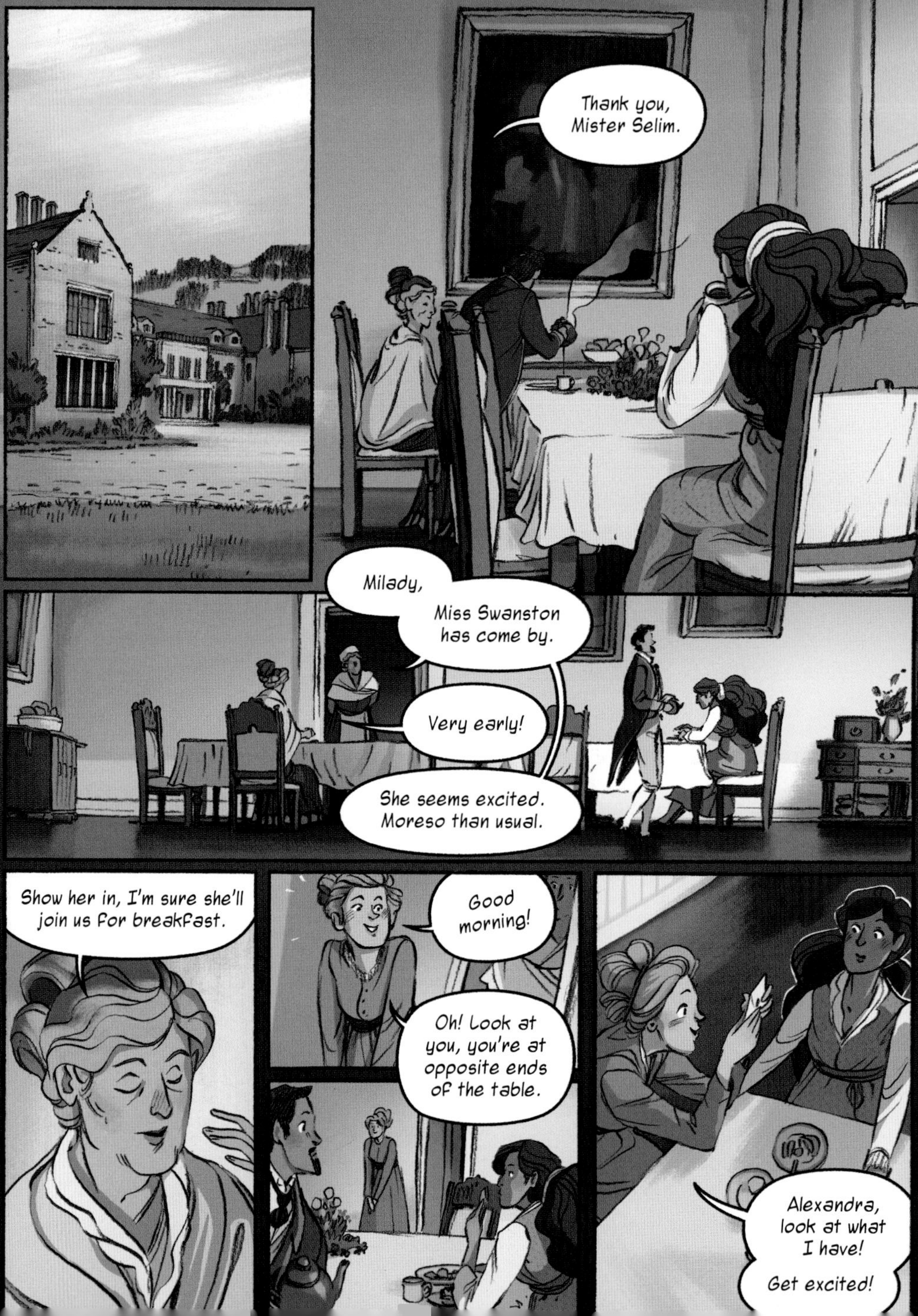
Thank you, Mister Selim.
Milady,
Miss Swanston has come by.
Very early!
She seems excited. Moreso than usual.
Show her in, I'm sure she'll join us for breakfast.
Good morning!
Oh! Look at you, you're at opposite ends of the table.
Alexandra, look at what I have!
Get excited!

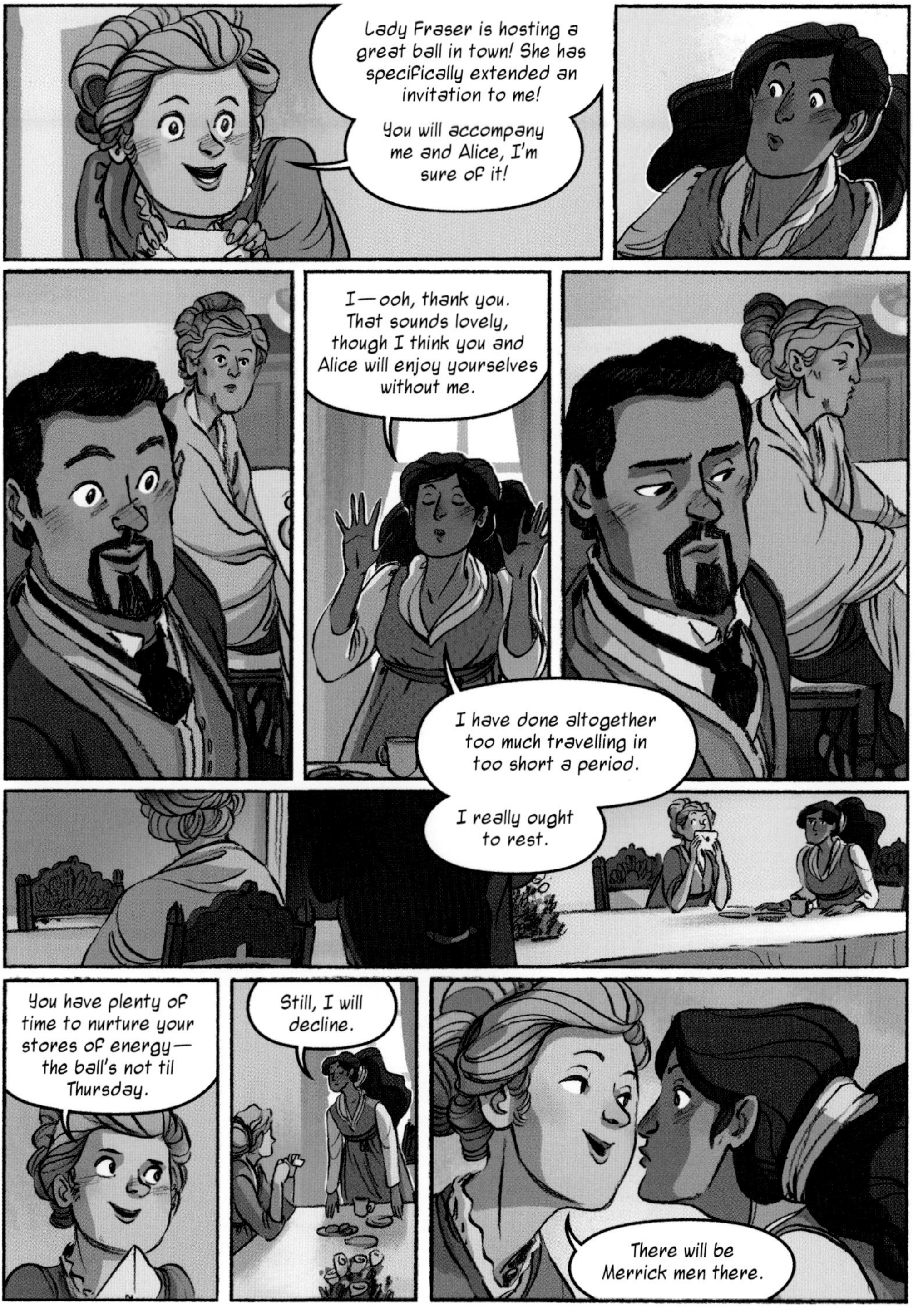
Lady Fraser is hosting a great ball in town! She has specifically extended an invitation to me!
You will accompany me and Alice, I'm sure of it!
I—ooh, thank you. That sounds lovely, though I think you and Alice will enjoy yourselves without me.
I have done altogether too much travelling in too short a period.
I really ought to rest.
You have plenty of time to nurture your stores of energy—the ball's not til Thursday.
Still, I will decline.
There will be Merrick men there.

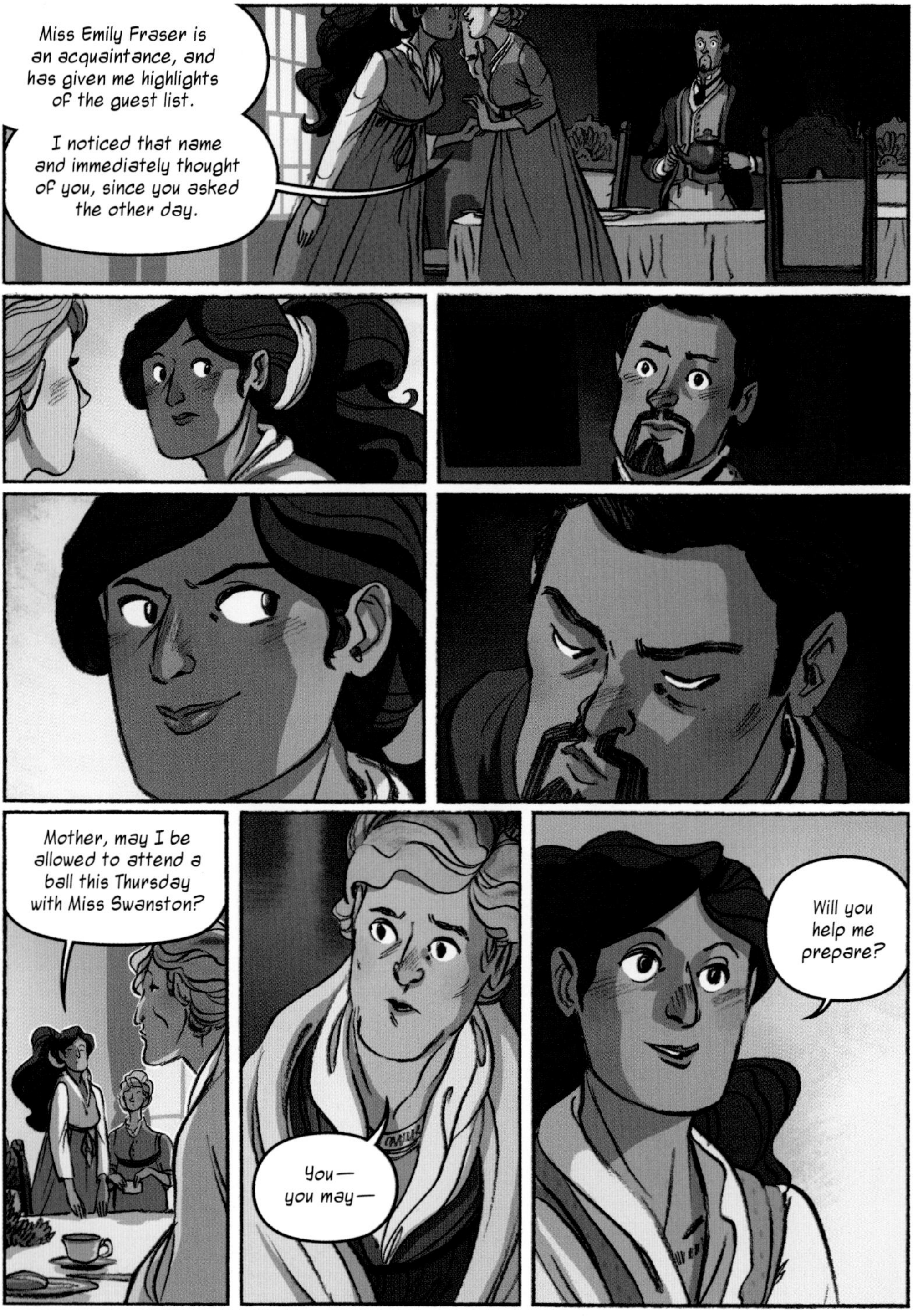
Miss Emily Fraser is an acquaintance, and has given me highlights of the guest list.
I noticed that name and immediately thought of you, since you asked the other day.
Mother, may I be allowed to attend a ball this Thursday with Miss Swanston?
You— you may—
Will you help me prepare?

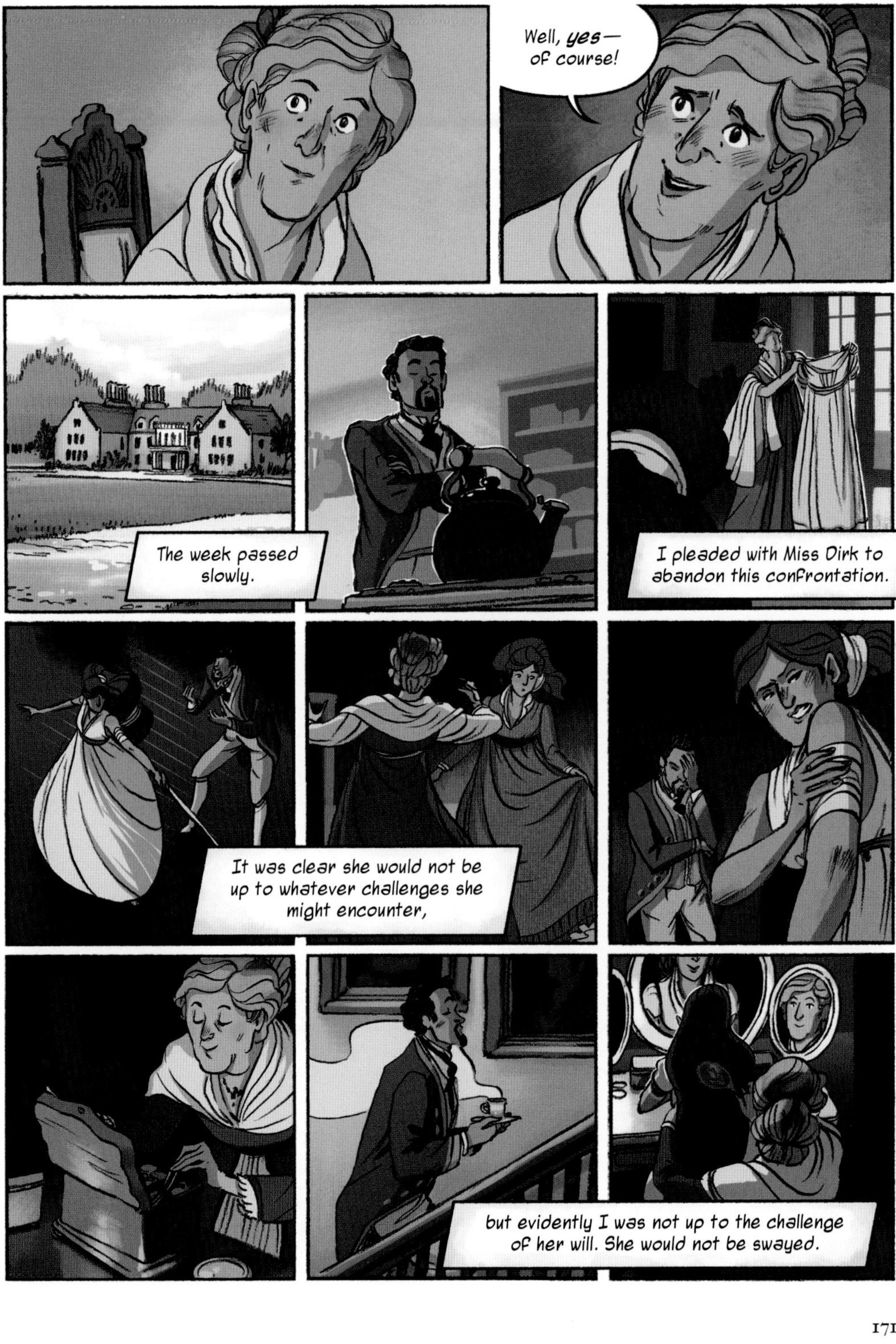
Well, yes—
of course!
The week passed slowly.
I pleaded with Miss Dirk to abandon this confrontation.
It was clear she would not be up to whatever challenges she might encounter,
but evidently I was not up to the challenge of her will. She would not be swayed.

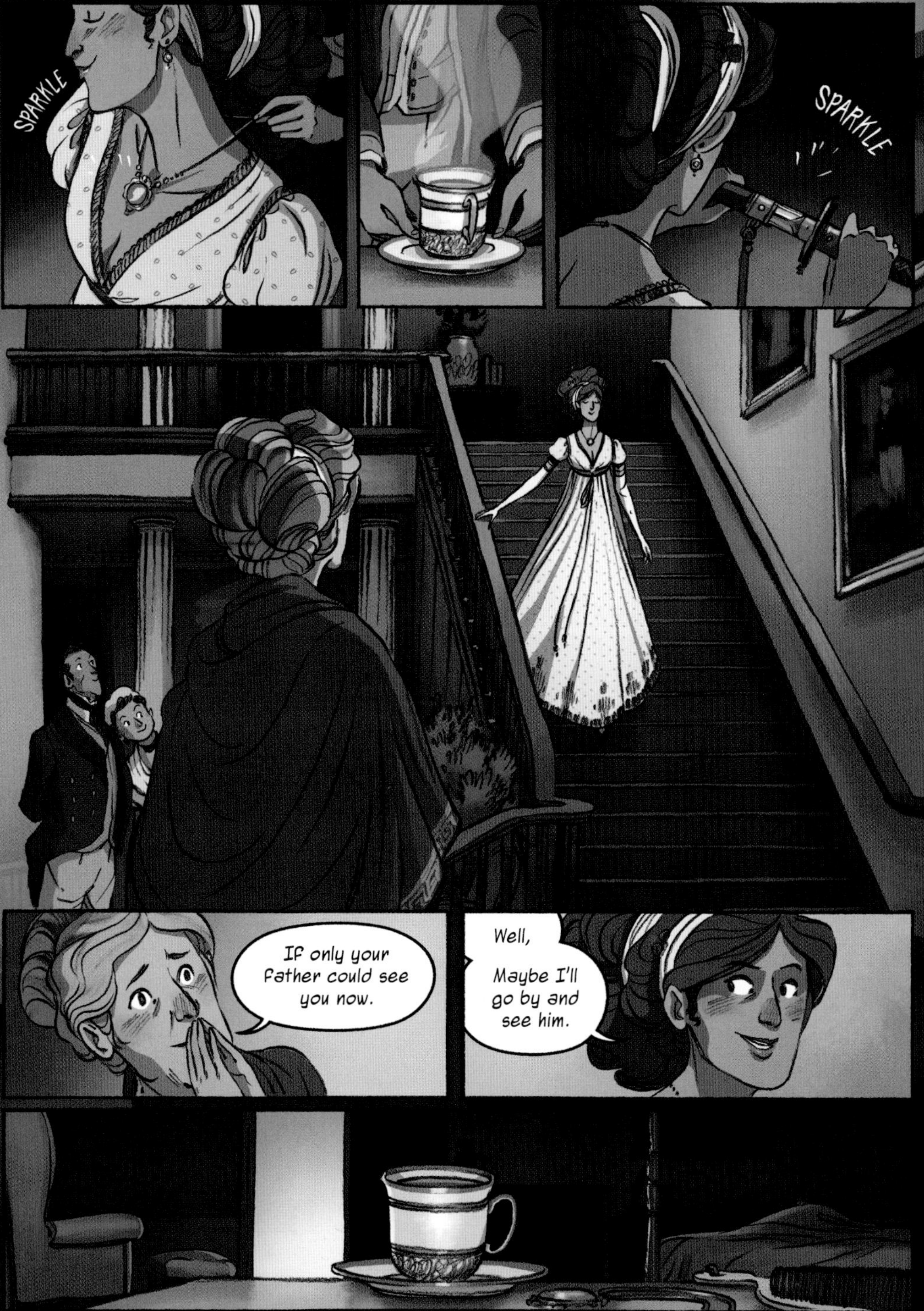
SPARKLE
SPARKLE
If only your father could see you now.
Well,
Maybe I'll go by and see him.

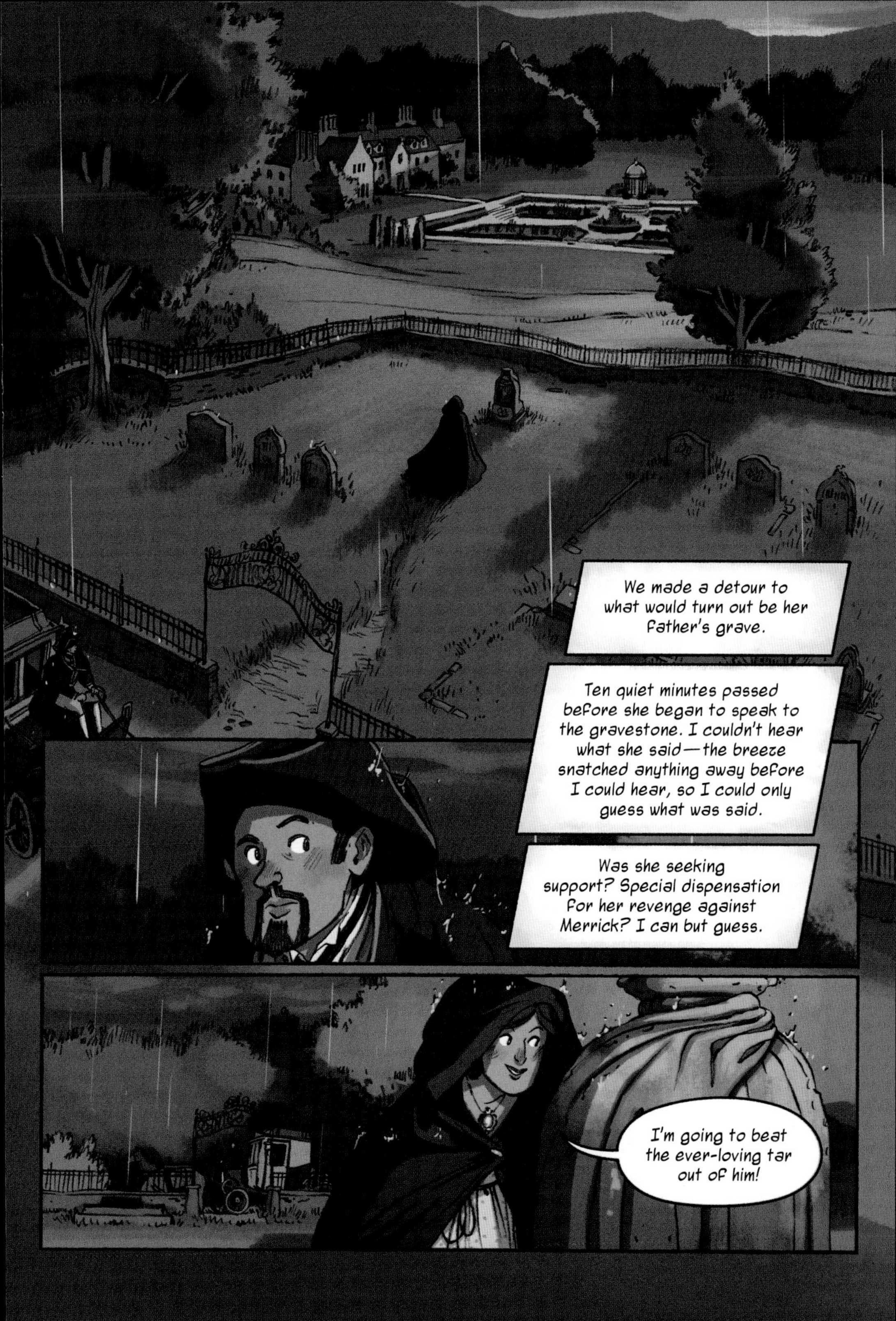

We made a detour to what would turn out be her father's grave.
Ten quiet minutes passed before she began to speak to the gravestone. I couldn't hear what she said—the breeze snatched anything away before I could hear, so I could only guess what was said.
Was she seeking support? Special dispensation for her revenge against Merrick? I can but guess.
I'm going to beat the ever-loving tar out of him!

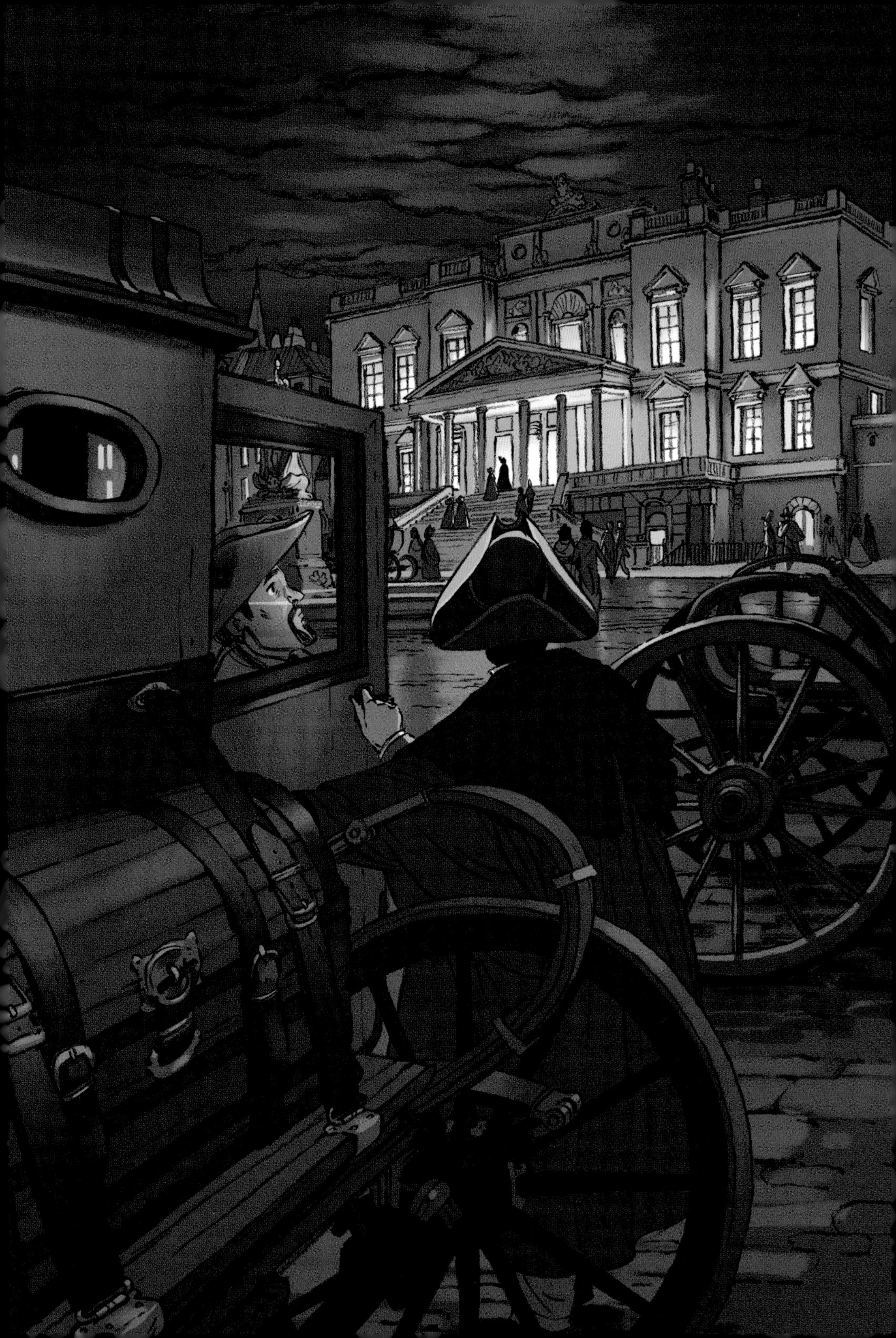

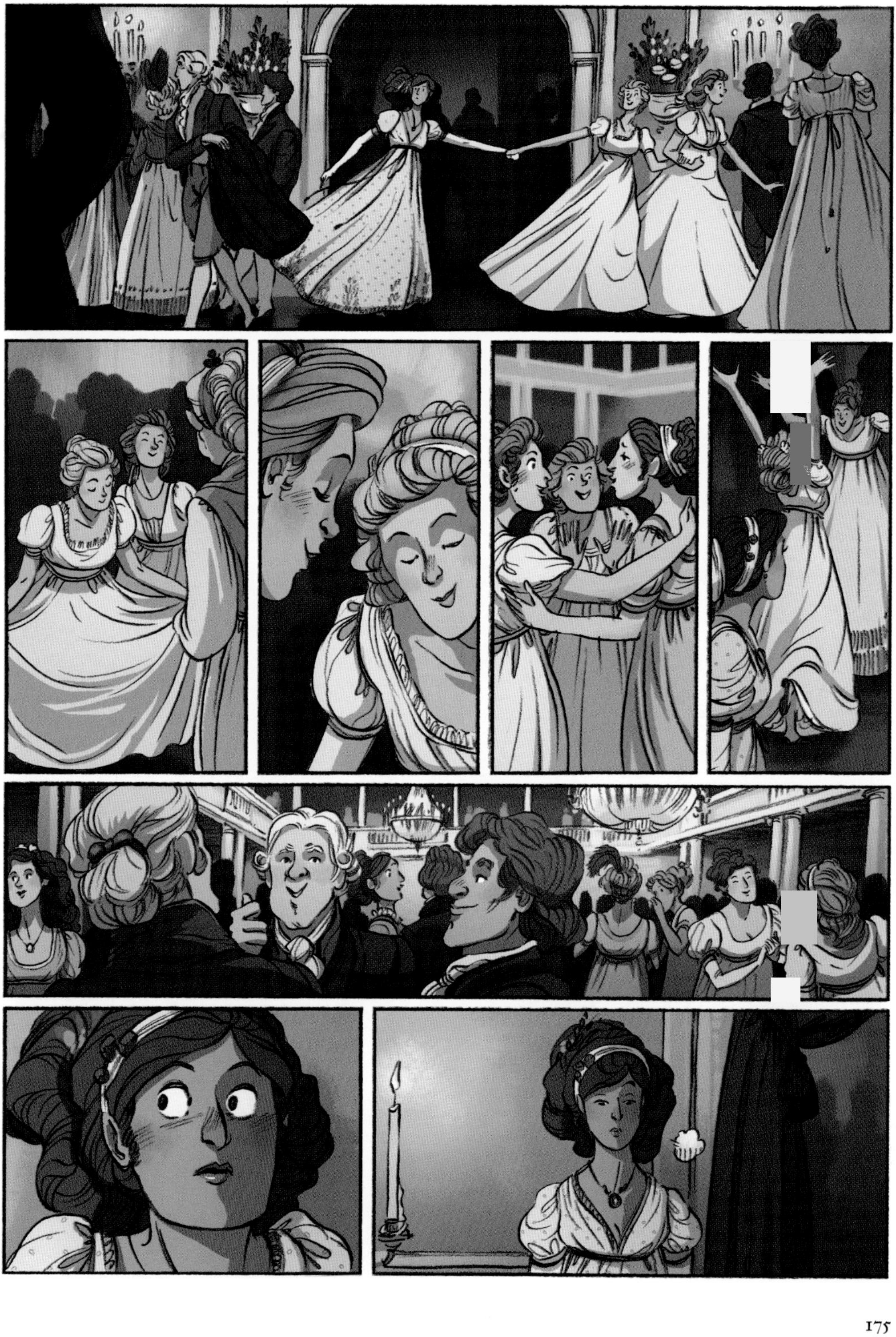

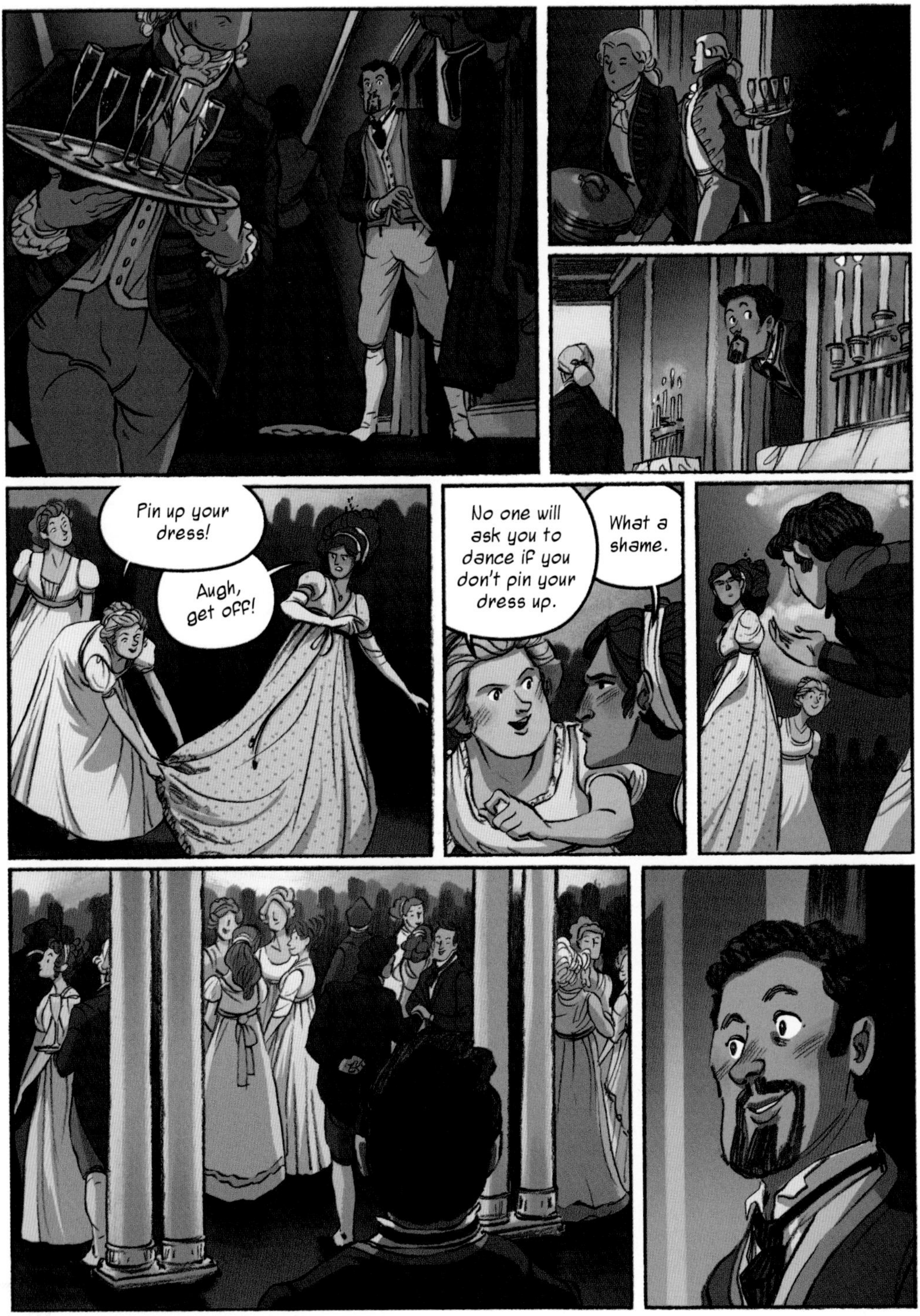
Pin up your dress!
Augh, get off!
No one will ask you to dance if you don't pin your dress up.
What a shame.

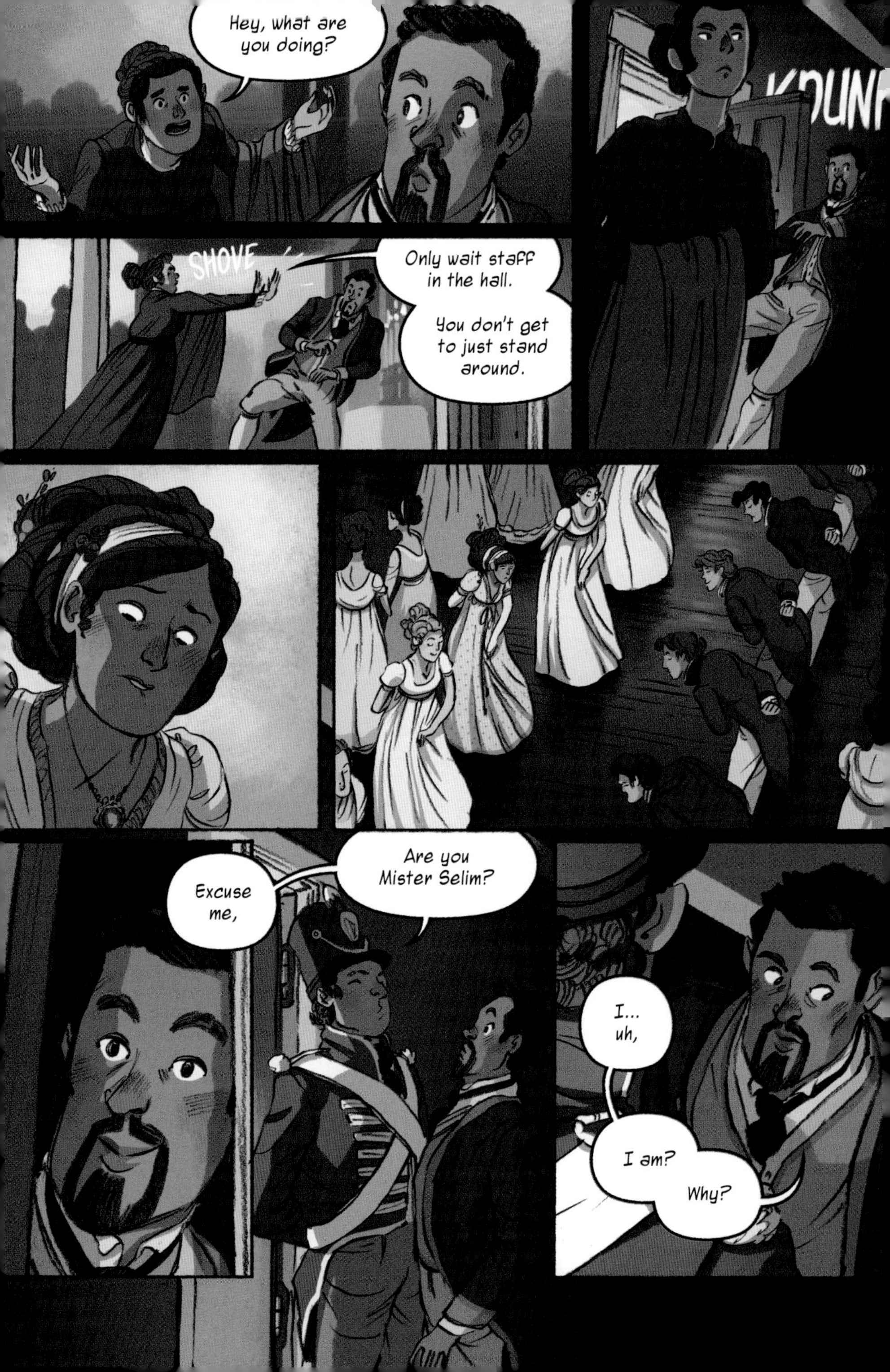
Hey, what are you doing?
KDUNK
SHOVE
Only wait staff in the hall.
You don't get to just stand around.
Excuse me,
Are you Mister Selim?
I... uh,
I am?
Why?

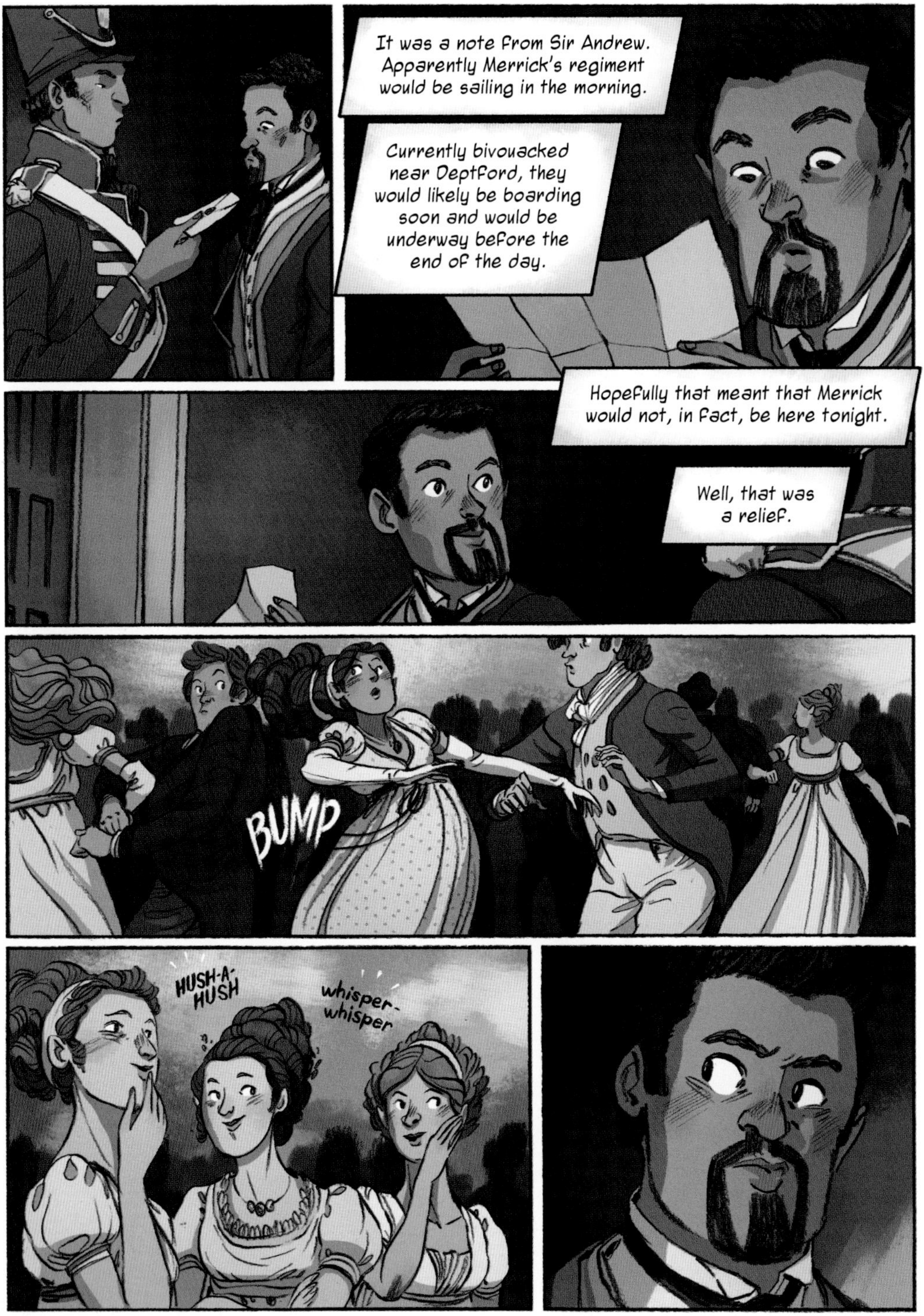
It was a note from Sir Andrew. Apparently Merrick's regiment would be sailing in the morning.
Currently bivouacked near Deptford, they would likely be boarding soon and would be underway before the end of the day.
Hopefully that meant that Merrick would not, in fact, be here tonight.
Well, that was a relief.
BUMP
HUSH-A-HUSH
whisper-whisper

SWIPP!

Perhaps I ought to have informed Miss Dirk of Merrick's absence.

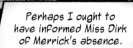

It might have been a kindness.

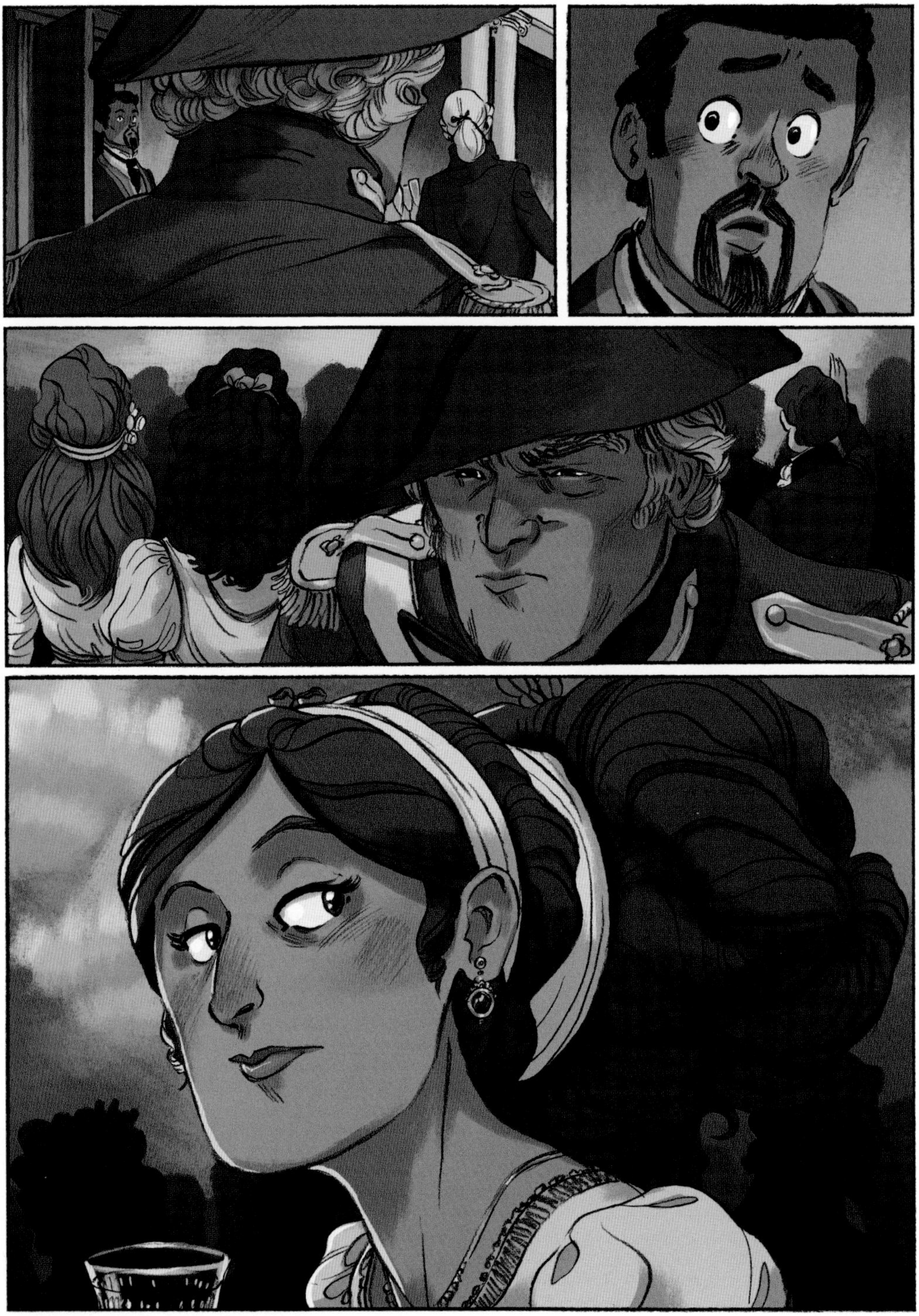

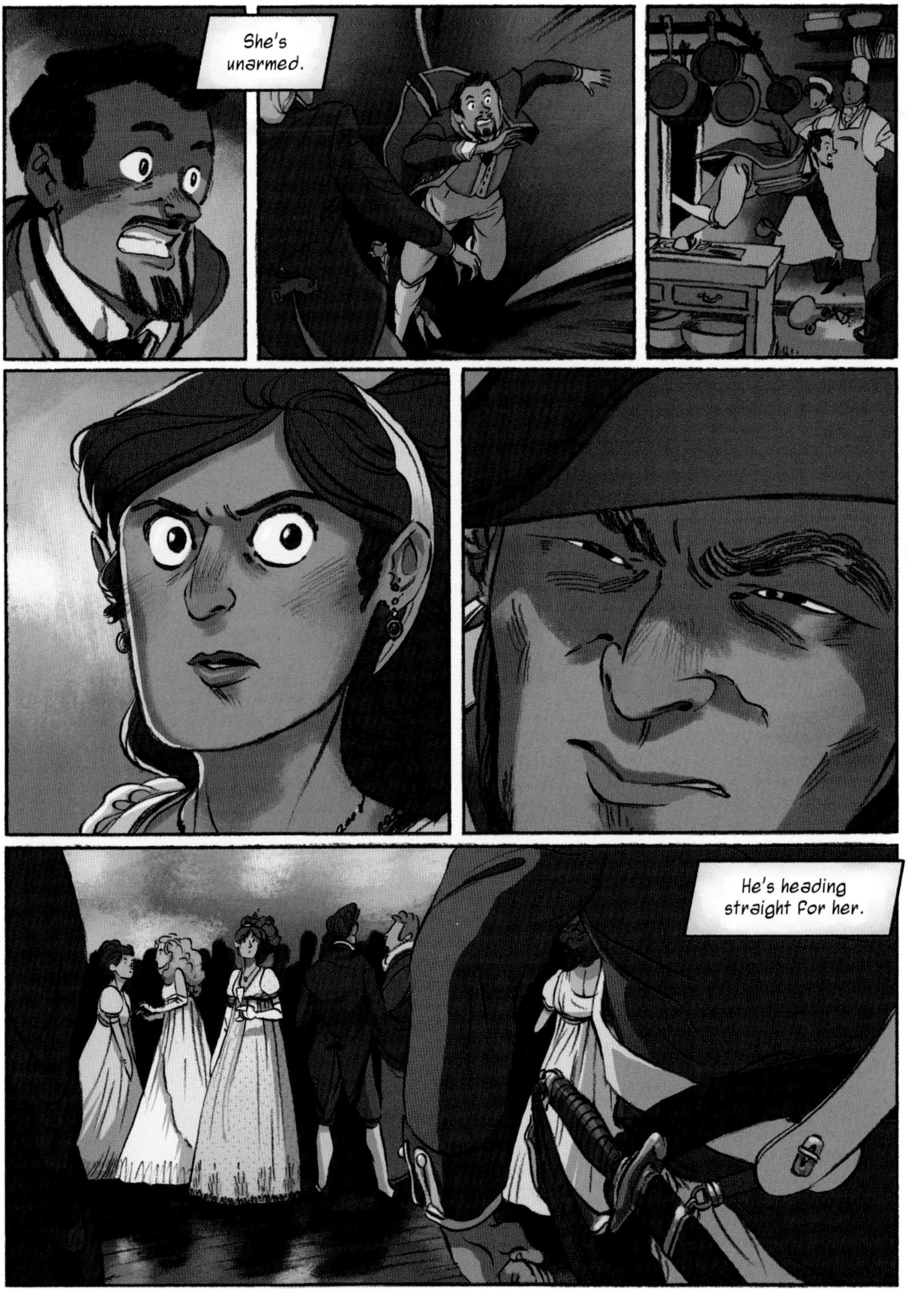
She's unarmed.
He's heading straight for her.

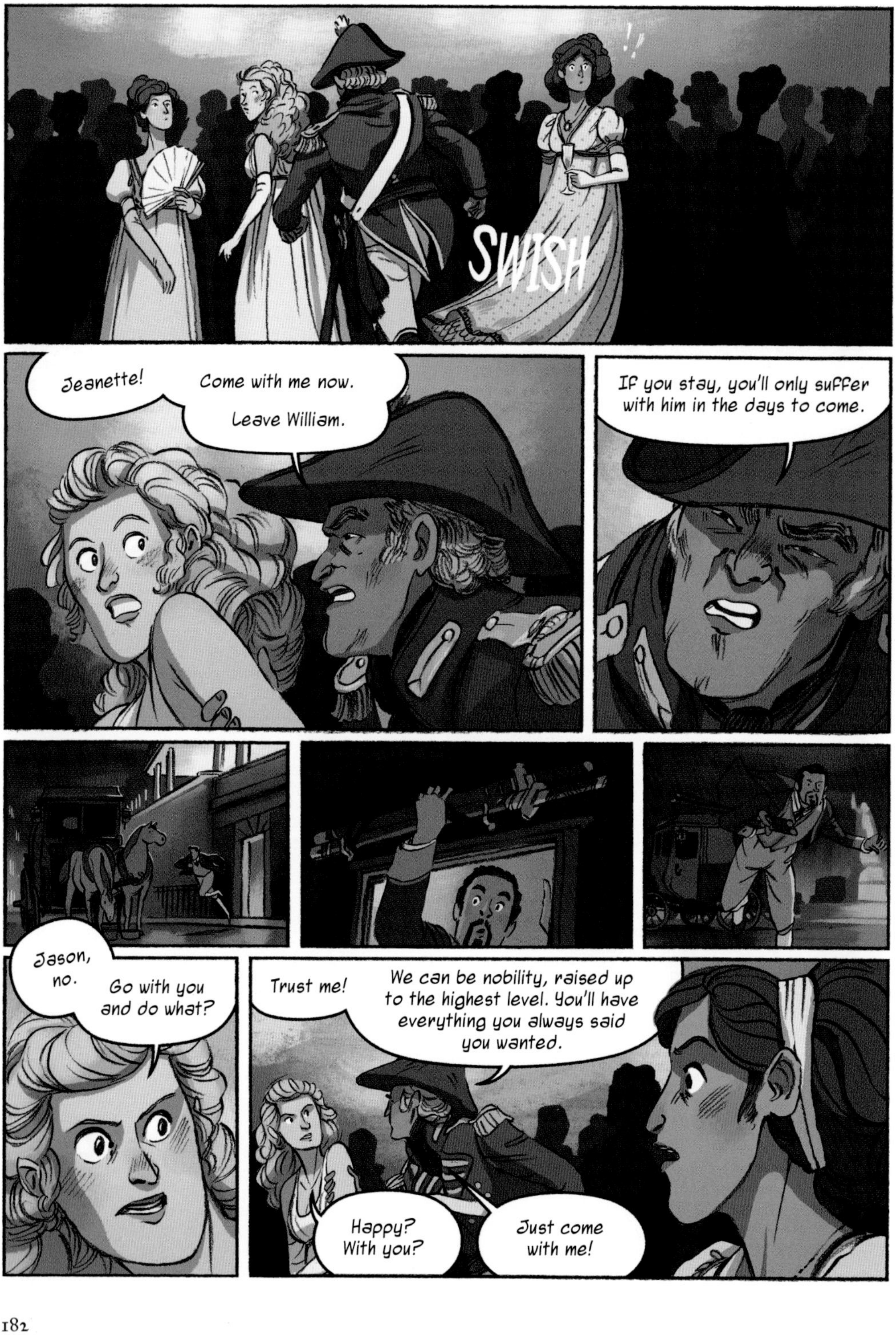
!!
SWISH
Jeanette!
Come with me now.
Leave William.
If you stay, you'll only suffer with him in the days to come.
Jason, no.
Go with you and do what?
Trust me!
We can be nobility, raised up to the highest level. You'll have everything you always said you wanted.
Happy? With you?
Just come with me!

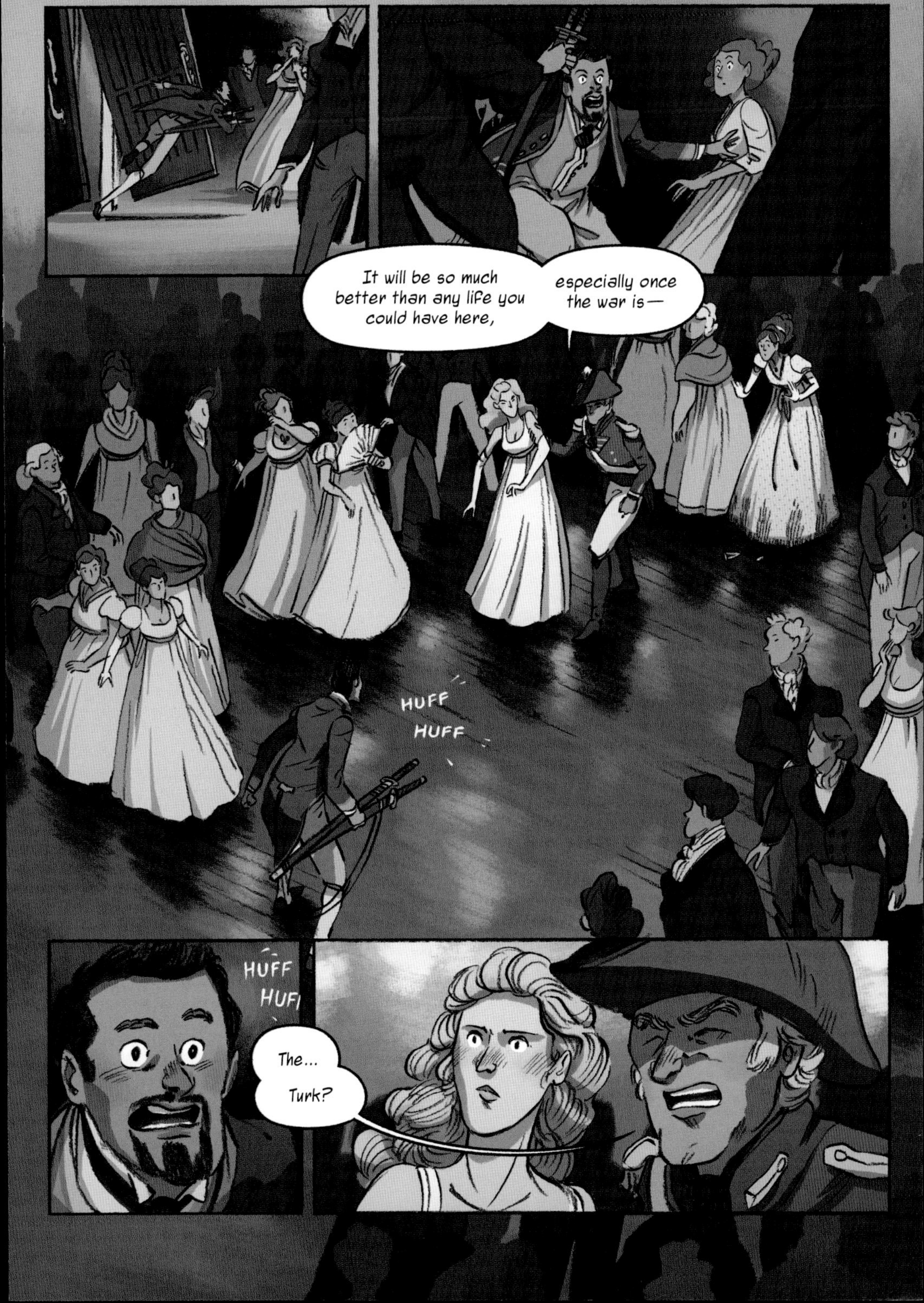
It will be so much better than any life you could have here,
especially once the war is—
HUFF
HUFF
HUFF
HUFF
The...
Turk?

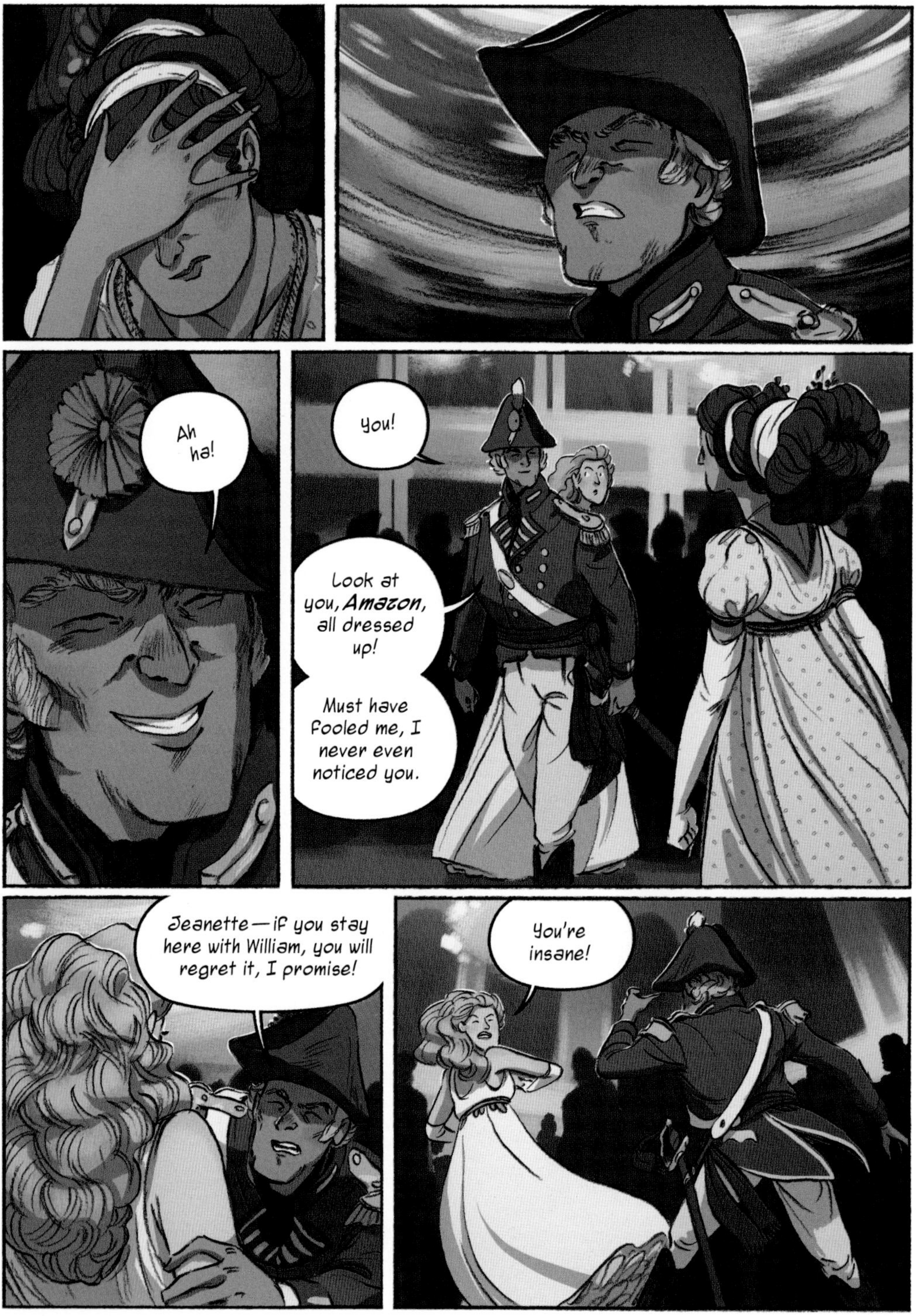
Ah ha!
You!
Look at you, Amazon, all dressed up!
Must have fooled me, I never even noticed you.
Jeanette—if you stay here with William, you will regret it, I promise!
You're insane!

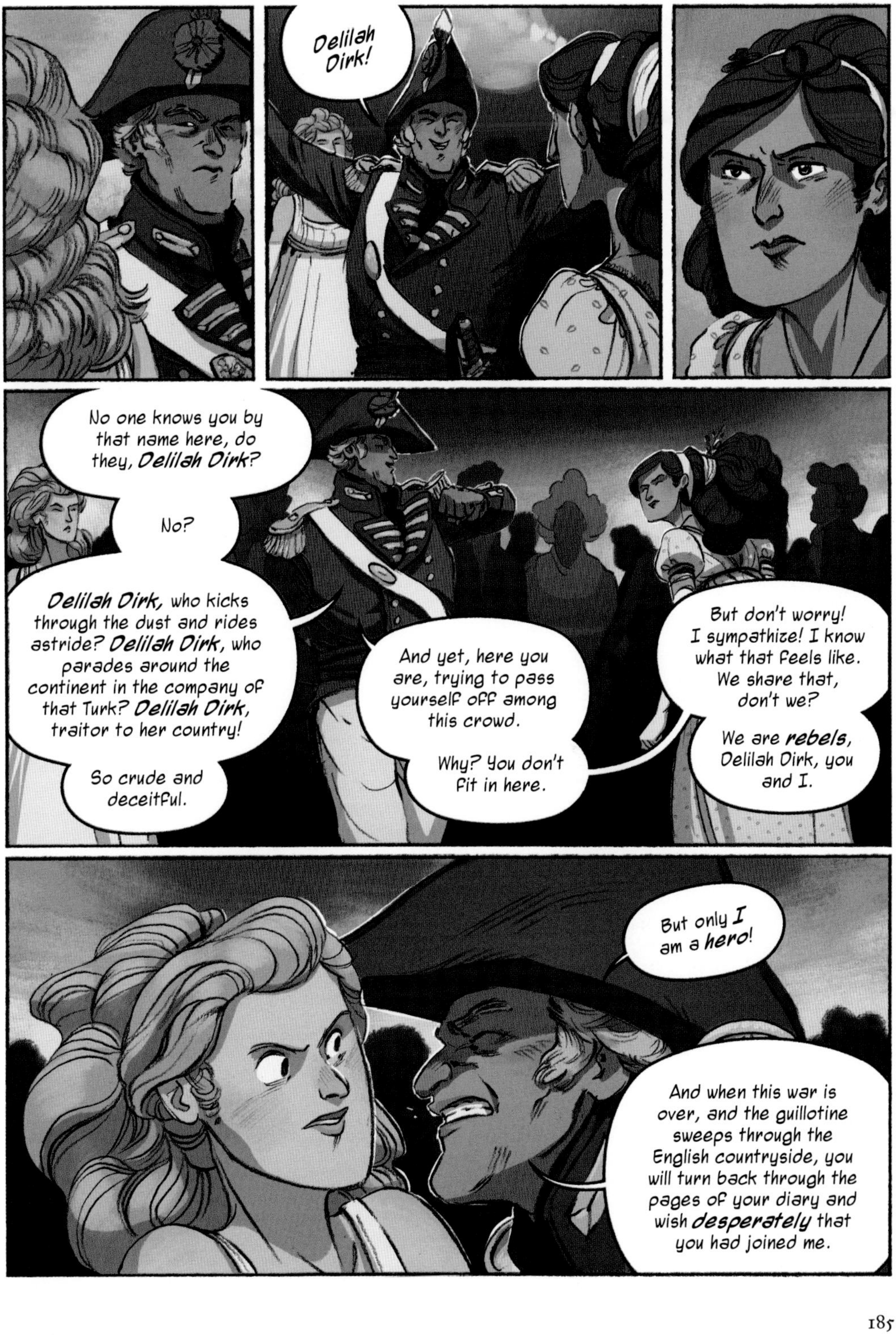
Delilah Dirk!
No one knows you by that name here, do they, Delilah Dirk?
No?
Delilah Dirk, who kicks through the dust and rides astride? Delilah Dirk, who parades around the continent in the company of that Turk? Delilah Dirk, traitor to her country!
So crude and deceitful.
And yet, here you are, trying to pass yourself off among this crowd.
Why? You don't fit in here.
But don't worry! I sympathize! I know what that feels like. We share that, don't we?
We are rebels, Delilah Dirk, you and I.
But only I am a hero!
And when this war is over, and the guillotine sweeps through the English countryside, you will turn back through the pages of your diary and wish desperately that you had joined me.

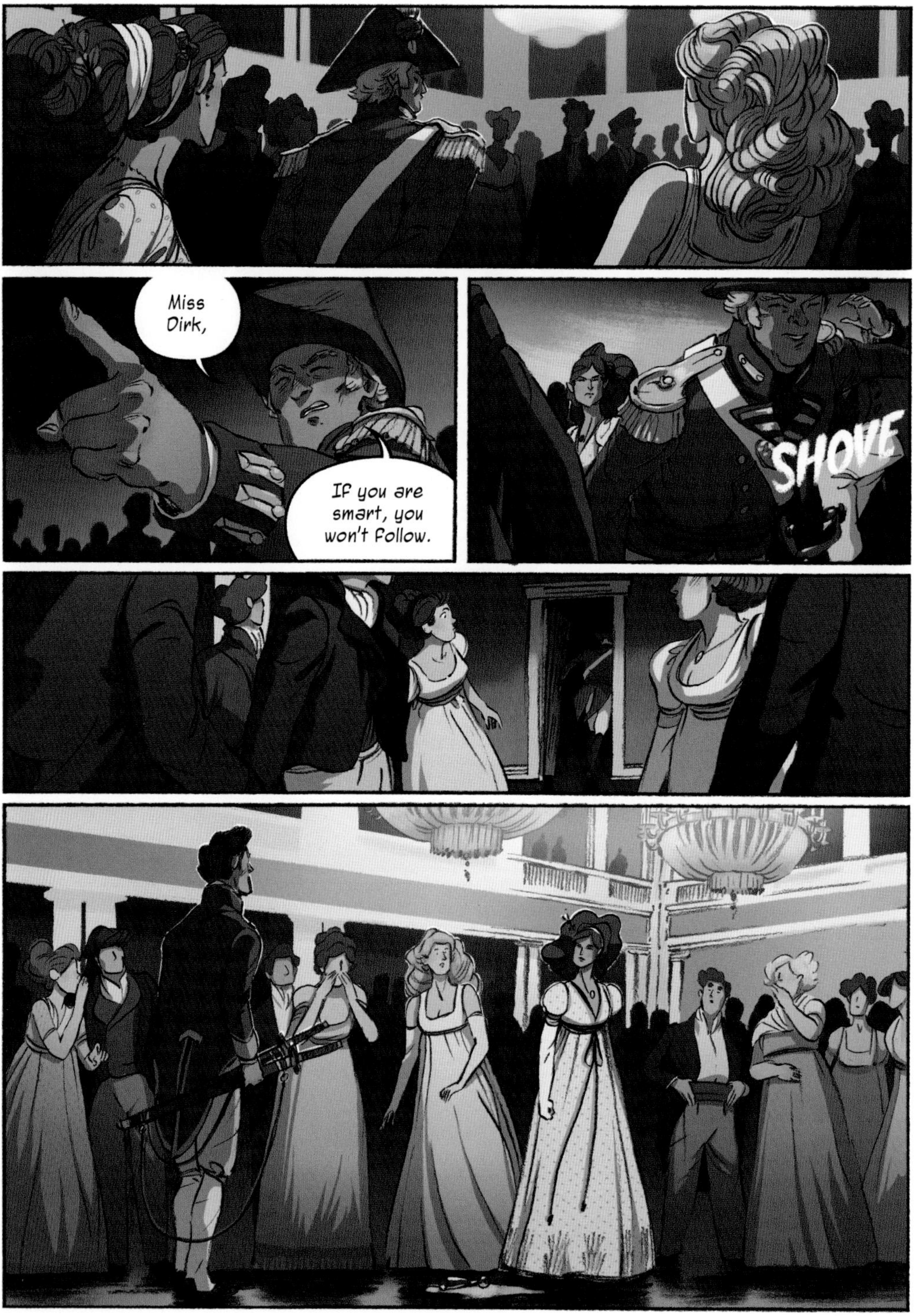
Miss Dirk,
If you are smart, you won't follow.
SHOVE

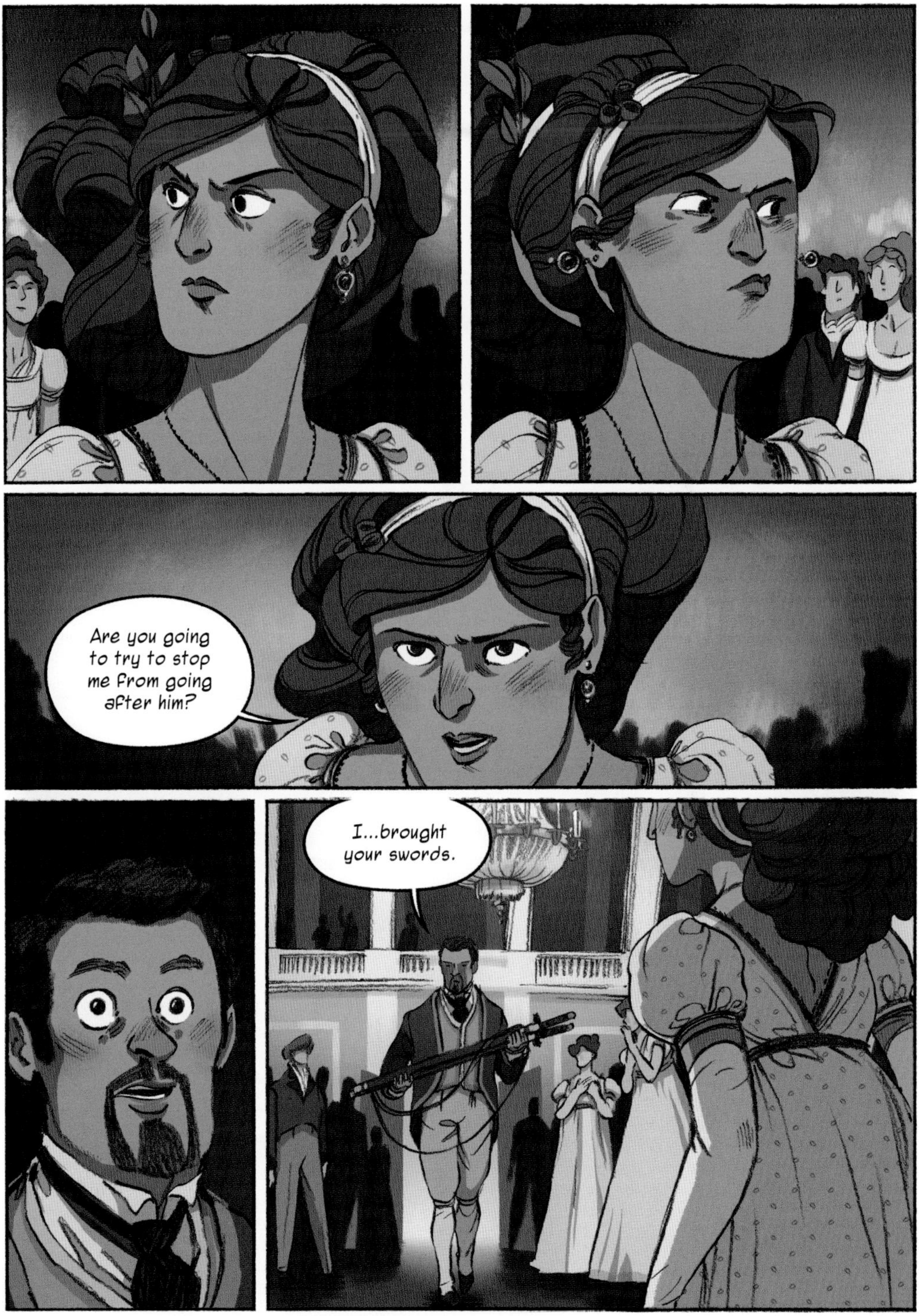
Are you going to try to stop me from going after him?
I...brought your swords.

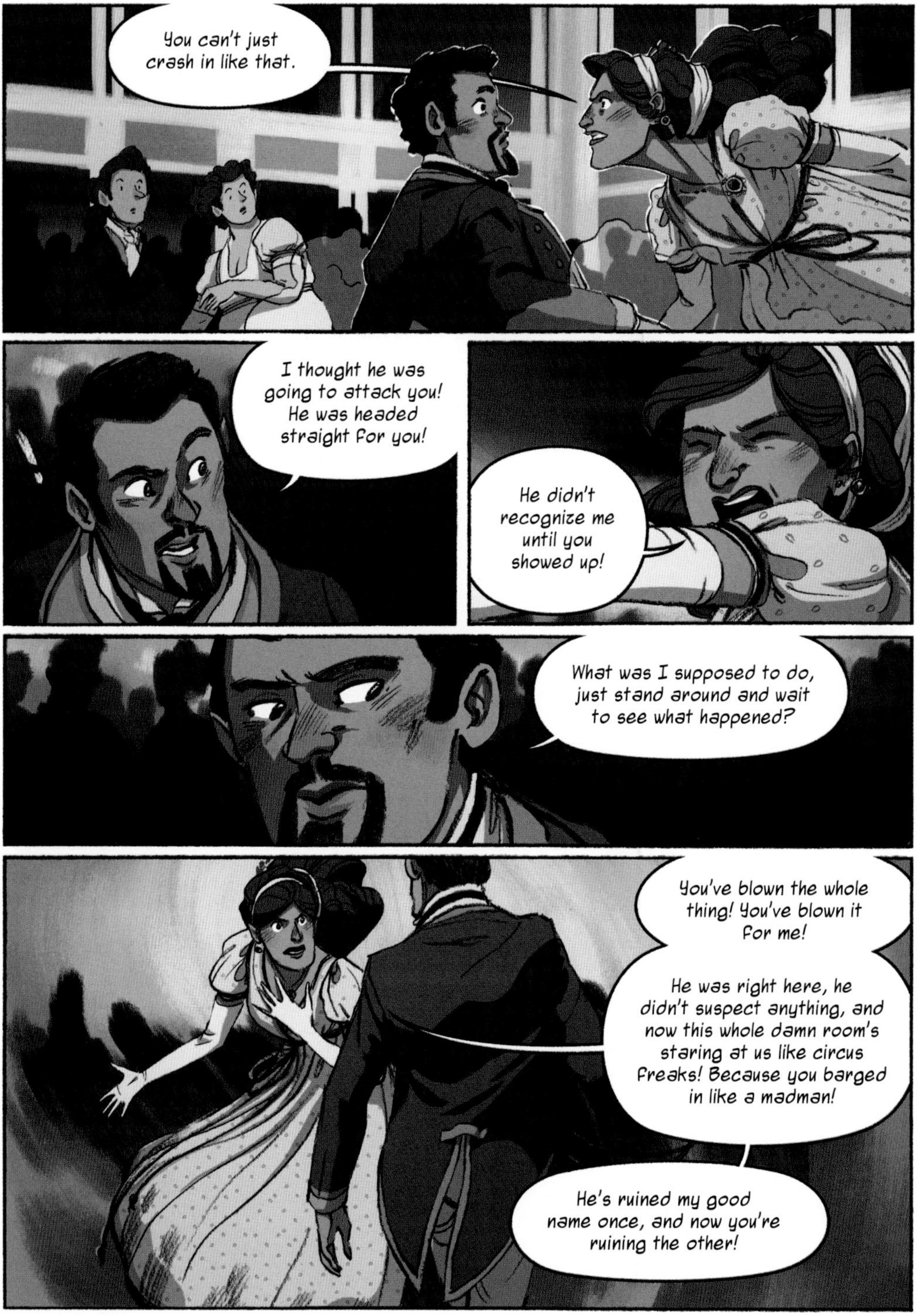
You can't just crash in like that.
I thought he was going to attack you! He was headed straight for you!
He didn't recognize me until you showed up!
What was I supposed to do, just stand around and wait to see what happened?
You've blown the whole thing! You've blown it for me!
He was right here, he didn't suspect anything, and now this whole damn room's staring at us like circus freaks! Because you barged in like a madman!
He's ruined my good name once, and now you're ruining the other!

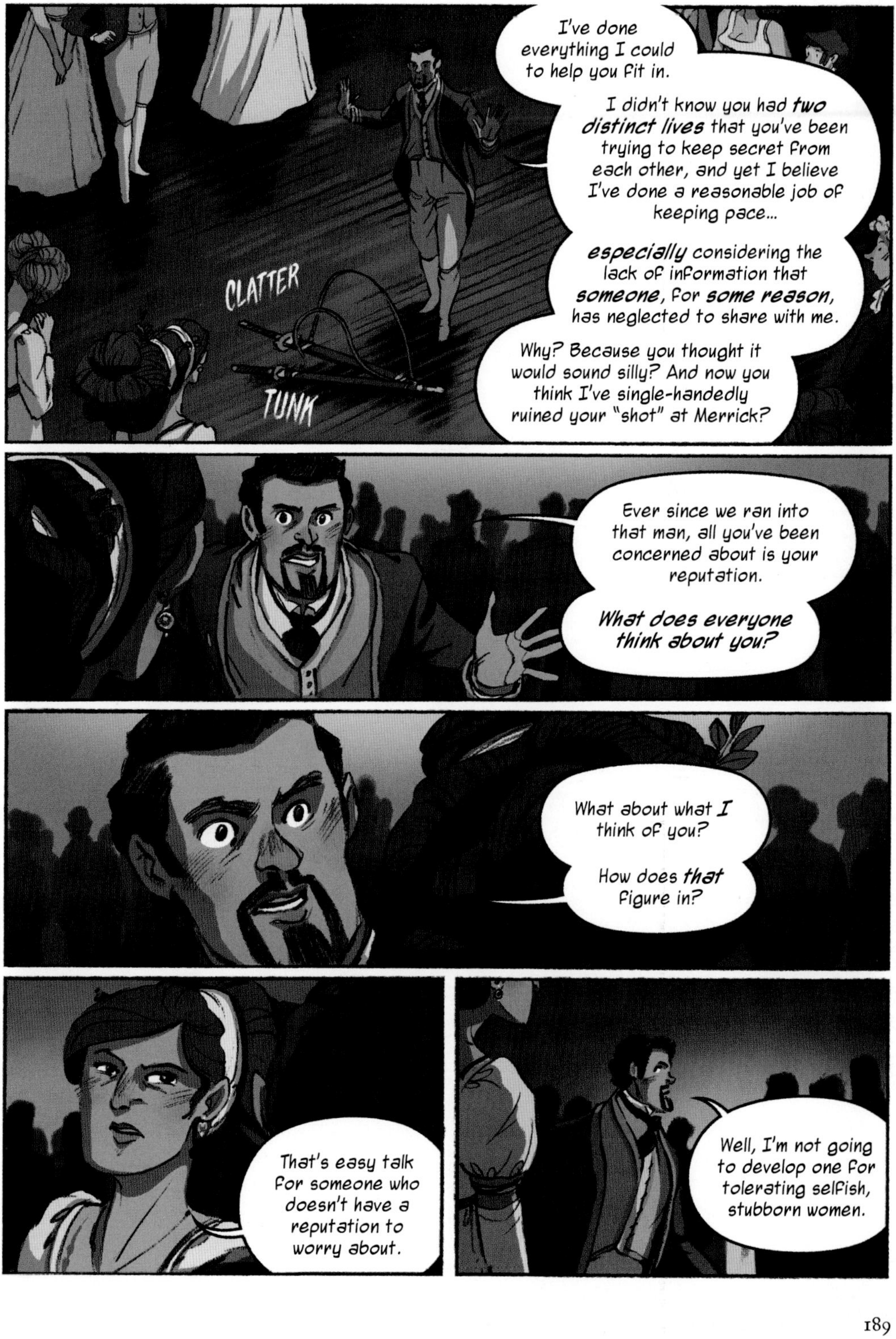
I've done everything I could to help you fit in.
I didn't know you had *two distinct lives* that you've been trying to keep secret from each other, and yet I believe I've done a reasonable job of keeping pace...
*especially* considering the lack of information that *someone*, for *some reason*, has neglected to share with me.
CLATTER
TUNK
Why? Because you thought it would sound silly? And now you think I've single-handedly ruined your "shot" at Merrick?
Ever since we ran into that man, all you've been concerned about is your reputation.
*What does everyone think about you?*
What about what *I* think of you?
How does *that* figure in?
That's easy talk for someone who doesn't have a reputation to worry about.
Well, I'm not going to develop one for tolerating selfish, stubborn women.

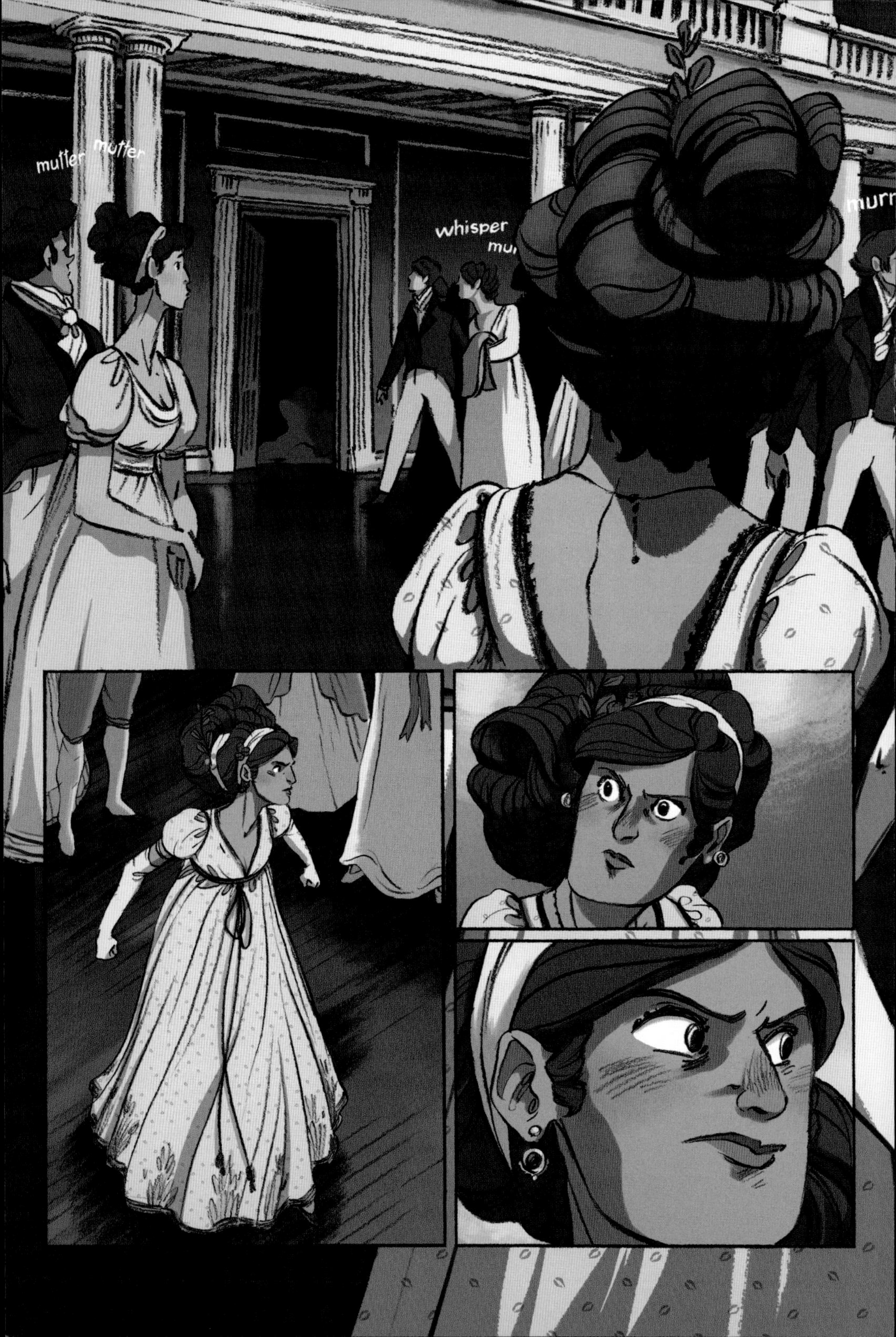
mutter
mutter
whisper

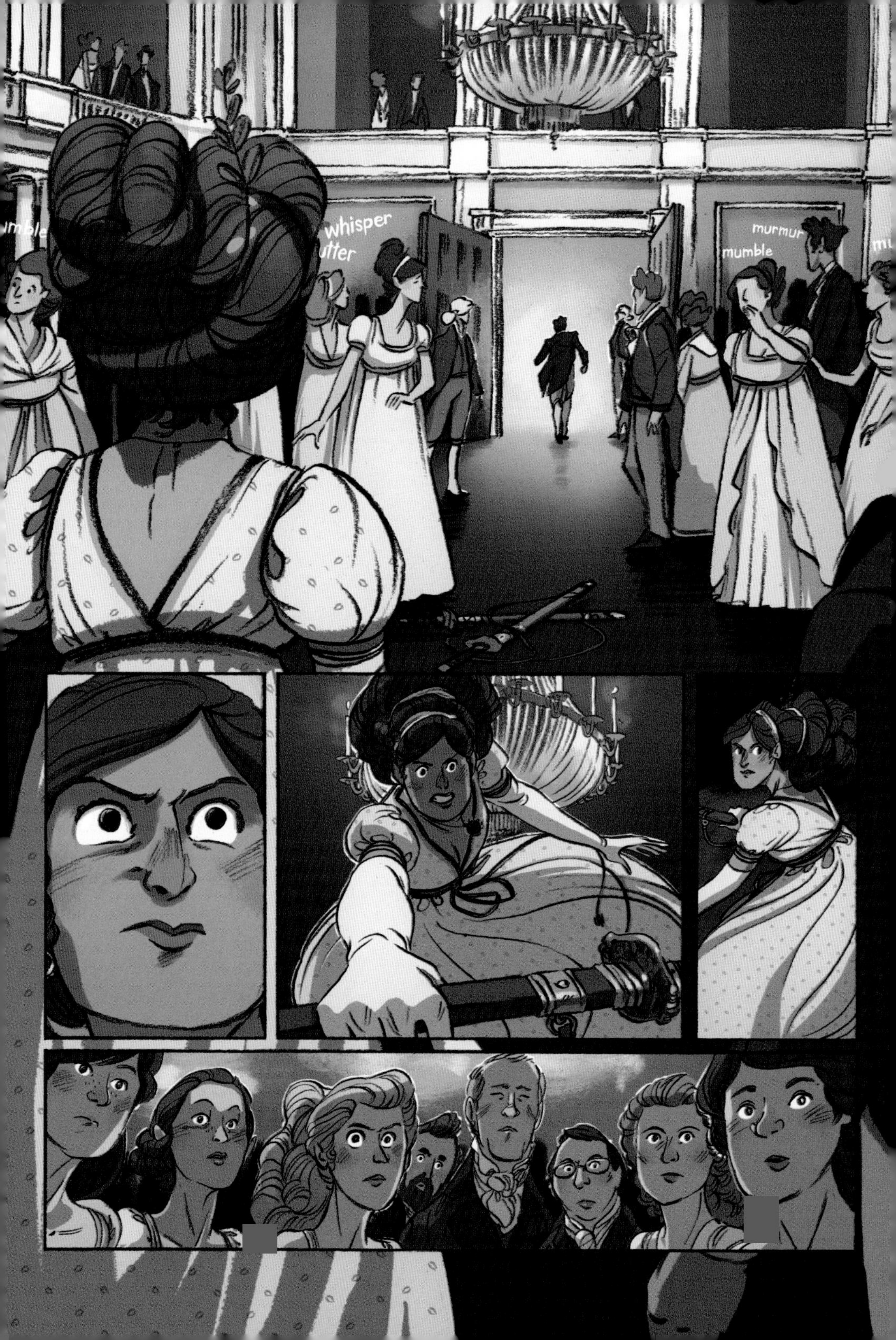
whisper
murmur
mumble

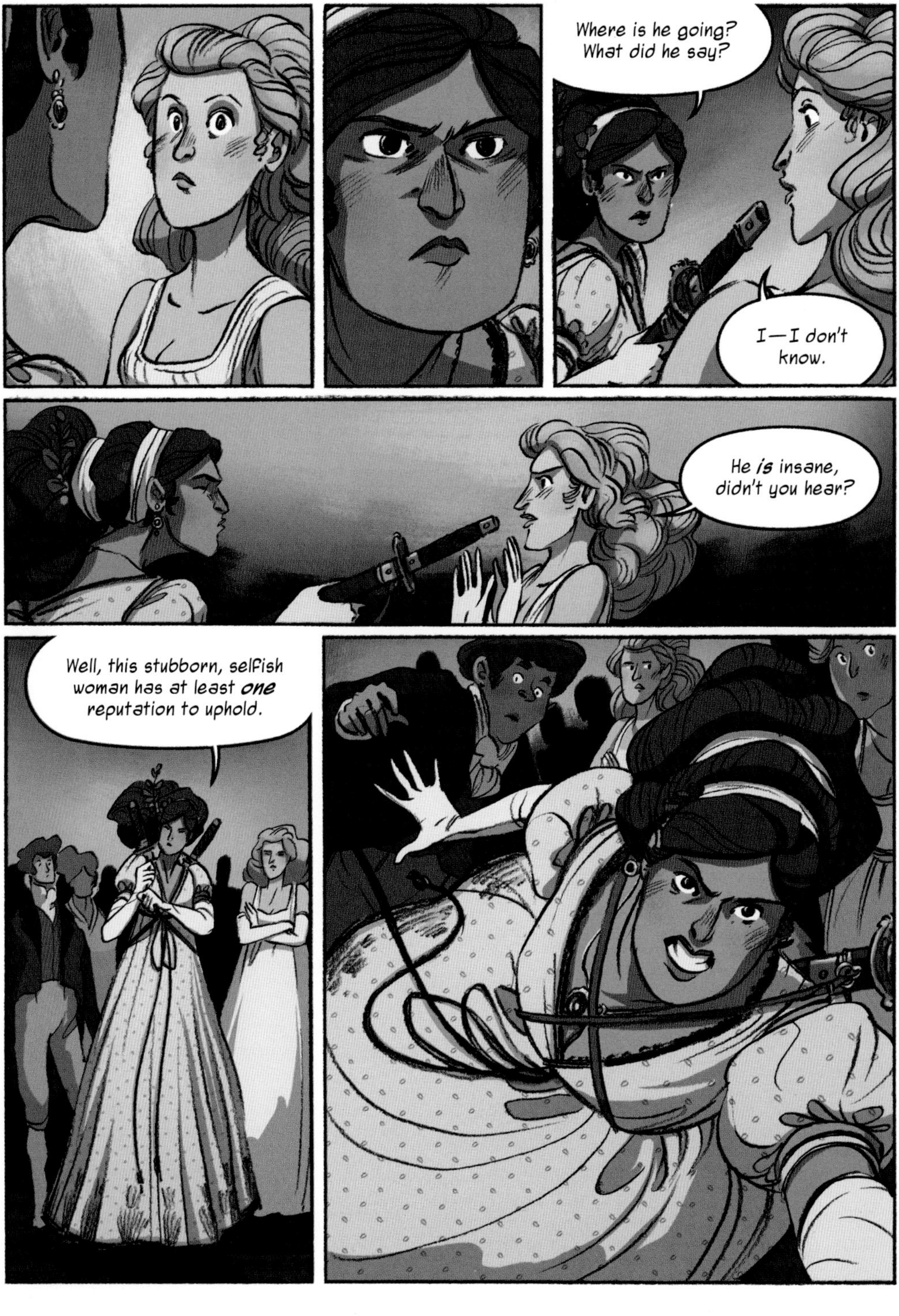
Where is he going? What did he say?
I—I don't know.
He *is* insane, didn't you hear?
Well, this stubborn, selfish woman has at least ***one*** reputation to uphold.

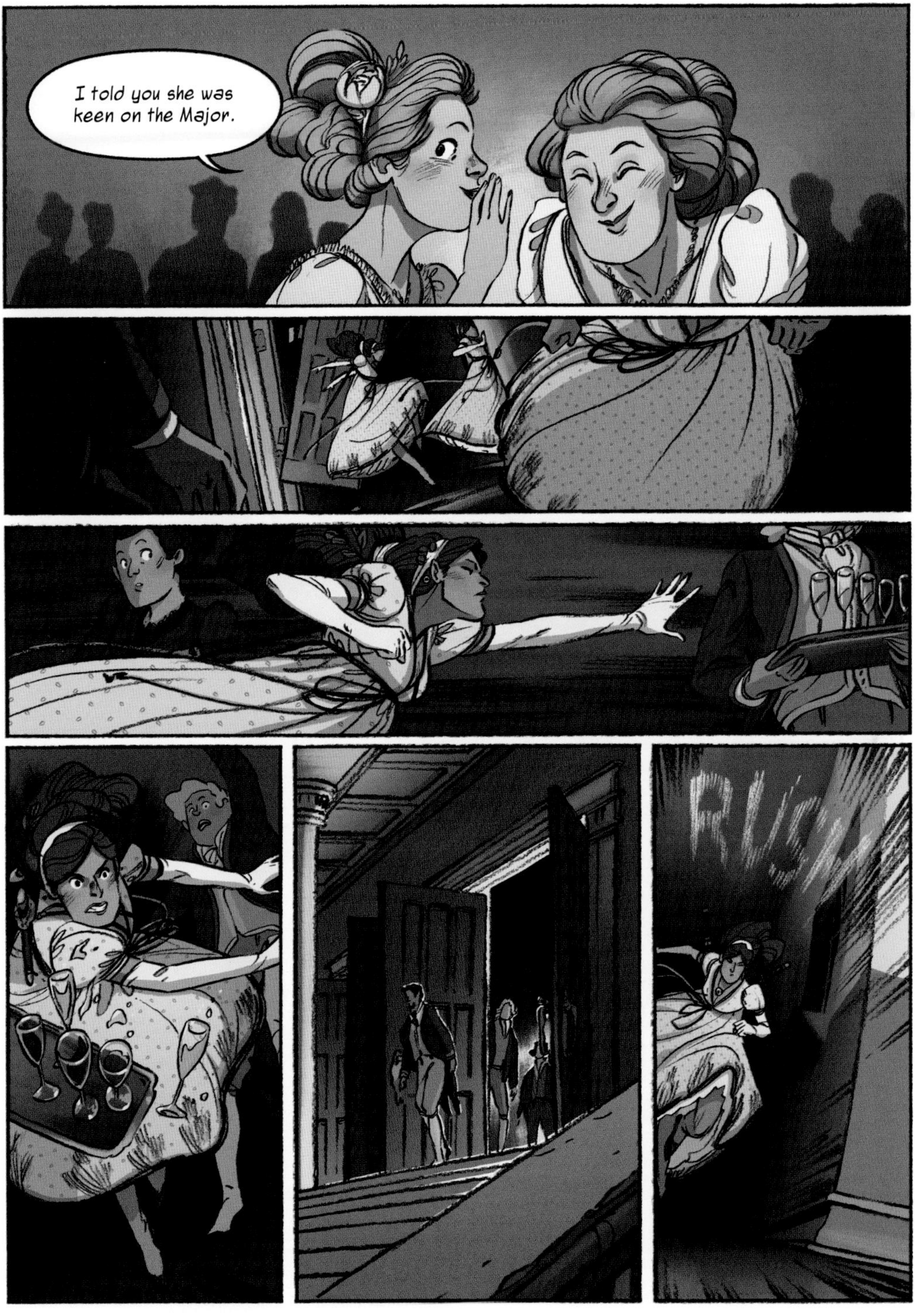
I told you she was keen on the Major.
RUSH

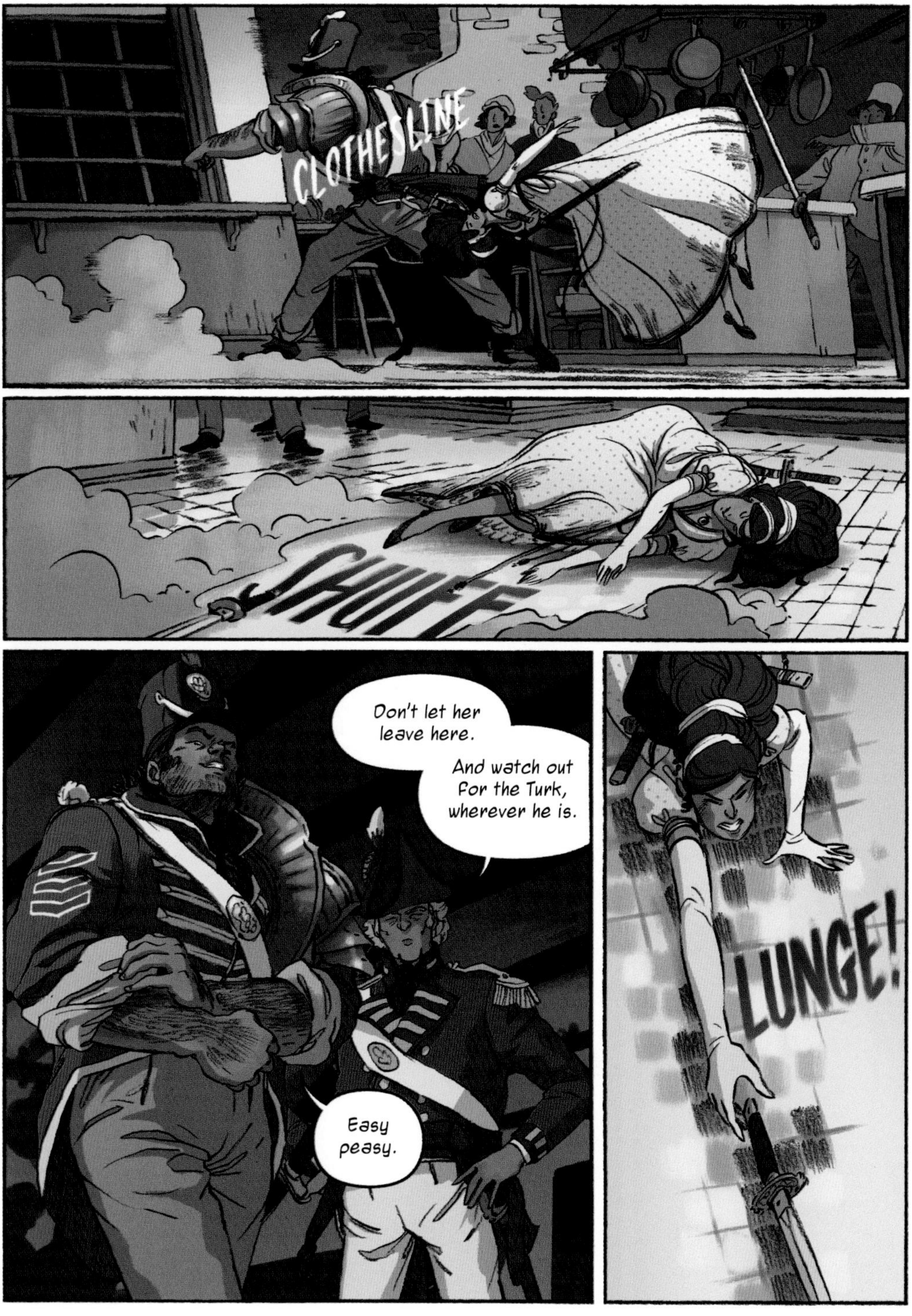
CLOTHESLINE
SCUFF
Don't let her leave here.
And watch out for the Turk, wherever he is.
Easy peasy.
LUNGE!

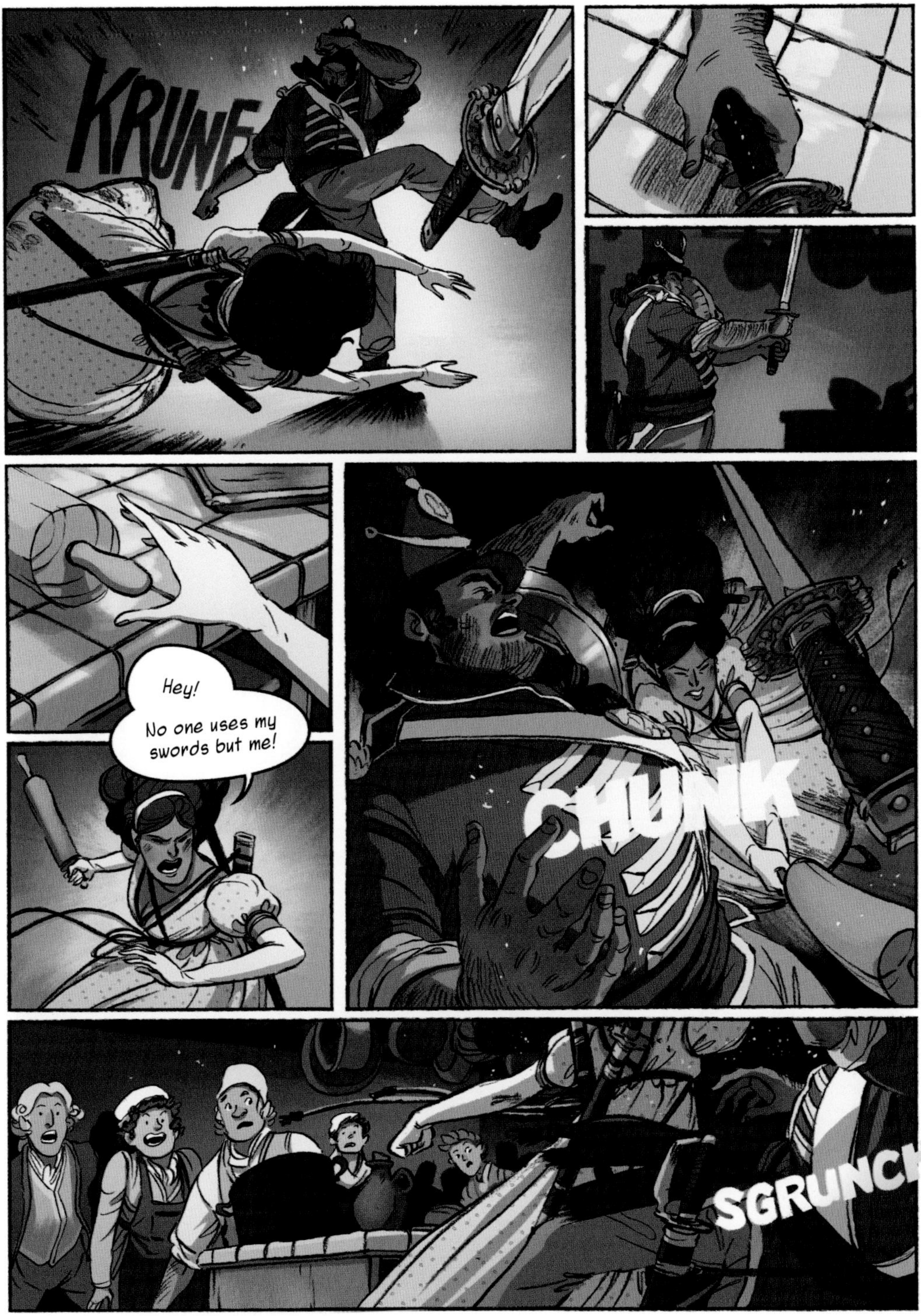
KRUNF
Hey!
No one uses my swords but me!
CHUNK
SGRUNCH

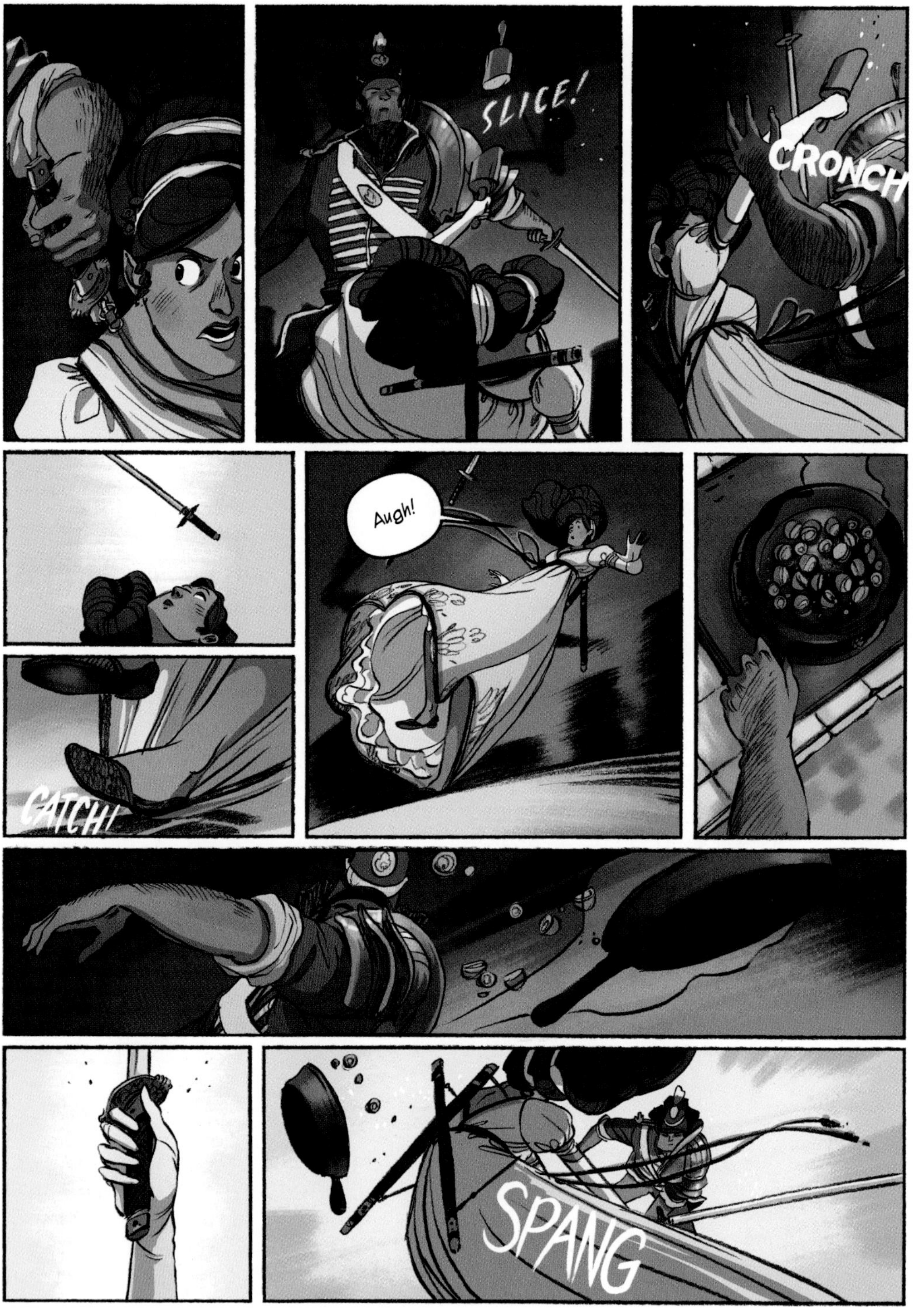
SLICE!
CRONCH
Augh!
CATCH!
SPANG

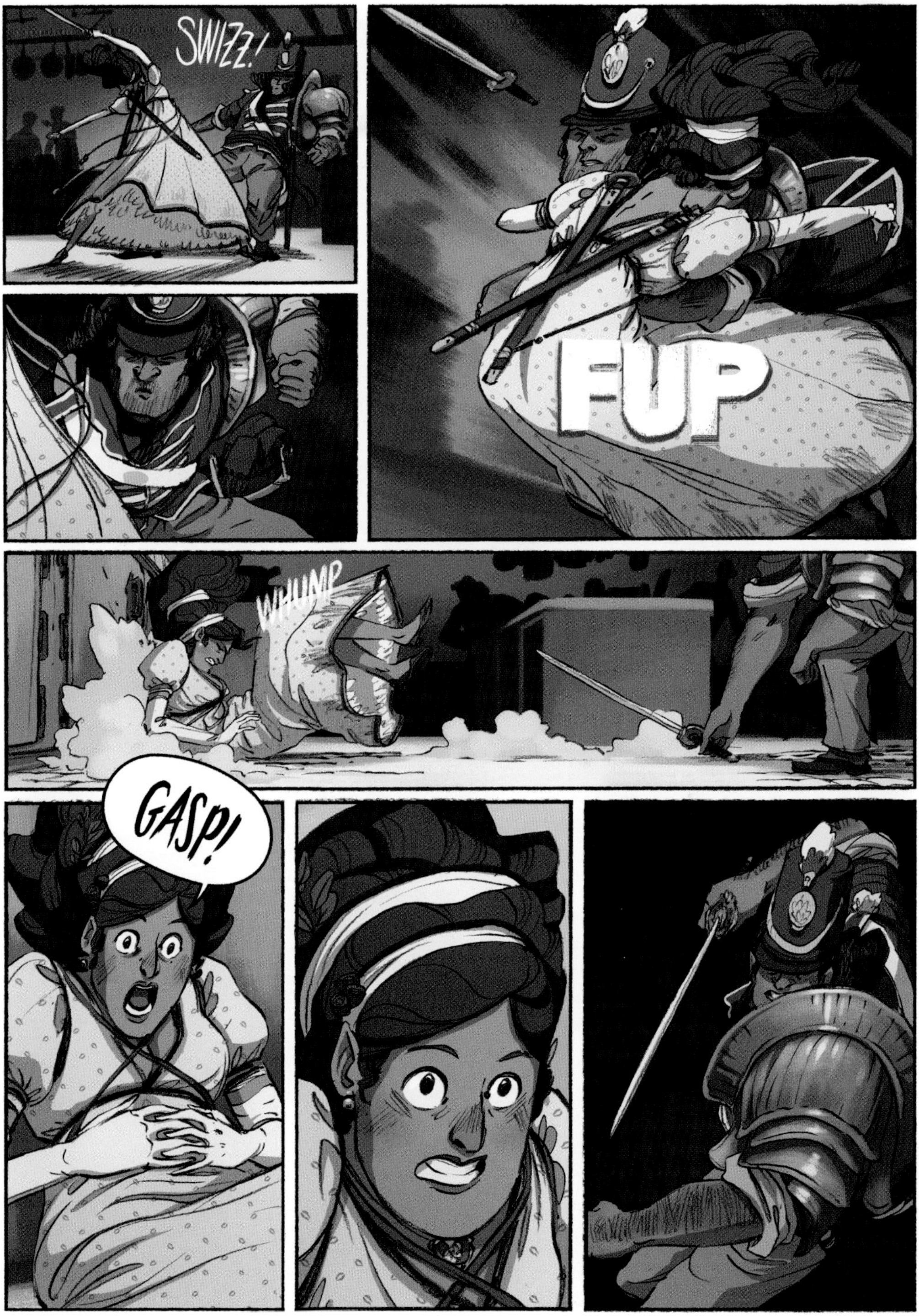
SWIZZ!
FUP
WHUMP
GASP!

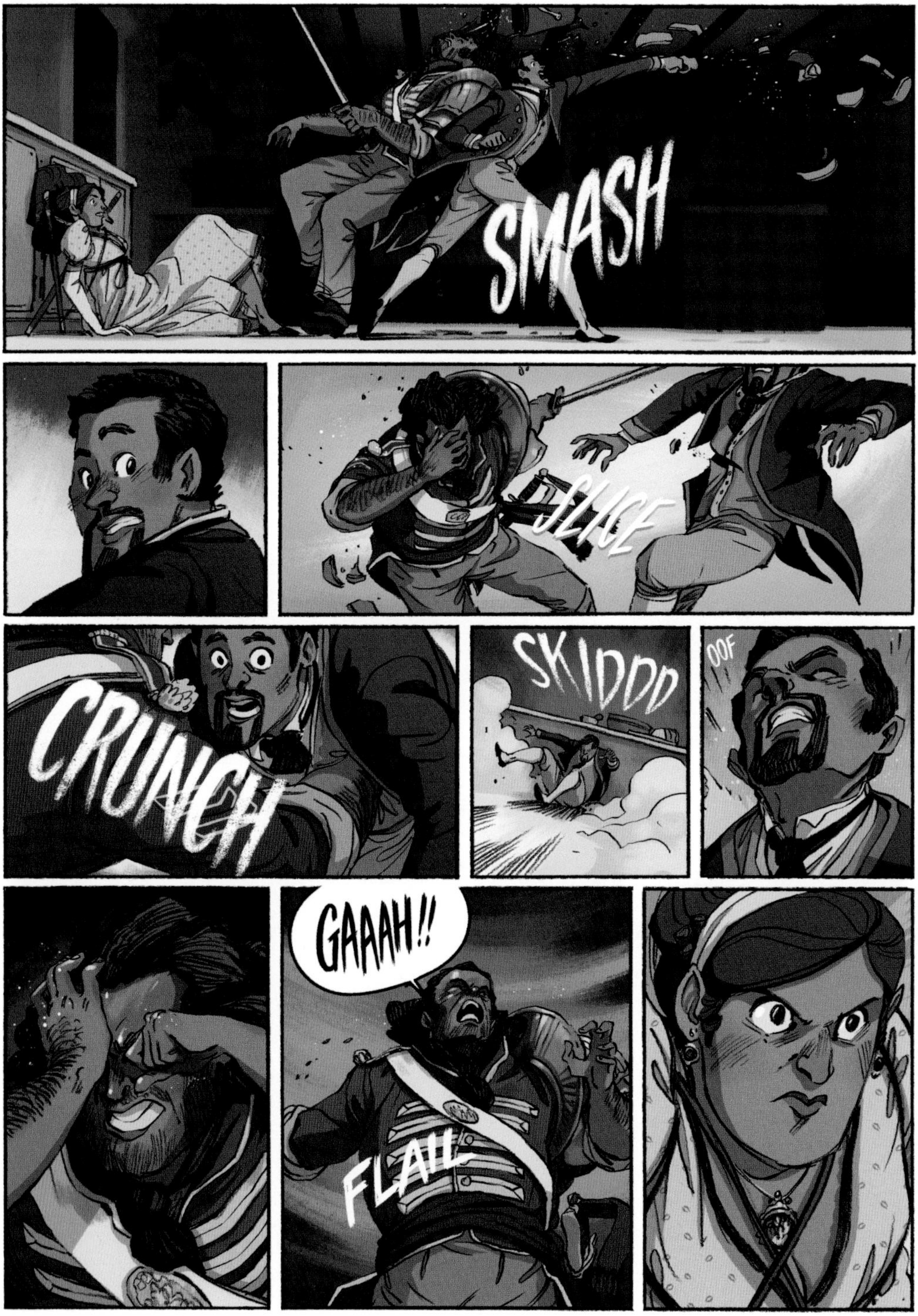
SMASH
SLICE
CRUNCH
SKIDDD
OOF
GAAAH!!
FLAIL

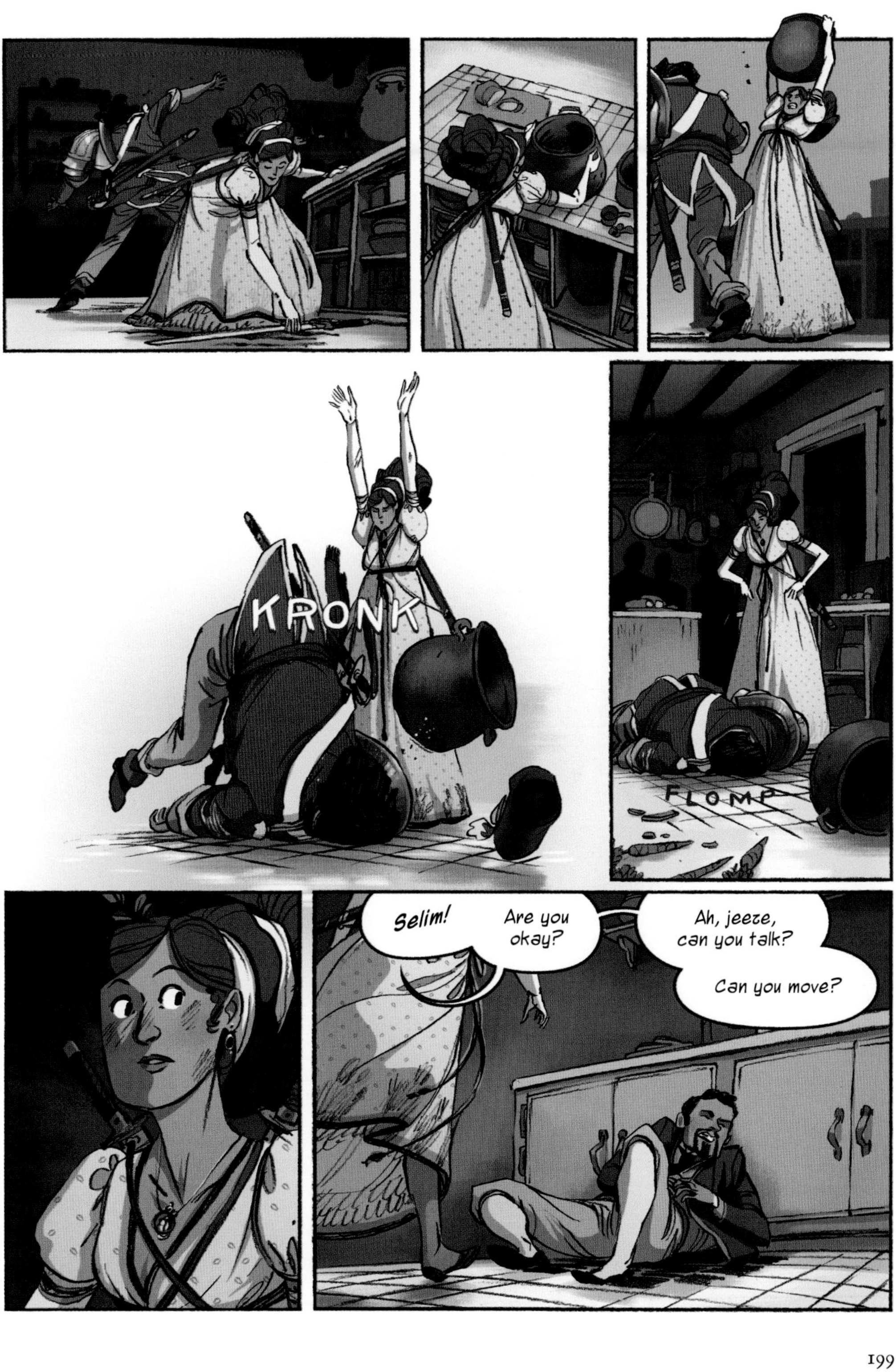
KRONK
FLOMP
Selim!
Are you okay?
Ah, jeeze, can you talk?
Can you move?

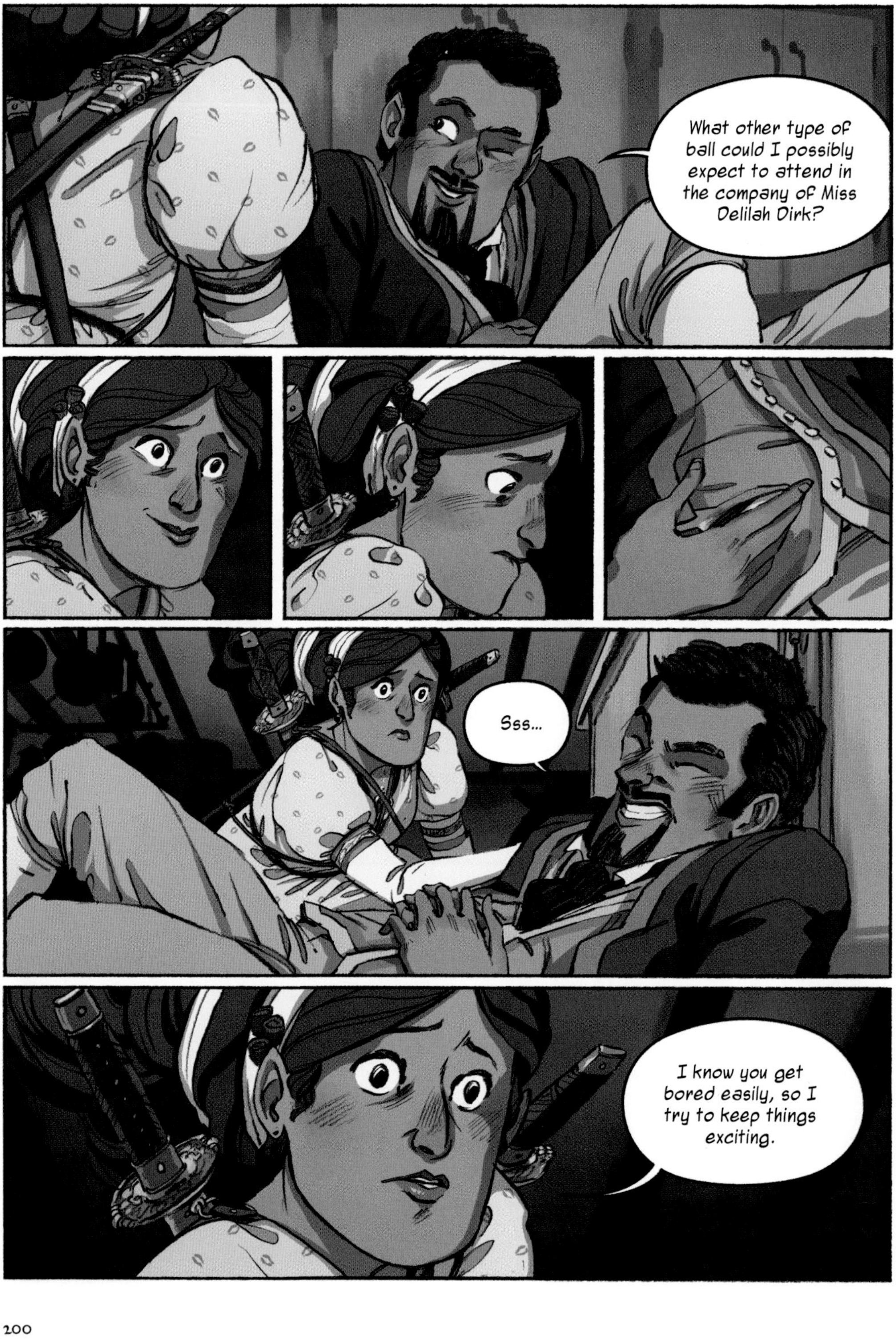
What other type of ball could I possibly expect to attend in the company of Miss Delilah Dirk?
Sss...
I know you get bored easily, so I try to keep things exciting.

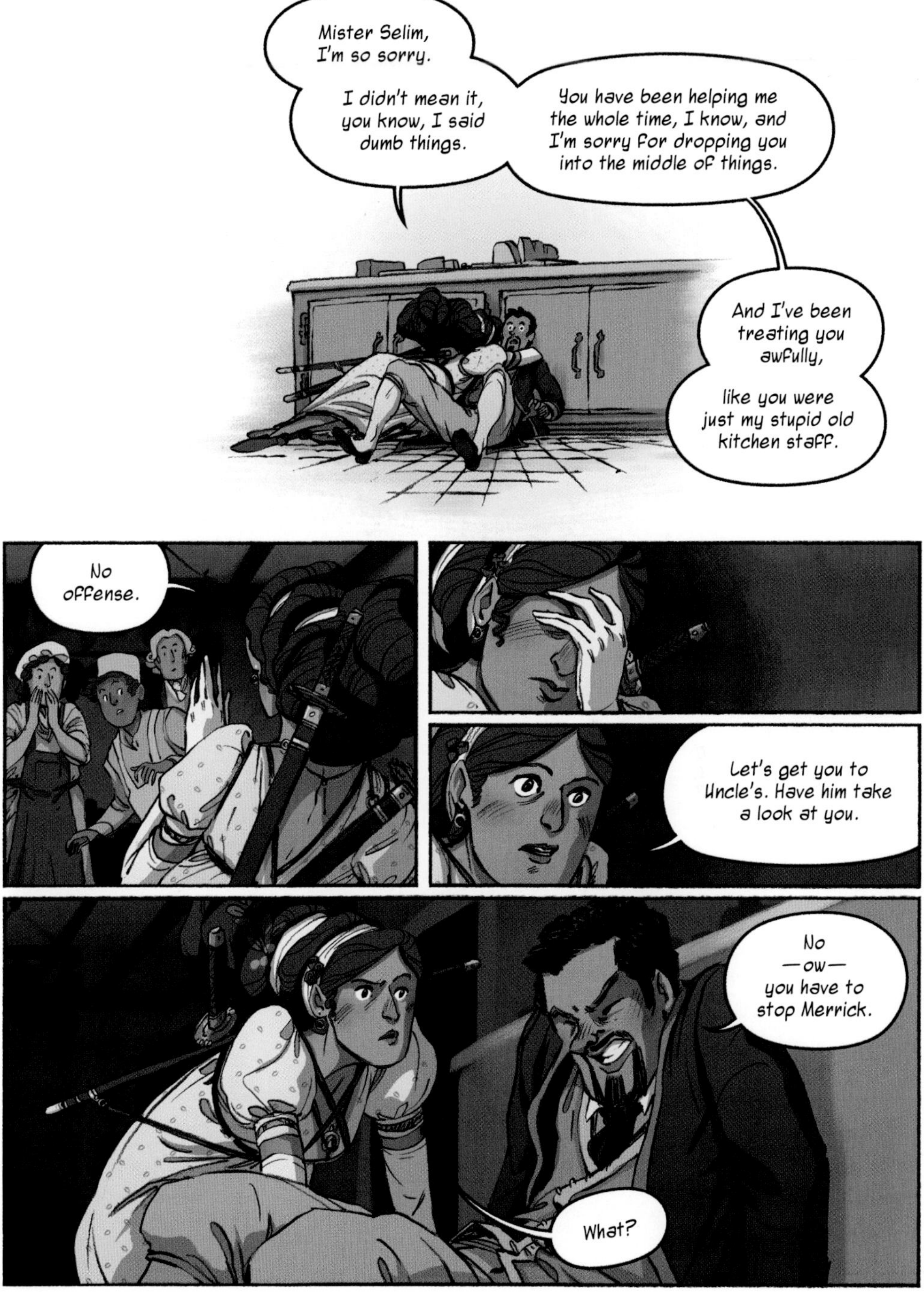
Mister Selim, I'm so sorry.
I didn't mean it, you know, I said dumb things.
You have been helping me the whole time, I know, and I'm sorry for dropping you into the middle of things.
And I've been treating you awfully,
like you were just my stupid old kitchen staff.
No offense.
Let's get you to Uncle's. Have him take a look at you.
No —ow— you have to stop Merrick.
What?

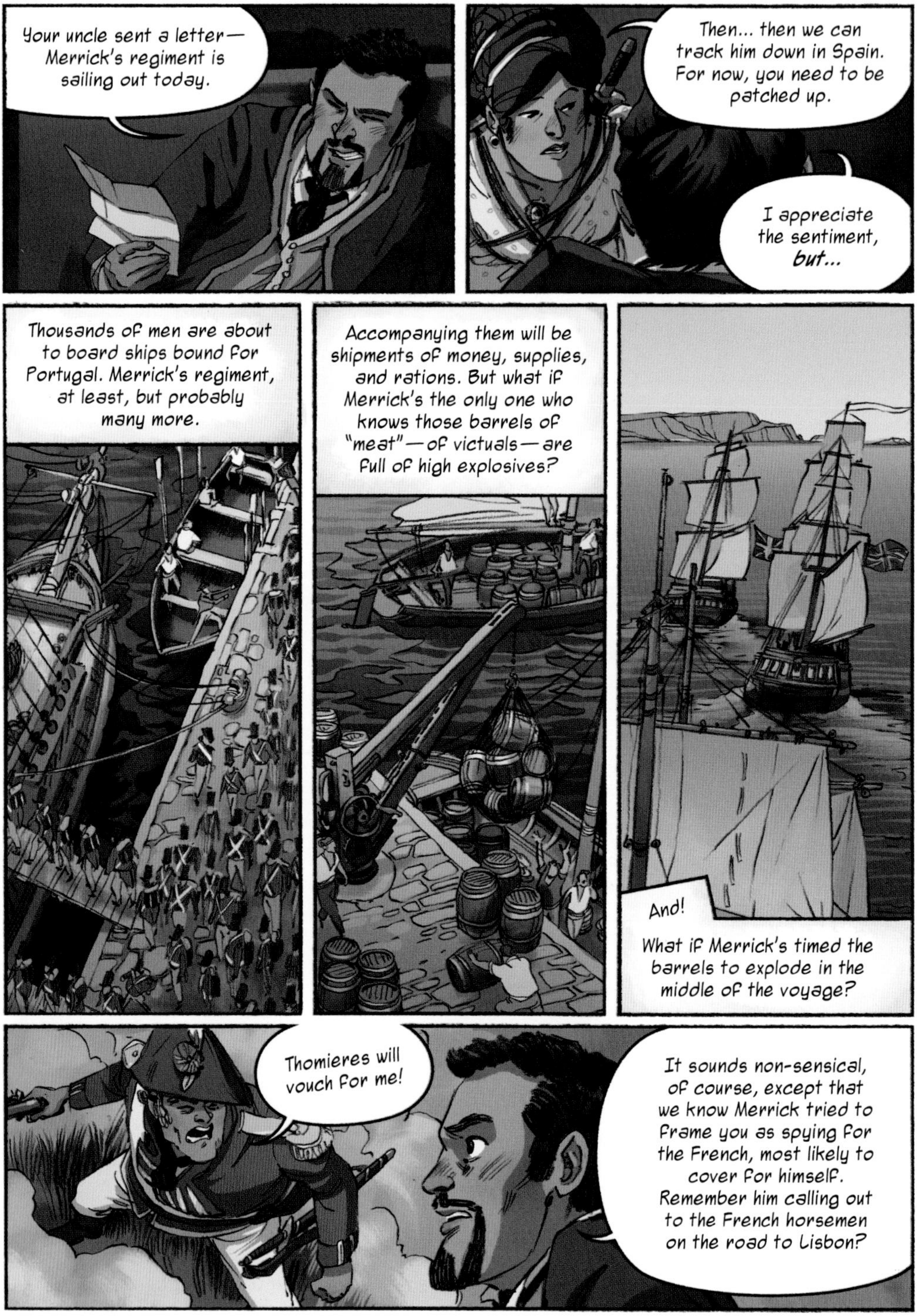

Your uncle sent a letter— Merrick's regiment is sailing out today.
Then... then we can track him down in Spain. For now, you need to be patched up.
I appreciate the sentiment, *but...*
Thousands of men are about to board ships bound for Portugal. Merrick's regiment, at least, but probably many more.
Accompanying them will be shipments of money, supplies, and rations. But what if Merrick's the only one who knows those barrels of "meat"—of victuals—are full of high explosives?
And!
What if Merrick's timed the barrels to explode in the middle of the voyage?
Thomieres will vouch for me!
It sounds non-sensical, of course, except that we know Merrick tried to frame you as spying for the French, most likely to cover for himself. Remember him calling out to the French horsemen on the road to Lisbon?

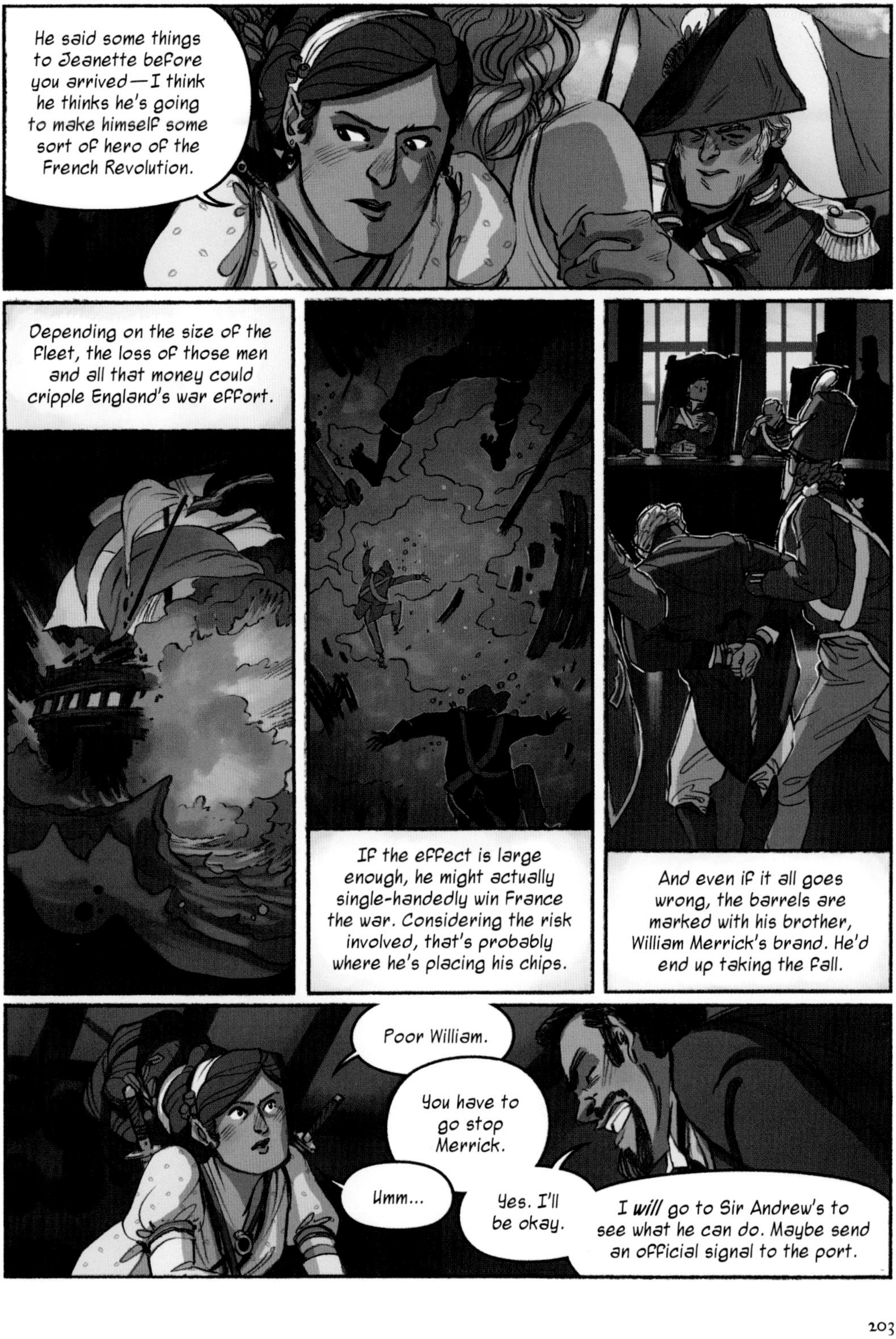
He said some things to Jeanette before you arrived—I think he thinks he's going to make himself some sort of hero of the French Revolution.
Depending on the size of the fleet, the loss of those men and all that money could cripple England's war effort.
If the effect is large enough, he might actually single-handedly win France the war. Considering the risk involved, that's probably where he's placing his chips.
And even if it all goes wrong, the barrels are marked with his brother, William Merrick's brand. He'd end up taking the fall.
Poor William.
You have to go stop Merrick.
Umm...
Yes. I'll be okay.
I *will* go to Sir Andrew's to see what he can do. Maybe send an official signal to the port.

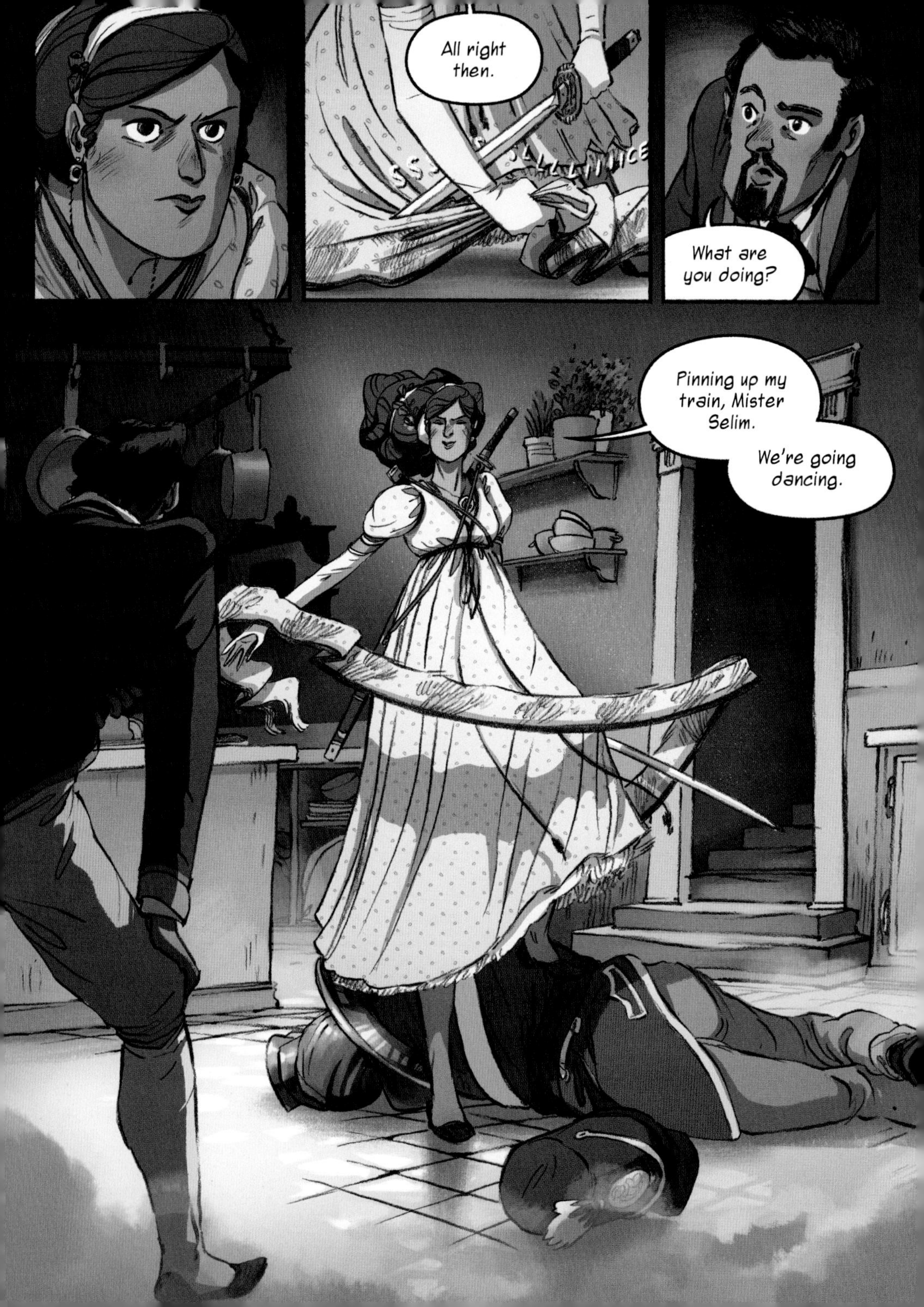
All right then.
What are you doing?
Pinning up my train, Mister Selim.
We're going dancing.

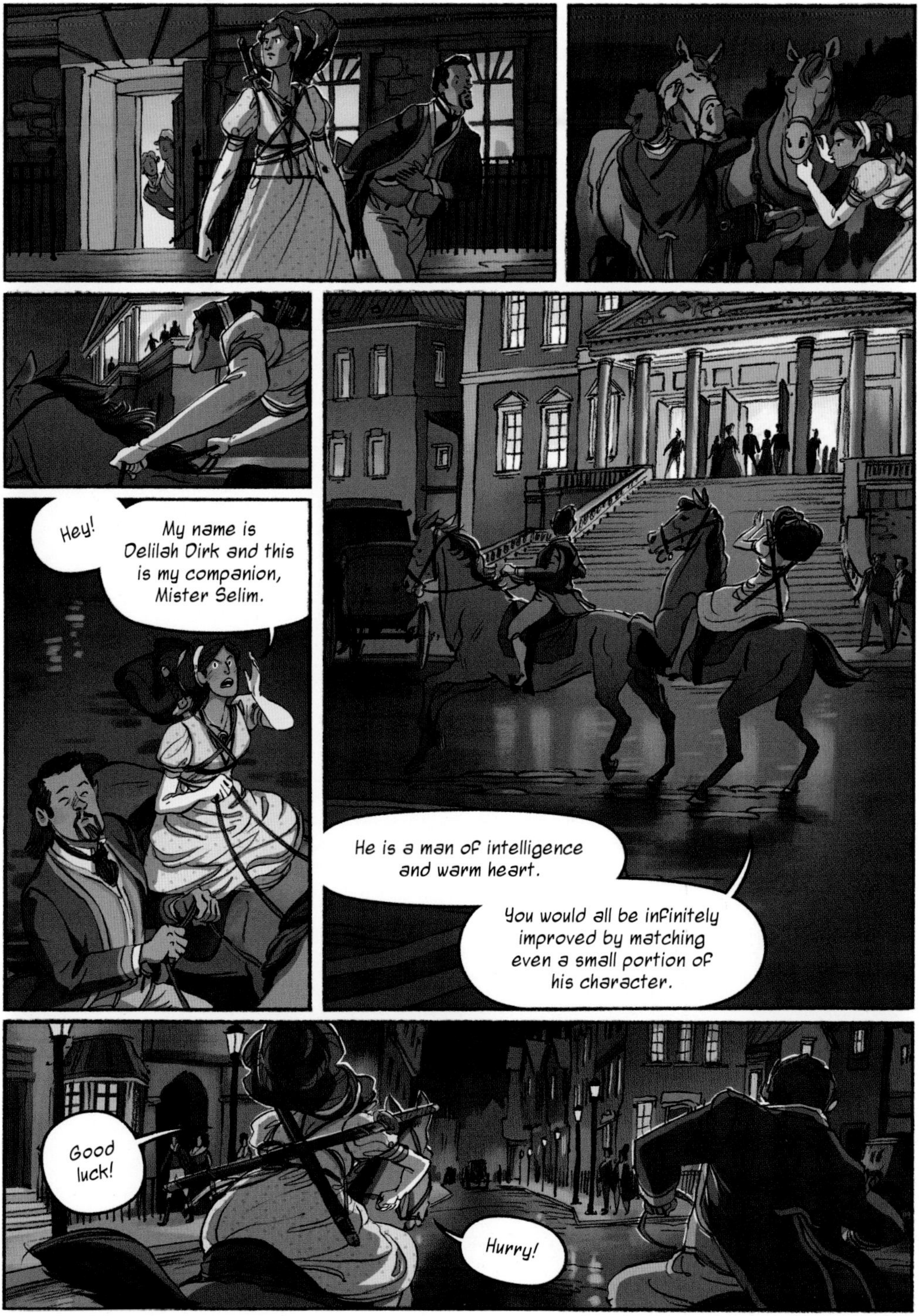
Hey!
My name is Delilah Dirk and this is my companion, Mister Selim.
He is a man of intelligence and warm heart.
You would all be infinitely improved by matching even a small portion of his character.
Good luck!
Hurry!

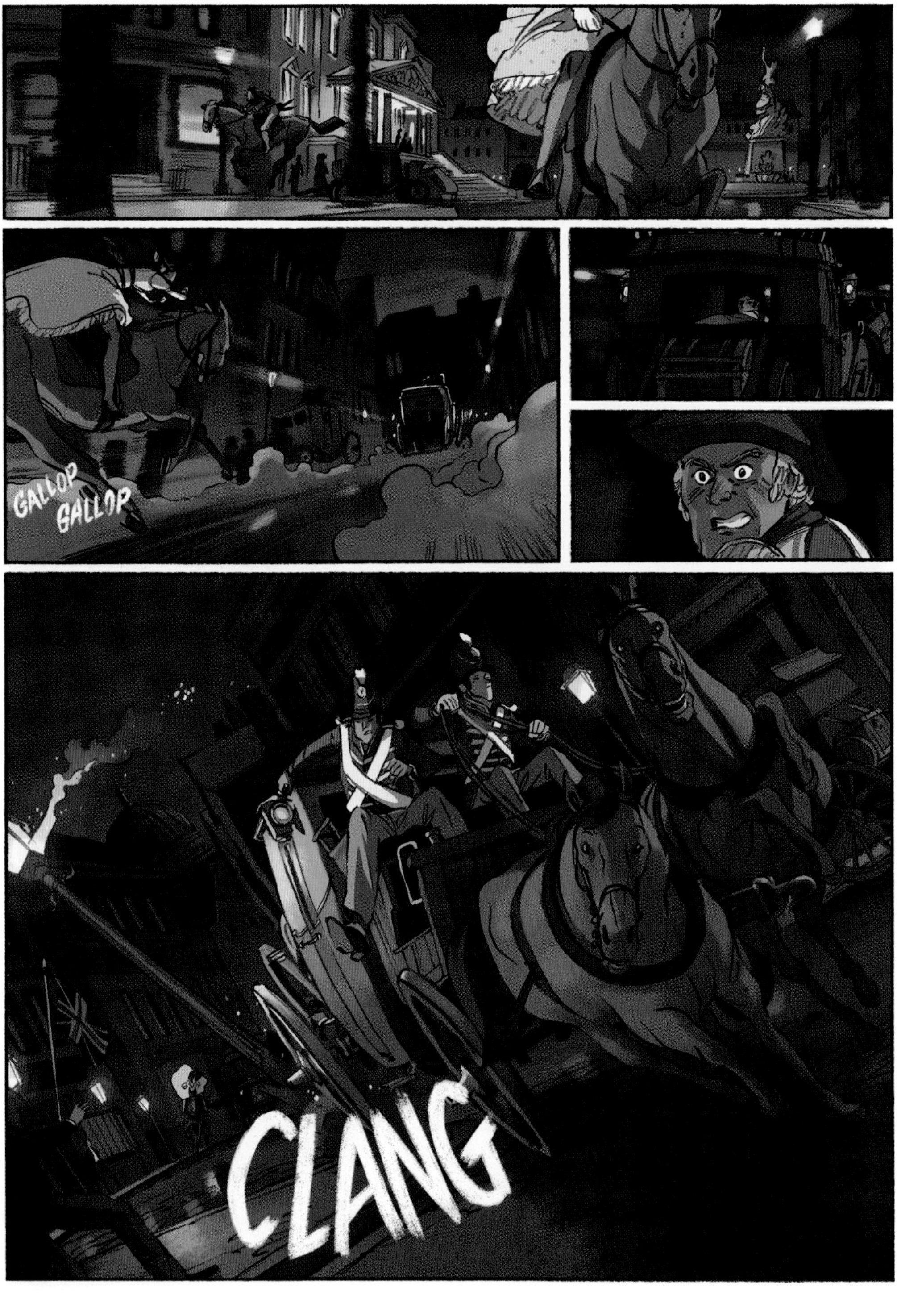
GALLOP GALLOP
CLANG

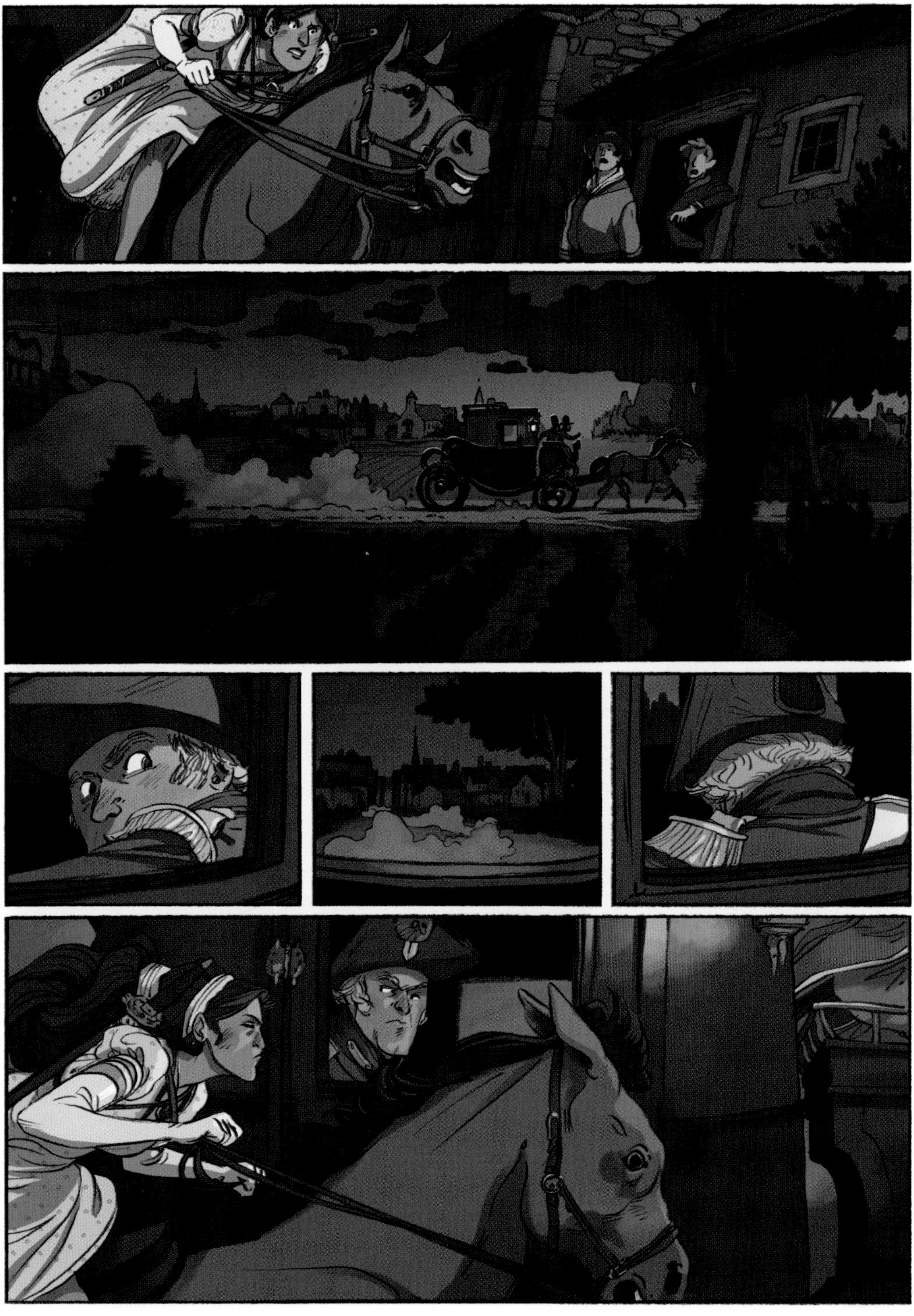

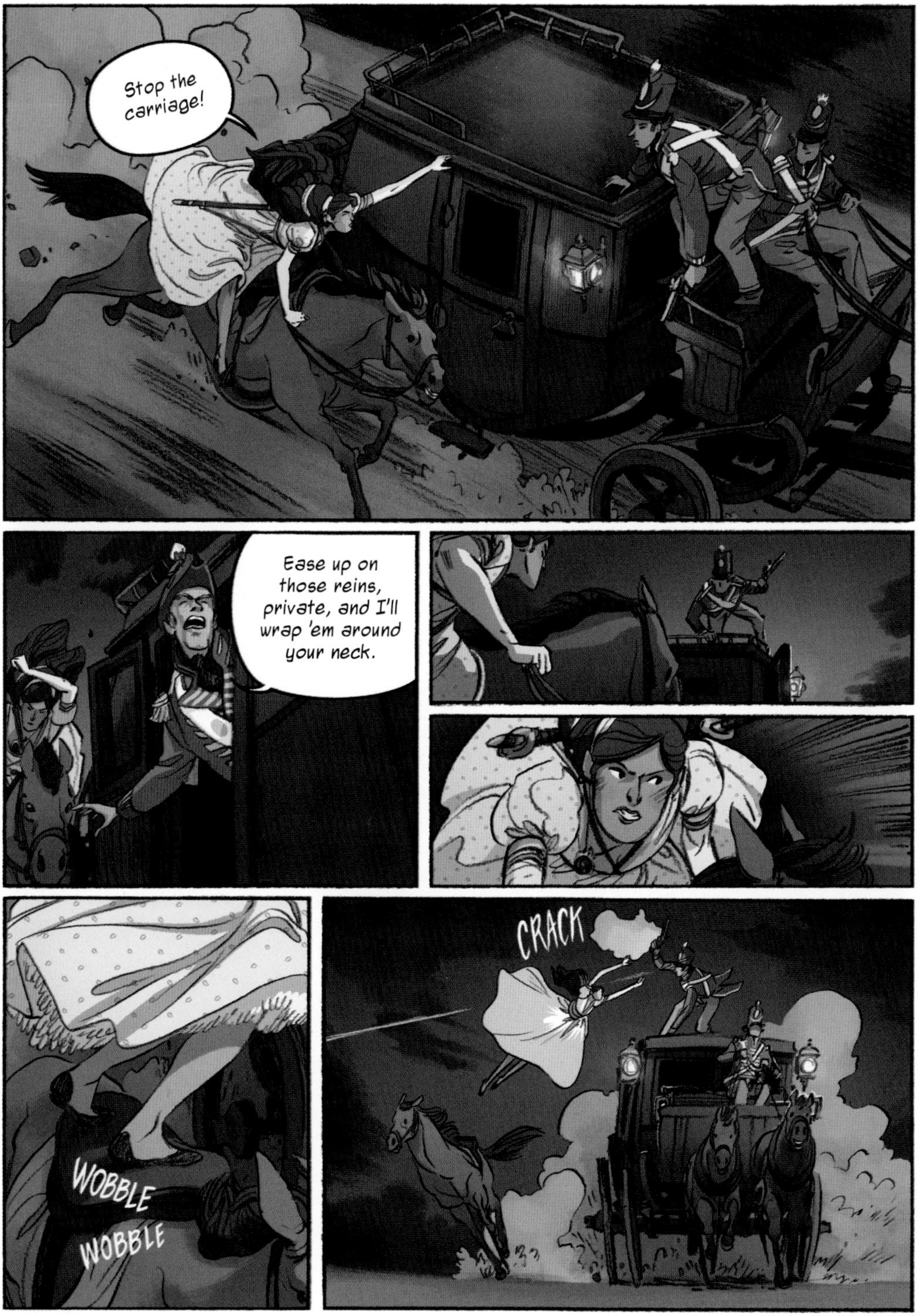
Stop the carriage!
Ease up on those reins, private, and I'll wrap 'em around your neck.
WOBBLE
WOBBLE
CRACK

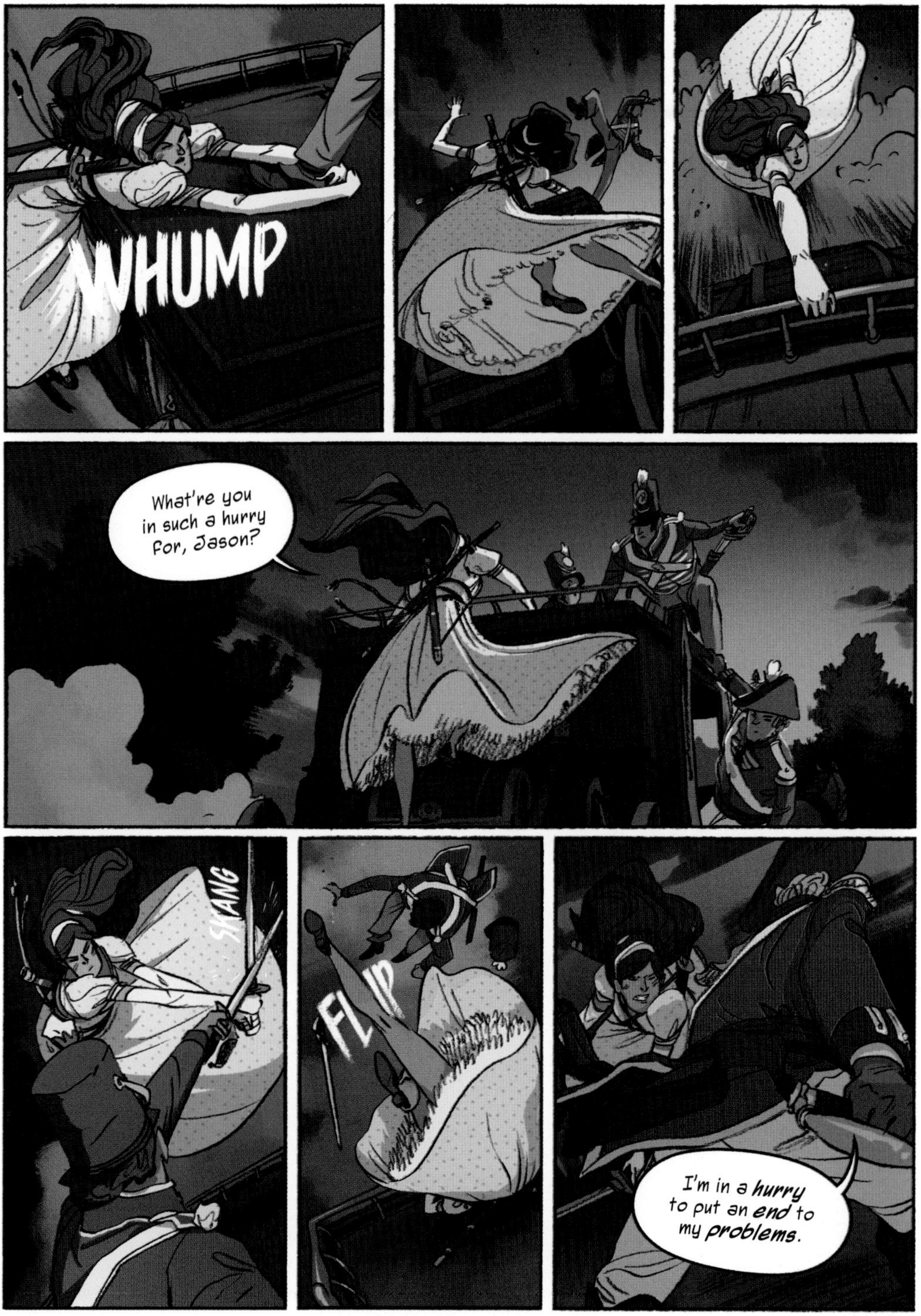
WHUMP
What're you in such a hurry for, Jason?
SKANG
FLIP
I'm in a *hurry* to put an *end* to my *problems*.

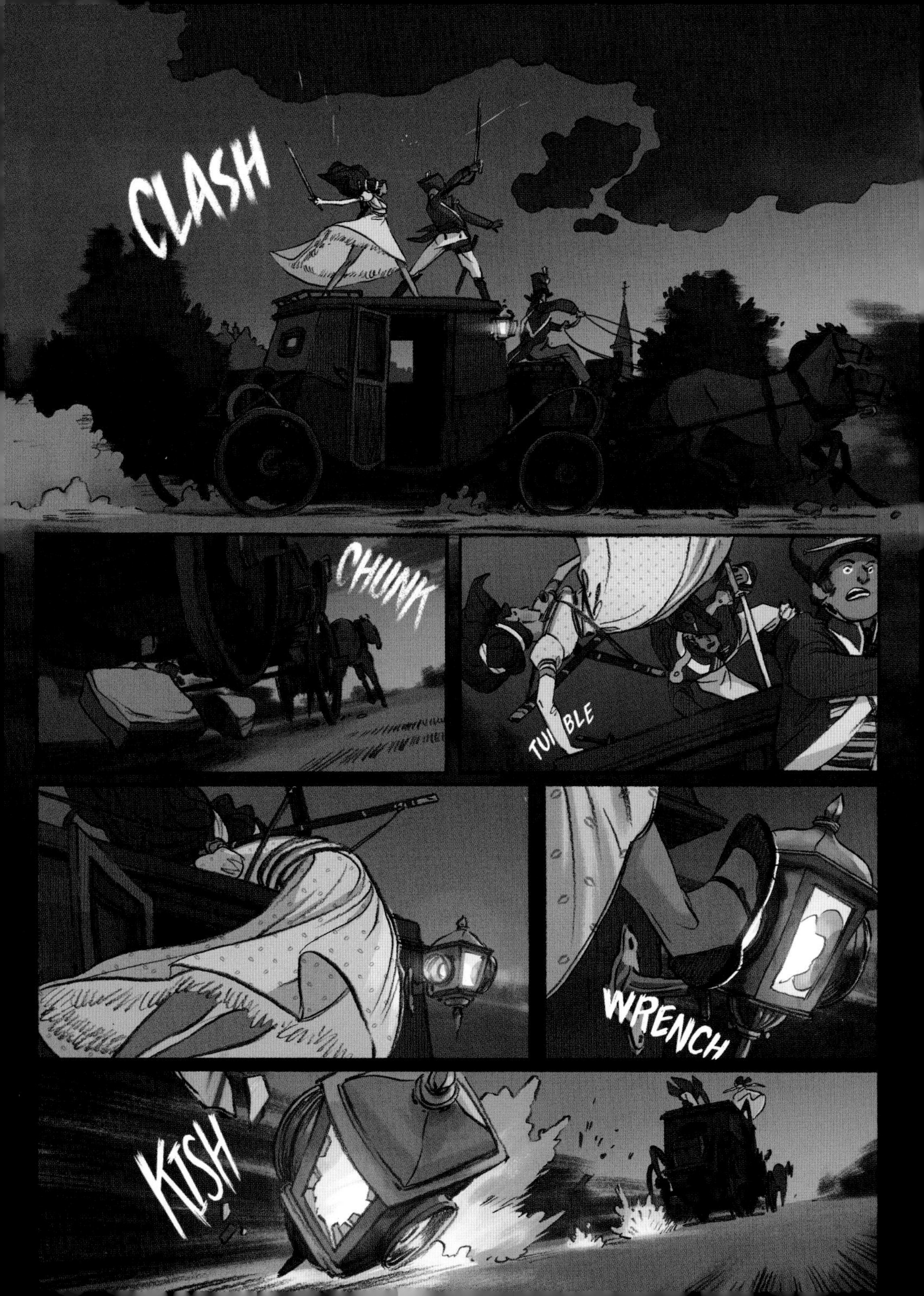
CLASH
CHUNK
TUMBLE
WRENCH
KISH

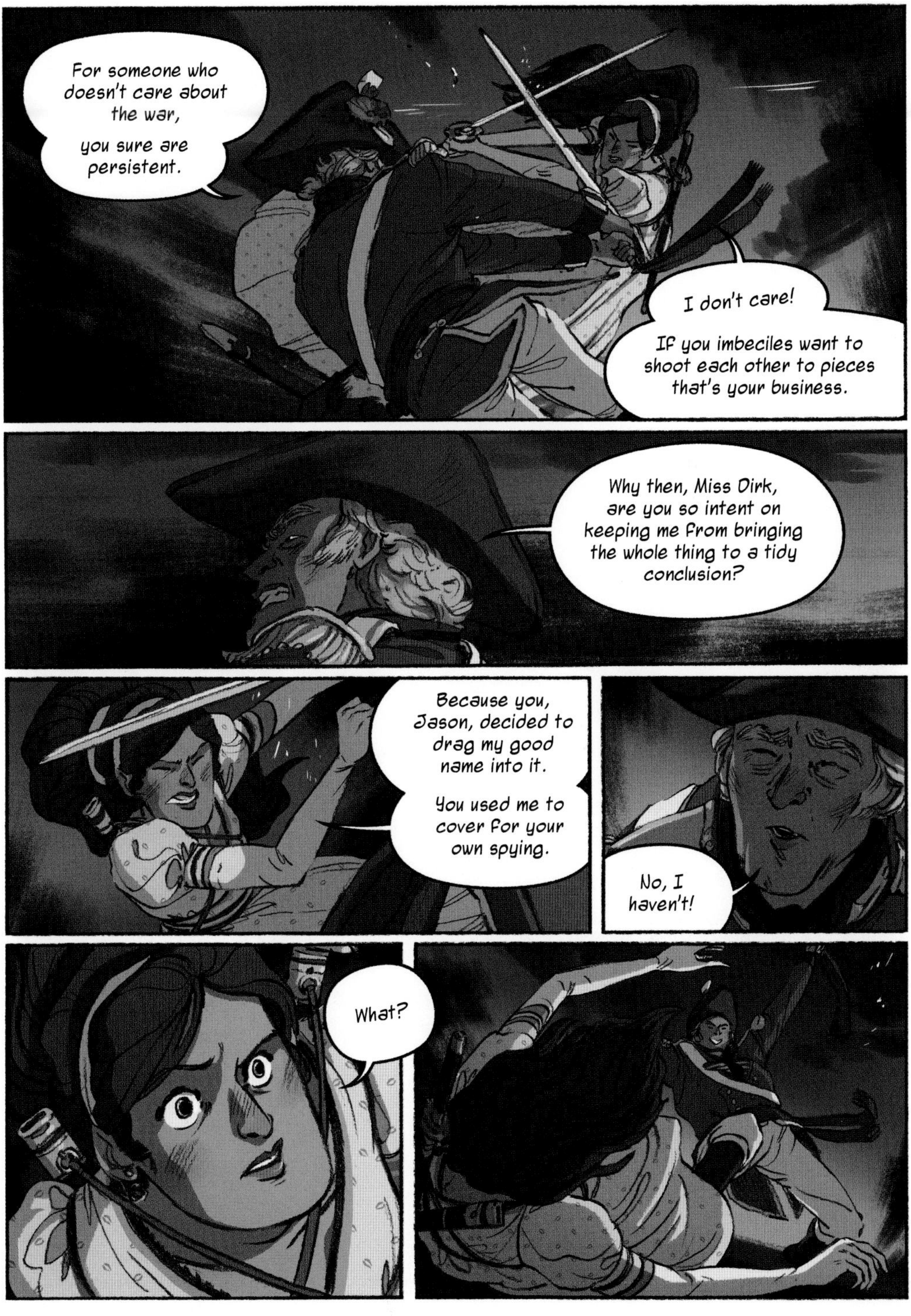
For someone who doesn't care about the war,
you sure are persistent.
I don't care!
If you imbeciles want to shoot each other to pieces that's your business.
Why then, Miss Dirk, are you so intent on keeping me from bringing the whole thing to a tidy conclusion?
Because you, Jason, decided to drag my good name into it.
You used me to cover for your own spying.
No, I haven't!
What?

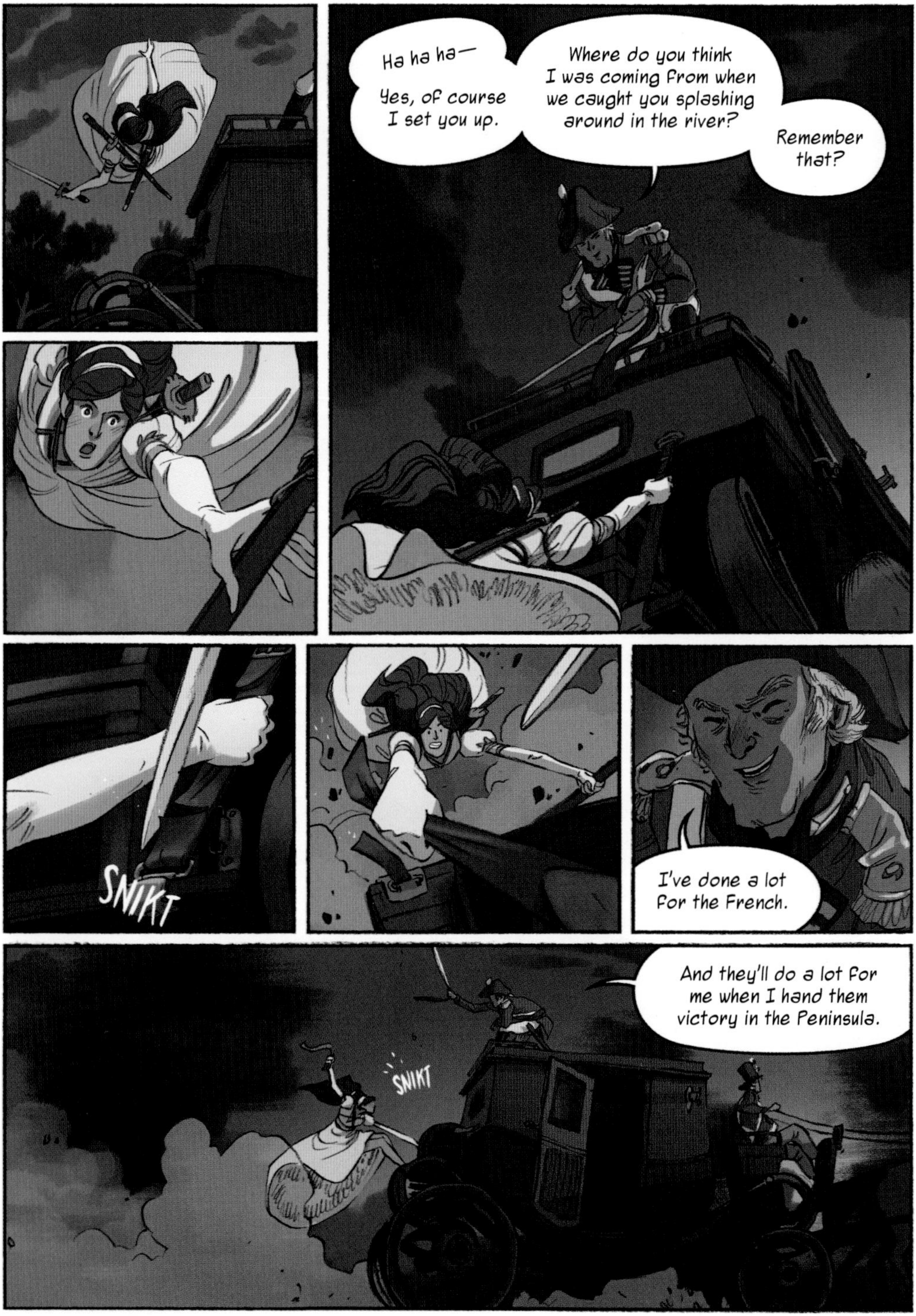
Ha ha ha—
Yes, of course I set you up.
Where do you think I was coming from when we caught you splashing around in the river?
Remember that?
SNIKT
I've done a lot for the French.
And they'll do a lot for me when I hand them victory in the Peninsula.
SNIKT

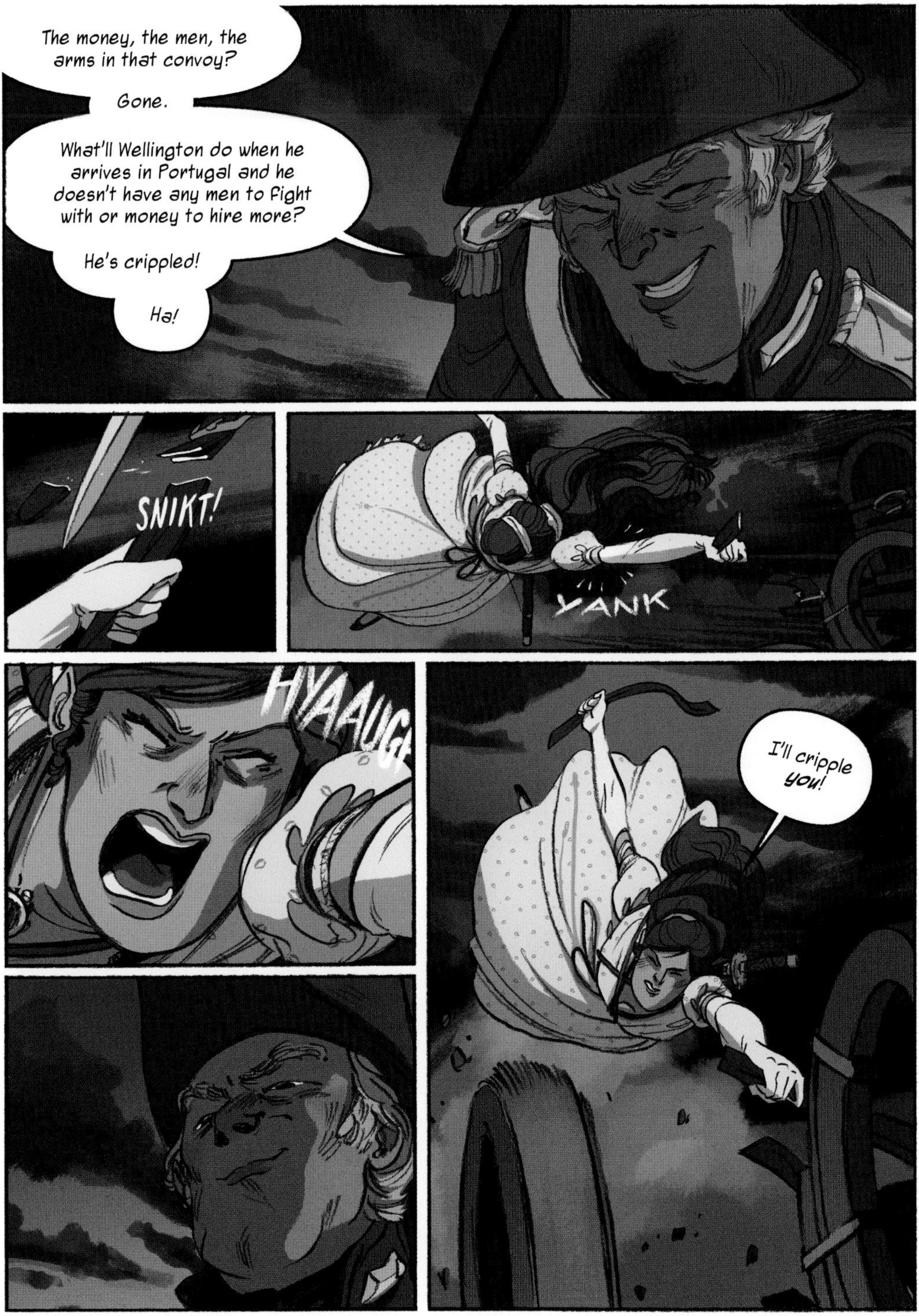
The money, the men, the arms in that convoy?
Gone.
What'll Wellington do when he arrives in Portugal and he doesn't have any men to fight with or money to hire more?
He's crippled!
Ha!
SNIKT!
YANK
HYAAUGH
I'll cripple you!

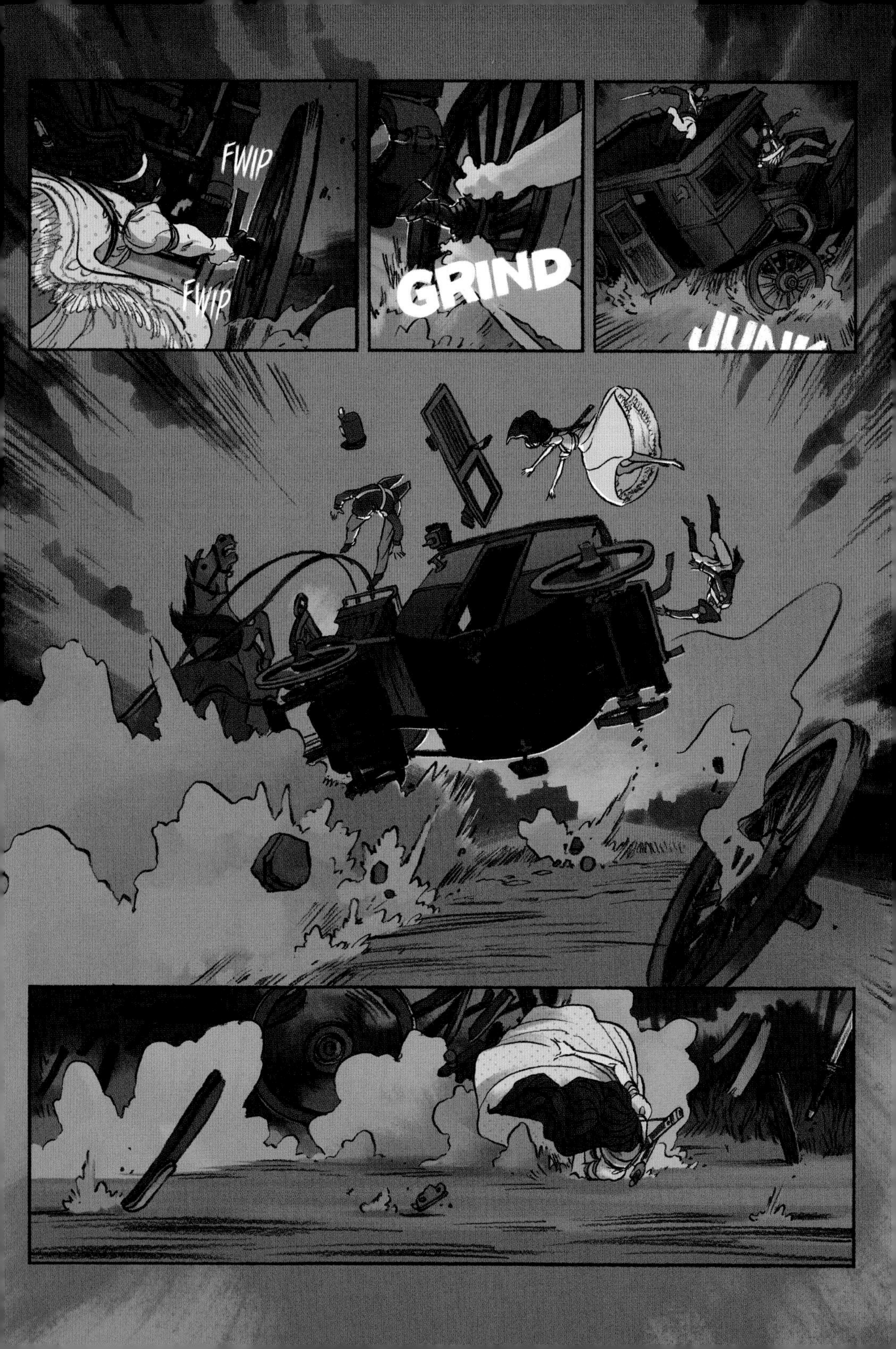
FWIP
FWIP
GRIND
JUNK

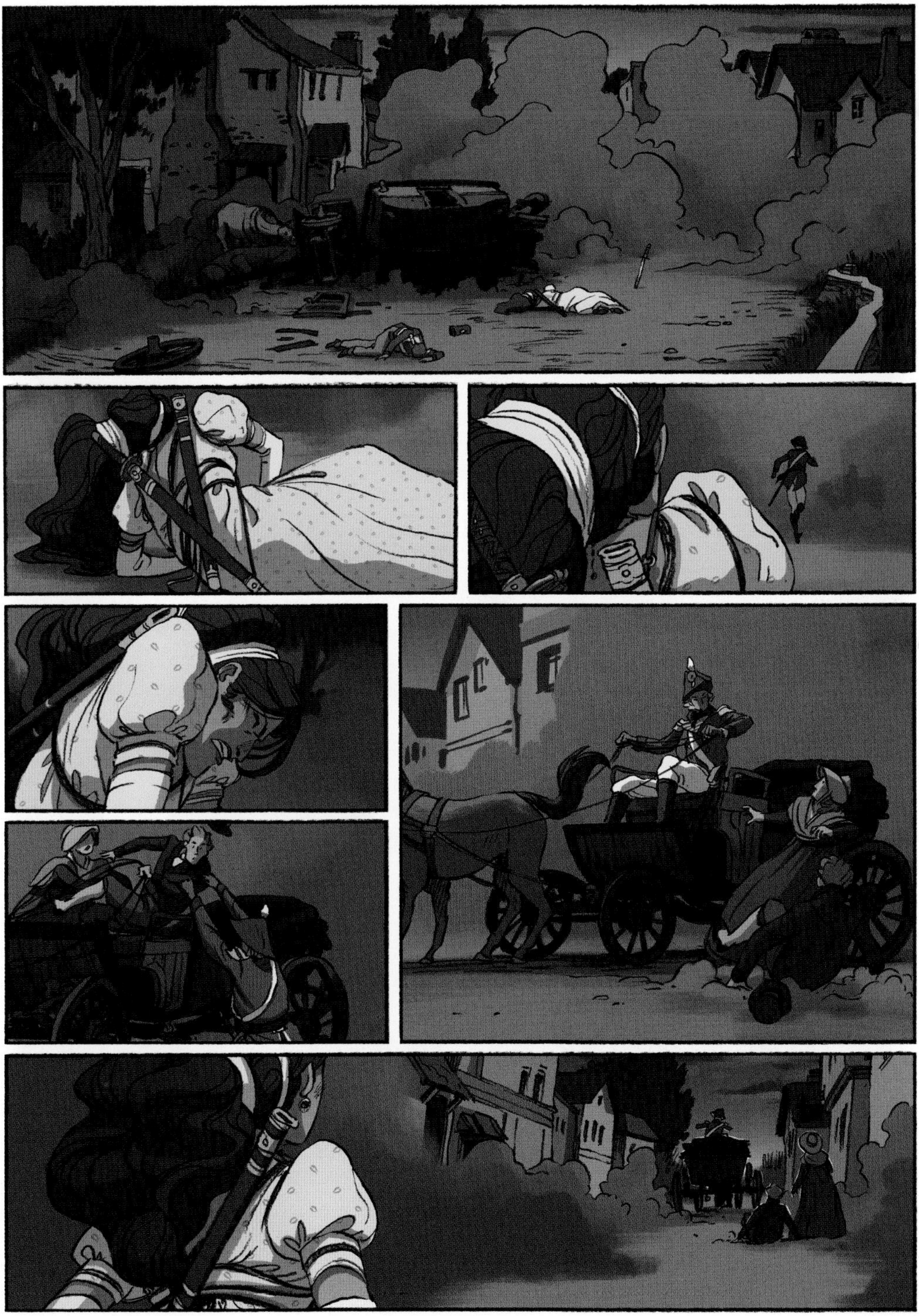

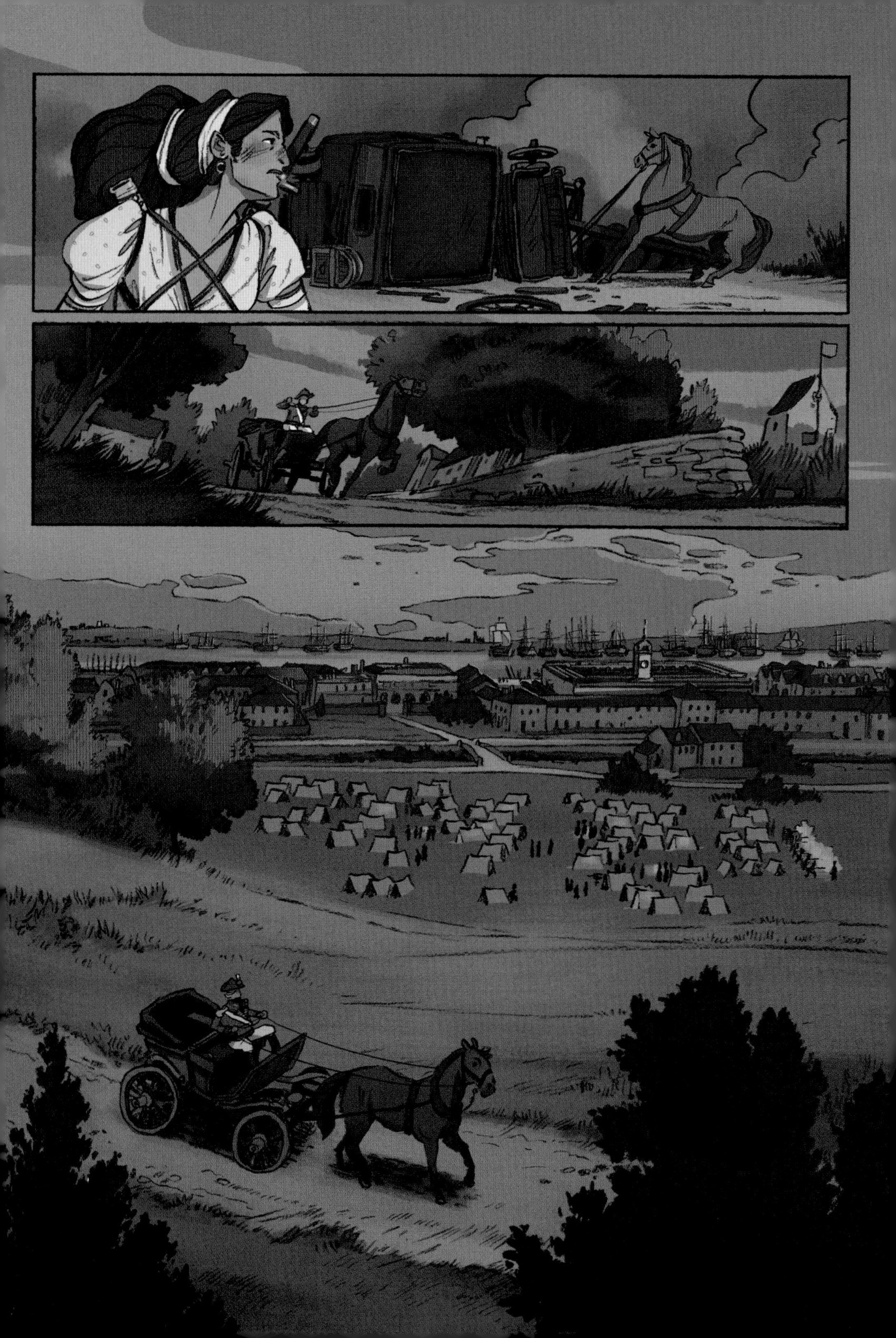

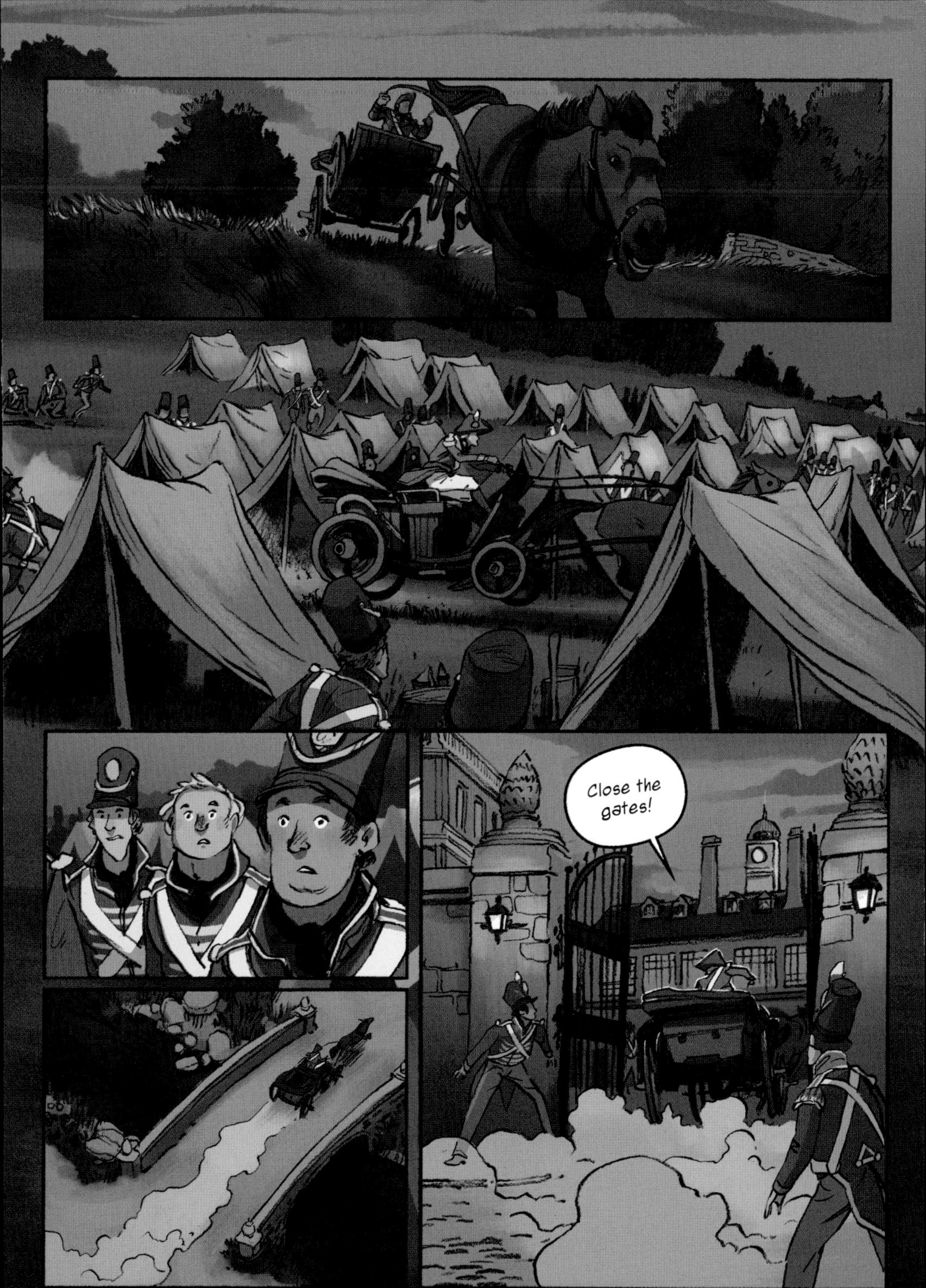
Close the gates!

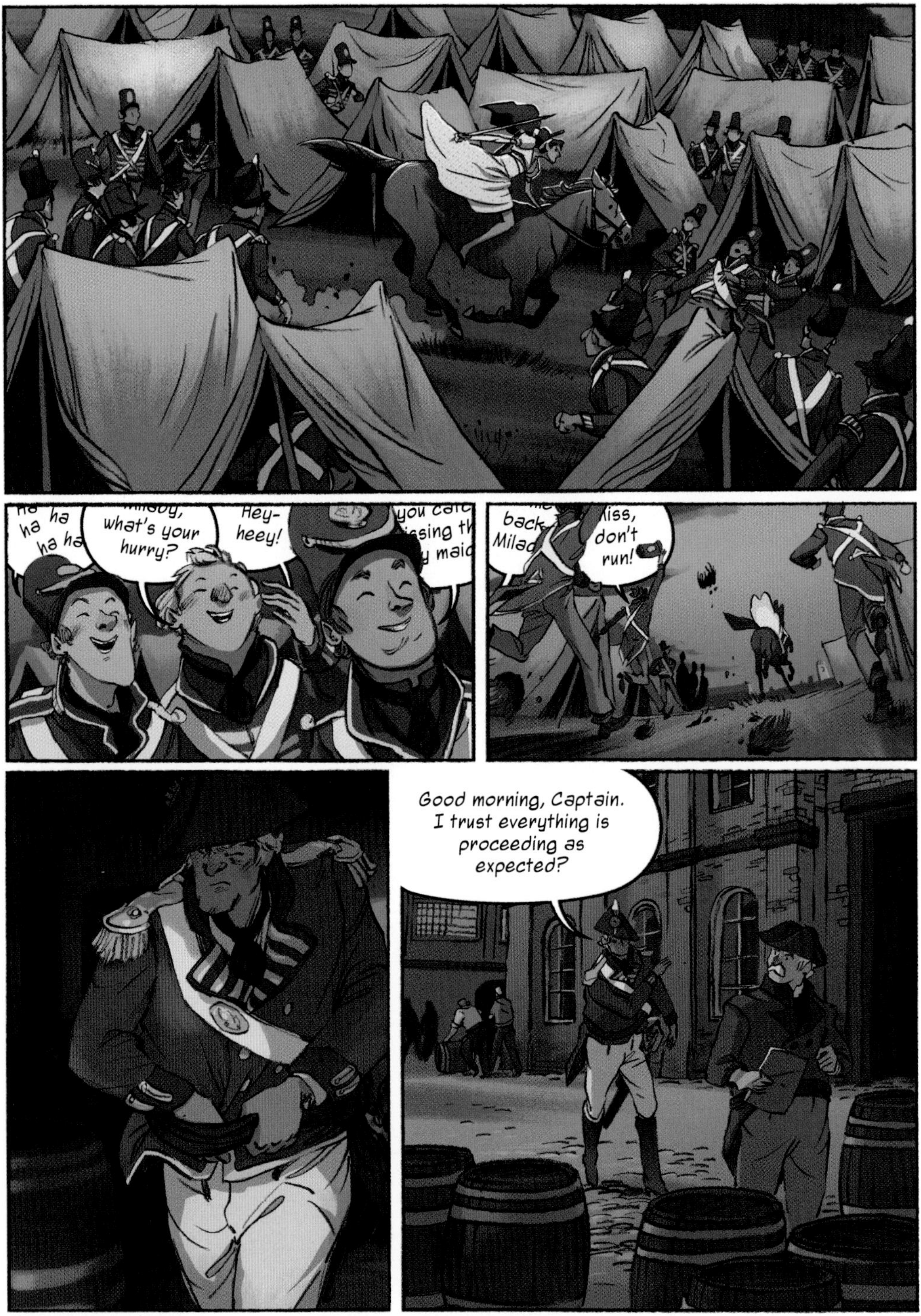
ha ha
ha ha
what's your hurry?
Hey-heey!
don't run!
Good morning, Captain. I trust everything is proceeding as expected?

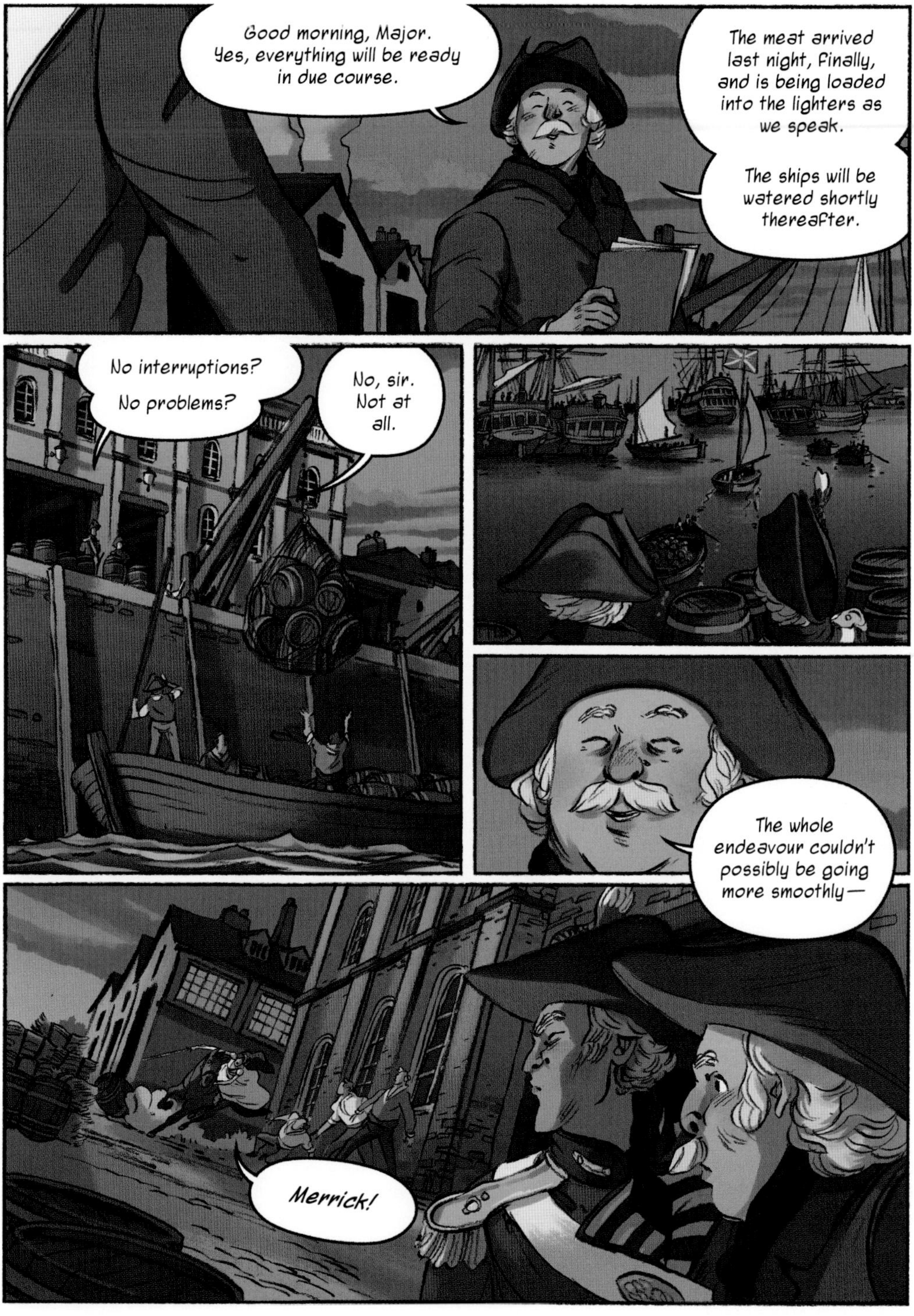
Good morning, Major. Yes, everything will be ready in due course.
The meat arrived last night, finally, and is being loaded into the lighters as we speak.
The ships will be watered shortly thereafter.
No interruptions?
No problems?
No, sir. Not at all.
The whole endeavour couldn't possibly be going more smoothly—
Merrick!

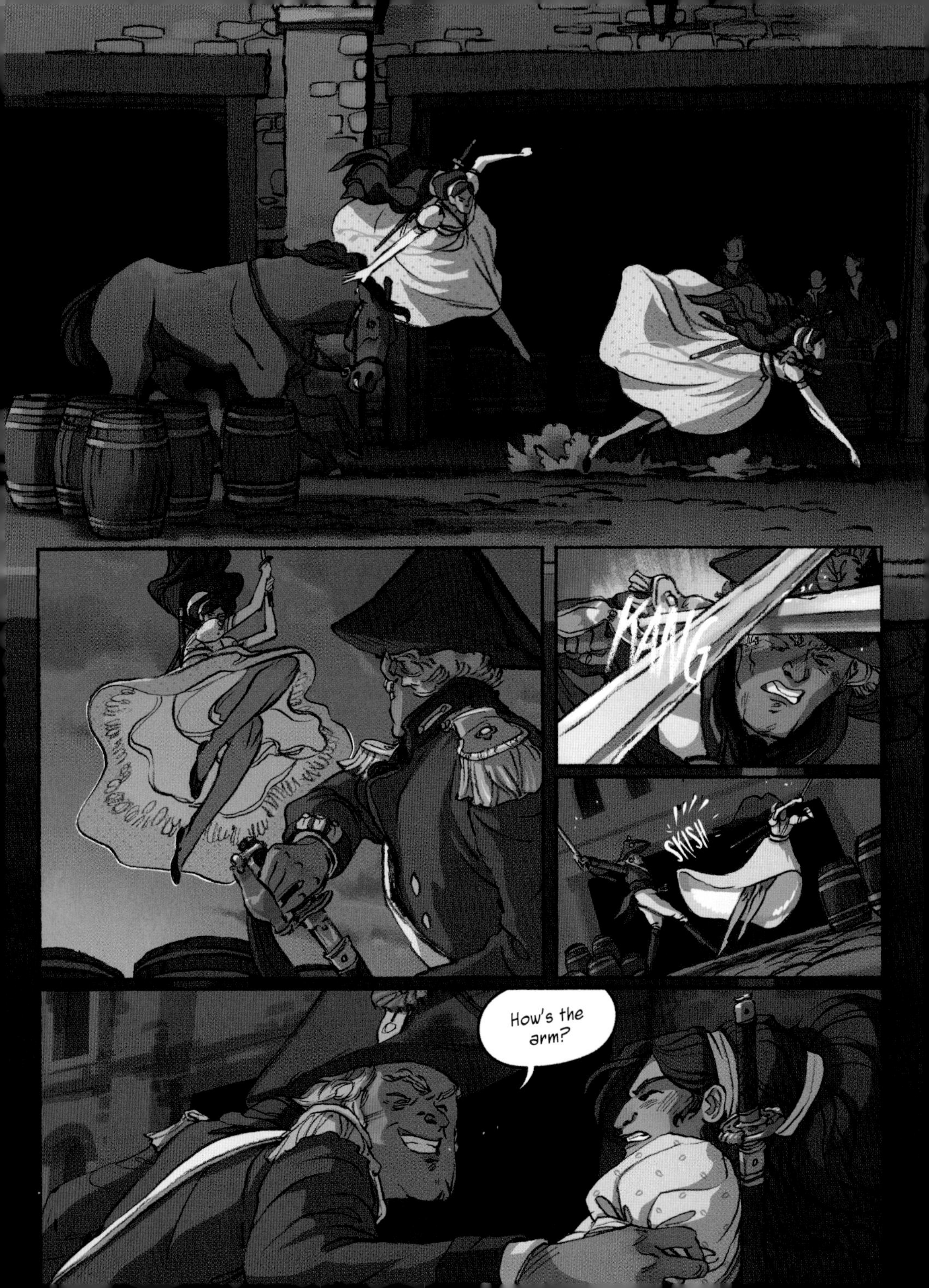
KANG
SKISH
How's the arm?

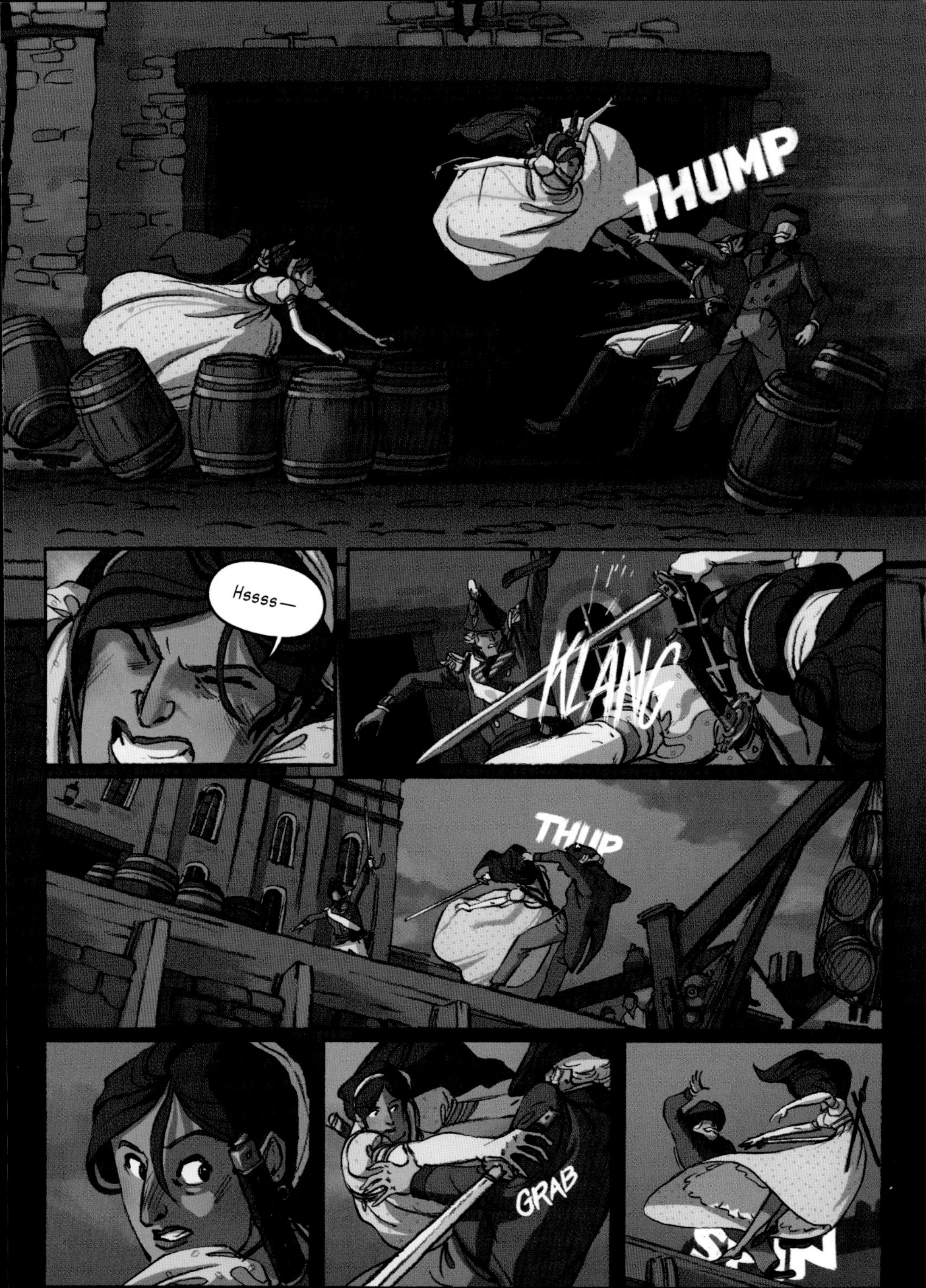
THUMP
Hssss—
KLANG
THUP
GRAB

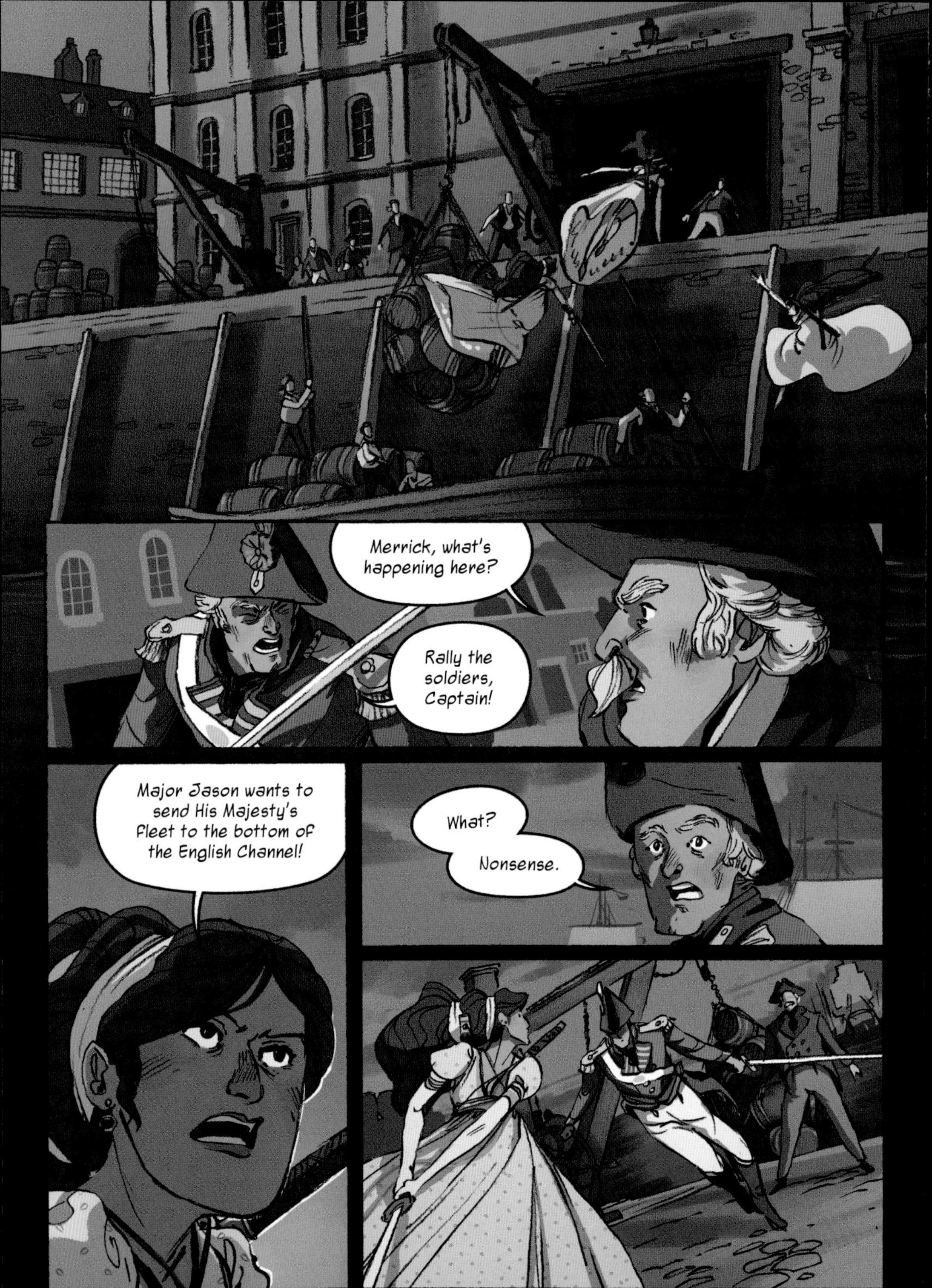

Merrick, what's happening here?
Rally the soldiers, Captain!
Major Jason wants to send His Majesty's fleet to the bottom of the English Channel!
What?
Nonsense.

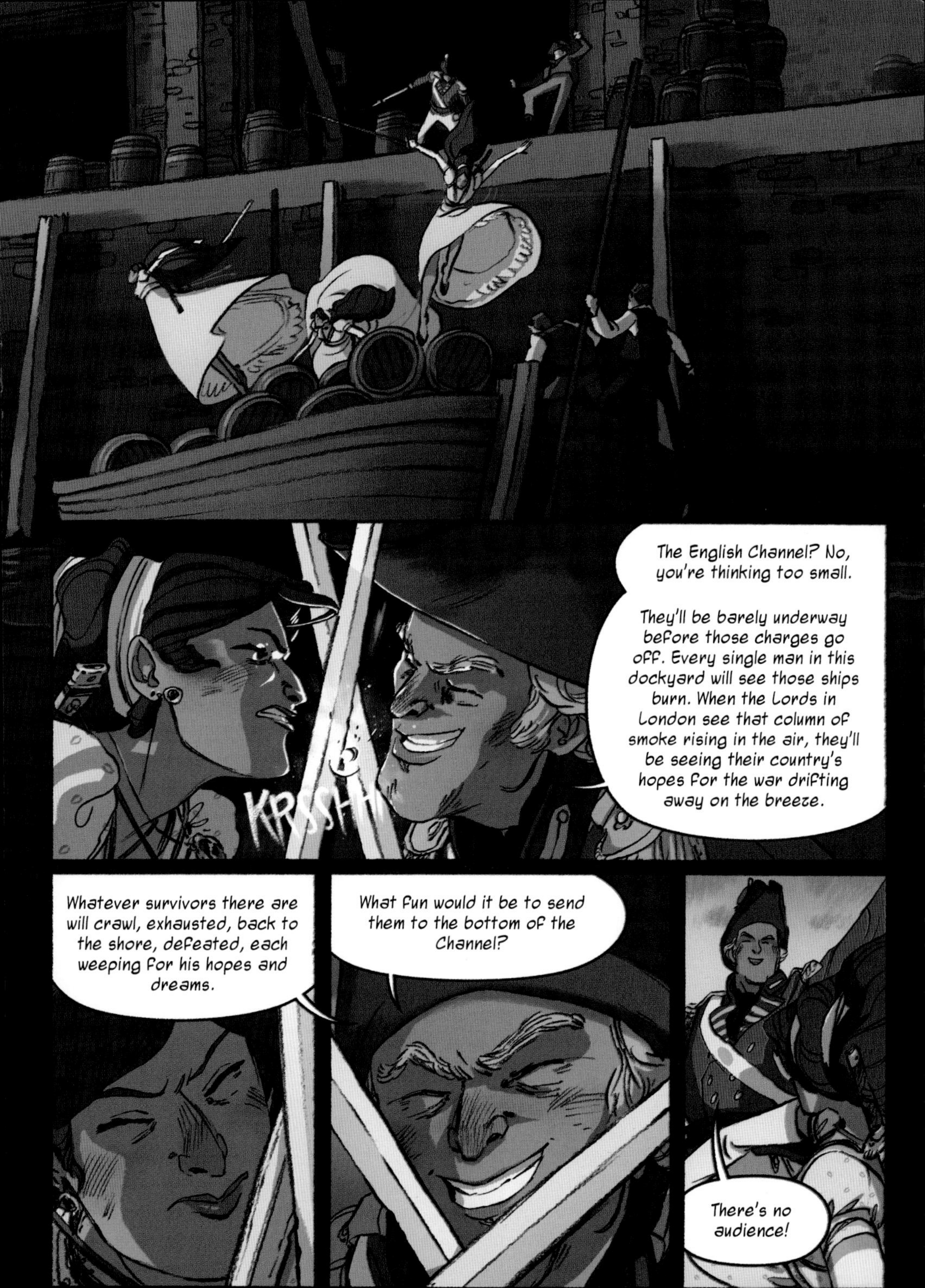

The English Channel? No, you're thinking too small.
They'll be barely underway before those charges go off. Every single man in this dockyard will see those ships burn. When the Lords in London see that column of smoke rising in the air, they'll be seeing their country's hopes for the war drifting away on the breeze.
KRSSHH
Whatever survivors there are will crawl, exhausted, back to the shore, defeated, each weeping for his hopes and dreams.
What fun would it be to send them to the bottom of the Channel?
There's no audience!

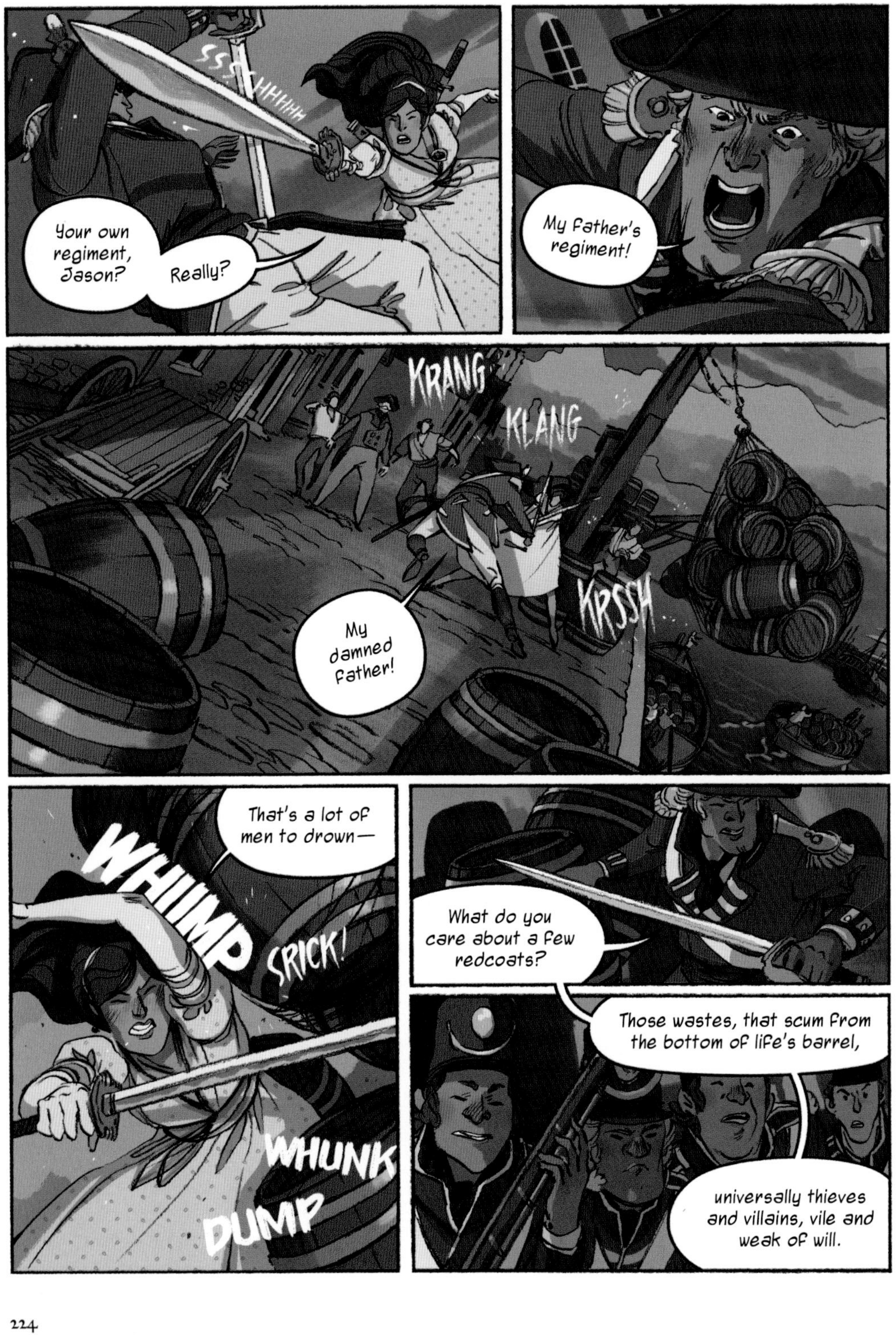
SSSHHHHHH
Your own regiment, Jason?
Really?
My father's regiment!
KRANG
KLANG
KRSSH
My damned father!
That's a lot of men to drown—
WHIMP
SRICK!
WHUNK
DUMP
What do you care about a few redcoats?
Those wastes, that scum from the bottom of life's barrel,
universally thieves and villains, vile and weak of will.

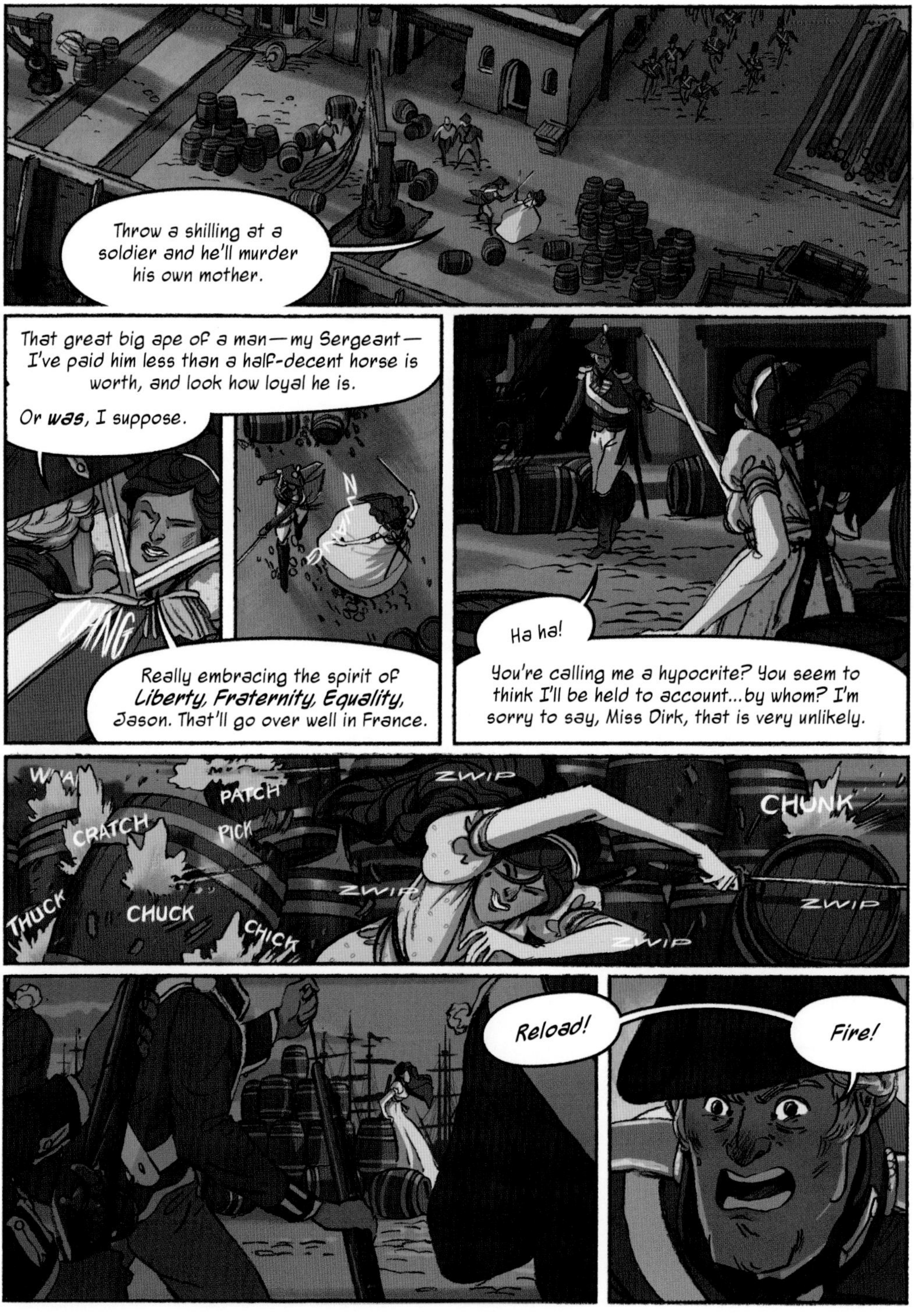

Throw a shilling at a soldier and he'll murder his own mother.
That great big ape of a man—my Sergeant—I've paid him less than a half-decent horse is worth, and look how loyal he is.
Or *was*, I suppose.
CLANG
Really embracing the spirit of *Liberty, Fraternity, Equality,* Jason. That'll go over well in France.
Ha ha!
You're calling me a hypocrite? You seem to think I'll be held to account...by whom? I'm sorry to say, Miss Dirk, that is very unlikely.
PATCH
CRATCH
PICK
THUCK
CHUCK
CHICK
ZWIP
ZWIP
CHUNK
ZWIP
ZWIP
Reload!
Fire!

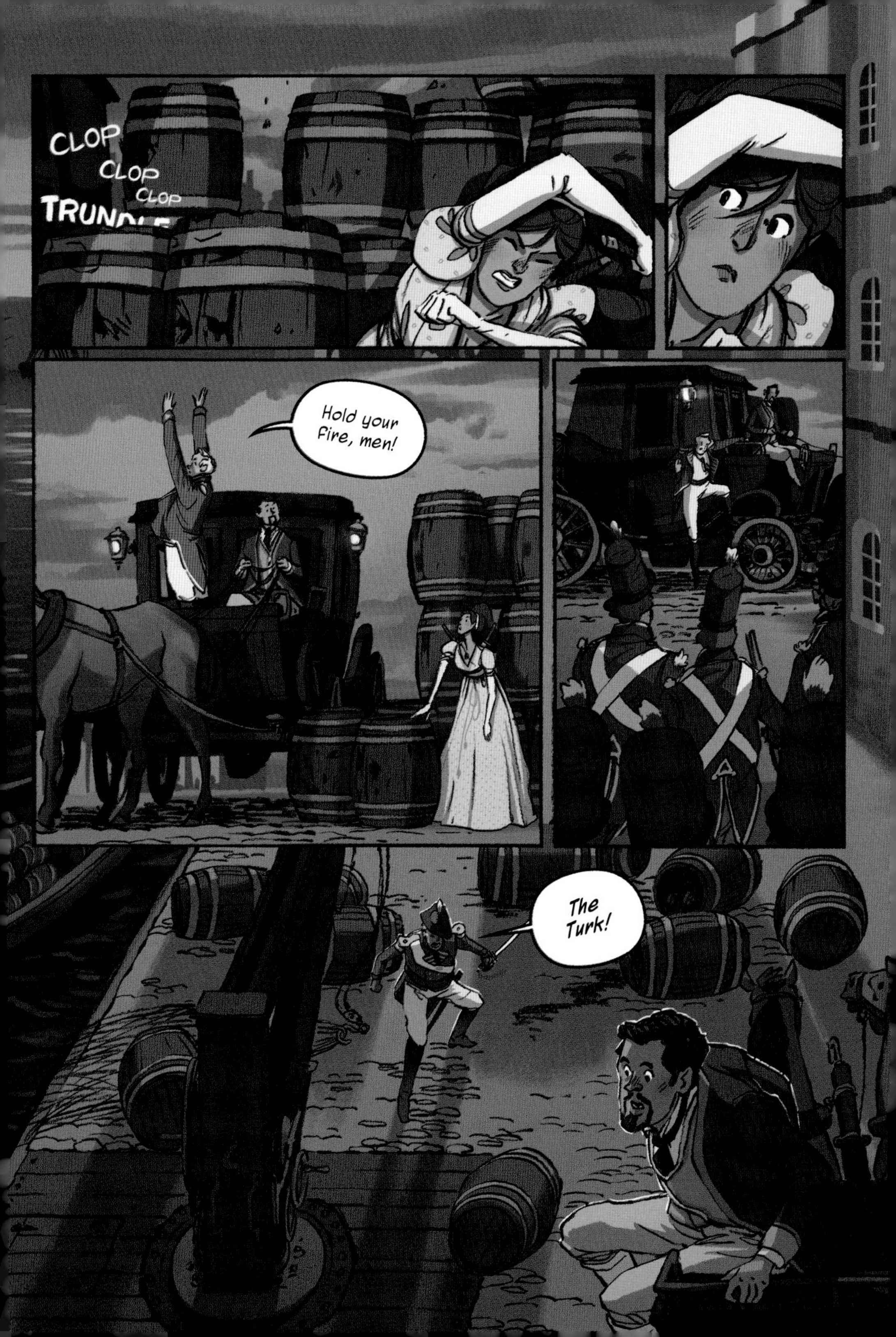
CLOP
CLOP
CLOP
TRUNDLE
Hold your fire, men!
The Turk!

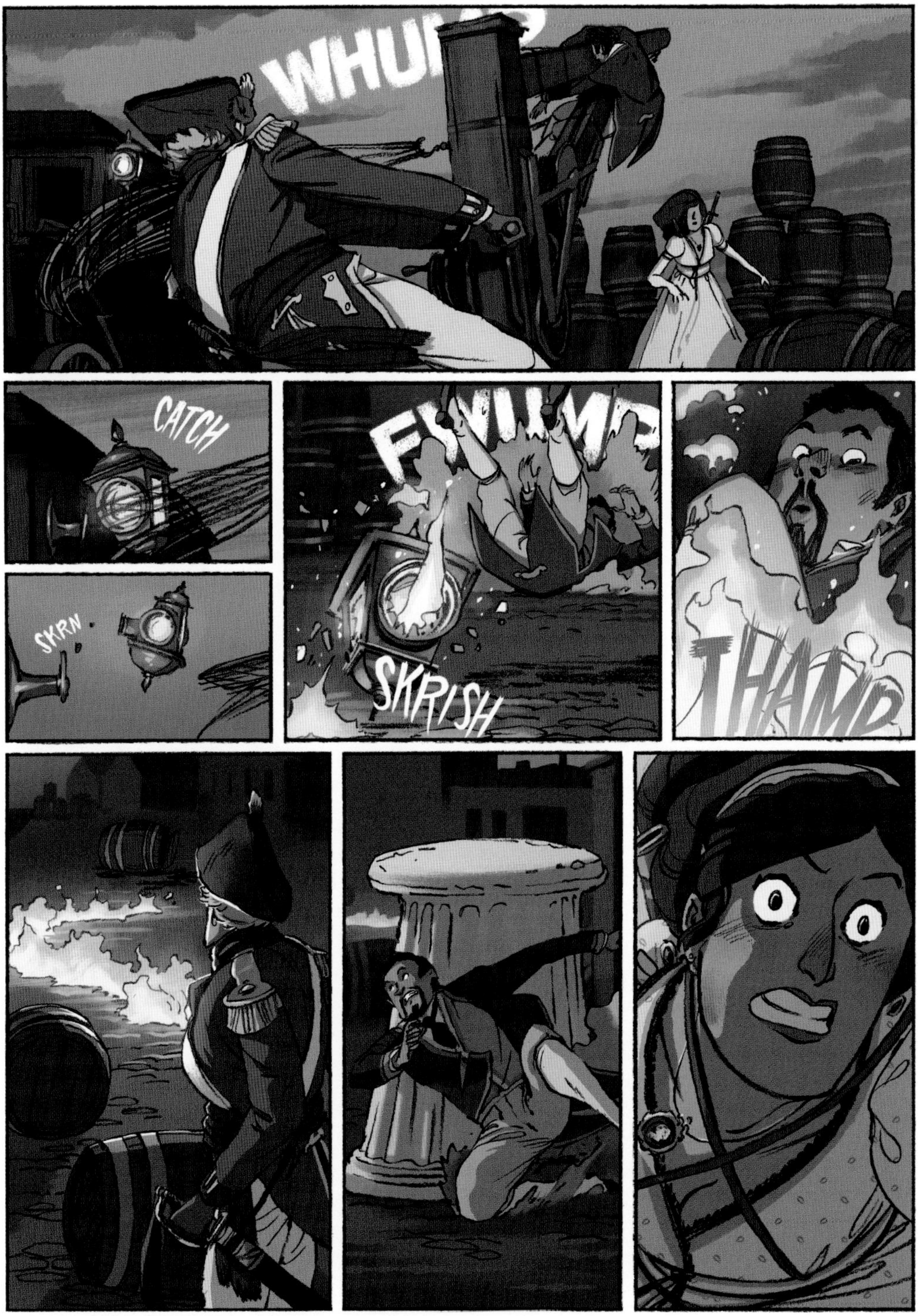

CATCH
SKRN
SKRISH
THAMP

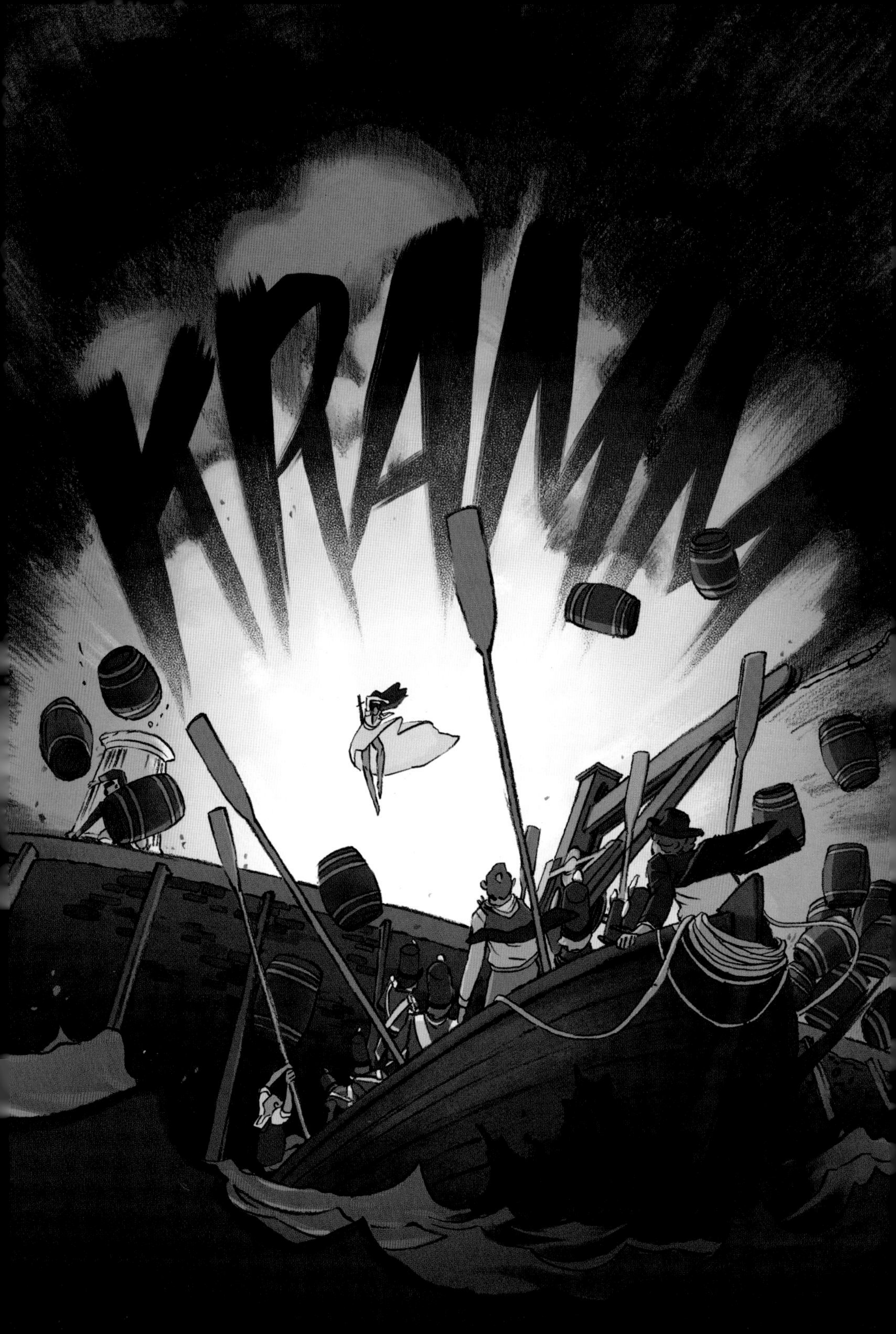

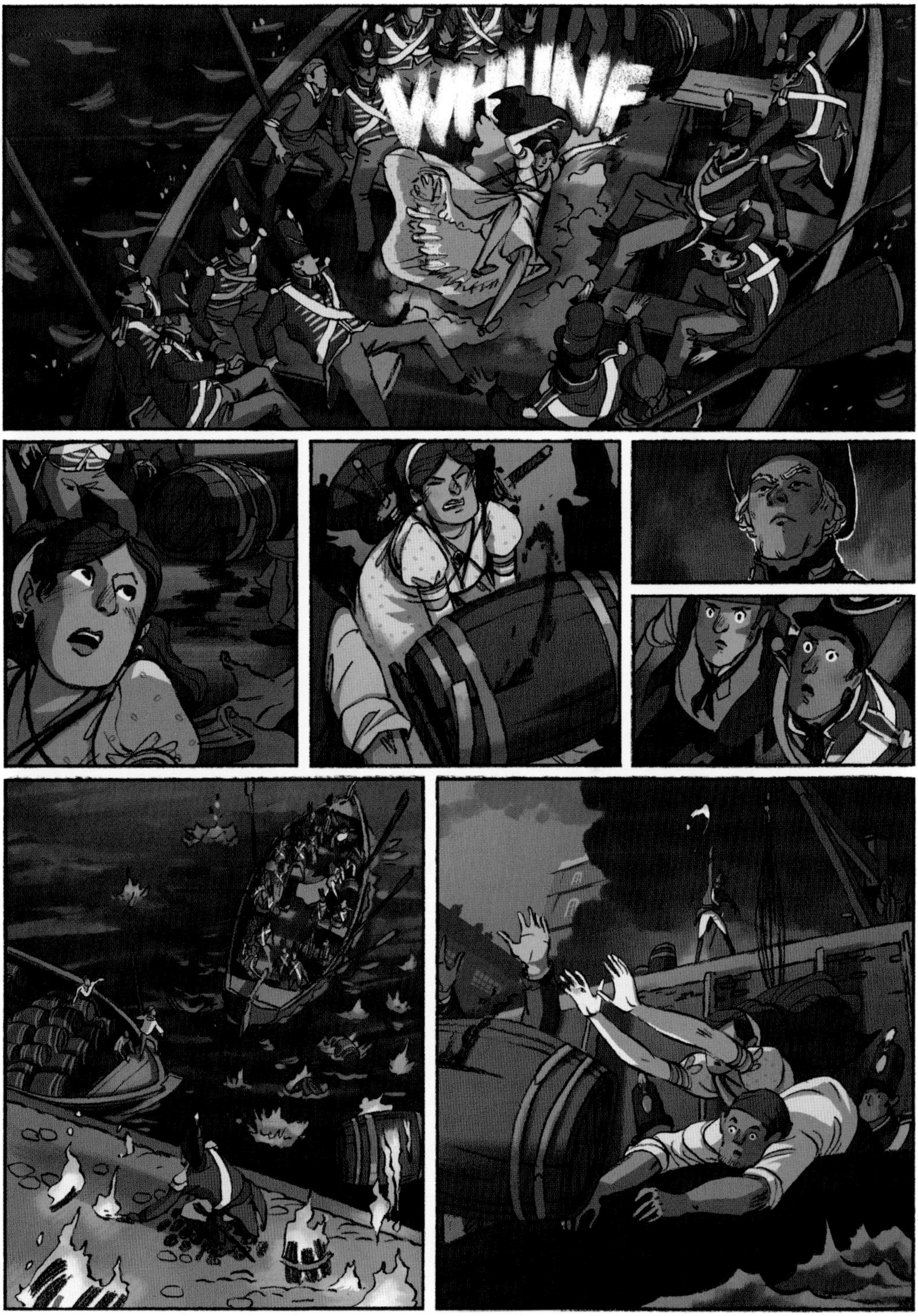
WHUNF

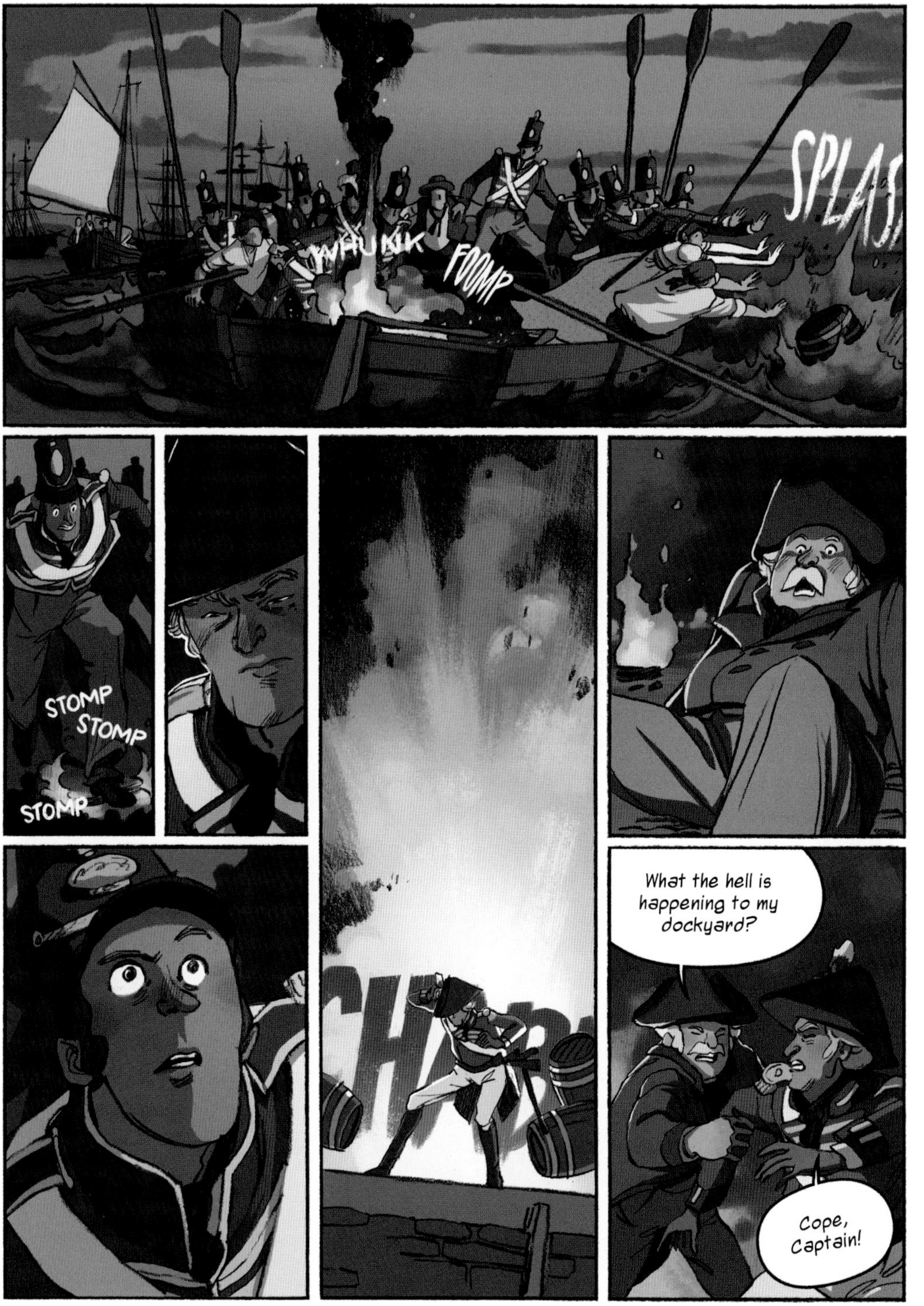
WHUNK
FOOMP
SPLAS
STOMP
STOMP
STOMP
What the hell is happening to my dockyard?
Cope, Captain!

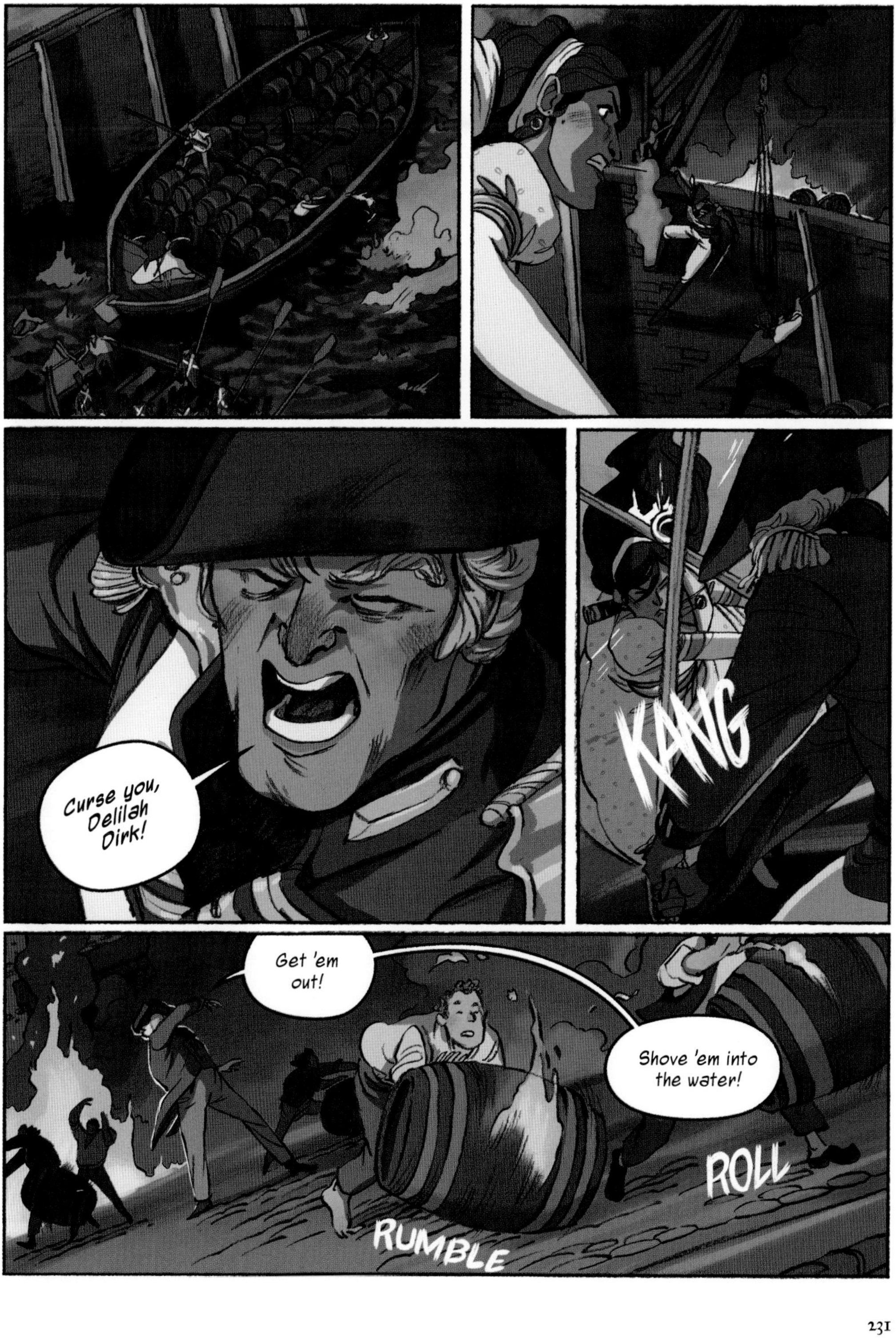
Curse you, Delilah Dirk!
KANG
Get 'em out!
Shove 'em into the water!
ROLL
RUMBLE

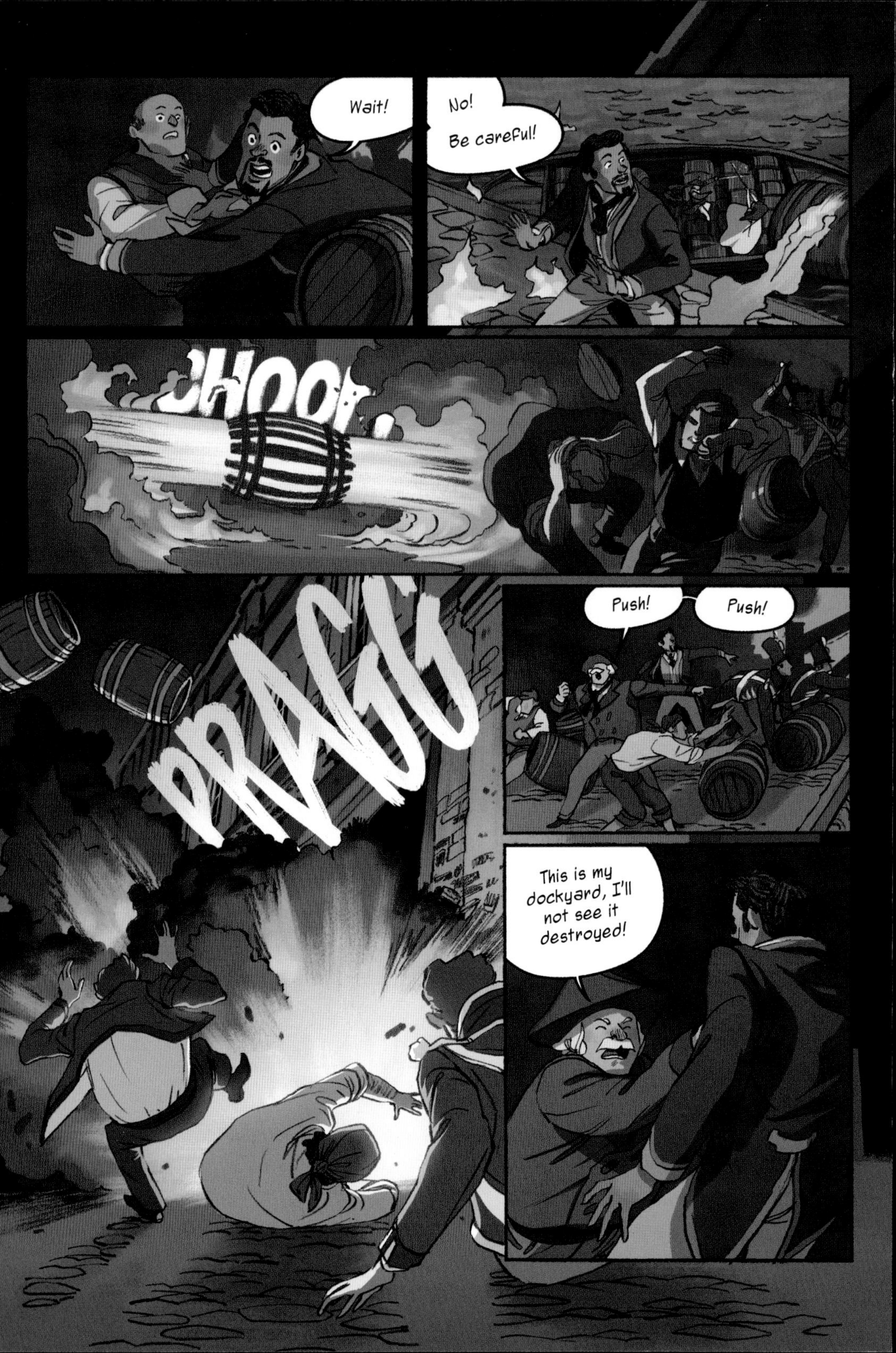
Wait!
No!
Be careful!
CHOOF
Push!
Push!
This is my dockyard, I'll not see it destroyed!

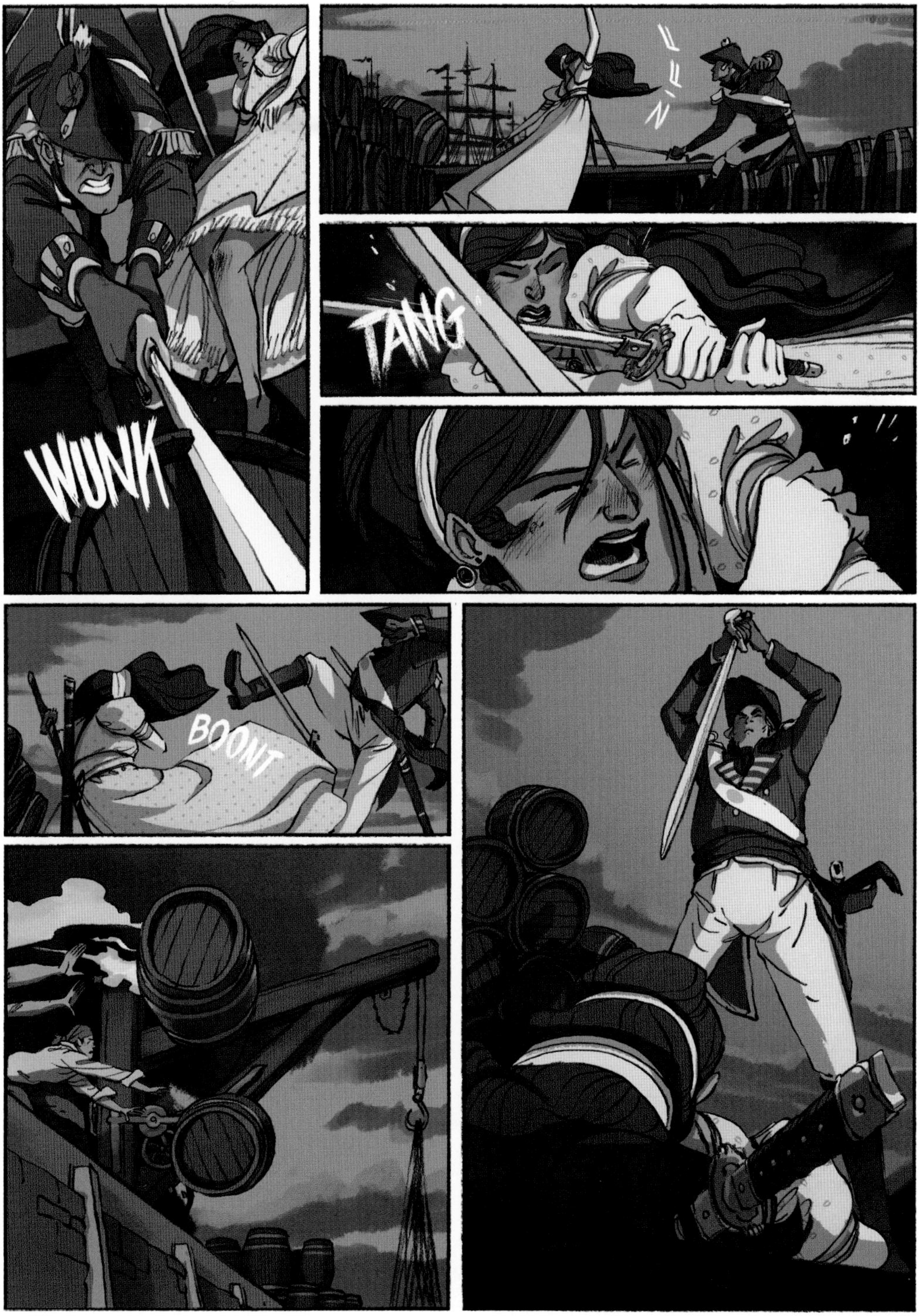
WUNK
ZIFF
TANG
BOONT

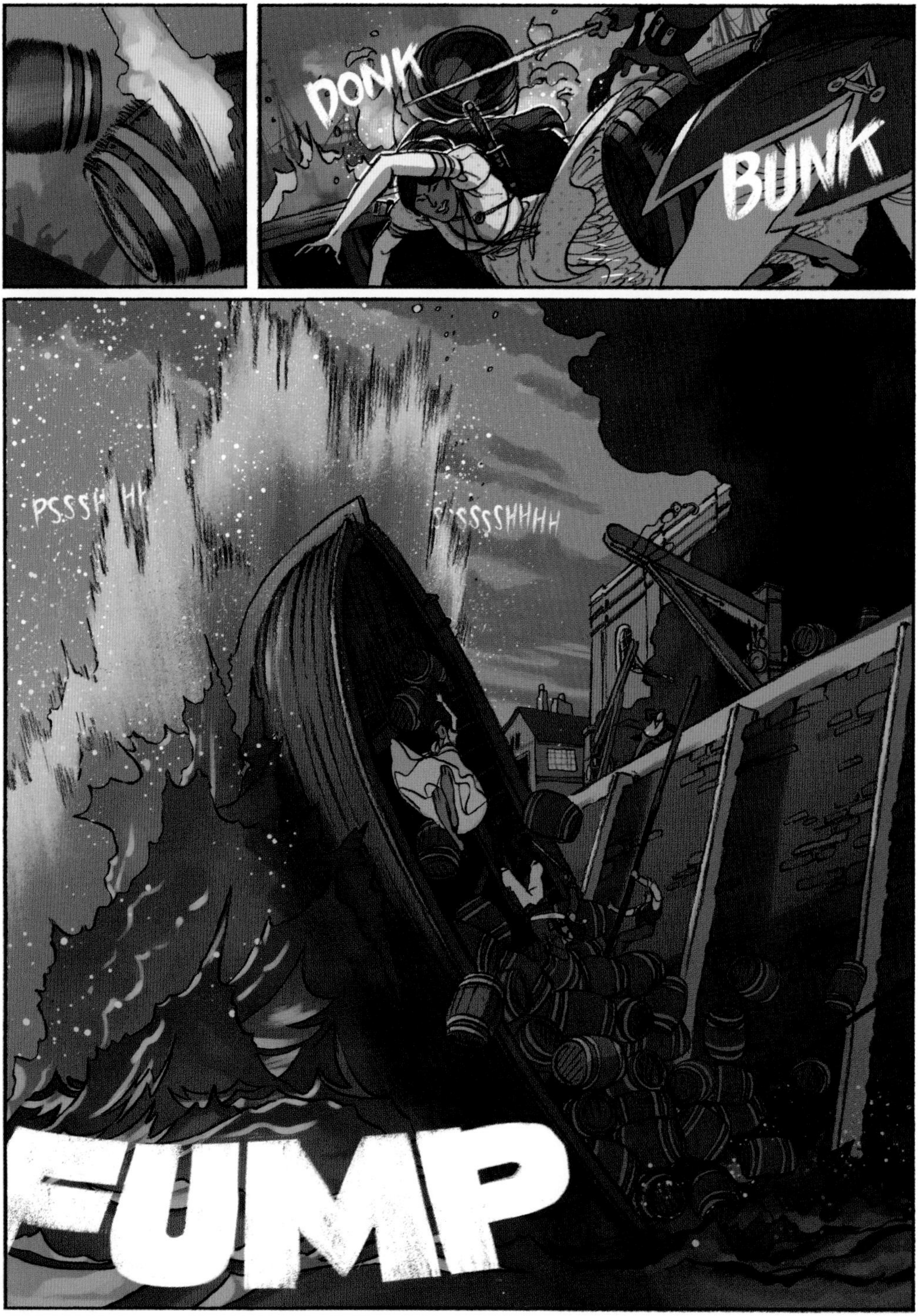
DONK
BUNK
PSSSHHH
SSSSHHHH
FUMP

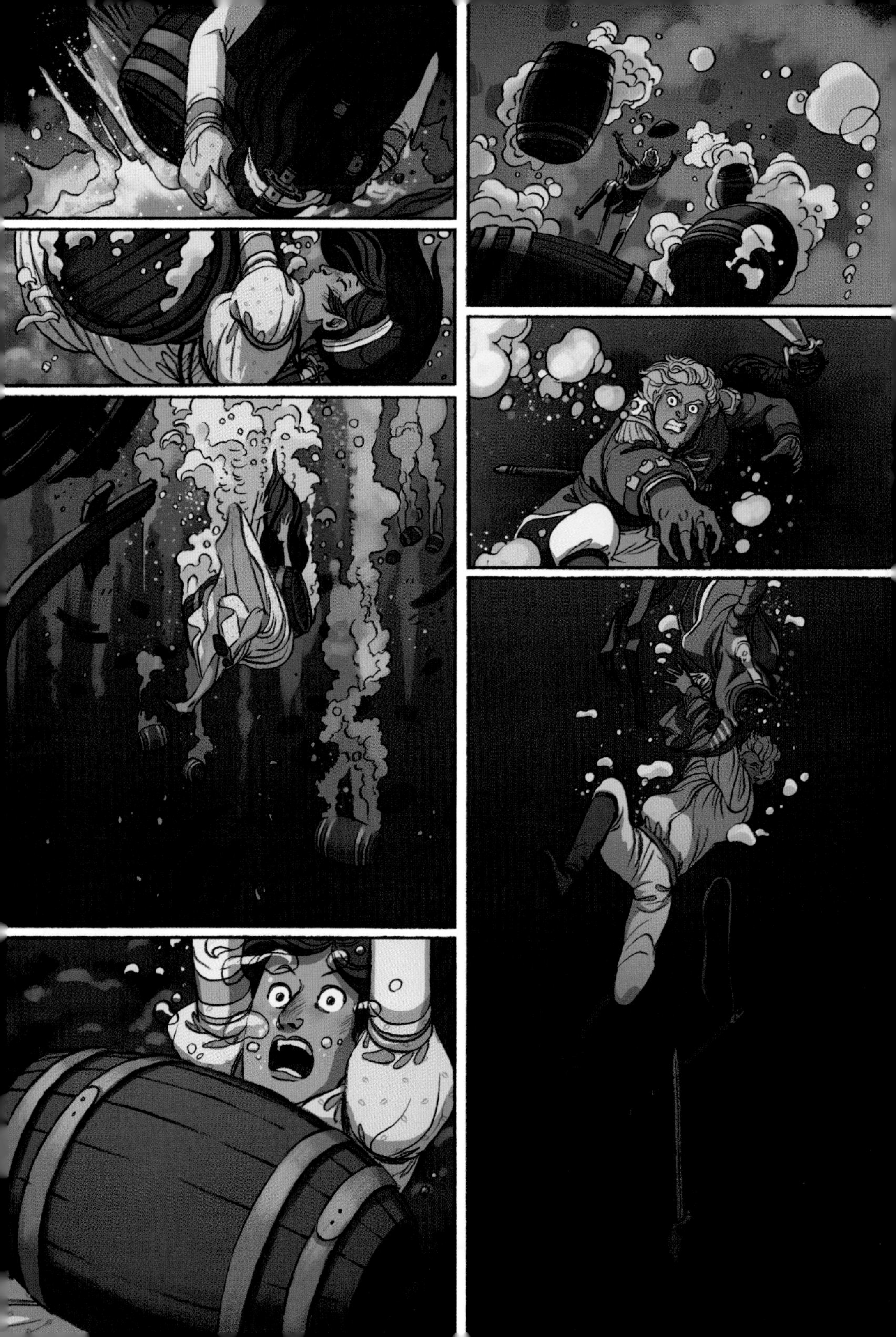

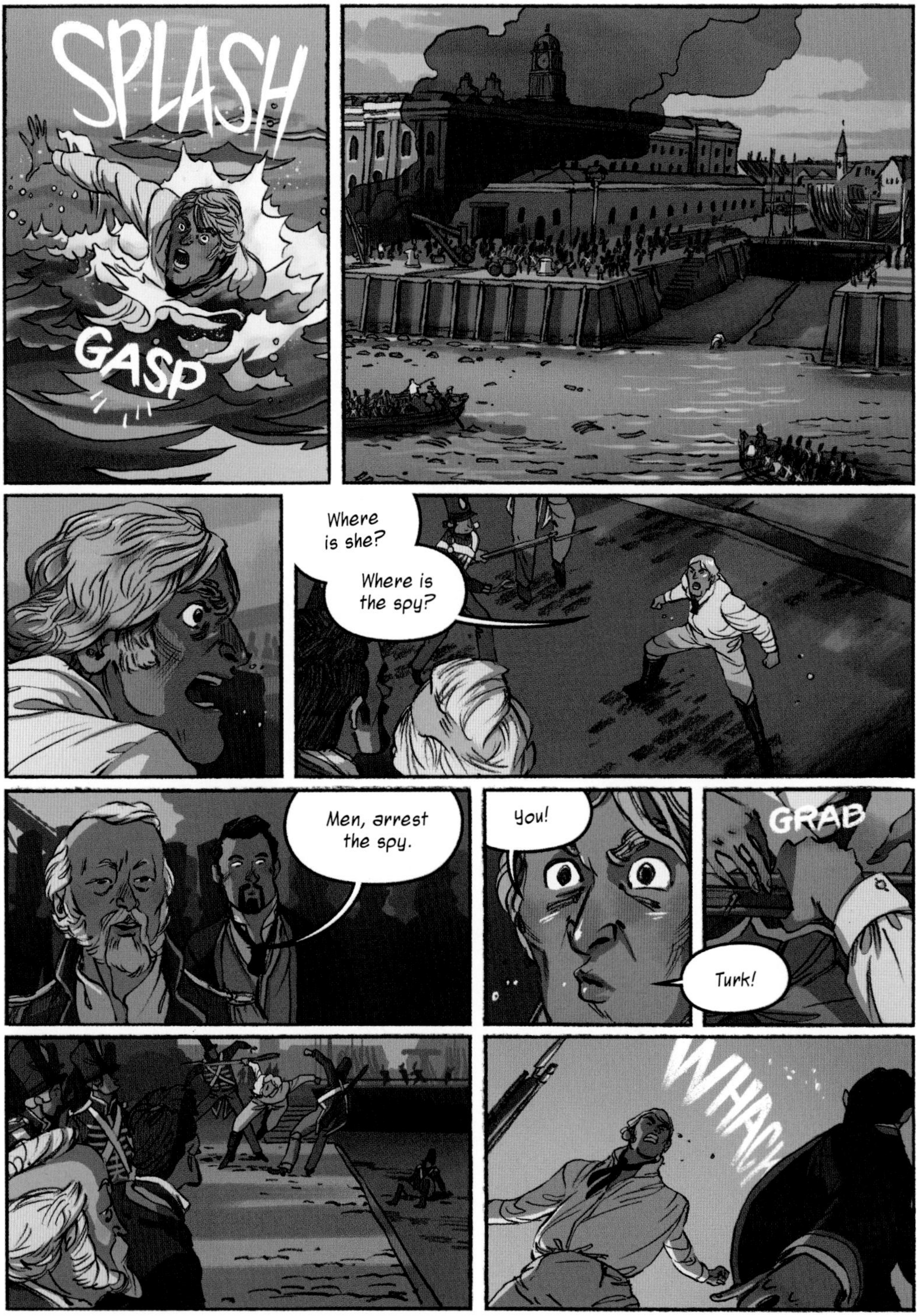
SPLASH
GASP
Where is she?
Where is the spy?
Men, arrest the spy.
You!
GRAB
Turk!
WHACK

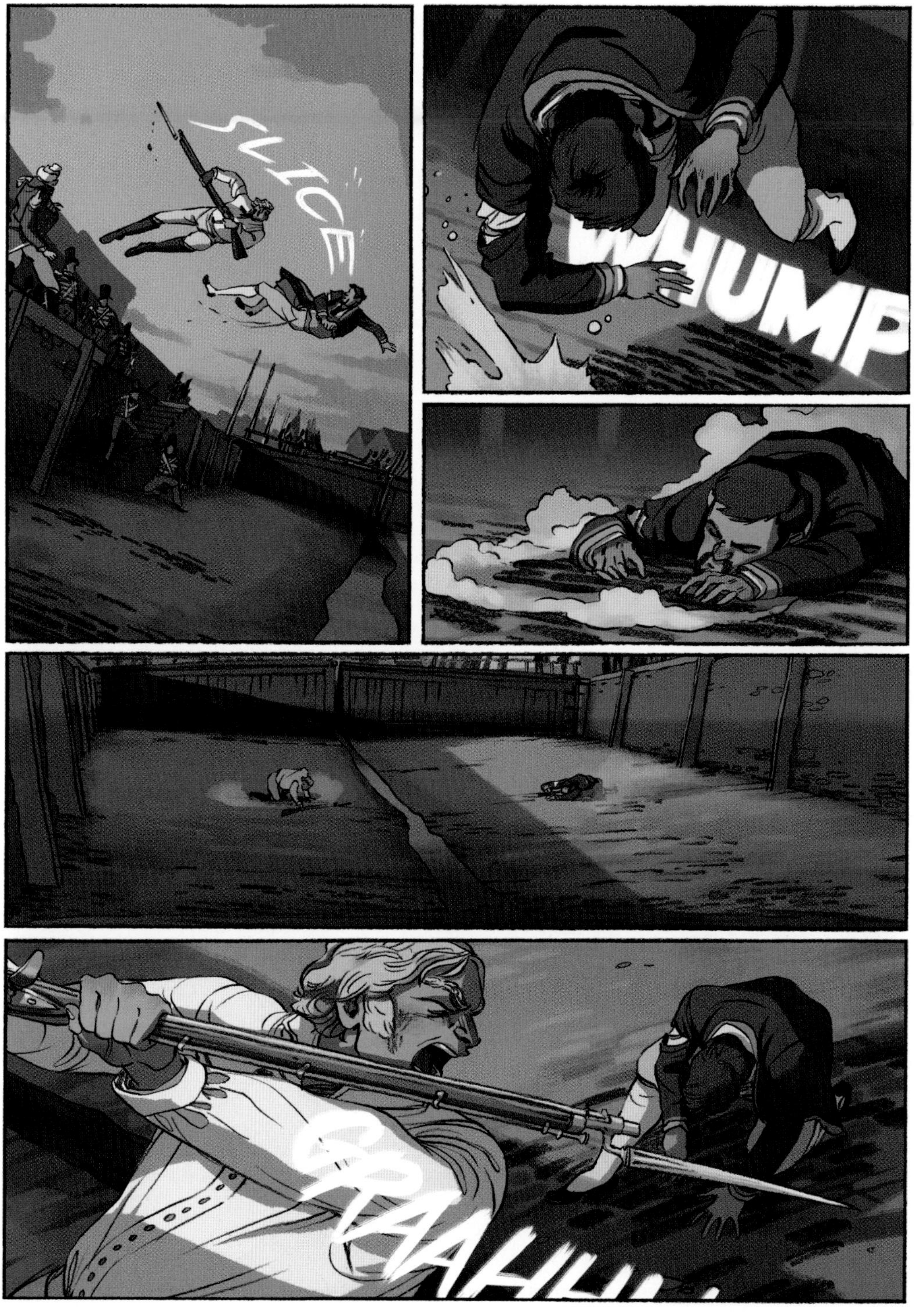
SLICE
WHUMP
GRAAHH

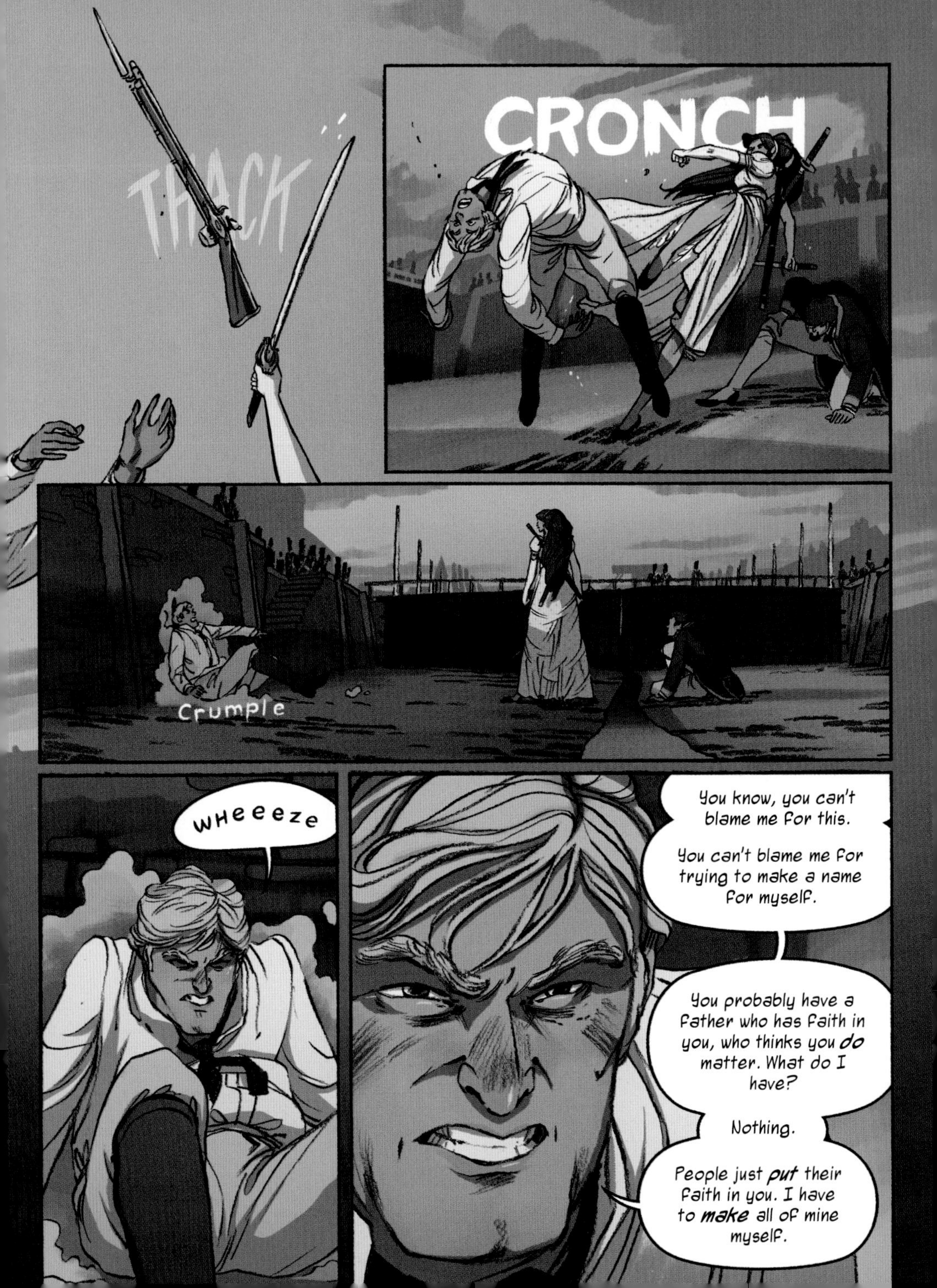
THACK
CRONCH
Crumple
WHEEEZE
You know, you can't blame me for this.
You can't blame me for trying to make a name for myself.
You probably have a father who has faith in you, who thinks you *do* matter. What do I have?
Nothing.
People just *put* their faith in you. I have to *make* all of mine myself.

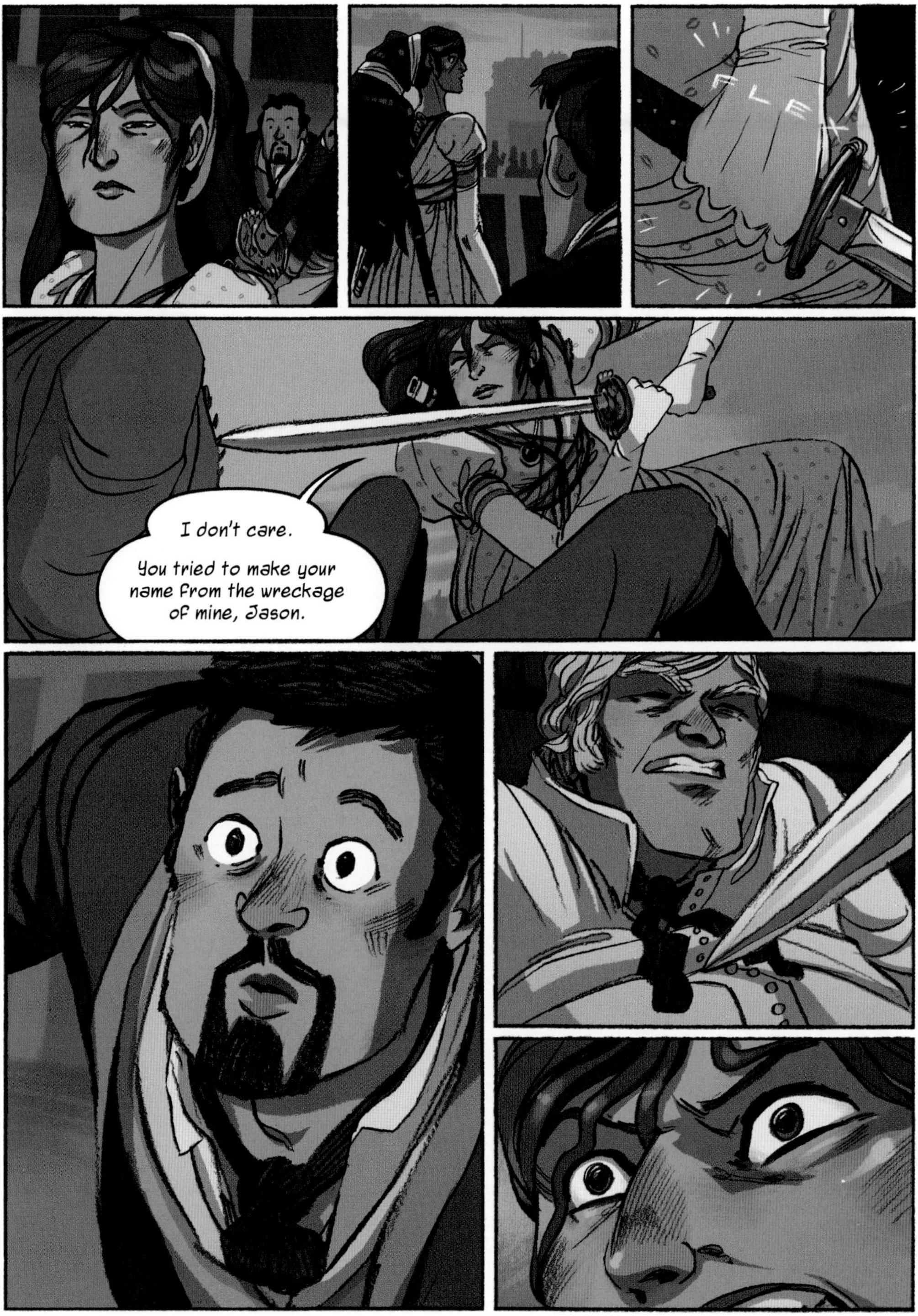
FLEX
I don't care.
You tried to make your name from the wreckage of mine, Jason.

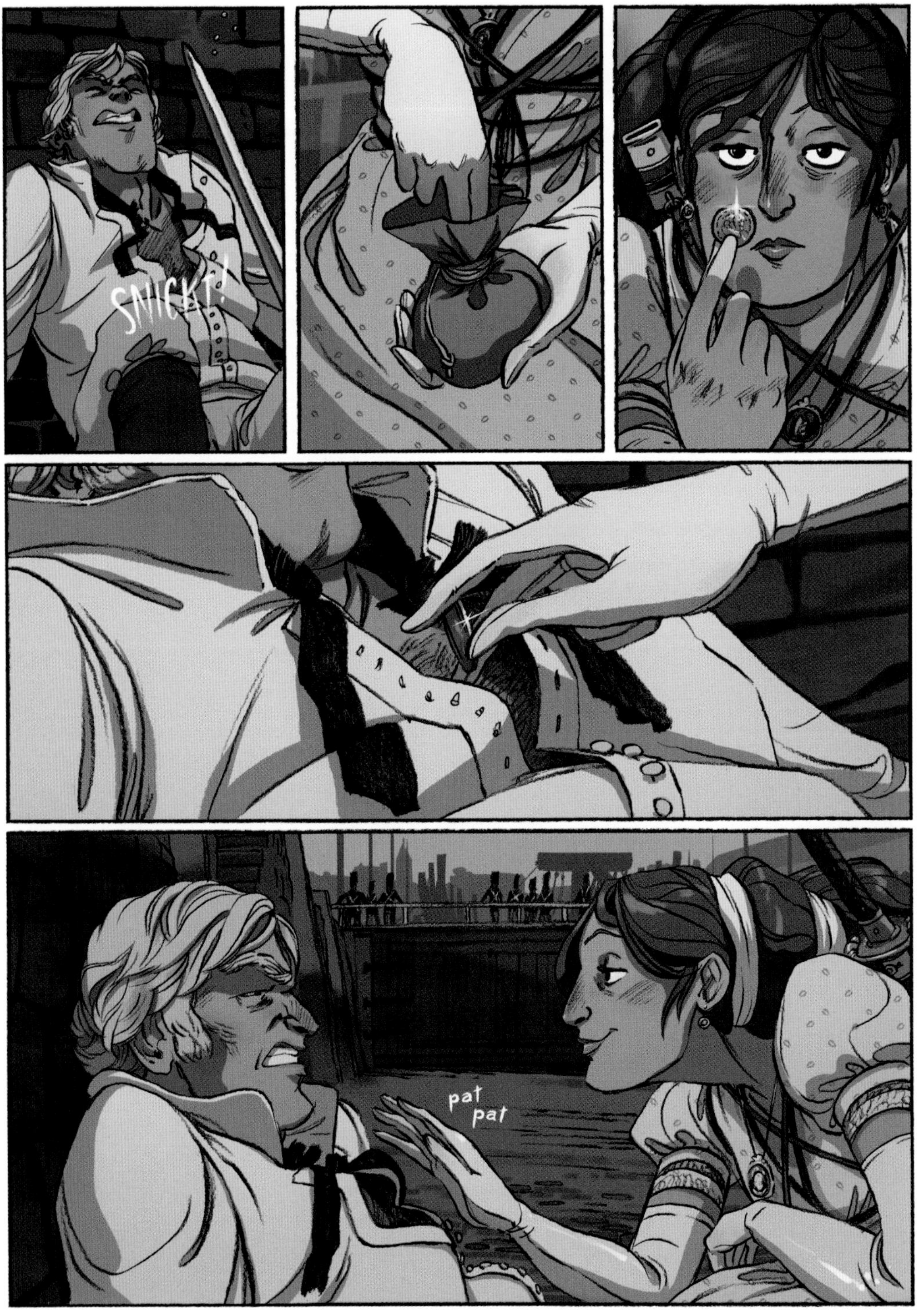
SNICKT!
pat
pat

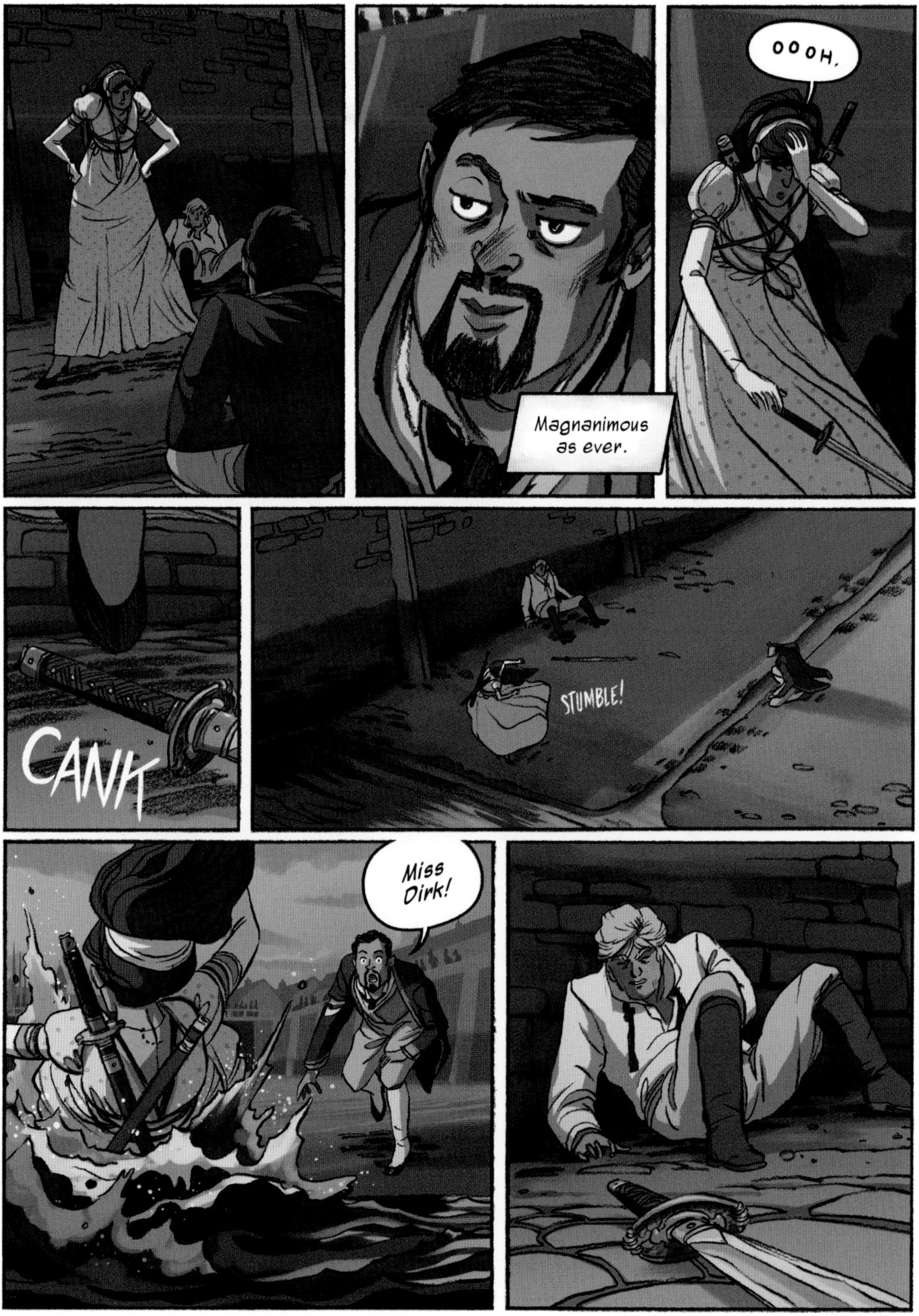
OOOH.
Magnanimous as ever.
CANK
STUMBLE!
Miss Dirk!

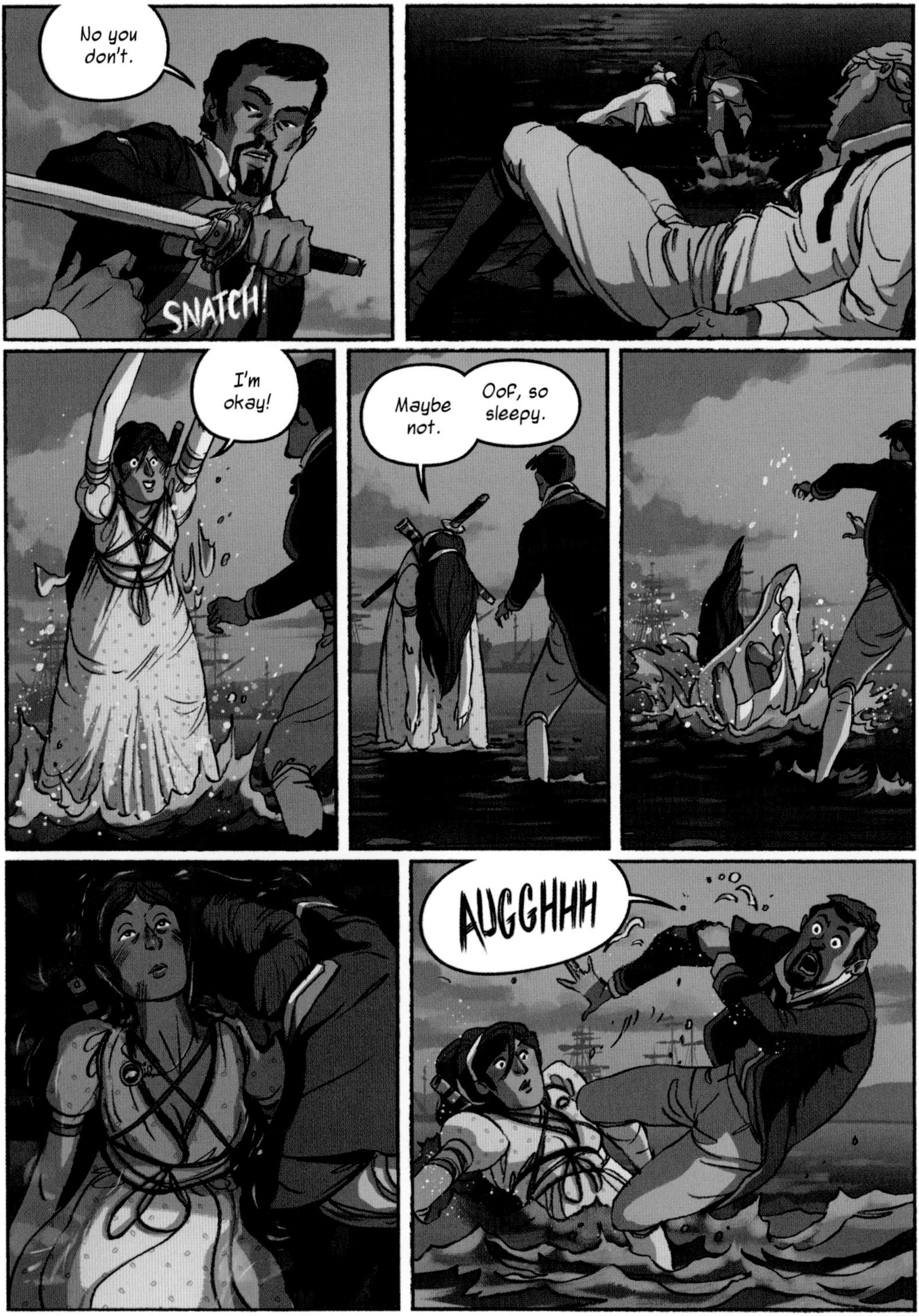
No you don't.
SNATCH!
I'm okay!
Maybe not.
Oof, so sleepy.
AUGGHHH

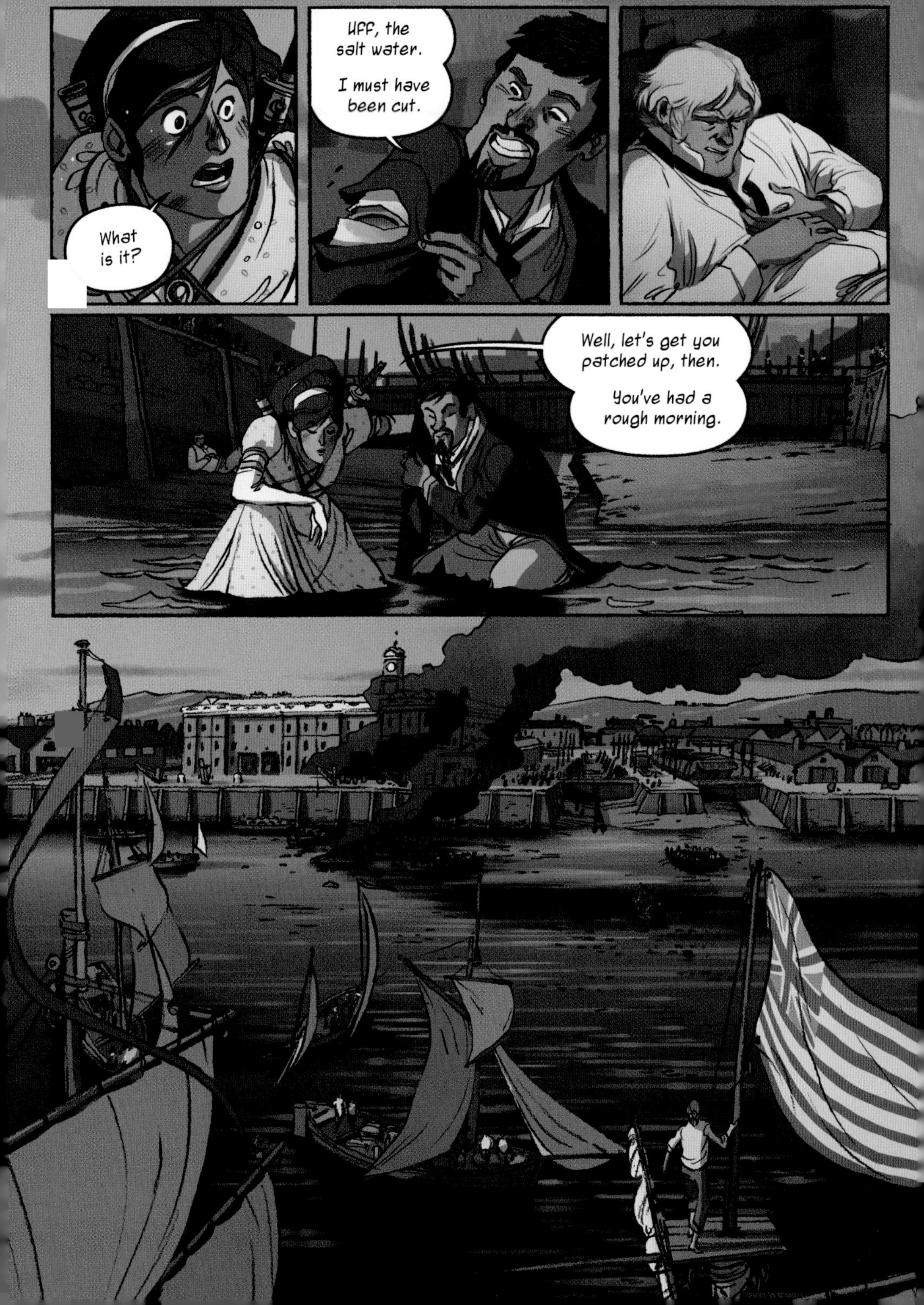
What is it?
Uff, the salt water.
I must have been cut.
Well, let's get you patched up, then.
You've had a rough morning.

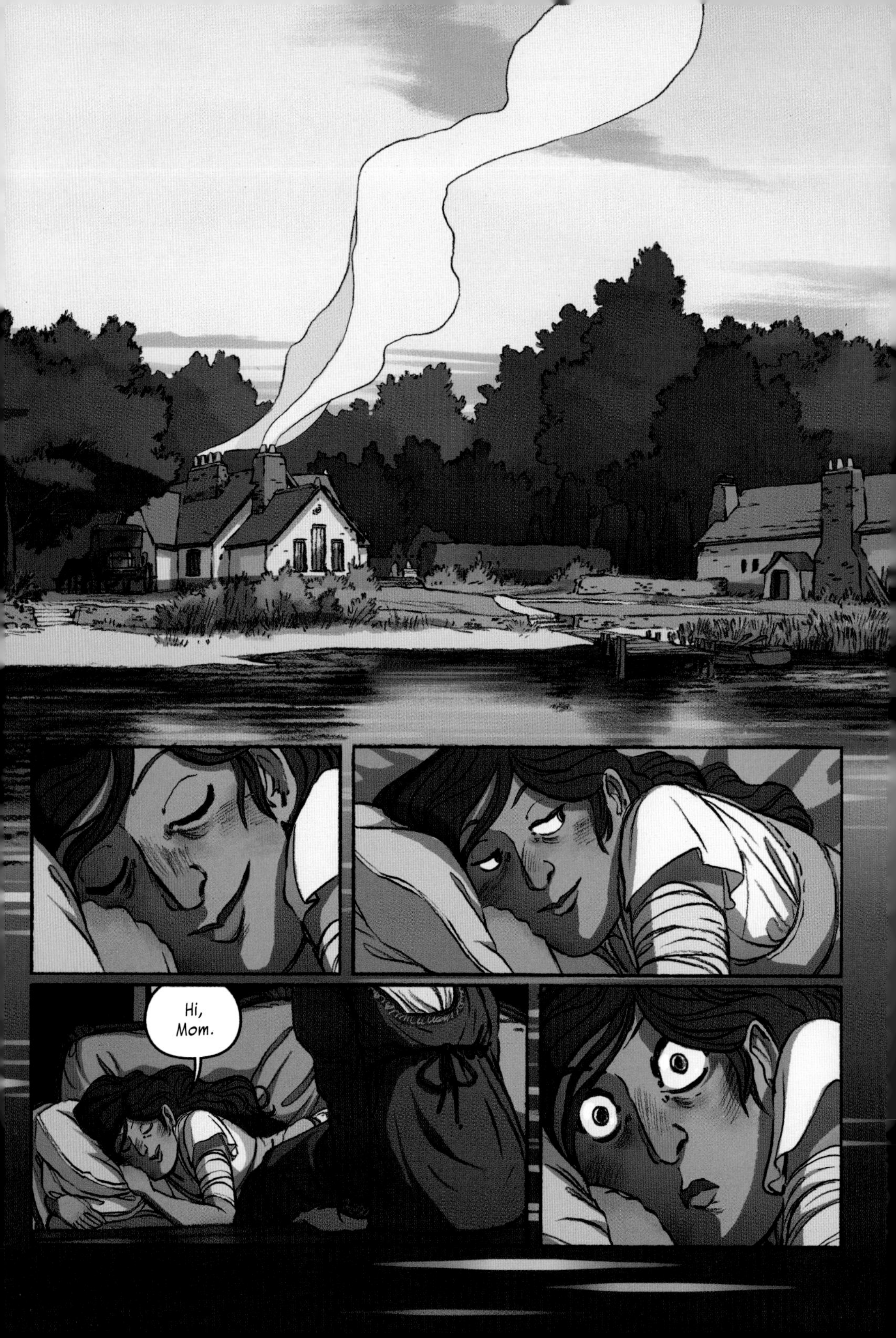
Hi, Mom.

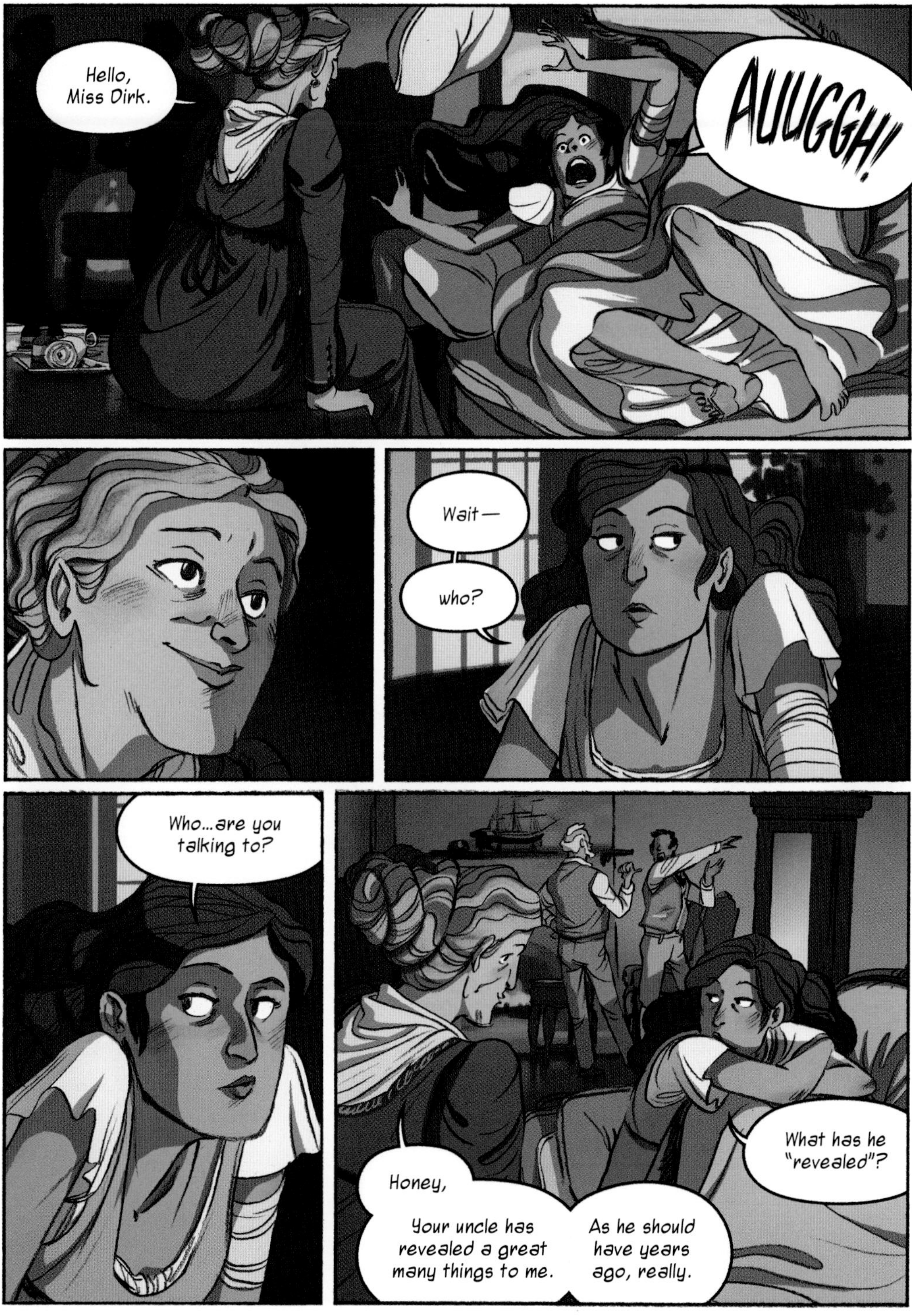
Hello, Miss Dirk.
AUUGGH!
Wait—
who?
Who...are you talking to?
Honey,
Your uncle has revealed a great many things to me.
As he should have years ago, really.
What has he "revealed"?

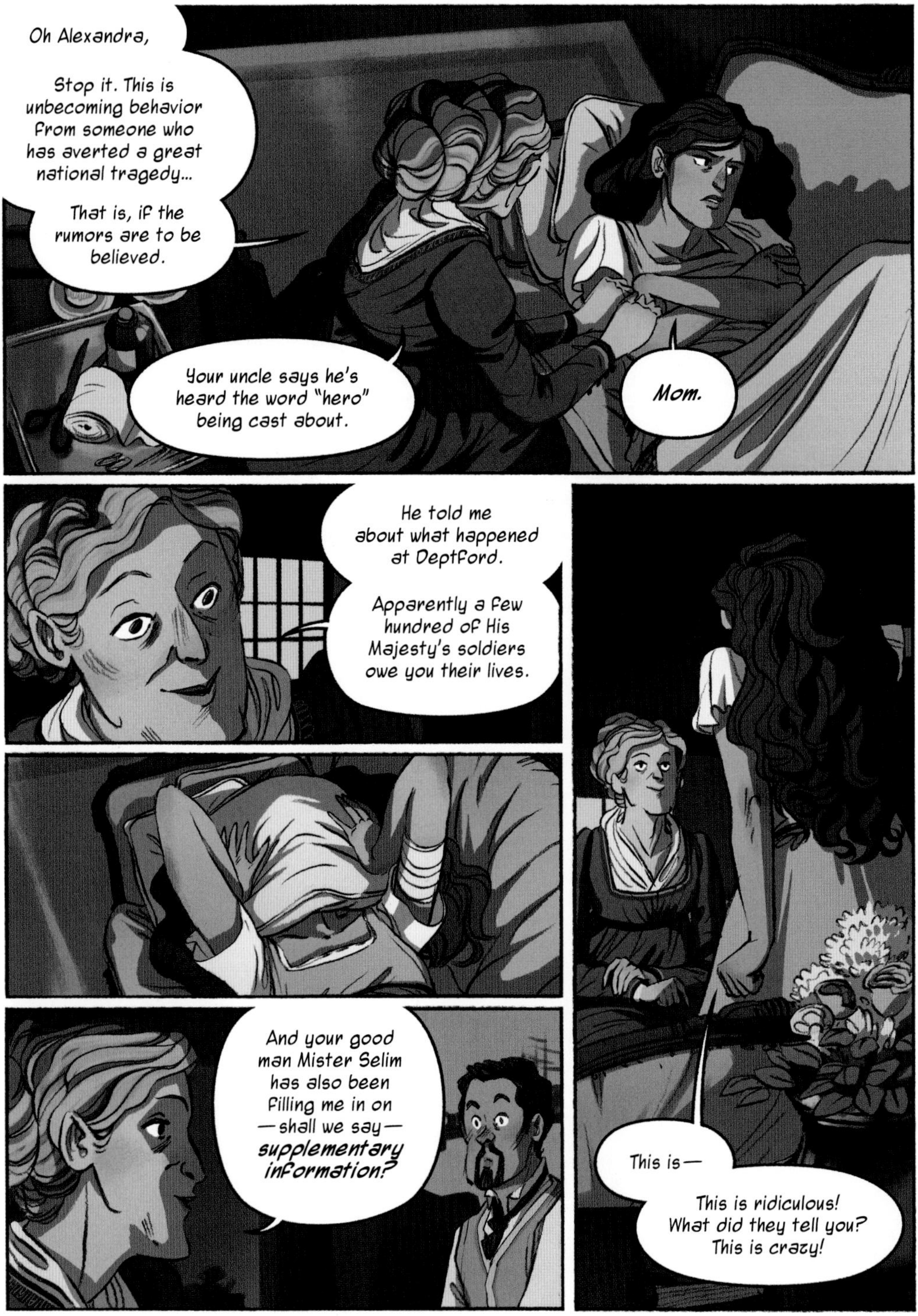

Oh Alexandra,
Stop it. This is unbecoming behavior from someone who has averted a great national tragedy...
That is, if the rumors are to be believed.
Your uncle says he's heard the word "hero" being cast about.
Mom.
He told me about what happened at Deptford.
Apparently a few hundred of His Majesty's soldiers owe you their lives.
And your good man Mister Selim has also been filling me in on —shall we say— supplementary information?
This is—
This is ridiculous! What did they tell you? This is crazy!

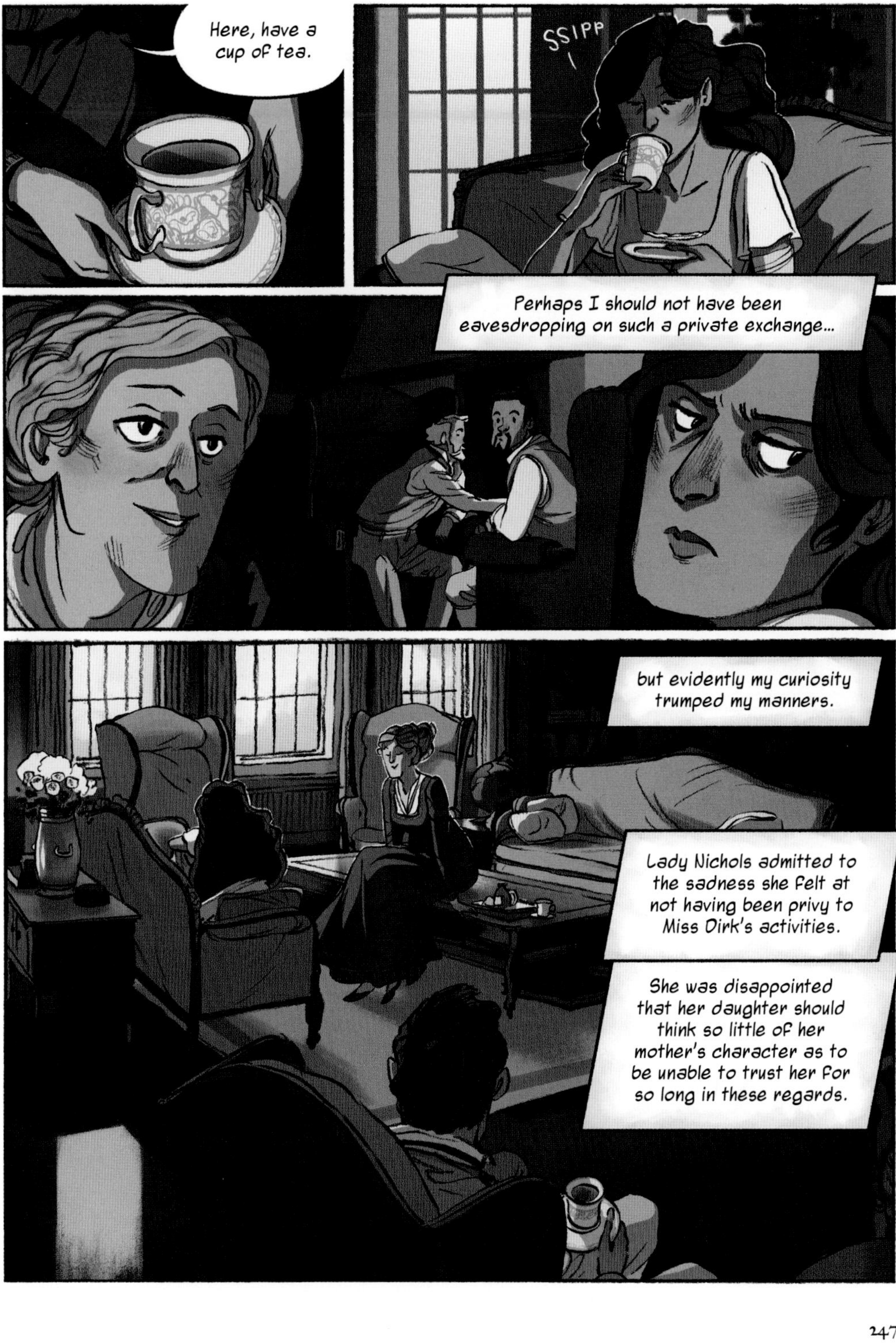
Here, have a cup of tea.
SSIPP
Perhaps I should not have been eavesdropping on such a private exchange...
but evidently my curiosity trumped my manners.
Lady Nichols admitted to the sadness she felt at not having been privy to Miss Dirk's activities.
She was disappointed that her daughter should think so little of her mother's character as to be unable to trust her for so long in these regards.

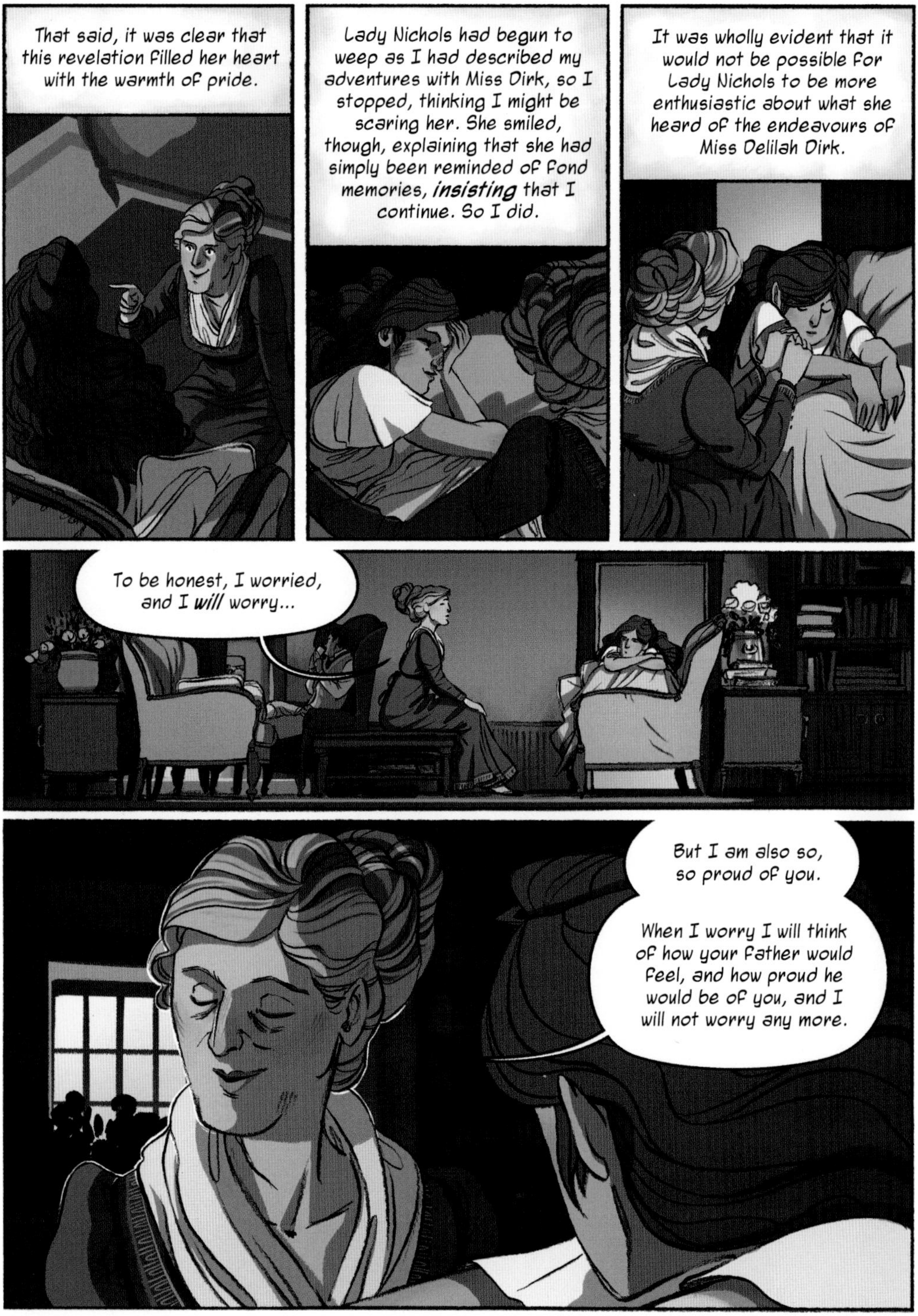
That said, it was clear that this revelation filled her heart with the warmth of pride.
Lady Nichols had begun to weep as I had described my adventures with Miss Dirk, so I stopped, thinking I might be scaring her. She smiled, though, explaining that she had simply been reminded of fond memories, *insisting* that I continue. So I did.
It was wholly evident that it would not be possible for Lady Nichols to be more enthusiastic about what she heard of the endeavours of Miss Delilah Dirk.
To be honest, I worried, and I *will* worry...
But I am also so, so proud of you.
When I worry I will think of how your father would feel, and how proud he would be of you, and I will not worry any more.

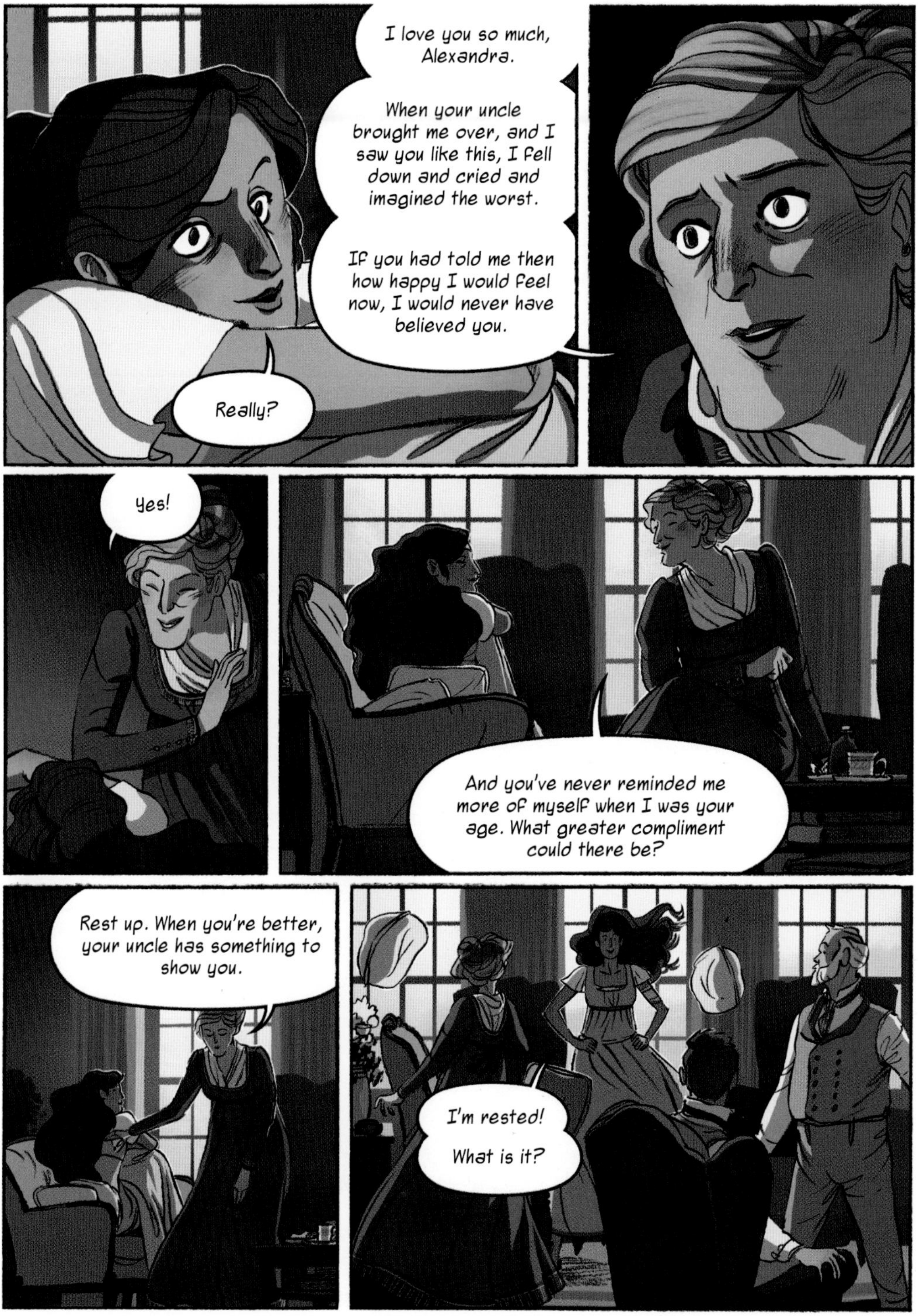
I love you so much, Alexandra.
When your uncle brought me over, and I saw you like this, I fell down and cried and imagined the worst.
If you had told me then how happy I would feel now, I would never have believed you.
Really?
Yes!
And you've never reminded me more of myself when I was your age. What greater compliment could there be?
Rest up. When you're better, your uncle has something to show you.
I'm rested!
What is it?

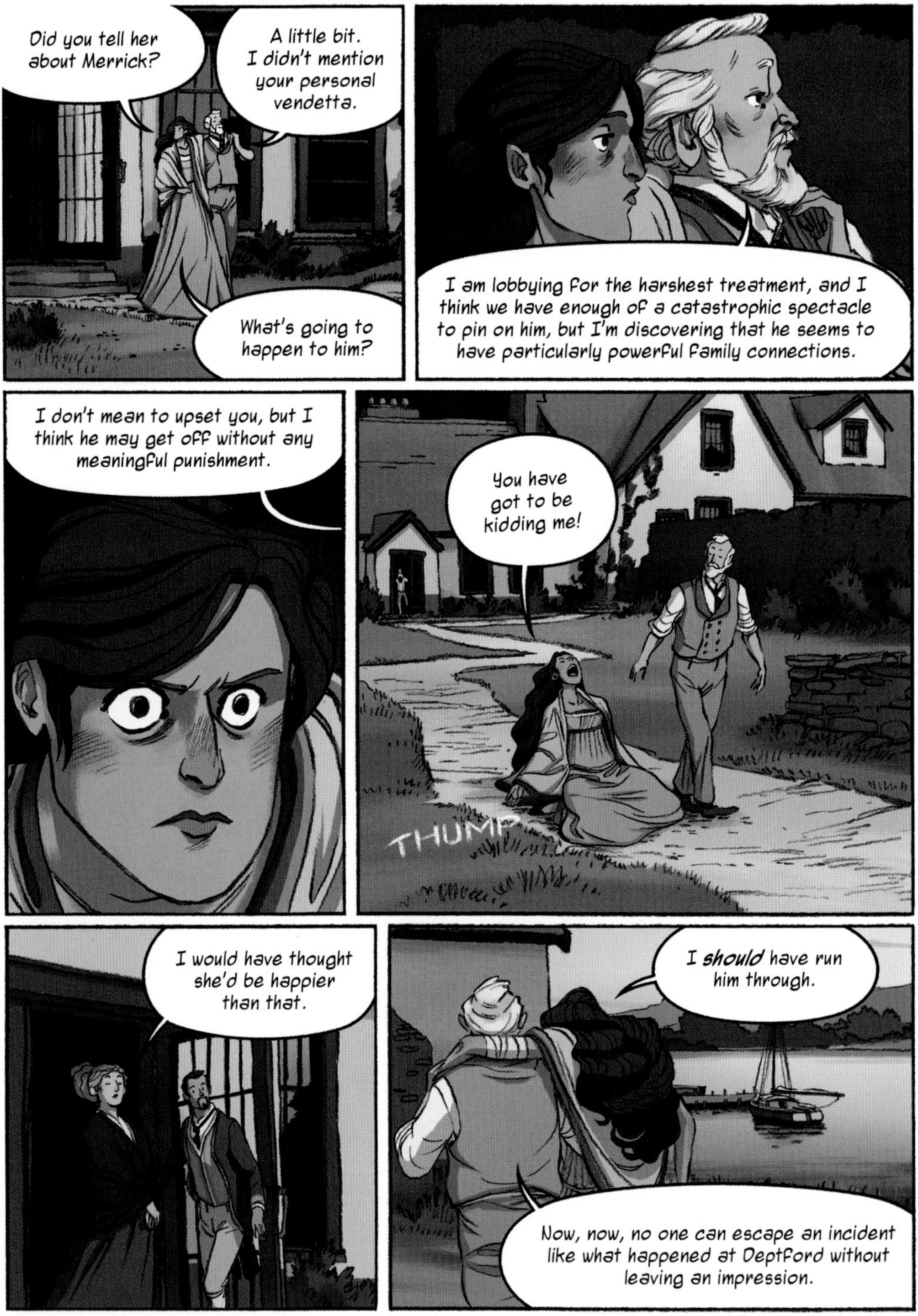
Did you tell her about Merrick?
A little bit. I didn't mention your personal vendetta.
What's going to happen to him?
I am lobbying for the harshest treatment, and I think we have enough of a catastrophic spectacle to pin on him, but I'm discovering that he seems to have particularly powerful family connections.
I don't mean to upset you, but I think he may get off without any meaningful punishment.
You have got to be kidding me!
THUMP
I would have thought she'd be happier than that.
I *should* have run him through.
Now, now, no one can escape an incident like what happened at Deptford without leaving an impression.

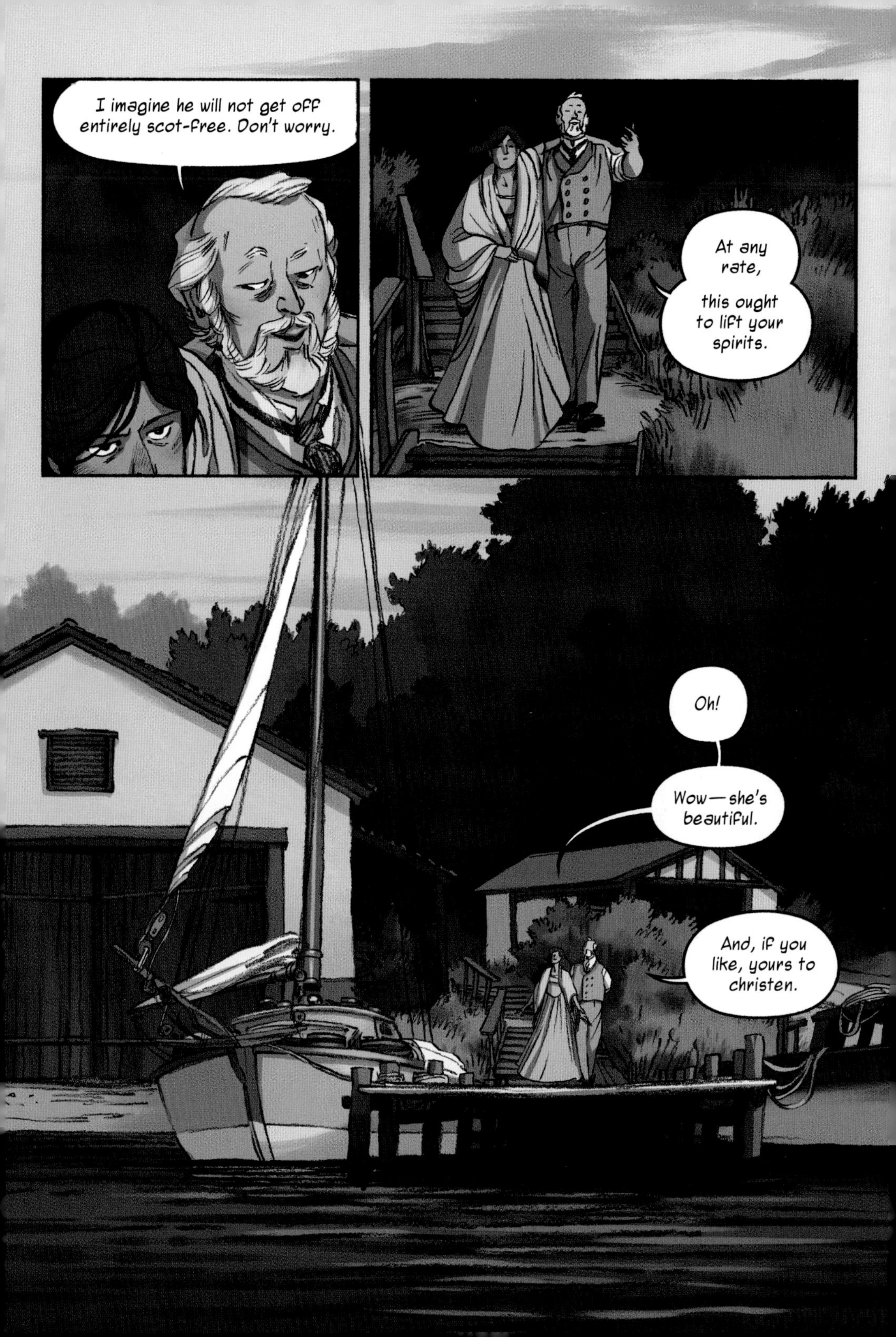
I imagine he will not get off entirely scot-free. Don't worry.
At any rate,
this ought to lift your spirits.
Oh!
Wow—she's beautiful.
And, if you like, yours to christen.

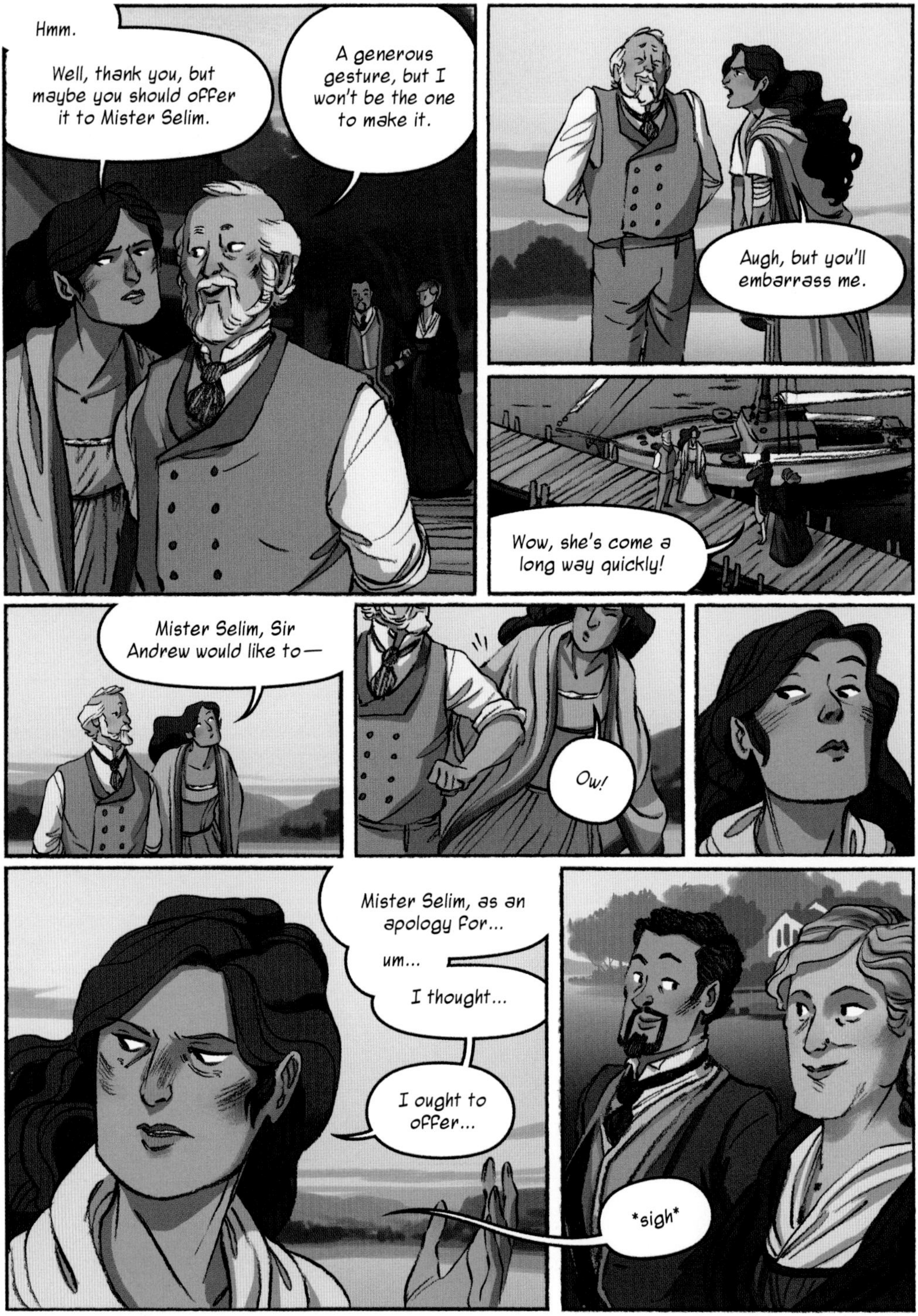
Hmm.
Well, thank you, but maybe you should offer it to Mister Selim.
A generous gesture, but I won't be the one to make it.
Augh, but you'll embarrass me.
Wow, she's come a long way quickly!
Mister Selim, Sir Andrew would like to—
Ow!
Mister Selim, as an apology for...
um...
I thought...
I ought to offer...
*sigh*

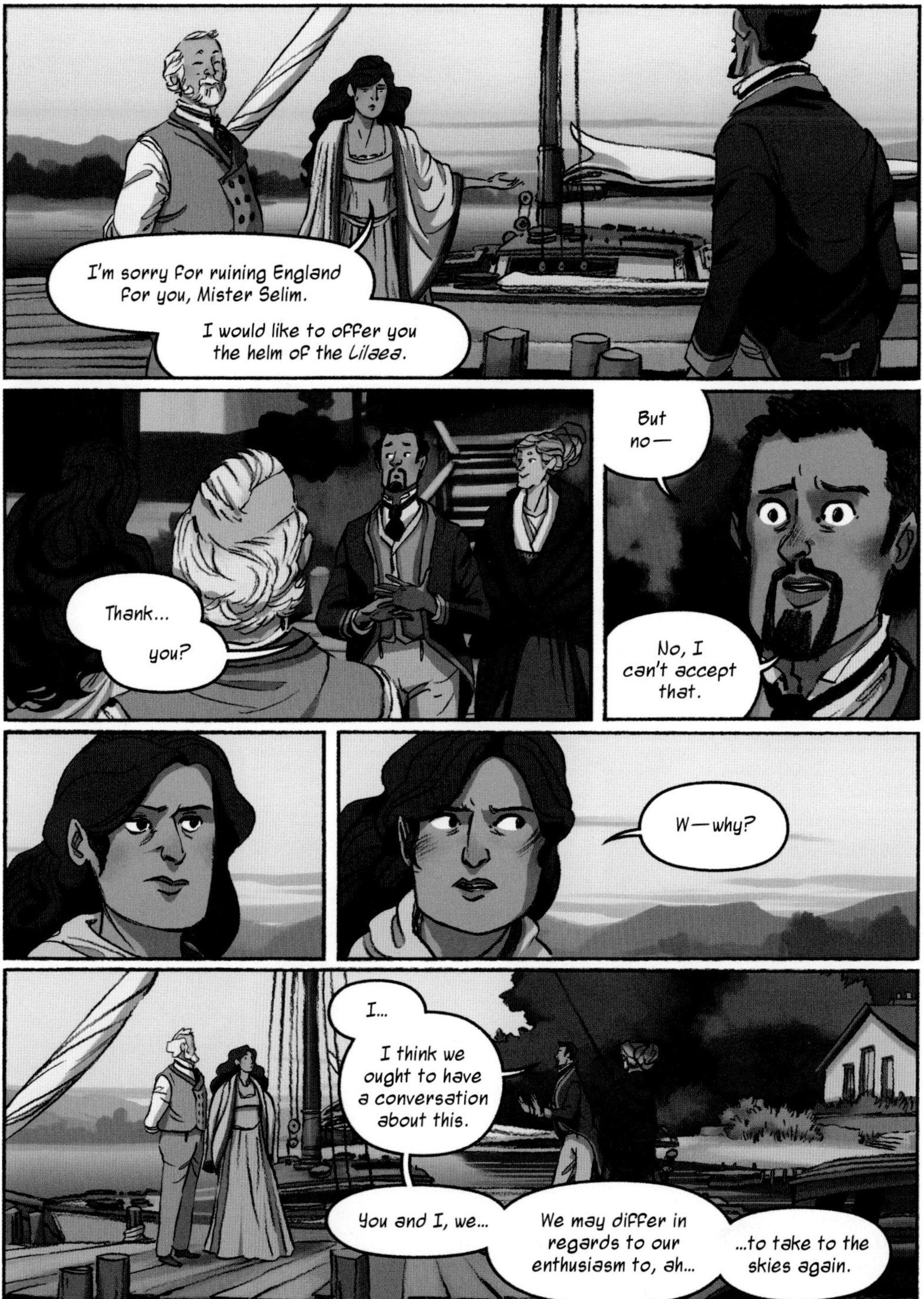
I'm sorry for ruining England for you, Mister Selim.
I would like to offer you the helm of the *Lilaea*.
Thank... you?
But no—
No, I can't accept that.
W—why?
I...
I think we ought to have a conversation about this.
You and I, we...
We may differ in regards to our enthusiasm to, ah...
...to take to the skies again.

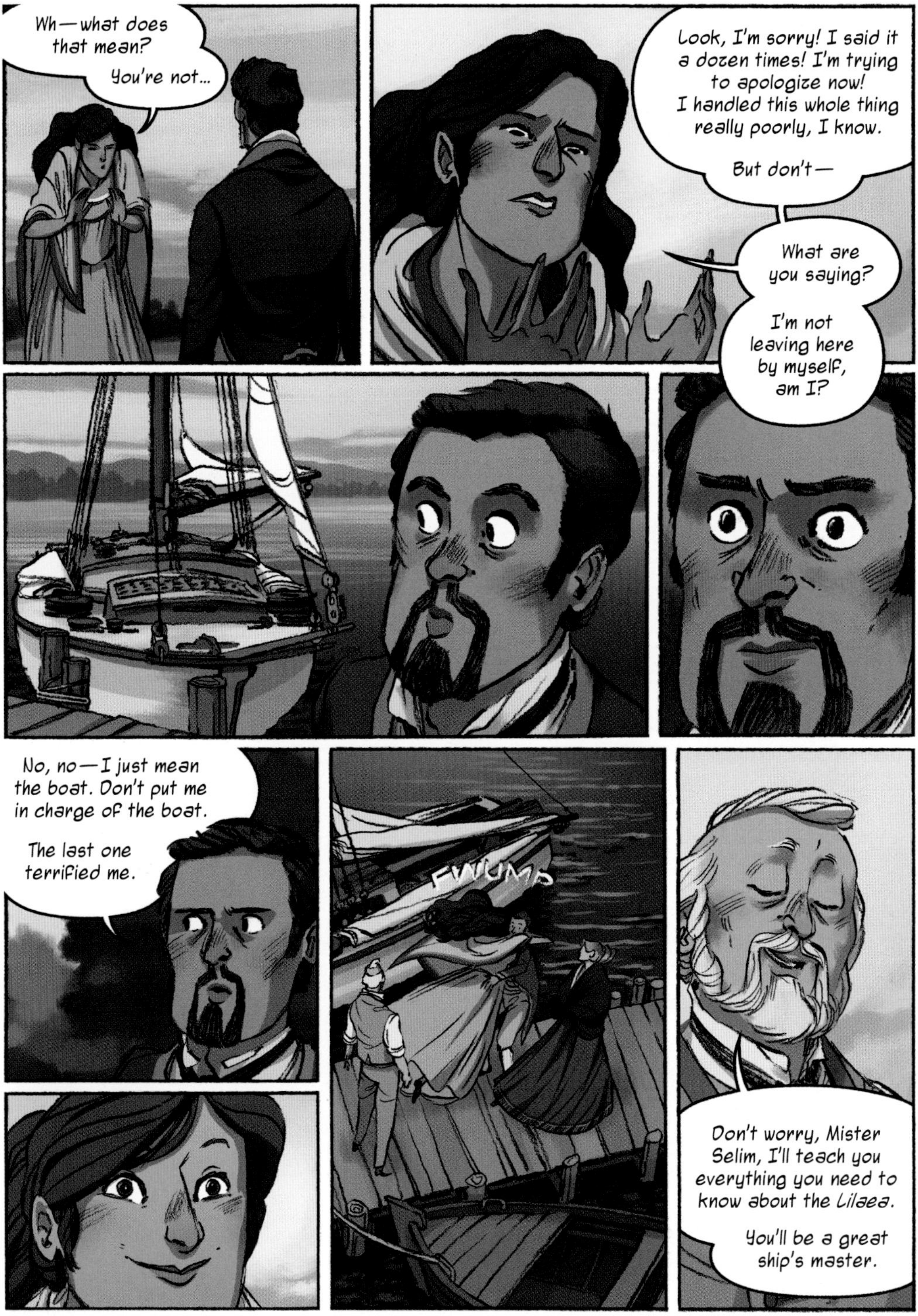
Wh—what does that mean?
You're not...
Look, I'm sorry! I said it a dozen times! I'm trying to apologize now! I handled this whole thing really poorly, I know.
But don't—
What are you saying?
I'm not leaving here by myself, am I?
No, no—I just mean the boat. Don't put me in charge of the boat.
The last one terrified me.
FWUMP
Don't worry, Mister Selim, I'll teach you everything you need to know about the *Lilaea*.
You'll be a great ship's master.

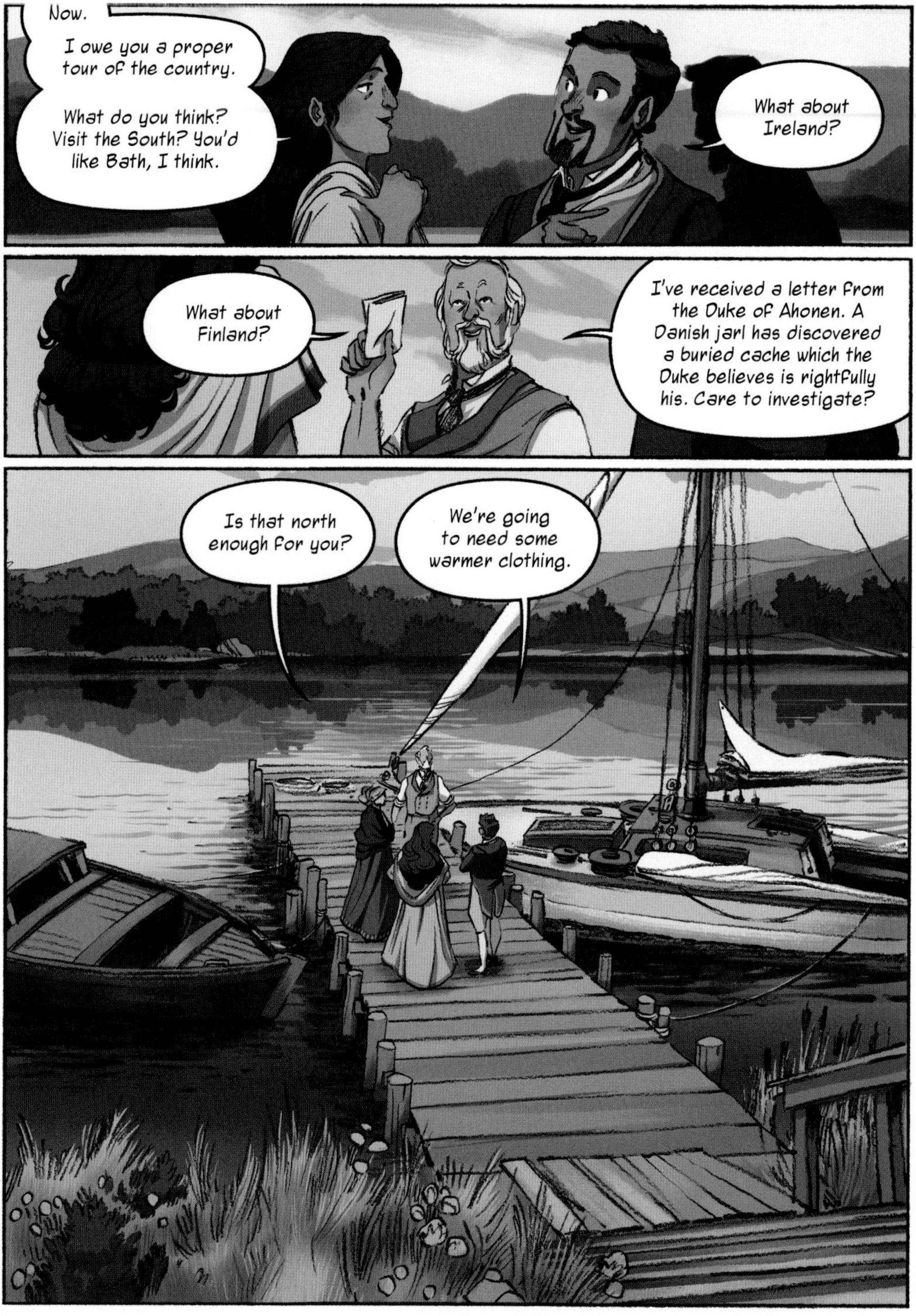
Now.
I owe you a proper tour of the country.
What do you think? Visit the South? You'd like Bath, I think.
What about Ireland?
What about Finland?
I've received a letter from the Duke of Ahonen. A Danish jarl has discovered a buried cache which the Duke believes is rightfully his. Care to investigate?
Is that north enough for you?
We're going to need some warmer clothing.

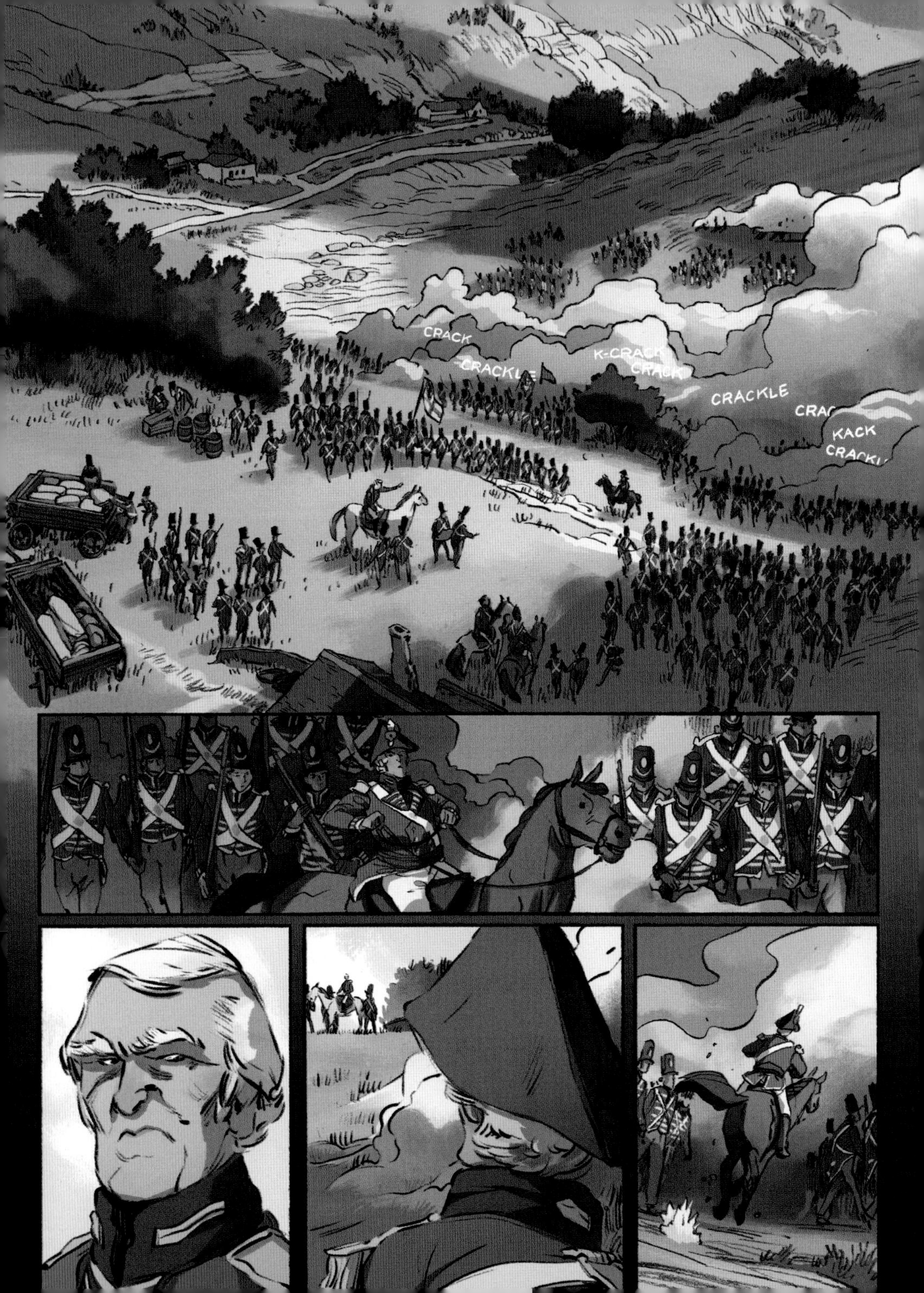
CRACK
CRACKLE
K-CRACK
CRACKLE
KACK

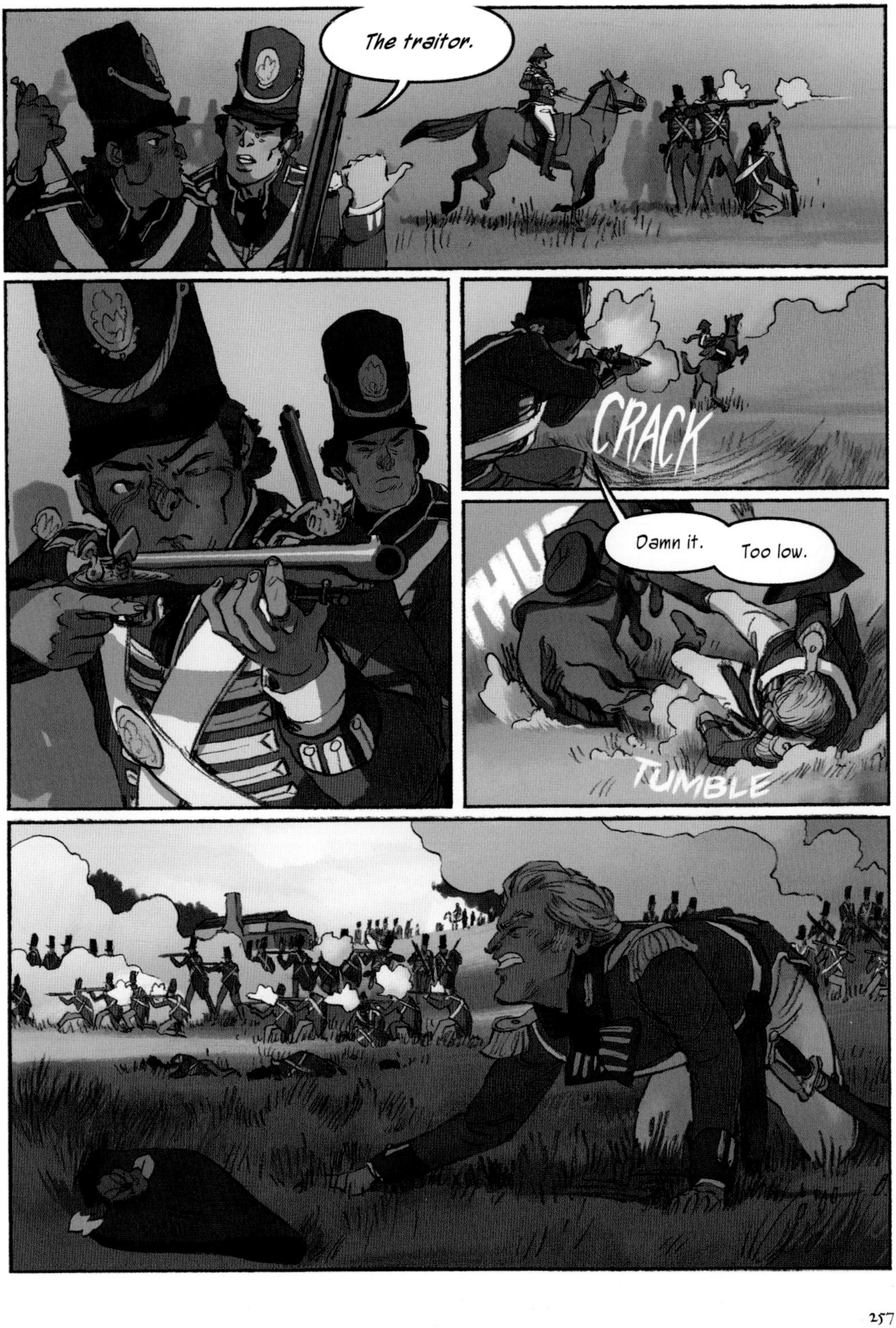
The traitor.
CRACK
Damn it.
Too low.
TUMBLE

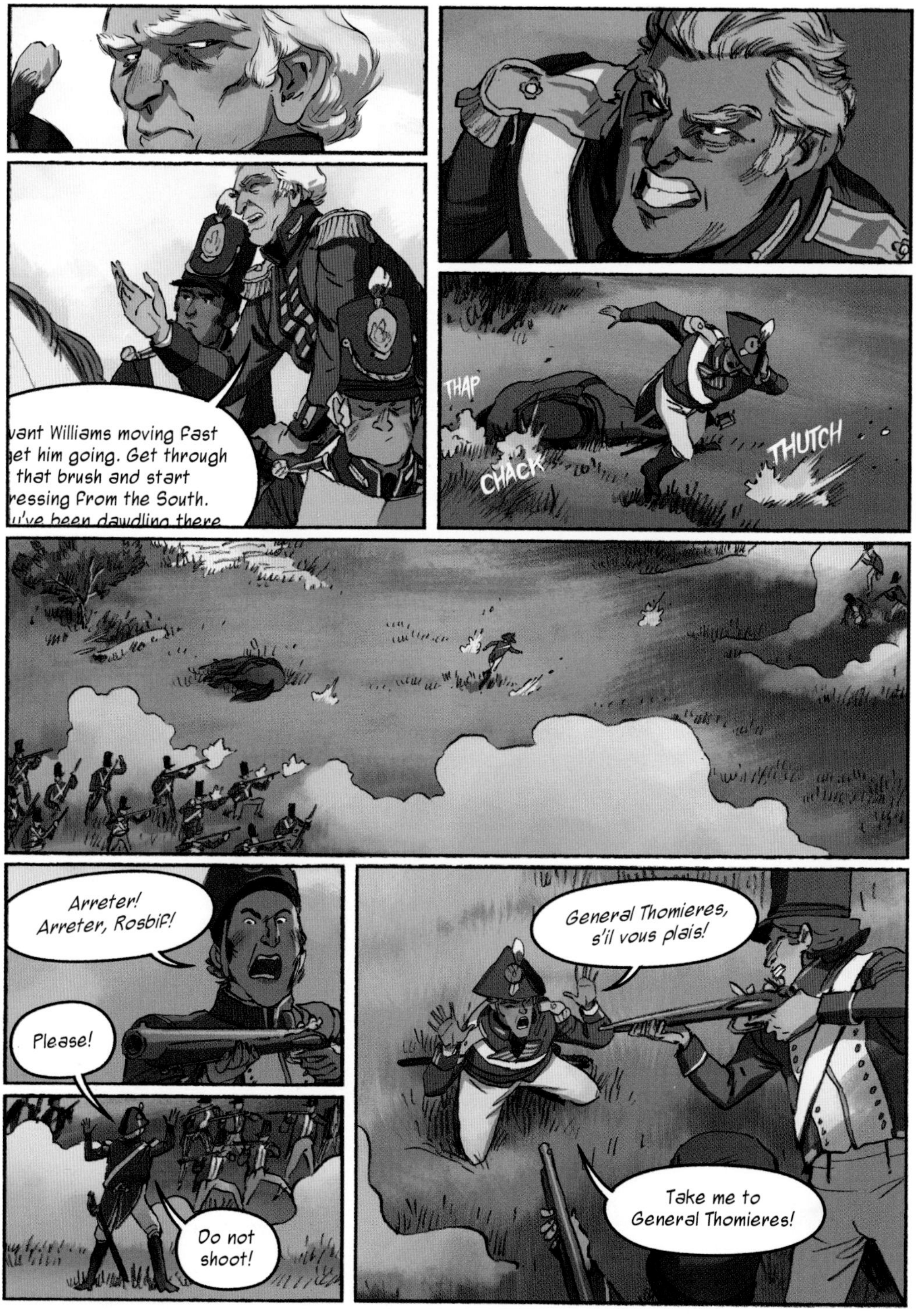
vant Williams moving fast
get him going. Get through
that brush and start
ressing from the South.
THAP
CHACK
THUTCH
Arreter!
Arreter, Rosbif!
Please!
Do not
shoot!
General Thomieres,
s'il vous plais!
Take me to
General Thomieres!

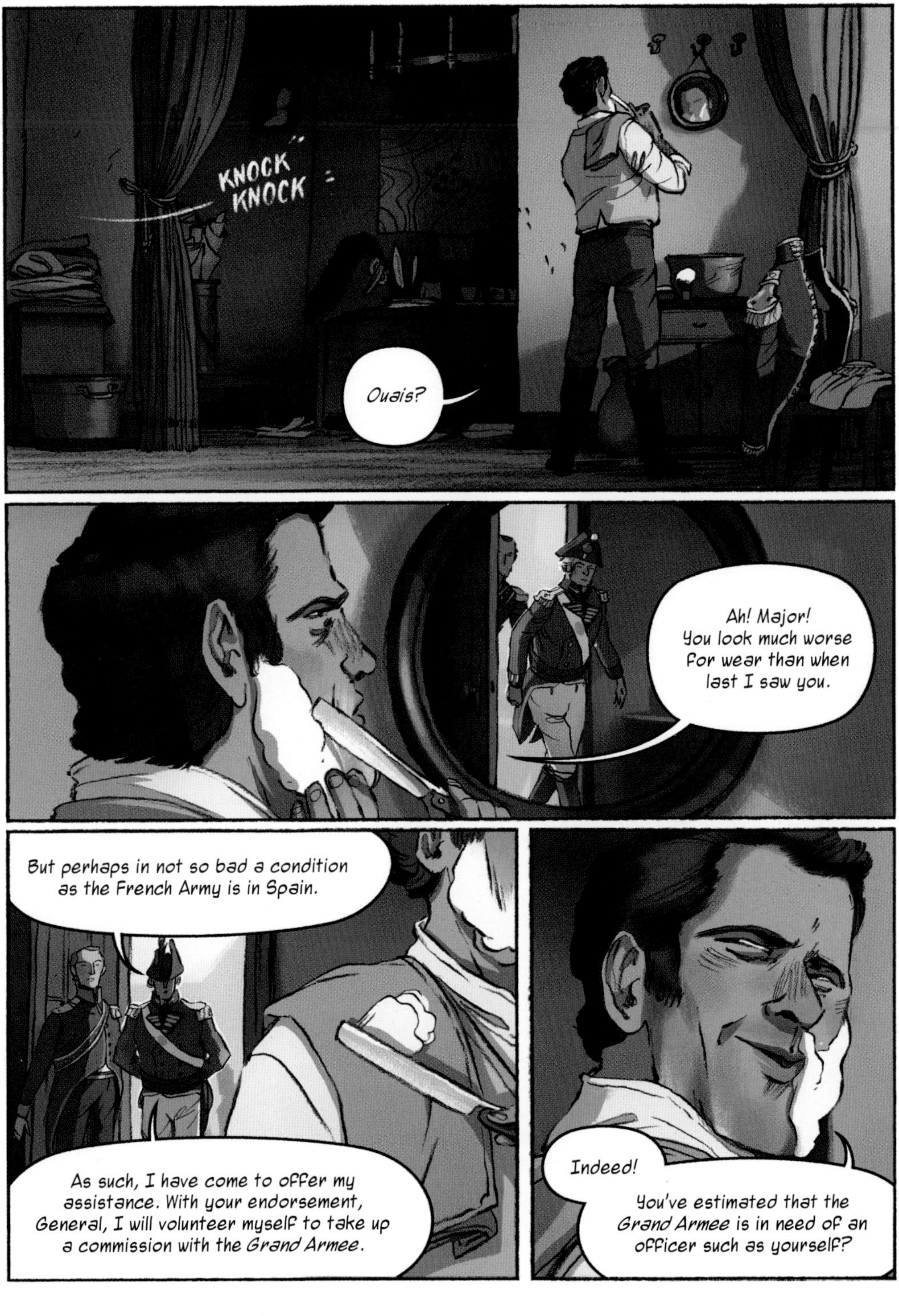
KNOCK KNOCK
Ouais?
Ah! Major! You look much worse for wear than when last I saw you.
But perhaps in not so bad a condition as the French Army is in Spain.
As such, I have come to offer my assistance. With your endorsement, General, I will volunteer myself to take up a commission with the *Grand Armee*.
Indeed!
You've estimated that the *Grand Armee* is in need of an officer such as yourself?

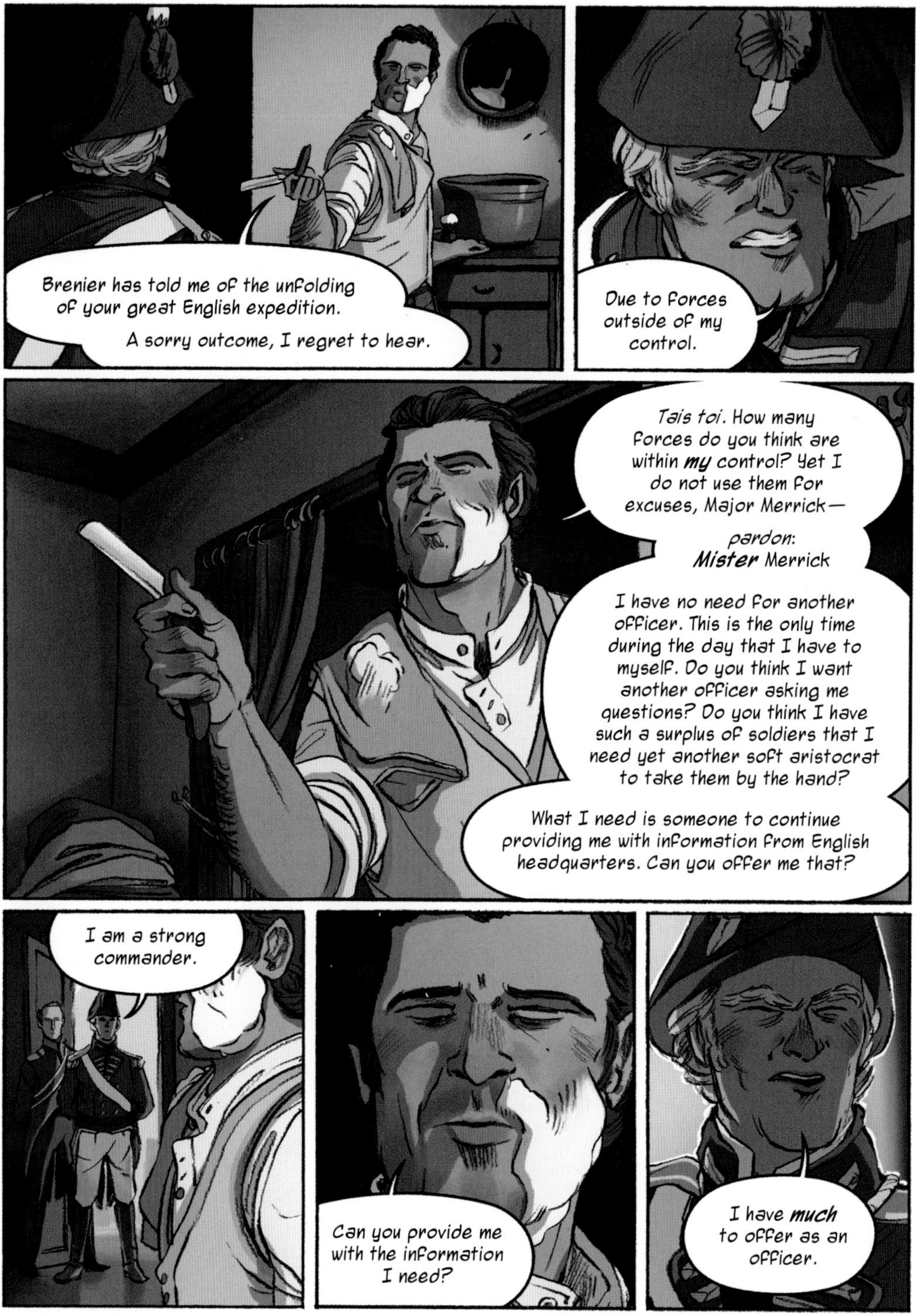
Brenier has told me of the unfolding of your great English expedition.
A sorry outcome, I regret to hear.
Due to forces outside of my control.
*Tais toi*. How many forces do you think are within ***my*** control? Yet I do not use them for excuses, Major Merrick—
*pardon*: ***Mister*** Merrick
I have no need for another officer. This is the only time during the day that I have to myself. Do you think I want another officer asking me questions? Do you think I have such a surplus of soldiers that I need yet another soft aristocrat to take them by the hand?
What I need is someone to continue providing me with information from English headquarters. Can you offer me that?
I am a strong commander.
Can you provide me with the information I need?
I have ***much*** to offer as an officer.

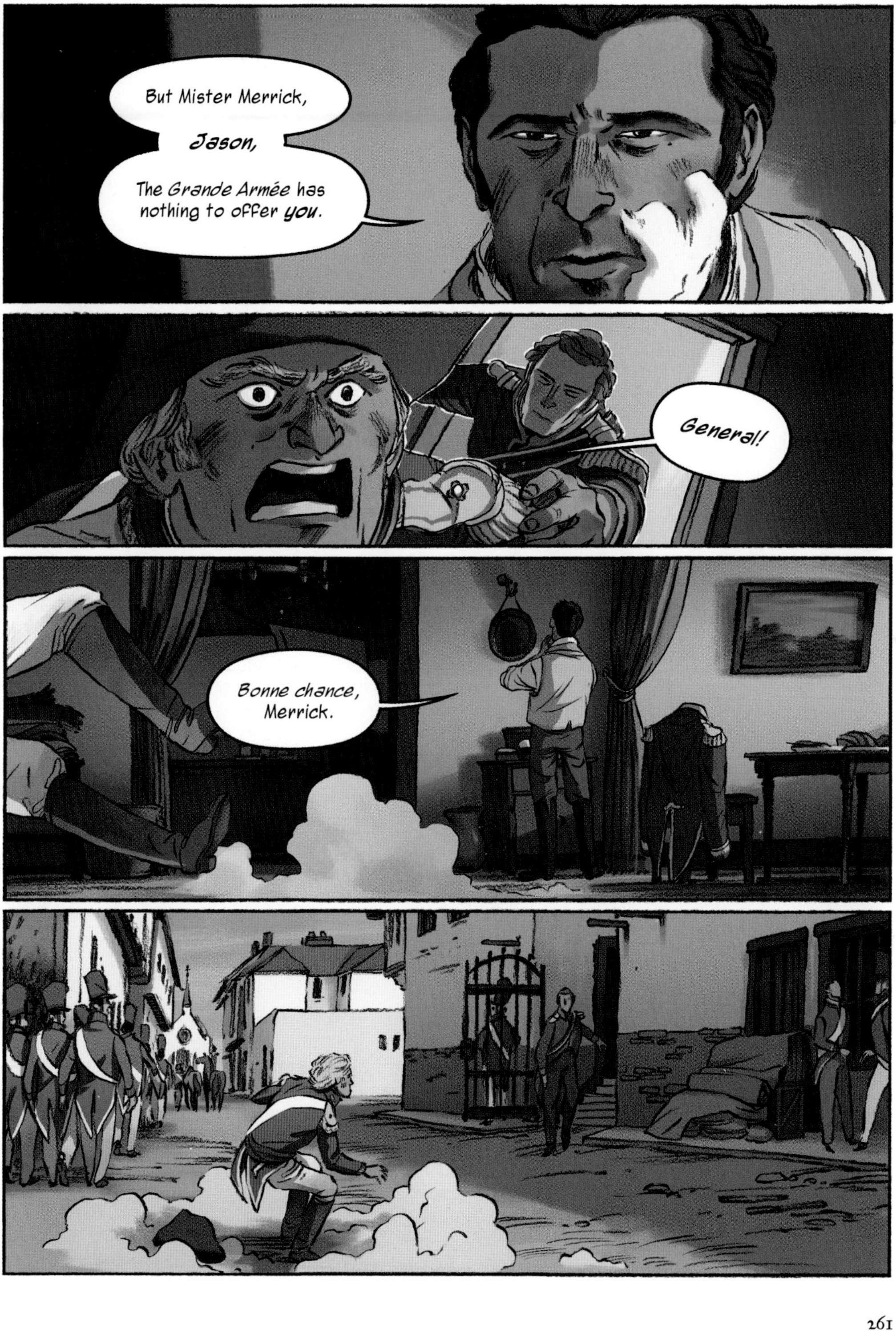
But Mister Merrick,
Jason,
The Grande Armée has nothing to offer you.
General!
Bonne chance, Merrick.

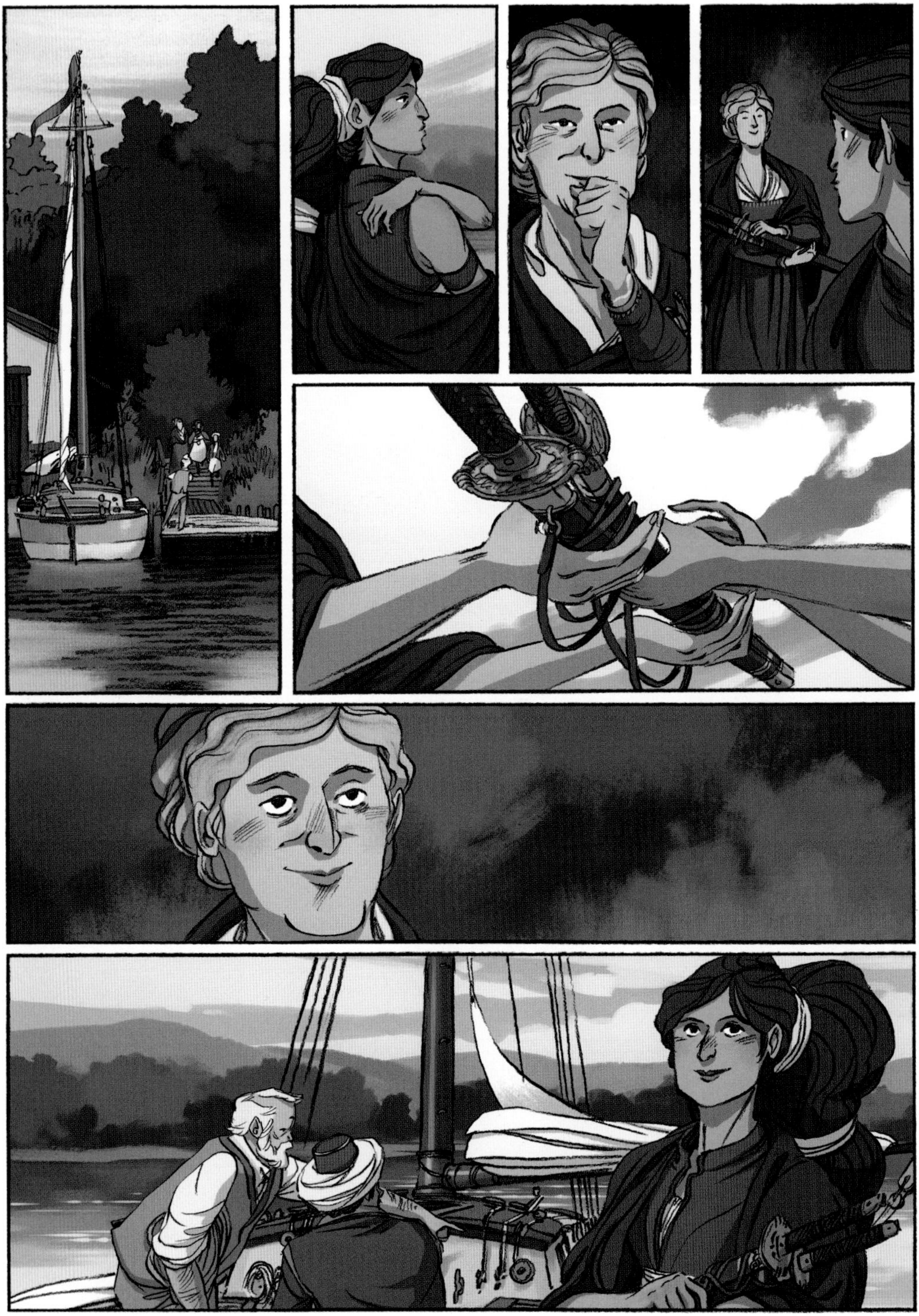

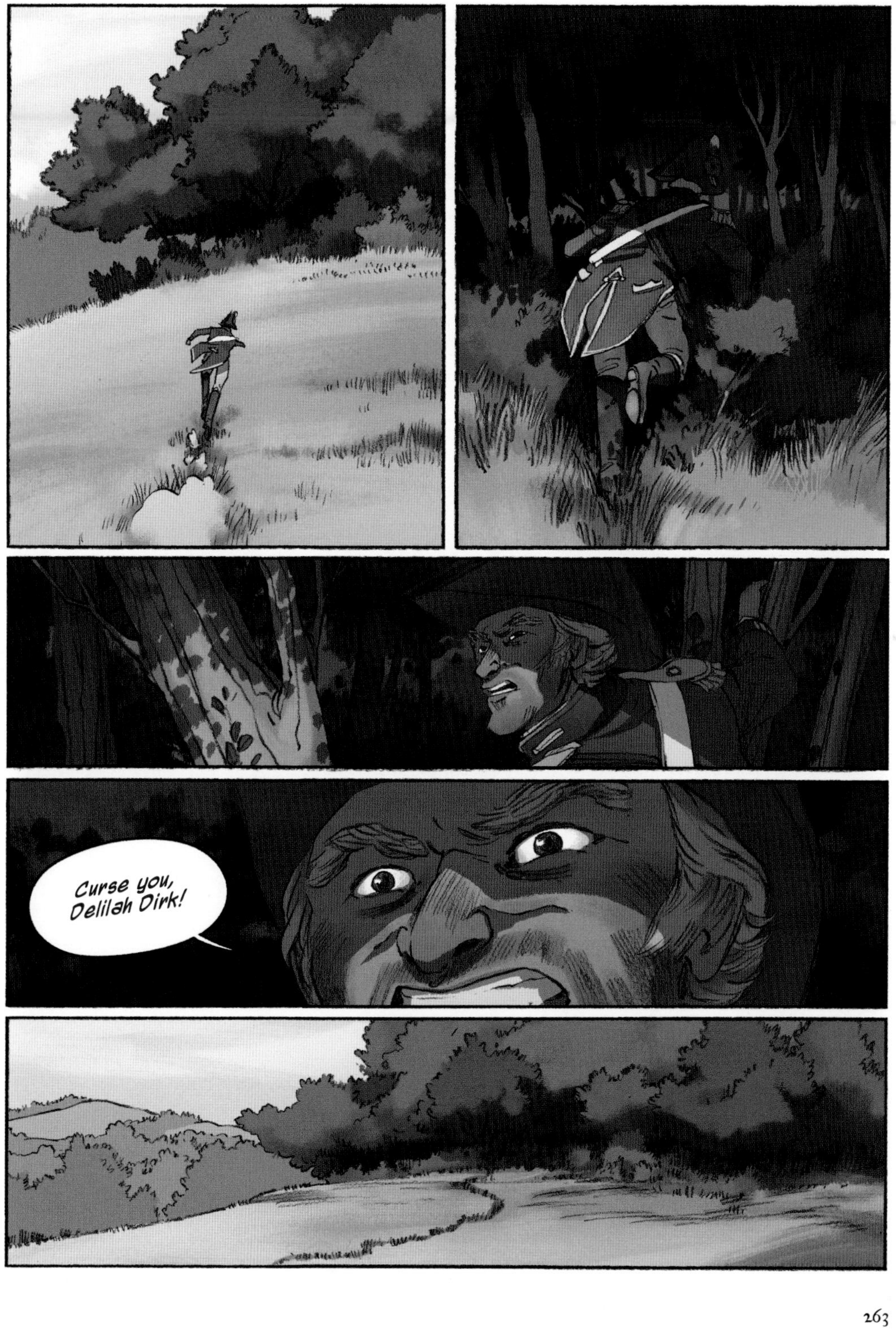
Curse you, Delilah Dirk!

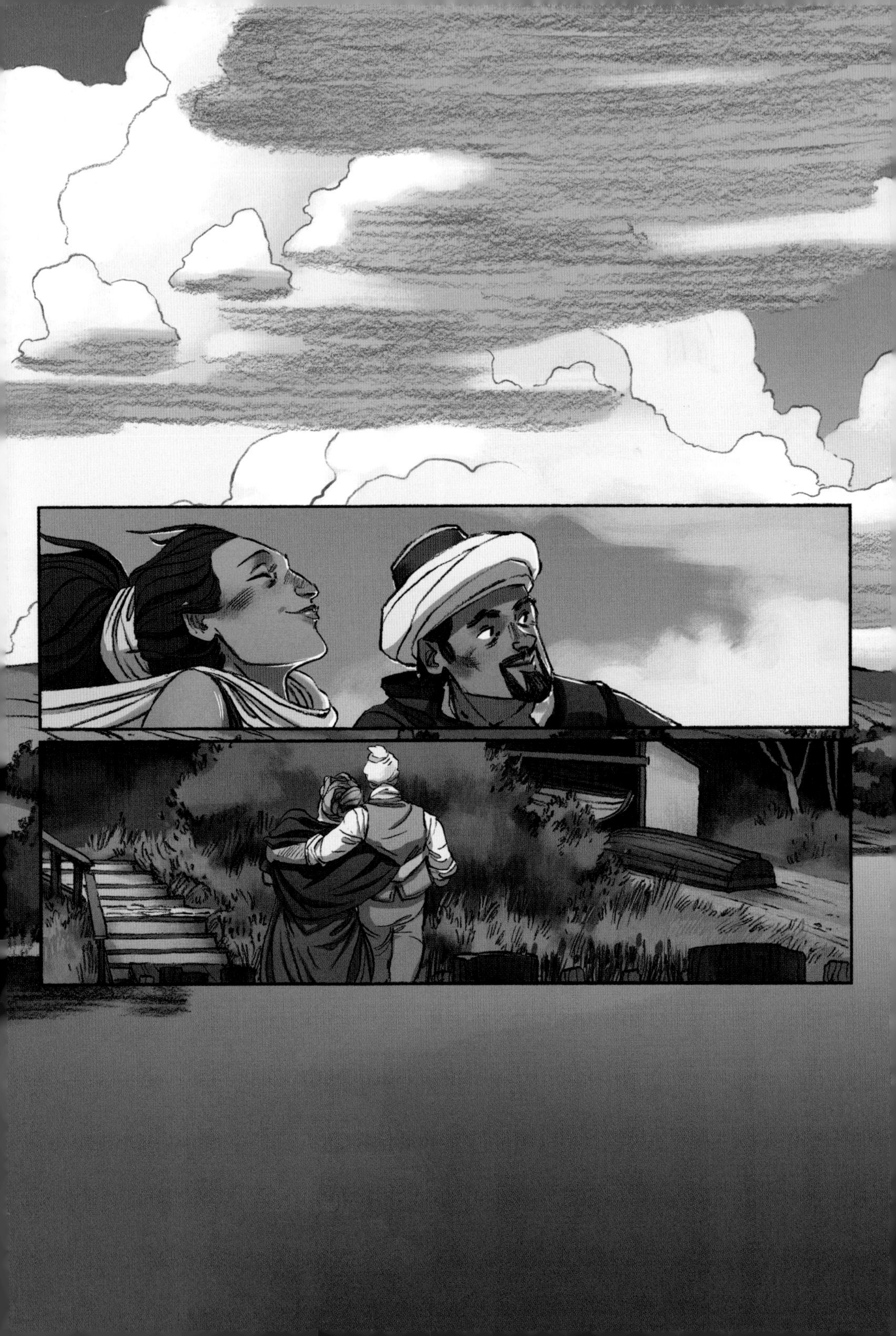

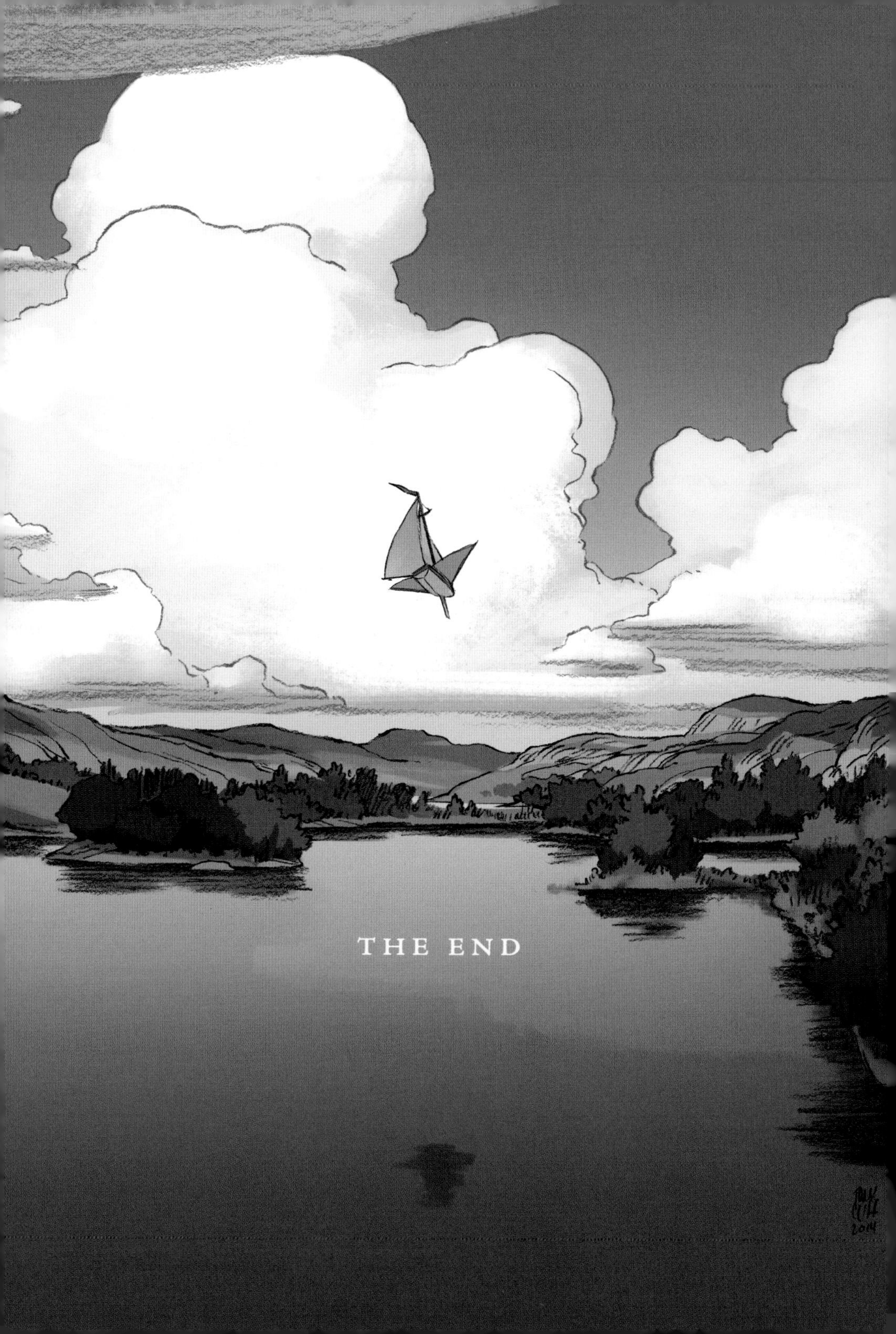
THE END

## A NOTE ON THE TOPIC OF HISTORICAL ACCURACY

This is not a history book. You already knew that, though, because it has been fun and easy to read.

I am, of course, being facetious. A good many very talented authors have written both entertainingly *and* accurately on historical subjects, and it is their achievements I have tried to emulate. However, despite my best efforts, there will inevitably be some elements of my depiction of 19th-century Europe that will conflict with the astute reader's knowledge of that time and place. Set aside obviously fantastical pieces such as Delilah's flying ship and wholly fictional imaginings such as names and personalities. Outside that territory, I'm certain there are elements which ought to have been depicted accurately but which were not. Perhaps I did not have enough concrete reference at hand and so resorted to using my best guess, or perhaps I just made a mistake. In other areas I have intentionally discarded accuracy in favor of other qualities; for example, Delilah gets around England much more rapidly than she ought to, even on horseback.

If you have found yourself caught upon such conflicts, I hope that you will accept my humble apologies and forgive my intentional historical infringements, and that none of this has adversely affected your enjoyment of *The King's Shilling*.

If, like me, you wish to see greater historical accuracy in future Deliah Dirk stories and you are able to assist me in my research and discovery, I encourage you to contact me via one of the many means available at **WWW.DELILAHDIRK.COM**.

## ACKNOWLEDGMENTS

For providing perspective, fresh eyes, and thoughtful notes, I am grateful to Kenny Park, Michael Swanston, Katy Campbell, Kean Soo, Tory Woollcott, and Sarah Airriess.

I had the great pleasure of corresponding with Lucy Bellwood, Paul Guinan, and most especially Dr. James Davey of the National Maritime Museum, London, UK, about victualling yards, shipping convoys, sailing ships of the period, Merrick's explosive-barrel plot, and many other nautical details. They were kind enough to supply me with very detailed historical information and I was cruel enough to disregard whole swathes of it. I hope my generous historical advisors will be forgiving.

Don Perro of Capilano University's Animation program and Kevin Gamble of Titmouse Canada lent me their time and technical assistance, speeding up production and keeping my stress levels low.

For her honesty, generosity, and assistance I am grateful to my agent, Bernadette Baker Baughman.

Calista Brill, Delilah's editor at First Second, provided heartfelt, invaluable course-correction. Her creative guidance ensured that a select few very important values from the first book were consistently reproduced in this, the second.

I am thankful to my parents, Anne and Brian Cliff, whose support has been as practical and immediate as it has been immeasurably foundational.

Finally, I am grateful to Sarah Haddleton, for reassurance, insight, and for effectively keeping me from turning into a desiccated, pencil-clutching husk of a former human. She is the living embodiment of care and understanding.